Lady on the Case

ABOUT THE EDITORS

MARCIA MULLER has published fourteen mystery novels, three of them with Bill Pronzini, as well as numerous short stories, articles, and book reviews. In addition, she has co-edited nine mystery and suspense anthologies, including *The Web She Weaves*.

BILL PRONZINI has published more than 40 novels, most in the mystery/suspense field, as well as three collections of short stories and three nonfiction books (including *1001 Midnights: The Aficionado's Guide to Mystery & Detective Fiction,* with Marcia Muller). He has also edited or co-edited numerous anthologies in a wide variety of categories. His awards include three from the Private Eye Writers of America: two Shamuses (for Best Novel of 1981 and Best Short Story of 1983) and a Life Achievement Award presented in 1987.

MARTIN H. GREENBERG has by now published more than 280 books, the majority of them anthologies. He is co-editor (with Bill Pronzini) of *Baker's Dozen™: 13 Short Detective Novels* and *101 Mystery Stories, Manhattan Mysteries* (with Bill Pronzini and Carol-Lynn Rössel Waugh), and *A Treasury of American Mystery Stories* (with Charles Waugh and Frank McSherry, Jr.), among many others.

Lady on the Case

Marcia Muller,
Bill Pronzini, and
Martin H. Greenberg

BONANZA BOOKS
NEW YORK

Publisher's Note: Selections in this work contain racial references and language the modern reader may find offensive. These references and language are part of the time period and environment written about, and do not reflect the attitudes of the editors or publisher of this current edition.

First published in 1988 by Bonanza Books, distributed by Crown Publishers, Inc., 225 Park Avenue South, New York, New York 10003, by arrangement with Marcia Muller, Bill Pronzini and Martin H. Greenberg.

Manufactured in the United States of America

Library of Congress Cataloging-in-Publication Data
Lady on the case / edited by Marcia Muller, Bill Pronzini, and Martin H. Greenberg.

1. Women detectives—Fiction. 2. Detective and mystery stories, American. 3. Detective and mystery stories, English. I. Muller, Marcia. II. Pronzini, Bill. III. Greenberg, Martin Harry.
PS648.D4L3 1988
813'.0872'08—dc19

88-6338
CIP

ISBN: 0-517-66715-0
h g f e d c b a

ACKNOWLEDGMENTS

CONTENTS

INTRODUCTION

The female detective—whether the snoopy maiden lady of the Golden Age, the modern career woman, or any number of other incarnations—has held a position of prominence in mystery and detective fiction virtually from the genre's beginnings. For it was in the early 1860s, two decades after Edgar Allan Poe wrote the first detective stories and more than two decades before the debut of Sherlock Holmes, that an anonymously created Mrs. Paschal of London solved several baffling mysteries in *The Revelations of a Lady Detective*.

And yet the fictional woman sleuth, up to and including the present time, has generally been regarded as a curiosity, set apart from her male colleagues. She is a woman who, whether armed with a .38 revolver or a pair of knitting needles, has defied convention by leaving home and hearth and venturing into dangerous territory. Such special attention is unfair, of course, both to male characters who don't receive it, and to female characters who are all too often dismissed as merely "eccentric" or "exceptional."

Ideally, this volume will help to dispel that outlook. The stories we've selected demonstrate the evolution of the female sleuth over the past hundred years—the wide variety of professionals and amateurs, of the cases they investigate, and of the methods they use to solve those cases. Taken as a whole, the stories also demonstrate that the woman detective is, and always has been, an integral part of the mainstream of criminous fiction.

In addition, these selections are highly reflective of the changes in the status of women in general over the past century. Early professional female detectives entered into their pursuits for basically the same reasons as Gothic heroines took jobs as governesses: because they were in reduced circumstances and needed to provide for themselves. Their more fortunate sisters engaged in amateur detection as a sort of frivolous hobby. The Golden Age of Detective Fiction (1920–40) brought us the intellectual who delighted in the challenge of working out a conundrum, preferably one involving a "bloodless" murder. During that same period, the more earthy women crime-solvers who made infrequent appearances in such pulp magazines as *Detective Fiction Weekly* and *Clues* had more interesting but often less believable motivations: they were eager for excitement. In recent years the female investigator and her *raison d'etre* have evolved into two basic categories: the paid professional who may or may not have a personal commitment in her cases; and the amateur who is caught up in solving a crime for strong personal reasons (and who would probably rather be safe at home reading a mystery story instead of living one). What all of these sleuths have in common besides their gender is a strong need to uncover the truth and see justice done.

The earliest female detective included here is Loveday Brooke, heroine of C. L. Pirkis's "The Murder at Troyte's Hill" (1894) and a former English society woman whose employment by a Fleet Street investigative agency brought the scorn of her high-toned former friends. Such employment (though not such scorn) makes her a rarity indeed for her time. Other early women sleuths represented in these pages are Anna Katharine Green's Violet Strange and Baroness Orczy's Lady Molly of Scotland Yard.

Of course no anthology such as this would be complete without a mystery solved by Miss Jane Marple, Agatha Christie's lovable amateur detective. Miss Marple draws upon her circumscribed knowledge of the inhabitants of her home village of St. Mary's Mead, applying it to the larger world into which she ventures. In "The Four Suspects," one of her best cases, she uses this rather personalized form of logic with great success.

The full-length novel we've provided, Stuart Palmer's *Murder on Wheels,* features Miss Hildegarde Withers—a maiden lady but hardly a Jane Marple clone. The heroine of fourteen novels and numerous short stories, Miss Withers is a schoolteacher of formidable presence, highly independent, and, we suspect, not entirely immune to the charms of the opposite sex. This early adventure set in her home base of New York City vividly showcases her keen intelligence and amusing ingenuity.

Among the other female detectives, both professional and amateur, you'll find here are a taxi dancer (Cornell Woolrich's "dancing detective"); a stylish young mystery writer (Mignon Eberhart's Susan Dare); a wise Jewish mother who always knows best (James Yaffe's "Mom") and one English mother (G.D.H. and Margaret Cole's Mrs. Warrender); a detecting nun (Anthony Boucher's Sister Ursula); and other such diverse individuals as a cab driver, a newspaper reporter, a consulting psychiatrist, a criminal-turned-detective, a retired theatrical performer, two policewomen, three private eyes, a Washington D.C. socialite and counterspy, and a Umatilla Indian animal-control officer.

Puzzling and provocative, these stories are some of the most entertaining that mystery fiction has to offer. And that makes them—and the women whose deductive talents are featured in each—very good indeed.

Pleasant reading.

Marcia Muller and Bill Pronzini
September 1988

Lady on the Case

THE MURDER AT TROYTE'S HILL

C. L. Pirkis

"Griffiths, of the Newcastle Constabulary, has the case in hand," said Mr. Dyer. "Those Newcastle men are keenwitted, shrewd fellows, and very jealous of outside interference. They only sent to me under protest, as it were, because they wanted your sharp wits at work inside the house."

"I suppose throughout I am to work with Griffiths, not with you?" said Miss Brooke.

"Yes; when I have given you in outline the facts of the case, I simply have nothing more to do with it, and you must depend on Griffiths for assistance of any sort that you may require."

Here, with a swing, Mr. Dyer opened his big ledger and turned rapidly over its leaves till he came to the heading "Troyte's Hill" and the date "September 6th."

"I am all attention," said Loveday, leaning back in her chair in the attitude of a listener.

"The murdered man," resumed Mr. Dyer, "is a certain Alexander Henderson—usually known as old Sandy—lodge-keeper to Mr. Craven, of Troyte's Hill, Cumberland. The lodge consists merely of two rooms on the ground floor, a bedroom and a sitting room; these Sandy occupied alone, having neither kith nor kin of any degree. On the morning of September sixth, some children, going up to the house with milk from the farm, noticed that Sandy's bedroom window stood wide open. Curiosity prompted them to peep in; and then, to their horror, they saw old Sandy, in his nightshirt, lying dead on the floor, as if he had fallen backwards from the window. They raised an alarm; and on examination it was found that death had ensued from a heavy blow on the temple, given either by a strong fist or some blunt instrument. The room, on being entered, presented a curious appearance. It was as if a herd of monkeys had been turned into it and allowed to work their impish will. Not an article of furniture remained in its place: the bedclothes had been rolled into a bundle and stuffed into the chimney; the bedstead—a small iron one—lay on its side; the one chair in the room stood on the top of the table; fender and fire irons lay across the washstand, whose basin was to be found in a farther corner, holding bolster and pillow. The clock stood on its head in the middle of the mantelpiece; and the small vases and ornaments, which flanked it on either side, were walking, as it were, in a straight line towards the door. The old man's clothes had been rolled into a ball and thrown on the top of a high cupboard in which he kept his savings and whatever valuables he had. This cupboard, however, had not been meddled with, and its contents remained intact, so it was evident that robbery was not the motive for the crime. At the inquest, subsequently held, a verdict of 'wilful murder' against some person or persons unknown was returned. The local police are diligently investigating the affair, but, as yet, no arrests have been made. The opinion that at present prevails in the neighborhood is that the crime has been perpetrated by some lunatic, escaped or otherwise, and inquiries are being made at the local asylums as to missing or lately released inmates. Griffiths, however, tells me that his suspicions set in another direction."

"Did anything of importance transpire at the inquest?"

"Nothing specially important. Mr. Craven broke down in giving his evidence when he alluded to the confidential relations that had always subsisted between Sandy and himself, and spoke of the last time that he had seen him alive. The evidence of the butler, and one or two of the female servants, seems clear enough, and they let fall something of a hint that Sandy was not altogether a favorite among them, on account of the overbearing manner in which he used his influence with his master. Young Mr. Craven, a youth of about twenty, home from Oxford for the long vacation, was not present at the inquest; a doctor's certificate was put in stating that he was suffering from typhoid fever, and could not leave his bed without risk to his life. Now this young man is a thoroughly bad sort, and as much a gentleman-blackleg as it is possible for such a young fellow to be. It seems to Griffiths that there is something suspicious about this illness of his. He came back from Oxford on the verge of delirium tremens, pulled round from that, and then suddenly, on the day after the murder, Mrs. Craven rings the bell, announces that he has developed typhoid fever, and orders a doctor to be sent for."

"What sort of man is Mr. Craven senior?"

"He seems to be a quiet old fellow, a scholar and learned philologist. Neither his neighbors nor his family see much of him; he almost lives in his study, writing a treatise, in seven or eight volumes, on comparative philology. He is not a rich man. Troyte's Hill, though it carries position in the county, is not a paying property, and Mr. Craven is unable to keep it up properly. I am told he has had to cut down expenses in all directions in order to send his son to college, and his daughter, from first to last, has been entirely educated by her mother. Mr. Craven was originally intended for the Church, but for some reason or other, when his college career came to an end, he did not present himself for ordination—went out to Natal instead, where he obtained some civil appointment, and where he remained for about fifteen years. Henderson was his servant during the latter portion of his Oxford career, and must have been greatly respected by him, for although the remuneration derived from his appointment at Natal was small, he paid Sandy a regular yearly allowance out of it. When, about ten years ago, he succeeded to Troyte's Hill, on the death of his elder brother, and returned home with his family, Sandy was immediately installed as lodge-keeper, and at so high a rate of pay that the butler's wages were cut down to meet it."

"Ah, that wouldn't improve the butler's feelings towards him," ejaculated Loveday.

Mr. Dyer went on: "But, in spite of his high wages, he doesn't appear to have troubled much about his duties as lodge-keeper, for they were performed, as a rule, by the gardener's boy, while he took his meals and passed his time at the house, and, speaking generally, put his finger into every pie. You know the old adage respecting the servant of twenty-one years' standing: 'Seven years my servant, seven years my equal, seven years my master.' Well, it appears to have held good in the case of Mr. Craven and Sandy. The old gentleman, absorbed in his philological studies, evidently let the reins slip through his fingers, and Sandy seems to have taken easy possession of them. The servants frequently had to go to him for orders, and he carried things, as a rule, with a high hand."

"Did Mrs. Craven never have a word to say on the matter?"

"I've not heard much about her. She seems to be a quiet sort of person. She is a Scotch missionary's daughter; perhaps she spends her time working for the Cape mission and that sort of thing."

"And young Mr. Craven: did he knock under to Sandy's rule?"

"Ah, now you're hitting the bull's-eye and we come to Griffith's theory. The young man and Sandy appear to have been at loggerheads ever since the Cravens took possession of Troyte's Hill. As a schoolboy

Master Harry defied Sandy and threatened him with his hunting crop; and subsequently, as a young man, has used strenuous endeavors to put the old servant in his place. On the day before the murder, Griffiths says, there was a terrible scene between the two, in which the young gentleman, in the presence of several witnesses, made use of strong language and threatened the old man's life. Now, Miss Brooke, I have told you all the circumstances of the case so far as I know them. For fuller particulars I must refer you to Griffiths. He, no doubt, will meet you at Grenfell—the nearest station to Troyte's Hill—and tell you in what capacity he has procured for you an entrance into the house. By the way, he has wired to me this morning that he hopes you will be able to save the Scotch express tonight."

Loveday expressed her readiness to comply with Mr. Griffiths' wishes.

"I shall be glad," said Mr. Dyer, as he shook hands with her at the office door, "to see you immediately on your return—that, however, I suppose, will not be yet awhile. This promises, I fancy, to be a longish affair?" This was said interrogatively.

"I haven't the least idea on the matter," answered Loveday. "I start on my work without theory of any sort—in fact, I may say, with my mind a perfect blank."

And any one who had caught a glimpse of her blank, expressionless features, as she said this, would have taken her at her word.

Grenfell, the nearest post town to Troyte's Hill, is a fairly busy, populous little town—looking south toward the Black Country, and northward to low, barren hills. Pre-eminent among these stands Troyte's Hill, famed in the old days as a border keep, and possibly at a still earlier date as a Druid stronghold.

At a small inn at Grenfell, dignified by the title of "The Station Hotel," Mr. Griffiths, of the Newcastle Constabulary, met Loveday, and still further initiated her into the mysteries of the Troyte's Hill murder.

"A little of the first excitement has subsided," he said, after preliminary greetings had been exchanged; "but still the wildest rumors are flying about and repeated as solemnly as if they were Gospel truths. My chief here and my colleagues generally adhere to their first conviction, that the criminal is some suddenly crazed tramp or else an escaped lunatic, and they are confident that sooner or later we shall come upon his traces. Their theory is that Sandy, hearing some strange noise at the park gates, put his head out of the window to ascertain the cause, and immediately had his death-blow dealt him; then they suppose that the lunatic scrambled into the room through the window and exhausted his frenzy by turning things generally upside down. They refuse altogether to share my suspicions respecting young Mr. Craven."

Mr. Griffiths was a tall, thin-featured man, with iron-gray hair, cut so close to his head that it refused to do anything but stand on end. This gave a somewhat comic expression to the upper portion of his face, and clashed oddly with the melancholy look that his mouth habitually wore.

"I have made all smooth for you at Troyte's Hill," he presently went on. "Mr. Craven is not wealthy enough to allow himself the luxury of a family lawyer, so he occasionally employs Messrs. Wells and Sugden, lawyers in this place, and who, as it happens, have, off and on, done a good deal of business for me. It was through them I heard that Mr. Craven was anxious to secure the assistance of an amanuensis. I immediately offered your services, stating that you were a friend of mine, a lady of impoverished means, who would gladly undertake the duties for the munificent sum of a guinea a month, with board and lodging. The old gentleman at once jumped at the offer, and is anxious for you to be at Troyte's Hill as soon as possible."

Loveday expressed her satisfaction with the program that Mr. Griffiths had sketched for her; then she had a few questions to ask.

"Tell me," she said, "what led you, in the first instance, to suspect young Mr. Craven of the crime?"

"The footing on which he and Sandy stood toward each other, and the terrible scene that occurred between them only the day before the murder," answered Griffiths promptly. "Nothing of this, however, was elicited at the inquest, where a very fair face was put on Sandy's relations with the whole of the Craven family. I have subsequently unearthed a good deal respecting the private life of Mr. Harry Craven, and, among other things, I have found out that on the night of the murder he left the house shortly after ten o'clock, and no one, so far as I have been able to ascertain, knows at what hour he returned. Now I must draw your attention, Miss Brooke, to the fact that at the inquest the medical evidence went to prove that the murder had been committed between ten and eleven at night."

"Do you surmise, then, that the murder was a planned thing on the part of this young man?"

"I do. I believe that he wandered about the grounds until Sandy shut himself in for the night, then aroused him by some outside noise, and, when the old man looked out to ascertain the cause, dealt him a blow with a bludgeon or loaded stick that caused his death."

"A cold-blooded crime that, for a young fellow of twenty!"

"Yes. He's a good-looking, gentlemanly youngster, too, with manners as mild as milk, but from all accounts is as full of wickedness as an egg is full of meat. Now, to come to another point—if, in connection with these ugly facts, you take into consideration the suddenness of his illness, I think you'll admit that it bears a suspicious appearance, and might reasonably give rise to the surmise that it was a plant on his part in order to keep out of the inquest."

"Who is the doctor attending him?"

"A man called Waters; not much of a practitioner, from all accounts, and no doubt he feels himself highly honored in being summoned to Troyte's Hill. The Cravens, it seems, have no family doctor. Mrs. Craven, with her missionary experience, is half a doctor herself, and never calls in one except in a serious emergency."

"The certificate was in order, I suppose?"

"Undoubtedly. And, as if to give color to the gravity of the case, Mrs. Craven sent a message down to the servants, that if any of them were afraid of the infection they could at once go to their homes. Several of the maids, I believe, took advantage of her permission, and packed their boxes. Miss Craven, who is a delicate girl, was sent away with her maid to stay with friends at Newcastle, and Mrs. Craven isolated herself with her patient in one of the disused wings of the house."

"Has any one ascertained whether Miss Craven arrived at her destination at Newcastle?"

Griffiths drew his brows together in thought.

"I did not see any necessity for such a thing," he answered. "I don't quite follow you. What do you mean to imply?"

"Oh, nothing. I don't suppose it matters much: it might have been interesting as a side-issue." She broke off for a moment, then added:

"Now tell me a little about the butler, the man whose wages were cut down to increase Sandy's pay."

"Old John Hales? He's a thoroughly worthy, respectable man; he was butler for five or six years to Mr. Craven's brother, when he was master of Troyte's Hill, and then took duty under this Mr. Craven. There's no ground for suspicion in that quarter. Hales's exclamation when he heard of the murder is quite enough to stamp him as an innocent man: 'Serve the old idiot right!' he cried: 'I couldn't pump up a tear for him if I tried for a month of Sundays!' Now I take it, Miss Brooke, a guilty man wouldn't dare make such a speech as that!"

"You think not?"

Griffiths stared at her. "I'm a little disappointed in her," he thought. "I'm afraid her powers have been slightly exaggerated if she can't see such a straightforward thing as that."

Aloud he said, a little sharply, "Well, I don't stand alone in my thinking. No one yet has breathed a word against Hales, and if they did I've no doubt he could prove an alibi without any trouble, for he lives in the house, and every one has a good word for him."

"I suppose Sandy's lodge has been put into order by this time?"

"Yes; after the inquest, and when all possible evidence had been taken, everything was put straight."

"At the inquest it was stated that no marks of footsteps could be traced in any direction?"

"The long drought we've had would render such a thing impossible, let alone the fact that Sandy's lodge stands right on the graveled drive, without flowerbeds or grass borders of any sort around it. But look here, Miss Brooke, don't you be wasting your time over the lodge and its surroundings. Every iota of fact on that matter has been gone through over and over again by me and my chief. What we want you to do is to go straight into the house and concentrate attention on Master Harry's sickroom, and find out what's going on there. What he did outside the house on the night of the sixth, I've no doubt I shall be able to find out for myself. Now, Miss Brooke, you've asked me no end of questions, to which I have replied as fully as it was in my power to do; will you be good enough to answer one question that I wish to put, as straightforwardly as I have answered yours? You have had fullest particulars given you of the condition of Sandy's room when the police entered it on the morning after the murder. No doubt, at the present moment, you can see it all in your mind's eye—the bedstead on its side, the clock on its head, the bedclothes halfway up the chimney, the little vases and ornaments walking in a straight line towards the door?"

Loveday inclined her head.

"Very well. Now will you be good enough to tell me what this scene of confusion recalls to your mind before anything else?"

"The room of an unpopular Oxford freshman after a raid upon it by undergrads," answered Loveday promptly.

Mr. Griffiths rubbed his hands.

"Quite so!" he ejaculated. "I see, after all, we are one at heart in this matter, in spite of a little surface disagreement of ideas. Depend upon it, by and by, like the engineers tunneling from different quarters under the Alps, we shall meet at the same point and shake hands. By the way, I have arranged for daily communication between us through the postboy who takes the letters to Troyte's Hill. He is trustworthy, and any letter you give him for me will find its way into my hands within the hour."

It was about three o'clock in the afternoon when Loveday drove in through the park gates of Troyte's Hill, past the lodge where old Sandy had met with his death. It was a pretty little cottage, covered with Virginia creeper and wild honeysuckle, and showed no outward sign of the tragedy that had been enacted within.

The park and pleasure grounds of Troyte's Hill were extensive, and the house itself was a somewhat imposing red brick structure, built, possibly, at the time when Dutch William's taste had grown popular in the country. Its frontage presented a somewhat forlorn appearance, its center windows—a square of eight—alone seeming to show signs of occupation. With the exception of two windows at the extreme end of the bedroom floor of the north wing, where, possibly, the invalid and his mother were located, and two windows at the extreme end of the ground floor of the south wing, which Loveday ascertained subsequently were those of Mr. Craven's study, not a single window in either wing owned blind or curtain. The wings were extensive, and it was easy to understand that at the extreme end of the one the fever patient would be isolated from the rest of the household, and that at the extreme end of the other Mr. Craven could secure the quiet and freedom from interruption which, no doubt, were essential to the due prosecution of his philological studies.

Alike on the house and on the ill-kept grounds were present the stamp of the smallness of the income of the master and owner of the place. The terrace, which ran the length of the house in front, and on to which every window on the ground floor opened, was miserably out of repair: not a lintel or doorpost, window ledge or balcony, but what seemed to cry aloud for the touch of the painter. "Pity me! I have seen better days," Loveday could fancy written as a legend across the red brick porch that gave entrance to the old house.

The butler, John Hales, admitted Loveday, shouldered her portmanteau, and told her he would show her to her room. He was a tall, powerfully built man, with a ruddy face and dogged expression of countenance. It was easy to understand that, off and on, there must have been many a sharp encounter between him and old Sandy. He treated Loveday in an easy, familiar fashion, evidently considering that an amanuensis took much the same rank as a nursery governess—that is to say, a little below a lady's maid and a little above a housemaid.

"We're short of hands, just now," he said, in broad Cumberland dialect, as he led the way up the wide staircase. "Some of the lasses downstairs took fright at the fever and went home. Cook and I are singlehanded, for Moggie, the only maid left, has been told off to wait on Madam and Master Harry. I hope you're not afeared of fever?"

Loveday answered that she was not, and asked if the room at the extreme end of the north wing was the one assigned to "Madam and Master Harry."

"Yes," said the man; "it's convenient for sick nursing; there's a flight of stairs runs straight down from it to the kitchen quarters. We put all Madam wants at the foot of those stairs and Moggie comes down and fetches it. Moggie herself never enters the sickroom. I take it you'll not be seeing Madam for many a day, yet awhile."

"When shall I see Mr. Craven? At dinner tonight?"

"That's what naebody could say," answered Hales. "He may not come out of his study till past midnight; sometimes he sits there till two or three in the morning. Shouldn't advise you to wait till he wants his dinner—better have a cup of tea and a chop sent up to you. Madam never waits for him at any meal."

As he finished speaking he deposited the portmanteau outside one of the many doors opening into the gallery.

"This is Miss Craven's room," he went on; "Cook and me thought you'd better have it, as it would want less getting ready than the other rooms, and work is work when there are so few hands to do it. Oh, my stars! I do declare there is cook putting it straight for you now."

The last sentence was added as the opened door laid bare to view the cook, with duster in her hand, polishing a mirror; the bed had been made, it is true, but otherwise the room must have been much as Miss Craven had left it, after a hurried packing up.

To the surprise of the two servants Loveday took the matter very lightly.

"I have a special talent for arranging rooms, and would prefer getting this one straight for myself," she said. "Now, if you will go and get ready that chop and cup of tea we were talking about just now, I shall think it much kinder than if you stayed here doing what I can so easily do for myself."

When, however, the cook and butler had departed in company, Loveday showed no disposition to exercise the "special talent" of which she had boasted.

She first carefully turned the key in the lock, and then proceeded to make a thorough and minute investigation of every corner of the room. Not an article of furniture, not an ornament or toilet accessory, but what was lifted from its place and carefully scrutinized. Even the ashes in the grate, the debris of the last fire made there, were raked over and well looked through.

This careful investigation of Miss Craven's late surroundings occupied in all about three-quarters of an hour, and Loveday, with her hat in her hand, descended the stairs to see Hales crossing the hall to the dining room with the promised cup of tea and chop.

In silence and solitude she partook of the simple repast in a dining hall that could with ease have banqueted a hundred and fifty guests.

"Now for the grounds before it gets dark," she said to herself, as she noted that already the outside shadows were beginning to slant.

The dining hall was at the back of the house; and here, as in the front, the windows, reaching to the ground, presented easy means of egress. The flower garden was on this side of the house, and sloped downhill to a pretty stretch of well-wooded country.

Loveday did not linger here even to admire, but passed at once round the south corner of the house to the windows which she had ascertained, by a careless question to the butler, were those of Mr. Craven's study.

Very cautiously she drew near them, for the blinds were up, the curtains drawn back. A side glance, however, relieved her apprehensions, for it showed her the occupant of the room, seated in an easy chair, with his back to the windows. From the length of his outstretched limbs he was evidently a tall man. His hair was silvery and curly, the lower part of his face was hidden from her view by the chair, but she could see that one hand was pressed tightly across his eyes and brows. The whole attitude was that of a man absorbed in deep thought. The room was comfortably furnished, but presented an appearance of disorder from the books and manuscripts scattered in all directions. A whole pile of torn fragments of foolscap sheets, overflowing from a wastepaper basket beside the writing table, seemed to proclaim the fact that the scholar had of late grown weary of or else dissatisfied with his work, and had condemned it freely.

Although Loveday stood looking in at this window for over five minutes, not the faintest sign of life did that tall, reclining figure give, and it would have been as easy to believe him locked in sleep as in thought.

From here she turned her steps in the direction of Sandy's lodge. As Griffiths had said, it was graveled up to its doorstep. The blinds were closely drawn, and it presented the ordinary appearance of a disused cottage.

A narrow path beneath overarching boughs of cherrylaurel and arbutus, immediately facing the lodge, caught her eye, and down this she at once turned her footsteps.

This path led, with many a wind and turn, through a belt of shrubbery that skirted the frontage of Mr. Craven's grounds, and eventually, after much zigzagging, ended in close proximity to the stables. As Loveday entered it, she seemed literally to leave daylight behind her.

"I feel as if I were following the course of a circuitous mind," she said to herself as the shadows closed around her. "I could fancy the great Machiavelli himself delighting in such a wind-about alley as this!"

The path showed grayly in front of her out of the dimness. On and on she followed it; here and there the roots of the old laurels, struggling out of the ground, threatened to trip her up. Her eyes, however, had now grown accustomed to the half-gloom, and not a detail of her surroundings escaped her as she went along.

A bird flew from out the thicket on her right hand with a startled cry. A dainty little frog leaped out of her way into the shriveled leaves lying below the laurels. Following the movements of this frog, her eye was caught by something black and solid among those leaves. What was it? A bundle—a shiny black coat? Loveday knelt down, and using her hands to assist her eyes, found that they came into contact with the dead, stiffened body of a beautiful black retriever. She parted, as well as she was able, the lower boughs of the evergreens, and minutely examined the poor animal. Its eyes were still open, though glazed and bleared, and its death had, undoubtedly, been caused by the blow of some blunt, heavy instrument, for on one side its skull was almost battered in.

"Exactly the death that was dealt to Sandy," she thought, as she groped hither and thither beneath the trees in hopes of lighting upon the weapon of destruction.

She searched until increasing darkness warned her that search was useless. Then, still following the zigzagging path, she made her way out by the stables and thence back to the house.

She went to bed that night without having spoken to a soul beyond the cook and butler. The next morning, however, Mr. Craven introduced himself to her across the breakfast table. He was a man of really handsome personal appearance, with a fine carriage of the head and shoulders, and eyes that had a forlorn, appealing look in them. He entered the room with an air of great energy, apologized to Loveday for the absence of his wife, and for his own remissness in not being in the way to receive her on the previous day. Then he bade her make herself at home at the breakfast table, and expressed his delight in having found a coadjutor in his work.

"I hope you understand what a great—a stupendous work it is?" he added, as he sank into a chair. "It is a work that will leave its impress upon thought in all the ages to come. Only a man who has studied comparative philology as I have for the past thirty years could gauge the magnitude of the task I have set myself."

With the last remark, his energy seemed spent, and he sank back in his chair, covering his eyes with his hand in precisely the same attitude as that in which Loveday had seen him overnight, and utterly oblivious of the fact that breakfast was before him and a stranger-guest seated at table. The butler entered with another dish. "Better go on with your breakfast," he whispered to Loveday; "he may sit like that for another hour."

He placed his dish in front of his master.

"Captain hasn't come back yet, sir," he said, making an effort to arouse him from his reverie.

"Eh, what?" said Mr. Craven, for a moment lifting his hand from his eyes.

"Captain, sir—the black retriever," repeated the man.

The pathetic look in Mr. Craven's eyes deepened.

"Ah, poor Captain!" he murmured; "the best dog I ever had."

Then he again sank back in his chair, putting his hand to his forehead.

The butler made one more effort to arouse him.

"Madam sent you down a newspaper, sir, that she thought you would like to see," he shouted almost into his master's ear, and at the same time laid the morning's paper on the table beside his plate.

"Confound you! leave it there," said Mr. Craven irritably. "Fools! dolts that you all are! With your trivialities and interruptions you are sending me out of the world with my work undone!"

And again he sank back in his chair, closed his eyes, and became lost to his surroundings.

Loveday went on with her breakfast. She changed her place at table to one on Mr. Craven's right hand, so that the newspaper sent down for his persual lay between his plate and hers. It was folded into an oblong shape, as if it were wished to direct attention to a certain portion of a certain column.

A clock in a corner of the room struck the hour with a loud, resonant stroke. Mr. Craven gave a start and rubbed his eyes.

"Eh, what's this?" he said. "What meal are we at?" He looked around with a bewildered air. "Eh!—who are you?" he went on, staring hard at Loveday. "What are you doing here? Where's Nina?—Where's Harry?"

Loveday began to explain, and gradually recollection seemed to come back to him.

"Ah, yes, yes," he said. "I remember; you've come to assist me with my great work. You promised, you know, to help me out of the hole I've got into. Very enthusiastic, I remember they said you were, on certain abstruse points in comparative philology. Now, Miss—Miss—I've forgotten your name—tell me a little of what you know about the elemental sounds of speech that are common to all languages. Now, to how many would you reduce those elemental sounds—to six, eight, nine? No, we won't discuss the matter here, the cups and saucers distract me. Come into my den at the other end of the house; we'll have perfect quiet there."

And, utterly ignoring the fact that he had not as yet broken his fast, he rose from the table, seized Loveday by the wrist, and led her out of the room and down the long corridor that led through the south wing to his study.

But seated in that study his energy once more speedily exhausted itself.

He placed Loveday in a comfortable chair at his writing table, consulted her taste as to pens, and spread a sheet of foolscap before her. Then he settled himself in his easy chair, with his back to the light, as if he were about to dictate folios to her.

In a loud, distinct voice he repeated the title of his learned work, then its subdivision, then the number and heading of the chapter that was at present engaging his attention. Then he put his hand to his head. "It's the elemental sounds that are my stumbling-block," he said. "Now, how on earth is it possible to get a notion of a sound of agony that is not in part a sound of terror? or a sound of surprise that is not in part a sound of either joy or sorrow?"

With this his energies were spent, and although Loveday remained seated in that study from early morning till daylight began to fade, she had not ten sentences to show for her day's work as amanuensis.

Loveday in all spent only two clear days at Troyte's Hill.

On the evening of the first of those days Detective Griffiths received, through the trustworthy postboy, the following brief note from her:

I have found out that Hales owed Sandy close upon a hundred pounds, which he had borrowed at various times. I don't know whether you will think this fact of any importance.—L.B.

Mr. Griffiths repeated the last sentence blankly. "If Harry Craven were put upon his defense, his counsel, I take it, would consider the fact of first importance," he muttered. And for the remainder of that day Mr. Griffiths went about his work in a perturbed state of mind, doubtful whether to hold or to let go his theory concerning Harry Craven's guilt.

The next morning there came another brief note from Loveday, which ran thus:

As a matter of collateral interest, find out if a person, calling himself Harold Cousins, sailed two days ago from London Docks for Natal in the Bonnie Dundee.

To this missive Loveday received in reply the following somewhat lengthy despatch:

I do not quite see the drift of your last note, but have wired to our agents in London to carry out its suggestion. On my part, I have important news to communicate. I have found out what Harry Craven's business out of doors was on the night of the murder, and at my instance a warrant has been issued for his arrest. This warrant it will be my duty to serve on him in the course of today. Things are beginning to look very black against him, and I am convinced his illness is all a sham. I have seen Waters, the man who is supposed to be attending him, and have driven him into a corner and made him admit that he has only seen young Craven once—on the first day of his illness—and that he gave his certificate entirely on the strength of what Mrs. Craven told him of her son's condition. On the occasion of this, his first and only visit, the lady, it seems, also told him that it would not be necessary for him to continue his attendance, as she felt herself quite competent to treat the case, having had so much experience in fever cases among the blacks at Natal.

As I left Waters's house, after eliciting this important information, I was accosted by a man who keeps a low-class inn in the place, McQueen by name. He said that he wished to speak to me on a matter of importance. To make a long story short, this McQueen stated that on the night of the sixth, shortly after eleven o'clock, Harry Craven came to his house, bringing him a val-

uable piece of plate—a handsome epergne—and requested him to lend him a hundred pounds on it, as he hadn't a penny in his pocket. McQueen complied with his request to the extent of ten sovereigns, and now, in a fit of nervous terror, comes to me to confess himself a receiver of stolen goods and play the honest man! He says he noticed that the young gentleman was very much agitated as he made the request, and he also begged him to mention his vist to no one. Now, I am curious to learn how Master Harry will get over the fact that he passed the lodge at the hour at which the murder was most probably committed; or how he will get out of the dilemma of having repassed the lodge on his way back to the house, and not noticed the wide-open window with the full moon shining down on it?

Another word! Keep out of the way when I arrive at the house, somewhere between two and three in the afternoon, to serve the warrant. I do not wish your professional capacity to get wind, for you will most likely yet be of some use to us in the house.—S.G.

Loveday read this note, seated at Mr. Craven's writing table, with the old gentleman himself reclining motionless beside her in his easy chair. A little smile played about the corners of her mouth as she read over again the words—"for you will most likely yet be of some use to us in the house."

Loveday's second day in Mr. Craven's study promised to be as unfruitful as the first. For fully an hour after she had received Griffiths' note, she sat at the writing table with her pen in her hand, ready to transcribe Mr. Craven's inspirations. Beyond, however, the phrase, muttered with closed eyes—"It's all here, in my brain, but I can't put it into words"—not a half-syllable escaped his lips.

At the end of that hour the sound of footsteps on the outside gravel made her turn her head towards the window. It was Griffiths approaching with two constables. She heard the hall door opened to admit them, but beyond that not a sound reached her ear, and she realized how fully she was cut off from communication with the rest of the household at the farther end of this unoccupied wing.

Mr. Craven, still reclining in his semi-trance, evidently had not the faintest suspicion that so important an event as the arrest of his only son on a charge of murder was about to be enacted in the house.

Meantime, Griffiths and his constables had mounted the stairs leading to the north wing, and were being guided through the corridors to the sickroom by the flying figure of Moggie, the maid.

"Hoot, mistress!" cried the girl, "here are three men coming up the stairs—policemen, every one of them—will ye come and ask them what they be wanting?"

Outside the door of the sickroom stood Mrs. Craven—a tall, sharp-featured woman with sandy hair going rapidly to gray.

"What is the meaning of this? What is your business here?" she said haughtily, addressing Griffiths, who headed the party.

Griffiths respectfully explained what his business was, and requested her to stand on one side that he might enter her son's room.

"This is my daughter's room; satisfy yourself of the fact," said the lady, throwing back the door as she spoke.

And Griffiths and his confreres entered, to find pretty Miss Craven, looking very white and scared, seated beside a fire in a long, flowing *robe-de-chambre*.

Griffiths departed in haste and confusion, without the chance of a professional talk with Loveday. That afternoon saw him telegraphing wildly in all directions, and despatching messengers in all quarters. Finally, he spent over an hour drawing up an elaborate report to his chief at Newcastle, assuring him of the identity of one Harold Cousins, who had sailed in the *Bonnie Dundee* for Natal, with Harry Craven, of Troyte's Hill, and advising that the police authorities in that faraway district should be immediately communicated with.

The ink had not dried on the pen with which this report was written before a note, in Loveday's writing, was put into his hand.

Loveday evidently had had some difficulty in finding a messenger for this note, for it was brought by a gardener's boy, who informed Griffiths that the lady had said he would receive a gold sovereign if he delivered the letter all right.

Griffiths paid the boy and dismissed him, and then proceeded to read Loveday's communication.

It was written hurriedly in pencil, and ran as follows:

> *Things are getting critical here. Directly you receive this, come up to the house with two of your men, and post yourselves anywhere in the grounds where you can see and not be seen. There will be no difficulty in this, for it will be dark by the time you are able to get there. I am not sure whether I shall want your aid tonight, but you had better keep in the grounds until morning, in case of need; and, above all, never once lose sight of the study windows. [This was underscored.] If I put a lamp with a green shade in one of those windows, do not lose a moment in entering by that window, which I will contrive to keep unlocked.*

Griffiths rubbed his forehead—rubbed his eyes, as he finished reading this.

"Well, I daresay it's all right," he said, "but I'm bothered, that's all, and for the life of me I can't see one step of the way she is going."

He looked at his watch; the hands pointed to a quarter past six. The short September day was drawing rapidly to a close. A good five miles lay between him and Troyte's Hill—there was evidently not a moment to lose.

At the very moment that Griffiths, with his two constables, were once more starting along the Grenfell High Road behind the best horse they could procure, Mr. Craven was rousing himself from his long slumber, and beginning to look around him. That slumber, however, though long, had not been a peaceful one, and it was sundry of the old gentleman's muttered exclamations, as he had started uneasily in his sleep, that had caused Loveday to pen, and then to creep out of the room to despatch, her hurried note.

What effect the occurrence of the morning had had upon the household generally, Loveday, in her isolated corner of the house, had no means of ascertaining. She only noted that when Hales brought in her tea, as he did precisely at five o'clock, he wore a particularly ill-tempered expression of countenance, and she heard him mutter, as he set down the tea tray with a clatter, something about being a respectable man, and not used to such "goings on."

It was not until nearly an hour and a half after this that Mr. Craven had awakened with a sudden start, and, looking wildly around him, had questioned Loveday as to who had entered the room.

Loveday explained that the butler had brought in lunch at one, and tea at five, but that since then no one had come in.

"Now that's false," said Mr. Craven, in a sharp, unnatural sort of voice; "I saw him sneaking round the room, the whining, canting hypocrite, and you must have seen him, too. Didn't you hear him say, in his squeaky old voice, 'Master, I knows your secret—' " He broke off abruptly, looking wildly round. "Eh, what's this?" he cried. "No, no, I'm all wrong—Sandy is dead and buried—they held an inquest on him, and we all praised him up as if he were a saint."

"He must have been a bad man, that old Sandy," said Loveday sympathetically.

"You're right! you're right!" cried Mr. Craven, springing up excitedly from his chair and seizing her by the hand. "If ever a man deserved his death, he did. For thirty years he held that rod over my head, and then—ah, where was I?"

He put his hand to his head, and again sank, as if exhausted, into his chair.

"I suppose it was some early indiscretion of yours at college that he knew of?" said Loveday, eager to get at as much of the truth as possible while the mood for confidence held sway in the feeble brain.

"That was it! I was fool enough to marry a disreputable girl—a barmaid in the town—and Sandy was present at the wedding, and then—" Here his eyes closed again and his mutterings became incoherent.

For ten minutes he lay back in his chair, muttering thus. "A yelp—a groan," were the only words Loveday could distinguish among those mutterings, then, suddenly, slowly and distinctly, he said, as if answering some plainly put question: "A good blow with the hammer and the thing was done."

"I should like amazingly to see that hammer," said Loveday; "do you keep it anywhere at hand?"

His eyes opened with a wild, cunning look in them.

"Who's talking about a hammer? I did not say I had one. If any one says I did it with a hammer, they're telling a lie."

"Oh, you've spoken to me about the hammer, two or three times," said Loveday calmly; "the one that killed your dog, Captain, and I should like to see it, that's all."

The look of cunning died out of the old man's eye. "Ah, poor Captain! splendid dog that! Well, now, where were we? Where did we leave off? Ah, I remember, it was the elemental sounds of speech that bothered me so that night. Were you here then? Ah, no! I remember. I had been trying all day to assimilate a dog's yelp of pain to a human groan, and I couldn't do it. The idea haunted me—followed me about wherever I went. If they were both elemental sounds, they must have something in common, but the link between them I could not find; then it occurred to me, would a well-bred, well-trained dog like my Captain in the stables, there, at the moment of death give an unmitigated currish yelp; would there not be something of a human note in his death cry? The thing was worth putting to the test. If I could hand down in my treatise a fragment of fact on the matter, it would be worth a dozen dogs' lives. So I went out into the moonlight—ah! but you know all about it—now, don't you?"

"Yes. Poor Captain! did he yelp or groan?"

"Why, he gave one loud, long, hideous yelp, just as if he had been a common cur. I might just as well have let him alone; it only set that other brute opening his window and spying out on me, and saying in his cracked old voice, 'Master, what are you doing out here at this time of night?' "

Again he sank back in his chair, muttering incoherently with half-closed eyes.

Loveday let him alone for a minute or so; then she had another question to ask.

"And that other brute—did he yelp or groan when you dealt him his blow?"

"What, old Sandy—the brute? He fell back. Ah, I remember, you said you would like to see the hammer that stopped his babbling old tongue—now, didn't you?"

He rose a little unsteadily from his chair, and seemed to drag his long limbs with an effort across the room to a cabinet at the farther end. Opening a drawer in this cabinet, he produced, from amidst some specimens of strata and fossils, a large-sized geological hammer.

He brandished it for a moment over his head, then paused with his finger on his lip.

"Hush!" he said, "we shall have the fools creeping in to peep at us if we don't take care." And to Loveday's horror he suddenly made for the door, turned the key in the lock, withdrew it, and put it into his pocket.

She looked at the clock; the hands pointed to half-past seven. Had Griffiths received her note at the proper time, and were the men now in the grounds? She could only pray that they were.

"The light is too strong for my eyes," she said, and, rising from her chair, she lifted the green-shaded lamp and placed it on a table that stood at the window.

"No, no, that won't do," said Mr. Craven; "that would show every one outside what we're doing in here." He crossed to the window as he spoke and removed the lamp thence to the mantelpiece.

Loveday could only hope that in the few seconds it had remained in the window it had caught the eye of the outside watchers.

The old man beckoned to Loveday to come near and examine his deadly weapon. "Give it a good swing round," he said, suiting the action to the word, "and down it comes with a splendid crash." He brought the hammer round within an inch of Loveday's forehead.

She started back.

"Ha, ha!" he laughed harshly and unnaturally, with the light of madness dancing in his eyes now; "did I frighten you? I wonder what sort of sound you would make if I were to give you a little tap just there." Here he lightly touched her forehead with the hammer. "Elemental, of course, it would be, and—"

Loveday steadied her nerves with difficulty. Locked in with this lunatic, her only chance lay in gaining time for the detectives to reach the house and enter through the window.

"Wait a minute," she said, striving to divert his attention; "you have not yet told me what sort of an elemental sound old Sandy made when he fell. If you'll give me pen and ink, I'll write down a full account of it all, and you can incorporate it afterwards in your treatise."

For a moment a look of real pleasure flitted across the old man's face, then it faded. "The brute fell back dead without a sound," he answered; "it was all for nothing, that night's work; yet not altogether for nothing. No, I don't mind owning I would do it all over again to get the wild thrill of joy at my heart that I had when I looked down into that old man's dead face and felt myself free at last! Free at last!" his voice rang out excitedly—once more he brought his hammer round with an ugly swing.

"For a moment I was a young man again; I leaped into his room—the moon was shining full in through the window—I thought of my old college days and the fun we used to have at Pembroke—topsy-turvy I turned everything—" He broke off abruptly, and drew a step nearer to Loveday. "The pity of it all was," he said, suddenly dropping from his high, excited tone to a low, pathetic one, "that he fell without a sound of any sort." Here he drew another step nearer. "I wonder—" he said, then broke off again, and came close to Loveday's side. "It has only this moment occurred to me," he said, now with his lips close to Loveday's ear, "that a woman, in her death agony, would be much more likely to give utterance to an elemental sound than a man."

He raised his hammer, and Loveday fled to the window, which was at that moment opened from the outside by three pairs of strong arms.

"I thought I was conducting my very last case—I never had such a narrow escape before!" said Loveday, as she stood talking with Mr. Griffiths on the Grenfell platform, awaiting the train to carry her back to London. "It seems strange that no one before suspected the old gentleman's sanity—I suppose, however, people were so used to his eccentricities that they did not notice how they had deepened into positive lunacy. His cunning evidently stood him in good stead at the inquest."

"It is possible," said Griffiths thoughtfully, "that he did not absolutely cross the very slender line that divides eccentricity from madness until after the murder. The excitement consequent upon the discovery of the crime may just have pushed him over the border. Now, Miss Brooke, we have exactly ten minutes before your train comes in. I should feel greatly obliged to you if you would explain one or two things that have a professional interest for me."

"With pleasure," said Loveday. "Put your questions in categorical order and I will answer them."

"Well, then, in the first place, what suggested to your mind the old man's guilt?"

"The relations that subsisted between him and Sandy seemed to me to savor too much of fear on the one side and power on the other. Also the income paid to Sandy during Mr. Craven's absence in Natal bore, to my mind, an unpleasant resemblance to hush-money."

"Poor wretched being! And I hear that, after all, the woman he married in his wild young days died soon afterwards of drink. I have no doubt, however, that Sandy sedulously kept up the fiction of her existence, even after his master's second marriage. Now for another question: How was it you knew that Miss Craven had taken her brother's place in the sick-room?"

"On the evening of my arrival I discovered a rather long lock of fair hair in the unswept fireplace of my room, which, as it happened, was usually occupied by Miss Craven. It at once occurred to me that the young lady had been cutting off her hair, and that there must be some powerful motive to induce such a sacrifice. The suspicious circumstances attending her brother's illness soon supplied me with such a motive."

"Ah! that typhoid fever business was very cleverly done. Not a servant in the house, I verily believe, but who thought Master Harry was upstairs, ill in bed, and Miss Craven away at her friends' in Newcastle. The young fellow must have got a clear start off within an hour of the murder. His sister, sent away the next day to Newcastle, dismissed her maid there, I hear, on the plea of no accommodation at her friends' house—sent the girl to her own home for a holiday, and herself returned to Troyte's Hill in the middle of the night, having walked the five miles from Grenfell. No doubt her mother admitted her through one of those easily opened front windows, cut her hair, and put her to bed to personate her brother without delay. With Miss Craven's strong likeness to Master Harry, and in a darkened room, it is easy to understand that the eyes of a doctor, personally unacquainted with the family, might easily be deceived. Now, Miss Brooke, you must admit that with all this elaborate chicanery and double-dealing going on, it was only natural that my suspicions should set in strongly in that quarter."

"I read it all in another light, you see," said Loveday. "It seemed to me that the mother, knowing her son's evil proclivities, believed in his guilt in spite, possibly, of his assertions of innocence. The son, most likely, on his way back to the house after pledging the family plate, had met old Mr. Craven with the hammer in his hand. Seeing, no doubt, how impossible it would be for him to clear himself without incriminating his father, he preferred flight to Natal to giving evidence at the inquest."

"Now about his alias?" said Mr. Griffiths briskly, for the train was at that moment steaming into the station. "How did you know that Harold Cousins was identical with Harry Craven, and had sailed in the *Bonnie Dundee?*"

"Oh, that was easy enough," said Loveday, as she stepped into the train; "a newspaper sent down to Mr. Craven by his wife was folded so as to direct his attention to the shipping list. In it I saw that the *Bonnie Dundee* had sailed two days previously for Natal. Now it was only natural to connect Natal with Mrs. Craven, who had passed the greater part of her life there; and it was easy to understand her wish to get her scapegrace son among her early friends. The alias under which he sailed came readily enough to light. I found it scribbled all over one of Mr. Craven's writing pads in his study; evidently it had been drummed into his ears by his wife as his son's alias, and the old gentleman had taken this method of fixing it in his memory. We'll hope that the young fellow, under his new name, will make a new reputation for himself—at any rate, he'll have a better chance of doing so with the ocean between him and his evil companions. Now it's good-bye, I think."

"No," said Mr. Griffiths; "it's *au revoir,* for you'll have to come back again for the assizes, and give the evidence that will shut old Mr. Craven in an asylum for the rest of his life."

THE MAN IN THE INVERNESS CAPE

Baroness Orczy

Well, you know, some say she is the daughter of a duke, others that she was born in the gutter, and that the handle has been soldered onto her name in order to give her style and influence.

I could say a lot, of course, but "my lips are sealed," as the poets say. All through her successful career at the Yard she honored me with her friendship and confidence, but when she took me in partnership, as it were, she made me promise that I would never breathe a word of her private life, and this I swore on my Bible oath—"wish I may die," and all the rest of it.

Yes, we always called her "my lady," from the moment that she was put at the head of our section; and the chief called her "Lady Molly" in our presence. We of the Female Department are dreadfully snubbed by the men, though don't tell me that women have not ten times as much intuition as the blundering and sterner sex; my firm belief is that we shouldn't have half so many undetected crimes if some of the so-called mysteries were put to the test of feminine investigation.

Many people say—people, too, mind you, who read their daily paper regularly—that it is quite impossible for any one to "disappear" within the confines of the British Isles. At the same time these wise people invariably admit one great exception to their otherwise unimpeachable theory, and that is the case of Mr. Leonard Marvell, who, as you know, walked out one afternoon from the Scotia Hotel in Cromwell Road and has never been seen or heard of since.

Information had originally been given to the police by Mr. Marvell's sister Olive, a Scotchwoman of the usually accepted type: tall, bony, with sandy-colored hair, and a somewhat melancholy expression in her blue-gray eyes.

Her brother, she said, had gone out on a rather foggy afternoon. I think it was the third of February, just about a year ago. His intention had been to go and consult a solicitor in the City—whose address had been given him recently by a friend—about some private business of his own.

Mr. Marvell had told his sister that he would get a train at South Kensington Station to Moorgate Street, and walk thence to Finsbury Square. She was to expect him home by dinner time.

As he was, however, very irregular in his habits, being fond of spending his evenings at restaurants and music halls, the sister did not feel the least anxious when he did not return home at the appointed time. She had her dinner in the *table d'hôte* room, and went to bed soon after ten.

She and her brother occupied two bedrooms and a sitting-room on the second floor of the little private hotel. Miss Marvell, moreover, had a maid always with her, as she was somewhat of an invalid. This girl, Rosie Campbell, a nice-looking Scotch lassie, slept on the top floor.

It was only on the following morning, when Mr. Leonard did not put in an appearance at breakfast, that Miss Marvell began to feel anxious. According to her own account, she sent Rosie in to see if anything was the matter, and the girl, wide-eyed and not a little frightened, came back with the news that Mr. Marvell was not in his room, and that his bed had not been slept in that night.

With characteristic Scottish reserve, Miss Olive said nothing about the matter at the time to any one, nor did she give information to the police until two days later, when she herself had exhausted every means in her power to discover her brother's whereabouts.

She had seen the lawyer to whose office Leonard Marvell had intended going that afternoon, but Mr. Statham, the solicitor in question, had seen nothing of the missing man.

With great adroitness Rosie, the maid, had made inquiries at South Kensington and Moorgate Street Stations. At the former, the booking clerk, who knew Mr. Marvell by sight, distinctly remembered selling him a first-class ticket to one of the City stations in the early part of the afternoon; but at Moorgate Street, which is a very busy station, no one recollected seeing a tall, red-haired Scotchman in an Inverness cape—such was the description given of the missing man. By that time the fog had become very thick in the City; traffic was disorganized, and every one felt fussy, ill-tempered, and self-centered.

These, in substance, were the details which Miss Marvell gave to the police on the subject of her brother's strange disappearance.

At first she did not appear very anxious; she seemed to have great faith in Mr. Marvell's power to look after himself; moreover, she declared positively that her brother had neither valuables nor money about his person when he went out that afternoon.

But as day succeeded day and no trace of the missing man had yet been found, matters became more serious, and the search instituted by our fellows at the Yard waxed more keen.

A description of Mr. Leonard Marvell was published in the leading London and provincial dailies. Unfortunately, there was no good photograph of him extant, and descriptions are apt to prove vague.

Very little was known about the man beyond his disappearance, which had rendered him famous. He and his sister had arrived at the Scotia Hotel about a month previously, and subsequently they were joined by the maid Campbell.

Scotch people are far too reserved ever to speak of themselves or their affairs to strangers. Brother and sister spoke very little to any one at the hotel. They had their meals in their sitting room, waited on by the maid, who messed with the staff. But, in face of the present terrible calamity, Miss Marvell's frigidity relaxed before the police inspector, to whom she gave what information she could about her brother.

"He was like a son to me," she explained with scarcely restrained tears, "for we lost our parents early in life, and as we were left very, very badly off, our relations took but little notice of us. My brother was years younger than I am—and though he was a little wild and fond of pleasure, he was as good as gold to me, and has supported us both for years by journalistic work. We came to London from Glasgow about a month ago, because Leonard got a very good appointment on the staff of the *Daily Post*."

All this, of course, was soon proved to be true; and although, on minute inquiries being instituted in Glasgow, but little seemed to be known about Mr. Leonard Marvell in that city, there seemed no doubt that he had done some reporting for the *Courier*, and that latterly, in response to an advertisement, he had applied for and obtained regular employment on the *Daily Post*.

The latter enterprising halfpenny journal, with characteristic magnanimity, made an offer of £50 reward to any of its subscribers who gave information which would lead to the discovery of the whereabouts of Mr. Leonard Marvell.

But time went by, and that £50 remained unclaimed.

Lady Molly had not seemed as interested as she usually was in cases of this sort. With strange flippancy—wholly unlike herself—she remarked that one Scotch journalist more or less in London did not vastly matter.

I was much amused, therefore, one morning about three weeks after the mysterious disappearance of Mr. Leonard Marvell, when Jane, our little parlor maid, brought in a card accompanied by a letter.

The card bore the name MISS OLIVE MARVELL. The letter was the usual formula from the chief, asking Lady Molly to have a talk with the lady in question, and to come and see him on the subject after the interview.

With a smothered yawn my dear lady told Jane to show in Miss Marvell.

"There are two of them, my lady," said Jane, as she prepared to obey.

"Two what?" asked Lady Molly with a laugh.

"Two ladies, I mean," explained Jane.

"Well! Show them both into the drawing room," said Lady Molly, impatiently.

Then, as Jane went off on this errand, a very funny thing happened; funny, because during the entire course of my intimate association with my dear lady, I had never known her act with such marked indifference in the face of an obviously interesting case. She turned to me and said:

"Mary, you had better see these two women, whoever they may be; I feel that they would bore me to distraction. Take note of what they say, and let me know. Now, don't argue," she added with a laugh, which peremptorily put a stop to my rising protest, "but go and interview Miss Marvell and Co."

Needless to say, I promptly did as I was told, and the next few seconds saw me installed in our little drawing room, saying polite preliminaries to the two ladies who sat opposite to me.

I had no need to ask which of them was Miss Marvell. Tall, ill-dressed in deep black, with a heavy crepe veil over her face, and black cotton gloves, she looked the uncompromising Scotchwoman to the life. In strange contrast to her depressing appearance, there sat beside her an over-dressed, much behatted, peroxided young woman, who bore the stamp of the theatrical profession all over her pretty, painted face.

Miss Marvell, I was glad to note, was not long in plunging into the subject which had brought her here.

"I saw a gentleman at Scotland Yard," she explained, after a short preamble, "because Miss—er—Lulu Fay came to me at the hotel this very morning with a story which, in my opinion, should have been told to the police directly my brother's disappearance became known, and not three weeks later."

The emphasis which she laid on the last few words, and the stern look with which she regarded the golden-haired young woman beside her, showed the disapproval with which the rigid Scotchwoman viewed any connection which her brother might have had with the lady, whose very name seemed unpleasant to her lips.

Miss—er—Lulu Fay blushed even through her rouge, and turned a pair of large, liquid eyes imploringly upon me.

"I—I didn't know. I was frightened," she stammered.

"There's no occasion to be frightened now," retorted Miss Marvell, "and the sooner you try and be truthful about the whole matter, the better it will be for all of us."

And the stern woman's lips closed with a snap, as she deliberately turned her back on Miss Fay and began turning over the leaves of a magazine which happened to be on a table close to her hand.

I muttered a few words of encouragement, for the little actress looked ready to cry. I spoke as kindly as I could, telling her that if indeed she could throw some light on Mr. Marvell's present whereabouts it was her duty to be quite frank on the subject.

She "hem"-ed and "ha"-ed for a while, and her simpering ways were just beginning to tell on my nerves, when she suddenly started talking very fast.

"I am principal boy at the Grand," she explained with great volubility, "and I knew Mr. Leonard Marvell well—in fact—er—he paid me a good deal of attention and—"

"Yes—and—" I queried, for the girl was obviously nervous.

There was a pause. Miss Fay began to cry.

"And it seems that my brother took this young—er—lady to supper on the night of February 3rd, after which no one has ever seen or heard of him again," here interposed Miss Marvell, quietly.

"Is that so?" I asked.

Lulu Fay nodded, whilst heavy tears fell upon her clasped hands.

"But why did you not tell this to the police three weeks ago?" I ejaculated, with all the sternness at my command.

"I—I was frightened," she stammered.

"Frightened? Of what?"

"I am engaged to Lord Mountnewte and—"

"And you did not wish him to know that you were accepting the attentions of Mr. Leonard Marvell—was that it? Well," I added, with involuntary impatience, "what happened after you had supper with Mr. Marvell?"

"Oh! I hope—I hope that nothing happened," she said through more tears. "We had supper at the Trocadero, and he saw me into my brougham. Suddenly, just as I was driving away, I saw Lord Mountnewte standing quite close to us in the crowd."

"Did the two men know one another?" I asked.

"No," replied Miss Fay. "At least, I didn't think so, but when I looked back through the window of my carriage I saw them standing on the curb talking to each other for a moment, and then walk off together towards Piccadilly Circus. That is the last I have seen of either of them," continued the little actress with a fresh flood of tears. "Lord Mountnewte hasn't spoken to me since, and Mr. Marvell has disappeared with my money and my diamonds."

"Your money and your diamonds?" I gasped in amazement.

"Yes; he told me he was a jeweler, and that my diamonds wanted resetting. He took them with him that evening, for he said that London jewelers were clumsy thieves, and that he would love to do the work for me himself. I also gave him two hundred pounds which he said he would want for buying the gold and platinum required for the settings. And now he has disappeared—and my diamonds—and my money! Oh! I have been very—very foolish—and—"

Her voice broke down completely. Of course, one often hears of the idiocy of girls giving money and jewels unquestioningly to clever adventurers who know how to trade upon their inordinate vanity. There was, therefore, nothing very out of the way in the story just told me by Miss—er—Lulu Fay, until the moment when Miss Marvell's quiet voice, with its marked Scotch burr, broke in upon the short silence which had followed the actress's narrative.

"As I explained to the chief detective inspector at Scotland Yard," she said calmly, "the story which this young—er—lady tells is only partly true. She may have had supper with Mr. Leonard Marvell on the night of February 3rd, and he may have paid her certain attentions; but he never deceived her by telling her that he was a jeweler, nor did he obtain possession of her diamonds and her money through false statements. My brother was the soul of honor and loyalty. If, for some reason which Miss—er—Lulu Fay chooses to keep secret, he had her jewels and money in his possession on the fatal February 3rd, then I think his disappearance is accounted for. He has been robbed and perhaps murdered."

Like a true Scotchwoman she did not give way to tears, but even her harsh voice trembled slightly when she thus bore witness to her brother's honesty, and expressed the fears which assailed her as to his fate.

Imagine my plight! I could ill forgive my dear lady for leaving me in this unpleasant position—a sort of peacemaker between two women who evidently hated one another, and each of whom was trying her best to give the other "the lie direct."

I ventured to ring for our faithful Jane and to send her with an imploring message to Lady Molly, begging her to come and disentangle the threads of this muddled skein with her clever fingers; but Jane returned with a curt note from my dear lady, telling me not to worry about such a silly case, and to bow the two women out of the flat as soon as possible and then come for a nice walk.

I wore my official manner as well as I could, trying not to betray the 'prentice hand. Of course, the interview lasted a great deal longer, and there was considerably more talk than I can tell you of in a brief narrative. But the gist of it all was just as I have said. Miss Lulu Fay stuck to every point of the story which she had originally told Miss Marvell. It was the latter uncompromising lady who had immediately marched the younger woman off to Scotland Yard in order that she might repeat her tale to the police. I did not wonder that the chief promptly referred them both to Lady Molly.

Anyway, I made excellent shorthand notes of the conflicting stories which I heard; and I finally saw, with real relief, the two women walk out of our little front door.

Our fellows at the Yard were abnormally active. It seemed, on the face of it, impossible that a man, healthy, vigorous, and admittedly sober, should vanish in London between Piccadilly Circus and Cromwell Road without leaving the slightest trace of himself or of the valuables said to have been in his possession.

Of course, Lord Mountnewte was closely questioned. He was a young Guardsman of the usual pattern, and, after a great deal of vapid talk which irritated Detective Inspector Saunders not a little, he made the following statement:

"I certainly am acquainted with Miss Lulu Fay. On the night in question I was standing outside the Troc, when I saw this young lady at her own carriage window talking to a tall man in an Inverness cape. She had, earlier in the day, refused my invitation to supper, saying that she was not feeling very well, and would go home directly after the theater; therefore I felt, naturally, a little vexed. I was just about to hail a taxi, meaning to go on to the club, when, to my intense astonishment, the man in the Inverness cape came up to me and asked me if I could tell him the best way to get back to Cromwell Road."

"And what did you do?" asked Saunders.

"I walked a few steps with him and put him on his way," replied Lord Mountnewte, blandly.

In Saunders's own expressive words, he thought that story "fishy." He could not imagine the arm of coincidence being quite so long as to cause these two men—who presumably were both in love with the same girl, and who had just met at a moment when one of them was obviously suffering pangs of jealousy—to hold merely a topographical conversation with one another. But it was equally difficult to suppose that the eldest son and heir of the Marquis of Loam should murder a successful rival and then rob him in the streets of London.

Moreover, here came the eternal and unanswerable questions: If Lord Mountnewte had murdered Leonard Marvell, where and how had he done it, and what had he done with the body?

I dare say you are wondering by this time why I have said nothing about the maid, Rosie Campbell.

Well, plenty of very clever people (I mean those who write letters to the papers and give suggestions to every official department in the kingdom) thought that the police ought to keep a very strict eye upon that pretty Scotch lassie. For she was very pretty, and had quaint, demure ways which rendered her singularly attractive, in spite of the fact that, for most masculine tastes, she would have been considered too tall. Of course, Saunders and Danvers kept an eye on her—you may be sure of that—and got a good deal of information about her from the people at the hotel. Most of it, unfortunately, was irrelevant to the case. She was maid-attendant to Miss Marvell, who was feeble in health, and who went out but little. Rosie waited on her master and mistress upstairs, carrying their meals to their private room, and doing their bedrooms. The rest of the day she was fairly free, and was quite sociable downstairs with the hotel staff.

With regard to her movements and actions on that memorable 3rd of February, Saunders—though he worked very hard—could glean but little useful information. You see, in a hotel of that kind, with an average of thirty to forty guests at one time, it is extremely difficult to state positively what any one person did or did not do on that particular day.

Most people at the Scotia remembered that Miss Marvell dined in the *table d'hôte* room on that 3rd of February; this she did about once a fortnight, when her maid had an evening "out."

The hotel staff also recollected fairly distinctly that Miss Rosie Campbell was not in the steward's room at supper time that evening, but no one could remember definitely when she came in.

One of the chambermaids who occupied the bedroom adjoining hers, said that she heard her moving about soon after midnight; the hall porter declared that he saw her come in just before half-past twelve when he closed the doors for the night.

But one of the ground-floor valets said that, on the morning of the 4th, he saw Miss Marvell's maid, in hat and coat, slip into the house and upstairs, very quickly and quietly, soon after the front doors were opened, namely, about 7:00 A.M.

Here, of course, was a direct contradiction between the chambermaid and hall porter on the one side, and the valet on the other, whilst Miss Marvell said that Campbell came into her room and made her some tea long before seven o'clock every morning, including that of the 4th.

I assure you our fellows at the Yard were ready to tear their hair out by the roots, from sheer aggravation at this maze of contradictions which met them at every turn.

The whole thing seemed so simple. There was nothing "to it" as it were, and but very little real suggestion of foul play, and yet Mr. Leonard Marvell had disappeared, and no trace of him could be found.

Everyone now talked freely of murder. London is a big town, and this would not have been the first instance of a stranger—for Mr. Leonard Marvell was practically a stranger in London—being enticed to a lonely part of the city on a foggy night, and there done away with and robbed, and the body hidden in an out-of-the-way cellar, where it might not be discovered for months to come.

But the newspaper-reading public is notably fickle, and Mr. Leonard Marvell was soon forgotten by every one save the chief and the batch of our fellows who had charge of the case.

Thus I heard through Danvers one day that Rosie Campbell had left Miss Marvell's employ, and was living in rooms in Findlater Terrace, near Walham Green.

I was alone in our Maida Vale flat at the time, my dear lady having gone to spend the weekend with the Dowager Lady Loam, who was an old friend of hers; nor, when she returned, did she seem any more interested in Rosie Campbell's movements than she had been hitherto.

Yet another month went by, and I for one had absolutely ceased to think of the man in the Inverness cape, who had so mysteriously and so completely vanished in the very midst of busy London, when, one morning early in January, Lady Molly made her appearance in my room, looking more like the landlady of a disreputable gambling house than anything else I could imagine.

"What in the world—" I began.

"Yes! I think I look the part," she replied, surveying with obvious complacency the extraordinary figure which confronted her in the glass.

My dear lady had on a purple cloth coat and skirt of a peculiarly vivid hue, and of a singular cut, which made her matchless figure look like a sack of potatoes. Her soft brown hair was quite hidden beneath a "transformation," of that yellow-reddish tint only to be met with in very cheap dyes.

As for her hat—I won't attempt to describe it. It towered above and around her face, which was plentifully covered with brick-red and with that kind of powder which causes the cheeks to look a deep mauve.

My dear lady looked, indeed, a perfect picture of appalling vulgarity.

"Where are you going in this elegant attire?" I asked in amazement.

"I have taken rooms in Findlater Terrace," she replied lightly. "I feel that the air of Walham Green will do us both good. Our amiable, if somewhat slatternly, landlady expects us in time for luncheon. You will have to keep rigidly in the background, Mary, all the while we are there. I said that I was bringing an invalid niece with me, and, as a preliminary, you may as well tie two or three thick veils over your face. I think I may safely promise that you won't be dull."

And we certainly were not dull during our brief stay at 34 Findlater Terrace, Walham Green. Fully equipped, and arrayed in our extraordinary garments, we duly arrived there, in a rickety four-wheeler, on the top of which were perched two seedy-looking boxes.

The landlady was a toothless old creature, who apparently thought washing a quite unnecessary proceeding. In this she was evidently at one with every one of her neighbors. Findlater Terrace looked unspeakably squalid; groups of dirty children congregated in the gutters and gave forth discordant shrieks as our cab drove up.

Through my thick veils I thought that, some distance down the road, I spied a horsy-looking man in ill-fitting riding breeches and gaiters, who vaguely reminded me of Danvers.

Within half an hour of our installation, and whilst we were eating a tough steak over a doubtful tablecloth, my dear lady told me that she had been waiting a full month, until rooms in this particular house happened to be vacant. Fortunately the population in Findlater Terrace is always a shifting one, and Lady Molly had kept a sharp eye on No. 34, where, on the floor above, lived Miss Rosie Campbell. Directly the last set of lodgers walked out of the ground-floor rooms, we were ready to walk in.

My dear lady's manners and customs, whilst living at the above aristocratic address, were fully in keeping with her appearance. The shrill, rasping voice which she assumed echoed from attic to cellar.

One day I heard her giving vague hints to the landlady that her husband, Mr. Marcus Stone, had had a little trouble with the police about a small hotel which he had kept somewhere near Fitzroy Square, and where "young gentlemen used to come and play cards of a night." The landlady was also made to understand that the worthy Mr. Stone was now living temporarily at His Majesty's expense, whilst Mrs. Stone had to live a somewhat secluded life, away from her fashionable friends.

The misfortunes of the pseudo Mrs. Stone in no way marred the amiability of Mrs. Tredwen, our landlady. The inhabitants of Findlater Terrace care very little about the antecedents of their lodgers, so long as they pay their week's rent in advance, and settle their "extras" without much murmur.

This Lady Molly did, with a generosity characteristic of an ex-lady of means. She never grumbled at the quantity of jam and marmalade which we were supposed to have consumed every week, and which anon reached titanic proportions. She tolerated Mrs. Tredwen's cat, tipped Ermyntrude—the tousled lodging-house slavey—lavishly, and lent the upstairs lodger her spirit lamp and curling tongs when Miss Rosie Campbell's got out of order.

A certain degree of intimacy followed the loan of those curling tongs. Miss Campbell, reserved and demure, greatly sympathized with the lady who was not on the best of terms with the police. I kept steadily in the background. The two ladies did not visit each other's rooms, but they held long and confidential conversations on the landings, and I gathered, presently, that the pseudo Mrs. Stone had succeeded in persuading Rosie Campbell that, if the police were watching No. 34 Findlater Terrace at all, it was undoubtedly on account of the unfortunate Mr. Stone's faithful wife.

I found it a little difficult to fathom Lady Molly's intentions. We had been in the house over three weeks, and nothing whatever had happened. Once I ventured on a discreet query as to whether we were to expect the sudden reappearance of Mr. Leonard Marvell.

"For if that's what it's about," I argued, "then surely the men from the Yard could have kept the house in view, without all this inconvenience and masquerading on our part."

But to this tirade my dear lady vouchsafed no reply.

She and her newly acquired friend were, about this time, deeply interested in the case known as the "West End Shop Robberies," which no doubt you recollect, since they occurred such a very little while ago. Ladies who were shopping in the large drapers' emporiums during the crowded and busy sale time lost reticules, purses, and valuable parcels without any trace of the clever thief being found.

The drapers, during sale time, invariably employ detectives in plain clothes to look after their goods, but in this case it was the customers who were robbed, and the detectives, attentive to every attempt at "shoplifting," had had no eyes for the more subtle thief.

I had already noticed Miss Rosie Campbell's keen look of excitement whenever the pseudo Mrs. Stone discussed these cases with her. I was not a bit surprised, therefore, when, one afternoon at about tea time, my dear lady came home from her habitual walk, and, at the top of her shrill voice, called out to me from the hall:

"Mary! Mary! They've got the man of the shop robberies. He's given the silly police the slip this time, but they know who he is now, and I suppose they'll get him presently. 'Tisn't anybody I know," she added, with that harsh, common laugh which she had adopted for her part.

I had come out of the room in response to her call, and was standing just outside our own sitting-room door. Mrs. Tredwen, too, bedraggled and unkempt, as usual, had sneaked up the area steps, closely followed by Ermyntrude.

But on the half-landing just above us the trembling figure of Rosie Campbell, with scared white face and dilated eyes, looked on the verge of a sudden fall.

Still talking shrilly and volubly, Lady Molly ran up to her, but Campbell met her half way, and the pseudo Mrs. Stone, taking vigorous hold of her wrist, dragged her into our own sitting room.

"Pull yourself together, now," she said with rough kindness. "That owl Tredwen is listening, and you needn't let her know too much. Shut the door, Mary. Lor' bless you, m'dear, I've gone through worse scares than these. There! You just lie down on this sofa a bit. My niece'll make you a cup o'tea; and I'll go and get an evening paper, and see what's going on. I suppose you are very interested in the shop-robbery man, or you wouldn't have took on so."

Without waiting for Campbell's contradiction to this statement, Lady Molly flounced out of the house.

Miss Campbell hardly spoke during the next ten minutes that she and I were left alone together. She lay on the sofa with eyes wide open, staring up at the ceiling, evidently still in a great state of fear.

I had just got tea ready when Lady Molly came back. She had an evening paper in her hand, but threw this down on the table directly she came in.

"I could only get an early edition," she said breathlessly, "and the silly thing hasn't got anything in it about the matter."

She drew near to the sofa, and, subduing the shrillness of her voice, she whispered rapidly, bending down towards Campbell:

"There's a man hanging about at the corner down there. No, no; it's not the police," she added quickly, in response to the girl's sudden start of alarm. "Trust me, my dear, for knowing a 'tec when I see one! Why, I'd smell one half a mile off. No; my opinion is that it's your man, my dear, and that he's in a devil of a hole."

"Oh! He oughtn't to come here," ejaculated Campbell in great alarm. "He'll get me into trouble and do himself no good. He's been a fool!" she added, with a fierceness wholly unlike her usual demure placidity, "getting himself caught like that. Now I suppose we shall have to hook it—if there's time."

"Can I do anything to help you?" asked the pseudo Mrs. Stone. "You know I've been through all this myself, when they was after Mr. Stone. Or perhaps Mary could do something."

"Well, yes," said the girl, after a slight pause, during which she seemed to be gathering her wits together. "I'll write a note, and you shall take it, if you will, to a friend of mine—a lady who lives in the Cromwell Road. But if you still see a man lurking about at the corner of the street, then, just as you pass him, say the word 'Campbell,' and if he replies 'Rosie,' then give *him* the note. Will you do that?"

"Of course I will, my dear. Just you leave it all to me."

And the pseudo Mrs. Stone brought ink and paper and placed them on the table. Rosie Campbell wrote a brief note, and then fastened it down with a bit of sealing wax before she handed it over to Lady Molly. The note was addressed to Miss Marvell, Scotia Hotel, Cromwell Road.

"You understand?" she said eagerly. "Don't give the note to the man unless he says 'Rosie' in reply to the word 'Campbell.' "

"All right—all right!" said Lady Molly, slipping the note into her reticule. "And you go up to your room, Miss Campbell; it's no good giving that old fool Tredwen too much to gossip about."

Rosie Campbell went upstairs, and presently my dear lady and I were walking rapidly down the badly lighted street.

"Where is the man?" I whispered eagerly as soon as we were out of earshot of No. 34.

"There is no man," replied Lady Molly, quickly.

"But the West End shop thief?" I asked.

"He hasn't been caught yet, and won't be either, for he is far too clever a scoundrel to fall into an ordinary trap."

She did not give me time to ask further questions, for presently, when we had reached Reporton Square, my dear lady handed me the note written by Campbell, and said:

"Go straight on to the Scotia Hotel, and ask for Miss Marvell; send up the note to her, but don't let her see you, as she knows you by sight. I must see the chief first, and will be with you as soon as possible. Having delivered the note, you must hang about outside as long as you can. Use your wits; she must not leave the hotel before I see her."

There was no hansom to be got in this elegant quarter of the town, so, having parted from my dear lady, I made for the nearest Underground station, and took a train for South Kensington.

Thus it was nearly seven o'clock before I reached the Scotia. In answer to my inquiries for Miss Marvell, I was told that she was ill in bed and could see no one. I replied that I had only brought a note for her, and would wait for a reply.

Acting on my dear lady's instructions, I was as slow in my movements as ever I could be, and was some time in finding the note and handing it to a waiter, who then took it upstairs.

Presently he returned with the message: "Miss Marvell says there is no answer."

Whereupon I asked for pen and paper at the office, and wrote the following brief note on my own responsibility, using my wits as my dear lady had bidden me to do.

Please, madam, I wrote, *will you send just a line to Miss Rosie Campbell? She seems very upset and frightened at some news she has had.*

Once more the waiter ran upstairs, and returned with a sealed envelope, which I slipped into my reticule.

Time was slipping by very slowly. I did not know how long I should have to wait about outside in the cold, when, to my horror, I heard a hard voice, with a marked Scotch accent, saying:

"I am going out, waiter, and shan't be back to dinner. Tell them to lay a little cold supper upstairs in my room."

The next moment Miss Marvell, with coat, hat, and veil, was descending the stairs.

My plight was awkward. I certainly did not think it safe to present myself before the lady; she would undoubtedly recollect my face. Yet I had orders to detain her until the appearance of Lady Molly.

Miss Marvell seemed in no hurry. She was putting on her gloves as she came downstairs. In the hall she gave a few more instructions to the porter, whilst I, in a dark corner in the background, was vaguely planning an assault or an alarm of fire.

Suddenly, at the hotel entrance, where the porter was obsequiously holding open the door for Miss Marvell to pass through, I saw the latter's figure stiffen; she took one step back as if involuntarily, then, equally quickly, attempted to dart across the threshold, on which a group—composed of my dear lady, of Saunders, and of two or three people scarcely distinguishable in the gloom beyond—had suddenly made its appearance.

Miss Marvell was forced to retreat into the hall; already I had heard Saunders's hurriedly whispered words:

"Try and not make a fuss in this place, now. Everything can go off quietly, you know."

Danvers and Cotton, whom I knew well, were already standing one each side of Miss Marvell, whilst suddenly amongst this group I recognized Fanny, the wife of Danvers, who is one of our female searchers at the Yard.

"Shall we go up to your own room?" suggested Saunders.

"I think that is quite unnecessary," interposed Lady Molly. "I feel convinced that *Mr.* Leonard Marvell will yield to the inevitable quietly, and follow you without giving any trouble."

Marvell, however, did make a bold dash for liberty. As Lady Molly had said previously, he was far too clever to allow himself to be captured easily. But my dear lady had been cleverer. As she told me subsequently, she had from the first suspected that the trio who lodged at the Scotia Hotel were really only a duo—namely, Leonard Marvell and his wife, Rosie Campbell. The latter impersonated a maid most of the time; but among these two clever people the three characters were interchangeable. *Of course, there was no Miss Marvell at all!* Leonard was alternately dressed up as man or woman, according to the requirements of his villainies.

"As soon as I heard that Miss Marvell was very tall and bony," said Lady Molly, "I thought that there might be a possibility of her being merely a man in disguise. Then there was the extraordinarily suggestive fact—but little dwelt on by either the police or public—that no one seems ever to have seen brother and sister together, nor was the entire trio ever seen at one and the same time.

"On that 3rd of February Leonard Marvell went out. No doubt he changed his attire in a lady's waiting room at one of the railway stations; subsequently he came home, now dressed as Miss Marvell, and had dinner in the *table d'hôte* room so as to set up a fairly plausible alibi. But ultimately it was his wife, Rosie Campbell, who stayed indoors that night, whilst he, Leonard Marvell, when going out after dinner, impersonated the maid until he was clear of the hotel; then he reassumed his male clothes once more, no doubt in the deserted waiting room of some railway station, and met Miss Lulu Fay at supper, subsequently returning to the hotel in the guise of the maid.

"You see the game of criss-cross, don't you? This interchanging of characters was bound to baffle every one. Many clever scoundrels have assumed disguises, sometimes impersonating members of the opposite sex, but never before have I known *two people play the part of three!* Thus, endless contradictions followed as to the hour when Campbell the maid went out and when she came in, for at one time it was she herself who was seen by the valet, and at another it was Leonard Marvell dressed in her clothes."

He was also clever enough to accost Lord Mountnewte in the open street, thus bringing further complications into this strange case.

After the successful robbery of Miss Fay's diamonds, Leonard Marvell and his wife parted for a while. They were waiting for an opportunity to get across the Channel and there turn their booty into solid cash. Whilst Mrs. Marvell, alias Rosie Campbell, led a retired life in Findlater Terrace, Leonard kept his hand in with West End shop robberies.

Then Lady Molly entered the lists. As usual, her scheme was bold and daring; she trusted her own intuition and acted accordingly.

When she brought home the false news that the author of the shop robberies had been spotted by the police, Rosie Campbell's obvious terror confirmed her suspicions. The note written by the latter to the so-called

Miss Marvell, though it contained nothing in any way incriminating, was the crowning certitude that my dear lady was right, as usual, in all her surmises.

And now Mr. Leonard Marvell will be living for two years at the tax payers' expense; he has "disappeared" temporarily from the public eye.

DEATH IN THE SUN

G.D.H. and Margaret Cole

1

"It really is beautiful here. Thank you so much for bringing me, James dear," said Mrs. Warrender, leaning back and sipping her glass of very mild Portuguese white wine with a smile of pleased satisfaction. "I've never known a place where it was so beautifully warm at night without being a bit too hot in the daytime."

She turned to look through the open loggia behind her at the still waters of the Bay of Funchal, the curving line of lights that marked the mole of the tiny harbor, the spangled black hill on the farther side of the bay, and the garish illumination of a liner at anchor.

"Umph!" said her son, with a grunt and a creak of his dress shirt. "It was hot enough down in the town this morning, anyhow."

"I'm sure it must have been, dear," his mother said. "It's too bad you should have to go down there in such horrid stuffy places. But it's lucky for me, because if you didn't we shouldn't be getting this lovely holiday. And it's quite cool now, isn't it?"

"Cool enough, but damnably noisy," James Warrender answered. He and his mother were sitting on the very edge of the Grand Hotel's open dance-and-dining room, finishing their dinner at one of the tables which encircled the dance floor. The soft evening breeze of Madeira came up to them from the sea below.

Mrs. Warrender gazed happily at the dancers swirling past their table.

"Oh, James!" she exclaimed. "Look how beautifully those two are dancing! They're from the party that came in to dinner, aren't they?"

The couple in question were doing a kind of exhibition display. The man was about twenty-five, tall, beautifully proportioned, with short curling black hair, a sun-tanned face, and a profile which was certainly in the first photographic rank. His partner, only three or four inches shorter, slender and aquiline, made in color a perfect contrast. Her pale golden hair was only the merest shade darker in tone than her faintly sun-flushed skin, and against his evening clothes her sheath of silver lamé shone like a moon. But it was not the color combination so much as the perfect timing and finish of their dancing that arrested attention. They moved like a single creature, executing complicated maneuvers amid the other dancers without a second's mistiming or hesitation.

"They *can* dance!" Mrs. Warrender repeated, with a sigh of satisfaction.

"Well, she ought to be able to, at any rate," James said with a faint hint of sourness. "She's the dancing and swimming instructress from Wright's Hotel. I wonder they let her out to come and show off at a one-horse place like this."

"Perhaps it's her evening off," said Mrs. Warrender dreamily. "It must be nice for her if she can get taken out herself sometimes. Do you know who the young man is, dear? He's wonderfully good-looking."

"Not an idea. By his looks and his clothes he must come from Wright's too. It's the only place where gilded youths of his type stay. Or perhaps he's landed off a summer cruise—no, I forgot it's tomorrow the *Armadilla* comes in. D'you mind if I leave you, mother? I want to go through those papers properly again, before I go to bed. I ought to know what's in them by tomorrow, and I can't attend to anything with this racket going on. You won't mind, will you? Get yourself some coffee, or a drink, or anything else you like."

"Of course not, dear. I shall be perfectly happy; I don't want anything at all," said his mother, and leaned back in her chair while the waiter cleared away the debris, looking with half-shut eyes at the dancers, and thinking how lucky she was, at sixty-five, to be enjoying this holiday in Madeira and how entirely unexpected it had been, even though it did mean that poor James had to go and argue with Portuguese in stuffy offices in the heat.

Mrs. Warrender was not at all wealthy. Her tiny income would certainly not have stretched to a holiday in Madeira had not James, in his capacity of private enquiry agent, been given a lucrative if tiresome commission which involved his going out to Madeira and spending a great deal of time interviewing shipping and wine companies. Fortunately, the client was lavish, and James who was always generous—even if he did sometimes fidget and demand his money's worth—had announced that the fees would easily cover both their expenses, if they shut up the house in Hampstead for the time.

So there she was, after a voyage of delirious excitement for a lady who had never been out of Europe, sitting on an almost open terrace at nine in the evening by an almost tropical sea. She lapsed into a reverie.

But not for long. By an accident which none of the Grand Hotel's usually efficient staff had noticed, the people at the table nearest hers had, in rising, knocked over a beaker of salad dressing which was slowly spreading in a greasy pool over the floor. Into this pool swept the girl from Wright's and her partner, in a magnificent sea-gull swoop—and instantly skidded.

They made a great effort to recover themselves, but they were going too fast and with too much abandon. After cannoning off the table from which the oil had come, they shot straight into that of the Warrenders, and sent it crashing on its side. The girl tripped over Mrs. Warrender's feet and fell helter-skelter into the chair which James had been occupying. The young man, graceful even in disaster, dropped back on his heels and came to rest, almost in a squatting position, with his arms encircling Mrs. Warrender, chair and all, and his dark eyes looking up into her face with a comic expression of dismay.

"Good heavens!" he exclaimed, rising swiftly. "What a clumsiness! I'm so sorry. I do hope we haven't hurt you much."

"Not a bit," said Mrs. Warrender, while the girl extricated herself from the chair. "It wasn't your fault at all. Somebody spilt some oil on the floor."

"Why, so they did," said the young man, in great relief. "That lets me out a bit—except that anybody who could dance at all oughtn't to slip on a patch of grease."

"But if you're dancing the way you two were—not just walking, but moving so beautifully—you couldn't possibly help it. It was so lovely to watch you," said Mrs. Warrender eagerly.

"Oh, but how charming of you!" the young man said. "I do hope we haven't spilt anything that matters."

"Nothing at all, thank you," said Mrs. Warrender. "There wasn't anything there to spill."

"Oh, but there ought to be! You will have a drink with me, won't you? It's the least I can do, after throwing partners and tables all over you. Some champagne?" Mrs. Warrender shook her head. "But you must!" And, turning to the girl in silver, "*You* tell her she ought to, Florence."

"Do, please," said the girl. She had a low, pleasant voice, though possibly she was not as young as she appeared to be at a distance. She was beautifully *soignée,* and the lift of her head was clear and even defiant; but anybody who looked close could detect a weary, indeed almost a wary, look in her eyes, as though life were beginning to press hard. Mrs. Warrender glanced at her with a sudden feeling of sympathy, but shook her head again.

"But, please—oh, I'm sorry. This is somebody's chair, isn't it?" the girl said.

"No, indeed. I'm all by myself."

"But you mustn't be! That's all wrong," said the young man, "and on so lovely an evening too. It makes people come and bump into your table and send it flying. You are sure you're not hurt? Florence didn't tear your stockings with her new sharpened heels, did she?" And, as Mrs. Warrender smiled and shook her head, "Then you really must have a drink with us. Look, we're all abandoned; our friends have swep' out and gone to the bar and we've got no one to play with. Don't you like champagne? Will you have a veesky-soda? I believe that's the correct drink for modern matrons, isn't it?"

"I really won't have anything like that, thank you," Mrs. Warrender smiled. "But if you would like me to—I *would* enjoy a little coffee—"

"Splendid!" said the young man, and clapped his hands for a waiter.

She found him charming, like something out of a very pleasant dream, as he stood inclining his shapely dark head. With the tail of her always maternal eye, she considered and approved his companion.

"Surely you are not here all by yourself?" he asked when the waiter had come and he had secured a chair.

"Oh, no. My son is with me—"

"How nice for him," the young man replied softly.

Mrs. Warrender, who in her far-off girlhood had been famous for her dimples, produced an unexpected one at the corner of her cheek. "He was dining with me, only he had to go and do some work. You're not staying here, are you?"

"No. We're at Wright's," he answered. "This is Miss Florence Truman, and my name's Jeremy Haydon. We've come here for a night out, away from all the financiers and colonial governors at Wright's. There are two others with us, Terry Gordon and Clare Ferrers. I'll introduce them directly; but as I said they've gone off to the bar. And you?"

"Our name's Warrender. My son is James Warrender."

"I say! You don't mean *the* James Warrender, do you? The man who's a great big private detective and agent—whom everybody's heard of?"

Mrs. Warrender nodded in pride, thinking what a pity it was that James couldn't be there to hear. He would never believe it if she told him; he always said, when she tried to pass on compliments, that she must have misheard and that nobody ever said nice things of him behind his back. James was cynical about the world.

"But, in that case . . . you must be the wonderful woman who is back of him, who always gets the hunches—"

"Oh, no! That's not true at all," Mrs. Warrender said, hoping now that James would *not* suddenly appear. "I don't have anything to do with his work."

"But, you see, I've got a sort of uncle—isn't it extraordinary that everybody you meet always knows somebody else? I know that sounds silly, but you know what I mean."

"Like me knowing your sister," Florence Truman put in.

"Exactly." (But Mrs. Warrender noticed a cloud cross his face, and felt rather than saw, that Miss Truman had noticed it also.)

"As I was saying, my uncle is a Magistrate somewhere in London, and I'm quite certain I remember him telling me about a burglary in Hampstead at the house of *the* James Warrender, where he—Mr. Warrender, I mean—hadn't been able to do anything about it, but his mother solved it and caught the criminal and all."

"Oh, but that's ridiculous," Mrs. Warrender said, dimpling again. "It was only, you see, that I happened to know Gladys."

"Gladys! Who's Gladys? Oh, do tell us."

"Why, Gladys was our maid. You see," said Mrs. Warrender, "I went away for the weekend, and when I came back I found James very cross, because all the silver had been stolen in the night. And he said Gladys had been woken by the burglar and had gone and screamed at the front door instead of calling him or anything. But I knew Gladys wouldn't have done a silly thing like stand and scream at the front door—unless she knew that somebody was getting away through the back door. So I told the inspector to go and see Gladys's young man, and he did, and found he was the thief. But—no, no," as they began to laugh and applaud, "that wasn't being a detective at all. It was only that I happened to know something about Gladys and of course James didn't."

"Well, I think it's superb," Jeremy Haydon began. "Hi!" he broke off, as his eye caught some people in the distance. "Hi! Come over here, you two. Meet Mrs. Warrender, mother of the great detective, and a four-flusher on her own. Mrs. Warrender—Miss Ferrers, Terry Gordon. Have a drink, you-all."

"Pleased to meet you," Terry Gordon said, without interest. Mrs. Warrender thought that she liked this pair much less than her previous companions. The young man was sleek, fair, and sinuous. He had a long narrow head, eyes set too close together, and a sulky mouth with a drooping lower lip. The girl was young, but what James would have called "hard boiled." Her hair was waved tight and close; she had long jade earrings, eyebrows plucked and replaced at an impossible angle, and blood-red nails ending in sharp points. And she twitched. Her eyelids twitched, and her mouth twitched, and her fingers fidgeted and tapped on anything within reach.

"Of course I want a drink," she said, motioning young Gordon to find her a chair. "But not here, in this lousy place. Let's get off and pub-crawl."

"It's nicer here," Jeremy said. "Cooler. Besides, we can't pub-crawl unless Terry's got any cash, and I don't suppose he has." Terry shook his head emphatically.

"Oh, are you broke? What a curse. Can't you borrow on your expectations or something?"

Again the cloud crossed Jeremy's face, and Florence Truman shifted suddenly on her chair.

Mrs. Warrender took a small decision, and rose to her feet.

"I must go and see what my son's doing," she said. "Good night, Mr. Haydon; good night, Miss Truman. And thank you so much for a pleasant evening."

"Thank you," Jeremy said. "And, I say, won't you return the call some time? Come over to Wright's tomorrow morning and bathe, won't you? About eleven. We've quite a decent bathing pool there. And I'll find you some coconut oil."

"I bet you will," said Clare Ferrers to the company at large. "Jeremy's a perfect old woman about his bathing. Lies in the sun for hours and cooks himself by the clock both sides—ten minutes either way—basting himself like a spring chicken."

"Of course I do," said Jeremy, not at all put out. "Madeira sun's fierce, and I don't want to go home covered with sores, whatever anybody else may do. But you will come, won't you?" to Mrs. Warrender.

"I don't know that I will bathe, thank you," Mrs. Warrender said. "I bathe here early, and I think that is enough for an old lady. But I should like very much to come and call on you both some time. And now I really must say good night." She extricated herself, but not too soon to hear Clare Ferrers remark, "Well, you have got catholic tastes, haven't you? What is it you're vamping now, gigolo?"

Upstairs she found her son, his work finished, wondering whether filial duty demanded that he should return again to the dance room, and very relieved to find that it would not be necessary.

"Hullo!" he said. "Had a nice time?"

"Very, thank you, dear," his mother replied. "I made the acquaintance of that young couple—you know, the girl you said was a dancing instructor at Wright's, and the young man. His name's Jeremy Haydon;

he's a charming boy. . . . Why, James, do you know him?" For his brow had knitted in a surprised scowl.

"Not him. But I know about him, a bit. He's the son of old Haydon, the banker, who died a year or two ago. He's got a sister who married that rotter Maurice Benoni. That's how I came to know about it, because Haydon asked me to look into Benoni. So I did, and I didn't find anything, though I never had any doubt that there was something shady about him. But I never heard any more of it, so maybe it turned out all right. Is this chap staying at Wright's?"

"Yes. Why?"

"It's what I should expect. Money to burn and nothing to do. At least I don't suppose he's got control of it yet, from what the old man told me, but I dare say he can drink himself to death on his expectations."

"I thought he was such a nice boy. I didn't care for some of his friends, though. There was a girl—quite pretty, but, oh, so disageeable and restless. She made me quite jumpy," Mrs. Warrender said.

"Drugs, probably. They're a sodden lot in these places," said James. "Well, how about a spot of bed, mother?"

"The big German boat's gone," said Mrs. Warrender, looking out of the window towards the bay.

"Left half an hour ago," James said. "The British cruise comes in tomorrow. Well, good night, ma mère."

2

"Look, James, isn't it curious, the way people turn up!" Mrs. Warrender, eating her breakfast on the terrace in the sun two days later, was fluttering in a pleased way over an envelope that had just been delivered by hand. She was very happy this morning; she had had a perfect bathe, and had even, with the encouragement of an amiable Portuguese gentleman, ventured into the open sea beyond the pool. And now here was a note, and from Wright's Hotel, asking her and James to pay a visit.

"Lang? Who's Lang? Pernicia Lang—what a name!" James said.

"It isn't Pernicia, dear, it's Persis, only her writing is always so bad."

"Well, who's Pernicious Lang, then?" James grunted.

"Oh, James dear, you know Dr. Lang—Hubert Lang. It's him and his wife. They're staying at Wright's—I'm sure I don't know how they came to know we were here."

"Oh, them," James looked at the letter again. "Well, I can't go today. I don't want to waste all the morning."

"No, dear, I know you don't. But I thought, perhaps, if I went round in the morning and had a little chat with them you might spare time to come over to lunch. They would be so pleased to see you, if you're not too busy. And, after all, you must have lunch somewhere, mustn't you?"

"Um-m. Well, perhaps I might," said James graciously.

"I'll just run along and tell them now," his mother said.

So it happened that, at midday, Mrs. Elizabeth Warrender was sitting, in a chair of bright steel and scarlet canvas, alongside Mrs. Persis Lang amid the plumbago and hibiscus of the gardens of Wright's Hotel, looking out over the bay. The bathing pool, where Dr. Lang and his son and daughter were disporting themselves, lay just below them at the bottom of the cliffs; but the two ladies had not bathed.

"I bathe before my breakfast," Mrs. Lang was saying in a voice that would have carried easily to the bathing pool and beyond; "and that's enough for me. I don't fancy lying about there in the sun with all those young things and everybody looking at me and calculating exactly how big a splash I'll make when I go in." She gave a huge reverberating guffaw, which shook her all over.

Mrs. Hubert Lang accepted the occasional inconveniences of her size with loud and cheerful comment, secure in the fact that her personality easily dominated her family, and that her very comfortable income not only served to give them holidays at the best hotel in Funchal, but had also raised her husband—a little hurried and hesitant man whom nature had obviously designed for a struggling G.P.—to the comparative dignity of a practice in Harley Street. Her two children appeared to be both proud and fond of her, though Mrs. Warrender did sometimes, when she allowed herself to entertain so uncharitable a thought, wonder whether Jocelyn Lang ever shivered in anticipation when her mother's figure came and sat down beside her—even more, whether any of Jocelyn's young men ever shivered.

"But that's no reason why you shouldn't have a bathe, my dear," Mrs. Lang continued. "Are you sure you won't? Geoffrey and Jocelyn would be delighted to see you—they're in and out of the water all the time, and they're pretty nearly making Hubert a duck between them."

"No, really, thank you," Mrs. Warrender said. "I've got so used to having just my early bathe that I don't want another. And you seem to have to do such a lot of lying in the sun and rubbing yourself with oil; I'm sure I should do it wrong and get a bad burn—and it isn't as though it was any use to *me* to have a nice brown back—"

"Well, that's true, too."

"—Besides, it is so pleasant here, looking at the sea and your lovely garden."

"Let's look at a bit more of it, shall we?" said Mrs. Lang, beginning to heave herself out of her chair. "They've really done it pretty well. It's worth seeing and though I'm large I'm not immovable yet. Besides, I shall have to go down to the pool sooner or later, to drag the others up to lunch. It wouldn't ever occur to them to come out of the water if I didn't fetch them. And I think you ought to see our pool; it's really rather prettily arranged. So let's walk down through the gardens, and we'll call Hubert out of the water and have a nice John Collins before lunch."

"I met such a charming young man from your hotel the other evening," said Mrs. Warrender, stopping to bury her appreciative nose in a great bush of frangipanni. "He was over dining in ours with some friends. He said his name was Jeremy Haydon." Mrs. Lang nodded in qualified approval.

"*I* think he's a nice boy," she said, "though I can't say as much for some of his friends here, and they do racket about a lot and drink like fishes. Hubert keeps on worrying that they will pick up Geoffrey and do him some harm; but what I say is, if Geoffrey's going to be a fool, a fool he'll be and much better do it here, where he can get away and forget all about it in a month, than in London or somewhere like that. Not that it's very likely; Geoffrey's much too like Hubert—afraid of getting his underpants wet.

"Young Haydon's got really pretty manners, that's what I like about him," she continued after a pause. "He may be a ne'er-do-well—dare say he is—but he doesn't treat a fat old woman as if she was just an ugly bit of furniture left over from last spring cleaning. And whatever you may say of him he's not a snob; he's just as nice to the hotel dancing partner as he is to any of his own friends—and I dare say she could do with it, poor girl."

"Doesn't she have a very pleasant time, then?" Mrs. Warrender enquired.

"Not too good. Some of the old wretches here," Mrs. Lang bellowed almost in the ear of a very frail old gentleman who was climbing shakily down a short flight of steps, "think they've bought the world because they're paying twice as much for their drinks as they would anywhere else. And old Lewis—that's the manager—is a skinflint and a bully. I've heard him ticking off the girl once or twice in a way that's made my blood boil. But young Haydon's always charming to her."

"He's very good-looking," Mrs. Warrender said. "He must look beautiful in the water."

"Well, you'll be able to judge of that yourself in a minute," said Mrs. Lang, turning into a steep path which appeared to lead direct to the pool, "in the water or out of it. He's pretty certain to be down at the pool; he generally spends most of the morning there, swimming or sunbathing." She paused to chuckle. "He's very particular about his tan, I must say, and goes about it most scientifically. His friends teased him about it so much—though I must say the result's worth looking at in my opinion—that he generally goes and lies by himself on a bit of rock and won't talk to anybody. Matter of fact, I seem to remember seeing him there early this morning, when we came down. So perhaps he won't be there now."

"Is he a good swimmer?" Mrs. Warrender asked.

"Beautiful. We'll have to get him to dive for you, if he's there, before we go up to lunch." By now they had arrived at the pool, a great shining expanse of clear green water, flanked by terraced rocks on which various half-clad figures lay bathing in the sun. "Geoffrey!"

"Adsum!" A young man in a black bathing slip climbed out of the pool at their feet.

"Where's your father?"

"In the sea. Trying to climb on a rubber horse," Geoffrey chuckled.

"Call him out, will you? It's time, if we're to have a drink before lunch. And, Geoffrey!" as the young man turned to obey. "Is Jeremy Haydon down, do you know? Mrs. Warrender wants him to dive for her."

"Oh, but I didn't mean—" Mrs. Warrender went faintly pink, but neither took any notice of her.

"I think so. Yes, that's him, over there on his rock. I haven't seen him in the water since I came down, so I dare say he'll be about ready for another dip. Go and ask him, won't you, Mrs. Warrender, while I whistle up father."

And Geoffrey sprang off, with a cry of "Hi! Jos! Come and haul the old man in," while Mrs. Lang waddled purposefully in the direction of the pavilion.

Left to herself, Mrs. Warrender found herself moving slowly, and not without a tiny tremor of excitement, in the direction of the solitary figure lying on its face on a brilliant orange mattress of rubber. After all, he *had* invited her to come and see him, and he was always charming to old ladies, so that he wouldn't be rude to her, even if he did prefer to be alone. Perhaps he might even be pleased that she had come. She quickened her steps a little, glad to be going to meet Jeremy Haydon again.

He was lying all alone on the farthest of the rock terraces. He was lying at full length, his head pillowed on his arms, and nothing on his finely shaped body but a pair of bright blue bathing-trunks, which showed up perfectly the deep bronze tan of his skin. Nothing of his head was visible; it was concealed by one of the huge striped Madeiran straw hats, which covered his shoulders as well, and was presumably protecting him from sunstroke. He lay very still, not moving a muscle at her approach. Was it wise, her maternal mind wondered, to lie so fast asleep in the full sub-tropical sun?

She stood looking at him for a moment, noticing subconsciously a faint tinge of green in the bronze of his back, and wondering what trick of light could have caused it.

It seemed a shame to disturb him; he looked so peaceful. But it would be nice to talk to him a little and perhaps he, too, would like a drink before lunch. And, anyway, she was sure he oughtn't to go on sleeping there in the glare. So she called his name, softly at first, and then louder, "Mr. Haydon!" but he did not stir.

Suddenly, as she looked, her heart gave a sickening leap, and the bright blue sea turned momentarily to a grayish-black. For a second she stood, with her eyes painfully screwed up, verifying what she had seen. Then she turned, trembling, back in the direction of the pool. For she had seen flies walking on his bare skin—and he had not even moved to brush them away.

Her heart thumping, she walked as quickly as she could back to the pool and there was fortunate enough to find her host, just out of the water.

"Dr. Lang! Could you come a moment, please? I think—perhaps—Mr. Haydon may be ill over there." She spoke in a low voice—even in panic Mrs. Warrender could never have brought herself to shout.

"He's lying so still," she explained, following the doctor. "It looks—he might have fainted or had a sunstroke."

"Righto. We'll see," said Dr. Lang cheerfully. "Now you mention it, I haven't seem him about much today, and it isn't too safe to lie too long in this sun." By now he had reached the young man, and whipped the hat from his head, disclosing the dark hair and the crooked elbows. Certainly he had not been in the water for some time; his hair was perfectly dry.

Dr. Lang knelt down beside him in his dripping suit, and laid a hand on his back. Immediately his face changed, and he half lifted the limp figure and slipped a hand under the shoulder. For a second he kept it there, then turned to Mrs. Warrender. In a peremptory bark which she would hardly have recognized he said, "Fetch Geoffrey, will you? Quick, please."

How Mrs. Warrender got back she hardly knew, but somehow she did, and managed, after some delay, to extract Geoffrey Lang from the dressing box into which he had disappeared.

"My *dear!*" Mrs. Lang, who had been a surprised spectator of her frenzied search for Geoffrey, boomed suddenly in her ear. "Are you ill? You've gone as white as a sheet. Is anything—*what's the matter?*"

"I don't know! . . . It's Mr. Haydon. I *must* go and see!" Shaking all over, Mrs. Warrender hurried on; and the large lady followed her at a slower pace. The sound of her voice had disturbed a number of the sunbathers, who began to sit up and look round, and there was a slow drift of the more active among them in the same direction.

When Mrs. Warrender got back to the rock, she found that Dr. Lang and his son had turned young Haydon over, and the former was still on his knees making an examination. He raised a hand to keep her back, but she paid no attention, approaching as near as she could to the boy. He lay on his back now, with his eyes wide open and staring straight into the sun, and the greenish tinge of the bronze tan was far more noticeable in his face. Mrs. Warrender had never seen anyone quite that color before, and for a second she closed her eyes.

"Is he . . .?" she said, hoping against hope that she did not know the answer to her question.

"Yes. He's dead," Dr. Lang almost snapped, seeming not to realize to whom he was speaking. Then he glanced up and saw the slow trek of people approaching. "Good Lord!" he said. "Geoffrey, go and keep that lot back, and send somebody for the manager quick. We don't want anyone here. No, Mrs. Warrender," in a gentler, though still preoccupied tone, "it's no good your coming. There's nothing to be done for him."

"But surely," Mrs. Warrender protested faintly, "there must be something—aren't you going to try and bring him round? He may be only in a bad faint."

"Good God!" the doctor suddenly barked. "He's been dead for hours, I tell you! He's as cold as a stone, except where the sun's got at him. Been lying here all night, most likely."

"Oh!" said Mrs. Warrender, and swayed.

"Hold up," said Geoffrey Lang. "Look here, sit down a bit." He guided her to a niche in the rock, where she sank down with her hands over her eyes to shut out the sight and the understanding. "*Oh!*" she said as the tears came seeping through her hands. "The poor boy. The *poor* boy."

3

It seemed hours before she could endure to remove her hands from her face, and look again at the rock at her feet, and the still blue sea, with the white awnings of the fishing boats making a pattern on the horizon. For some reason, the thought of Jeremy Haydon's dead body lying out all night, and for half the day, uncared for and unnoticed by those around him, struck at her heart even more deeply than his death, though that was shock enough. How *could* people, she raged to herself, how could they be so cold and uninterested as not even to have seen that he had not moved for hours, not even to have noticed that he had not been for a swim, not even to have asked him to come and dive for them? For, if they had, if somebody had come over to speak to him—Dr. Lang might have been wrong, and it might not have been too late. They might have done something for him, revived him, before he had got so cold—so cold that even the Madeira sun could not warm him through the chill. And then, suddenly, a fresh realization overcame her that Jeremy Haydon, the lithe dancer who had overset her table little more than thirty-six hours before and had squatted on his heels apologizing in his nice voice and asking her to come and bathe with him, would never dance or upset anything again, and once more the easy tears of old age burnt her cheeks.

She roused herself, at the sound of harsh argumentative voices, and opened her eyes again. Nothing had changed very much since she had shut them. The body of Jeremy Haydon still lay sprawled on its orange mattress on the rock, against a cascade of red bougainvillea—curious that she had not noticed that before—which was falling down from the cliff edges. But a number of new people had appeared. One, a short dark man with a fleshy nose, and an obviously corseted figure, was making most of the noise which had aroused her. He was shouting directions at two or three men in long white coats and black trousers, and at the same time, it would appear, conducting an argument with the doctor. Possibly he was the manager of the hotel. She sat up, in order to see better what was happening, and as she did so her foot struck against a small object that was lying on the rock, at which she automatically turned to look. She was not four feet from the mattress on which the body was lying.

"It's no use trying to bully me," Dr. Lang was saying with a truculence that she never expected to hear from him. "I'm not going to give you any opinion until I've had time to make a proper examination, and I can't do that in this blazing sun without any clothes on. You get him to his own room, and I'll come up directly and look into it properly."

"He hasn't got any room," the manager said, "not that he's paid for. It's more than a fortnight now since he's paid me a penny for his keep or the drinks he and his friends mopped up. If I hadn't believed he's got friends and money in the background somewhere I'd have told him to clear out. Now he's dead—"

"Yes, he's dead; and if you think that is a way to behave when a guest of yours dies in your bathing pool, I'll soon inform you that you're mistaken!" Dr. Lang stormed. "Get him up, I tell you, and I'll tell you directly everything you need to know. If you don't and if you say another word, I'll lodge a complaint with the British Consul in half an hour from now. Get a move on, I tell you! Where's your stretcher? Well, then, put him on. You needn't handle him like glass, man; you can't do him any harm now."

With excruciating slowness, like the dreariest of educational films, the white-coated men produced a stretcher, and on to it loaded the corpse. Slowly they moved back along the rocks; and Dr. Lang heaved a sigh, and reclaimed the large bathing towel which his wife was dutifully holding for him.

"Have to get back quick and dress," he observed. "Can't do anything like this. Mrs. Warrender all right? Good God!" with a sudden change of tone. "What are you doing with that? Put it down quick! Where'd you find it?"

Mrs. Warrender dropped, as if it were red-hot, the small object against which her foot had struck. "It was just here, by me," she said feebly. "I touched it, and picked it up. I'm sorry; I didn't know it mattered."

"It's a hypodermic," exclaimed Dr. Lang. "Better let me have it, and not touch it again. You see," he swallowed hard, "one can't tell how he died. People don't die like that, from lying out all night, when there isn't even any sun. And a hypodermic syringe—an injection—that might tell us."

"Oh!" said Mrs. Warrender, surrendering the syringe. "Perhaps you'd better have that little bottle too." She pointed to one a yard or two away, which had rolled into the shadow of the rock wall. "It looks like coconut oil, and he told me that he always had plenty of it, so I suppose it may have been his."

"Yes, I'll take it." Dr. Lang dived and secured it with his handkerchief. "Thanks, m'dear," turning to his wife. "I'd better get up. Can't tell how long this will take, but I'll be along as soon as I can. You'll be all right? Better start lunch without waiting for me."

Mrs. Warrender and Mrs. Lang, clinging together like two stricken madonnas, crawled back to the hotel, where they found Mrs. Warrender's son, who had just witnessed the body of Jeremy Haydon being carried through the hotel door, and had heard of the tragedy. He was, in fact, already putting two and two together, rather callously, the Langs thought.

"There doesn't seem much doubt," he informed them, when they were seated in the dining room, "that the young fellow committed suicide."

There was a shower of startled exclamations. "What? But why on earth?"

"How do you know?" said Geoffrey Lang.

"Lord, what a blow!" said his sister.

Mrs. Lang said, "Nonsense! That nice cheerful boy kill himself. I don't believe it for a single minute."

Mrs. Warrender, after her first cry, said nothing at all. She was remembering Dr. Lang's face when he spoke to her after the body had gone. He had seemed oddly worried; had he thought then that something was wrong? But surely—to kill oneself one must be terribly unhappy. Could he—Jeremy—have been so unhappy, and still talked to her so lightly? Or was he—had something disastrous happened to him since?

"It isn't nonsense, you know," James said. "I wouldn't say it if it were. And he wasn't as bright and cheerful as all that—at least he oughtn't to have been. He was getting into deep water. He'd been running up bills here for a couple of weeks and more—pretty hefty bills too—I gather he let his friends sponge on him right and left; and I dare say they'll find he had more owing in the town. Anyway, the point is that he'd no means of paying them, as far as we know. The fellows whom he was banking with here—according to the manager—said that instructions from England were strict not to let him anticipate his allowance by more than a certain amount, and I understand, also from the manager, that he'd already got to that limit. So, you see, he was pretty well due for a showdown in a day or so. Just the sort of thing a lad like that, who'd been throwing his weight about and cutting a dash, wouldn't like to have to face."

"But then, how? I mean, how did he do it?" Geoffrey Lang asked.

"Oh, that. Well, you see, it wasn't a natural death. Your husband, Mrs. Lang, is quite sure of that. He's just making a final examination, and he'll probably call for a p.m.; but he told *me* he hadn't any doubts it would turn out to be morphine poisoning. I understand somebody or other found a hypodermic just close to his body. They'll probably find he was an addict, when they come to investigate. Lots of these fly-by-night young people are. All bright and starry-eyed when they've got their dope, and heavy as lead and fretted to fiddle strings as soon as it's worn off."

Mrs. Warrender very quietly, hoping her action would not be noticed, put down the mouthful that was choking her. It couldn't be—that bright gaiety *couldn't* be produced by drug taking. But then, she realized sadly, quiet old ladies don't really know much about the effect of drugs.

"Added to which," James was saying, "the manager's been on to that dancing girl he brought over to our place the other night—you remember, mother, I think you were talking to them—and she's let out that the young man has seemed pretty much under the weather the last day or two. Hullo, mother, what's up?"

"You ought to be more careful what you say, James! Frightening your mother like that," said Mrs. Lang indignantly. "Here, waiter, a cognac, quickly."

Mrs. Warrender leaned back, apologizing in a faint voice, though in reality it was not James's words that had startled her, but the sudden sight of a tall girl with a white, absolutely stricken face passing the doors of the dining room. Florence Truman, at least, was not indifferent to Haydon's death. Nobody else, however, appeared to have noticed her; and as Dr. Lang appeared almost immediately and showed a marked disinclination to discuss the case, Mrs. Warrender was mercifully left to toy with her lunch in peace.

"Well, mother, how about getting along home?" James suggested when he had finished. "I've got a good lot of things to do, and I suggest you ought to lie down and have a rest. You look pretty played out, and you'll want to be in decent trim when you've got to give evidence."

"Oh, *no!* I shan't, shall I? Shall I have to?"

" 'Fraid so, at the inquest, or whatever it is they have in this country. You see, it was you who found him. She will, won't she?" to Dr. Lang.

"Maybe. Might be arranged. No need to bother about it now," the doctor grunted. He scribbled on a bit of paper in his pocket. "Here, Warrender, take this and get your hotel to make it up pronto, and give it to Mrs. Warrender. You take things easy," he said to her, "and don't go sitting in the sun."

"No, I won't," said Mrs. Warrender with a faint, wilted smile. "It's—it's rather dangerous isn't it?"

He looked at her with a glance of comprehension, but all he said was, "Only need to be a bit carefull—that's all. But you—had a shock—don't knock yourself up. Bad business, anyway."

"Dr. Lang, I don't want to ask things I shouldn't. But do you really think it was that—that he poisoned himself?"

" 'Fraid so. From all I could see. 'Course it's not official, yet, but—bad business," said Dr. Lang again. "Nice-looking lad."

"Thank you! But I can't—I can't believe it," Mrs. Warrender thought to herself as she passed on James's arm out of the hotel and along the cobbled, palm-lined road which she had traversed so happily three hours before.

4

"Better tuck yourself up and have a bit of a shuteye, mother," said James when they had got back to the Grand Hotel and the prescription had been handed to the chemist. "No use knocking yourself up."

"No, dear. But I don't think I'll go to bed, if you don't mind," his mother said. "It's so hot in my bedroom in the afternoon, and I've got rather a headache. I think I'll just go and sit quietly in the garden."

It was not, however, the heat, but sleep, that she was afraid of. By keeping her eyes firmly open, she was just able not to see that scene on the rocks, with the blood-red bougainvillea hanging down to within a foot of the boy's head; but once she shut them she knew that it would all come vividly back. So she made her way, with a half-knitted sock of James's, to a hard iron seat in the Grand Hotel's back garden, under an extraordinarily twisted kind of tree whose name she had never discovered. It was hot, however, even in the garden; the knitting needles felt sticky in her hands, and the restless lizards running to and fro dazzled her eyes. After a very little effort she laid down the knitting and fixed her gaze on the bright green fronds of a banana plantation in the distance, just by which a white sheet or garment of some sort was fluttering in the air. She kept her eyes sternly fastened on it until sheer strain forced her to close them, and when she opened them again it seemed that the white object had moved. She stared until she was certain she was right: not only had it moved, but it was still moving. It was coming straight towards her, flapping its sides—no, its wings. It was an enormous bird.

It was all rather extraordinary. She had not noticed any gulls in Madeira, and this seemed a particularly large one—and what was it doing in the grounds of the hotel? It was circling about—it seemed to be looking for something. She rather hoped it would not come near; it was such a big bird, and in some unreasonable way it frightened her.

But it did come near. It came quite close, and then rose straight above her head, so that she could see it perfectly clearly; it was a fierce predatory bird with a great beak, and it looked hungry. She gave a little shiver of fright—could it be going to attack her? But no. With a hoarse cry it swooped past her, just to her feet, and she screamed in sheer terror as she realized what it was doing—tearing with a hungry beak at something below her—something which lay naked and defenseless on the sun-baked rock. . . .

"I beg your pardon, madam. Are you not well?"

Mrs. Warrender lifted her head with a start. No—how ridiculous! Of course this was the hotel garden, with the flowers and the lizards, just as usual. There was nothing else there, no rock, no hungry bird of prey. Even the washing had been taken from the banana plantation; and there was a hotel servant standing beside her seat, looking at her with an expression of concern, and telling her, as far as she could make out, that she was wanted on the telephone. How stupid of her—what could she have been imagining?

She was a little surprised that there was anyone in Madeira who could want to telephone to her; but she got up and went obediently if rather shakily into the telephone-box.

" 'Allo," she said, trying ineffectively to answer like a foreigner.

"Is that Mrs. Warrender?" a strained voice answered her. "Mrs. Warrender, it's Florence Truman speaking, from Wright's Hotel. I don't know if you'll remember me—"

"Indeed I do."

"Mrs. Warrender, I'm afraid it's a lot to ask, but could you possibly come over and see me? I'd come to you, but I can't get away—not now. They'll be watching me . . . and I *must* talk to somebody. *Could* you?"

"Why, of course, if you really want me. . . ."

"You know what it's about," Florence Truman went on urgently. "I can't—I daren't talk to you much on the phone, but—Mrs. Warrender, he *didn't* kill himself, and they're trying to make me say he did!"

"What?" said Mrs. Warrender. The world seemed to be turning upside down again.

"He didn't! I mean, he couldn't have. Oh, please, will you come and see me? I must talk to somebody, and—you did like him, didn't you? The night we came over to your place?"

"I thought he was one of the most charming people I had ever seen," said Mrs. Warrender sincerely. "It's terrible."

"Then you'll come. Please!" Florence's voice cut her short. "Believe me, I'd come to you, but I daren't. If you could get over to Wright's this evening about half-past six, and we could go to my room . . . Oh, *please*. I daren't go on talking, or somebody will hear."

"Yes, of course I will," Mrs. Warrender said, startled by the urgency of the strained voice at the other end of the phone. For a time she sat in her chair motionless; then she went to her room to tidy herself, and descended for tea on the terrace.

"James," she said to her son when he joined her, "do you think it's really certain that that poor boy committed suicide?"

"How you do go on. Really, I didn't think you could be so interested in somebody you'd only met for a few minutes," said James. But he did not say it unkindly; perhaps Dr. Lang had given him a hint not to be too rough. At any rate his voice was unusually gentle as he added, "I'm afraid there's very little doubt about it, my dear. Lang says it looks as though he must have taken a whacking great dose."

"But he did seem so cheerful—so almost happy—when he was over here. It seems so extraordinary."

"You only saw him for an hour or so," James reminded her. "And they go up and down very quickly, change a lot, when they're like that. Besides, you don't know what happened after he left here. Something may have turned up to upset him."

"But I can't think what it could have been," Mrs. Warrender murmured.

"Well, how should you? You didn't know him. I can think of half a dozen things it might have been, if you ask me."

"What?"

"Well, suppose he found he'd got himself into trouble with that girl he was dancing with. It's common talk that he made a lot of quite unsuitable fuss about her, and a girl in her position's very likely to fasten on a fool of a young man who looks as though he has money. Suppose she suddenly cut up nasty? Don't look like that; I dare say it does shock you, but people do do that sort of thing, you know. And you asked me about it—I wasn't going to have told you."

"It wasn't that, quite," said Mrs. Warrender. "But, James, even if he did—die of poisoning, it needn't have been suicide, need it? Surely people do, accidentally, take too much?"

"If Lang's right in what he says, you can put that clean out of your head," her son replied. "Nobody would take as huge a shot as he thinks it was, by mistake. No, if you're determined to say he didn't do it himself, you'll have to think of somebody who did it for him. Murder, in fact. And murder with a hypodermic."

5

Mrs. Warrender, although she had a son who was a well-known detective, had never succeeded in accustoming herself to the terms and processes of the law; and the calm way in which James let fall the word "murder" had given her a shock—more particularly because of the introduction, in the same conversation, of suggestions about the relationships between the Haydon boy and Florence Truman. She was feeling very nervous, and in doubt what to say, as she made her way to the lounge of Wright's Hotel, where Florence, who had obviously been waiting anxiously for her to appear, beckoned her hastily out and led the way to a small uncomfortable bedroom on the top floor where the westering sun streamed uncomfortably in. She looked more white and more strained, if possible, than in the short glimpse at lunch time, and was clearly on the verge of a breakdown. But her first words cleared up at least one complication.

"There's one thing," she began, locking the door of the little room on them, and standing with her chin held high, "that I'd like to say to you before anything else. I know what everybody's saying about this—that Jeremy killed himself because he'd been making passes at me, and I'd fallen for him and was trying to make things difficult. It isn't true."

"But, my dear," said Mrs. Warrender, hoping she had successfully suppressed her start of surprise, "why? Why should anybody say anything so unkind?"

"Oh, it's obvious," the girl said with a curl of her lip. "Because he was decent and friendly to me—and you know it doesn't pay to be 'too free with the servants'—they think you mean more than you do and begin to take liberties. I'm sorry," seeing her guest's expression of distress. "I didn't mean to bother you. I don't really mind; it's the kind of thing some people always say in places like this, when a man treats a hired dancer like me as if she was a human creature. But I'd like *you* to know it wasn't true. I wasn't making love to him and I wasn't trying to get hold of him in any way. I—I was fond of him; he was damned decent to me, and I'd cry my eyes out now if I thought it would be any sort of good to him. He was a *nice* lad: he got one, like that. But there wasn't a single thing more to it. You believe that, don't you?"

"Indeed!" said Mrs. Warrender, though she did not feel quite certain whether it was a denial or a renunciation to which she had listened. "Indeed I do. But, are you sure—that he—didn't—"

"Not on your life," Florence said. "Matter of fact, I don't think he'd ever fallen for a woman at all. I believe, if you ask me, that he'd got so fed up with girls throwing themselves at his head because he was good looking and splashed his money about that he just wasn't having any. I think he cared for his sister more than for any creature in the world—at any rate"—she turned her back and swallowed for a second—"he certainly wasn't in love with me, though he did talk to me a bit about himself now and again—more than he did to any of the lot here. That's why."

"Why what?"

"Oh, don't you *see?*" Florence turned and faced her. "I thought—when we met you the other night—that you sounded as if you knew about knowing people. I mean . . . you were telling us about Gladys and the silver and how you knew what had happened because you knew what sort of things Gladys could do and what she couldn't. You see what I mean? . . . Well, I *did* know Jeremy, and I do know that he wouldn't—couldn't kill himself. Especially not now."

"Not on purpose," Mrs. Warrender said. "But couldn't he have done it accidentally?" She was still clinging to her small hope, the more so since Florence seemed to have no suspicion of the possibility of murder.

"Accidentally? How do you mean? He got a great shot of morphia out of a hypodermic."

"Yes, but . . . Isn't it easy to take too much, sometimes?"

"*Sometimes?* What do you mean? . . . Oh! Are people saying that—that Jeremy was a morphia addict?"

Mrs. Warrender gave an infinitesimal nod.

"It's a lie! It's a *damned* lie! He never drugged in his life. I ought to know all about addicts, living in places like this, and I tell you he never did! Besides, if you don't believe me, you've only to ask the doctor. If Jeremy had been in the habit of dosing himself with morphia out of a hypodermic, do you know what his skin would have been like? All over punctures. And I've seen him bathing often enough—he hadn't a mark on his body."

"He hadn't got diabetes, had he, or anything like that?" Mrs. Warrender asked.

"Diabetes? No, I'm sure he hadn't. He was as fit as anything. But why on earth—?"

"Oh, just something I thought of," said Mrs. Warrender, looking rather puzzled. There was a minute's silence. "But there was something you were going to tell me—some reason why you know he couldn't have killed himself," she said.

"Yes . . . Only I don't quite know how to start," said Florence. "Because, you see, I'm quite certain that, apart from that, he couldn't. He wasn't that kind—he was too happy, and—and, sort of damn-it-all, something will turn up. I *know,* but I know nobody will believe me—it's just knowing, and who takes any notice of that?"

"It's what matters, though," said Mrs. Warrender. The girl gave her a grateful look.

"Well, anyway, look here. He *was* bothered, this last day or two, and he did tell me about it. It was about his sister. I told you I thought he always cared for his sister more than for any other woman—well, what he told me was that his sister'd got married, a few years ago, to a fellow whom he simply couldn't stand and thought was a real bad hat; only he was only a kid at the time—she's older than him—and he couldn't do anything about it.

"After a while his sister began to find out about her husband—but kept it to herself. It wasn't till the other day, when he got a letter from her, that he realized that it had been merry hell for her for months back, but she hadn't said a thing. In fact, she'd only written to him when she did because she'd made up her mind to try and get a divorce, and the man she'd married had rushed off round the world or something like that, and she thought she might as well use the chance to talk about it a bit. She's the kind, I understand, that would go on sticking rather anything than have a row in the home—there's a baby, you see, and all that sort of thing."

Mrs. Warrender, having the gift of silence, made no superfluous comment. The girl went on, jerkily.

"So she'd just written asking him if he'd please come home before Maurice—that's the husband—got back. They're orphans, you see, without anybody to go to except some sort of old trustee who'd let anything pass rather than have a fuss. And she asked him, *please*—like that—to come back on the next boat, and he couldn't."

"Because he'd got no money?" Mrs. Warrender hazarded.

"Because he hadn't a bean! Because he'd been letting a whole lot of cheapskates sponge on him here, and because a fellow he'd lent nearly all his last quarter's allowance to, and who'd solemnly promised to let him have it back three months ago, hadn't let him have a farthing. That's why he was so miserable underneath—why some people thought him a moody neurotic. He *wanted* to get back to England, to see if there wasn't a chance of making things all right for his sister before this Maurice man could get back."

"So he was really worried?" Mrs. Warrender spoke quietly.

"Yes, fearfully. He was talking to me about it two nights ago, the evening we met you at the Grand—wondering if the man he'd lent the money to wouldn't pay by the next post, or if he could squeeze the bank for a bit extra, if he told them all about it—only he didn't want to have to, because of his sister. But he said, if everything went wrong, he'd stow away on one of the Union Castle liners, and work his passage back, because there wasn't anywhere they could put him off till Southampton. Or he'd get a passage on a yacht that wanted an extra hand—he thought he'd rather like that. Oh, don't you *see?*" said Florence Truman. "I mean, he wasn't a bit in despair, as that beast Lewis was trying to make me say. He didn't for a minute think he wasn't going to get there somehow, only he was bothered because he didn't see how to do it without getting into an awful tangle. Only he'd never, never have just faded out and left his sister to tackle it all alone. I mayn't know much, but I do know that!"

She stopped, and there was silence for two full minutes. Then she turned suddenly on Mrs. Warrender. "Say something, can't you? Say that I'm a liar, and you don't believe a word I say. Only do say something!"

"My dear, I do believe you," Mrs. Warrender said gently. "Only, I was just thinking—"

"What?"

"Sit down," said Mrs. Warrender; and, somewhat to her surprise, the girl sat. "You see, I'm quite sure you're telling me the truth, and I think you know a great deal about Mr. Haydon, because you were so fond of him. No, dear, I don't mean anything you wouldn't like me to mean, and anyhow I think affection gives one a great deal clearer insight into people than just falling in love—I'm afraid I don't express myself very well, but perhaps you see what I mean. I'm sure you know, if you say Mr. Haydon wasn't going to kill himself. But if he wasn't, and you say he couldn't have killed himself by accident—wait a moment, dear—don't you see, somebody must have killed him?"

"I don't. . . . You mean, he was *murdered?*" Florence Truman said.

"That's what my son said, this afternoon, and he's got a great deal of experience. He said, 'If he didn't do it himself, you'll have to think of somebody who did it for him.' My *dear,* don't!"

"I wasn't. I'm not going to cry. Only," said Florence, "I never thought of it. Do you mean—somebody *murdered* Jeremy? Killed him, like that?"

"It's dreadful, I know," said Mrs. Warrender. "Only—I don't see anything else."

"If they did," said the girl, clenching her thin hands very slowly and staring until her eyes came out of her head, "I won't do a thing else—I won't eat or sleep or do anything, until I've made them pay for it. It—it's like killing a baby, to hurt any thing as decent and happy as Jeremy. Don't you think so?" Mrs. Warrender nodded.

Florence Truman walked up and down the room for a few seconds, muttering a little to herself. Then she turned and faced her visitor. "You're right," she said. "You must be right. God knows why I didn't think of it myself, only I was a fool and got into a rage. He *was* murdered. *Jeremy Haydon was murdered*. . . . Listen." She stood, staring straight at Mrs. Warrender, and spoke in a low determined voice. "I swear—now—by Almighty God that if it costs me all I have and all I hope for I will see that his murderers are punished. But," she added, "you've got to help me."

"I? But, dear—"

"Don't you see," said Florence in the same quiet tone, "there are just the two of us, you and I, who know that he was murdered. I know because I know he couldn't have killed himself, and you know because you believed me when I said so and because you saw that there was nothing else that could have happened. But nobody else knows it except us two. Lewis, and the doctor, and his bank, they all believe he killed himself—and I'll bet anything your son thinks so too, doesn't he? . . . I thought as much. So, you see, they won't do anything about it—they'll just have an inquest and bury him quick out of the way, so that Lewis won't lose his summer visitors, and it'll all be forgotten, and if I say anything I'll be fired, and that'll be that. Oh, don't you understand? You *can't* do nothing; you couldn't go home when your holiday's over and know he'd been murdered and you hadn't said a word. You might meet his sister some day in England—I met her once. And he was nice to you, wasn't he? It isn't for me I'm asking. It's because we're the only two who *know*."

"My dear," said Mrs. Warrender, very much moved, "of course I'll do anything I can to help. But what *can* an old lady like me do?"

"I don't know." The light faded out of Florence's eyes, and she dropped into a chair. "I don't know what either of us can do, really. But there is—there must be *something*."

"You see," said Mrs. Warrender, picking her words slowly, "if he was really killed, it must have been—he must have been killed by somebody. And the question is—who?"

"Yes," Florence echoed dully. *"Who?"*

" 'A murderer—with a hypodermic' " Mrs. Warrender quoted, half under her breath. "My dear, what is it?" For Florence had stiffened and was staring at her as if she had seen a ghost.

"My heavens, do you know everything? That girl—the one you saw—Clare Ferrers—and her boy friend—they dope like fiends. How did you know?"

"I didn't," said Mrs. Warrender. "It was only something my son said."

"She'd have enough morphia to sink a battleship. But I don't know why she should want to kill him. She sucked him dry. I'd have killed *her* half a dozen times for the asking. She didn't like his consorting with the lower classes," Florence said bitterly. She paused a moment, and an ugly look came over her face. "If it was, I'll—I'll jolly well have the hide off her! She's going to get what's coming to her some day, anyhow, the mean, spiteful little—"

"Please! Just a minute," Mrs. Warrender interrupted. "I mean—we mustn't be in too much of a hurry, must we?" She hesitated, putting her thought into shape. "You see, my dear, it's a question of what we *know*, isn't it, just as you said? I *knew* about Gladys, and you *know* about Mr. Haydon—I think you're right, I think I would have known too, if I'd seen a little more of him. Now, you know these friends of his you were talking about, and I've only seen two of them and that just for two minutes. So I must rely on you. Do you know—do you think, quite honestly—that one of them, Miss Ferrers, perhaps, would be a—murderer? It's very important, you see, to be quite certain. Lots of people can be very unpleasant and not be murderers."

Florence looked up quickly, and flushed a little. "Meaning, don't be a cat, and let your private spites come in. I get you. . . . No-o. I suppose, if I'm being honest," she said reluctantly, "I don't see Clare Ferrers murdering anybody. I hate her like poison, but, as you say, that's not the point. And if she wasn't, there isn't any one of them that would. They're a poor greedy sponging lot—and I know some of them pretty well, a lot better, really, than Jeremy did. But I *don't* feel they're murderers. That's a lot of help, isn't it?"

"Well, then," said Mrs. Warrender, "it was somebody else."

"But who? *Who?* That's what I can't think. He didn't know anybody else, unless you count barmen and shopkeepers down the town, and the bank manager, but why should they kill him? Unless you're going to say there was a lunatic walking around."

"I don't think lunatics generally have hypodermics full of morphia," said Mrs. Warrender.

"I suppose they don't—anyway there aren't any here, that I'm aware of. Why did you want to know if Jeremy had diabetes, by the way?"

"Only a funny little thing I noticed," said Mrs. Warrender. "You know, it was I who picked up the syringe." She screwed up her eyes for a moment, the recollection of that scene was still too near the surface of consciousness. "I happened to notice the name on it, because it was my own chemists—Loxley's in Baker Street. They're very good, but they're not a big firm, and I should be very surprised if you could buy one of their hypodermics in Funchal."

"What difference does it make where it was bought?"

"Don't you see, dear, if Mr. Haydon had had one of his own—if he'd been in the habit of taking morphia—or if he'd had diabetes or anything you have to take injections for—he might quite likely have bought the syringe in London. But you tell me he didn't—"

"And I'll swear that's true."

"I'm sure you're right, my dear. Well, if he hadn't got one, and had suddenly decided to commit suicide, he might have bought one in the town, but I'm sure it wouldn't have been one from Loxley's. So it looks as though it might have been somebody else's."

"That's clever of you," the girl said, rather wearily; "but I don't see that it gets us anywhere much. Unless it means that we should look for a homicidal lunatic, who had a syringe from Baker Street and hasn't got it now."

"I don't think it could have been a homicidal lunatic," Mrs. Warrender said. "I'm sure Mr. Haydon wouldn't have waited while a strange madman stuck a syringe into him. He'd have fought him. It must have been someone he knew quite well. Someone he knew but you didn't, perhaps."

Florence shook her head.

"Oh, but, my dear, you didn't know everybody he knew. You weren't with him all the time." Mrs. Warrender's voice was gentle. "For instance, the day before he died—what was he doing then?"

"I don't really know. I didn't see much of him that day. He was out somewhere a good bit of the time."

"With his friends?"

"No. They'd all gone off in a car somewhere. I think myself he was glad to be shut of them for a bit."

"Then he might have met somebody. Look here," said Mrs. Warrender, "don't you feel that's what we ought to do? Try to find out what he was doing the day before, and see whether that doesn't tell us anything?"

"It wasn't the day before; matter of fact, it was the same day."

"Oh!" Mrs. Warrender had forgotten, for the moment, Dr. Lang's words.

"I heard the doctor saying to one of the policemen, 'between ten and twelve last night.' Anyway, his bed wasn't slept in. He must have been lying out there all night. That's one of the things that's sickening to think of, though I suppose it doesn't matter to him. You die pretty quickly of a shot of morphia, don't you?"

"I'm sure you don't feel or notice anything," Mrs. Warrender reassured her. "But isn't it queer that nobody noticed him there?"

"Not so much as you'd think. People lie there all day, off and on. They turn over, of course, and oil themselves; but unless you were looking you would quite likely not notice if they didn't. And his place was right at the end, and he never cared much to talk to people while he was sunbathing. If you hadn't come this morning, I expect he'd be there now—or until something or somebody noticed him," said Florence with a shudder.

"My dear, you mustn't!" Mrs. Warrender turned pale, finding that others could imagine large white birds with beaks. "Don't—we *can't* stop to think of horrors."

"Sorry," said the girl. "Maybe I'm going crazy."

"We know," Mrs. Warrender went on, in the desire to shut out visions thinking with a rapidity unusual to her, "we know that he was killed by the pool sometime between ten and twelve."

"Perhaps he wasn't killed there."

"Oh, I think he must have been. I'm sure nobody would have tried to carry a big man like Mr. Haydon—and in a bathing suit. They would have been sure to be seen. I wonder if anyone did see them—or see Mr. Haydon down there? Was he in the hotel for dinner, do you know?"

"Yes, I saw him. But he went upstairs pretty soon, and then I didn't see him again."

"Would anybody have been likely to see him down there? At about ten or eleven?"

"Not very likely," the girl said, "unless they'd been bathing, and I shouldn't think it was very likely that any one was. You see, it was gala night at your hotel, and you've got a big pool, so most of our people would have gone there, if they wanted to bathe. The hotels take turns for gala nights."

"Still, he *was* bathing, so I suppose the other person probably was too, and somebody might have seen them. I wonder if he had a visitor that evening. No, that was silly of me. Anybody who wanted to murder him wouldn't come walking up to the door and ask for him. I wonder if he'd made an appointment with the other man."

"You seem very sure there *was* another man."

"But, of course, there must have been. Or else he couldn't have been killed, could he?" said Mrs. Warrender. She wrinkled her brows. "Did he have a letter, or a note or anything, in the morning, do you know?"

"I don't. But I should think the porter would. I could ask him."

"If he had, and he didn't throw it away, it would be in his rooms or his clothes, I suppose."

"They won't let you in to look there. I tried and they threw me out," said Florence.

"Or he may have made an appointment when he went down to the town. I do wonder where he went. You're sure you haven't any idea?"

"I don't *know* where he went, of course. But if he did what he ordinarily did, I know where he might have been part of the time."

"Where?"

"At that big café—Joao's, it's called; I don't know if you know it—down on the waterfront, just opposite the jetty where the launches land."

"Yes, I know it. With the big awnings, and the golden sun on top of it."

"That's right. Well, Jeremy used to go into Joao's in the afternoon, practically every day that he was down in the town, and sit there often quite a long time looking at the harbor. He was great pals with a waiter there, a nice lad called Tomas, and they used to have long talks."

"So, if he'd been going to meet anybody, he might have met them there. . . . Does Mr. Tomas speak any English?"

"Oh, yes. Badly, but he does speak it. Otherwise, Jeremy wouldn't have been able to talk to him—he was just lazy about learning foreign languages. I once or twice helped him out with some Portuguese, because I pick lingoes up like a monkey. But with Tomas it really wasn't necessary. Why?"

"Well, I thought perhaps he would know and could tell us if Mr. Haydon met anybody there yesterday."

"Do you mean go and ask him?"

Mrs. Warrender nodded.

"What, now?"

Mrs. Warrender looked at her watch, and gave a little squeal. "My dear, I'm so sorry! I'd no idea it was so late. And, of course, you've got to go on duty."

"I didn't mean that. I needn't go on till nine o'clock, and anyhow it doesn't matter much to me now. If old Lewis gives me any of his lip, I'll tell him to go and fry himself in his own fat—I expect he's intending to give me the sack anyway. I was thinking of you. Oughtn't you to go back and have some dinner? Wouldn't be any good to have you knocking yourself up."

"I don't feel I want any dinner. I had a good tea, and I'm not really very hungry in the evenings," Mrs. Warrender said. "I would *much* rather go on and find out something, if there is anything to find out. But I think perhaps, if I'm not going back, I ought to send a message to my son, or he might be worrying. Perhaps I could telephone—or get somebody to telephone for me"—Mrs. Warrender had never got over her fear of telephones, and foreign telephones were particularly terrifying—"just so that he knows I'm all right. I expect you could find me a little something to eat when we've finished? That is, if you are sure you really ought to manage it. I would much rather have somebody with me than go and talk to Mr. Tomas all alone; but I shouldn't like you to lose your post."

"My post, as you call it, isn't worth worrying about. I'll lose it now or at the end of the season, and I can't say I care which," the girl said listlessly. "I'll come along if you like; it's better than doing nothing and wondering what people are saying. Let's go, shall we?"

"You haven't got a—a photograph of Mr. Haydon anywhere, have you?" asked Mrs. Warrender. She was not at all sure why she should ask for a photograph; but she had a vague idea that detectives always carried photographs about with them.

"As it happens, I've got quite a nice one, though it's only a snap," Florence said. "Here it is. You can have it if you like. I'd like to have it back some time, though."

"Of *course,* dear. Of course you shall," said Mrs. Warrender, stowing the print away in her handbag.

"Did you say you wanted to telephone?"

"I think—I think I'd like to ask Dr. Lang to send a message, if we could find his room," Mrs. Warrender said. Florence stared a little, but prepared to comply. She was not aware that Mrs. Warrender's investigation of her handbag had discovered yet another reason for consulting Dr. Lang. James, alleging that she always muddled the change, hardly ever let her have any money, and she was sure, though she did not know the market rate for information in Madeira, that detectives always had to pay for it. And of course Florence mustn't be allowed to pay, even if she had the money, which was very unlikely.

So, guided by Florence, she came to the door of the Langs' suite, and was very much relieved to find Dr. Lang himself in the corridor about ten yards off. It was much easier to ask him questions when Persis's roaring geniality was not within hearing. Trying very hard, but without much success, not to seem agitated, she explained that she was staying to have dinner with Miss Truman, and would Dr. Lang be so very kind as to telephone a message to James, because she couldn't manage the telephone? And further, would Dr. Lang be even more kind, and lend her five pounds in Portuguese currency. (She thought that should cover contingencies, not realizing how joyfully any Madeiran would leap at a handful of British small change.) For she had stupidly come out without any, and would want some after dinner. The doctor looked at her for an instant, but immediately produced the funds requested.

Then, trying to make her voice sound only like that of an inquisitive tourist, she said, "Oh, Dr. Lang! You saw poor Mr. Haydon, didn't you? Can you tell me—could it be true, what they're saying? That he'd taken a lot of drugs, often—I mean, that he was in the habit of it?"

"Not by injection, he didn't," the doctor said, "and you can tell anybody that you like. Of course, if he'd swallowed them or sniffed cocaine, say, that wouldn't show. But I'd be prepared to bet he didn't; looked a thoroughly healthy fellow."

"Oh, I'm so glad," said Mrs. Warrender. "What—" she tried to find a plausible way of disguising her question, and gave it up—"I wonder what happened to the syringe."

"The police, or whatever they call themselves here, took it with the bottle you found. I suppose they're keeping it somewhere," said Dr. Lang, lifting his eyebrows a trifle. "Come in and see Persis, won't you, if you're not in a hurry. She was resting, but she'll be up now."

"Oh, thank you very much, but I *really* must go; I'll be keeping Miss Truman waiting," said Mrs. Warrender; and fled. If he thought her an elderly ghoul she could not help it. Actually, Dr. Lang stared after her for a minute or two in indecision. She looked, he thought, rather queer and overexcited; and he was sure that it would not be good for her to be in the company of that dancing girl, who was probably pretty much upset herself, poor thing.

6

Mrs. Warrender found her way back to Florence, and so to the hotel entrance, where, feeling unusually competent, she hailed a taxi to take them to the waterfront. They spoke little on the way down. Florence seemed sunk in her thoughts, and Mrs. Warrender, beyond one timid pat on her knee, refrained from interrupting.

When they reached Joao's, on the waterfront, Florence appeared suddenly to wake up, and to begin to take command. "I'll tell you what we're going to do," she said, "we're going to sit down and order omelettes, before we even try to get hold of Tomas. It's quite silly, your thinking you can go and talk to people without having anything to eat, and I haven't been sacked yet—I've got enough for that."

"Oh, my dear—but I couldn't *dream* of letting you pay. I've got *heaps* of money," said Mrs. Warrender, displaying it proudly. "I thought we might need some for Mr. Tomas. So I borrowed it."

Florence laughed—Mrs. Warrender had not heard her laugh for forty-eight hours.

"You really are a darling," she said. "Tomas won't need tipping. But you must eat something."

"If you say so, dear," Mrs. Warrender acquiesced, and looked out towards the bay, along the short stone jetty with its groups of idle strollers. But there were no snorting little launches there to take passengers to and fro from the liners, for there was no big ship anchored there that evening. Florence secured omelettes, one of which she ate rapidly, while Mrs. Warrender picked politely at the other.

Eventually, Florence beckoned to a small waiter with a monkey face, and said, "*Deux cognacs—*"

"But, please, I don't want brandy," said Mrs. Warrender.

"Then I'll drink both of them," said Florence.

When the waiter came back with the cognacs, Florence said, "Wait a minute, Tomas. You know me?"

The man nodded.

"And you have heard—what's happened?"

"Oh, si! Yahs, yess. It is veree sad, yahs?" He really did look distressed, even if his English was not equal to the occasion.

"It is. It was so—sudden," said Florence with a wry face. "You saw him yesterday, perhaps? He went to the town."

"Yes, indeed I see him. He was having his drink here, like always, and I serve him, yahs, like always."

"What time?"

"But I do not know. The same time, like always."

"Was he with a friend?"

"Oh, no," said Tomas. Their faces fell. "Indeed, no. I know his friends well indeed. He was not a friend, no."

"What?" Both spoke simultaneously, but Mrs. Warrender yielded.

"He did have somebody with him then?" Florence said.

"Oh, yahs. But not his friend."

"Who was it?"

"Oh, I do not know. It was a man. He come walking past, and he say, 'Fahnsee you here,' and the señor say, 'Yes, I am here, like always. You have a drink, yes—no?' So they have two—three."

"You didn't hear what they said?" Mrs. Warrender intervened.

"Yahs. Some I hear. But not understand. I understand ze English only so, when I listen, like always." Tomas smiled ingratiatingly.

"And you weren't listening then."

"No. I have many peoples, because of the big ship. I cannot listen. I only hear when zey say, 'Well, so long. Ten-thirty at ze hotel.' Pardon, señora, they call me," and Tomas shot away, unaware of the sensation his words had made.

"You were right." Florence stared at Mrs. Warrender. "And I thought you were dreaming. He *did* meet somebody here, somebody I didn't know—"

"By chance, you know," replied Mrs. Warrender. "He said, 'Fancy seeing you here.' "

"And he was going to meet him again, at Wright's, at ten-thirty. Oh, Lord," said Florence, "you're a witch. Look here, let's pay Tomas—I think he gets double tip, don't you?—and go back. Can you run to another taxi?"

"If he came," said Mrs. Warrender in the taxi—she was now nearly as excited as her companion—"how did he get in, without being seen? You said Mr. Haydon hadn't had any visitors."

"Oh, I suppose Jeremy walked up the drive and met him. Or he could have come in at the side entrance—that's not locked till ten forty-five. But what could he do when he got there?" Her eyes were shining, and her lips moving; she looked a different girl.

"Bathe," said Mrs. Warrender. "Mr. Haydon was bathing."

"Oh, yes. He might have gone straight to the pool, of course. But how do we know?"

"What do you do when you bathe?" Mrs. Warrender asked.

"Why, undress, I suppose."

"Yes, but then? I mean, I'm sorry if I'm putting it stupidly; but, if Mr. Haydon wanted a bathing suit and a towel, where would he get it from?"

"From his locker."

"And if his friend did too—I mean, people don't generally come out in the evening carrying bathing suits, do they?"

"He'd have to get one out of the store. Oh, I see! . . . No." Florence's face clouded over. "I'm afraid that's a washout. You see, there's somebody on duty at the store most of the day, but he goes off at ten, unless it's a gala night. And the residents have keys, in case they might want to entertain a friend suddenly. So Jeremy would just have had to unlock the door, and fish a costume out, and nobody would have known.

"What is odder," she said after a pause, "is how on earth the man got out again."

"Why?"

"Well, if he came in through the side gate, okay. But that gate's locked at 10:45, and unless he'd been very quick, he couldn't have bathed *and* killed Jeremy and got up again, all in a quarter of an hour, could he?"

"Couldn't he have gone straight out, by the ordinary way?"

"We-ell. There's a man on there, every night, to check up who comes in and who goes out. They had some sort of row with the police, I believe; and that was why they put him on. Anyway he was there. Besides, you think the man came incog., don't you? So he wouldn't want to go away in a blaze of publicity. But how on earth *did* he get away?"

By now they were at the entrance to Wright's Hotel.

"I think I'll go down to the pool store," Florence said. "It isn't ten yet, and José's rather a friend of mine. I might get something out of him. Will you wait here?"

"No, I think I'll come down with you," said Mrs. Warrender. "It will be cooler by the pool, and I would like to know if you find out anything."

While Florence went to talk to the bathing attendant, Mrs. Warrender proceeded down the farthest flight of steps which led to the pool itself, and stood for a long time at the point on its rim where a stairway led down to a rope ladder which in turn led down to the sea. Across the still black water the lights of Funchal pricked the darkness.

"Mrs. Warrender! Mrs. Warrender!" Florence, all excited, came springing down the steps to her. "José doesn't know about anybody having bathed last night. But, what do you think, he's lost a bathing costume out of the store! And he knows it was there yesterday. What's that mean? But you aren't listening!"

"Yes, I am, dear," said Mrs. Warrender. "But just come here for a minute." She took her to the lip of the pool, and pointed to where, very near owing to the curve of the bay, the bathing pool of the Grand Hotel projected into the sea. "I shouldn't think the Grand Hotel pool is as much as a quarter of a mile from here, and look how beautifully calm it is. If he was a good swimmer, he could make his own clothes into a bundle, and swim there carrying them, and nobody would ever know he'd been here."

"My God! And then he'd go back and mix with the Grand Hotel crowd." Florence stared across the motionless water.

"You remember it was a gala night," said Mrs. Warrender. "There would be quite a lot of people there. I think, my dear, we'd better walk over to the Grand Hotel, don't you? It isn't far, if you can spare the time."

"What shall we do there?"

"Oh, see if we can find his bathing dress. I don't suppose he would have wanted to keep it longer than he needed, do you?"

When they had reached the Grand Hotel, Mrs. Warrender led the way to the bathing pool, and inquired, in her gentlest voice, of the attendant on duty whether she could be allowed to have the keys of all the bathing boxes.

"*All,* madam?" asked he, surprised.

"Well, you see," said Mrs. Warrender, "we think we may have left a bathing dress in one of them, and we can't remember which. What color was it, dear?"

"Orange," said Florence.

"There *was* an orange bathing dress found this morning, in Number 51, but I am afraid it wasn't yours. It belonged to Wright's Hotel. So we're sending it back there. I'm sorry."

"But it might have been—thank you so much—it might have been the one I mean. My friend didn't say where he'd got it," said Mrs. Warrender, "only where he'd left it, and he might have come over from Wright's."

"Perhaps in the boat," the official agreed. "I saw people were using the boat last night."

"Boat?" said Florence.

"There's a boat just by the pool, miss. People use it to row out to that island. Anybody can use it, if they know how to undo it."

"If you haven't actually sent back the bathing dress, might I see it?" said Mrs. Warrender. "I might just know, from looking, whether it was the one my friend was wearing—he's the kind of man who would never know where it came from." And as he turned to get it, she whispered rapidly to Miss Truman, "Look at it all you can, my dear: you may be able to notice something."

"I didn't get anything but its number, which may be worth knowing," Florence Truman said. "But, honestly, you're a living marvel. I didn't believe a bit in this other man when you suggested him, but now you've not only proved that he existed, but that he swam over from Wright's last evening—"

"Rowed, dear," said Mrs. Warrender. "Much quicker, and less splashy. It was silly of me not to think of it before."

"What do we do now, then?"

"I suppose," said Mrs. Warrender, "we go up to the hotel, and see whether there is any one staying there who would possibly fit."

Her voice faltered a little on the last words; it was a long pull up from the pool to the hotel, and she suddenly felt very tired. But Florence Truman was buoyant.

"Ends of the earth, if you say so," she said. "Gosh, but you don't know what a difference all this makes! It's like being in a new world. Hi, don't trip over the cobbles."

They arrived, at length, in the foyer of the Grand Hotel, and casually inspected the register. But they found nothing of interest.

"There's nobody arrived at all," said Mrs. Warrender. "But I'm sure, from the way Tomas was talking, that this man had only just come."

"Then he must have come on that German boat, the day before," Florence observed. "There's no English liner calling round about now— What's the matter?"

"Oh, but I'm so *silly!*" Mrs. Warrender exclaimed. "The *Armadilla*—that big cruising ship. If you please"—she addressed the porter, with some little difficulty, because he seemed to have turned into two or three porters, and it was so awkward not to know which one you ought to look at—"could you tell me what time the *Armadilla* left, yesterday? And where was she going?"

"She left at twelve-thirty, madam," said the porter. "Making for Buenos Aires."

"Oh? And passengers went ashore?"

"Oh, yes, madam, quite a lot. The launches were running quite late, taking them back."

"Launches. We ought to go and see all the l-launches," said Mrs. Warrender; and suddenly collapsed in a small heap on the floor.

7

Mrs. Warrender woke the next morning from a long and sound sleep, with the feeling that one occasionally has that something important has happened, but one cannot imagine what it is.

She lay still, slowly collecting her wits, and wondering a little why she felt so limp. Then her eye was caught by her clothes, lying on a chair, and she looked at them again in mild perplexity. What had she been thinking of, to leave them like that when she came to bed? Reflecting on this, she was surprised to find that she had no recollection of taking off her clothes when she came to bed, or, indeed, of coming to bed at all. Now how could that be? At this point in her reflections there was a knock on the door, and James came in.

"Good morning, dear," said Mrs. Warrender cheerfully. "It looks like another nice day. Why, James, is anything the matter? You look quite worried."

"I should think so!" her son burst out. "What do you suppose, when you gave us such a fright last night? Going and fainting in the foyer, with everybody looking at you!" He said the last words with indignation, as though the publicity added to the offense.

"Oh!" It all began to come back. Joao's, the pool, the orange bathing dress, and asking about the sailing time of the *Armadilla*. And, of course, she had been meaning to find out about the launches. Mrs. Warrender sat up in bed with a feeling of determination. What a pity she had been so foolish as to faint, and to cause James, doubtless, a lot of inconvenience.

"I *am* so sorry, dear," she said. "It was *very* silly of me, and so tiresome for you. It was nothing—only that I was a little tired—"

"No wonder, going all over the place with that girl, and having practically no dinner!" James said. "If Lang hadn't happened to be over here I should have had to get some dago doctor from the hotel! But he carried you up, and we phoned for his wife to come over and put you to bed, and Lang gave you a sleeping draught."

"Oh, dear, what a nuisance I've been! And a sleeping draught too! That must be why I slept so soundly. I feel *perfectly* well now," Mrs. Warrender said.

"That's as may be. But you'll stop in bed today and have no gallivanting about," said James severely.

"Yes, dear," meekly. "Do you know what happened to Miss Truman?"

"I don't. I gave her a piece of my mind, and packed her off to her own place. And I hope the manager ticked her off properly. Pure selfishness!" said James. His mother gave a small sigh, but was too experienced to attempt a defense. "Well, mother, shall I ring for your breakfast?"

"If you please, dear. Oh, James," as he turned to go, "I wonder if you could spare me a little time. I've something rather important I want to ask you."

"If you want to, by all means. I suppose this afternoon would do; I must do some work now. Mind, you're not to get up today—Lang says so."

"No, dear. Thank you very much." Poor James, his case seemed to be very troublesome.

During the interval, while she was waiting for her breakfast and eating it, Mrs. Warrender strove to set her recollections in order. Jeremy Haydon had met a man in the town on the afternoon of his death, a stranger to the place, and one who seemed surprised to see him. He had made an appointment with this man at Wright's Hotel for ten-thirty that evening, and by midnight, at latest, he was dead—in his bathing suit. This, she said to herself, was quite certain, quite proved. Then there was the rest, which she believed was certain but which James would certainly say was not proved; that the unknown came to Wright's not by land, but in the boat from the Grand Hotel's bathing pool, that he bathed in an orange bathing dress taken by Jeremy from the store at Wright's, and that he subsequently, having killed Jeremy, rowed back to the Grand Hotel and dressed, leaving his borrowed bathing dress in one of their boxes.

Why not dress before he went back? Because, Mrs. Warrender argued to herself, somebody *might* have turned up at any moment, and he have been seen. Then—it must be true—he had hurried down to the harbor and got on a launch going to the *Armadilla,* and was now on his way to Buenos Aires—the cruel, callous brute! But—who *was* he? And why did he want to murder Jeremy Haydon?

What could she do? She could try and find out if a strange man had gone away late on a launch, though she had hoped that James would do that for her. It was so difficult, not knowing at all what he looked like. Of course, she might ask Tomas that. Or she could take the photograph of Jeremy, which Florence had given to her, and see whether anybody—the bank manager, perhaps—had seen him about with a strange man.

She reached for the snapshot, which lay on the table beside her. But, when she got it, she found to her surprise that it was two snapshots, which must have got stuck together. The top one was of Jeremy Haydon, leaning against the rail of the pool and drinking a long drink. The other was of a group: Jeremy, a woman looking rather like him, but a few years older, and another man. Mrs. Warrender stared long and seriously at the second photograph. An idea—an idea which startled her both by its incredibility and by the way in which it seemed to fit—had come to her. She put the photograph down and got out of bed with determination. For James's instructions she had ceased to care; this was life or death.

She dressed, feeling a little more shaky than she would have liked to own, and made her way downstairs. There she bearded the porter—who looked at her sympathetically and tried to start a conversation about the heat—and made him ring up Wright's Hotel and get Florence Truman on the telephone. For a time there was a slight confusion of courtesies, as she enquired after Florence's job and Florence expressed anxiety about her health; but at length this was resolved and she managed to put her question about the photograph.

"Oh, I didn't know you'd got it," Florence said. "It must have stuck. Yes, of course, it's him and his sister—Mrs. Benoni—and the other man's her husband."

"I thought that might be it," said Mrs. Warrender. "Tell me—I thought you said Mr. Benoni was out of England."

"So he is. Cruising somewhere, Jeremy told me. But—oh, I say—you don't think——?"

"Hush, my dear! *Don't* say anything. Not on the telephone. I will tell you, but I must think. Goodbye, my dear." And Mrs. Warrender, literally trembling with agitation, rang off.

No more delay. Regardless of the heat, and a certain inconvenient lightheadness, Mrs. Warrender found a hat, and a taxi, and set off for the town. She alighted at the offices of the firm which acted as general tourist agency for the whole of Madeira, and asked the clerk if she could see the passenger list of the *Armadilla*.

There, however, she met a check. The clerk—he was a bored, unintelligent underling—said that the passenger list of the *Armadilla* was private. She was not a liner; she was on a pleasure cruise, and it was no business of casual callers to know who was on board her.

"Oh, but it's very important to me! I do want to know if—if a friend of mine is on her," Mrs. Warrender quavered.

"Sorry, madam. We cannot help that. I have no authority," said the clerk, and disappeared somewhere into the back of the office.

"Oh, dear!" Mrs. Warrender sat down rather suddenly on a very worn leather seat, and looked at an advertisement of winter tours to the Amazon, wishing very much that she did not feel so inclined to cry. At this moment the entrance door behind her opened, and an indignant bark said: "Mrs. Warrender! What on earth are you doing down here? Surely James told you—"

"Oh, Dr. Lang!" Mrs. Warrender cried, forgetful of everything, but that here was a port in a storm. "Dr. Lang! *Please* help me. The man at the counter won't let me see the passenger list of the *Armadilla,* and it's really dreadfully important that I should. Can't you make him, please, Dr. Lang? I know you must think I've gone quite mad—but I must see it! No, no!" as he tried to soothe her, and take her away. "I can't help what James or you or anybody thinks. I must see that list, and I can't go away from here until I do."

An alarmed Englishman, particularly if he barks when alarmed, has a remarkable effect in Madeira; and Dr. Lang was at the moment decidedly alarmed. He had an affection for Mrs. Warrender of which she was hardly aware; he was genuinely distressed to see her pale face and excited eyes, and he understood that a Portuguese official was the proximate cause of them. So he banged on the counter, and bellowed at the Portuguese official in his most imperialist manner, until the latter, cowed into believing that he was about to create an "international incident," apologized and yielded up the precious document. Mrs. Warrender followed its length with a quivering finger until, with what was almost a hiccup of excitement, she found the name she sought.

"Oh, *thank* you, Dr. Lang!" she said.

"That all you want? And now," said the doctor with determination, "will you please allow me to take you back to the hotel and put you straight into bed?"

"It's so very kind of you," said Mrs. Warrender, obeying, "and I'm afraid I've been very tiresome and taken up a great deal of your time."

"Not at all. My job. But you will go and rest now, won't you?" the doctor said.

"Oh, I will! But—do you think you could ask James to come and see me first? I know he's busy; but I wouldn't keep him more than a minute or two. And I should be so much happier."

"I'll see he does," Dr. Lang promised.

In a very few minutes after their arrival at the hotel, James Warrender duly appeared, looking distinctly cross. Anxiety always made James Warrender cross.

"Well, mother, here I am," he said. "Lang said you wanted to see me."

"James, can you tell me about old Mr. Haydon's money?"

"*Haydon's?* Why on earth—what do you want to know?"

"Who got it, when he died?"

"Why, the children, so far as I know. That young chap who killed himself, and his sister."

"But to spend, did they? I mean, I thought you told me young Mr. Haydon couldn't get at the capital. Or something like that."

"Oh, I see. Yes, I believe that was so. I'm not absolutely certain," said James after a pause, "but I'm nearly sure they each got the interest on their share of the estate until they were twenty-five or until they married."

"And suppose one of them died?"

"The other got the lot. I know that."

"Are you sure that they, either of them, got it all when they married?"

"Yes, I am sure. I remember that particularly, because I thought old Haydon was a fool to put it that way. Was sure that Maurice Benoni was a scamp, and that he'd get hold of his wife's money, somehow, if it was absolutely hers. I advised the old man to tie it up on the girl and her children; but he never listened to anything anybody said—Why?"

"Only," said Mrs. Warrender, feeling she had at last come to the end of her nightmare, "I think Maurice Benoni must have murdered Mr. Haydon."

"*Murdered?* My dear mother, you're mad." James Warrender looked properly scandalized at such wild leaping to conclusions.

"No, dear. You see, he was here, the other day. He came on the *Armadilla,* and I'm almost certain he met Mr. Haydon. No, dear, just a minute, I'm not being silly, if you'd only just listen." And she unfolded the story of the two days' research, ending with the discovery of the name of Maurice Benoni on the passenger list of the *Armadilla*.

"You see, dear," she finished, "I've got a photograph of him here, and I meant to have asked Mr. Tomas, the waiter, if it was the same man, only I got rather tired. But I'm quite sure, if *you* asked him, you'd find out; and if he got back to the ship so late, just before it was going to sail, some of those men who run the launches would remember taking him. If that photograph's at all right, he must be quite a funny-looking man—the sort of person people would remember."

"I dare say," said James thoughtfully. "Yes, I'll certainly look into it. You leave it to me, mother. Don't you worry your head."

"Indeed I won't," said Mrs. Warrender. "I just—thought you'd like to—know." And, much to her subsequent shame, she then and there fell asleep.

"Not at all a bad job, though I say it as shouldn't," said James a little while afterwards, when after intensive enquiries, the necessary identification had been secured, and an extradition warrant issued for Maurice Benoni. "Quite sharp of you, mother, to have spotted that that syringe couldn't have been got in Madeira. I don't mind saying that had quite slipped my notice. But I think, on the whole, we didn't do too badly over that case. Of course, there's no direct money in it; but that sort of thing rather helps. Gets you known, and all that."

"I'm so glad, dear," said Mrs. Warrender. "But, James—I'm so sorry, but I quite forgot. I borrowed five pounds from Dr. Lang and I never gave it back. Could you pay it? I've got quite a lot of it still left, so it isn't so much as it sounds."

"*Five pounds?* What on earth did you want five pounds for?" said James.

THE SECOND BULLET

Anna Katharine Green

"You must see her."

"No. No."

"She's a most unhappy woman. Husband and child both taken from her in a moment; and now, all means of living as well, unless some happy thought of yours—some inspiration of your genius—shows us a way of re-establishing her claims to the policy voided by this cry of suicide."

But the small wise head of Violet Strange continued its slow shake of decided refusal.

"I'm sorry," she protested, "but it's quite out of my province. I'm too young to meddle with so serious a matter."

"Not when you can save a bereaved woman the only possible compensation left her by untoward fate?"

"Let the police try their hand at that."

"They have had no success with the case."

"Or you?"

"Nor I either."

"And you expect—"

"Yes, Miss Strange. I expect *you* to find the missing bullet which will settle the fact that murder and not suicide ended George Hammond's life. If you cannot, then a long litigation awaits this poor widow, ending, as such litigation usually does, in favor of the stronger party. There's the alternative. If you once saw her—"

"But that's what I'm not willing to do. If I once saw her I should yield to her importunities and attempt the seemingly impossible. My instincts bid me say no. Give me something easier."

"Easier things are not so remunerative. There's money in this affair, if the insurance company is forced to pay up. I can offer you—"

"What?"

There was eagerness in the tone despite her effort at nonchalance. The other smiled imperceptibly, and briefly named the sum.

It was larger than she had expected. This her visitor saw by the way her eyelids fell and the peculiar stillness which, for an instant, held her vivacity in check.

"And you think I can earn that?"

Her eyes were fixed on his in an eagerness as honest as it was unrestrained.

He could hardly conceal his amazement, her desire was so evident and the cause of it so difficult to understand. He knew she wanted money–that was her avowed reason for entering into this uncongenial work. But to want it *so much!* He glanced at her person; it was simply clad but very expensively–how expensively it was his business to know. Then he took in the room in which they sat. Simplicity again, but the simplicity of high art–the drawing room of one rich enough to indulge in the final luxury of a highly cultivated taste, viz.: unostentatious elegance and the subjection of each carefully chosen ornament to the general effect.

What did this favored child of fortune lack that she could be reached by such a plea, when her whole being revolted from the nature of the task he offered her? It was a question not new to him; but one he had never heard answered and was not likely to hear answered now. But the fact remained that the consent he had thought dependent upon sympathetic interest could be reached much more readily by the promise of large emolument–and he owned to a feeling of secret disappointment even while he recognized the value of the discovery.

But his satisfaction in the latter, if satisfaction it were, was of very short duration. Almost immediately he observed a change in her. The sparkle which had shone in the eye whose depths he had never been able to penetrate, had dissipated itself in something like a tear and she spoke up in that vigorous tone no one but himself had ever heard, as she said:

"No. The sum is a good one and I could use it; but I will not waste my energy on a case I do not believe in. The man shot himself. He was a speculator, and probably had good reason for his act. Even his wife acknowledges that he has lately had more losses than gains."

"See her. She has something to tell you which never got into the papers."

"You say that? You know that?"

"On my honor, Miss Strange."

Violet pondered; then suddenly succumbed.

"Let her come, then. Prompt to the hour. I will receive her at three. Later I have a tea and two party calls to make."

Her visitor rose to leave. He had been able to subdue all evidence of his extreme gratification, and now took on a formal air. In dismissing a guest, Miss Strange was invariably the society belle and that only. This he had come to recognize.

The case (well known at the time) was, in the fewest possible words, as follows:

On a sultry night in September, a young couple living in one of the large apartment houses in the extreme upper portion of Manhattan were so annoyed by the incessant crying of a child in the adjoining suite, that they got up, he to smoke, and she to sit in the window for a possible breath of cool air. They were congratulating themselves upon the wisdom they had shown in thus giving up all thought of sleep–for the child's crying had not ceased–when (it may have been two o'clock and it may have been a little later) there came from somewhere near, the sharp and somewhat peculiar detonation of a pistol shot.

He thought it came from above; she, from the rear, and they were staring at each other in the helpless wonder of the moment, when they were struck by the silence. The baby had ceased to cry. All was as still in the adjoining apartment as in their own–too still–much too still. Their mutual stare turned to one of horror. "It came from there!" whispered the wife. "Some accident has occurred to Mr. or Mrs. Hammond–we ought to go—"

Her words–very tremulous ones–were broken by a shout from below. They were standing in their window and had evidently been seen by a passing policeman. "Anything wrong up there?" they heard him cry. Mr. Saunders immediately looked out. "Nothing wrong here," he called down. (They were but two stories from the pavement.) "But I'm not so sure about the rear apartment. We thought we heard a shot. Hadn't you better come up, officer? My wife is nervous about it. I'll meet you at the stairhead and show you the way."

The officer nodded and stepped in. The young couple hastily donned some wraps, and, by the time he appeared on their floor, they were ready to accompany him.

Meanwhile, no disturbance was apparent anywhere else in the house, until the policeman rang the bell of the Hammond apartment. Then, voices began to be heard, and doors to open above and below, but not the one before which the policeman stood.

Another ring, and this time an insistent one–and still no response. The officer's hand was rising for the third time when there came a sound of fluttering from behind the panels against which he had laid his ear, and finally a choked voice uttering unintelligible words. Then a hand began to struggle with the lock, and the door, slowly opening, disclosed a woman clad in a hastily donned wrapper and giving every evidence of extreme fright.

"Oh!" she explaimed, seeing only the compassionate faces of her neighbors. "You heard it, too! a pistol shot from there–*there* my husband's room. I have not dared to go–I–I–Oh, have mercy and see if anything is wrong! It is so still–so still, and only a moment ago the baby was crying. Mrs. Saunders, Mrs. Saunders, why is it so still?"

She had fallen into her neighbor's arms. The hand with which she had pointed out a certain door had sunk to her side and she appeared to be on the verge of collapse.

The officer eyed her sternly, while noting her appearance, which was that of a woman hastily risen from bed.

"Where were you?" he asked. "Not with your husband and child, or you would know what had happened there."

"I was sleeping down the hall," she managed to gasp out. "I'm not well–I–Oh, why do you all stand still and do nothing? My baby's in there. Go! go!" and, with a sudden energy, she sprang upright, her eyes wide open and burning, her small well-featured face white as the linen she sought to hide.

The officer demurred no longer. In another instant he was trying the door at which she was again pointing.

It was locked.

Glancing back at the woman, now cowering almost to the floor, he pounded at the door and asked the man inside to open.

No answer came back.

With a sharp turn he glanced again at the wife.

"You say that your husband is in this room?"

She nodded, gasping faintly, "And the child!"

He turned back, listened, then beckoned to Mr. Saunders. "We shall have to break our way in," said he. "Put your shoulder well to the door. *Now!*"

The hinges of the door creaked; the lock gave way (this special officer weighed two hundred and seventy-five, as he found out, next day), and a prolonged and sweeping crash told the rest.

Mrs. Hammond gave a low cry; and, straining forward from where she crouched in terror on the floor, searched the faces of the two men for some hint of what they saw in the dimly lighted space beyond.

Something dreadful, something which made Mr. Saunders come rushing back with a shout:

"Take her away! Take her to our apartment, Jennie. She must not see—"

Not see! He realized the futility of his words as his gaze fell on the young woman who had risen up at his approach and now stood gazing at him without speech, without movement, but with a glare of terror in her eyes, which gave him his first realization of human misery.

His own glance fell before it. If he had followed his instinct he would have fled the house rather than answer the question of her look and the attitude of her whole frozen body.

Perhaps in mercy to his speechless terror, perhaps in mercy to herself, she was the one who at last found the word which voiced their mutual anguish.

"Dead?"

No answer. None was needed.

"And my baby?"

Oh, that cry! It curdled the hearts of all who heard it. It shook the souls of men and women both inside and outside the apartment; then all was forgotten in the wild rush she made. The wife and mother had flung herself upon the scene, and, side by side with the not unmoved policeman, stood looking down upon the desolation made in one fatal instant in her home and heart.

They lay there together, both past help, both quite dead. The child had simply been strangled by the weight of his father's arm which lay directly across the upturned little throat. But the father was a victim of the shot they had heard. There was blood on his breast, and a pistol in his hand.

Suicide! The horrible truth was patent. No wonder they wanted to hold the young widow back. Her neighbor, Mrs. Saunders, crept in on tiptoe and put her arms about the swaying, fainting woman; but there was nothing to say–absolutely nothing.

At least, they thought not. But when they saw her throw herself down, not by her husband, but by the child, and drag it out from under that strangling arm and hug and kiss it and call out wildly for a doctor, the officer endeavored to interfere and yet could not find the heart to do so, though he knew the child was dead and should not, according to all the rules of the coroner's office, be moved before that official arrived. Yet because no mother could be convinced of a fact like this, he let her sit with it on the floor and try all her little arts to revive it, while he gave orders to the janitor and waited himself for the arrival of doctor and coroner.

She was still sitting there in wide-eyed misery, alternately fondling the little body and drawing back to consult its small set features for some sign of life, when the doctor came, and, after one look at the child, drew it softly from her arms and laid it quietly in the crib from which its father had evidently lifted it but a short time before. Then he turned back to her, and found her on her feet, upheld by her two friends. She had understood his action, and without a groan had accepted her fate. Indeed, she seemed incapable of any further speech or action. She was staring down at her husband's body, which she, for the first time, seemed fully to see. Was her look one of grief or of resentment for the part he had played so unintentionally in her child's death? It was hard to tell; and when, with slowly rising finger, she pointed to the pistol so tightly clutched in the other outstretched hand, no one there–and by this time the room was full–could foretell what her words would be when her tongue regained its usage and she could speak.

What she did say was this:

"Is there a bullet gone? Did he fire off that pistol?" A question so manifestly one of delirium that no one answered it, which seemed to surprise her, though she said nothing till her glance had passed all around the walls of the room to where a window stood open to the night, its lower sash being entirely raised. "There! look there!" she cried, with a commanding accent, and, throwing up her hands, sank a dead weight into the arms of those supporting her.

No one understood; but naturally more than one rushed to the window. An open space was before them. Here lay the fields not yet parceled out into lots and built upon; but it was not upon these they looked, but upon the strong trellis which they found there, which, if it supported no vine, formed a veritable ladder between this window and the ground.

Could she have meant to call attention to this fact; and were her words expressive of another idea than the obvious one of suicide?

If so, to what lengths a woman's imagination can go! Or so their combined looks seemed to proclaim, when to their utter astonishment they saw the officer, who had presented a calm appearance up till now, shift his position and with a surprised grunt direct their eyes to a portion of the wall just visible beyond the half-drawn curtains of the bed. The mirror hanging there showed a star-shaped breakage, such as follows the sharp impact of a bullet or a fiercely projected stone.

"He fired two shots. One went wild; the other straight home."

It was the officer delivering his opinion.

Mr. Saunders, returning from the distant room where he had assisted in carrying Mrs. Hammond, cast a look at the shattered glass, and remarked forcibly:

"I heard but one; and I was sitting up, disturbed by that poor infant.

Jennie, did you hear more than one shot?" he asked, turning toward his wife.

"No," she answered, but not with the readiness he had evidently expected. "I heard only one, but that was not quite usual in its tone. I'm used to guns," she explained, turning to the officer. "My father was an army man, and he taught me very early to load and fire a pistol. There was a prolonged sound to this shot; something like an echo of itself, following close upon the first ping. Didn't you notice that, Warren?"

"I remember something of the kind," her husband allowed.

"He shot twice and quickly," interposed the policeman sententiously. "We shall find a spent bullet back of that mirror."

But when, upon the arrival of the coroner, an investigation was made of the mirror and the wall behind, no bullet was found either there or anywhere else in the room, save in the dead man's breast. Nor had more than one been shot from his pistol, as five full chambers testified. The case which seemed so simple had its mysteries, but the assertion made by Mrs. Saunders no longer carried weight, nor was the evidence offered by the broken mirror considered as indubitably establishing the fact that a second shot had been fired in the room.

Yet it was equally evident that the charge which had entered the dead speculator's breast had not been delivered at the close range of the pistol found clutched in his hand. There were no powder marks to be discerned on his pajama jacket, or on the flesh beneath. Thus anomaly confronted anomaly, leaving open but one other theory: that the bullet found in Mr. Hammond's breast came from the window and the one he shot went out of it. But this would necessitate his having shot his pistol from a point far removed from where he was found; and his wound was such as made it difficult to believe that he would stagger far, if at all, after its infliction.

Yet, because the coroner was both conscientious and alert, he caused a most rigorous search to be made of the ground overlooked by the above mentioned window; a search in which the police joined, but which was without any result save that of rousing the attention of people in the neighborhood and leading to a story being circulated of a man seen some time the night before crossing the fields in a great hurry. But as no further particulars were forthcoming, and not even a description of the man to be had, no emphasis would have been laid upon this story had it not transpired that the moment a report of it had come to Mrs. Hammond's ears (why is there always some one to carry these reports?) she roused from the torpor into which she had fallen, and in wild fashion exclaimed:

"I knew it! I expected it! He was shot through the window and by that wretch. He never shot himself." Violent declarations which trailed off into the one continuous wail, "Oh, my baby! my poor baby!"

Such words, even though the fruit of delirium, merited some sort of attention, or so this good coroner thought, and as soon as opportunity offered and she was sufficiently sane and quiet to respond to his questions, he asked her whom she had meant by *that wretch,* and what reason she had, or thought he had, of attributing her husband's death to any other agency than his own disgust with life.

And then it was that his sympathies, although greatly roused in her favor began to wane. She met the question with a cold stare followed by a few ambiguous words out of which he could make nothing. Had she said *wretch?* She did not remember. They must not be influenced by anything she might have uttered in her first grief. She was well-nigh insane at the time. But of one thing they might be sure: her husband had not shot himself; he was too much afraid of death for such an act. Besides, he was too happy. Whatever folks might say he was too fond of his family to wish to leave it.

Nor did the coroner or any other official succeed in eliciting anything further from her. Even when she was asked, with cruel insistence, how she explained the fact that the baby was found lying on the floor instead of in its crib, her only answer was: "His father was trying to soothe it. The child was crying dreadfully, as you have heard from those who were kept awake by him that night, and my husband was carrying him about when the shot came which caused George to fall and overlay the baby in his struggles."

"Carrying a baby about with a loaded pistol in his hand?" came back in stern retort.

She had no answer for this. She admitted when informed that the bullet extracted from her husband's body had been found to correspond exactly with those remaining in the five chambers of the pistol taken from his hand, that he was not only the owner of this pistol but was in the habit of sleeping with it under his pillow; but, beyond that, nothing; and this reticence, as well as her manner which was cold and repellent, told against her.

A verdict of suicide was rendered by the coroner's jury, and the life insurance company, in which Mr. Hammond had but lately insured himself for a large sum, taking advantage of the suicide clause embodied in the policy, announced its determination of not paying the same.

Such was the situation, as known to Violet Strange and the general public, on the day she was asked to see Mrs. Hammond and learn what might alter her opinion as to the justice of this verdict and the stand taken by the Shuler Life Insurance Company.

The clock on the mantel in Miss Strange's rose-colored boudoir had struck three, and Violet was gazing in some impatience at the door, when there came a gentle knock upon it, and the maid (one of the elderly, not youthful, kind) ushered in her expected visitor.

"You are Mrs. Hammond?" she asked, in natural awe of the too-black figure outlined so sharply against the deep pink of the seashell room.

The answer was a slow lifting of the veil which shadowed the features she knew only from the cuts she had seen in newspapers.

"You are–Miss Strange?" stammered her visitor, "the young lady who—"

"I am," chimed in a voice as ringing as it was sweet. "I am the person you have come here to see. And this is my home. But that does not make me less interested in the unhappy, or less desirous of serving them. Certainly you have met with the two greatest losses which can come to a woman–I know your story well enough to say that–but what have you to tell me in proof that you should not lose your anticipated income as well? Something vital, I hope, else I cannot help you; something which you should have told the coroner's jury–and did not."

The flush which was the sole answer these words called forth did not take from the refinement of the young widow's expression, but rather added to it; Violet watched it in its ebb and flow and, seriously affected by it (why, she did not know, for Mrs. Hammond had made no other appeal either by look or gesture), pushed forward a chair and begged her visitor to be seated.

"We can converse in perfect safety here," she said. "When you feel quite equal to it, let me hear what you have to communicate. It will never go any further. I could not do the work I do if I felt it necessary to have a confidant."

"But you are so young and so–so—"

"So inexperienced you would say and so evidently a member of what New Yorkers call 'society.' Do not let that trouble you. My inexperience is not likely to last long and my social pleasures are more apt to add to my efficiency than to detract from it."

With this Violet's face broke into a smile. It was not the brilliant one so often seen upon her lips, but there was something in its quality which carried encouragement to the widow and led her to say with obvious eagerness:

"You know the facts?"

"I have read all the papers."

"I was not believed on the stand."

"It was your manner—"

"I could not help my manner. I was keeping something back, and, being unused to deceit, I could not act quite naturally."

"Why did you keep something back? When you saw the unfavorable impression made by your reticence, why did you not speak up and frankly tell your story?"

"Because I was ashamed. Because I thought it would hurt me more to speak than to keep silent. I do not think so now; but I did then–and so made my great mistake. You must remember not only the awful shock of my double loss, but the sense of guilt accompanying it; for my husband and I had quarreled that night, quarreled bitterly–that was why I had run away into another room and not because I was feeling ill and impatient of the baby's fretful cries."

"So people have thought." In saying this, Miss Strange was perhaps cruelly emphatic. "You wish to explain that quarrel? You think it will be doing any good to your cause to go into that matter with me now?"

"I cannot say; but I must first clear my conscience and then try to convince you that quarrel or no quarrel, *he* never took his own life. He was not that kind. He had an abnormal fear of death. I do not like to say it but he was a physical coward. I have seen him turn pale at the least hint of danger. He could no more have turned that muzzle upon his own breast than he could have turned it upon his baby. Some other hand shot him, Miss Strange. Remember the open window, the shattered mirror; and *I think I know that hand*."

Her head had fallen forward on her breast. The emotion she showed was not so eloquent of grief as of deep personal shame.

"You think you know the *man?*" In saying this, Violet's voice sunk to a whisper. It was an accusation of murder she had just heard.

"To my great distress, yes. When Mr. Hammond and I were married," the widow now proceeded in a more determined tone, "there was another man–a very violent one–who vowed even at the church door that George and I should never live out two full years together. We have not. Our second anniversary would have been in November."

"But—"

"Let me say this: the quarrel of which I speak was not serious enough to occasion any such act of despair on his part. A man would be mad to end his life on account of so slight a disagreement. It was not even on account of the person of whom I've just spoken, though that person had been mentioned between us earlier in the evening, Mr. Hammond having come across him face to face that very afternoon in the subway. Up to this time neither of us had seen or heard of him since our wedding day."

"And you think this person whom you barely mentioned, so mindful of his old grudge that he sought out your domicile, and, with the intention of murder, climbed the trellis leading to your room and turned his pistol upon the shadowy figure which was all he could see in the semi-obscurity of a much lowered gas jet."

"A man in the dark does not need a bright light to see his enemy when he is intent upon revenge."

Miss Strange altered her tone.

"And your husband? You must acknowledge that he shot off his pistol whether the other did or not."

"It was in self-defense. He would shoot to save his own life–or the baby's."

"Then he must have heard or seen—"

"A man at the window."

"And would have shot there?"

"Or tried to."

"Tried to?"

"Yes; the other shot first–oh, I've thought it all out–causing my husband's bullet to go wild. It was his which broke the mirror."

Violet's eyes, bright as stars, suddenly narrowed.

"And what happened then?" she asked. "Why cannot they find the bullet?"

"Because it went out of the window—glanced off and went out of the window." Mrs. Hammond's tone was triumphant, her look spirited and intense.

Violet eyed her compassionately.

"Would a bullet glancing off from a mirror, however hung, be apt to reach a window so far on the opposite side?"

"I don't know; I only know that it did," was the contradictory, almost absurd, reply.

"What *was* the cause of the quarrel you speak of between your husband and yourself? You see, I must know the exact truth and all the truth to be of any assistance to you."

"It was–it was about the care I gave, or didn't give, the baby. I feel awfully to have to say it, but George did not think I did my full duty by the child. He said there was no need of its crying so; that if I gave it the proper attention it would not keep the neighbors and himself awake half the night. And I–I got angry and insisted that I did the best I could; that the child was naturally fretful and that if he wasn't satisfied with my way of looking after it, he might try his. All of which was very wrong and unreasonable on my part, as witness the awful punishment which followed."

"And what made you get up and leave him?"

"The growl he gave me in reply. When I heard that, I bounded out of bed and said I was going to the spare room to sleep; and if the baby cried he might just try what he could do himself to stop it."

"And he answered?"

"This, just this–I shall never forget his words as long as I live–'If you go, you need not expect me to let you in again no matter what happens.' "

"He said that?"

"And locked the door after me. You see I could not tell all that."

"It might have been better if you had. It was such a natural quarrel and so unprovocative of actual tragedy."

Mrs. Hammond was silent. It was not difficult to see that she had no very keen regrets for her husband personally. But then he was not a very estimable man nor in any respect her equal.

"You were not happy with him," Violet ventured to remark.

"I was not a fully contented woman. But for all that he had no cause to complain of me except for the reason I have mentioned. I was not a very intelligent mother. But if the baby were living now–Oh, if he were living now–with what devotion I should care for him."

She was on her feet, her arms were raised, her face impassioned with feeling. Violet, gazing at her, heaved a little sigh. It was perhaps in keeping with the situation, perhaps extraneous to it, but whatever its source, it marked a change in her manner. With no further check upon her sympathy, she said very softly: "It is well with the child."

The mother stiffened, swayed, and then burst into wild weeping.

"But not with me," she cried, "not with me. I am desolate and bereft. I have not even a home in which to hide my grief and no prospect of one."

"But," interposed Violet, "surely your husband left you something? You cannot be quite penniless?"

"My husband left nothing," was the answer, uttered without bitterness, but with all the hardness of fact. "He had debts. I shall pay those debts. When these and other necessary expenses are liquidated, there will be but little left. He made no secret of the fact that he lived close up to his means. That is why he was induced to take on a life insurance. Not a friend of his but knows his improvidence. I–I have not even jewels. I have only my determination and an absolute conviction as to the real nature of my husband's death."

"What is the name of the man you secretly believe to have shot your husband from the trellis?"

Mrs. Hammond told her.

It was a new one to Violet. She said so and then asked:

"What else can you tell me about him?"

"Nothing, but that he is a very dark man and has a club foot."

"Oh, what a mistake you've made."

"Mistake? Yes, I acknowledge that."

"I mean in not giving this last bit of information at once to the police. A man can be identified by such a defect. Even his footsteps can be traced. He might have been found that very day. Now, what have we to go upon?"

"You are right, but not expecting to have any difficulty about the insurance money I thought it would be generous in me to keep still. Besides, this is only surmise on my part. I feel certain that my husband was shot by another hand than his own, but I know of no way of proving it. Do you?"

Then Violet talked seriously with her, explaining how their only hope lay in the discovery of a second bullet in the room which had already been ransacked for this very purpose and without the shadow of a result.

A tea, a musicale, and an evening dance kept Violet Strange in a whirl for the remainder of the day. No brighter eye nor more contagious wit lent brilliance to these occasions, but with the passing of the midnight hour no one who had seen her in the blaze of electric lights would have recognized this favored child of fortune in the earnest figure sitting in the obscurity of an uptown apartment, studying the walls, the ceilings, and the floors by the dim light of a lowered gas jet. Violet Strange in society was a very different person from Violet Strange under the tension of her secret and peculiar work.

She had told them at home that she was going to spend the night with a friend; but only her old coachman knew who that friend was. Therefore a very natural sense of guilt mingled with her emotions at finding herself alone on a scene whose gruesome mystery she could solve only by identifying herself with the place and the man who had perished there.

Dismissing from her mind all thought of self, she strove to think as he thought, and act as he acted on the night when he found himself (a man of but little courage) left in this room with an ailing child.

At odds with himself, his wife, and possibly with the child screaming away in its crib, what would he be apt to do in his present emergency? Nothing at first, but as the screaming continued he would remember the old tales of fathers walking the floor at night with crying babies, and hasten to follow suit. Violet, in her anxiety to each his inmost thought, crossed to where the crib had stood, and, taking that as a start, began pacing the room in search of the spot from which a bullet, if shot, would glance aside from the mirror in the direction of the window. (Not that she was ready to accept this theory of Mrs. Hammond, but that she did not wish to entirely dismiss it without putting it to the test.)

She found it in an unexpected quarter of the room and much nearer the bed head than where his body was found. This, which might seem to confuse matters, served, on the contrary, to remove from the case one of its most serious difficulties. Standing here, he was within reach of the pillow under which his pistol lay hidden, and if startled, as his wife believed him to have been by a noise at the other end of the room, had but to crouch and reach behind him in order to find himself armed and ready for a possible intruder.

Imitating his action in this as in other things, she had herself crouched low at the bedside and was on the point of withdrawing her hand from under the pillow when a new surprise checked her movement and held her fixed in her position, with eyes staring straight at the adjoining wall. She had seen there what he must have seen in making this same turn—the dark bars of the opposite windowframe outlined in the mirror—and understood at once what had happened. In the nervousness and terror of the moment, George Hammond had mistaken this reflection of the window for the window itself, and shot impulsively at the man he undoubtedly saw covering him from the trellis without. But while this explained the shattering of the mirror, how about the other and still more vital question, of where the bullet went afterward? Was the angle at which it had been fired acute enough to send it out of a window diagonally opposed? No; even if the pistol had been held closer to the man firing it than she had reason to believe, the angle still would be oblique enough to carry it on to the further wall.

But no sign of any such impact had been discovered on this wall. Consequently, the force of the bullet had been expended before reaching it, and when it fell—

Here, her glance, slowly traveling along the floor, impetuously paused. It had reached the spot where the two bodies had been found, and unconsciously her eyes rested there, conjuring up the picture of the bleeding father and the strangled child. How piteous and how dreadful it all was. If she could only understand—Suddenly she rose straight up, staring and immovable in the dim light. Had the idea–the explanation–the only possible explanation covering the whole phenomena come to her at last?

It would seem so, for as she so stood, a look of conviction settled over her features, and with this look, evidences of a horror which for all her fast accumulating knowledge of life and its possibilities made her appear very small and very helpless.

A half-hour later, when Mrs. Hammond, in her anxiety at hearing nothing more from Miss Strange, opened the door of her room, it was to find, lying on the edge of the sill, the little detective's card with these words hastily written across it:

I do not feel as well as I could wish, and so have telephoned to my own coachman to come and take me home. I will either see or write you within a few days. But do not allow yourself to hope. I pray you do not allow yourself the least hope; the outcome is still very problematical.

When Violet's employer entered his office the next morning it was to find a veiled figure awaiting him which he at once recognized as that of his little deputy. She was slow in lifting her veil and when it finally came free he felt a momentary doubt as to his wisdom in giving her just such a matter as this to investigate. He was quite sure of his mistake when he saw her face, it was so drawn and pitiful.

"You have failed," said he.

"Of that you must judge," she answered; and drawing near she whispered in his ear.

"No!" he cried in his amazement.

"Think," she murmured, "think. Only so can all the facts be accounted for."

"I will look into it; I will certainly look into it," was his earnest reply. "If you are right—But never mind that. Go home and take a horseback ride in the Park. When I have news in regard to this I will let you know. Till then forget it all. Hear me, I charge you to forget everything but your balls and your parties."

And Violet obeyed him.

Some few days after this, the following statement appeared in all the papers:

"Owing to some remarkable work done by the firm of —&—, the well-known private detective agency, the claim made by Mrs. George Hammond against the Shuler Life Insurance Company is likely to be allowed without further litigation. As our readers will remember, the contestant has insisted from the first that the bullet causing her husband's death came from another pistol than the one found clutched in his own hand. But while reasons were not lacking to substantiate this assertion, the failure to discover more than the disputed track of a second bullet led to a verdict of suicide, and a refusal of the company to pay.

"But now that bullet has been found. And where? In the most startling place in the world, viz.: in the larynx of the child found lying dead upon the floor beside his father, strangled as was supposed by the weight of that father's arm. The theory is, and there seems to be none other, that the father, hearing a suspicious noise at the window, set down the child he was endeavoring to soothe and made for the bed and his own pistol, and, mistaking a reflection of the assassin for the assassin himself, set his shot sidewise at a mirror just as the other let go the trigger which drove a similar bullet into his breast. The course of the one was straight and fatal and that of the other deflected. Striking the mirror at an oblique angle, the bullet fell to the floor where it was picked up by the crawling child, and, as was most natural, thrust at once into his mouth. Perhaps it felt hot to the little tongue; perhaps the child was simply frightened by some convulsive movement of the father who evidently spent his last moment in an endeavor to reach the child, but, whatever the cause, in the quick gasp it gave, the bullet was drawn into the larynx, strangling him.

"That the father's arm, in his last struggle, should have fallen directly across the little throat is one of those anomalies which confounds reason and misleads justice by stopping investigation at the very point where truth lies and mystery disappears.

"Mrs. Hammond is to be congratulated that there are detectives who do not give too much credence to outward appearances.

"We expect soon to hear of the capture of the man who sped home the death-dealing bullet."

The Stripper

Anthony Boucher

He was called Jack the Stripper because the only witness who had seen him and lived (J. F. Flugelbach, 1463 N. Edgemont) had described the glint of moonlight on bare skin. The nickname was inevitable.

Mr. Flugelbach had stumbled upon the fourth of the murders, the one in the grounds of City College. He had not seen enough to be of any help to the police; but at least he had furnished a name for the killer heretofore known by such routine cognomens as "butcher," "werewolf," and "vampire."

The murders in themselves were enough to make a newspaper's fortune. They were frequent, bloody, and pointless, since neither theft nor rape was attempted. The murderer was no specialist, like the original Jack, but rather an eclectic, like Kürten the Düsseldorf Monster, who struck when the mood was on him and disregarded age and sex. This indiscriminate taste made better copy; the menace threatened not merely a certain class of unfortunates but every reader.

It was the nudity, however, and the nickname evolved from it, that made the cause truly celebrated. Feature writers dug up all the legends of naked murderers—Courvoisier of London, Durrant of San Francisco, Wallace of Liverpool, Borden of Fall River—and printed them as sober fact, explaining at length the advantages of avoiding the evidence of bloodstains.

When he read this explanation, he always smiled. It was plausible, but irrelevant. The real reason for nakedness was simply that it felt better that way. When the color of things began to change, his first impulse was to get rid of his clothing. He supposed that psychoanalysts could find some atavistic reason for that.

He felt the cold air on his naked body. He had never noticed that before. Noiselessly he pushed the door open and tiptoed into the study. His hand did not waver as he raised the knife.

The Stripper case was Lieutenant Marshall's baby, and he was going nuts. His condition was not helped by the constant allusions of his colleagues to the fact that his wife had once been a stripper of a more pleasurable variety. Six murders in three months, without a single profitable lead, had reduced him to a state where a lesser man might have gibbered, and sometimes he thought it would be simpler to be a lesser man.

He barked into phones nowadays. He hardly apologized when he realized that his caller was Sister Ursula, that surprising nun who had once planned to be a policewoman and who had extricated him from several extraordinary cases. But that was just it; those had been extraordinary, freak locked-room problems, while this was the horrible epitome of ordinary, clueless, plotless murder. There was no room in the Stripper case for the talents of Sister Ursula.

He was in a hurry and her sentences hardly penetrated his mind until he caught the word "Stripper." Then he said sharply, "So? Backtrack please, Sister. I'm afraid I wasn't listening."

"He says," her quiet voice repeated, "that he thinks he knows who the Stripper is, but he hasn't enough proof. He'd like to talk to the police about it; and since he knows I know you, he asked me to arrange it, so that you wouldn't think him just a crank."

"Which," said Marshall, "he probably is. But to please you, Sister . . . What did you say his name is?"

"Flecker. Harvey Flecker. Professor of Latin at the University."

Marshall caught his breath. "Coincidence," he said flatly. "I'm on my way to see him now."

"Oh. Then he did get in touch with you himself?"

"Not with me," said Marshall. "With the Stripper."

"God rest his soul. . . ." Sister Ursula murmured.

"So. I'm on my way now. If you could meet me there and bring his letter—"

"Lieutenant, I know our order is a singularly liberal one, but still I doubt if Reverend Mother—"

"You're a material witness," Marshall said authoritatively. "I'll send a car for you. And don't forget the letter."

Sister Ursula hung up and sighed. She had liked Professor Flecker, both for his scholarly wit and for his quiet kindliness. He was the only man who could hold his agnostic own with Father Pearson in disputatious sophistry, and he was also the man who had helped keep the Order's soup-kitchen open at the depth of the Depression.

She took up her breviary and began to read the office for the dead while she waited for the car.

"It is obvious," Professor Lowe enunciated, "that the Stripper is one of the three of us."

Hugo Ellis said, "Speak for yourself." His voice cracked a little, and he seemed even younger than he looked.

Professor de' Cassis said nothing. His huge hunchbacked body crouched in the corner and he mourned his friend.

"So?" said Lieutenant Marshall. "Go on, Professor."

"It was by pure chance," Professor Lowe continued, his lean face alight with logical satisfaction, "that the back door was latched last night. We have been leaving it unfastened for Mrs. Carey since she lost her key; but Flecker must have forgotten that fact and inadvertently reverted to habit. Ingress by the front door was impossible, since it was not only secured by a spring lock but also bolted from within. None of the windows shows any sign of external tampering. The murderer presumably counted upon the back door to make plausible the entrance of an intruder; but Flecker had accidentally secured it, and that accident," he concluded impressively, "will strap the Tripper."

Hugo Ellis laughed, and then looked ashamed of himself.

Marshall laughed too. "Setting aside the Spoonerism, Professor, your statement of the conditions is flawless. This house was locked tight as a drum. Yes, the Stripper is one of the three of you." It wasn't amusing when Marshall said it.

Professor de' Cassis raised his despondent head. "But why?" His voice was guttural. "Why?"

Hugo Ellis said, "Why? With a madman?"

Professor Lowe lifted one finger as though emphasizing a point in a lecture. "Ah, but is this a madman's crime? There is the point. When the Stripper kills a stranger, yes, he is mad. When he kills a man with whom he lives . . . may he not be applying the technique of his madness to the purpose of his sanity?"

"It's an idea," Marshall admitted. "I can see where there's going to be some advantage in having a psychologist among the witnesses. But there's another witness I'm even more anxious to—" His face lit up as Sergeant Raglan came in. "She's here, Rags?"

"Yeah," said Raglan. "It's the sister. Holy smoke, Loot, does this mean this is gonna be another screwy one?"

Marshall had said *she* and Raglan had said *the sister*. These facts may serve as sufficient characterization of Sister Felicitas, who had accompanied her. They were always a pair, yet always spoken of in the singular. Now Sister Felicitas dozed in the corner where the hunchback had crouched, and Marshall read and reread the letter which seemed like the posthumous utterance of the Stripper's latest victim:

My dear Sister:

I have reason to fear that someone close to me is Jack the Stripper.

You know me, I trust, too well to think me a sensationalist striving to be a star witness. I have grounds for what I say. This individual, whom I shall for the moment call "Quasimodo" for reasons that might particularly appeal to you, first betrayed himself when I noticed a fleck of blood behind his ear—a trifle, but suggestive. Since then I have religiously observed his comings and goings, and found curious coincidences between the absence of Quasimodo and the presence elsewhere of the Stripper.

I have not a conclusive body of evidence, but I believe that I do have sufficient to bring to the attention of the authorities. I have heard you mention a Lieutenant Marshall who is a close friend of yours. If you will recommend me to him as a man whose word is to be taken seriously, I shall be deeply obliged.

I may, of course, be making a fool of myself with my suspicions of Quasimodo, which is why I refrain from giving you his real name. But every man must do what is possible to rid this city a negotio perambulante in tenebris.

Yours respectfully,
Harvey Flecker

"He didn't have much to go on, did he?" Marshall observed. "But he was right, God help him. And he may have known more than he cared to trust to a letter. He must have slipped somehow and let Quasimodo see his suspicions. . . . What does that last phrase mean?"

"Lieutenant! And you an Oxford man!" exclaimed Sister Ursula.

"I can translate it. But what's its connotation?"

"It's from St. Jerome's Vulgate of the ninetieth psalm. The Douay version translates it literally: *of the business that walketh about in the dark;* but that doesn't convey the full horror of that nameless prowling *negotium*. It's one of the most terrible phrases I know, and perfect for the Stripper."

"Flecker was a Catholic?"

"No, he was a resolute agnostic, though I have always had hopes that Thomist philosophy would lead him into the Church. I almost think he refrained because his conversion would have left nothing to argue with Father Pearson about. But he was an excellent Church Latinist and knew the liturgy better than most Catholics."

"Do you understand what he means by Quasimodo?"

"I don't know. Allusiveness was typical of Professor Flecker; he delighted in British crossword puzzles, if you see what I mean. But I think I could guess more rapidly if he had not said that it might particularly appeal to me. . . ."

"So? I can see at least two possibilities—"

"But before we try to decode the Professor's message, Lieutenant, tell me what you have learned here. All I know is that the poor man is dead, may he rest in peace."

Marshall told her. Four university teachers lived in this ancient (for Southern California) two-story house near the Campus. Mrs. Carey came in every day to clean for them and prepare dinner. When she arrived this morning at nine, Lowe and de' Cassis were eating breakfast and Hugo Ellis, the youngest of the group, was out mowing the lawn. They were not concerned over Flecker's absence. He often worked in the study till all hours and sometimes fell asleep there.

Mrs. Carey went about her work. Today was Tuesday, the day for changing the beds and getting the laundry ready. When she had finished that task, she dusted the living room and went on to the study.

The police did not yet have her story of the discovery. Her scream had summoned the others, who had at once called the police and, sensibly, canceled their classes and waited. When the police arrived, Mrs. Carey was still hysterical. The doctor had quieted her with a hypodermic, from which she had not yet revived.

Professor Flecker had had his throat cut and (Marshall skipped over this hastily) suffered certain other butcheries characteristic of the Stripper. The knife, an ordinary kitchen knife, had been left by the body as usual. He had died instantly, at approximately one in the morning, when each of the other three men claimed to be asleep.

More evidence than that of the locked doors proved that the Stripper was an inmate of the house. He had kept his feet clear of the blood which bespattered the study, but he had still left a trail of small drops which revealed themselves to the minute police inspection—blood which had bathed his body and dripped off as he left his crime.

This trail led upstairs and into the bathroom, where it stopped. There were traces of watered blood in the bathtub and on one of the towels—Flecker's own.

"Towel?" said Sister Ursula. "But you said Mrs. Carey had made up the laundry bundle."

"She sends out only sheets and such—does the towels herself."

"Oh." The nun sounded disappointed.

"I know how you feel, Sister. You'd welcome a discrepancy anywhere, even in the laundry list. But that's the sum of our evidence. Three suspects, all with opportunity, none with an alibi. Absolutely even distribution of suspicion, and our only guidepost is the word *Quasimodo*. Do you know any of these three men?"

"I have never met them, Lieutenant, but I feel as though I know them rather well from Professor Flecker's descriptions."

"Good. Let's see what you can reconstruct. First, Ruggiero de' Cassis, professor of mathematics, formerly of the University of Turin, voluntary exile since the early days of Fascism."

Sister Ursula said slowly, "He admired de' Cassis, not only for his first-rate mind, but because he seemed to have adjusted himself so satisfactorily to life despite his deformity. I remember he said once, 'De' Cassis has never known a woman, yet every day he looks on Beauty bare.' "

"On Beauty . . .? Oh yes. Millay. *Euclid alone* . . . All right. Now Marvin Lowe, professor of psychology, native of Ohio, and from what I've seen of him a prime pedant. According to Flecker . . .?"

"I think Professor Lowe amused him. He used to tell us the latest Spoonerisms; he swore that flocks of students graduated from the University believing that modern psychology rested on the researches of two men named Frung and Jeud. Once Lowe said that his favorite book was Max Beerbohm's *Happy Hypocrite;* Professor Flecker insisted that was because it was the only one he could be sure of pronouncing correctly."

"But as a man?"

"He never said much about Lowe personally; I don't think they were intimate. But I do recall his saying, 'Lowe, like all psychologists, is the physician of Greek proverb.' "

"Who was told to heal himself? Makes sense. That speech mannerism certainly points to something a psychiatrist could have fun with. All right. How about Hugo Ellis, instructor in mathematics, native of Los Angeles?"

"Mr. Ellis was a child prodigy, you know. Extraordinary mathematical feats. But he outgrew them, I almost think deliberately. He made himself into a normal young man. Now he is, I gather, a reasonably good young instructor—just run of the mill. An adult with the brilliance which he had as a child might be a great man. Professor Flecker turned the French proverb around to fit him: 'If youth could, if age knew. . . .' "

"So. There they are. And which," Marshall asked, "is Quasimodo?"

"Quasimodo . . ." Sister Ursula repeated the word, and other words seemed to follow it automatically. "*Quasimodo geniti infantes . . .*" She paused and shuddered.

"What's the matter?"

"I think," she said softly, "I know. But like Professor Flecker, I fear making a fool of myself—and worse, I fear damning an innocent man. . . . Lieutenant, may I look through this house with you?"

He sat there staring at the other two and at the policeman watching them. The body was no longer in the next room, but the blood was. He had never before revisited the scene of the crime; that notion was the nonsense of legend. For that matter he had never known his victim.

He let his mind go back to last night. Only recently had he been willing to do this. At first it was something that must be kept apart, divided from his normal personality. But he was intelligent enough to realize the danger of that. It could produce a seriously schizoid personality. He might go mad. Better to attain complete integration, and that could be accomplished only by frank self-recognition.

It must be terrible to be mad.

"Well, where to first?" asked Marshall.

"I want to see the bedrooms," said Sister Ursula. "I want to see if Mrs. Carey changed the sheets."

"You doubt her story? But she's completely out of the—all right. Come on."

Lieutenant Marshall identified each room for her as they entered it. Harvey Flecker's bedroom by no means consorted with the neatness of his mind. It was a welter of papers and notes and hefty German works on Latin philology and puzzle books by Torquemada and Caliban and early missals and codices from the University library. The bed had been changed and the clean upper sheet was turned back. Harvey Flecker would never soil it.

Professor de' Cassis's room was in sharp contrast—a chaste monastic cubicle. His books—chiefly professional works, with a sampling of Leopardi and Carducci and other Italian poets and an Italian translation of Thomas à Kempis—were neatly stacked in a case, and his papers were out of sight. The only ornaments in the room were a crucifix and a framed picture of a family group, in clothes of 1920.

Hugo Ellis's room was defiantly, almost parodistically the room of a normal, healthy college man, even to the University banner over the bed. He had carefully avoided both Flecker's chaos and de' Cassis's austerity; there was a precisely calculated normal litter of pipes and letters and pulp magazines. The pin-up girls seemed to be carrying normality too far, and Sister Ursula averted her eyes.

Each room had a clean upper sheet.

Professor Lowe's room would have seemed as normal as Ellis's, if less spectacularly so, if it were not for the inordinate quantity of books. Shelves covered all wall space that was not taken by door, window, or bed. Psychology, psychiatry, and criminology predominated; but there was a selection of poetry, humor, fiction for any mood.

Marshall took down William Roughead's *Twelve Scots Trials* and said, "Lucky devil! I've never so much as seen a copy of this before." He smiled at the argumentative pencilings in the margins. Then as he went to replace it, he saw through the gap that there was a second row of books behind. Paperbacks. He took one out and put it back hastily. "You wouldn't want to see that, Sister. But it might fit into that case we were proposing about repressions and word-distortions."

Sister Ursula seemed not to heed him. She was standing by the bed and said, "Come here."

Marshall came and looked at the freshly made bed.

Sister Ursula passed her hand over the mended but clean lower sheet. "Do you see?"

"See what?"

"The answer," she said.

Marshall frowned. "Look, Sister—"

"Lieutenant, your wife is one of the most efficient housekeepers I've ever known. I thought she had, to some extent, indoctrinated you. Think. Try to think with Leona's mind."

Marshall thought. Then his eyes narrowed and he said, "So . . ."

"It is fortunate," Sister Ursula said, "that the Order of Martha of Bethany specializes in housework."

Marshall went out and called downstairs. "Raglan! See if the laundry's been picked up from the back porch."

The Sergeant's voice came back. "It's gone, Loot. I thought there wasn't no harm—"

"Then get on the phone quick and tell them to hold it."

"But what laundry, Loot?"

Marshall muttered. Then he turned to Sister Ursula. "The men won't know of course, but we'll find a bill somewhere. Anyway, we won't need that till the preliminary hearing. We've got enough now to settle Quasimodo."

He heard the Lieutenant's question and repressed a startled gesture. He had not thought of that. But even if they traced the laundry, it would be valueless as evidence without Mrs. Carey's testimony. . . .

He saw at once what had to be done.

They had taken Mrs. Carey to the guest room, that small downstairs bedroom near the kitchen which must have been a maid's room when this was a large family house. There were still police posted outside the house, but only Raglan and the lieutenant inside.

It was so simple. His mind, he told himself, had never been functioning more clearly. No nonsense about stripping this time; it was not for pleasure. Just be careful to avoid those crimson jets. . . .

The Sergeant wanted to know where he thought he was going. He told him.

Raglan grinned. "You should've raised your hand. A teacher like you ought to know that."

He went to the back porch toilet, opened and closed its door without going in. Then he went to the kitchen and took the second best knife. The best had been used last night.

It would not take a minute. Then he would be safe and later when the body was found what could they prove? The others had been out of the room too.

But as he touched the knife it began to happen. Something came from the blade up his arm and into his head. He was in a hurry, there was no time—but holding the knife, the color of things began to change. . . .

He was half naked when Marshall found him.

Sister Ursula leaned against the jamb of the kitchen door. She felt sick. Marshall and Raglan were both strong men, but they needed help to subdue him. His face was contorted into an unrecognizable mask like a demon from a Japanese tragedy. She clutched the crucifix of the rosary that hung at her waist and murmured a prayer to the Archangel Michael. For it was not the physical strength of the man that frightened her, nor the glint of his knife, but the pure quality of incarnate evil that radiated from him and made the doctrine of possession a real terror.

As she finished her prayer, Marshall's fist connected with his jaw and he crumpled. So did Sister Ursula.

"I don't know what you think of me," Sister Ursula said as Marshall drove her home. (Sister Felicitas was dozing in the back seat.) "I'm afraid I couldn't ever have been a policewoman after all."

"You'll do," Marshall said. "And if you feel better now, I'd like to run over it with you. I've got to get my brilliant deductions straight for the press."

"The fresh air feels good. Go ahead."

"I've got the sheet business down pat, I think. In ordinary middle-class households you don't change both sheets every week; Leona never does, I remembered. You put on a clean upper sheet, and the old upper becomes the lower. The other three bedrooms each had one clean sheet—the upper. His had two—upper and lower; therefore his upper sheet had been stained in some unusual way and had to be changed. The hasty bath, probably in the dark, had been careless, and there was some blood left to stain the sheet. Mrs. Carey wouldn't have thought anything of it at the time because she hadn't found the body yet. Right?"

"Perfect, Lieutenant."

"So. But now about Quasimodo . . . I still don't get it. He's the one it *couldn't* apply to. Either of the others—"

"Yes?"

"Well, who is Quasimodo? He's the Hunchback of Notre Dame. So it could mean the deformed de' Cassis. Who wrote Quasimodo? Victor Hugo. So it could be Hugo Ellis. But it wasn't either; and how in heaven's name could it mean Professor Lowe?"

"Remember, Lieutenant: Professor Flecker said this was an allusion that might particularly appeal to me. Now I am hardly noted for my devotion to the anticlerical prejudices of Hugo's *Notre-Dame de Paris*. What is the common meeting-ground of my interests and Professor Flecker's?"

"Church liturgy?" Marshall ventured.

"And why was your Quasimodo so named? Because he was born—or found or christened, I forget which—on the Sunday after Easter. Many Sundays, as you may know, are often referred to by the first word of their introits, the beginning of the proper of the Mass. As the fourth Sunday in Lent is called *Laetare* Sunday, or the third in Advent *Gaudete* Sunday. So the Sunday after Easter is known as *Quasimodo* Sunday, from its introit *Quasimodo geniti infantes* . . . 'As newborn babes.' "

"But I still don't see—"

"The Sunday after Easter," said Sister Ursula, "is more usually referred to as *Low* Sunday."

"Oh," said Marshall. After a moment he added refectively, "*The Happy Hypocrite . . .*"

"You see that too? Beerbohm's story is about a man who assumes a mask of virtue to conceal his depravity. A schizoid allegory. I wonder if Professor Lowe dreamed that he might find the same happy ending."

Marshall drove on a bit in silence. Then he said, "He said a strange thing while you were out."

"I feel as though he were already dead," said Sister Ursula. "I want to say, 'God rest his soul.' We should have a special office for the souls of the mad."

"That cues into my story. The boys were taking him away and I said to Rags, 'Well, this is once the insanity plea justifies itself. He'll never see the gas chamber.' And he turned on me—he'd quieted down by then—and said, "Nonsense, sir! Do you think I would cast doubt on my sanity merely to save my life?' "

"Mercy," said Sister Ursula. At first Marshall thought it was just an exclamation. Then he looked at her face and saw that she was not talking to him.

THE CLARET STICK

Mignon Eberhart

Susan Dare rose from the stage and brushed dust from her skirt. Death in its primary form is never pleasant, and this death was particularly ugly. She felt a queer desire to move the man at her feet so that his battered head no longer hung over into the footlights.

She felt ill and terribly shaken. No wonder that Adelaide Cholster was uttering one hysterical sob after another.

Adelaide Cholster. Susan's eyes went thoughtfully to the small group huddled at the other side of the stage. Adelaide was the faded little blonde—sister, was it?—of the murdered man.

The brown-faced woman in the dark knitted suit, who was so terribly controlled, was his wife, then. Jane they had called her. Jane Cholster.

Susan looked again at the man sprawled upon the stage. He was a large man, heavy but well proportioned. He was blond and probably older than his sister and wife. Of course, the heavy make-up on his mouth and chin was a little confusing.

Susan forced herself to look at his face again. His face was unpowdered, and his eyes had not been touched; his mouth, however, was strongly outlined in soft crimson, and a small beard made of crêpe hair had been fastened to his chin. He had been, then, ready for rehearsal when he was murdered. The blow that had killed him had to be one of enormous power.

"Killed by blunt instrument," thought Susan and looked around the stage. It was set simply for an exterior, a balcony scene, with two long French windows opening at either side upon the balcony of which the footlights defined the limits.

There were a table and two chairs near one of the windows, but neither table nor chairs were heavy enough to deal the blow that had crushed out that hearty, strong life.

She looked again at the small group across the stage. Adelaide was sobbing now in the arms of the slim, dark young man—the one who had called himself Clare Dickenson and whom the others called Dickie.

Jane Cholster was lighting a cigarette, and her brown face, outlined clearly in the small light that the other man was holding for her, looked set. Her full-lipped, strong mouth, however, puffed steadily, her topaz eyes reflected a gleam from the light; Susan realized suddenly that she was an extremely attractive woman, although the charm lay in something aside from beauty. She glanced at the sobbing Adelaide and turned again to the man next her. "How much longer do you think it will be, Tom? Surely, they've had time to find the murderer. He must be somewhere in the theater."

Tom (he had given his name to the constable as Tom Remy, Susan remembered) shrugged and lit a cigarette for himself. "No telling," he said.

Beyond the footlights was a brightly lighted cavern that contained rows and rows of empty seats. Away at the back stood a man on guard—a townsman hastily deputized by the undeniably flustered constable. Below the stage now and then could be heard a rumble of heavy voices, or the bang of a door, or footsteps. They were searching the dressing rooms, the furnace and storage rooms, then.

The Little Theater movement, thought Susan rather dryly, must have been very successful to permit the use of so large a theater—large, at least, for the size of the town. And ambitious! She remembered the placards she had seen in the crowded little drugstore where she and Jim had stopped for directions to reach the theater—large handsomely printed placards announcing the Little Theater's newest production which was to be *Private Lives* and which was to open the following night for a three-night run.

Well, it wouldn't open.

The Cholsters—the murdered man, Jane Cholster, the sister—were all of them exactly the type to go in strongly and rather cleverly for amateur theatricals. They were quite evidently people of means, of leisure, and probably an intelligent understanding of the arts, including the art of play-making.

The man they called Dickie was the director. He would be, then, professional: a man of experience as an actor and a director, paid probably a generous sum by the members of the Little Theater group. He had a thin dark face; clever dark eyes, and an air of quick authoritative efficiency.

Tom Remy, who stood quietly smoking, was a little more difficult to orient. He was tall, stooped, grayish around the temples, and so far had said practically nothing.

All of the faces except the director's showed signs of make-up, though Jane Cholster had wiped her face thoroughly with her handkerchief. Adelaide lifted her head and sobbed, and Jane Cholster said rather sharply: "Stop that, Adelaide."

"Why don't they get a doctor?" sobbed Adelaide.

"There's no use getting a doctor now," said Tom Remy quietly. "The constable is doing everything he can."

"They're trying to get the murderer before he has a chance to escape," said Dickie quickly and in an efficient manner. "He must be somewhere in the building. The only possible way of escape would have been by the front door, and he didn't go that way."

Adelaide turned a small puffy face, on which heavy make-up was grotesquely streaked with tears, toward the other side of the stage and saw Susan. "Who's that?" she said.

Jane's topaz eyes gave Susan a cool glance.

"She came in with the reporter."

"Reporter!" cried Adelaide. "What reporter?"

"The reporter from the *Record*. He was in Kittiwake for a story about something or other—spring floods probably, nothing else has happened here—and heard about the murder."

Dickie turned quickly to Tom Remy.

"Oh, is he the fellow that came in with the constable?" His quick clever eyes darted to meet Susan's. "Are you a reporter, too?"

"No. My name is Dare." She looked at Jane. "May I do anything to help you?"

"Nothing, thank you," said Jane. She glanced at the others and said, as if not wholly conscious of them or of Susan: "Miss Cholster. Mr. Remy. Mr. Dickenson."

Something banged heavily below, and Adelaide cried: "What *are* they doing?" There were footsteps on the stairway off toward their right, resounding heavily and rousing dull murmurs that were echoes.

"I wonder if they've found anybody," said Tom Remy. And then the three men were in the wings and approaching the stage again, the constable, red and puffing a bit, in the lead, an assistant (also, Susan suspected, hastily deputized) following him, and Jim Byrne bringing up the rear.

Jim took off his hat, and as the constable, puffing and clutching his revolver, addressed himself to Mrs. Cholster, Jim drew Susan aside.

"My God, Sue," he said under his breath, "what a case! The whole theater's locked up tight. The sheriff's at the other end of the county. And I'll bet my hat the murderer's right here. Have I got a story or have I got a story?"

"You've got a story," said Susan rather somberly. She glanced toward the sprawled gray figure, and Jim caught the look in her eyes. "I know, Sue," he said. "But, after all, it happened."

He stopped abruptly, struck by something the constable was saying, and Susan listened also.

"—And so the sheriff said over the telephone to keep you all here till he got back. He said he'd start right off quick. Now, I'm sorry about this, Mrs. Cholster; but it can't be helped."

"But this is preposterous!" Jane exclaimed. "Do you realize that while you are holding us here my husband's murderer is escaping?"

"Well," said the constable slowly, "we ain't so sure about that."

"What do you mean by that?" she demanded.

"That's easy to answer, ma'am. According to this Dickenson fellow, nobody went out the front door of the theater. And the stage entrance is bolted on the inside. So it stands to reason that the murderer's still here."

"Do you mean to say that you will not even permit my husband's body to be cared for? I insist upon calling Dr. Marks. And also my lawyer."

"Now, Mrs. Cholster," the constable said, "there ain't no call for you to talk like that. The sheriff said to hold you here, and that's what I'm going to do. He's got to see the body just as it is, and we can't move it till he looks at it and till the coroner looks at it. And I got to go ahead with my inquiry. That's my duty, and I'd advise you folks not to resist the law. I got two deputies here with me, and all of us is armed."

Jane's eyes flashed dangerously. "Did the sheriff say to allow reporters here?" she asked sharply.

"Reporters," said the constable largely, "is always permitted. Dunc, you might take something and cover Mr. Cholster."

Tom Remy stepped forward. "Let's get this straight," he said. "Are you holding us for murder?"

Adelaide blinked and gave a little scream, and the constable said: "Well, there ain't anybody else around, is there?"

There was, not unnaturally, an abrupt silence.

Jane Cholster's face was ashy again under the brown, but set and guarded. Tom Remy's eyes retreated, and Adelaide blinked and gasped and balled her handkerchief at her mouth, and Dickenson's handsome dark face became an impassive mask with only his quick dark eyes alive.

Around them the old theater was very still. Its stage that night already had played a strange and tragic drama, and Susan felt eerily that it was waiting for the play to go on, to play itself out. Below were passages and empty dressing rooms. Above was a dim loft extending mysteriously upward.

The constable's voice broke the silence. "I reckon," he said, "I'd better ask you some questions. And I reckon I don't need to tell you that you'd better tell the truth. Now, then, there's some chairs back there somewhere. Dunc," he continued, "bring them out. We may as well be comfortable." The little deputy disappeared, and the constable turned and shouted toward the bulky, dark figure standing at the back of the house. "Don't let anybody in, Wid, till the sheriff gets here."

"Here's a chair, miss," said Dunc's small voice to Susan, and she accepted it.

She looked at the other people seating themselves in a kind of circle on the stage.

Was Jane Cholster's character so strong that she could indefinitely withhold any signs of grief and shock? Was Adelaide so loving and so tender that she must collapse frequently into sobs? Was either of these women physically strong enough to deal the crushing blow that had been dealt Brock Cholster?

Jane was slender and brown and looked as if her muscles were hard. She must have, too, a tremendous reserve of nerve power. She sat now quietly erect and graceful—but under her quiet you felt that muscles might be gathered ready to spring.

Jane was only of medium height, but Adelaide looked small beside her. She huddled in the armchair that the deputy had given her. Her faded blonde curls were pushed up away from her puffy little face. She was older than Susan had surmised, for there were definite little pouches under her eyes and in the corners of her chin. Susan was vaguely aware that Jim and the constable were talking in a low murmur, there near the body; her eyes traveled on to the nervous, dark young director and to Tom Remy.

Either of the men might have been physically capable of that blow, providing a suitable weapon were at hand. ("Weapon?" thought Susan parenthetically. "What happened to it? And what *was* it?")

Neither, however, looked exactly athletic, although you couldn't measure the strength that sheer emotion might give to inadequate muscular force.

Tom Remy was smoking again; his eyes were narrowed into lines that made them look sharp and very observant and yet altogether unfathomable. As Susan watched, he gave Jane Cholster a long look which she returned, and Susan had a curious feeling that there was an unspoken communication between them, although neither face changed at all.

The dark young director passed a hand over his smooth black hair and said suddenly: "Who put the curtain up?"

"Curtain?" said Jane slowly. The constable turned abruptly to join the small circle, and Jim followed him, and the man Dickenson said quickly:

"Curtain, of course. It was down when I arrived, for I glanced at the stage. I didn't put it up. Who did?"

No one replied, and the constable said:

"What's all this about a curtain? You mean the fire curtain? It's a village ordinance that it—"

"Exactly. Of course. I know." Dickenson's interruptions were sharp and quick. "Certainly it was down. And when I came out of the office down there—" he motioned, with the nervous quickness that characterized his gestures, toward the door leading to the foyer—"and walked up here, the curtain was up."

"It was you that discovered the body?"

"Of course. You know that. I told you when I telephoned for you."

"When did you know it was Mr. Cholster?"

"I—" he closed his eyes for an instant as if to recall and Susan could see a little flutter of his eyeballs under his thin dark lids—"I believe I was only aware that the curtain was up and that there was something humped up there. But I hurried up to the switchboard and turned on the lights and saw it was Mr. Cholster. I thought, of course, he'd fainted or something and ran out on the stage. And I stopped about there and knew—what had happened."

"Then what did you do?"

"I—I think I called out. Everybody else, you know, was downstairs getting ready for rehearsal. Then I ran back to the telephone in the office again. When I came out, Tom and Mrs. Cholster and Adelaide were all on the stage—"

"You had the main door locked when I got here," said the constable. "How was that? When did you lock it?"

"I had locked it as soon as everybody got here. Locked it simply because we needed a good last rehearsal, and if I had left the door unlocked we'd have been continually interrupted. A lot of Kittiwake residents prefer sneaking in to dress rehearsal to coming around the next night and paying for their tickets."

Jim cleared his throat gently, and the constable cleared his also and said politely: "Did you say something, Mr. Byrne?"

"I was only wondering," said Jim, "why you didn't use the stage entrance. It would seem more convenient."

"Well, it isn't," said the young director rather snappishly. "There's no key to the thing extant, and you have to bolt it on the inside. It's bolted now."

"Then the only exit for the murderer was the door that the deputy is guarding now?"

"Yes," said Dickenson.

"And the door to the office is just at right angles to it there in the foyer, isn't it?"

"Yes, of course."

"Then you must have seen anyone entering or leaving the theater?"

"Why, I—" His quick dark eyes swept around the circle and he said—"that's what I thought when you first questioned me. But I suppose I could have been mistaken."

The constable cleared his throat again and looked at Jim, who said:

"I hope you don't mind letting me get this straight? You told the constable you arrived at the theater at about twenty minutes to eight?"

"Yes."

"You had called a dress rehearsal at eight?"

"I had said make-up at eight sharp. Rehearsal at eight-fifteen."

"Was it customary to make up for dress rehearsal?" asked Jim, Irish honey on his tongue. "I thought that was only to get used to properties—all that."

"Well," said the director hesitating, "it is. But you see—" he paused, and then said with abrupt candor—"but you know how it is with amateurs. They like the smell of grease paint." Dickenson stopped rather short and said: "Are you conducting this inquiry or getting a story for your paper?"

Jim said: "You unlocked the theater when you arrived?"

"Certainly. That is, I unlocked that one door."

"Who arrived next?"

"Jane—Mrs. Cholster, and—Brock. They came together."

Jim turned to Jane Cholster.

"Mrs Cholster, do you know of anything that was worrying your husband? Was he quite as usual tonight?"

"Quite," said Jane Cholster steadily. "He was a little sleepy, owing to having been gardening most of the afternoon. If you are trying to make out that my husband had any enemies, you are wasting your time. He had none."

The constable spoke suddenly. "Now, Mrs. Cholster," he said, "you and Miss Adelaide, there, living so close to him all in the same house—and Mr. Remy the next-door neighbor—between you, you ought to be able to give some sort of helpful evidence. This murder had a motive. It wasn't an accident. And it wasn't robbery. Nothing's been taken from Mr. Cholster. You'd ought to be more helpful, Mrs. Cholster."

"*But I tell you—*" Jane paused to control the impatience in her voice—

"I tell you there is nothing," she said. "Nothing. He was in no quarrel. He had no enemies."

"The village has it that he's a rich man."

"Not rich," said Jane. "He was no millionaire."

"Did he leave any insurance?"

"Really, Mr. Lambrikin," said Jane, the dangerous light flaring in her eyes again. "You'll have to ask our lawyer about that. I can tell you, however, that my husband was always very generous with me and with Adelaide. It is true that he controlled all the Cholster money—my money and Adelaide's inheritance, as well as his own. But he gave us anything we wanted. His will is no secret either: our own money was to revert to each of us and to each of us half of Brock's estate. I assure you that there is no motive for murder there. If either of us wanted money we had only to ask for it at any time."

"After Mr. and Mrs. Cholster arrived at the theater, what happened? Did they stop to speak to you?" It was Jim again, all his Celtic grace so smoothly to the fore that even Dickenson did not question his right to inquire.

"They stopped there in the doorway, and we chatted a moment. Then they said they were going down to the dressing rooms to make up, and Brock said he'd decided it would change his appearance more to an audience of townspeople if he wore a beard, and he'd got one already made. He handed Mrs. Cholster his make-up box and cap, and she went on into the theater while Brock showed me the beard—it's there on his chin now—and then he went on."

"I arrived next," said Tom Remy suddenly. "I stopped, too, and spoke to Dickie, and then went directly through the house—up those steps and, without even glancing out on the stage, to the dressing rooms. The stage was dark. And I do remember that the curtain was down."

"Did you see the Cholsters downstairs?" asked the constable quickly.

"I saw Mrs. Cholster," said Tom Remy slowly. "She stood there in her dressing-room door. I spoke to her a moment and went on to my own dressing room. But I do not believe that Mrs. Cholster left her dressing room at all until we heard Dickie shouting for us from up here."

"Why do you think that?" said Jim.

"Because," said Tom Remy, "I could hear her voice."

"Her voice?" cried the constable. "You mean she was talking to somebody? That would be Mr. Cholster, then. Was that—"

"No," said Jane. "I was not talking to my husband. I never saw him again alive after I left him at the door of the office back there." She stopped—deliberately, Susan thought—after throwing out the word "office." The constable's eyes went to Dickenson, who looked suddenly white.

Jim said: "To whom were you talking, Mrs. Cholster?"

Susan caught a tiny flame in Jane's eyes. She said: "I was rehearsing my lines."

Dickenson had got his breath.

"If you think that I killed Brock and dragged him up here to the stage you are wrong. I couldn't have lifted him. It's physically impossible."

"Maybe," said the constable. "But as to that, I don't know as any of you could have lifted him. Or struggled with him, for that matter. He was easy stronger than any one of you. Any one of you." He looked speculative and added: "Of course, two of you—"

"The wound," said Jim in a voice without any inflection at all, "was in the forehead. Somebody had to be very close to him. And directly in front of him. Therefore someone he knew and did not fear."

Jane leaped to her feet. "How dare you say such things! It is not true."

"Jane—Jane—" said Tom Remy, with again a guarded note of warning in his voice. "Look here, Constable, I am sure that Mrs. Cholster was in her dressing room downstairs from the time I arrived to the time we heard Dickie shouting for us here on the stage."

"We ain't saying Mrs. Cholster is the murderer," said the constable. "But Brock Cholster's dead, ain't he? Now then, Dickenson, you claimed that you saw everybody that entered the theater tonight."

"I thought so," he said rapidly. "But now that I've had time to think of it I realize that someone might have entered without my knowledge—"

"You said you were in the office the whole time from your arrival till everybody was here. Who came last? Miss Adelaide?"

"Yes, Adelaide. Yes, I said that in the haste of the moment when you arrived, Constable. But now I realize that someone must have slipped past the office door when I wasn't looking."

"And then slipped out again after he'd murdered Brock Cholster?" inquired the constable heavily.

"Exactly," said Dickenson eagerly. "That's what must have happened. There's no other explanation."

"It's pretty late for it, Dickenson," said the constable. "And it ain't reasonable to suppose that you saw everybody else that entered the theater and were sitting right there by the door from the time you unlocked it until you locked it again, and yet the murderer got past you twice without your seeing him. No, it ain't reasonable. Now, Miss Adelaide, what's your story?"

"Why, I—I came in, as Dickie said. And I went along the aisle there at the side and up those steps—just as the others did, I suppose, and then immediately down to my dressing room. That's all I know. That is, till I heard Dickie calling for us up here on the stage, and we all hurried upstairs and saw—" she gave a convulsive shudder and finished—"saw him."

"Was the curtain up when you came along the aisle?"

She blinked, hesitated, and then was certain.

"I don't know. I really don't know. I don't remember it at all."

"Was the stage dark?"

"Yes. Yes, it must have been."

Jim coughed lightly, and the constable looked at him, and Jim said: "Odd that no one heard any noise—"

"Did anyone hear a noise?" asked the constable directly.

No one replied, and the small silence grew oppressive. Again Susan was acutely conscious of the empty waiting theater, of the spaces, of the shadows, of the empty passages and rooms below them. Behind them, of course, was the balcony set with its French doors, and wings jutting out that looked like brick walls with vines over them. She glanced up and over her shoulder into what she could see of the loft. It, too, was dim in spite of lights, and hung with great ghostly ropes that stretched hazily upward into darkness.

She wondered if anyone could conceal himself up there in the dim reaches of the loft, clinging somehow to perilous ropes, and decided that it was not possible. She did not, however, like those mysterious dark spaces above and out in the wings.

The constable sighed and said: "Mrs. Cholster, didn't you hear anything?"

Jane Cholster moistened her lips.

"I heard nothing like—like a blow," she said as if forcing out the words. "I did hear someone on the stage. Arranging it, I thought, and supposed it was Mr. Dickenson. I didn't give it much attention."

"Mr. Remy?"

"Why, I—I didn't hear anything like a blow, either. Could we have heard that?"

The constable glanced toward the heap under its covering and said: "I think you could have heard it. Did you hear anyone on the stage?"

"I don't know," said Tom Remy. "I remember thinking that Dickie was getting the stage ready, but I don't know why I thought that—must have heard some sound, I suppose. Certainly," he added, as if making amends to Dickenson, "I had no reason to think it was Dickenson except that he usually arranged the stage for us. And it was only a vague recognition of someone moving about above us. Then there was, too, a sort of rumbling sound."

"A rumbling sound—"

"That was the ventilator," said Dickenson at once. "I had turned it on—the switch is in the office—to see how it worked. It's a recent addition and wasn't made for old theaters. It makes a lot of noise here. We can only use it between acts and when the theater is empty. But I was not arranging the stage."

"What time was the ventilator going?"

"I don't know exactly. Around eight, I suppose."

"Did *you* hear anything? Anything besides the—ventilator?"

"No," said Dickenson. "Nothing. But I'd like to know who put the curtain up."

Again no one spoke, and again the old theater waited. Someone behind Susan sighed: it was the little deputy. Jane Cholster was biting her lips, and Adelaide was staring upward in her turn into the mysterious ghostly reaches of the fly loft. Tom Remy blew out beige smoke, and quite suddenly there was a small skittering sound. Though it was faint, everyone started.

Then Dickenson said softly: "Mice," and Adelaide screamed raggedly but softly and pulled up her feet and jerked her skirt tighter over her legs.

Mere nerves, of course. They were all terribly aware, as Susan herself was aware, that murder had walked that stage.

And the murderer was still at large—or at least still undiscovered. Which of those taut, unrevealing faces concealed murder?

Or was it possible that the search of the theater had left some dark corner unseen?

"Then some time between ten minutes till eight and ten minutes after eight the murder occurred," said the constable suddenly. "Did you say they were to put this stuff on their faces at eight, Dickenson?"

Dickenson shrugged.

"Oh—I said make-up at eight," he said. "But that doesn't mean that Brock Cholster went down to his dressing room at exactly eight and then came up here again."

"But he was in his dressing room at some time," pressed the constable.

"Must have been."

"And he was murdered after he was made up?"

"Well, obviously. And obviously he wasn't murdered in his dressing room. Nobody could have got him up that stairway."

"When was your husband in his dressing room, Mrs. Cholster?"

"I—don't know."

"You didn't hear him at all?"

"No."

"But you know Mr. Remy was there?"

It was then that the storm growing behind Jane Cholster's lambent eyes burst into fury. She rose with a lithe movement and faced the constable.

"Constable," she said furiously. "This is an outrage. You are keeping us in this horrible place, frightening us—inquiring; and we have no recourse but to stay here and wait for the sheriff. But we can refuse to talk, and I do so now. I will not answer another question. And I will wait for the sheriff how and where I please."

She whirled and walked off the stage, turning aside beyond the switchboard. They could hear her quick footsteps as she went down the steps leading to the outside aisle of the house.

"Hey, there," cried the constable, standing. "You can't leave."

The trim dark figure did not turn. They watched as she coolly selected a seat and sat down in it, leaning her head on her hand.

Tom Remy, Adelaide, and Dickenson had risen, too, as if Jane's action had inspired them also to defiance, and were drifting toward the wings, Adelaide supported solicitously by the sleek young director.

"Well, let 'em go," said the constable to the deputy, who looked troubled. "Guess there's nothing much to do but wait for the sheriff."

"What do you think of it?" said Jim.

"Well," said the constable, "looks very much as if the deed was done around eight o'clock. Probably between eight and eight-ten. I figure it took Mr. Cholster a few minutes to get that stuff on his face. Then for some reason he came back here on the stage. Mr. Remy and Mrs. Cholster sort of alibi each other, but alibis ain't always certain. Miss Adelaide didn't hardly have time to kill him without an awful lot of luck before this Dickenson fellow locked the door and came straight up to the stage. I figure it wasn't more than a minute. I—"

"What's that?" It was Dickenson beside them suddenly, and Jim said:

"The constable and I were just saying that you must have followed Miss Adelaide into the theater almost at once."

"I did. I spoke to her, and she came on in, and I turned off the ventilator, locked the door, and followed."

"She must have put on her make-up very quickly," said Susan.

Dickenson's quick dark eyes gave her a very sharp look.

"Why, yes, I suppose she was hurrying. Probably hadn't finished when I found Cholster and called. If you're figuring whether she had time to—to kill him and then get down to her dressing room and get make-up on, why she didn't. And I realize that that leaves me the only one without an alibi; but I didn't kill him."

The constable said something again about the uncertainty of alibis, and Susan drifted away.

No one looked at the small figure in brown that unobtrusively crossed the stage, rounded the end of the set, and found herself in the dim world backstage. Now Susan could see the fly loft more clearly, though it was still a mysterious dark realm draped in a ghostly etching of ropes. Away up there were—what did they call them? Grids, was it?—great pulleys, anyway, over which the ropes passed. And nearer but still far away, flys and borders and drops and even empty battens were hanging motionless in the musty air. A theater has, as if distilled within it, a life of its own, and Susan, standing backstage, was strongly aware of that sentience. Voices drifted to her, and Susan turned and made her way toward the railed stairway that descended to the dressing rooms.

The air was colder and felt dank, and the musty smells were heavier. As she reached the last step she reminded herself that the whole place had been thoroughly searched.

The narrow passage ran up and down, with doors opening from it. It was lighted, of course; they had turned on every light in the theater. The light, however, rather emphasized its dreariness. There were six dressing rooms. Two of them were empty; the other four had, each of them, a make-up box on the table below the mirror. Susan entered swiftly one after another.

The first was probably Adelaide's, for a beige coat was flung hurriedly over the chair, and the top layer of the make-up box (Susan paused to remark the extremely nice make-up box that Adelaide had chosen to supply herself with for use merely as an amateur) had been removed, as if hastily, and lay on the bare table with its sticks of grease paint spilling. Pink powder lay open, also spilling, and a box of rouge. Susan looked carefully at the many sticks and pencils—liners, weren't they called?—and their colors and went on to the next dressing room. It was empty except for a gray cap and a make-up box—the make-up box was open and was much like Adelaide's. Because of the cap, Susan felt reasonably certain that it was the room the dead man was supposed to have used.

The other two dressing rooms were across the narrow passage and past an expanse of white-washed wall and were not directly opposite the first two rooms. The first one held another handsome make-up box, identical with the other two. It was closed, but there was a towel on the table with wisps of powder on it, and two or three cigarette ends and ashes were on the floor. Probably that was Jane's room, and she had apparently finished her make-up and closed the box. In the remaining room there was no make-up box at all, although on the table lay a box of tan power, a black eyebrow liner, and a stick of carmine lip paste. Tom Remy, then, used only the barest essentials. Susan pulled her loose pigskin glove over her hand and picked up the stick of lip paste. And just then something flickered in the wavery mirror before her.

Susan stared and whirled.

The doorway was bare and there was only whitewashed wall opposite. Surely there had been a motion there at the door. Surely—she put down the carmine paste and was at the door. The passage was dreary and empty.

But she realized suddenly that she could no longer hear voices from above.

Well, she had seen what she came to see. She would return. The passage, however, was rather dark. And certainly very quiet. And the door to the room that had had the gray tweed cap in it was closed.

She stopped abruptly.

She had left it open. She was sure of that.

Quite suddenly and absurdly, she was frightened and wanted to scream. And just then there was a rustle in the room and a quick metallic click. The door swung wide, and Tom Remy stood on the threshold and saw her.

He said calmly: "Oh, Miss—er—Dare. You look frightened."

"I—I didn't know you were here," said Susan.

His eyes retreated to dark, enigmatic slits, and for a long moment he stood there looking at her. Then he said finally and very slowly: "Yes, I—I came down to get Miss Adelaide's coat."

"What is your profession, Mr. Remy?" She was relieved to find that her question sounded quite steady.

"I'm a painter."

"Landscape?" inquired Susan.

"Portraits," he said. "Why?"

"There's a beige coat in the dressing room nearest the stairs," said Susan. "Did you—"

A figure emerged rather promptly from Adelaide's dressing room. It had the beige coat over its arm and was Dickenson. He looked at them and said: "I've got her coat, Tom."

"Why, I—" said Tom Remy and stopped abruptly and said: "Oh, I see."

Which was it, thought Susan, preceding the two men up the stairway, who had been watching her? And why? At the top of the stairs she paused to look at the door that was the stage entrance.

"Here, Tom," said Dickenson suddenly. "Take this coat on to Adelaide, will you? I'll—er—be there in a minute, tell her."

"All right," said Remy briefly.

"This is the stage entrance?" murmured Susan.

"Certainly. Bolted up tight. Not even the cat could get in."

"Of course," said Susan. "I see. She looked at the bolt, then lifted it and put her gloved hand on the under side of the heavy latch. The door opened, and night air swept in, and a stalwart figure loomed out of the darkness beyond.

"Hey, there," it said truculently. "Shut that door and stay in there, miss."

"Well guarded," said Dickenson. His thin lips smiled, but his eyes looked worried, and Susan let the bolt fall back into place. He turned as she turned, and walked toward the stage beside her.

"That," said Susan, "is, of course, the switchboard?" She indicated the panel set into the wall.

He nodded. "Here's the signal for the asbestos curtain," he volunteered. "It's the only curtain or drop in the theater that's controlled by an electric switch. The rest of these are lights."

She walked out on the stage. Jane Cholster was still sitting coolly in the seat she had chosen. Tom Remy was bending over her, and both were talking.

Adelaide, wrapped now in her beige coat, was sitting near them, staring at nothing.

Away at the back, the constable was having a conference with the deputy on guard at the door. The other deputy—Dunc—was sitting on the stage looking thin and disconsolate. Jim was nowhere to be seen.

Susan approached the deputy, and he sprang up with a startled look and put his hand on his revolver. Dickenson was watching her from the wings with steady, knowing black eyes. She said in a low voice to the deputy: "Have any of those people down there moved about the theater much?"

"Huh?" He had pale blue eyes which opened in surprise. "No, I guess not. That is, Tom Remy went downstairs a few minutes ago. And this young Dickenson fellow, too."

"Which one first?"

"Dickenson, I think."

Susan said slowly: "I believe that one of them is going to try to hide something. Something that's important. Do you—"

"Sure! I get it! I'll watch every move they make." His eyes had lighted up, and her tone must have carried conviction, for he did not question her, which was as well, for Dickenson was crossing the stage to her side. She turned toward the French doors, and again he turned with her, followed her as she went through them and stopped when she stopped.

Furniture for a drawing room was crowded in space between the two sets. A light couch, several chairs, a table.

"It's for the second act," said Dickenson, watching her. Curious, said something in the back of Susan's mind, how quickly we are removed from the deputy—from the people sitting out there in the house. It's almost as if we were entirely alone. She moved a little away from the slender, dark figure but he moved also. She was acutely conscious of his dark eyes, and of his shoulder all but touching her own as she bent closer to scrutinize the couch.

"They looked here for a weapon, I suppose," she said.

"Yes, I—I think so."

She moved around the couch, and he followed her. She was aware of his silent graceful tread behind her as she walked out into the wings again and around behind the second act set. She was plunged at once into a dark world of empty spaces that seemed, somehow, not empty. She looked up again into the shadowy loft.

Against the dark old wall and about thirty feet above the stage was a small wooden platform. Narrow wooden steps led upward to it, and ropes from away overhead dropped in long taut lines to its railing . . . Susan turned toward it, and the man at her side said suddenly:

"See here, you aren't going up in the fly gallery, are you?"

"Why not?" said Susan, wondering what he would say.

"Well, it's—it's against union rules, you know. Nobody but stage crew is permitted up there. And—and then there must be two men; I mean to manipulate the ropes, you know. It's—rather dangerous. Nearly had an accident myself once—fellow let down what looked like an empty rope, not realizing it held a weight. Came very near to hitting me. Since then, believe me, I warn my casts to stay away from the gallery. These amateurs— I say, what in the world do you want to go up there for? There's nothing there."

He wasn't as quick-witted as somehow she had expected him to be; otherwise his objections would have been more forceful.

She put her hand on the railing of the steps and was glad it was there, for Susan had never liked a ladder or anything remotely resembling it.

"Union rules aren't applying tonight," she said lightly and started upward.

It was not a pleasant climb. The steps were very narrow and very steep, and she was altogether too acutely aware that he was still following her. Step by step, just there below her heels. Oh, well—she could always call out to the people below. That is, if there were need. But she rather wished she had waited for Jim.

And when she reached the small gallery it seemed very much farther to the floor of the stage than the same distance had seemed looking up. She closed her eyes against a momentary dizziness and clung to the heavy railing.

"If you're looking for clues," said Dickenson's suave voice at her side, "there's nothing at all here. Don't you think you'd better go down again? I can't have you fainting on my hands up here."

Susan opened her eyes.

"I'm not fainting," she said. "What are these things called?" She touched one of a line of long wooden pegs fastened along the railing, from which extended the ropes.

"Pins," he said briefly. "Ropes pass over those pulleys up there and are looped in a half-hitch around these. Holds them. It takes an expert to manipulate these things. The flys and drops are very heavy, you know. The new theaters have everything controlled by electricity. It's grand when you get in a place like that." His eyes slid toward her face, and he said: "I shouldn't dare to work one of these myself; though, of course, I've done it now and then in rehearsals. But the weight is much heavier than you'd think. Knew of a fellow once that got his ankle twisted in one of the coils, the thing got away from him, and he was carried clear up to the grids—an eighty-foot drop below." He looked at her more fully and said very slowly and markedly: "It's very dangerous."

He knows that I know, thought Susan.

She looked downward. The back part of the stage was spread out below her as if it were on a platter. But the exterior set and the border above it cut off, except for a band of brighter light, a view of the deputy and of the seats. There were people near—yet no one was to be seen. And no one knew where she was.

It looked a long distance to the floor below. How easy an accident would be—how easy a slip and a fall!

It was just then that she saw the loops of rope. The loops that were not quite like those other loops—the loops that were irregular and lacked entirely the sureness that marked those about the other pins. For her life she could not have refrained from putting out her hand and clutching the rope above that pin.

"Look out," said Dickenson in a swift hard voice.

Susan was looking upward through the dimness of the loft. It was dust that made it so dim—a lazy fog of dust hanging up there, moving in its own mysterious course. What did that rope support in the midst of the masking dusk?

Dickenson's hands, like steel, were on her own.

"Stop that," he said. And then Susan knew that someone was moving on the floor below. It was a small figure in a beige coat, and it looked up and said: "Dickie. Dickie, darling, what *are* you doing?"

Susan could feel Dickenson's muscles jerk at the sound of Adelaide's voice. But he did not relinquish his grip, although he called out in a strange voice:

"Go back to Jane, Adelaide. And stay there. Go on—"

But Adelaide too was staring upward into the purple fog of dust. Susan, fascinated, watched her small face become rigid and her eyes become fixed and black and horrified.

"*Dickie—*" screamed Adelaide and turned blindly and fell in a huddled queer heap.

Dickenson released Susan's hands and was climbing down the steps. The deputy reached Adelaide first, and then Jane came hurrying from somewhere, and Tom Remy followed. By the time they had moved Adelaide to the couch and pushed things about to give her air, the constable and Jim were there, too.

Susan clung to the railing and watched. The figures below were foreshortened and queer, but every word floated up to her ears.

So that was the weapon. But what was the motive?

Her knees were unsteady, and she glanced at the steep narrow steps at her side and did not want to undertake that descent. It was always easier to climb a ladder than to go down it again. Jim, below, was looking for her.

She whistled softly, and he saw her, though no one else looked away from the couch where Adelaide was lying. His eyes looked relieved, and he walked directly under the gallery and said softly:

"Come down."

Susan looked at the ladder-like steps again and shook her head. "Can't."

He started to speak, stopped, and decided to join her. Her breath began to come more evenly as she watched his gray shoulders come nearer and nearer.

He emerged onto the gallery and said rather grimly: "I was looking for you."

"And high time," said Susan unsteadily. "Take a girl for a ride, plunge her into murder, and leave her there, scared half to death."

"Nonsense," said Jim simply. "See here, Susan, what do you make of all this? And why did that woman down there faint?"

"Because I know what the weapon was that killed Brock Cholster," said Susan. "And she knows, too."

"Weapon?" said Jim.

Susan looked at the couch and then upward again into the purple dusk.

"Jim," she said slowly. "I'm going to put myself in the place of the murderer for a moment. And I want you to listen. Suppose I want to murder Brock Cholster—perhaps have wanted to for a long time, or perhaps quite suddenly want to more overwhelmingly than I have ever wanted to before. Suppose I come up on the stage and the asbestos curtain is down and thus no one can see and for some reason I stop there and discover that Cholster is there, too. That he is sleepy and drowsy, for he's been gardening all day—that he is lying at full length on the couch down there."

"Susan—"

"Wait. I stand there perhaps and look at him and hate him. Hate him as I've never done before. Hate him until it is almost insupportable. For he stands in the way of something I must have. And I wish that he were dead. But the wish isn't enough to kill him, and perhaps it's accident—or perhaps it's some memory of danger from above that makes me look upward. And way up there, hanging like a sword of Damocles I see a weapon—wait, Jim, don't talk—

"It's hanging there as if it were waiting for me. And it looks as if Cholster has actually chosen to put himself directly under it—as if fate itself were offering the weapon ready for my hand. I look at it and think only of that weapon at last ready for me and that no one will know—or dream of looking up there. There isn't much time, so I hurry up to this gallery. And I find the rope that holds that weight. So I—I let down the rope—slowly, perhaps, *until I discover that it is actually,* as it looked from down there, *directly above his head*. And when I'm sure of that I let it fall. Heavily."

She stopped and this time Jim did not offer to speak. He was staring upward, and his face looked white and grim. He said finally: "And then what?"

"Then," said Susan. "I jerked the thing up again. I loop the rope hurriedly around this pin. I hurry down the steps. He is dead, and the thing is done. Suddenly the nervous tension of that awful emotion collapses, and I am terrified. How can I hide my own part in what has happened? How can I confuse things—make them seem different—somehow change things? The lack of a weapon will lead suspicion away from the people now in the theater and thus from myself. Fortunately he is on the couch, and the couch—Jim, you remember the rumbling sound they heard?"

Jim looked at her. "The ventilator?"

"Perhaps it was going, too, but the sound of someone arranging the stage was the sound of that light couch being pushed across the stage. (It's got casters and would move readily; I looked to be sure.) It would not be difficult to pull the body off the couch and return the couch to its place. And as the body lay when it was discovered, there was nothing but proscenium and ceiling above it, for it was far out over the footlights. It was simple enough to put up the absestos curtain and thus allow the body to project beyond the curtain line."

Jim shook his head slowly.

"But the murderer couldn't have known that Cholster would be exactly there."

"The murderer *didn't* know! Of course, he didn't know. That's the key to the whole affair. The crime wasn't planned at all. All that stored-up hatred didn't, perhaps, even reach the point of murder until the murderer saw the man and the weapon. Victim and weapon together, at a time when for some reason the murderer was worked up to a frenzy—all three combined like chemicals and produced murder."

Susan's grave low voice came to a stop. In the silence, she could hear the crisp flap of a newspaper with which Jane was fanning Adelaide and the murmur of Tom Remy's voice speaking to Dickenson.

Jim sighed and said very soberly and deliberately:

"I believe you're right, Sue. The weight will show it under analysis. And of course, if it didn't come exactly over his head it would have been a simple matter to fasten the rope, run down to him without waking him and swing the thing so that it—accomplished its purpose. The weight itself isn't much, but the momentum makes it deadly. Yes, Sue, I think you're right. But any one of them could have done it. Who had a motive?"

"The motive must have been actually desire," said Susan slowly. "Desire so strong that it produced a smoldering, gathering hatred. All ready to be lashed into frenzy. But I don't know." She paused, wishing she could seek objectively instead of subjectively through all those currents of feeling and motives and consciousness that are handily put together and labeled personality. Or character. Jim was more reasonable and more definite than she was; she could only push out blind tentacles of something that was perilously like intuition.

"I don't know," she said sadly, "what that lashing was."

Jim said thoughtfully: "Revenge might come into it. A grudge. The constable says Cholster had really a wicked temper. Town gossip has it that he was nothing short of a tyrant in his own home."

"Does the constable's knowledge extend to Jane Cholster's reaction?"

"I asked about that. He knew of nothing, except that she was a bit high-handed. But if there was trouble between them, the constable hadn't heard of it. Oh, by the way, Sue—this young Dickenson isn't altogether honest in his statement about what he was doing back there in the office. He was actually talking over long distance."

"Talking!"

"Exactly. To some woman. I went back to telephone my story. Had to make a long distance call, and the girl asked if I wanted the charge reversed again. I said, 'Again?' and she said, 'Oh I thought it was Mr. Dickenson. You're at the Majestic, aren't you?' (The Majestic, dear Susan, is the name of this theater.) It took only a minute or two to get it out of her. At ten minutes to eight o'clock he was talking to a girl in Springfield. It lasted only a few minutes, so it isn't an alibi. And from what central, who obligingly listened in, says, it was an extremely loving conversation. Why are you looking so queer?"

"Queer?" said Susan vaguely. "Oh—nothing. Except that there's the weapon, you see. And the murderer. And—odd, isn't it, if that telephone conversation hadn't taken place there would have been no murder."

"What—"

"Oh, yes, of course. It couldn't have been any other way. But—oh, look—look, Jim, quick—down there! See, she's becoming conscious again. She's opening her eyes—she's looking—she's remembering."

Jim, watching, saw the figure in the beige coat stir, sit upright, and fumble suddenly at the bottom of the coat.

Susan was leaning forward, her face white and her eyes frightened. "Quick, Jim, get the coat. Somehow—anyhow—"

After all, she did not even remember going down that narrow, steep flight of steps. She didn't know either what Jim said to the others. She only knew that he thrust the coat into her hands.

The pockets were empty, but she found it in the bottom of the coat between the lining and the soft beige wool. She worked the small hard object up until it emerged from a torn bit of the lining of a pocket and was in her fingers.

"What are you doing?" demanded Jane Cholster. Her face was pasty gray and her eyes blazing.

Susan did not reply. Instead she crossed the stage, and Jim was beside her when she knelt there at the body. It was he who thrust Tom Remy out of the way when he would have snatched at the thing that Susan held. Somebody—the constable it was—seized Remy and held him struggling, and the guard at the door and the little deputy were both running toward them.

Then Susan covered the face again.

"What—" said Jim. "Who did it?"

Susan felt ill and wished she had never heard of Kittiwake. She said to Jane: "Did you put the make-up box and cap in his dressing room?"

"Yes, of course," said Jane slowly. "I left it open and ready for him."

"You knew that he objected," said Susan after a long moment. "You knew he refused."

"God forgive me," said Jane suddenly looking old and tired. "I knew—I think we all knew—"

Susan nodded to Jim. "I wasn't sure," she said, "until Mrs. Cholster admitted it just now. That is, I wasn't sure of the motive. The rest of it was terribly simple."

She held out her hand toward the constable. "Here it is," she said. "The lipstick that was used on his mouth by the murderer."

"Lip—" said the constable and after a long time added—"stick." And away at the back someone was suddenly pounding on the doors—pounding so loud that the sound echoed in waves that all but submerged those on the stage.

The constable turned to the deputy.

"Open the door for the sheriff," he said.

The group moved and wavered. The sound and motion left Jim and Susan for a moment as if on a small remote island.

"Are you sure?" said Jim.

Susan nodded. "The face was made up for only one motive, and that had to be to give the impression that it had been made up before the murder; thus that the murder had been done after, approximately, eight o'clock—the time set for make-up. Therefore, it must have been done before eight or thereabouts. Therefore it had to be done by someone who was here at eight—Dickenson—Jane—Tom Remy."

"Wait. How do you know the face was made up by the murderer?"

"There was no powder on it and no cream. That would have been put on first. And the lipstick on his mouth was not matched in color or in quality by any of the lip paste in the make-up boxes downstairs. Of course, there were a hundred places to hide the lipstick. But it was not hidden till too late."

The pounding stopped and there was a sound of voices—inquiring, explaining.

Jim glanced over Susan's shoulder and said tersely: "Go on. Quick."

"Well, then—since the murder wasn't planned, there must be inconsistencies—things that changed somehow in the very act of being done. Blunders. I tried again to follow what I should have done in the murderer's place: frantic, trying to confuse things again—changing the position of the body, putting on the beard—Cholster had it there in his hand, probably, and it must have suggested that attempt at make-up. Yet there was no time to open a make-up box and do it thoroughly. Besides, the power would have spilled. The beard and lipstick were enough, anyway."

"Yes—yes—"

"Well, then, I would have turned and—and passed the switchboard and put up the asbestos curtain—perhaps, as I said before, so the body could be dragged out near the footlights, perhaps merely from that frantic blind desire to confuse, to make things opposite to what they had been. I don't know. But after that I would have gone down to the dressing room. And *on the way* I would have passed the stage entrance. And I would have known suddenly of another change—of another inconsistency. That I could walk out that door, wait outside for a few moments, walk slowly around to the front of the theater, enter again, and—this time—be very sure that I was seen by the man in the office. Then, in going down to the dressing room again, I could bolt that door, on the inside, as it had been."

Jim's eyes looked dark and shining. The confused voices of sheriff and men were coming closer.

Jim said, whispering: "*Adelaide.*"

"No one else entered after eight o'clock. If she had had time to plan, she wouldn't have made up Cholster. But she was frantic, excited, obliged to snatch at defense. This time she snatched at an alibi. Dickenson discovered the murder only a moment or two after her arrival. But it was her second arrival. He really hadn't seen her at first. He was too intent on the girl in Springfield probably."

"But the motive?"

"Remember Cholster controlled her money and thus actually controlled her. He was tyrannical and violent-tempered. It seemed to me that her sobs were more frightened petulance than sorrow. And that she was much more concerned about Dickenson than anything else. That's what I meant and what Jane meant when she replied. Probably Dickenson talked marriage: Cholster objected; refused to give Adelaide money that was rightfully her own; and Dickenson—I don't suppose he wanted her without money."

"And then she heard the telephone conversation—"

"Yes," said Susan soberly. "She entered the theater and heard that. And jealousy—rage—the fury of a woman who sees the only thing she wants denied her (a vain woman, clutching at youth)—all of it swept to a climax. She walked up to the stage and saw Cholster lying there asleep. And *at the same instant* saw a weapon for her vengeance and for her release hanging there over his head."

"It's her lipstick?"

"Yes. It was in her coat pocket; that's why she sent for her coat. Jane uses none. Adelaide does, and you can see a smear of it on her lips now. It's called claret—a rather soft crimson. Any woman would note the exact shade. And Tom Remy saw it, too. He was looking in Cholster's make-up box to see if there was a stick of lip paste of that shade of soft crimson. And without the odor of grease paints. But then," said Susan slowly, "perhaps they all knew in their hearts who did it—and why. Jane admitted that. And—for proof there are fingerprints on the bolt of the stage door where Adelaide had to touch it."

The sheriff reached the footlights and stopped.

Without looking Susan could see the group at the other side of the stage.

"So," said the sheriff, "there's a murder here."

Jim's hand touched Susan's shoulder.

"The car's outside at the corner where we left it. Go on and wait for me there."

THE FOUR SUSPECTS

Agatha Christie

The conversation hovered round undiscovered and unpunished crimes. Everyone in turn vouchsafed an opinion: Colonel Bantry, his plump amiable wife, Jane Helier, Dr. Lloyd, and even old Miss Marple. The one person who did not speak was the one best fitted in most people's opinion to do so. Sir Henry Clithering, ex-Commissioner of Scotland Yard, sat silent, twisting his moustache—or rather stroking it—and half smiling, as though at some inward thought that amused him.

"Sir Henry," said Mrs. Bantry at last, "if you don't say something, I shall scream. Are there a lot of crimes that go unpunished, or are there not?"

"You're thinking of newspaper headlines, Mrs. Bantry. SCOTLAND YARD AT FAULT AGAIN. And a list of unsolved mysteries to follow."

"Which really, I suppose, form a very small percentage of the whole?" said Dr. Lloyd.

"Yes, that is so. The hundreds of crimes that are solved and the perpetrators punished are seldom heralded and sung. But that isn't quite the point at issue, is it? When you talk of undiscovered crimes and unsolved crimes, you are talking of two different things. In the first category come all the crimes that Scotland Yard never hears about, the crimes that no one even knows have been committed."

"But I suppose there aren't very many of those?" said Mrs. Bantry.

"Aren't there?"

"Sir Henry! You don't mean there are?"

"I should think," said Miss Marple thoughtfully, "that there must be a very large number."

The charming old lady, with her old-world, unruffled air, made her statement in a tone of the utmost placidity.

"My dear Miss Marple," said Colonel Bantry.

"Of course," said Miss Marple, "a lot of people are stupid. And stupid people get found out, whatever they do. But there are quite a number of people who aren't stupid, and one shudders to think of what they might accomplish unless they had very strongly rooted principles."

"Yes," said Sir Henry, "there are a lot of people who aren't stupid. How often does some crime come to light simply by reason of a bit of unmitigated bungling, and each time one asks oneself the question: If this hadn't been bungled, would anyone ever have known?"

"But that's very serious, Clithering," said Colonel Bantry. "Very serious, indeed."

"Is it?"

"What do you mean, is it? Of course it's serious."

"You say crime goes unpunished, but does it? Unpunished by the law perhaps, but cause and effect works outside the law. To say that every crime brings its own punishment is by way of being a platitude, and yet in my opinion nothing can be truer."

"Perhaps, perhaps," said Colonel Bantry. "But that doesn't alter the seriousness—the—er—seriousness—" He paused, rather at a loss.

Sir Henry Clithering smiled.

"Ninety-nine people out of a hundred are doubtless of your way of thinking," he said. "But you know, it isn't really guilt that is important—it's innocence. That's the thing that nobody will realize."

"I don't understand," said Jane Helier.

"I do," said Miss Marple. "When Mrs. Trent found half a crown missing from her bag, the person it affected most was the daily woman, Mrs. Arthur. Of course the Trents thought it was her, but being kindly people and knowing she had a large family and a husband who drinks, well—they naturally didn't want to go to extremes. But they felt differently toward her, and they didn't leave her in charge of the house when they went away, which made a great difference to her; and other people began to get a feeling about her too. And then it suddenly came out that it was the governess. Mrs. Trent saw her through a door reflected in a mirror. The purest chance—though I prefer to call it Providence. And that, I think, is what Sir Henry means. Most people would be only interested in who took the money, and it turned out to be the most unlikely person—just like in detective stories! But the real person it was life and death to was poor Mrs. Arthur, who had done nothing. That's what you mean, isn't it, Sir Henry?"

"Yes, Miss Marple, you've hit off my meaning exactly. Your charwoman person was lucky in the instance you relate. Her innocence was shown. But some people may go through a lifetime crushed by the weight of a suspicion that is really unjustified."

"Are you thinking of some particular instance, Sir Henry?" asked Mrs. Bantry shrewdly.

"As a matter of fact, Mrs. Bantry, I am. A very curious case. A case where we believe murder to have been committed, but with no possible chance of ever proving it."

"Poison, I suppose," breathed Jane. "Something untraceable."

Dr. Lloyd moved restlessly and Sir Henry shook his head.

"No, dear lady. Not the secret arrow poison of the South American Indians! I wish it were something of that kind. We have to deal with something much more prosaic—so prosaic, in fact, that there is no hope of bringing the deed home to its perpetrator. An old gentleman who fell downstairs and broke his neck; one of those regrettable accidents which happen every day."

"But what happened really?"

"Who can say?" Sir Henry shrugged his shoulders. "A push from behind? A piece of cotton or string tied across the top of the stairs and carefully removed afterward? That we shall never know."

"But you do think that it—well, wasn't an accident? Now why?" asked the doctor.

"That's rather a long story, but—well, yes, we're pretty sure. As I said, there's no chance of being able to bring the deed home to anyone—the evidence would be too flimsy. But there's the other aspect of the case—the one I was speaking about. You see, there were four people who might have done the trick. One's guilty, but the other three are innocent. And unless the truth is found out, those three are going to remain under the terrible shadow of doubt."

"I think," said Mrs. Bantry, "that you'd better tell us your long story."

"I needn't make it so very long after all," said Sir Henry. "I can at any rate condense the beginning. That deals with a German secret society—the *Schwartze Hand*—something after the lines of the Camorra or what is most people's idea of the Camorra. A scheme of blackmail and terrorization. The thing started quite suddenly after the war and spread to an amazing extent. Numberless people were victimized by it. The authorities were not successful in coping with it, for its secrets were jealously guarded, and it was almost impossible to find anyone who could be induced to betray them.

"Nothing much was ever known about it in England, but in Germany it was having a most paralyzing effect. It was finally broken up and dispersed through the efforts of one man, a Dr. Rosen, who had at one time been very prominent in Secret Service work. He became a member, penetrated its inmost circle, and was, as I say, instrumental in bringing about its downfall.

"But he was, in consequence, a marked man, and it was deemed wise that he should leave Germany—at any rate for a time. He came to England, and we had letters about him from the police in Berlin. He came and had a personal interview with me. His point of view was both dispassionate and resigned. He had no doubts of what the future held for him.

" 'They will get me, Sir Henry,' he said. 'Not a doubt of it.' He was a big man with a fine head and a very deep voice, with only a slight guttural intonation to tell of his nationality. 'That is a foregone conclusion. It does not matter, I am prepared. I faced the risk when I undertook this business. I have done what I set out to do. The organization can never be gotten together again. But there are many members of it at liberty, and they will take the only revenge they can—my life. It is simply a question of time, but I am anxious that that time should be as long as possible. You see, I am collecting and editing some very interesting material—the result of my life's work. I should like, if possible to be able to complete my task.'

"He spoke very simply, with a certain grandeur which I could not but admire. I told him we would take all precautions, but he waved my words aside.

" 'Some day, sooner or later, they will get me,' he repeated. 'When that day comes, to not distress yourself. You will, I have no doubt, have done all that is possible.'

"He then proceeded to outline his plans which were simple enough. He proposed to take a small cottage in the country where he could live quietly and go on with his work. In the end he selected a village in Somerset—King's Gnaton, which was seven miles from a railway station and singularly untouched by civilization. He bought a very charming cottage, had various improvements and alterations made, and settled down there most contentedly. His household consisted of his niece, Greta; a secretary; an old German servant who had served him faithfully for nearly forty years; and an outside handy man and gardener who was a native of King's Gnaton."

"The four suspects," said Dr. Lloyd softly.

"Exactly. The four suspects. There is not much more to tell. Life went on peacefully at King's Gnaton for five months and then the blow fell. Dr. Rosen fell down the stairs one morning and was found dead about half an hour later. At the time the accident must have taken place, Gertrud was in her kitchen with the door closed and heard nothing—so she says.

Fräulein Greta was in the garden, planting some bulbs—again, so she says. The gardener, Dobbs, was in the small potting shed having his elevenses—so he says; and the secretary was out for a walk, and once more there is only his own word for it. No one had an alibi—no one can corroborate anyone else's story. But one thing is certain. No one from outside could have done it, for a stranger in the little village of King's Gnaton would be noticed without fail. Both the back and the front doors were locked, each member of the household having his own key. So you see it narrows down to those four. And yet each one seems to be above suspicion. Greta, his own brother's child. Gertrud, with forty years of faithful service. Dobbs, who has never been out of King's Gnaton. And Charles Templeton, the secretary—"

"Yes," said Colonel Bantry, "what about him? He seems the suspicious person to my mind. What do you know about him?"

"It is what I knew about him that put him completely out of court—at any rate, at the time," said Sir Henry gravely. "You see, Charles Templeton was one of my own men."

"Oh!" said Colonel Bantry, considerably taken aback.

"Yes. I wanted to have someone on the spot, and at the same time I didn't want to cause talk in the village. Rosen really needed a secretary. I put Templeton on the job. He's a gentleman, he speaks German fluently, and he's altogether a very able fellow."

"But, then, which do you suspect?" asked Mrs. Bantry in a bewildered tone. "They all seem so—well, impossible."

"Yes, so it appears. But you can look at the thing from another angle. Fräulein Greta was his niece and a very lovely girl, but the war has shown us time and again that brother can turn against sister, or father against son, and so on, and the loveliest and gentlest of young girls did some of the most amazing things. The same thing applies to Gertrud, and who knows what other forces might be at work in her case? A quarrel, perhaps, with her master, a growing resentment all the more lasting because of the long faithful years behind her. Elderly women of that class can be amazingly bitter sometimes. And Dobbs? Was he right outside it because he had no connection with the family? Money will do much. In some way Dobbs might have been approached and bought.

"For one thing seems certain: Some message or some order must have come from outside. Otherwise, why five months' immunity? No, the agents of the society must have been at work. Not yet sure of Rosen's perfidy, they delayed till the betrayal had been traced to him beyond any possible doubt. And then, all doubts set aside, they must have sent their message to the spy within the gates—the message that said, 'Kill.' "

"How nasty!" said Jane Helier, and shuddered.

"But how did the message come? That was the point I tried to elucidate—the one hope of solving my problem. One of those four people must have been approached or communicated with in some way. There would be no delay—I knew that; as soon as the command came, it would be carried out. That was a peculiarity of the *Schwartze Hand*.

"I went into the question, went into it in a way that will probably strike you as being ridiculously meticulous. Who had come to the cottage that morning? I eliminated nobody. Here is the list."

He took an envelope from his pocket and selected a paper from its contents.

"The butcher, bringing some neck of mutton. Investigated and found correct.

"The grocer's assistant, bringing a packet of corn flour, two pounds of sugar, a pound of butter, and a pound of coffee. Also investigated and found correct.

"The postman, bringing two circulars for Fräulein Rosen, a local letter for Gertrud, three letters for Dr. Rosen, one with a foreign stamp, and two letters for Mr. Templeton, one also with a foreign stamp."

Sir Henry paused and then took a sheaf of documents from the envelope.

"It may interest you to see these for yourself. They were handed me by the various people concerned or collected from the wastepaper basket. I need hardly say they've been tested by experts for invisible ink, et cetera. No excitement of that kind is possible."

Everyone crowded round to look. The catalogues were respectively from a nurseryman and from a prominent London fur establishment. The two bills addressed to Dr. Rosen were a local one for seeds for the garden and one from a London stationery firm. The letter addressed to him ran as follows:

> *My Dear Rosen—Just back from Dr. Helmuth Spath's. I saw Edgar Jackson the other day. He and Amos Perry have just come back from Tsingtau. In all Honesty I can't say I envy them the trip. Let me have news of you soon. As I said before: Beware of a certain person. You know who I mean, though you don't agree.*
>
> *—Yours,*
> *Georgina.*

"Mr. Templeton's mail consisted of this bill which, as you see, is an account rendered from his tailor, and a letter from a friend in Germany," went on Sir Henry. "The latter, unfortunately, he tore up while out on his walk. Finally we have the letter received by Gertrud."

Dear Mrs. Swartz,—We're hoping as how you be able to come the social on friday evening. the vicar says has he hopes you will—one and all being welcome. The resipy for the ham was very good, and I thanks you for it. Hoping as this finds you well and that we shall see you friday i remain

Yours faithfully,
Emma Greene.

Dr. Lloyd smiled a little over this and so did Mrs. Bantry.

"I think the last letter can be put out of court," said Dr. Lloyd.

"I thought the same," said Sir Henry, "but I took the precaution of verifying that there was a Mrs. Greene and a church social. One can't be too careful, you know."

"That's what our friend Miss Marple always says," said Dr. Lloyd, smiling. "You're lost in a daydream, Miss Marple. What are you thinking out?"

Miss Marple gave a start.

"So stupid of me," she said. "I was just wondering why the word Honesty in Dr. Rosen's letter was spelled with a capital H."

Mrs. Bantry picked it up.

"So it is," she said. "Oh!"

"Yes, dear," said Miss Marple. "I thought you'd notice!"

"There's a definite warning in that letter," said Colonel Bantry. "That's the first thing caught my attention. I notice more than you'd think. Yes, a definite warning—against whom?"

"There's rather a curious point about that letter," said Sir Henry. "According to Templeton, Dr. Rosen opened the letter at breakfast and tossed it across to him, saying he didn't know who the fellow was from Adam."

"But it wasn't a fellow," said Jane Helier. "It was signed 'Georgina.' "

"It's difficult to say which it is," said Dr. Lloyd. "It might be Georgey, but it certainly looks more like Georgina. Only it strikes me that the writing is a man's."

"You know, that's interesting," said Colonel Bantry. "His tossing it across the table like that and pretending he knew nothing about it. Wanted to watch somebody's face. Whose face—the girl's? Or the man's?"

"Or even the cook's?" suggested Mrs. Bantry. "She might have been in the room bringing in the breakfast. But what I don't see is . . . it's most peculiar—"

She frowned over the letter. Miss Marple drew closer to her. Miss Marple's finger went out and touched the sheet of paper. They murmured together.

"But why did the secretary tear up the other letter?" asked Jane Helier suddenly. "It seems—oh, I don't know—it seems queer. Why should he have letters from Germany? Although, of course, if he's above suspicion, as you say—"

"But Sir Henry didn't say that," said Miss Marple quickly, looking up from her murmured conference with Mrs. Bantry. "He said four suspects. So that shows that he includes Mr. Templeton. I'm right, am I not, Sir Henry?"

"Yes, Miss Marple. I have learned one thing through bitter experience. Never say to yourself that anyone is above suspicion. I gave you reasons just now why three of these people might after all be guilty, unlikely as it seemed. I did not at that time apply the same process to Charles Templeton. But I came to it at last through pursuing the rule I have just mentioned. And I was forced to recognize this: That every army and every navy and every police force has a certain number of traitors within its ranks, much as we hate to admit the idea. And I examined dispassionately the case against Charles Templeton.

"I asked myself very much the same questions as Miss Helier has just asked. Why should he, alone of all the house, not be able to produce the letter he had received—a letter, moreover, with a German stamp on it. Why should he have letters from Germany?

"The last question was an innocent one, and I actually put it to him. His reply came simply enough. His mother's sister was married to a German. The letter had been from a German girl cousin. So I learned something I did not know before—that Charles Templeton had relations with people in Germany. And that put him definitely on the list of suspects—very much so. He is my own man—a lad I have always liked and trusted; but in common justice and fairness I must admit that he heads that list.

"But there it is—I do not know! I do not know. . . . And in all probability I never shall know. It is not a question of punishing a murderer. It is a question that to me seems a hundred times more important. It is the blighting, perhaps, of an honorable man's whole career . . . because of suspicion—a suspicion that I dare not disregard."

Miss Marple coughed and said gently:

"Then, Sir Henry, if I understand you rightly, it is this young Mr. Templeton only who is so much on your mind?"

"Yes, in a sense. It should, in theory, be the same for all four, but that is not actually the case. Dobbs, for instance—suspicion may attach to him in my mind, but it will not actually affect his career. Nobody in the village has ever had any idea that old Dr. Rosen's death was anything but an accident. Gertrud is slightly more affected. It must make, for instance, a difference in Fräulein Rosen's attitude toward her. But that, possibly, is not of great importance to her.

"As for Greta Rosen—well, here we come to the crux of the matter. Greta is a very pretty girl and Charles Templeton is a good-looking young man, and for five months they were thrown together with no outer distractions. The inevitable happened. They fell in love with each other—even if they did not come to the point of admitting the fact in words.

"And then the catastrophe happens. It is three months ago now, and a day or two after I returned, Greta Rosen came to see me. She had sold the cottage and was returning to Germany, having finally settled up her uncle's affairs. She came to me personally, although she knew I had retired, because it was really about a personal matter she wanted to see me. She beat about the bush a little, but at last it all came out. What did I think? That letter with the German stamp—she had worried about it and worried about it—the one Charles had torn up. Was it all right? Surely it must be all right. Of course she believed his story, but—oh, if she only knew! If she knew—for certain.

"You see? The same feeling: the wish to trust—but the horrible lurking suspicion, thrust resolutely to the back of the mind, but persisting nevertheless. I spoke to her with absolute frankness and asked her to do the same. I asked her whether she had been on the point of caring for Charles and he for her.

" 'I think so,' she said. 'Oh yes, I know it was so. We were so happy. Every day passed so contentedly. We knew—we both knew. There was no hurry—there was all the time in the world. Some day he would tell me he loved me, and I should tell him that I, too—Ah! But you can guess! And now it is all changed. A black cloud has come between us—we are constrained, when we meet we do not know what to say. It is, perhaps, the same with him as with me. . . . We are each saying to ourselves, "If I were sure!" That is why, Sir Henry, I beg of you to say to me, "You may be sure, whoever killed your uncle, it was not Charles Templeton!" Say it to me! Oh, say it to me! I beg—I beg!'

"I couldn't say it to her. They'll drift farther and farther apart, those two—with suspicion like a ghost between them—a ghost that can't be laid."

He leaned back in his chair; his face looked tired and grey. He shook his head once or twice despondently.

"And there's nothing more can be done, unless—" He sat up straight again and a tiny whimsical smile crossed his face.—"unless Miss Marple can help us. Can't you, Miss Marple? I've a feeling that letter might be in your line, you know. The one about the church social. Doesn't it remind you of something or someone that makes everything perfectly plain? Can't you do something to help two helpless young people who want to be happy?"

Behind the whimsicality there was something earnest in his appeal. He had come to think very highly of the mental powers of this frail, old-fashioned maiden lady. He looked across at her with something very like hope in his eyes.

Miss Marple coughed and smoothed her lace.

"It does remind me a little of Annie Poultny," she admitted. "Of course the letter is perfectly plain—both to Mrs. Bantry and myself. I don't mean the church-social letter, but the other one. You living so much in London and not being a gardener, Sir Henry, would not have been likely to notice."

"Eh?" said Sir Henry. "Notice what?"

Mrs. Bantry reached out a hand and selected a catalogue. She opened it and read aloud with gusto:

" 'Dr. Helmuth Spath. Pure lilac, a wonderfully fine flower, carried on exceptionally long and stiff stem. Splendid for cutting and garden decoration. A novelty of striking beauty.

" 'Edgar Jackson. Beautifully shaped chrysanthemum-like flower of a distinct brick-red color.

" 'Amos Perry. Brilliant red, highly decorative.

" 'Tsingtau. Brilliant orange-red, showy garden plant and lasting cut flower.

" 'Honesty—' "

"With a capital H, you remember," murmured Miss Marple.

" 'Honesty. Rose and white shades, enormous perfect-shaped flower.' "

Mrs. Bantry flung down the catalogue and said with immense explosive force:

"Dahlias!"

"And their initial letters spell 'Death,' " explained Miss Marple.

"But the letter came to Dr. Rosen himself," objected Sir Henry.

"That was the clever part of it," said Miss Marple. "That and the warning in it. What would he do, getting a letter from someone he didn't know, full of names he didn't know. Why, of course, toss it over to his secretary."

"Then, after all—"

"Oh no!" said Miss Marple. "Not the secretary. Why, that's what makes it so perfectly clear that it wasn't him. He'd never have let that letter be found if so. And equally he'd never have destroyed a letter to himself with a German stamp on it. Really, his innocence is—if you'll allow me to use the word—just shining."

"Then who—"

"Well, it seems almost certain—as certain as anything can be in this world. There was another person at the breakfast table, and she would—

quite naturally under the circumstances—put out her hand for the letter and read it. And that would be that. You remember that she got a gardening catalogue by the same post—"

"Greta Rosen," said Sir Henry slowly. "Then her visit to me—"

"Gentlemen never see through these things," said Miss Marple. "And I'm afraid they often think we old women are—well, cats, to see things the way we do. But there it is. One does know a great deal about one's own sex, unfortunately. I've no doubt there was a barrier between them. The young man felt a sudden inexplicable repulsion. He suspected, purely through instinct, and couldn't hide the suspicion. And I really think that the girl's visit to you was just pure spite. She was safe enough really, but she just went out of her way to fix your suspicions definitely on poor Mr. Templeton. You weren't nearly so sure about him until after her visit."

"I'm sure it was nothing that she said—" began Sir Henry.

"Gentlemen," said Miss Marple calmly, "never see through these things."

"And that girl—" He stopped. "She commits a cold-blooded murder and gets off scot-free!"

"Oh no, Sir Henry," said Miss Marple. "Not scot-free. Neither you nor I believe that. Remember what you said not long ago. No. Greta Rosen will not escape punishment. To begin with, she must be in with a very queer set of people—blackmailers and terrorists—associates who will do her no good and will probably bring her to a miserable end. As you say, one mustn't waste thoughts on the guilty—it's the innocent who matter. Mr. Templeton, who I daresay will marry that German cousin, his tearing up her letter looks—well, it looks suspicious—using the word in quite a different sense from the one we've been using all the evening. A little as though he were afraid of the other girl noticing or asking to see it? Yes, I think there must have been some little romance there. And then there's Dobbs—though, as you say, I daresay it won't much matter to him. His elevenses are probably all he thinks about. And then there's that poor old Gertrud—the one who reminded me of Annie Poultny. Poor Annie Poultny. Fifty years' faithful service and suspected of making away with Miss Lamb's will, though nothing could be proved. Almost broke the poor creature's faithful heart. And then after she was dead it came to light in the secret drawer of the tea caddy where old Miss Lamb had put it herself for safety. But too late then for poor Annie.

"That's what worries me so about that poor old German woman. When one is old, one becomes embittered very easily. I felt much more sorry for her than for Mr. Templeton, who is young and good-looking and evidently a favorite with the ladies. You will write to her, won't you, Sir Henry, and just tell her that her innocence is established beyond doubt? Her dear old master dead, and she no doubt brooding and feeling herself suspected of . . . Oh! It won't bear thinking about!"

"I will write, Miss Marple," said Sir Henry. He looked at her curiously. "You know, I shall never quite understand you. Your outlook is always a different one from what I expect."

"My outlook, I'm afraid, is a very petty one," said Miss Marple humbly. "I hardly ever go out of St. Mary Mead."

"And yet you have solved what may be called an international mystery," said Sir Henry. "For you have solved it. I am convinced of that."

Miss Marple blushed, then bridled a little.

"I was, I think, well educated for the standard of my day. My sister and I had a German governess—a Fräulein. A very sentimental creature. She taught us the language of flowers—a forgotten study nowadays, but most charming. A yellow tulip, for instance, means 'Hopeless Love,' while a China aster means 'I Die of Jealousy at Your Feet.' That letter was signed Georgina, which I seem to remember as dahlia in German, and that of course made the whole thing perfectly clear. I wish I could remember the meaning of dahlia, but alas, that eludes me. My memory is not what it was."

"At any rate, it didn't mean 'Death.' "

"No, indeed. Horrible, is it not? There are very sad things in the world."

"There are," said Mrs. Bantry with a sigh. "It's lucky one has flowers and one's friends."

"She puts us last, you observe," said Dr. Lloyd.

"A man used to send me purple orchids every night to the theater," said Jane dreamily.

" 'I Await Your Favors'—that's what that means," said Miss Marple brightly.

Sir Henry gave a peculiar sort of cough and turned his head away.

Miss Marple gave a sudden exclamation.

"I've remembered. Dahlias mean 'Treachery and Misrepresentation.' "

"Wonderful," said Sir Henry. "Absolutely wonderful."

And he sighed.

THE BROKEN MEN

Marcia Muller

1

Dawn was breaking when I returned to the Diablo Valley Pavilion. The softly rounded hills that encircled the amphitheater were edged with pinkish gold, but their slopes were still dark and forbidding. They reminded me of a herd of humpbacked creatures huddling together while they waited for the warmth of the morning sun; I could imagine them stretching and sighing with relief when its rays finally touched them.

I would have given a lot to have daylight bring me that same sense of relief, but I doubted that would happen. It had been a long, anxious night since I'd arrived here the first time, over twelve hours before. Returning was a last-ditch measure, and a long shot at best.

I drove up the blacktop road to where it was blocked by a row of posts and got out of the car. The air was chill; I could see my breath. Somewhere in the distance a lone bird called, and there was a faint, monotonous whine that must have had something to do with the security lights that topped the chain link fence at intervals, but the overall silence was heavy, oppressive. I stuffed my hands into the pockets of my too-light suede jacket and started toward the main entrance next to the box office.

As I reached the fence, a stocky, dark-haired man stepped out of the adjacent security shack and began unlocking the gate. Roy Canfield, night supervisor for the pavilion. He'd been dubious about what I'd suggested when I'd called him from San Francisco three quarters of an hour ago, but had said he'd be glad to cooperate if I came back out here. Canfield swung the gate open and motioned me through one of the turnstiles that had admitted thousands to the Diablo Valley Clown Festival the night before.

He said, "You made good time from the city."

"There's no traffic at five A.M. I could set my own speed limit."

The security man's eyes moved over me appraisingly, reminding me of how rumpled and tired I must look. Canfield himself seemed as fresh and alert as when I'd met him before last night's performance. But then, *he* hadn't been chasing over half the Bay Area all night, hunting for a missing client.

"Of course," I added, "I was anxious to get here and see if Gary Fitzgerald might still be somewhere on the premises. Shall we take a look around?"

Canfield looked as dubious as he'd sounded on the phone. He shrugged and said, "Sure we can, but I don't think you'll find him. We check every inch of the place after the crowd leaves. No way anybody could still be inside when we lock up."

There had been a note of reproach in his words, as if he thought I was questioning his ability to do his job. Quickly I said, "It's not that I don't believe you, Mr. Canfield. I just don't have any place else left to look."

He merely grunted and motioned for me to proceed up the wide concrete steps. They led uphill from the entrance to a promenade whose arms curved out in opposite directions around the edge of the amphitheater. As I recalled from the night before, from the promenade the lawn sloped gently down to the starkly modernistic concert shell. Its stage was wide—roughly ninety degrees of the circle—with wings and dressing rooms built back into the hill behind it. The concrete roof, held aloft by two giant pillars, was a curving slab shaped like a warped arrowhead, its tip pointing to the northeast, slightly off center. Formal seating was limited to a few dozen rows in a semi-circle in front of the stage; the pavilion had been designed mainly for the casual type of concert-goer who prefers to lounge on a blanket on the lawn.

I reached the top of the steps and crossed the promenade to the edge of the bowl, then stopped in surprise.

The formerly pristine lawn was now mounded with trash. Paper bags, cups and plates, beer cans and wine bottles, wrappers and crumpled programs and other indefinable debris were scattered in a crazy-quilt pattern. Trash receptacles placed at strategic intervals along the promenade had overflowed, their contents cascading to the ground. On the low wall between the formal seating and the lawn stood a monumental pyramid of Budweiser cans. In some places the debris was only thinly scattered, but in others it lay deep, like dirty drifted snow.

Canfield came up behind me, breathing heavily from the climb. "A mess, isn't it?" he said.

"Yes. Is it always like this after a performance?"

"Depends. Shows like last night, where you get a lot of young people, families, picnickers, it gets pretty bad. A symphony concert, that's different."

"And your maintenance crew doesn't come on until morning?" I tried not to sound disapproving, but allowing such debris to lie there all night was faintly scandalous to a person like me, who had been raised to believe that not washing the supper dishes before going to bed just might constitute a cardinal sin.

"Cheaper that way—we'd have to pay overtime otherwise. And the job's easier when it's light anyhow."

As if in response to Canfield's words, daylight—more gold than pink now—spilled over the hills in the distance, slightly to the left of the stage. It disturbed the shadows on the lawn below us, making them assume different, distorted forms. Black became gray, gray became white; short shapes elongated, others were truncated; fuzzy lines came into sharp focus. And with the light a cold wind came gusting across the promenade.

I pulled my jacket closer, shivering. The wind rattled the fall-dry leaves of the young poplar trees—little more than saplings—planted along the edge of the promenade. It stirred the trash heaped around the receptacles, then swept down the lawn, scattering debris in its wake. Plastic bags and wads of paper rose in an eerie dance, settled again as the breeze passed. I watched the undulation—a paper wave upon a paper sea—as it rolled toward the windbreak of cypress trees to the east.

Somewhere in the roiling refuse down by the barrier between the lawn and the formal seating I spotted a splash of yellow. I leaned forward, peering toward it. Again I saw the yellow, then a blur of blue and then a flicker of white. The colors were there, then gone as the trash settled.

Had my eyes been playing tricks on me in the half-light? I didn't think so, because while I couldn't be sure of the colors, I was distinctly aware of a shape that the wind's passage had uncovered—long, angular, solid-looking. The debris had fallen in a way that didn't completely obscure it.

The dread that I had held in check all night spread through me. After a frozen moment, I began to scramble down the slope toward the spot I'd been staring at. Behind me, Canfield called out, but I ignored him.

The trash was deep down by the barrier, almost to my knees. I waded through bottles, cans, and papers, pushing their insubstantial mass aside, shoveling with my hands to clear a path. Shoveled until my fingers encountered something more solid . . .

I dropped to my knees and scooped up the last few layers of debris, hurling it over my shoulder.

He lay on his back, wrapped in his bright yellow cape, his baggy blue plaid pants and black patent leather shoes sticking out from underneath it. His black beret was pulled halfway down over his white clown's face hiding his eyes. I couldn't see the red vest that made up the rest of the costume because the cape covered it, but there were faint red stains on the irridescent fabric that draped across his chest.

I yanked the cape aside and touched the vest. It felt sticky, and when I pulled my hand away it was red too. I stared at it, wiped it off on a scrap of newspaper. Then I felt for a pulse in his carotid artery, knowing all the time what a futile exercise it was.

"Oh, Jesus!" I said. For a moment my vision blurred and there was a faint buzzing in my ears.

Roy Canfield came thrashing up behind me, puffing with exertion. "What . . . Oh, my God!"

I continued staring down at the clown; he looked broken, an object that had been used up and tossed on a trash heap. After a moment, I touched my thumb to his cold cheek, brushed at the white makeup. I pushed the beret back, looked at the theatrically blackened eyes. Then I tugged off the flaxen wig. Finally I pulled the fake bulbous nose away.

"Gary Fitzgerald?" Canfield asked.

I looked up at him. His moonlike face creased in concern. Apparently the shock and bewilderment I was experiencing showed.

"Mr. Canfield," I said, "this man is wearing Gary's costume, but it's not him. I've never seen him before in my life."

2

The man I *was* looking for was half of an internationally famous clown act, Fitzgerald and Tilby. The world of clowning, like any other artistic realm, has its various levels—from the lowly rodeo clown whose chief function is to keep bull riders from being stomped on, to circus clowns such as Emmett Kelly and universally acclaimed mimes like Marcel Marceau. Fitzgerald and Tilby were not far below Kelly and Marceau in that hierarchy and gaining on them every day. Instead of merely employing the mute body language of the typical clown, the two Britishers combined it with a subtle and sophisticated verbal comedy routine. Their fame had spread beyond aficionados of clowning in the late seventies when they had made a series of artful and entertaining television commercials for one of the Japanese auto makers, and subsequent ads for, among others, a major U.S. airline, one of the big insurance companies, and a computer firm had assured them of a place in the hearts of humor-loving Americans.

My involvement with Fitzgerald and Tilby came about when they agreed to perform at the Diablo Valley Clown Festival, a charity benefit co-sponsored by the Contra Costa County Chamber of Commerce and KSUN, the radio station where my friend Don Del Boccio works as a disc jockey. The team's manager, Wayne Kabalka, had stipulated only two conditions to their performing for free: that they be given star billing, and that they be provided with a bodyguard. Since Don was to be emcee of the show, he was in on all the planning, and when he heard of Kabalka's second stipulation, he suggested me for the job.

As had been the case ever since I'd bought a house near the Glen Park district of San Francisco the spring before, I was short of money at the time. And All Souls Legal Cooperative, where I am staff investigator, had no qualms about me moonlighting provided it didn't interfere with any of the co-op's cases. Since things had been slack at All Souls during September, I felt free to accept. Bodyguarding isn't my idea of challenging work, but I had always enjoyed Fitzgerald and Tilby, and the idea of meeting them intrigued me. Besides, I'd be part of the festival and get paid for my time, rather than attending on the free pass Don had promised me.

So on that hot Friday afternoon in late September, I met with Wayne Kabalka in the lounge at KSUN's San Francisco studios. As radio stations go, KSUN is a casual operation, and the lounge gives full expression to this orientation. It is full of mismatched Salvation Army reject furniture, the posters on the walls are torn and tattered, and the big coffee table is always littered with rumpled newspapers, empty Coke cans and coffee cups, and overflowing ashtrays. On this particular occasion, it was also graced with someone's half-eaten Big Mac.

When Don and I came in, Wayne Kabalka was seated on the very edge of one of the lumpy chairs, looking as if he were afraid it might have fleas. He saw us and jumped as if one had just bitten him. *His* orientation was anything but casual: in spite of the heat, he wore a tan three-piece suit that almost matched his mane of tawny hair, and a brown striped tie peeked over the V of his vest. Kabalka and his clients might be based in L.A., but he sported none of the usual Hollywoodish accoutrements—gold chains, diamond rings, or Adidas running shoes. Perhaps his very correct appearance was designed to be in keeping with his clients, Englishmen with rumored connections to the aristocracy.

Don introduced us and we all sat down, Kabalka again doing his balancing act on the edge of his chair. Ignoring me, he said to Don, "I didn't realize the bodyguard you promised would be female."

Don shot me a look, his shaggy black eyebrows raised a fraction of an inch.

I said, "Please don't let my gender worry you, Mr. Kabalka. I've been a private investigator for nine years, and before that I worked for a security firm. I'm fully qualified for the job."

To Don he said, "But has she done this kind of work before?"

Again Don looked at me.

I said, "Bodyguarding is only one of any number of types of assignments I've carried out. And one of the most routine."

Kabalka continued looking at Don. "Is she licensed to carry firearms?"

Don ran his fingers over his thick black mustache, trying to hide the beginnings of a grin. "I think," he said, "that I'd better let the two of you talk alone."

Kabalka put out a hand as if to stay his departure, but Don stood. "I'll be in the editing room if you need me."

I watched him walk down the hall, his gait surprisingly graceful for such a tall, stocky man. Then I turned back to Kabalka. "To answer your question, sir, yes, I'm firearms qualified."

He made a sound halfway between clearing his throat and a grunt. "Uh . . . then you have no objection to carrying a gun on this assignment?"

"Not if it's necessary. But before I can agree to that, I'll have to know why you feel your clients require an armed bodyguard."

"I'm sorry?"

"Is there some threat to them that indicates the guard should be armed?"

"Threat. Oh . . . no."

"Extraordinary circumstances, then?"

"Extraordinary circumstances. Well, they're quite famous, you know. The TV commercials—you've seen them?"

I nodded.

"Then you know what a gold mine we have here. We're due to sign for three more within the month. Bank of America, no less. General Foods is getting into the act. Mobil Oil is hedging, but they'll sign. Fitzgerald and Tilby are important properties; they must be protected."

Properties, I thought, not people. "That still doesn't tell me what I need to know."

Kabalka laced his well-manicured fingers together, flexing them rhythmically. Beads of perspiration stood out on his high forehead; no wonder, wearing that suit in this heat. Finally he said, "In the past couple of years we've experienced difficulty with fans when the boys have been on tour. In a few instances, the crowds got a little too rough."

"Why haven't you hired a permanent bodyguard, then? Put one on staff?"

"The boys were opposed to that. In spite of their aristocratic connections, they're men of the people. They didn't want to put any more distance between them and their public than necessary."

The words rang false. I suspected the truth of the matter was that Kabalka was too cheap to hire a permanent guard. "In a place like the Diablo Valley Pavilion, the security is excellent, and I'm sure that's been explained to you. It hardly seems necessary to hire an armed guard when the pavilion personnel—"

He made a gesture of impatience. "Their security force will have dozens of performers to protect, including a number who will be wandering throughout the audience during the show. My clients need extra protection."

I was silent, watching him. He shifted his gaze from mine, looking around with disproportionate interest at the tattered wall posters. Finally I said, "Mr. Kabalka, I don't feel you're being quite frank with me. And I'm afraid I can't take on this assignment unless you are."

He looked back at me. His eyes were a pale blue, washed out—and worried. "The people here at the station speak highly of you," he said after a moment.

"I hope so. They—especially Mr. Del Boccio—know me well." Especially Don; we'd been lovers for more than six months now.

"When they told me they had a bodyguard lined up, all they said was that you were a first-rate investigator. If I was rude earlier because I was surprised by your being a woman, I apologize."

"Apology accepted."

"I assume by first-rate, one of the things they mean is that you are discreet."

"I don't talk about my cases, if that's what you want to know."

He nodded. "All right, I'm going to entrust you with some information. It's not common knowledge, and you're not to pass it on, gossip about it to your friends—"

Kabalka was beginning to annoy me. "Get on with it, Mr. Kabalka. Or find yourself another bodyguard." Not easy to do, when the performers needed to arrive at the pavilion in about three hours.

His face reddened, and he started to retort, but bit back the words. He looked down at his fingers, still laced together and pressing against one another in a feverish rhythm. "All right. Once again I apologize. In my profession you get used to dealing with such scumbags that you lose perspective—"

"You were about to tell me . . .?"

He looked up, squared his shoulders as if he were about to deliver a state secret to an enemy agent. "All right. There *is* a reason why my clients require special security precautions at the Diablo Valley Pavilion.

They—Gary Fitzgerald and John Tilby—are originally from Contra Costa County."

"What? I thought they were British."

"Yes, of course you did. And so does almost everyone else. It's part of the mystique, the selling power."

"I don't understand."

"When I discovered the young men in the early seventies, they were performing in a cheap club in San Bernardino, in the valley east of L.A. They were cousins, fresh off the farm—the ranch, in their case. Tilby's father was a dairy rancher in the Contra Costa hills, near Clayton; he raised both boys—Gary's parents had died. When old Tilby died, the ranch was sold and the boys ran off to seek fortune and fame. Old story. And they'd found the glitter doesn't come easy. Another old story. But when I spotted them in that club, I could see they were good. Damned good. So I took them on and made them stars."

"The oldest story of all."

"Perhaps. But now and then it does come true."

"Why the British background?"

"It was the early seventies. The mystique still surrounded such singing groups as the Rolling Stones and the Beatles. What could be better than a British clown act with aristocratic origins? Besides, they were already doing the British bit in their act when I discovered them, and it worked."

I nodded, amused by the machinations of show business. "So you're afraid someone who once knew them might get too close out at the pavilion tonight and recognize them?"

"Yes."

"Don't you think it's a long shot—after all these years?"

"They left there in sixty-nine. People don't change all that much in sixteen years."

That depended, but I wasn't about to debate the point with him. "But what about makeup? Won't that disguise them?" Fitzgerald and Tilby wore traditional clown white-face.

"They can't apply the makeup until they're about to go on—in other circumstances, it might be possible to put it on earlier, but not in this heat."

I nodded. It all made sense. But why did I feel there was something Kabalka wasn't telling me about his need for an armed guard? Perhaps it was the way his eyes had once again shifted from mine to the posters on the walls. Perhaps it was the nervous pressing of his laced fingers. Or maybe it was only that sixth sense that sometimes worked for me: what I called a detective's instinct and others—usually men—labeled woman's intuition.

"All right, Mr. Kabalka," I said, "I'll take the job."

3

I checked in with Don to find out when I should be back at the studios, then went home to change clothing. We would arrive at the pavilion around four; the show—an early one because of its appeal for children—would begin at six. And I was certain that the high temperature—sure to have topped 100 in the Diablo Valley—would not drop until long after dark. Chambray pants and an abbreviated tank top, with my suede jacket to put on in case of a late evening chill were all I would need. That, and my .38 special, tucked in the outer compartment of my leather shoulderbag.

By three o'clock I was back at the KSUN studios. Don met me in the lobby and ushered me to the lounge where Kabalka, Gary Fitzgerald, and John Tilby waited.

The two clowns were about my age—a little over thirty. Their British accents might once have been a put-on, but they sounded as natural now as if they'd been born and raised in London. Gary Fitzgerald was tall and lanky, with straight dark hair, angular features that stopped just short of being homely, and a direct way of meeting one's eye. John Tilby was shorter, sandy haired—the type we used to refer to in high school as "cute." His shy demeanor was in sharp contrast to his cousin's straightforward greeting and handshake. They didn't really seem like relatives, but then neither do I in comparison to my four siblings and numerous cousins. All of them resemble one another—typical Scotch-Irish towheads—but I have inherited all the characteristics of our one-eighth Shoshone Indian blood. And none of us are similar in personality or outlook, save for the fact we care a great deal about one another.

Wayne Kabalka hovered in the background while the introductions were made. The first thing he said to me was, "Did you bring your gun?"

"Yes, I did. Everything's under control."

Kabalka wrung his hands together as if he only wished it were true. Then he said, "Do you have a car, Ms. McCone?"

"Yes."

"Then I suggest we take both yours and mine. I have to swing by the hotel and pick up my wife and John's girlfriend."

"All right. I have room for one passenger in mine. Don, what about you? How are you getting out there?"

"I'm going in the Wonder Bus."

I rolled my eyes. The Wonder Bus was a KSUN publicity ploy—a former schoolbus painted in rainbow hues and emblazoned with the station call letters. It traveled to all KSUN-sponsord events, plus to anything else where management deemed its presence might be beneficial. As far as I was concerned, it was the most outrageous in a panoply of the station's brazen efforts at self-promotion, and I took every opportunity to expound this viewpoint to Don. Surprisingly, Don—a quiet classical musician who hated rock-and-roll and the notoriety that went with being a D.J.—never cringed at riding the Wonder Bus. If anything, he took an almost perverse pleasure in the motorized monstrosity.

Secretly, I had a shameful desire to hitch a ride on the Wonder Bus myself.

Wayne Kabalka looked somewhat puzzled at Don's statement. "Wonder Bus?" he said to himself. Then, "Well, if everyone's ready, let's go."

I turned to Don and smiled in a superior fashion. "Enjoy your ride."

We trooped out into the parking lot. Heat shimmered off the concrete paving. Kabalka pulled a handkerchief from his pocket and wiped his brow. "Is it always this hot here in September?"

"This is the month we have our true summer in the city, but no, this is unusual." I went over and placed my bag carefully behind the driver's seat of my MG convertible.

When John Tilby saw the car, his eyes brightened; he came over to it, running a hand along one of its battle-scarred flanks as if it were a brand new Porsche. "I used to have one of these."

"I'll bet it was in better shape than this one."

"Not really." A shadow passed over his face and he continued to caress the car in spite of the fact that the metal must be burning hot to the touch.

"Look," I said, "if you want to drive it out to the pavilion, I wouldn't mind being a passenger for a change."

He hesitated, then said wistfully, "That's nice of you, but I can't . . . I don't drive. But I'd like to ride along—"

"John!" Kabalka's voice was impatient behind us. "Come on, we're keeping Corinne and Nicole waiting."

Tilby gave the car a last longing glance, then shrugged. "I guess I'd better ride out with Wayne and the girls." He turned and walked off to Kabalka's new-looking Seville that was parked at the other side of the lot.

Gary Fitzgerald appeared next to me, a small canvas bag in one hand, garment bag in the other. "I guess you're stuck with me," he said, smiling easily.

"That's not such a bad deal."

He glanced back at Tilby and Kabalka, who were climbing into the Cadillac. "Wayne's right to make John go with him. Nicole would be jealous if she saw him drive up with another woman." His tone was slightly resentful. Of Nicole? I wondered. Perhaps the girlfriend has caused dissension between the cousins.

"Corinne is Wayne's wife?" I asked as we got into the MG.

"Yes. You'll meet both of them at the performance; they're never very far away." Again I heard the undertone of annoyance.

We got onto the freeway and crossed the Bay Bridge. Commuter traffic out of the city was already getting heavy; people left their offices early on hot Fridays in September. I wheeled the little car in and out from lane to lane, bypassing trucks and A.C. Transit buses. Fitzgerald didn't speak. I glanced at him a couple of times to see if my maneuvering bothered him, but he sat slumped against the door, his almost-homely features shadowed with thought. Pre-performance nerves, possibly.

From the bridge, I took Highway 24 east toward Walnut Creek. We passed through the outskirts of Oakland, smog-hazed and sprawling—ugly duckling of the Bay Area. Sophisticates from San Francisco scorned Oakland, repeating Gertrude Stein's overused phrase, "There is no there there," but lately there had been a current of unease in their mockery. Oakland's thriving port had stolen much of the shipping business from her sister city across the Bay; her politics were alive and spirited; and on the site of former slums, sleek new buildings had been put up. Oakland was at last shedding her pinfeathers, and it made many of my fellow San Franciscans nervous.

From there we began the long ascent through the Berkeley Hills to the Caldecott Tunnel. The MG's aged engine strained as we passed lumbering trucks and slower cars, and when we reached the tunnel—three tunnels, actually, two of them now open to accommodate the eastbound commuter rush—I shot into the far lane. At the top of the grade midway through the tunnel, I shifted into neutral to give the engine a rest. Arid heat assailed us as we emerged; the temperature in San Francisco had been nothing compared to this.

The freeway continued to descend, past brown sunbaked hills covered with live oak and eucalyptus. Then houses began to appear, tucked back among the trees. The air was scented with dry leaves and grass and dust. Fire danger, I thought. One spark and those houses become tinderboxes.

The town of Orinda appeared on the right. On the left, in the center of the freeway, a BART train was pulling out of the station. I accelerated and tried to outrace it, giving up when my speedometer hit eighty and waving at some schoolkids who were watching from the train. Then I dropped back to sixty and glanced at Fitzgerald, suddenly embarrassed by my childish display. He was sitting up straighter and grinning.

I said, "The temptation was overwhelming."

"I know the feeling."

Feeling more comfortable now that he seemed willing to talk, I said, "Did Mr. Kabalka tell you that he let me in on where you're really from?"

For a moment he looked startled, then nodded.

"Is this the first time you've been back here in Contra Costa County?"

"Yes."

"You'll find it changed."

"I guess so."

"Mainly there are more people. Places like Walnut Creek and Concord have grown by leaps and bounds in the last ten years."

The county stretched east from the ridge of hills we'd just passed over, toward Mount Diablo, a nearly 4,000-foot peak which had been developed into a 15,000-acre state park. On the north side of the county was the Carquinez Strait, with its oil refineries, Suisun Bay, and the San Joaquin River which separated Contra Costa from Sacramento County and the Delta. The city of Richmond and environs, to the west, were also part of the county, and their inclusion had always struck me as odd. Besides being geographically separated by the expanse of Tilden Regional Park and San Pablo Reservoir, the mostly black industrial city was culturally light years away from the rest of the suburban, upwardly mobile county. With the exception of a few towns like Pittsburgh or Antioch, this was affluent, fast-developing land; I supposed one day even those north-county backwaters would fall victim to expensive residential tracts and shopping centers full of upscale boutiques.

When Fitzgerald didn't comment, I said, "Does it look different to you?"

"Not really."

"Wait till we get to Walnut Creek. The area around the BART station is all highrise buildings now. They're predicting it will become an urban center that will eventually rival San Francisco."

He grunted in disapproval.

"About the only thing they've managed to preserve out here is the area around Mount Diablo. I suppose you know it from when you were a kid."

"Yes."

"I went hiking in the park last spring, during wildflower season. It was really beautiful that time of year. They say if you climb high enough you can see thirty-five counties from the mountain."

"This pavilion," Fitzgerald said, "is it part of the state park?"

For a moment I was surprised, then realized the pavilion hadn't been in existence in 1969, when he'd left home. "No, but near it. The land around it is relatively unspoiled. Horse and cattle ranches, mostly. They built it about eight years ago, after the Concord Pavilion became such a success. I guess that's one index of how this part of the Bay Area has grown, that it can support two concert pavilions."

He nodded. "Do they ever have concerts going at the same time at both?"

"Sure."

"It must really echo off these hills."

"I imagine you can hear it all the way to Port Chicago." Port Chicago was where the Naval Weapons Station was located, on the edge of Suisun Bay.

"Well, maybe not all the way to Chicago."

I smiled at the feeble joke, thinking that for a clown, Fitzgerald really didn't have much of a sense of humor, then allowed him to lapse back into his moody silence.

4

When we arrived at the pavilion, the parking lot was already crowded, the gates having opened early so people could picnic before the show started. An orange-jacketed attendant directed us to a far corner of the lot which had been cordoned off for official parking near the performers' gate. Fitzgerald and I waited in the car for about fifteen minutes, the late afternoon sun beating down on us, until Wayne Kabalka's Seville pulled up alongside. With the manager and John Tilby were two women: a chic, fortyish redhead, and a small, dark-haired woman in her twenties. Fitzgerald and I got out and went to greet them.

The redhead was Corinne Kabalka; her strong handshake and level gaze made me like her immediately. I was less sure about Nicole Leland; the younger woman was beautiful, with short black hair sculpted close to her head and exotic features, but her manner was very cold. She nodded curtly when introduced to me, then took Tilby's arm and let him off toward the performer's gate. The rest of us trailed behind.

Security was tight at the gate. We met Roy Canfield, who was personally superintending the check-in, and each of us was issued a pass. No one, Canfield told us, would be permitted backstage or through the gate without showing his pass. Security personnel would also be stationed in the audience to protect those clowns who, as part of the show, would be performing out on the lawn.

We were then shown to a large dressing room equipped with a couch, a folding card table and chairs. After everyone was settled there I took Kabalka aside and asked him if he would take charge of the group for about fifteen minutes while I checked the layout of the pavilion. He nodded distractedly and I went out front.

Stage personnel were scurrying around, setting up sound equipment and checking the lights. Don had already arrived, but he was conferring with one of the other KSUN jocks and didn't look as if he could be disturbed. The formal seating was empty, but the lawn was already crowded. People lounged on blankets, passing around food, drink and an occasional joint. Some of the picnics were elaborate—fine china, crystal wineglasses, ice buckets, and in one case, a set of lighted silver candelabra; others were of the paper-plate and plastic-cup variety. I spotted the familiar logos of Kentucky Fried Chicken and Jack-in-the-Box here and there. People called to friends, climbed up and down the hill to the restroom and refreshment facilities, dropped by other groups' blankets to see what goodies they had to trade. Children ran through the crowd, an occasional frisbee sailed through the air. I noticed a wafting trail of irridescent soap bubbles, and my eyes followed it to a young woman in a red halter top who was blowing them, her face aglow with childlike pleasure.

For a moment I felt a stab of envy, realizing that if I hadn't taken on this job I could be out front, courtesy of the free pass Don had promised me. I could have packed a picnic, perhaps brought along a woman friend, and Don could have dropped by to join us when he had time. But instead, I was bodyguarding a pair of clowns who—given the pavilion's elaborate security measures—probably didn't need me. And in addition to Fitzgerald and Tilby, I seemed to be responsible for an entire group. I could see why Kabalka might want to stick close to his clients, but why did the wife and girlfriend have to crowd into what was already a stuffy, hot dressing room? Why couldn't they go out front and enjoy the performance? It complicated my assignment, having to contend with an entourage, and the thought of those complications made me grumpy.

The grumpiness was probably due to the heat, I decided. Shrugging it off, I familiarized myself with the layout of the stage and the points at which someone could gain access. Satisfied that pavilion security could deal with any problems that might arise there, I made my way through the crowd—turning down two beers, a glass of wine, and a pretzel—and climbed to the promenade. From there I studied the stage once more, then raised my eyes to the sun-scorched hills to the east.

The slopes were barren, save for an occasional outcropping of rock and live oak trees, and on them a number of horses with riders stood. They clustered together in groups of two, four, six and even at this distance, I sensed they shared the same camaraderie as the people on the lawn. They leaned toward one another, gestured, and occasionally passed objects—perhaps they were picnicking too—back and forth.

What a great way to enjoy a free concert, I thought. The sound, in this natural echo chamber, would easily carry to where the watchers were stationed. How much more peaceful it must be on the hill, free of crowds and security measures. Visibility, however, would not be very good. . . .

And then I saw a flare of reddish light and glanced over to where a lone horseman stood under the sheltering branches of a live oak. The light flashed again, and I realized he was holding binoculars which had caught the setting sun. Of course—with binoculars or opera glasses, visibility would not be bad at all. In fact, from such a high vantage point it might even be better than from many points on the lawn. My grumpiness returned; I'd have loved to be mounted on a horse on that hillside.

Reminding myself that I was here on business that would pay for part of the new bathroom tile, I turned back toward the stage, then started when I saw Gary Fitzgerald. He was standing on the lawn not more than six feet from me, looking around with one hand forming a visor over his eyes. When he saw me he started too, and then waved.

I rushed over to him and grabbed his arm. "What are you doing out here? You're supposed to stay backstage!"

"I just wanted to see what the place looks like."

"Are you out of your mind? Your manager is paying good money for me to see that people stay away from you. And here you are, wandering through the crowd—"

He looked away, at a family on a blanket next to us. The father was wiping catsup from the smallest child's hands. "No one's bothering me."

"That's not the point." Still gripping his arm, I began steering him toward the stage. "Someone might recognize you, and that's precisely what Kabalka hired me to prevent."

"Oh, Wayne's just being a worrywart about that. No one's going to recognize anybody after all this time. Besides, it's common knowledge in the trade that we're not what we're made out to be."

"In the trade, yes. But your manager's worried about the public." We got to the stage, showed our passes to the security guard, and went back to the dressing room.

At the door Fitzgerald stopped. "Sharon, would you mind not mentioning my going out there to Wayne?"

"Why shouldn't I?"

"Because it would only upset him, and he's nervous enough before a performance. Nothing happened—except that I was guilty of using bad judgment."

His smile was disarming, and I took the words as an apology. "All right. But you'd better go get into costume. There's only half an hour before the grand procession begins."

5

The next few hours were uneventful. The grand procession—a parade through the crowd in which all the performers participated—went off smoothly. After they returned to the dressing room, Fitzgerald and Tilby removed their makeup—which was already running in the intense heat—and the Kabalkas fetched supper from the car—deli food packed in hampers by their hotel. There was a great deal of grumbling about the quality of the meal, which was not what one would have expected of the St. Francis, and Fitzgerald teased the others because he was staying at a small bed-and-breakfast establishment in the Haight-Ashbury which had better food at half the price.

Nicole said, "Yes, but your hotel probably has bedbugs."

Fitzgerald glared at her, and I was reminded of the disapproving tone of voice in which he'd first spoken of her. "Don't be ignorant. Urban chic has come to the Haight-Ashbury."

"Making it difficult for you to recapture your misspent youth there, no doubt."

"Nicole," Kabalka said.

"That *was* your intention in separating from the rest of us, wasn't it, Gary?" Nicole added.

Fitzgerald was silent.

"Well, Gary?"

He glanced at me. "You'll have to excuse us for letting our hostilities show."

Nicole smiled nastily. "Yes, when a man gets to a certain age, he must try to recapture—"

"Shut up, Nicole," Kabalka said.

She looked at him in surprise, then picked up her sandwich and nibbled daintily at it. I could understand why she had backed off; there was something in Kabalka's tone that said he would put up with no more from her.

After the remains of supper were packed up, everyone settled down. None of them displayed the slightest inclination to go out front and watch the show. Kabalka read—one of those slim volumes that claim you can make a financial killing in spite of the world economic crisis. Corinne crocheted—granny squares. Fitzgerald brooded. Tilby played solitaire. Nicole fidgeted. And while they engaged in these activities, they also seemed to be watching one another. The covert vigilant atmosphere puzzled me; after a while I concluded that maybe the reason they all stuck together was that each was afraid to leave the others alone. But why?

Time crawled. Outside, the show was going on; I could hear music, laughter, and—occasionally—Don's enthusiastic voice as he introduced the acts. Once more I began to regret taking this job.

After a while Tilby reshuffled the cards and slapped them on the table. "Sharon, do you play gin rummy?"

"Yes."

"Good. Let's have a few hands."

Nicole frowned and made a small sound of protest.

Tilby said to her, "I offered to teach you. It's not my fault you refused."

I moved my chair over to the table and we played in silence for a while. Tilby was good, but I was better. After about half an hour, there was a roar from the crowd and Tilby raised his head. "Casey O'Connell must be going on."

"Who?" I said.

"One of our more famous circus clowns."

"There really is quite a variety among the performers in your profession, isn't there?"

"Yes, and quite a history: clowning is an old and honored art. They had clowns back in ancient Greece. Wandering entertainers, actually, who'd show up at a wealthy household and tell jokes, do acrobatics, or juggle for the price of a meal. Then in the Middle Ages, mimes appeared on the scene."

"That long ago?"

"Uh-huh. They were the cream of the crop back then. Most of the humor in the Middle Ages was kind of basic; they loved buffoons, jesters, simpletons, that sort of thing. But they served the purpose of making people see how silly we really are."

I took the deuce he'd just discarded, then lay down my hand to show I had gin. Tilby frowned and slapped down his cards; nothing matched. Then he grinned. "See what I mean—I'm silly to take this game so seriously."

I swept the cards together and began to shuffle. "You seem to know a good bit about the history of clowning."

"Well, I've done some reading along those lines. You've heard the term *commedia dell'arte?*"

"Yes."

"It appeared in the late 1500s, an Italian brand of the traveling comedy troupe. The comedians always played the same role—a Harlequin or a Pulcinella or a Pantalone. Easy for the audience to recognize."

"I know what a Harlequin is, but what are the other two?"

"Pantalone is a personification of the overbearing father figure. A stubborn, temperamental old geezer. Pulcinella was costumed all in white, usually with a dunce's cap; he assumed various roles in the comedy—lawyer, doctor, servant, whatever—and was usually greedy, sometimes pretty coarse. One of his favorite tricks was urinating onstage."

"Good Lord!"

"Fortunately we've become more refined since then. The British contributed a lot, further developing the Harlequin, creating the Punch and Judy shows. And of course, the French had their Figaro. The Indians created the *vidushaka*—a form of court jester. The entertainers at the Chinese court were known as *Chous,* after the dynasty in which they originated. And Japan has a huge range of comic figures appearing in their *Kyogen* plays—the humorous counterpart of the *Noh* play."

"You really have done your homework."

"Well, clowning's my profession. Don't you know about the history of yours?"

"What I know is mostly fictional; private investigation is more interesting in books than in real life, I'm afraid."

"Gin." Tilby spread his cards on the table. "Your deal. But back to what I was saying, it's the more contemporary clowns that interest me. And I use the term 'clown' loosely."

"How so?"

"Well, do you think of Will Rogers as a clown?"

"No."

"I do. And Laurel and Hardy, Flip Wilson, Mae West, Woody Allen, Lucille Ball. As well as the more traditional figures like Emmett Kelly, Charlie Chaplin, and Marceau. There's a common denominator among all those people: they're funny and, more important, they all make the audience take a look at humanity's foibles. They're as much descended from those historical clowns as the white-face circus performer."

"The whiteface is the typical circus clown, right?"

"Well, there are three basic types. Whiteface is your basic slaphappy fellow. The Auguste—who was created almost simultaneously in Germany and France—usually wears pink or blackface and is the one you see falling all over himself in the ring, often sopping wet from having buckets of water thrown at him. The Grotesque is usually a midget or a dwarf, or has some other distorted feature. And there are performers whom you can't classify because they've created something unique, such as Kelly's Weary Willie, or Russia's Popov, who is such an artist that he doesn't even need to wear makeup."

"It's fascinating. I never realized there was such variety. Or artistry."

"Most people don't. They think clowning is easy, but a lot of the time it's just plain hard work. Especially when you have to go on when you aren't feeling particularly funny." Tilby's mouth drooped as he spoke, and I wondered if tonight was one of those occasions for him.

I picked up a trey and said, "Gin," then tossed my hand on the table and watched as he shuffled and dealt. We fell silent once more. The sounds of the show went on, but the only noise in the dressing room was the slap of the cards on the table. It was still uncomfortably hot. Moths fluttered around the glaring bare bulbs of the dressing tables. At about ten-thirty, Fitzgerald stood up.

"Where are you going?" Kabalka said.

"The men's room. Do you mind?"

I said, "I'll go with you."

Fitzgerald smiled faintly. "Really, Sharon, that's above and beyond the call of duty."

"I mean, just to the door."

He started to protest, then shrugged and picked up his canvas bag.

Kabalka said, "Why are you taking that?"

"There's something in it I need."

"What?"

"For Christ's sake, Wayne!" He snatched up his yellow cape, flung it over one shoulder.

Kabalka hesitated. "All right, go. But Sharon goes with you."

Fitzgerald went out into the hall and I followed. Behind me, Nicole said, "Probably Maalox or something like that for his queasy stomach. You can always count on Gary to puke at least once before a performance."

Kabalka said, "Shut up, Nicole."

Fitzgerald started off, muttering, "Yes, we're one big happy family."

I followed him and took up a position next to the men's room door. It was ten minutes before I realized he was taking too long a time, and when I did I asked one of the security guards to go in after him. Fitzgerald had vanished, apparently through an open window high off the floor—a trash receptacle had been moved beneath it, which would have allowed him to climb up there. The window opened onto the pavilion grounds rather than outside of the fence, but from there he could have gone in any one of a number of directions—including out the performers' gate.

From then on, all was confusion. I told Kabalka what had happened and again left him in charge of the others. With the help of the security personnel, I combed the backstage area—questioning the performers, stage personnel, Don, and the other people from KSUN. No one had seen Fitzgerald. The guards in the audience were alerted, but no one in baggy plaid pants, a red vest, and a yellow cape was spotted. The security man on the performers' gate knew nothing; he'd only come on minutes ago, and the man he had relieved had left the grounds on a break.

Fitzgerald and Tilby were to be the last act to go on—at midnight, as the star attraction. As the hour approached, the others in their party grew frantic and Don and KSUN people grew grim. I continued to search systematically. Finally I returned to the performers' gate; the guard had returned from his break and Kabalka had buttonholed him. I took over the questioning. Yes, he remembered Gary Fitzgerald. He'd left at about ten thirty, carrying his yellow cape and a small canvas bag. But wait—hadn't he returned just a few minutes ago, before Kabalka had come up and started asking questions? But maybe that wasn't the same man, there had been something different. . . .

Kabalka was on the edge of hysterical collapse. He yelled at the guard and only confused him further. Maybe the man who had just come in had been wearing a red cape . . . maybe the pants were green rather than blue . . . no, it wasn't the same man after all. . . .

Kabalka yelled louder, until one of the stage personnel told him to shut up, he could be heard out front. Corinne appeared and momentarily succeeded in quieting her husband. I left her to deal with him and went back to the dressing room. Tilby and Nicole were there. His face was pinched, white around the mouth. Nicole was pale and—oddly enough—had been crying. I told them what the security guard had said, cautioned them not to leave the dressing room.

As I turned to go, Tilby said, "Sharon, will you ask Wayne to come in here?"

"I don't think he's in any shape—"

"Please, it's important."

"All right. But why?"

Tilby looked at Nicole. She turned her tear-streaked face away toward the wall.

He said, "We have a decision to make about the act."

"I hardly think so. It's pretty clear cut. If Gary doesn't turn up, you simply can't go on."

He stared bleakly at me. "Just ask Wayne to come in here."

Of course the act didn't go on. The audience was disappointed, the KSUN people were irate, and the Fitzgerald and Tilby entourage were grim—a grimness that held a faint undercurrent of tightly reined panic. No one could shed any light on where Fitzgerald might have gone, or why—at least, if anyone had suspicions, he was keeping it to himself. The one thing everyone agreed on was that his disappearance wasn't my fault; I hadn't been hired to prevent treachery within the ranks. I myself wasn't so sure of my lack of culpability.

So I'd spent the night chasing around, trying to find a trace of him. I'd gone to San Francisco: to Fitzgerald's hotel in the Haight-Ashbury, to the St. Francis where the rest of the party were staying, even to the KSUN studios. Finally I went back to the Haight, to a number of the after-hours places I knew of, in the hopes Fitzgerald was there recapturing his youth, as Nicole had termed it earlier. And I still hadn't found a single clue to his whereabouts.

Until now. I hadn't located Gary Fitzgerald, but I'd found his clown costume. On another man. A dead man.

6

After the county sheriff's men had finished questioning me and said I could go, I decided to return to the St. Francis and talk to my clients once more. I wasn't sure if Kabalka would want me to keep searching for Fitzgerald now, but he—and the others—deserved to hear from me about the dead man in Gary's costume, before the authorities contacted them. Besides, there were things bothering me about Fitzgerald's disappearance, some of them obvious, some vague. I hoped talking to Kabalka and company once more would help me bring the vague ones into more clear focus.

It was after seven by the time I had parked under Union Square and entered the hotel's elegant, dark-paneled lobby. The few early risers who clustered there seemed to be tourists, equipped with cameras and anxious to get on with the day's adventures. A dissipated-looking couple in evening clothes stood waiting for an elevator, and a few yards away in front of the first row of expensive shops, a maid in the hotel uniform was pushing a vacuum cleaner with desultory strokes. When the elevator came, the couple and I rode up in silence; they got off at the floor before I did.

Corinne Kabalka answered my knock on the door of the suite almost immediately. Her eyes were deeply shadowed, she wore the same white linen pantsuit—now severely rumpled—that she'd had on the night before, and in her hand she clutched her crocheting. When she saw me, her face registered disappointment.

"Oh," she said, "I thought . . ."

"You hoped it would be Gary."

"Yes. Well, any of them, really."

"Them? Are you alone?"

She nodded and crossed the sitting room to a couch under the heavily draped windows, dropping onto it with a sigh and setting down the crocheting.

"Where did they go?"

"Wayne's out looking for Gary. He refuses to believe he's just . . . vanished. I don't know where John is, but I suspect he's looking for Nicole."

"And Nicole?"

Anger flashed in her tired eyes. "Who knows?"

I was about to ask her more about Tilby's unpleasant girlfriend when a key rattled in the lock, and John and Nicole came in. His face was pulled into taut lines, reflecting a rage more sustained than Corinne's brief flare-up. Nicole looked haughty, tight-lipped, and a little defensive.

Corinne stood. "Where have you two been?"

Tilby said, "*I* was looking for Nicole. It occurred to me that we didn't want to lose another member of this happy party."

Corinne turned to Nicole. "And you?"

The younger woman sat on a spindly chair, studiously examining her plum-colored fingernails. "I was having breakfast."

"Breakfast?"

"I was hungry, after that disgusting supper last night. So I went around the corner to a coffee shop—"

"You could have ordered from room service. Or eaten downstairs where John could have found you more easily."

"I needed some air."

Now Corinne drew herself erect. "Always thinking of Nicole, aren't you?"

"Well, what of it? Someone around here has to act sensibly."

In their heated bickering, they all seemed to have forgotten I was there. I remained silent, taking advantage of the situation; one could learn very instructive things by listening to people's unguarded conversations.

Tilby said, "Nicole's right, Corinne. We can't all run around like Wayne, looking for Gary when we have no idea where to start."

"Yes, *you* would say that. You never did give a damn about him, or anyone. Look how you stole Nicole from your own cousin—"

"Good God, Corinne! You can't *steal* one person from another."

"You did. You stole her and then you wrecked—"

"Let's not go into this, Corinne. Especially in front of an outsider." Tilby motioned at me.

Corinne glanced my way and colored. "I'm sorry, Sharon. This must be embarrassing for you."

On the contrary, I wished they would go on. After all, if John had taken Nicole from his cousin, Gary would have had reason to resent him—perhaps even to want to destroy their act.

I said to Tilby, "Is that the reason Gary was staying at a different hotel—because of you and Nicole?"

He looked startled.

"How long have you two been together?" I asked.

"Long enough." He turned to Corinne. "Wayne hasn't come back or called, I take it?"

"I've heard nothing. He was terribly worried about Gary when he left."

Nicole said, "He's terribly worried about the TV commercials and his cut of them."

"Nicole!" Corinne whirled on her.

Nicole looked up, her delicate little face all innocence. "You know it's true. All Wayne cares about is money. I don't know why he's worried, though. He can always get someone to replace Gary, Wayne's good at doing that sort of thing—"

Corinne stepped forward and her hand lashed out at Nicole's face, connecting with a loud smack. Nicole put a hand to the reddening stain on her cheekbone, eyes widening; then she got up and ran from the room. Corinne watched her go, satisfaction spreading over her handsome features. When I glanced at Tilby, I was surprised to see he was smiling.

"Round one to Corinne," he said.

"She had it coming." The older woman went back to the couch and sat, smoothing her rumpled pantsuit. "Well, Sharon, once more you must excuse us. I assume you came here for a reason?"

"Yes." I sat down in the chair Nicole had vacated and told them about the dead man at the pavilion. As I spoke, the two exchanged glances that were at first puzzled, then worried, and finally panicky.

When I had finished, Corinne said, "But who on earth can the man in Gary's costume be?" The words sounded theatrical, false.

"The sheriff's department is trying to make an identification. Probably his fingerprints will be on file somewhere. In the meantime, there are a few distinctive things about him which may mean something to you or John."

John sat down next to Corinne. "Such as?"

"The man had been crippled, probably a number of years ago, according to the man from the medical examiner's office. One arm was bent badly, and he wore a lift to compensate for a shortened leg. He would have walked with a limp."

The two of them looked at each other, and then Tilby said—too quickly—"I don't know anyone like that."

Corinne also shook her head, but she didn't meet my eyes.

I said, "Are you sure?"

"Of course we're sure." There was an edge of annoyance in Tilby's voice.

I hesitated, then went on, "The sheriff's man who examined the body theorizes that the dead man may have been from the countryside around there, because he had fragments of madrone and chapparal leaves caught in his shoes, as well as foxtails in the weave of his pants. Perhaps he's someone you knew when you lived in the area?"

"No, I don't remember anyone like that."

"He was about Gary's height and age, but with sandy hair. He must have been handsome once, in an elfin way, but his face was badly scarred."

"I said, I don't know who he is."

I was fairly certain he was lying, but accusing him would get me nowhere.

Corinne said, "Are you sure the costume was Gary's? Maybe this man was one of the other clowns and dressed similarly."

"That's what I suggested to the sheriff's man, but the dead man had Gary's pass in his vest pocket. We all signed our passes, remember?"

There was a long silence. "So what you're saying," Tilby finally said, "is that Gary *gave* his pass and costume to his man."

"It seems so."

"But why?"

"I don't know. I'd hoped you could provide me with some insight."

They both stared at me. I noticed Corinne's face had gone quite blank. Tilby was as white-lipped as when I'd come upon him and Nicole in the dressing room shortly after Fitzgerald's disappearance.

I said to Tilby, "I assume you each have more than one change of costume."

It was Corinne who answered. "We brought three on this tour. But I had the other two sent out to the cleaner when we arrived here in San Francisco. . . . Oh!"

"What is it?"

"I just remembered. Gary asked me about the other costumes yesterday morning. He called from that hotel where he was staying. And he was very upset when I told him they would be at the cleaner until this afternoon."

"So he planned it all along. Probably he hoped to give his extra costume to the man, and when he found he couldn't, he decided to make a switch." I remembered Fitzgerald's odd behavior immediately after we'd arrived at the pavilion—his sneaking off into the audience when he'd been told to stay backstage. Had he had a confederate out there? Someone to hand the things to? No. He couldn't have turned over either the costume or the pass to anyone, because the clothing was still backstage, and he'd needed his pass when we returned to the dressing room.

Tilby suddenly stood up. "The son of a bitch! After all we've done—"

"John!" Corinne touched his elbow with her hand.

"John," I said, "why was your cousin staying at the hotel in the Haight?"

He looked at me blankly for a moment. "What? Oh, I don't know. He claimed he wanted to see how it had changed since he'd lived there."

"I thought you grew up together on your father's ranch near Clayton and then went to Los Angeles."

"We did. Gary lived in the Haight before we left the Bay Area."

"I see. Now, you say he 'claimed' that was the reason. Was there something else?"

Tilby was silent, then looked at Corinne. She shrugged.

"I guess," he said finally, "he'd had about all he could take of us. As you may have noticed, we're not exactly a congenial group lately."

"Why is that?"

"Why is what?"

"That you're all at odds? It hasn't always been this way, has it?"

This time Tilby shrugged. Corinne was silent, looking down at her clasped hands.

I sighed, silently empathizing with Fitzgerald's desire to get away from these people. I myself was sick of their bickering, lies, backbiting, and evasions. And I knew I would get nowhere with them—at least not now.

Better to wait until I could talk with Kabalka, see if he were willing to keep on employing me. Then, if he was, I could start fresh.

I stood up, saying, "The Contra Costa authorities will be contacting you. I'd advise you to be as frank as possible with them."

To Corinne, I added, "Wayne will want a personal report from me when he comes back; ask him to call me at home." I took out a card with both my All Souls and home number, lay it on the coffee table, and started for the door.

As I let myself out, I glanced back at them. Tilby stood with his arms folded across his chest, looking down at Corinne. They were still as statues, their eyes locked, their expressions bleak and helpless.

7

Of course, by the time I got home to my brown-shingled cottage the desire to sleep had left me. It was always that way when I harbored nagging unanswered questions. Instead of going to bed and forcing myself to rest, I made coffee and took a cup of it out on the back porch to think.

It was a sunny, clear morning and already getting hot. The neighborhood was Saturday noisy: to one side, my neighbors, the Halls, were doing something to their backyard shed that involved a lot of hammering; on the other side, the Curleys' dog was barking excitedly. Probably, I thought, my cat was deviling the dog by prancing along the top of the fence, just out of his reach. It was Watney's favorite game lately.

Sure enough, in a few minutes there was a thump as Wat dropped down from the fence onto an upturned half barrel I'd been meaning to make into a planter. His black-and-white spotted fur was full of foxtails; undoubtedly he'd been prowling around in the weeds at the back of the Curleys' lot.

"Come here, you," I said to him. He stared at me, tail swishing back and forth. "Come here!" He hesitated, then galloped up. I managed to pull one of the foxtails from the ruff of fur over his collar before he trotted off again, his belly swaying pendulously, a great big horse of a cat. . . .

I sat staring at the foxtail, rolling it between my thumb and forefinger, not really seeing it. Instead, I pictured the hills surrounding the pavilion as I'd seen them the night before. The hills that were dotted with oak and madrone and chapparal . . . that were sprinkled with people on horses . . . where a lone horseman had stood under the sheltering branches of a tree, his binoculars like a signal flare in the setting sun. . . .

I got up and went inside to the phone. First I called the Contra Costa sheriff's deputy who had been in charge of the crime scene at the pavilion. No, he told me, the dead man hadn't been identified yet; the only personal item he had been carrying was a bus ticket—issued yesterday—from San Francisco to Concord which had been tucked into his shoe. While this indicated he was not a resident of the area, it told them nothing else. They were still hoping to get an identification on his fingerprints, however.

Next I called the pavilion and got the home phone number of Jim Hayes, the guard who had been on the performers' gate when Fitzgerald had vanished. When Hayes answered my call, he sounded as if I'd woken him, but he was willing to answer a few questions.

"When Fitzgerald left he was wearing his costume, right?" I asked.

"Yes."

"What about makeup?"

"No. I'd have noticed that; it would have seemed strange, him leaving with his face all painted."

"Now, last night you said you thought he'd come back in a few minutes after you returned from your break. Did he show you his pass?"

"Yes, everyone had to show one. But—"

"Did you look at the name on it?"

"Not closely. I just checked to see if it was valid for that date. Now I wish I *had* looked, because I'm not sure it was Fitzgerald. The costume seemed the same, but I just don't know."

"Why?"

"Well, there was something different about the man who came in. He walked funny. The guy you found murdered, he was crippled."

So that observation might or might not be valid. The idea that the man walked "funny" could have been planted in Hayes' mind by his knowing the dead man was a cripple. "Anything else?"

He hesitated. "I think . . . yes. You asked if Gary Fitzgerald was wearing makeup when he left. And he wasn't. But the guy who came in, he *was* made up. That's why I don't think it was Fitzgerald."

"Thank you, Mr. Hayes. That's all I need to know."

I hung up the phone, grabbed my bag and car keys, and drove back out to the pavilion in record time.

The heat-hazed parking lots were empty today, save for a couple of trucks that I assumed belonged to the maintenance crew. The gates were locked, the box office windows shuttered, and I could see no one. That didn't matter, however. What I was interested in lay outside the chain-link fence. I parked the MG near the trucks and went around the perimeter of the amphitheater to the area near the performers' gate, then looked up at the hill to the east. There was a fire break cut through the high wheat-colored grass, and I started up it.

Halfway to the top, I stopped, wiping sweat from my forehead and looking down at the pavilion. Visibility was good from here. Pivoting, I surveyed the surrounding area. To the west lay a monotonous grid-like pattern of tracts and shopping centers, broken here and there by hills and the upthrusting skyline of Walnut Creek. To the north I could see smoke billowing from the stacks of the paper plant at Antioch, and the bridge spanning the river toward the Sacramento Delta. Further east, the majestic bulk of Mount Diablo rose; between it and this foothill were more hills and hollows—ranch country.

The hill on which I stood was only lightly wooded, but there was an outcropping of rock surrounded by madrone and live oak about a hundred yards to the south, on a direct line from the tree where the lone horseman with the signal-like binoculars had stood. I left the relatively easy footing of the fire break and waded through the dry grass toward it. It was cool and deeply shadowed under the branches of the trees, and the air smelled of vegetation gone dry and brittle. I stood still for a moment, wiping the sweat away once more, then began to look around. What I was searching for was wedged behind a low rock that formed a sort of table: a couple of tissues smeared with makeup. Black and red and white greasepaint—the theatrical makeup of a clown.

The dead man had probably used this rock as a dressing table, applying what Fitzgerald had brought him in the canvas bag. I remembered Gary's insistence on taking the bag with him to the men's room; of course he needed it; the makeup was a necessary prop to their plan. While Fitzgerald could leave the pavilion without his greasepaint, the other man couldn't enter un-madeup; there was too much of a risk that the guard might notice the face didn't match the costume or the name on the pass.

I looked down at the dry leaves beneath my feet. Oak, and madrone, and brittle needles of chapparal. And the foxtails would have been acquired while pushing through the high grass between here and the bottom of the hills. That told me the route the dead man had taken, but not what had happened to Fitzgerald. In order to find that out, I'd have to learn where one could rent a horse.

I stopped at a feed store in the little village of Hillside, nestled in a wooded hollow southeast of the pavilion. It was all you could expect of a country store, with wood floors and big sacks and bins of feed. The weatherbeaten old man in overalls who looked up from the saddle he was polishing completed the rustic picture.

He said, "Help you with something?"

I took a closer look at the saddle, then glanced around at the hand-tooled leather goods hanging from the hooks on the far wall. "That's beautiful work. Do you do it yourself?"

"Sure do."

"How much does a saddle like that go for these days?" My experience with horses had ended with the lessons I'd taken in junior high school.

"Custom job like this, five hundred, thereabouts."

"Five hundred! That's more than I could get for my car."

"Well . . ." He glanced through the door at the MG.

"I know. You don't have to say another word."

"It runs, don't it?"

"Usually." Rapport established, I got down to business. "What I need is some information. I'm looking for a stable that rents horses."

"You want to set up a party or something?"

"I might."

"Well, there's MacMillan's, on the south side of town. I wouldn't recommend them, though. They've got some mean horses. This would be for a bunch of city folks?"

"I wasn't aware it showed."

"Doesn't, all that much. But I'm good at figuring out about folks. You don't look like a suburban lady, and you don't look country either." He beamed at me, and I nodded and smiled to compliment his deductive ability. "No," he went on, "I wouldn't recommend MacMillan's if you'll have folks along who maybe don't ride so good. Some of those horses are mean enough to kick a person from here to San Jose. The place to go is Wheeler's; they got some fine mounts."

"Where is Wheeler's?"

"South too, a couple of miles beyond MacMillan's. You'll know it by the sign."

I thanked him and started out. "Hey!" he called after me. "When you have your party, bring your city friends by. I got a nice selection of handtooled belts and wallets."

I said I would, and waved at him as I drove off.

About a mile down the road on the south side of the little hamlet stood a tumble-down stable with a hand-lettered sign advertising horses for rent. The poorly recommended MacMillan's, no doubt. There wasn't an animal, mean or otherwise, in sight, but a large, jowly woman who resembled a bulldog greeted me, pitchfork in hand.

I told her the story that I'd hastily made up on the drive: a friend of mine had rented a horse the night before to ride up on the hill and watch the show at the Diablo Valley Pavilion. He had been impressed with the horse and the stable it had come from, but couldn't remember the name of the place. Had she, by any chance, rented to him? As I spoke, the woman began to frown, looking more and more like a pugnacious canine every minute.

"It's not honest," she said.

"I'm sorry?"

"It's not honest, people riding up there and watching for free. Stealing's stealing, no matter what name you put on it. Your Bible tells you that."

"Oh." I couldn't think of any reply to that, although she was probably right.

She eyed me severely, as if she suspected me of pagan practices. "In answer to your question, no, I didn't rent to your friend. I wouldn't let a person near one of my horses if he was going to ride up there and watch."

"Well, I don't suppose my friend admitted what he planned to do—"

"Any decent person would be too ashamed to admit to a thing like that." She motioned aggressively with the pitchfork.

I took a step backwards. "But maybe you rented to him not knowing—"

"You going to do the same thing?"

"What?"

"Are you going to ride up there for tonight's concert?"

"Me? No, ma'am. I don't even ride all that well. I just wanted to find out if my friend had rented his horse from—"

"Well, he didn't get the horse from here. We aren't open evenings, don't want our horses out in the dark with people like you who can't ride. Besides, even if people don't plan it, those concerts are an awful temptation. And I can't sanction that sort of thing. I'm a born-again Christian, and I won't help people go against the Lord's word."

"You know," I said hastily, "I agree with you. And I'm going to talk with my friend about his behavior. But I still want to know where he got that horse. Are there any other stables around here besides yours?"

The woman looked somewhat mollified. "There's only Wheeler's. They do a big business—trail trips on Mount Diablo, hayrides in the fall. And, of course, folks who want to sneak up to that pavilion. They'd rent to a person who was going to rob a bank on horseback if there was enough money in it."

Stifling a grin, I started for my car. "Thanks for the information."

"You're welcome to it. But you remember to talk to your friend, tell him to mend his ways."

I smiled and got out of there in a hurry.

Next to MacMillan's, Wheeler's Riding Stables looked prosperous and attractive. The red barn was freshly painted, and a couple of dozen healthy, sleek horses grazed within white rail fences. I rumbled down a dirt driveway and over a little bridge that spanned a gully, and parked in front of a door labeled OFFICE. Inside, a blond-haired man in faded Levi's and a T-shirt lounged in a canvas chair behind the counter, reading a copy of *Playboy*. He put it aside reluctantly when I came in.

I was tired of my manufactured story, and this man looked like someone I could be straightforward with. I showed him the photostat of my license and said, "I'm cooperating with the county sheriff's department on the death at the Diablo Valley Pavilion last night. You've heard about it?"

"Yes, it made the morning news."

"I've got reason to believe that the dead man may have rented a horse prior to the show last night."

The man raised a sun-bleached eyebrow and waited, as economical with his words as the woman at MacMillan's had been spendthrift.

"Did you rent any horses last night?"

"Five. Four to a party, another later on."

"Who rented the single horse?"

"Tall, thin guy. Wore jeans and a plaid shirt. At first I thought I knew him."

"Why?"

"He looked familiar, like someone who used to live near here. But then I realized it couldn't be. His face was disfigured, his arm crippled up, and he limped. Had trouble getting on the horse, but once he was mounted, I could tell he was a good rider."

I felt a flash of excitement, the kind you get when things start coming together the way you've hoped they would. "That's the man who was killed."

"Well, that explains it."

"Explains what?"

"Horse came back this morning, riderless."

"What time?"

"Oh, around five, five-thirty."

That didn't fit the way I wanted it to. "Do you keep a record of who you rent the horses to?"

"Name and address. And we take a deposit that's returned when they bring the horses back."

"Can you look up the man's name?"

He grinned and reached under the counter for a looseleaf notebook. "I can, but I don't think it will help you identify him. I noted it at the time—Tom Smith. Sounded like a phony."

"But you still rented to him?"

"Sure. I just asked for double the deposit. He didn't look too prosperous, so I figured he'd be back. Besides, none of our horses are so terrific that anyone would trouble to steal one."

I stood there for a few seconds, tapping my fingers on the counter. "You said you thought he was someone you used to know."

"At first, but the guy I knew wasn't crippled. Must have been just a chance resemblance."

"Who was he?"

"Fellow who lived on a ranch near here back in the late sixties. Gary Fitzgerald."

I stared at him.

"But like I said, Gary Fitzgerald wasn't crippled."

"Did this Gary have a cousin?" I asked.

"Yeah, John Tilby. Tilby's dad owned a dairy ranch. Gary lived with them."

"When did Gary leave here?"

"After the old man died. The ranch was sold to pay the debts and both Gary and John took off. For southern California." He grinned again. "Probably had some cockeyed idea about getting into show business."

"By any chance, do you know who was starring on the bill at the pavilion last night?"

"Don't recall, no. It was some kind of kid show, wasn't it?"

"A clown festival."

"Oh." He shrugged. "Clowns don't interest me. Why?"

"No reason." Things definitely weren't fitting together the way I'd wanted them to. "You say the cousins took off together after John Tilby's father died."

"Yes."

"And went to Southern California."

"That's what I heard."

"Did Gary Fitzgerald ever live in the Haight-Ashbury?"

He hesitated. "Not unless they went there instead of L.A. But I can't see Gary in the Haight, especially back then. He was just a country boy, if you know what I mean. But what's all this about him and John? I thought—"

"How much to rent a horse?"

The man's curiosity was easily sidetracked by business. "Ten an hour. Twenty for the deposit."

"Do you have a gentle one?"

"You mean for you? Now?"

"Yes."

"Got all kinds, gentle or lively."

I took out my wallet and checked it. Luckily, I had a little under forty dollars. "I'll take the gentlest one."

The man pushed the looseleaf notebook at me, looking faintly surprised. "You sign the book, and then I'll go saddle up Whitefoot."

8

Once our transaction was completed, the stable man pointed out the bridle trail that led toward the pavilion, wished me a good ride, and left me atop one of the gentlest horses I'd ever encountered. Whitefoot—a roan who did indeed have one white fetlock—was so placid I was afraid he'd go to sleep. Recalling my few riding lessons, which had taken place sometime in my early teens, I made some encouraging clicking sounds and tapped his flanks with my heels. Whitefoot put his head down and began munching a clump of dry grass.

"Come on, big fellow," I said. Whitefoot continued to munch.

I shook the reins—gently, but with authority.

No response. I stared disgustedly down the incline of his neck, which made me feel I was sitting at the top of a long slide. Then I repeated the clicking and tapping process. The horse ignored me.

"Look, you lazy bastard," I said in a low, menacing tone, "get a move on!"

The horse raised his head and shook it, glancing back at me with one sullen eye. Then he started down the bridle trail in a swaying, lumbering walk. I sat up straighter in correct horsewoman's posture, feeling smug.

The trail wound through a grove of eucalyptus, then began climbing uphill through grassland. The terrain was rough, full of rocky outcroppings and eroded gullies, and I was thankful for both the well-traveled path and Whitefoot's slovenly gait. After a few minutes I began to feel secure enough in the saddle to take stock of my surroundings, and when we reached the top of a rise, I stopped the horse and looked around.

To one side lay grazing land dotted with brown-and-white cattle. In the distance, I spotted a barn and a corral with horses. To the other side, the vegetation was thicker, giving onto a canyon choked with manzanita, scrub oak, and bay laurel. This was the type of terrain I was looking for—the kind where a man can easily become disoriented and lost. Still, there must be dozens of such canyons in the surrounding hills; to explore all of them would take days.

I had decided to ride a little further before plunging into rougher territory, when I noticed a movement under the leafy overhang at the edge of the canyon. Peering intently at the spot, I made out a tall figure in light-colored clothing. Before I could identify it as male or female, it slipped back into the shadows and disappeared from view.

Afraid that the person would see me, I reined the horse to one side, behind a large sandstone boulder a few yards away. Then I slipped from the saddle and peered around the rock toward the canyon. Nothing moved there. I glanced at Whitefoot and decided he would stay where he was without being tethered; true to form, he had lowered his head and was munching contentedly. After patting him once for reassurance, I crept through the tall grass to the underbrush. The air there was chill and pungent with the scent of bay laurel—more reminiscent of curry powder than of the bay leaf I kept in a jar in my kitchen. I crouched behind the billowy bright green mat of a chapparal bush while my eyes became accustomed to the gloom. Still nothing stirred; it was as if the figure had been a creature of my imagination.

Ahead of me, the canyon narrowed between high rock walls. Moss coated them, and stunted trees grew out of their cracks. I came out of my shelter and started that way, over ground that was sloping and uneven. From my right came a trickling sound; I peered through the underbrush and saw a tiny stream of water falling over the outcropping. A mere dribble now, it would be a full cascade in the wet season.

The ground became even rougher, and at times I had difficulty finding a foothold. At a point where the mossy walls almost converged, I stopped, leaning against one of them, and listened. A sound, as if someone were thrashing through thick vegetation, came from the other side of the narrow space. I squeezed between the rocks and saw a heavily forested area. A tree branch a few feet from me looked as if it had recently been broken.

I started through the vegetation, following the sounds ahead of me. Pine boughs brushed at my face, and chapparal needles scratched my bare arms. After a few minutes, the thrashing sounds stopped. I stood still, wondering if the person I was following had heard me.

Everything was silent. Not even a bird stirred in the trees above me. I had no idea where I was in relation to either the pavilion or the stables. I wasn't even sure if I could find my way back to where I'd left the horse. Foolishly I realized the magnitude of the task I'd undertaken; such a search would better be accomplished with a helicopter than on horseback.

And then I heard the voices.

They came from the right, past a heavy screen of scrub oak. They were male, and from their rhythm I could tell they were angry. But I couldn't identify them or make out what they were saying. I edged around a clump of manzanita and started through the trees, trying to make as little sound as possible.

On the other side of the trees was an outcropping that formed a flat rock shelf that appeared to drop off sharply after about twenty feet. I clambered up on it and flattened onto my stomach, then crept forward. The voices were louder now, coming from straight ahead and below. I identified one as belonging to the man I knew as Gary Fitzgerald.

". . . didn't know he intended to blackmail anyone. I thought he just wanted to see John, make it up with him." The words were labored, twisted with pain.

"If that were the case, he could have come to the hotel." The second man was Wayne Kabalka. "He didn't have to go through all those elaborate machinations of sneaking into the pavilion."

"He told me he wanted to reconcile. After all, he was John's own cousin—"

"Come on, Elliott. You knew he had threatened us. You knew all about the pressure he'd put on us the past few weeks, ever since he found out the act would be coming to San Francisco."

I started at the strange name, even though I had known the missing man wasn't really Gary Fitzgerald. Elliott. Elliott who?

Elliott was silent.

I continued creeping forward, the mossy rock cold through my clothing. When I reached the edge of the shelf, I kept my head down until Kabalka spoke again. "You knew we were all afraid of Gary. That's why I hired the McCone woman; in case he tried anything, I wanted an armed guard there. I never counted on you playing the Judas."

Again Elliott was silent. I risked a look over the ledge.

There was a sheer drop of some fifteen or twenty feet to a gully full of jagged rocks. The man I'd known as Gary Fitzgerald lay at its bottom, propped into a sitting position, his right leg twisted at an unnatural angle. He was wearing a plaid shirt and jeans—the same clothing the man at the stables had described the dead man as having on. Kabalka stood in front of him, perhaps two yards from where I lay, his back to me. For a minute, I was afraid Elliott would see my head, but then I realized his eyes were glazed half blind with pain.

"What happened between John and Gary?" he asked.

Kabalka shifted his weight and put one arm behind his back, sliding his hand into his belt.

"Wayne, what happened?"

"Gary was found dead at the pavilion this morning. Stabbed. None of this would have happened if you hadn't connived to switch clothing so he could sneak backstage and threaten John."

Elliott's hand twitched, as if he wanted to cover his eyes but was too weak to lift it. "Dead." He paused. "I was afraid something awful had happened when he didn't come back to where I was waiting with the horse."

"Of course you were afraid. You knew what would happen."

"No . . ."

"You planned this for weeks, didn't you? The thing about staying at the fleabag in the Haight was a ploy, so you could turn over one of your costumes to Gary. But it didn't work, because Corinne had sent all but one to the cleaner. When did you come up with the scheme of sneaking out and trading places?"

Elliott didn't answer.

"I suppose it doesn't matter when. But why, Elliott? For God's sake, *why?*"

When he finally answered, Elliott's voice was weary. "Maybe I was sick of what you'd done to him. What we'd *all* done. He was so pathetic when he called me in L.A. And when I saw him . . . I thought maybe that if John saw him too, he might persuade you to help Gary."

"And instead he killed him."

"No. I can't believe that."

"And why not?"

"John loved Gary."

"John loved Gary so much he took Nicole away from him. And then he got into a drunken quarrel with him and crashed the car they were riding in and crippled him for life."

"Yes, but John's genuinely guilty over the accident. And he hates you for sending Gary away and replacing him with me. What a fraud we've all perpetrated—"

Kabalka's body tensed and he began balancing aggressively on the balls of his feet. "That fraud has made us a lot of money. Would have made us more until you pulled this stunt. Sooner or later they'll identify Gary's body and then it will all come out. John will be tried for the murder—"

"I still don't believe he killed him. I want to ask him about it."

Slowly Kabalka slipped his hand from his belt—and I saw the knife. He held it behind his back in his clenched fingers and took a step toward Elliott.

I pushed up with my palms against the rock. The motion caught Elliott's eye and he looked around in alarm. Kabalka must have taken the look to be aimed at him because he brought the knife up.

I didn't hesitate. I jumped off the ledge. For what seemed like an eternity I was falling toward the jagged rocks below. Then I landed heavily—directly on top of Kabalka.

As he hit the ground, I heard the distinctive sound of cracking bone. He went limp, and I rolled off of him—unhurt, because his body had cushioned my fall. Kabalka lay unconscious, his head against a rock. When I looked at Elliott, I saw he had passed out from pain and shock.

9

The room at John Muir Hospital in Walnut Creek was antiseptic white, with bright touches of red and blue in the curtains and a colorful spray of fall flowers on the bureau. Elliott Larson—I'd found out that was his full name—lay on the bed with his right leg in traction. John Tilby stood by the door, his hands clasped formally behind his back, looking shy and afraid to come any further into the room. I sat on a chair by the bed, sharing a split of smuggled-in wine with Elliott.

I'd arrived at the same time as Tilby, who had brought the flowers. He'd seemed unsure of a welcome, and even though Elliott had acted glad to see him, he was still keeping his distance. But after a few awkward minutes, he had agreed to answer some questions and had told me about the drunken auto accident five years ago in which he had been thrown clear of his MG and the real Gary Fitzgerald had been crippled. And about how Wayne Kabalka had sent Gary away with what the manager had termed an "ample settlement"—and which would have been except for Gary's mounting medical expenses, which eventually ate up all his funds and forced him to live on welfare in a cheap San Francisco hotel. Determined not to lose the bright financial future the comedy team had promised him, Kabalka had looked around for a replacement for Gary and found Elliott performing in a seedy Haight-Ashbury club. He'd put him into the act, never telling the advertisers who were clamoring for Fitzgerald and Tilby's services that one of the men in the whiteface was not the clown they had contracted with. And he'd insisted Elliott totally assume Gary's identity.

"At first," Elliott said, "it wasn't so bad. When Wayne found me, I was on a downslide. I was heavy into drugs, and I'd been kicked out of my place in the Haight and was crashing with whatever friends would let me. At first it was great making all that money, but after a while I began to realize I'd never be anything more than the shadow of a broken man."

"And then," I said, "Gary reappeared."

"Yes. He needed some sort of operation and he contacted Wayne in L.A. Over the years Wayne had been sending him money—hush money, I guess you could call it—but it was barely enough to cover his minimum expenses. Gary had been seeing all the ads on TV, reading about how well we were doing, and he was angry and demanding a cut."

"And rightly so," Tilby added. "I'd always thought Gary was well provided for, because Wayne took part of my earnings and said he was sending it to him. Now I know most of it was going into Wayne's pocket."

"Did Wayne refuse to give Gary the money for the operation?" I asked.

Tilby nodded. "There was a time when Gary would merely have crept back into the woodwork when Wayne refused him. But by then his anger and hurt had festered, and he wasn't taking no for an answer. He threatened Wayne, and continued to make daily threats by phone. We were all on edge, afraid of what he might do. Corinne kept urging Wayne to give him the money, especially because we had contracted to come to San Francisco, where Gary was, for the clown festival. But Wayne was too stubborn to give in."

Thinking of Corinne, I said, "How's she taking it, anyway?"

"Badly," Tilby said. "But she's a tough lady. She'll pull through."

"And Nicole?"

"Nicole has vanished. Was packed and gone by the time I went back to the hotel after Wayne's arrest." He seemed unconcerned; five years with Nicole had probably been enough.

I said, "I talked to the sheriff's department. Wayne hasn't confessed." After I'd revived Elliott out there in the canyon, I'd given him my gun and made my way back to where I'd left the horse. Then I'd ridden—the most energetic ride of old Whitefoot's life—back to the stables and summoned the sheriff's men. When we'd arrived at the gully, Wayne had regained consciousness and was attempting to buy Elliott off. Elliott seemed to be enjoying bargaining and then refusing.

Remembering the conversation I'd overheard between the two men, I said to Elliott, "Did Wayne have it right about you intending to loan Gary one of your spare costumes?"

"Yes. When I found I didn't have an extra costume to give him, Gary came up with the plan of signaling me from a horse on the hill. He knew the area from when he lived there and had seen a piece in the paper about how people would ride up on the hill to watch the concerts. You guessed about the signal?"

"I saw it happen. I just didn't put it together until later, when I thought about the fragments of leaves and needles they found in Gary's clothing." No need to explain about the catalyst to my thought process—the horse of a cat named Watney.

"Well," Elliott said, "that was how it worked. The signal with the field glasses was to tell me Gary had been able to get a horse and show me where he'd be waiting. At the prearranged time, I made the excuse about going to the men's room, climbed out the window, and left the pavilion. Gary changed and got himself into white face in a clump of trees with the aid of a flashlight. I put on his clothes and took the horse and waited, but he never came back. Finally the crowd was streaming out of the pavilion, and then the lights went out; I tried to ride down there, but I'm not a very good horseman, and I got turned around in the dark. Then something scared the horse and it threw me into that ravine and bolted. As soon as I hit the rocks I knew my leg was broken."

"And you lay there all night."

"Yes, half frozen. And in the morning I heard Wayne thrashing through the underbrush. I don't know if he intended to kill me at first, or if he planned to try to convince me that John had killed Gary and we should cover it up."

"Probably the latter, at least initially." I turned to Tilby. "What happened at the pavilion with Gary?"

"He came into the dressing room. Right off I knew it was him, by the limp. He was angry, wanted money. I told him I was willing to give him whatever he needed, but that Wayne would have to arrange for it. Gary hid in the dressing room closet and when you came in there, I asked you to get Wayne. He took Gary away, out into the audience, and when he came back, he said he'd fixed everything." He paused, lips twisting bitterly. "And he certainly had."

We were silent for a moment. Then Elliott said to me, "Were you surprised to find out I wasn't really Gary Fitzgerald?"

"Yes and no. I had a funny feeling about you all along."

"Why?"

"Well, first there was the fact you and John just didn't look like you were related. And then when we were driving through Contra Costa County, you didn't display much interest in it—not the kind of curiosity a man would have when returning home after so many years. And there was one other thing."

"What?"

"I said something about sound from the two pavilions being audible all the way to Port Chicago. That's the place where the Naval Weapons Station is, up on the Strait. And you said, 'Not all the way to Chicago.' You didn't know what Port Chicago was, but I took it to mean you were making a joke. I remember thinking that for a clown, you didn't have much of a sense of humor."

"Thanks a lot." But he grinned, unoffended.

I stood up. "So now what? Even if Wayne never confesses, they've got a solid case against him. You're out a manager, so you'll have to handle your own future plans."

They shrugged almost simultaneously.

"You've got a terrific act," I said. "There'll be some adverse publicity, but you can probably weather it."

Tilby said, "A couple of advertisers have already called to withdraw their offers."

"Others will be calling with new ones."

He moved hesitantly toward the chair I'd vacated. "Maybe."

"You can count on it. A squeaky clean reputation isn't always an asset in show business; your notoriety will hurt you in some ways, but help you in others." I picked up my bag and squeezed Elliott's arm, went toward the door, touching Tilby briefly on the shoulder. "At least think about keeping the act going."

As I went out, I looked back at them. Tilby had sat down in the chair. His posture was rigid, tentative, as if he might flee at any moment. Elliott looked uncertain, but hopeful.

What was it, I thought, that John had said to me about clowns when we were playing gin in the dressing room at the pavilion? Something to the effect that they were all funny but, more important, that they all made people take a look at their own foibles. John Tilby and Elliott Larson—in a sense both broken men like Gary Fitzgerald had been—knew more about those foibles than most people. Maybe there was a way they could continue to turn that sad knowledge into laughter.

THE INVISIBLE INTRUDER

Edward D. Hoch

Clients of the Libby Knowles Protection Service sometimes proved to be a bit paranoid, and at first Libby would have placed Frederick Warfer in that category. He was a balding man of around fifty who glanced over his shoulder even as he entered her outer office.

Libby's new secretary, Janice, was out to lunch at the time, and when he saw Libby at the reception desk, he jumped to the wrong conclusion. "I—I don't have an appointment. Do you suppose Miss Knowles could see me?"

Libby straightened up. "I'm Libby Knowles. My secretary is at lunch."

"Maybe I should come back later," he muttered. "I didn't realize it was lunchtime."

"No, come in. I've already had some yogurt."

He followed her into the inner office, a big square room with a wide window overlooking the busy traffic on Madison Street. The building was old, but the rent was reasonable, and that was what mattered to Libby in her first year of being in business on her own.

"Now what can I do for you, Mr.—?" She glanced at the card he'd handed her. "Warfer."

"Frederick Warfer. I'm an industrial consultant—an inventor of sorts. Companies come to me with technical problems and I try to find solutions for them."

"You want me to protect an invention of yours?"

"No, I want you to protect *me*. Someone's trying to kill me."

"Why do you think that?" Libby asked, sitting down behind her desk and indicating that he sit, too.

"Someone's been getting into my house at night," he said, perching on the one visitor's chair. "It sets off the alarms, but by the time the police arrive no one's there. There's never any sign of forced entry."

"Perhaps the alarm system's defective," Libby suggested.

"I've checked it completely and it's working perfectly." He hesitated. "I want you to come out and stay at the house with me."

"All right. That's my job, of course. But I don't share a room with male clients. Do you have a spare room?"

"Yes."

"Are you married, Mr. Warfer?" She'd started making notes on a yellow legal pad.

"I—no, not at the present. My wife left me two years ago."

"I see. Are you alone in the house? Do you have any children?"

"No, no children. I'm alone. My address is on my card there."

Libby studied it, then asked, "Who do you think might want to kill you?"

"A business competitor, maybe. I don't know. I just need protection. The police don't believe me any more. After a full week of that alarm going off, they're starting to think I'm doing it myself."

"Are you, Mr. Warfer?"

"No, of course not! But I'm afraid the police are going to stop coming out when the alarm goes off. Or else they'll take their time about it. And that's when he'll do it."

"He'll?"

"She'll! Whoever!"

"Do what?"

"Kill me."

"I see. All right, Mr. Warfer, I'll be there this evening."

"Will you be armed?"

"Yes. I'm a former policewoman. I know how to use a handgun responsibly."

Libby had arranged to meet Sergeant O'Bannion for a drink late that afternoon. He was a bulky man with a big face that seemed to crease itself into a gloomy expression at the least opportunity. People who didn't know him well thought he was perpetually unhappy, but Libby knew better. O'Bannion had been the one person who'd urged her to remain on the force after her lover, a vice-squad detective, had been caught in a cocaine scandal and killed himself in an auto crash while fleeing his fellow cops. She hadn't followed O'Bannion's advice, but he'd been good to her—and good for her—ever since, often sending business her way that the department couldn't handle on an official basis.

"I have a new client," she told him over drinks. "A man named Frederick Warfer. Do you know him?"

O'Bannion shook his head. "Should I?"

"His alarm's been ringing every night for a week. He's afraid the police will start ignoring him."

"I'll check the reports in the morning. Where does he live?"

"Maple Shade Drive. I'll be out there tonight."

"Take care of yourself, Libby. Lady bodyguards are hard to replace."

She smiled. "The biggest threat to my health so far has been starvation."

Warfer's home proved to be an expensive Moorish-looking place with a long curving driveway. Libby guessed it had probably been built back in the 1930s when the popularity of Moorish architecture had reached this part of the country. She'd expected to find her client alone in a darkened house, but the window showed plenty of light and he opened the door with an attractive blonde woman at his side.

"Come in, Miss Knowles. This is Helen Rodney, my neighbor from across the street."

Helen Rodney appeared to be in her late thirties, with the sort of eyes that stayed hard even when she smiled. "This is your bodyguard?" she asked him with a laugh. "What will she protect you from?"

"I'd like to have a look around the house," Libby told Warfer.

The June night had been warm and she'd worn only a light jacket over her blouse and slacks. She dropped it on top of her overnight bag in the entryway and followed after her client, turning her back decisively on the blonde neighbor. They stepped down into a large living room, dominated on its far end by a massive fieldstone fireplace. "That's lovely," Libby said, going and peering into it.

"I never use it. It's too much trouble."

"It's almost big enough for a man to hide in," Libby said, peering up into the chimney.

Warfer shook his head. "Not really. I checked it out."

The dining room was almost as large, with a table and ten chairs, and the kitchen was spacious and lavishly equipped. It was a house obviously designed for entertaining and Libby said as much.

"We did a great deal of entertaining before my wife left," Warfer said quietly.

He showed her the highly sophisticated burglar-alarm system that not only wired the doors and windows but also threw a pattern of invisible beams across rooms and doorways. "Once it's switched on, any movement in here, no matter how slight, triggers the alarm," he explained.

"I've seen only one alarm system this elaborate in my life," Libby told him, "and that was in a museum. What do you have here that's so valuable, anyway?"

"I told you, I'm an inventor. There are times when a small fortune in ideas, notes, and mock-ups can be found in this house."

Helen Rodney had followed along a few steps behind them, but when Warfer led Libby to the stairs to the second floor she said, "I think I'd better be going. If you get frightened of anything during the night, Frederick, just give me a call."

When she'd gone, Libby remarked, "I feel as if I'm coming between you two."

"No. Helen's just an old friend. A friend of my wife's, really. She's been trying to take care of me ever since Betty left."

"Your wife?"

He nodded, leading her into the master bedroom and indicating a framed color photograph on a bedside table. "Betty and I were married for twenty-one years. And then she just left."

"I'm sorry." The woman was smiling at the camera, but the picture was overexposed and she was squinting slightly into the sun. Her eyes were a stunning blue. The photo had obviously been blown up from a much smaller candid shot. "She's very attractive."

"She was."

When he added no more, she said, "Tell me about this intruder. What time does he usually arrive?"

"Shortly after I retire. Sometimes I'm still awake when the alarm goes off. See—" he showed her the mechanism "—it buzzes next to the bed, too."

"Midnight? One o'clock?"

"It varies. Closer to one, usually, but that may be because I go to bed late. The police have come and searched every inch of the house, but they've found no one. The intruder is invisible by night and nonexistent by day. But I have a terrible feeling he's getting closer to me every time."

"We'll see what happens tonight," Libby said.

Warfer showed her the guest room and she brought her bag up and unpacked what she needed. The .38-caliber snub-nosed revolver went under her pillow.

Warfer rapped at her door a few minutes after one, waking her. "The alarm just went off!" he told her anxiously.

Libby, who slept fully clothed when on a job, grabbed her gun from under the pillow and ran down the stairs ahead of him. Her left hand hit the living-room light switch as she went into a crouch in the doorway. "Hands up!" she shouted. "I have a gun!"

The room was empty, and so was the dining room. The entire first floor was empty.

"You can see for yourself that the doors and windows haven't been tampered with," Warfer said after they had both checked them. "It's just like the other times."

"Maybe you've got mice."

"Mice four feet tall? That's the height of these alarm beams that were broken."

A flashing red light suddenly lit up the wall opposite the front windows. "That'll be the police," Libby said. "I'll go out and talk to them."

There was a single officer in the squad car, a slim young man whose name tag read David Oakes. He was new since Libby's days on the force and she introduced herself.

"I know," the officer said wearily. "The alarm went off again and no one was here." His deep-set brown eyes took in the scene.

"Well, I was here this time, but I didn't set it off."

Oakes sighed and recorded the time on his call sheet. "They're talking about fining people with defective alarm systems. It wastes one hell of a lot of our time."

"He claims it's not defective. He's an inventor and he's checked all the wiring."

Frederick Warfer joined them. "I'm sorry, Officer. I had hoped that hiring Miss Knowles might solve the problem."

"Give me a chance," Libby countered. "It's only my first night."

A light went on in the house across the street and she saw Helen Rodney appear in the doorway. "Are you all right, Frederick?" she called.

"I'm fine, Helen," he called back. "Just another false alarm."

She wrapped her robe more tightly around her, waved, and went back inside.

"You'd better disconnect the alarm for tonight," Oakes suggested after taking a quick walk around the house, shining his flashlight at the windows and trying the doors.

"All right," Warfer told him. "I'll disconnect the call-in alarm that flashes at the police station, but I'll leave on the house alarm."

"Fine," Libby agreed.

Somehow she didn't think their unseen visitor would be back that night, and she was right. They spent the rest of the time till dawn in undisturbed slumber.

Since the bodyguard assignment was only for nighttime, Libby left Warfer's house and drove to her office in the morning as usual. She was going through the mail, dictating some replies to her secretary, when Sergeant O'Bannion phoned. "How'd it go last night, Libby?"

"The alarm went off but there was no one in the house. The same as before."

"I dug out the complaint file and checked on this guy Warfer. He's had a string of false alarms lately."

"I know. That's why he hired me."

"But there's more. Somebody flagged his file with a cross-index to Missing Persons."

"How come?"

"He had a wife named Monica Warfer."

"He told me she walked out on him." But he'd called her Betty.

"Maybe it's true. It was eleven years ago and she just disappeared one day. He said she went downtown to shop and never came back. We never found a trace of her. Some of the smart guys in the Bureau thought maybe he buried her in the back yard, but there was never any evidence of it."

"How old would she have been at the time?" Libby asked him. Warfer had told her Betty left him just two years ago.

"Somewhat younger than her husband. Only thirty-five. A good age for running off, I suppose."

"Any relatives?"

"A brother who still lives in town. Ralph Forrest. Want his address?"

"I think so, yes."

After lunch she tracked down Ralph Forrest at work. He was a used-car salesman at a lot near downtown. When she told him what she wanted, his manner turned into something resembling annoyance. "Monica's gone," he said. "She's been gone for eleven years. Why are you bothering me now?"

"You must have heard from her during that time—a postcard or something."

He shook his head. "We weren't very close toward the end."

"The end of what?"

"I mean before she went away. I'd be the last one she'd write to."

"Who'd be the first one?"

"Her husband, I suppose."

"Are you friendly with Frederick Warfer?"

"Not so's you'd notice. He came raving to me a few times after she left, but I haven't seen him in years."

"You think she ran away from him?"

"You met Warfer? What do you think? Me, I always thought she was crazy to marry him in the first place. Anything might have happened."

"He believes someone has been breaking into his house, trying to harm him."

"Who'd bother?"

"You don't think your sister could be back in the city, do you?"

The very idea seemed to startle him. He thought about it, but only for a moment. "No, she's not back. She's never coming back."

"Would you happen to have a picture of your sister?"

"I might have an old snapshot in my desk. Let me see."

Libby followed him into an office at the center of the lot. He rummaged through the drawers of a cluttered desk before coming up with a photograph of a solemn woman in her thirties with dark hair and eyes. It wasn't the same woman as the one in the photograph by Frederick Warfer's bed.

"Was your sister ever called Betty?"

"Betty? No—her name was Monica." He seemed about to say more, but Libby was in a hurry now.

"May I keep this picture for a bit?"

"Take it," he told her tiredly. "I don't need it."

Libby arrived promptly at eight o'clock to begin another night of guard duty. This time Warfer was alone and there was no sign of his neighbor from across the street.

"I'm going to sleep down here in the living room tonight," she told him.

His eyes widened a bit but he said nothing to dissuade her. Once more she searched the ground floor of the house and made certain the doors and windows were locked. It was a warm night, but she didn't want to risk opening a window. "Don't you have air-conditioning?" she asked.

"It's bad for your health," he said with conviction. "I leave the windows open upstairs. Do you want to change your mind and—"

Libby shook her head. "I'm more likely to hear someone trying to break in if I'm down here," she told him.

After he went up to bed, Libby read a little, then, before she turned out the lights, she switched on the alarm system so that a small red light would go on in the house but no signal would be transmitted to the police. It just might be that the arrival of the squad car was scaring away the invisible intruder.

Taking care to keep below the four-foot height of the electronic beams that criss-crossed the first floor, she settled down with a blanket, a flashlight and her revolver close at hand on the coffee table. She could hear Warfer moving around upstairs for a time and then there was silence. It was about midnight.

For the next half hour, nothing happened.

Remembering how quickly the alarm had sounded the previous night, Libby began to grow uneasy. She kept glancing at the alarm switch in the hallway, but no red light glowed. Then she remembered they hadn't retired until twelve-thirty last night and it had been a good half hour after that before the alarm had sounded.

She must have dozed momentarily. She awoke with a start, certain she'd felt something brush the air near her head. It was just before one by the glowing digits of her watch. She glanced toward the hallway and froze. The alarm light was showing red!

She rolled over on her back and quickly reached for the flashlight on the table. Holding it in her left hand, she picked up the revolver with her right. Then she felt it again, the feather-light rush of air. She snapped on the flashlight.

It was a bat, swooping and soaring about the room as if seeking an exit. Libby jumped to her feet and hit the light switch. Turning back, she saw the bat fly into the fieldstone fireplace and disappear.

The fireplace! Of course! It had gotten in there somehow a week ago and was unable to find its way back up the chimney! Every night, after the lights were turned out, it flew around the ground floor of the house seeking its freedom, then retreated up the chimney again when the lights went back on. It was as simple as that.

Libby was grinning as she ran up the stairs to break the good news to Frederick Warfer. The light was on in his room, as she knew it would be once the alarm light had shown. "It's all over," she announced, knocking at his half closed door, "I found our intruder."

The silence that greeted her was so ominous, she pushed the door open cautiously.

Frederick Warfer was slumped against the bed by the window. His throat had been cut and he was dead.

Libby had to steady herself against a chair as she looked down at the bloody sight. Then the wave of nausea passed and she looked around the room to make certain the killer wasn't hiding there. She checked the closet and under the bed. The window was open, but it was a good fifteen-foot drop to the ground.

The red alarm light on Warfer's bedside panel was still on. It reminded her of the police and she went to the phone to call them. In almost no time, she heard a squad car pull up.

There were two cars, actually, and Officer Oakes emerged from one. "We figured we'd hear from you tonight," he said.

"Mr. Warfer's been murdered," she told him. "He's upstairs, in his bedroom."

"What?"

"Someone cut his throat."

The young policeman ran up the stairs ahead of her with the two officers from the second car behind him. "So the intruder finally got to him," Oakes said after checking out the body for signs of life.

"No, the intruder who set off the alarm was a bat."

"Then who—?" He stared at her.

"I don't know. I was downstairs. He was alone up here."

There were other cars pulling up outside and she was thankful to see Sergeant O'Bannion climbing the stairs, followed by some other detectives. "What happened?" he asked.

She told him about the bat and about finding Warfer dead. "He was my client," she heard herself saying. "And now he's dead."

"We lose clients all the time, Libby. Every time a taxpayer is mugged or killed, it's a client we've failed."

"This is a first for me."

"Any ideas about it?" he asked as the lab technicians set about their business.

She glanced at the photograph of Warfer's wife. "Not right now."

"It looks as if the killer either came up the stairs or through the window. Go home and get some rest, Libby. We'll handle it from here."

"Don't you want a statement from me?"

"Come down to the office in the morning."

Still, she felt she had to remain until they took the body away. Frederick Warfer had paid her for the week and she hadn't earned it. Maybe she wouldn't really earn it if she found his killer, either, but it was the least she could try to do now.

On the way out to her car later, she saw Helen Rodney watching from behind her picture window across the street.

Libby stopped by the office in the morning before going to police headquarters. She wanted to look through the mail and tell her secretary what had happened, but instead she found a familiar-looking middle-aged woman waiting in the reception room.

"This is Mrs. Coxe," Janice said from behind her desk. "She'd like to talk with you."

Libby glanced at her watch. It wasn't yet ten and she had a few minutes. If only she could remember where she'd seen the woman before. "Come in, Mrs. Coxe. I have to go out again in ten minutes, but perhaps I can help you."

"I heard on the morning news that Frederick Warfer was killed last night while you were guarding him."

Then it clicked. "The photo in his bedroom! You're Betty Warfer!"

The woman smiled slightly. "Not any more," she said, taking the seat opposite Libby's desk. "That was over two years ago. In fact, I'm not really sure I ever was Mrs. Warfer legally. That's why I wanted to see you before I went to the police."

Libby took out the photograph of Monica Forrest. "I think you can help me clear something up. Frederick Warfer told me he'd been married to you for twenty-one years when you left him two years ago. But eleven years ago he had a wife whose maiden name was Monica Forrest—this woman—who disappeared and was never seen again."

Betty Coxe nodded. "I can explain it in one word—bigamy. Frederick had two wives at the same time."

"How did he manage that?"

"He and I lived in the house on Maple Shade Drive. He had another house well out in the suburbs where he lived with Monica. His consultant's business involved a great deal of travel—or so I was always led to believe. He kept up this double life for twenty years or more. I suspect he might have had a child by her. It was never clear which of us he married first, so I don't even know if my marriage was legal. My divorce was, though."

"How did you find out about his other marriage?"

"One day eleven years ago I wanted to use one of his credit cards for some shopping. We needed some yard equipment—a pruning hook for the trees and some shovels to dig up the rose garden and put in some new things. In his wallet I found a credit card in his name but with a different address out in Shady Heights. I asked him about it and he went to pieces. He confessed to a double life and begged me to forgive him. He promised he'd get rid of this other woman, Monica, and be faithful to me. A short time later he told me she'd run off, disappeared. He even filed a missing-persons report with the police but she never turned up."

"What happened to this child you mentioned?"

"Fred never admitted the boy was his. He said it happened about the same time we were married and she used her pregnancy to trap him into marrying her, too. After she disappeared, her brother raised him. I had believed everything Fred said, but about two years ago the brother, Ralph Forrest, came to see me. He told me for the first time that the police suspected Fred of *murdering* Monica. But they hadn't known about his double life and they never found her body. I was horrified."

"Why did her brother come to you at that late date?"

"He'd only just found out about me himself. He was clinging to the hope that Monica was still alive and might have contacted Fred. When I couldn't help him, he told me the police theory. Once he put it into words, I realized it might be true. That's when I decided to leave Fred. I got a divorce and have since remarried."

"You say you're going to the police now. For what reason?"

"To tell them what I know. If Monica's brother really suspected Fred of causing her death, he might have had a motive for killing him." She hesitated. "I just wondered—"

"What?" Libby asked.

"Well, Fred was never one to be without a woman. I wanted to make certain there wasn't another one around who might have had a reason to kill him. I don't want to get the police after Ralph Forrest without cause."

"There was no other woman that I know of," Libby answered. Then she remembered Helen Rodney across the street.

Sergeant O'Bannion listened to Betty Coxe's story and when she had gone he called Libby into his office. "What do you think about this, Libby?"

"I'm not on the force any more," she reminded him. "I don't have to think anything about it."

"Come on, Libby. Give me a break."

"All right—have you questioned the woman who lives across the street? Her name is Helen Rodney. She was at Frederick Warfer's house when I arrived two nights ago. He said she'd been trying to take care of him since Betty left him—"

"Rodney." He shuffled through the reports on his desk. "Sure—young Oakes talked to her last night. I'll read you his report: 'Arrived at Warfer home at one A.M. in response to burglar alarm. All seemed quiet outside the house but noted a neighbor, Helen Rodney, crossing her front yard at number 34. The Rodney woman reported she'd been walking her dog and thought she saw a light in the Warfer garage. Before I could investigate further, patrol car arrived in response to telephone call reporting dead man at Warfer home.' "

"So she was on the prowl last night," Libby said.

"Walking her dog. People do walk their dogs at night."

"A woman alone, at one in the morning?"

"Maybe it's a big attack dog."

"And maybe we should have a look at Warfer's garage."

O'Bannion grinned at her as he got to his feet. "I'll get you back on the force yet, Libby. Let's go. . . ."

When they reached the Warfer home, they found Oakes and a police officer named Skefski just coming out the front door with a large butterfly net. "We caught your bat," Oakes said. "It was in the chimney, all right."

Libby peered at it and made a face. "I hate those things."

She followed O'Bannion into the attached garage and watched while he looked over the accumulation of garden tools, automotive parts, and just plain junk. "The side door was unlocked," O'Bannion pointed out. "Anyone could have come in here. Maybe that woman across the street did see something."

Libby nodded. "The killer could have picked up a pair of garden shears, slipped up the stairs somehow, and killed Warfer."

"Except that the door to the kitchen and the rest of the house was locked on the inside. We need a better theory than that, Libby."

She'd walked over and was examining the long pruning hook leaning against one wall of the garage. It was in two sections that fastened together. Each was six feet long or more and the top section had a curved, saw-toothed blade at the top for cutting high limbs. Looking up at it now, the blade appeared a bit rusty from disuse. Ironic, Libby thought, remembering that it was the pruning hook Betty had been going to buy when she discovered her husband's double life.

"What is it?" O'Bannion asked, following her gaze.

"The garden," she said. "Betty Coxe was buying gardening supplies. They were digging, putting in new things. This was eleven years ago, remember, when she discovered the truth and Warfer promised to break it off. And then the other one, Monica, disappeared. Your officers thought he might have buried her in the back yard but there was no evidence of that. But suppose he put her body in the trunk of his car and drove back over here? Suppose he buried her in *this* back yard?"

O'Bannion was unconvinced. "Why would he do that?"

"They were digging here anyway. Betty told us that. And he'd been renting or selling the other house after Monica was gone. Much safer to have the unmarked grave here, where he could watch it."

"It makes sense, I suppose." He groaned wearily. "This is a big back yard."

"Not that big when you know what you're looking for." Libby led the way into the yard and headed for the back. "They were digging up the rose garden, she said."

O'Bannion stood staring at it for a full two minutes, then he gave a yell. "Skefski! Oakes! Grab a couple of shovels from the garage and come back here—we've got some digging to do!"

The two officers shed their Sam Browne belts and started digging up Frederick Warfer's rose garden. They'd been at it about ten minutes when Skefski's shovel encountered something besides roots. "A piece of canvas," he said, peering down into the excavation. "Pretty well rotted away."

"Go easy now," O'Bannion cautioned. "Use your hands."

Libby hated herself for what she was about to do.

"There are bones here," Officer Oakes said, his voice breaking.

"They belong to Monica Forrest," Libby said quite clearly. "They belong to your mother, Mr. Oakes. You thought all along that he killed her. That's why you murdered Frederick Warfer."

She was ready for him to come charging out of the newly uncovered grave in a murderous rage, swinging his shovel at her. Instead, he sank slowly to his knees and wept. "What is all this?" O'Bannion asked, bewildered.

Libby felt drained of emotion. "David Oakes is Monica Forrest's son. Maybe he's Warfer's son, too, but we'll probably never know that for sure. He looks very much like the picture of Monica that her brother gave me, especially his eyes. After his mother disappeared, David was brought up by his uncle, Ralph Forrest, and he changed his name before becoming a police officer. Maybe Forrest suggested Oakes to him. Warfer's double life began at least twenty years ago and Betty told me she thought Monica had a child by him early on. That would make the child in his or her early twenties."

While she spoke, Oakes remained kneeling. Skefski stood by him. Neither man spoke. "How do you know he killed Warfer?" O'Bannion asked quietly.

"In his written report about seeing Helen Rodney walking her dog, he said he came here in response to the burglar alarm. But no alarm sounded because I turned it off myself. The second car came in response to my call. He came here earlier for another reason, and when Helen Rodney saw him prowling around the house moments after he'd killed Warfer, he had to avoid suspicion by questioning her."

"How could he have entered the house?"

"He didn't enter it. Remember that pruning hook in the garage? The blade at the end seemed to me at first to have rust spots, but now I think they may be traces of dried blood. Officer Oakes must have noticed it when he searched the house for intruders earlier in the week—and he probably noticed Betty's picture upstairs, too, rather than his mother's. He would remember Warfer after eleven years even if Warfer didn't recognize him. He came here last night, assembled the two sections of the pruning hook in the garage, and went around to the back of the house. The thing is at least twelve feet long with a saw-toothed blade at the end. Held by a man, it could easily reach a second-floor window fifteen feet off the ground. He probably tapped on the window with the blade or threw pebbles at it. Warfer looked out and saw a police officer he knew standing in the yard, opened the window wider, stuck his head out—and got his throat ripped open with that saw-toothed blade."

"I always knew he'd killed her," Oakes said dreamily, still kneeling by the grave. "I was asleep that night but I woke up and heard them fighting. He was going to break it off and leave her. They fought a lot and I went back to sleep. Later he said she left him, but I knew it wasn't true. She'd never have left him without taking me along. My uncle Ralph thought so, too. I joined the police force thinking someday I could find the evidence against him, and when I got called out here this week and saw him, I—"

"I must caution you," O'Bannion interrupted, "that you're entitled to an attorney before making a statement."

"That's all right, Sergeant. I did it and I'd do it again."

O'Bannion motioned to Skefski. "Take him into custody. I'll get that pruning hook from the garage, then—"

"I think I'll go now," Libby said.

"Thanks to you," O'Bannion told her, "we've wrapped up two murders."

"But I wasn't successful in protecting my client's life," Libby said. "He's dead and I don't feel any triumph about finding his killer."

O'Bannion took her arm. "It was probably fate that brought Warfer and Oakes together again after eleven years."

"Fate," said Libby. "Or a bat caught in a chimney."

A DATE IN HELSINKI

Patricia McGerr

The international trade conference in Stockholm ended with a banquet on Friday evening. Selena, covering the event for her magazine, caught up with the American delegate as he left the ballroom and asked him to clarify the final statement.

"You know I can't do that," he told her. "Ambiguity is the heart of a joint communiqué. That's the only way we can all sign it and then go home to claim that we each won the most concessions for our country. Don't expect me to sacrifice that to clarity. When do you go back to Washington?"

"Tomorrow. On the noon flight."

"Great. So do I. We can talk on the plane."

"Ambiguously, I presume."

"Or off the record," he retorted. "You have a choice."

She went to the hotel desk for her key and with it was given a long white envelope.

"This was delivered by messenger," the clerk explained. "It came about an hour ago."

She thanked him and looked at the return address. Quest Travel Agency. Not one she had heard of. Probably nonexistent. The initial letter indicated a communication from the small secret intelligence unit headed by her husband and known to its operative as Section Q. Why were they sending her a message? Had something happened to Hugh? She felt a sudden rush of fear. Selena's first husband had been killed on a job for Q and there lurked always on the fringes of her mind the possibility of its happening again.

She moved swiftly to the elevator, stopping on the way to refuse an invitation to join several of her colleagues in the bar. The car rose with maddening slowness to the tenth floor while she gripped the envelope tightly. But she resisted the urge to open it until she was alone in her room.

There she found an airline ticket made out in her name. She was scheduled to fly from Stockholm to Helsinki on Finnair flight 792 at 11:25 the next morning. There was nothing else in the envelope. No instructions. No note of explanation. She thought of calling Hugh in Washington but at once dismissed the idea. They couldn't discuss Section Q's business on an insecure line. The plane ticket told her all she, at that moment, needed to know. She had an assignment in Helsinki.

Arriving at the airport an hour early, she checked in, left her luggage, and found a seat in the waiting area. Someone would have to tell her how to proceed after the plane landed and she had allowed ample time in case the briefing was programmed before takeoff.

Looking about at the other travelers she saw no one who seemed a likely contact. But experience had taught her to disregard appearances, so when a young man with a baby in a backpack stopped beside her she was prepared to hear a Q-initialed sentence identifying him as a fellow agent. Instead he asked, in a crisp New England accent, if she'd mind watching his daughter while he went to the men's room. Getting her consent, he put the backpack with its occupant on the seat beside her and hurried away. She rummaged in her handbag for her key chain, dangled it in front of the child, who reached for it, and, when it was pulled away, gurgled happily at the new game.

Will this, she reflected, confuse my Section Q contact? Whatever description Hugh gave him—or her—to aid in recognizing her, it certainly didn't include an infant. Or was the infant her assignment? Perhaps a putative father had permanently disappeared and it was Selena's job to take his little girl into Finland. But that guess was erased by the young man's return. And while he was rebuckling the pack on his back, flight 792 was announced. She was not, it appeared, to learn why she was flying to Helsinki until she arrived there.

Unless, she amended, as she took her assigned seat, she was to be briefed en route. But her seatmate was a plump blonde laden with parcels and bound, she told Selena, for a family reunion. A Finn married to a

Swede, she anticipated seeing not only her relatives who had remained at home but a brother who worked in Leningrad.

"Is it difficult to go from Leningrad to Helsinki?" Selena asked her.

"Oh, no. The roads are good. He can drive in a few hours. Of course, by air it is faster. Or for a tourist, you may enjoy to go by ship. Any route, it is an easy trip."

And that, Selena thought, may answer the question, Why Helsinki? Finland and the Soviet Union share a border. It's an unaligned country with political and economic links to both East and West. There can be many reasons to choose it as a meeting place, a delivery point, a communications center. But that doesn't answer the other question—Why me? Hugh is usually very unwilling to involve me in Section Q affairs. In any event, someone will have to give me all the answers very soon. The ticket has brought me this far, but once I'm off the plane I'll have no idea where to go or what to do. I'll just have to wait in the airport for them to find me.

The fifty-minute flight was soon over. She had only a short wait for her suitcase, showed her passport to a courteous official, and passed into the main part of the building. There she looked about for Q's representative. Who will it be? she wondered. A messenger bringing directions for me to carry out alone? Or a principal I'm to assist? And what—

As her eyes swept the entrance, she saw with a shock a familiar face.

"Hugh!"

"Selena!" He covered the distance between them in seconds. "Your plane was on time. That's a surprise. And you already have your luggage. Good. I've a cab waiting." He picked up the suitcase and turned toward the door. She followed, thoughts awhirl, trying to adjust to the new circumstances. She had talked to Hugh yesterday morning, told him her flight number and Washington arrival time, and he had promised to meet her at National Airport. Instead he had flown to Finland. It must have been a sudden decision.

She suppressed her curiosity in the taxi, followed Hugh's lead in talking about the flight, the weather, and other banalities fit for the driver to hear. And in the hotel to which he took her they were equally discreet. To assume that anyplace that can be bugged may be bugged was standard operating procedure.

"It's such a fine day," he announced, "I thought we'd buy a lunch and eat in the park across the street. I'm sure you're hungry."

"Yes, I am. Very." Her emphasis made clear that her hunger was more for information than for food. Out in the open air, with no chance of listening ears, they could at last talk freely.

A small pub-type restaurant near the hotel supplied fresh fish sandwiches and bottles of Finnish beer. In the park on the shores of a broad bay, they sat on a bench and spread the food between them. A warm sun filtered through the leaf-laden trees.

"Pleasant, isn't it?" Hugh asked. "A splendid way to unwind after a busy week."

"I may be unwinding," Selena returned, "but you're not. You came here for Section Q."

"True. But it was pure luck that the job coincided with your Stockholm meeting, so we can turn it into a holiday as well."

"Turn me into cover, you mean. You didn't change all my reservations just so we could have a picnic in Helsinki. Whatever the job is, you'll be less conspicuous as half of a touring couple than as an American traveling alone. Since I'm being used as camouflage, I've a right to know what it's about."

"I can't argue with that." He paused to take a bite of sandwich and a swallow of beer. "However—"

"However, it's against the rules." She finished his sentence, then recited, " 'All personnel operate on a need-to-know basis. There will be no exchange of nonessential information.' All right, I won't pressure you, since I know it's useless."

"However—" he wiped his mouth and continued as if there had been no interruption "—you don't need to persuade me. I'm about to tell you everything. Or almost everything. The problem is one you may be able to help solve. It has to do with a small but strategically important country."

"Whose name—" she smiled wryly "—I don't need to know."

"Right. Although you can probably make a good guess. The regime is friendly to us, or at least not openly hostile, and has great influence on its neighbors. There are a number of groups plotting its overthrow and we try to keep a close watch on them all. Most of them are small and disorganized but one has been growing in size and power and is almost ready to strike. If it does—well, it could be like lighting the first in a string of firecrackers. The entire region may explode."

"When is this due to happen?"

"That's the crucial question," he answered. "We were able to turn around a man in the rebels' top council. He's been sending out reports for several months. Until last week they were fairly routine. Then he sent word that they'd raised enough money to buy weapons and were in touch with a source that will supply everything they need for a small-scale revolution. He gave us most of the details. A list of the weapons, how and where the transfer will take place. All we lack is the delivery date. That's to be set by the supplier and unfortunately our man won't be able to pass it on to us. He was killed in a car crash two days ago."

"An accident?"

"It looked like one. He was confident no one suspected him, so it may have been. At any event, we've lost our informant when we need him most."

"If you know the delivery point, can't you set a watch until the weapons arrive?"

"That may be anytime in the next three weeks. Since it's in a remote mountain area, we can't put observers there without them being observed. Then the rebels would change their plans and we'd come up empty. Our only hope is to learn the date in advance and mount a surprise attack."

"Is that why we're here?"

"Yes." He crumbled bits of bread left from his sandwich and scattered it for the birds. "Helsinki, as neutral ground, was picked for the rendezvous. Our man's final report said that the arms merchant was working out a timetable and would send a messenger here today to let the buyers know when to expect shipment. Luckily for us, neither side trusts the other. And the rebels are especially wary of letting any outsider know who they are. Since they keep everything within the inner circle, one of the movement leaders is coming. According to our informant, they worked out a careful procedure for him to learn the date without revealing his own identity."

"How can he do that?"

"Our man didn't tell us. When he sent the report, it wasn't necessary. He expected to be at the next meeting, learn the date, and pass it on to us. But now he's dead and we've got to intercept the message here today."

"Do you know who is coming for it?"

"Yes, we even have his picture." He pulled from his pocket a sketch of a hawk-nosed man with a pointed beard. "His code name is Cactus and he's on a plane due to land in—" he checked his watch— "one hour and twenty minutes. One of our people is sitting behind him. Another will pick up his trail at the airport. There are two more based at the hotel where he has his reservation."

"The one where we're staying, I presume."

"Of course. We've been liberal with agents so that he won't see the same face too often and sense he's been followed. Since we don't know who's representing the seller or when they're to meet, we have to maintain constant surveillance."

"You can't follow him into his room," Selena pointed out. "Have you put a mike there and tapped his phone?"

"No. We're sure the meet will take place in the open. The entire transaction has been hedged with caution to keep the gun runners from identifying any of the rebels. They don't want them to add a blackmail bonus to the selling price."

"But if he uses an assumed name, how could they—Oh, I see. If they know his room number, someone can take his picture. But, good heavens, Hugh, they've set themselves an impossible goal. There's no way he can get his answer without risking recognition. Even if he's arranged to exchange a password at night in a dark alley, someone can follow him into the light. Even a dead drop isn't risk-free. He can't be sure there won't be someone with a camera waiting for him to pick it up. I don't see how it can be done."

"Neither do I." He put the bottles and sandwich wrappings into a paper bag and stood up. "But they found a way and we'd better match them before it's too late. If the arms shipment goes through, the whole area may be lost to us. Whereas if we get there in time to stop it, we'll earn gratitude with a great future value."

They strolled along the path through the trees, bought ice-cream cones at an open booth and continued their walk in silent thought. How can two strangers meet, Selena asked herself, so that X can give Z a message while both remain nameless and faceless? Or am I making it harder than it really is?

"Is anonymity imperative for both sides?" she asked Hugh.

"No, only for the rebel leader. The gun runners can hire someone to pass on the date without knowing what it means or who hired him. He can be in the open. Why?"

He studied her face with rising hope. "You have an idea how it can be done?"

"Sorry, no. I'm just trying to define the problem. It's not quite as unmanageable if only one of the parties has to stay under cover.

"They had a week to figure out a method. We have to do it in hours." Again he checked his watch. "We'd better get back to the hotel. I want to make sure everyone is in place."

Hugh stayed in the lobby where a display of picture postcards provided an observation post. Selena went on to their room. She wished they were really on holiday. It was a beautiful country and an interesting one, with no end of things to do and see. Even right here in the hotel. She picked up a card from the dressing table which listed services and attractions. There were three dining rooms, keyed to every taste and budget. Music for dancing in the roof garden from 7:00 P.M. to midnight. A ground-floor casino opened at 5:00 P.M. It was, the card informed her, run by the government with profits going to charity. A comfortable way to gamble, she mused. If I lose, the orphans win.

Returning to the lobby, she found that Hugh had moved to a couch and appeared to read a London newspaper. She stopped at the cashier's cage to change a traveler's check into Finnmarks before going to join him.

"Any news?"

She sat close to him and kept her voice low, though the couch was in a far corner with no one within earshot.

"Our friend checked in ten minutes ago. He's gone into his room. One of our people is in the hall outside. I'm watching the elevator. Have you any suggestions?"

"I'm going to try my luck in the casino."

"Oh?" His eyebrows tilted, seeking explanation.

"There are lots of numbers on a roulette wheel. Some people play their birthdays. Others may put their chips on a different kind of date."

"I like it," he said. "Perhaps we'll meet there later."

The casino was small with, at that early hour, only one table in use. Selena gave the operator a 20-Finnmark note and received ten orange chips. There were five other people at the table—a young man in jeans and a UCLA T-shirt, an elderly couple who conferred with each other in Spanish before placing their chips, a tall, turbanned East Indian, and a sharp-featured woman of about fifty in a gray-tweed tailored suit. As the wheel spun, Selena studied the table. UCLA's chips were blue—there was one on number 7. The Spaniards had green chips on 2, 12, and 20. The Indian had put his browns on even, black and 0. The woman's yellows were on black, 25 and 36.

Selena made a mental calculation. Today was July 24. Hugh said the shipment must take place within three weeks, which made August 14 the latest possible date. So the operative number for the month would be 7 or 8 and for the day between 25 and 31 or 1 and 14.

The wheel slowed, the little ball hovered near 7, then dropped on the red 18. The croupier added a brown chip to the one on even and swept away all the others. The Spaniards conferred again, agreed to play 3, 13, and 30. UCLA put one on 27. The Indian left his doubled stake on even, dropped two chips on each black and 0. The woman put chips on red 8 and 9. "Make your plays," the croupier repeated and Selena dropped a chip on odd a second before he said, "No more." Again the Indian was the only winner as the ball stopped on 22.

On the next dozen spins Selena, alternating odd and even, won only four times while she studied the other players' patterns. UCLA, his supply of chips dwindling, bet only one at a time, alternating 7 and 27. July 27? Day after the day after tomorrow? That was calling it very close but, if the arms shipment was already en route, not impossible. Yet the rebels had gone to such lengths to cover their trail and keep their plans secret it seemed out of character to make the date announcement so obvious.

But if not UCLA, who? The Spaniards, after a final conference, eliminated themselves by gathering up their chips and leaving. The gray-suited woman each time put down three chips, one on red or black, the other two on numbers. But the numbers seemed to be chosen at random, with her yellow chips roaming the table from high to low to middle and back again. Perhaps she was a professional gambler with an intricate system. If so, it wasn't working. She won a little more than she lost on red and black, but her numbers had not yet clicked. Yet she showed no sign of tension, seemed untroubled by her diminishing pile of chips. It was as if she played only to pass the time, unconcerned as to whether she won or lost. As if—

"How're you doing, hon?" Hugh had come up behind her, falling easily into the role of hearty American tourist. "Won enough to pay our hotel bill?"

"I'm afraid not." Selena pointed to her few remaining chips. At the end of the table two men had moved into the spaces left by the Spaniards. One was Japanese, the other the rebel leader whose picture she had seen. Cactus. The Japanese bought a hundred chips and put five on each of the numbered corners. The bearded man bought only ten and put one on the number nearest him. While most eyes followed the spinning wheel, Cactus, like Selena, studied the placement of the other players' chips. He lost, played the same number again. This time the ball stopped on 27. UCLA exclaimed "Bingo!" and the croupier pushed thirty-five chips toward him. Gathering them up, he beamed at the other players as if expecting them to share his joy. Only Selena smiled back as he left the table to cash them in.

She lost her last chips on the next two spins of the wheel. "I'm wiped out," she told Hugh. "Let's go."

"I'll stake you if you want to keep playing."

"No, I've had enough."

"You're sure?" His tone was doubtful.

"Positive."

"O.K., if you say so." He accepted her decision with reluctance and moved with her toward the door. His frown lifted when he reached the lobby and, looking back, saw the bearded man come out of the casino and head for the elevator.

"Shall we take a walk?" Selena suggested.

When they were once more in the open air, Hugh tucked her hand inside his arm and they walked at a brisk pace.

"Evidently you guessed right," he conceded. "But that quick passage of information is at odds with all we were told. California played his seven and twenty-seven, then left a few minutes after Cactus came in. So he must have recognized him. And in that case—well, no matter. The important thing is, we know the date—July twenty-seventh—and we'll have to move face to get our people in place before then."

"Not that fast," she countered. "The shipment isn't due until August eleventh."

"How do you figure that?"

"The young man left because his number finally came up. He wasn't the contact. It was the woman in gray."

"I watched her too," he returned. "She was dropping chips all over the board. It's true she had eight and eleven in combination once while Cactus was watching. But she also played eight and nine, seven and thirty-one, and eight and fifteen. So how could you—or Cactus, for that matter—settle on August eleventh as the significant date?"

"You weren't there long enough to catch her pattern," Selena explained. "Most of the time she played black and with it a variety of other numbers. But every fifth or sixth spin she put a chip on red and the numbers with it were always eight and eleven. Cactus didn't have to spend much time at the table, didn't even have to know who the contact was. Red was the key and as soon as he saw her play it twice with the same two numbers, he had his answer."

"A red-letter date," Hugh summed up. "So we have two weeks' lead time. Let's go back to the hotel and I'll put out the word. Then we can have a leisurely dinner and make it a real holiday."

Reversing direction, they almost collided with the young man in the UCLA shirt.

"My fault," he apologized. "Hey, I saw you in the casino. You're American, aren't you?"

"We are," Hugh agreed. "And you must be from California."

"I'll be glad to get back there too. I take off early in the morning."

"Then you'll be home for your birthday," Selena said.

"Hey, you some kind of detective?" He stared at her. "How'd you know?—Oh, sure, you saw me playing seven and twenty-seven. It paid off for me too." He patted his pocket. "Maybe next time you'll be lucky."

THE DANCING DETECTIVE

Cornell Woolrich

Patsy Marino was clocking us as usual when I barged in through the foyer. He had to look twice at his watch to make sure it was right when he saw who it was. Or pretended he had to, anyway. It was the first time in months I'd breezed in early enough to climb into my evening dress and powder up before we were due on the dance floor.

Marino said, "What's the matter, don't you feel well?"

I snapped, "D'ya have to pass a medical examination to get in here and earn a living?" and gave him a dirty look across the frayed alley-cat I wore on my shoulder.

"The reason I ask is you're on time. Are you sure you're feeling well?" he pleaded sarcastically.

"Keep it up and you won't be," I promised, but soft-pedaled it so he couldn't quite get it. He was my bread and butter after all.

The barn looked like a morgue. It always did before eight—or so I'd heard. They didn't have any of the "pash" lights on yet, those smoky red things around the walls that gave it atmosphere. There wasn't a cat in the box, just five empty gilt chairs and the coffin. They had all the full-length windows overlooking the main drag open to get some ventilation in, too. It didn't seem like the same place at all; you could actually breathe fresh air in it!

My high heels going back to the dressing room clicked hollowly in the emptiness, and my reflection followed me upside down across the waxed floor, like a ghost. It gave me a spooky feeling, like tonight was going to be a bad night. And whenever I get a spooky feeling, it turns out to be a bad night all right.

I shoved the dressing room door in and started, "Hey, Julie, why didn't you wait for me, ya getting too high-hat?" Then I quit again.

She wasn't here either. If she wasn't at either end, where the hell was she?

Only Mom Henderson was there, reading one of tomorrow morning's tabs. "Is it that late?" she wanted to know when she saw me.

"Aw, lay off," I said. "It's bad enough I gotta go to work on a empty stomach." I slung my cat-pelt on a hook. Then I sat down and took off my pumps and dumped some foot powder in them, and put them back on again.

"I knocked on Julie's door on my way over," I said, "and didn't get any answer. We always have a cup of Java together before we come to work. I don't know how I'm going to last the full fifteen rounds—"

An unworthy suspicion crossed my mind momentarily: Did Julie purposely dodge me to get out of sharing a cup of coffee with me like I always took with her other nights? They allowed her to make it in her rooming house because it had a fire escape; they wouldn't allow me to make it in mine. I put it aside as unfair. Julie wasn't that kind; you could have had the shirt off her back—only she didn't wear a shirt, just a brassière.

"Matter?" Mom sneered. "Didn't you have a nickel on you to buy your own?"

Sure I did. Habit's a funny thing, though. Got used to taking it with a sidekick and—I didn't bother going into it with the old slob.

"I got a feeling something's going to happen tonight," I said, hunching my shoulders.

"Sure," said Mom. "Maybe you'll get fired."

I thumbed my nose at her and turned the other way around on my chair. She went back to her paper. "There haven't been any good murders lately," she lamented. "Damn it, I like a good, juicy murder wanst in a while!"

"You're building yourself up to one right in here," I scowled into the mirror at her.

She didn't take offense; she wasn't supposed to, anyway. "Was you here when that thing happened to that Southern girl, Sally, I think, was her name?"

"No!" I snapped. "Think I'm as old as you? Think I been dancing here all my life?"

"She never showed up to work one night, and they found her— That was only, let's see now . . ." she figured it out on her fingers. . . . "Three years ago."

"Cut it out!" I snarled. "I feel low enough as it is!"

Mom was warming up now. "Well, for that matter, how about the Fredericks kid? That was only a little while before you come here, wasn't it?"

"I know," I cut her short. "I remember hearing all about it. Do me a favor and let it lie."

She parked one finger up alongside her mouth. "You know," she breathed confidentially, "I've always had a funny feeling one and the same guy done away with both of them."

"If he did, I know who I wish was third on his list!" I was glowering at her, when thank God the rest of the chain gang showed up and cut the deathwatch short. The blonde came in, and then the Raymond tramp, and the Italian frail, and all the rest of them—all but Julie.

I said, "She was never as late as this before!" and they didn't even know who or what I was talking about. Or care. Great bunch.

A slush-pump started to tune up outside, so I knew the cats had come in too.

Mom Henderson got up, sighed. "Me for the white tiles and rippling waters," and waddled out to her beat.

I opened the door on a crack and peeped out, watching for Julie. The pash lights were on now and there were customers already buying tickets over the bird cage. All the other taxi dancers were lining up—but not Julie.

Somebody behind me yelled, "Close that door! Think we're giving a free show in here?"

"You couldn't interest anyone in that second-hand hide of yours even with a set of dishes thrown in!" I squelched absent-mindedly, without even turning to find out who it was. But I closed it anyway.

Marino came along and banged on it and hollered, "Outside, you in there! What do I pay you for anyway?" and somebody yelled back, "I often wonder!"

The cats exploded into a razzmatazz just then with enough oompah to be heard six blocks away, so it would pull them in off the pave. Once they were in, it was up to us. We all came out single file, to a fate worse than death, me last. They were putting the ropes up, and the mirrored tops started to go around in the ceiling and scatter flashes of light all over everything, like silver rain.

Marino said, "Where you goin', Ginger?" and when he used your front name like that it meant he wasn't kidding.

I said, "I'm going to phone Julie a minute, find out what happened to her."

"You get out there and goona-goo!" he said roughly. "She knows what time the session begins! How long's she been working here, anyway?"

"But she'll lose her job, you'll fire her," I wailed.

He hinged his watch. "She is fired already," he said flatly.

I knew how she needed that job, and when I want to do a thing I do it. A jive artist was heading my way, one of those barnacles you can't shake off once they fasten on you. I knew he was a jive, because he'd bought enough tickets to last him all week; a really wise guy only buys them from stretch to stretch. The place might burn down for all he knows.

I grabbed his ticket and tore it quick, and Marino turned and walked away. So then I pleaded, "Gimme a break, will you? Lemme make a phone call first. It won't take a second."

The jive said, "I came in here to danst."

"It's only to a girl friend," I assured him. "And I'll smile pretty at you the whole time." *(Clink! Volunteer 8-IIII.)* "And I'll make it up to you later, I promise I will." I grabbed him quick by the sleeve. "Don't go way, stand here!"

Julie's landlady answered. I said, "Did Julie Bennett come back yet?"

"I don't know," she said. "I ain't seen her since yesterday."

"Find out for me, will ya?" I begged. "She's late and she'll lose her job over here."

Marino spotted me, came back and thundered, "I thought I told you—"

I waved the half ticket in his puss. "I'm working," I said. "I'm on this gentleman's time," and I goona-gooed the jive with teeth and eyes, one hand on his arm.

He softened like ice cream in a furnace. He said, "It's all right, Mac," and felt big and chivalrous or something. About seven cents worth of his dime was gone by now.

Marino went away again, and the landlady came down from the second floor and said, "She don't answer her door, so I guess she's out."

I hung up and I said, "Something's happened to my girlfriend. She ain't there and she ain't here. She wouldn'ta quit cold without telling me."

The goona-goo was beginning to wear off the jive by this time. He fidgeted, said, "Are you gonna danst or are you gonna stand there looking blue?"

I stuck my elbows out. "Wrap yourself around this!" I barked impatiently. Just as he reached, the cats quit and the stretch was on.

He gave me a dirty look. "Ten cents shot to hell!" and he walked off to find somebody else.

I never worry about a thing after it's happened, not when I'm on the winning end anyway. I'd put my call through, even if I hadn't found out anything. I got back under the ropes, and kept my fingers crossed to ward off garlic eaters.

By the time the next stretch began, I knew Julie wasn't coming any more that night. Marino wouldn't have let her stay even if she had, and I couldn't have helped her get around him any more, by then, myself. I kept worrying, wondering what had happened to her, and that creepy feeling about tonight being a bad night came over me stronger than ever, and I couldn't shake it off no matter how I goona-gooed.

The cold orangeade they kept buying me during the stretches didn't brace me up any either. I wasn't allowed to turn it down, because Marino got a cut out of the concession profits.

The night was like most of the others, except I missed Julie. I'd been more friendly with her than the rest of the girls, because she was on the square. I had the usual run of freaks.

"With the feet, with the feet," I said wearily, "lay off the belt-buckle crowding."

"What am I supposed to do, build a retaining wall between us?"

"You're supposed to stay outside the three-mile limit," I flared, "and not try to go mountain climbing in the middle of the floor. Do I look like an Alp?" And I glanced around to see if I could catch Marino's eye.

The guy quit pawing. Most of them are yellow like that. But on the other hand, if a girl complains too often, the manager begins to figure her for a troublemaker. "Wolf!" you know, so it don't pay.

It was about twelve when they showed up, and I'd been on the floor three and a half hours straight, with only one more to go. There are worse ways of earning a living. You name them. I knew it was about twelve because Duke, the front man, had just wound up "The Lady Is a Tramp," and I knew the sequence of his numbers and could tell the time of night by them, like a sailor can by bells. Wacky, eh? Half-past—"Limehouse Blues."

I gandered at them when I saw them come into the foyer, because customers seldom come in that late. Not enough time left to make it worth the general admission fee. There were two of them; one was a fat, bloated little guy, the kind we call a "belly-wopper," the other was a pip. He wasn't tall, dark and handsome because he was medium height, light haired and clean-cut looking without being pretty about it, but if I'd had any dreams left he coulda moved right into them. Well, I didn't, so I headed for the dressing room to count up my ticket stubs while the stretch was on; see how I was making out. Two cents out of every dime when you turn them in.

They were standing there sizing the barn up, and they'd called Marino over to them. Then the three of them turned around and looked at me just as I made the door, and Marino thumbed me. I headed over to find out what was up. Duke's next was a rhumba, and I said to myself, "If I draw the kewpie, I'm going to have kittens all over the floor."

Marino said, "Get your things, Ginger." I thought one of them was going to take me out; they're allowed to do that, you know, only they've got to make it up with the management for taking you out of circulation. It's not as bad as it sounds, you can still stay on the up and up, sit with them in some laundry and listen to their troubles. It's all up to you yourself.

I got the back-yard sable and got back just in time to hear Marino say something about, "Will I have to go bail for her?"

Fat said, "Naw, naw, we just want her to build up the background a little for us."

Then I tumbled, got jittery, squawked, "What is this, a pinch? What've I done? Where you taking me?"

Marino soothed, "They just want you to go with them, Ginger. You be a good girl and do like they ast." Then he said something to them I couldn't figure. "Try to keep the place here out of it, will you, fellas? I been in the red for six months, as it is."

I cowered along between them like a lamb being led to the slaughter, looking from one to the other. "Where you taking me?" I wailed, going down the stairs.

Maiden's Prayer answered, in the cab. "To Julie Bennett's, Ginger." They'd gotten my name from Marino, I guess.

"What's she done?" I half sobbed.

"May as well tell her now, Nick," Fat suggested. "Otherwise she'll take it big when we get there."

Nick said, quietly as he could, "Your friend Julie met up with some tough luck, babe." He took his finger and he passed it slowly across his neck.

I took it big right there in the cab, Fat to the contrary. "Ah, no!" I whispered, holding my head. "She was on the floor with me only last night! Just this time last night we were in the dressing room together having a smoke, having some laughs! No! She was my only friend." And I started to bawl like a two-year-old, straight down my makeup onto the cab floor.

Finally this Nick, after acting embarrassed as hell, took a young tent out of his pocket, said, "Have yourself a time on this, babe."

I was still working on it when I went up the rooming-house stairs sandwiched between them. I recoiled just outside the door. "Is she—is she still in there?"

"Naw, you won't have to look at her," Nick reassured me.

I didn't, because she wasn't in there anymore, but it was worse than if she had been. Oh God, that sheet, with one tremendous streak down it as if a chicken had been—! I swiveled, played puss-in-the-corner with the first thing I came up against, which happened to be this Nick guy's chest.

He sort of stood still like he liked the idea. Then he growled, "Turn that damn thing over out of sight, will you?"

The questioning, when I was calm enough to take it, wasn't a grill, don't get that idea. It was just, as they'd said, to fill out her background. "When was the last time you saw her alive? Did she go around much, y'know what we mean? She have any particular steady?"

"I left her outside the house door downstairs at one-thirty this morning, last night, or whatever you call it," I told them. "We walked home together from Joyland right after the session wound up. She didn't go around at all. She never dated the boys afterwards and neither did I."

The outside half of Nick's left eyebrow hitched up at this, like when a terrier cocks its ear at something. "Notice anyone follow the two of you?"

"In our racket they always do; it usually takes about five blocks to wear them out, though, and this is ten blocks from Joyland."

"You walk after you been on your pins all night?" Fat asked, aghast.

"We should take a cab, on our earnings! About last night, I can't swear no one followed us, because I didn't look around. That's a come-on, if you do that."

Nick said, "I must remember that," absent-mindedly.

I got up my courage, faltered, "Did it—did it happen right in here?"

"Here's how it went: She went out again after she left you the first time—"

"I knew her better than that!" I yipped. "Don't start that, Balloon Lungs, or I'll let you have this across the snout!" I swung my cat-piece at him.

He grabbed up a little box, shook it in my face. "For this," he said. "Aspirin! Don't try to tell us different, when we've already checked with the all-night drugstore over on Sixth!" He took a couple of heaves, cooled off, sat down again. "She went out, but instead of locking the house door behind her, she was too lazy or careless; shoved a wad of paper under it to hold it on a crack till she got back. In that five minutes or less, somebody who was watching from across the street slipped in and lay in wait for her in the upper hallway out here. He was too smart to go for her on the open street, where she might have had a chance to yell."

"How'd he know she was coming back?"

"The unfastened door woulda told him that; also the drug clerk tells us she showed up there fully dressed, but with her bare feet stuck in a pair of carpet slippers to cool 'em. The killer musta spotted that too."

"Why didn't she yell out here in the house, with people sleeping all around her in the different rooms?" I wondered out loud.

"He grabbed her too quick for that, grabbed her by the throat just as she was opening her room door, dragged her in, closed the door, finished strangling her on the other side of it. He remembered later to come out and pick up the aspirins which had dropped and rolled all over out there. All but one, which he overlooked and we found. She wouldn't've stopped to take one outside her door. That's how we know about that part of it."

I kept seeing that sheet, which was hidden now, before me all over again. I couldn't help it, I didn't want to know, but still I had to know. "But if he strangled her, where did all that blood—" I gestured sickly, "come from?"

Fat didn't answer, I noticed. He shut up all at once, as if he didn't want to tell me the rest of it, and looked kind of sick himself. His eyes gave him away. I almost could have been a detective myself, the way I pieced the rest of it together just by following his eyes around the room. He didn't know I was reading them, or he wouldn't have let them stray like that.

First they rested on the little portable phonograph she had there on a table. By using bamboo needles she could play it late at night, soft, and no one would hear it. The lid was up and there was a record on the turntable, but the needle was worn down half-way, all shredded, as though it had been played over and over.

Then his eyes went to a flat piece of paper, on which were spread out eight or ten shiny new dimes; I figured they'd been put aside like that, on paper, for evidence. Some of them had little brown flecks on them, bright as they were. Then lastly his eyes went down to the rug; it was all pleated up in places, especially along the edges, as though something heavy, inert, had been dragged back and forth over it.

My hands flew up to my head and I nearly went wacky with horror. I gasped it out because I hoped he'd say no, but he didn't so it was yes. "You mean he danced with her *after* she was gone? Gave her dead body a dime each time, stabbed her over and over while he did?"

There was no knife, or whatever it had been, left around, so either they'd already sent it down for prints or *he'd* taken it out with him again.

The thought of what must have gone on here in this room, of the death dance that must have taken place. . . . All I knew was that I wanted to get out of here into the open, couldn't stand it any more. Yet before I lurched out, with Nick holding me by the elbow, I couldn't resist glancing at the label of the record on the portable. "Poor Butterfly."

Stumbling out the door I managed to say, "She didn't put that on there. She hated that piece, called it a drip. I remember once I was up here with her and started to play it, and she snatched it off, said she couldn't stand it, wanted to bust it then and there but I kept her from doing it. She was off love and men, and it's a sort of mushy piece, that was why. She didn't buy it, they were all thrown in with the machine when she picked it up second hand."

"Then we know his favorite song, if that means anything. If she couldn't stand it, it would be at the bottom of the stack of records, not near the top. He went to the trouble of skimming through them to find something he liked."

"With her there in his arms, already!" That thought was about the finishing touch, on top of all the other horror. We were on the stairs going down, and the ground floor seemed to come rushing up to meet me. I could feel Nick's arm hook around me just in time, like an anchor, and then I did a clothespin act over it. And that was the first time I didn't mind being pawed.

When I could see straight again, he was holding me propped up on a stool in front of a lunch counter a couple doors down, holding a cup of coffee to my lips.

"How's Ginger?" he said gently.

"Fine," I dribbled mournfully all over my lap. "How's Nick?"

And on that note the night of Julie Bennett's murder came to an end.

Joyland dance hall was lonely next night. I came in late, and chewing cloves, and for once Marino didn't crack his whip over me. Maybe even he had a heart. "Ginger," was all he said as I went hurrying by, "don't talk about it while you're on the hoof, get me? If anyone asks you, you don't know nothing about it. It's gonna kill business."

Duke, the front man, stopped me on my way to the dressing room. "I hear they took you over there last night," he started.

"Nobody took nobody nowhere, schmaltz," I snapped. He wore feathers on his neck, that's why I called him that; it's the word for long-haired musicians in our lingo.

I missed her worse in the dressing room than I was going to later on out in the barn; there'd be a crowd out there around me, and noise and music, at least. In here it was like her ghost was powdering its nose alongside me at the mirror the whole time. The peg for hanging up her things still had her name penciled under it.

Mom Henderson was having herself a glorious time; you couldn't hear yourself think, she was jabbering away so. She had two tabloids with her tonight, instead of just one, and she knew every word in all of them by heart. She kept leaning over the gals' shoulders, puffing down their necks: "And there was a dime balanced on each of her eyelids when they found her, and another one across her lips, and he stuck one in each of her palms and folded her fingers over it, mind ye! D'ye ever hear of anything like it? Boy, he sure must've been down on you taxis—"

I yanked the door open, planted my foot where it would do the most good, and shot her out into the barn. She hadn't moved that fast from one place to another in twenty years. The other girls just looked at me, and then at one another, as much as to say, "Touchy, isn't she?"

"Get outside and break it down; what do I pay you for anyway?" Marino yelled at the door. A gob-stick tootled plaintively, out we trooped like prisoners in a lock step, and another damn night had started in.

I came back in again during the tenth stretch. ("Dinah" and "Have You Any Castles, Baby?") to take off my kicks a minute and have a smoke. Julie's ghost came around me again. I could still hear her voice in my ears, from night-before-last! "Hold that match, Gin. I'm trying to duck a cement-mixer out there. Dances like a slap-happy pug. Three little steps to the right, as if he were priming for a standing broad-jump. I felt like screaming, For Pete's sake, if you're gonna jump, jump!"

And me, "What're you holding your hand for, been dancing upside down?"

"It's the way he holds it. Bends it back on itself and folds it under. Like this, look. My wrist's nearly broken. And look what his ring did to me!" She had shown me a strawberry-sized bruise.

Sitting there alone, now, in the half-light, I said to myself, "I bet *he* was the one! I bet *that's* who it was! Oh, if I'd only gotten a look at him, if I'd only had her point him out to me! If he enjoyed hurting her that much while she was still alive, he'd have enjoyed dancing with her after she was dead." My cigarette tasted rotten, I threw it down and got out of there in a hurry, back into the crowd.

A ticket was shoved at me and I ripped it without looking up. Gliding backward, all the way around on the other side of the barn, a voice finally said a little over my ear, "How's Ginger?"

I looked up and saw who it was, said, "What're you doing here?"

"Detailed here," Nick said.

I shivered to the music. "Do you expect him to show up *again,* after what he's done already?"

"He's a dance-hall killer," Nick said. "He killed Sally Arnold and the Fredericks girl, both from this same mill, and he killed a girl in Chicago in between. The prints on Julie Bennett's phonograph records match those in two of the other cases, and in the third case—where there were no prints—the girl was holding a dime clutched in her hand. He'll show up again sooner or later. There's one of us cops detailed to every one of these mills in the metropolitan area tonight, and we're going to keep it up until he does."

"How do you know what he looks like?" I asked.

He didn't answer for a whole bar. "We don't," he admitted finally. "That's the hell of it. Talk about being invisible in a crowd! We only know he isn't through yet, he'll keep doing it until we get him!"

I said, "He was here that night, he was right up here on this floor with her that night, before it happened; I'm sure of it!" And I sort of moved in closer. Me, who was always griping about being held too tight. I told him about the impression the guy's ring had left on her hand, and the peculiar way he'd held it, and the way he'd danced.

"You've got something there," he said, and left me flat on the floor and went over to phone it in.

Nick picked me up again next dance.

He said, shuffling off, "That was him all right who danced with her. They found a freshly made impression still on her hand, a little offside from the first, which was almost entirely obliterated by then. Meaning the second had been made after death, and therefore stayed uneffaced, just like a pinhole won't close up in the skin after death. They made an impression of it with moulage, my lieutenant just tells me. Then they filled that up with wax, photographed it through a magnifying lens, and now we know what kind of a ring he's wearing. A seal ring shaped like a shield, with two little jewel splinters, one in the upper right-hand corner, the other in the lower left."

"Any initials on it?" I gaped, awestricken.

"Nope, but something just as good. He can't get it off, unless he has a jeweler or locksmith file it off, and he'll be afraid to do that now. The fact that it would press so deeply into her hand proves that he can't get it off, the flesh of his finger has grown around it; otherwise it would have had a little give to it, the pressure would have shifted the head of it around a little."

He stepped all over my foot, summed up, "So we know how he dances, know what his favorite song is, 'Poor Butterfly,' know what kind of ring he's wearing. And we know he'll be back sooner or later."

That was all well and good, but I had my own health to look out for; the way my foot was throbbing! I hinted gently as I could, "You can't do very much watching out for him, can you, if you keep dancing around like this?"

"Maybe you think I can't. And if I just stand there with my back to the wall it's a dead giveaway. He'd smell me a mile away and duck out again. Keep it quiet what I'm doing here, don't pass it around. Your boss knows, of course, but it's to his interest to cooperate. A screwball like that can put an awful dent in his receipts."

"You're talking to the original sphinx," I assured him. "I don't pal with the rest of these twists anyway. Julie was the only one I was ever chummy with."

When the session closed and I came downstairs to the street, Nick was hanging around down there with the other lizards. He came over to me and took my arm and steered me off like he owned me.

"What's this?" I said.

He said, "This is just part of the act, make it look like the McCoy."

"Are you sure?" I said to myself, and I winked to myself without him seeing me.

All the other nights from then on were just a carbon copy of that one, and they started piling up by sevens. Seven, fourteen, twenty-one. Pretty soon it was a month since Julie Bennett had died. And not a clue as to who the killer was, where he was, what he looked like. Not a soul had noticed him that night at Joyland, too heavy a crowd. Just having his prints on file was no good by itself.

She was gone from the papers long ago, and she was gone from the dressing room chatter, too, after a while, as forgotten as though she'd never lived. Only me, I remembered her, because she'd been my pal. And Nick Ballestier, he did because that was his job. I suppose Mom Henderson did too, because she had a morbid mind and loved to linger on gory murders. But outside of us three, nobody cared.

They did it the wrong way around, Nick's superiors at Homicide, I mean. I didn't try to tell him that, because he would have laughed at me. He would have said, "Sure! A dance-mill pony knows more about running the police department than the commissioner does himself! Why don't you go down there and show 'em how to do it?"

But what I mean is, the dance mills didn't need all that watching in the beginning, the first few weeks after it happened, like they gave them. Maniac or not, anyone would have known he wouldn't show up *that* soon after. They needn't have bothered detailing anyone at all to watch the first few weeks. He was lying low then. It was only after a month or so that they should have begun watching real closely for him. Instead they did it just the reverse. For a whole month Nick was there nightly. Then after that he just looked in occasionally, every second night or so, without staying through the whole session.

Then finally I tumbled that he'd been taken off the case entirely and was just coming for—er, the atmosphere. I put it up to him unexpectedly one night. "Are you still supposed to come around here like this?"

He got all red, admitted, "Naw, we were all taken off this duty long ago. I—er, guess I can't quit because I'm in the habit now or something."

"Oh, yeah?" I said to myself knowingly. I wouldn't have minded that so much, only his dancing didn't get any better, and the wear and tear on me was something awful. It was like trying to steer a steamroller around the place.

"Nick," I finally pleaded one night, when he pinned me down flat with one of his size twelves and then tried to push me out from under with the rest of him, "be a detective all over the place, only please don't ask me to dance anymore, I can't take it."

He looked innocently surprised. "Am I that bad?"

I tried to cover up with a smile at him. He'd been damn nice to me even if he couldn't dance.

When he didn't show up at all next night, I thought maybe I'd gone a little too far, offended him maybe. But the big hulk hadn't looked like the kind that was sensitive about his dancing, or anything else for that matter. I brought myself up short with a swift, imaginary kick in the pants at this point. "What the heck's the matter with *you?*" I said to myself. "You going soft? Didn't I tell you never to do that!" And I reached for the nearest ticket, and tore it, and I goona-gooed with a, "Grab yourself an armful, mister, it's your dime."

I got through that night somehow but I had that same spooky feeling the next night like I'd had *that* night—like tonight was going to be a bad night. Whenever I get that spooky feeling, it turns out to be a bad night all right. I tried to tell myself it was because Nick wasn't around. I'd got used to him, that was all, and now he'd quit coming, and the hell with it. But the feeling wouldn't go away. Like something was going to happen, before the night was over. Something bad.

Mom Henderson was sitting in there reading tomorrow morning's tab. "There hasn't been any good juicy murders lately," she mourned over the top of it. "Damn it, I like a good murder y'can get your teeth into wanst in awhile!"

"Ah, dry up, you ghoul!" I snapped. I took off my shoes and dumped powder into them, put them on again. Marino came and knocked on the door. "Outside, freaks! What do I pay you for anyway?"

Someone jeered, "I often wonder!" and Duke, the front man, started to gliss over the coffin, and we all came out single file, me last, to a fate worse than death.

I didn't look up at the first buyer, just stared blindly at a triangle of shirtfront level with my eyes. It kept on like that for a while; always that same triangle of shirtfront. Mostly white, but sometimes blue, and once it was lavender, and I wondered if I ought to lead. The pattern of the tie across it kept changing too, but that was all.

"Butchers and barbers and rats from the harbors
Are the sweethearts my good luck has brought me."

"Why so downcast, Beautiful?"

"If you were standing where I am, looking where you are, you'd be downcast too."

That took care of him. And then the stretch.

Duke went into a waltz, and something jarred for a minute. My timetable. This should have been a gut bucket (low-down swing music) and it wasn't. He'd switched numbers on me, that's what it was. Maybe a request. For waltzes they killed the pash lights and turned on a blue circuit instead, made the place cool and dim with those flecks of silver from the mirror-top raining down.

I'd had this white shirt-triangle with the diamond pattern before; I remembered the knitted tie, with one tier unraveled on the end. I didn't want to see the face, too much trouble to look up. I hummed the piece mentally, to give my blank mind something to do. Then words seemed to drop into it, fit themselves to it, of their own accord, without my trying, so they must have belonged to it. "Poor butterfly by the blossoms waiting."

My hand ached, he was holding it so darned funny. I squirmed it, tried to ease it, and he held on all the tighter. He had it bent down and back on itself. . . .

"The moments pass into hours—"

Gee, if there's one thing I hate it's a guy with a ring that holds your mitt in a straitjacket! And he didn't know the first thing about waltzing. Three funny little hops to the right, over and over and over. It was getting my nerves on edge. "If you're gonna jump, jump!" Julie's voice came back to me from long ago. She'd run into the same kind of a—

"I just must die, poor butterfly!"

Suddenly I was starting to get a little scared and a whole lot excited. I kept saying to myself, "Don't look up at him, you'll give yourself away." I kept my eyes on the knitted tie that had one tier unraveled. The lights went white and the stretch came on. We separated, he turned his back on me and I turned mine on him. We walked away from each other without a word. They don't thank you, they're paying for it.

I counted five and then I looked back over my shoulder, to try to see what he was like. He looked back at me at the same time, and we met each other's looks. I managed to slap on a smile, as though I'd only looked back because he'd made a hit with me, and that I hoped he'd come around again.

There was nothing wrong with his face, not just to look at anyway. It was no worse than any of the others around. He was about forty, maybe forty-five, hair still dark. Eyes speculative, nothing else, as they met mine. But he didn't answer my fake smile, maybe he could see through it. We both turned away again and went about our business.

I looked down at my hand, to see what made it hurt so. Careful not to raise it, careful not to bend my head, in case he was still watching. Just dropped my eyes to it. There was a red bruise the size of a small strawberry on it, from where his ring had pressed into it the whole time. I knew enough not to go near the box. I caught Duke's eye from where I was and hitched my head at him, and we got together sort of casually over along the wall.

"What'd you play 'Poor Butterfly' for that last time?" I asked.

"Request number," he said.

I said, "Don't point, and don't look around, but whose request was it?"

He didn't have to. "The guy that was with you the last two times. Why?" I didn't answer, so then he said, "I get it." He didn't at all. "All right, chiseler," he said, and handed me two dollars and a half, splitting a fiver the guy had slipped him to play it. Duke thought I was after a kickback.

I took it. It was no good to tell him. What could he do? Nick Ballestier was the one to tell. I broke one of the singles at the orangeade concession—for nickels. Then I started to work my way over toward the phone, slow and aimless. I was within a yard of it when the cats started up again!

And suddenly *he* was right next to me, he must have been behind me the whole time.

"Were you going anyplace?" he asked.

I thought I saw his eyes flick to the phone, but I wasn't positive. One thing sure, there wasn't speculation in them any more, there was—decision.

"No place," I said meekly. "I'm at your disposal." I thought, "If I can only hold him here long enough, maybe Nick'll show up."

Then just as we got to the ropes, he said, "Let's skip this. Let's go out to a laundry and sit a while."

I said, smooth on the surface, panic stricken underneath, "But I've already torn your ticket, don't you want to finish this one out at least?" And tried to goona-goo him for all I was worth, but it wouldn't take. He turned around and flagged Marino, to get his O.K.

His back was to me, and across his shoulder I kept shaking my head, more and more violently, to Marino—no, no, I don't want to go with him. Marino just ignored me. It meant more money in his pocket this way.

When I saw that the deal was going through, I turned like a streak, made the phone, got my buffalo in. It was no good trying to tell Marino, he wouldn't believe me, he'd think I was just making it up to get out of going out with the guy. Or if I raised the alarm on my own, he'd simply duck down the stairs before anyone could stop him and vanish again. Nick was the only one to tell, Nick was the only one who'd know how to nail him here.

I said, "Police headquarters, quick! Quick!" and turned and looked over across the barn. But Marino was already alone out there. I couldn't see where the guy had gone, they were milling around so, looking over their prospects for the next one.

A voice came on and I said, "Is Nick Ballestier there? Hurry up, get him for me."

Meanwhile Duke had started to break it down again; real corny. It must have carried over the open wire. I happened to raise my eyes, and there was a shadow on the wall in front of me, coming across my shoulders from behind me. I didn't move, held steady, listening.

I said, "All right, Peggy, I just wanted to know when you're gonna pay me back that five bucks you owe me," and I killed it.

Would he get it when they told him? They'd say, "A girl's voice asked for you, Nick, from somewhere where there was music going on, and we couldn't make any sense out of what she said, and she hung up without waiting." A pretty slim thread to hold all your chances on.

I stood there afraid to turn. His voice said stonily, "Get your things, let's go. Suppose you don't bother any more tonight about your five dollars." There was a hidden meaning, a warning, in it.

There was no window in the dressing room, no other way out but the way I'd come in, and he was right there outside the door. I poked around all I could, mourning, "Why don't Nick come?" and, boy, I was scared. A crowd all around me and no one to help me. He wouldn't stay; the only way to hang onto him for Nick was to go with him and pray for luck. I kept casing him through the crack of the door every minute or so. I didn't think he saw me, but he must have. Suddenly his heel scuffed at it brutally, and made me jump about an inch off the floor.

"Quit playing peek-a-boo, I'm waiting out here!" he called in sourly.

I grabbed up Mom Henderson's tab and scrawled across it in lipstick: "Nick: He's taking me with him, and I don't know where to. Look for my ticket stubs. Ginger."

Then I scooped up all the half tickets I'd accumulated all night long and shoved them loose into the pocket of my coat. Then I came sidling out to him. I thought I heard the phone on the wall starting to ring, but the music was so loud I couldn't be sure. We went downstairs and out on the street.

A block away I said, "There's a joint. We all go there a lot from our place," and pointed to Chan's. He said "Shut up!" I dropped one of the dance checks on the sidewalk. Then I began making a regular trail of them.

The neon lights started to get fewer and fewer, and pretty soon we were in a network of dark lonely sidestreets. My pocket was nearly empty now of tickets. My luck was he didn't take a cab. He didn't want anyone to remember the two of us together, I guess.

I pleaded, "Don't make me walk any more, I'm awfully tired."

He said, "We're nearly there, it's right ahead." The sign on the next corner up fooled me; there was a chop-suey joint, there, only a second-class laundry, but I thought that was where we were going.

But in between us and it there was a long dismal block, with tumble-down houses and vacant lots on it. And I'd run out of dance checks. All my take gone, just to keep alive. He must have worked out the whole set-up carefully ahead of time, known I'd fall for that sign in the distance that we *weren't* going to.

Sure, I could have screamed out at any given step of the way, collected a crowd around us. But you don't understand. Much as I wanted to get away from him, there was one thing I wanted even more: To hold him for Nick. I didn't just want him to slip away into the night, and then do it all over again at some future date. And that's what would happen if I raised a row. They wouldn't believe me in a pinch, they'd think it was some kind of a shakedown on my part. He'd talk himself out of it or scram before a cop came.

You have to live at night like I did to know the real callousness of passersby on the street, how seldom they'll horn in, lift a finger to help you. Even a harness cop wouldn't be much good, would only weigh my story against his, end up by sending us both about our business.

Maybe the thought came to me because I spotted a cop ahead just then, loitering toward us. I could hardly make him out in the gloom, but the slow steady walk told me. I didn't really think I was going to do it until we came abreast of him.

The three of us met in front of a boarded-up condemned house. Then, as though I saw my last chance slipping away—because Nick couldn't bridge the gap between me and the last of the dance checks any more, it was too wide—I stopped dead.

I began in a low tense voice, "Officer, this man here—"

Julie's murderer had involuntarily gone on a step without me. That put him to the rear of the cop. The whole thing was so sudden, it must have been one of those knives that shot out of their own hilts. The cop's eyes rolled, I could see them white in the darkness, and he coughed right in my face, warm, and he started to come down on top of me, slow and lazy. I sidestepped and he fell with a soft thud and rocked a couple of times with his own fall and then lay still.

But the knife was already out of him long ago, and its point was touching my side. And where the cop had been a second ago, *he* was now. We were alone together again.

He said in a cold, unexcited voice, "Go ahead, scream, and I'll give it to you right across him."

I didn't, I just pulled in all my breath.

He said, "Go ahead, down there," and steered me with his knife down a pair of steps into the dark areaway of the boarded-up house it had happened in front of. "Stand there, and if you make a sound—you know what I told you." Then he did something to the cop with his feet, and the cop came rolling down into the areaway after me.

I shrank back and my back was against the boarded-up basement door.

It moved a little behind me. I thought, "This must be where he's taking me. If it is, then it's open." I couldn't get out past him, but maybe I could get *in* away from him.

I turned and clawed at the door, and the whole framed barrier swung out a little, enough to squeeze in through. He must have been hiding out in here, coming and going through here, all these weeks. No wonder they hadn't found him.

The real basement door behind it had been taken down out of the way. He'd seen what I was up to, and he was already wriggling through the gap after me. I was stumbling down a pitch-black hallway by then.

I found stairs going up by falling down on top of them full length. I sobbed, squirmed up the first few on hands and knees, straightened up as I went.

He stopped to light a match. I didn't have any, but his helped me too, showed me the outline of things. I was on the first-floor hall now, flitting down it. I didn't want to go up too high, he'd only seal me in some dead end up there, but I couldn't stand still down here.

A broken-down chair grazed the side of my leg as I went by, and I turned, swung it up bodily, went back a step and pitched it down over the stairwell on top of him. I don't know if it hurt him at all but his match went out.

He said a funny thing then. "You always had a temper, Muriel."

I didn't stand there listening. I'd seen an opening in the wall farther ahead, before the match went out. Just a blackness. I dived through it and all the way across with swimming motions, until I hit a jutting mantel slab over some kind of fireplace. I crouched down and tucked myself in under it. It was one of those huge old-fashioned ones. I groped over my head and felt an opening there, lined with rough brickwork and furry with cobwebs, but it wasn't wide enough to climb up through. I squeezed into a corner of the fireplace and prayed he wouldn't spot me.

He'd lit another match, and it came into the room after me, but I could only see his legs from the fireplace opening, it cut him off at the waist. I wondered if he could see me; he didn't come near where I was.

The light got a little stronger, and he'd lit a candle stump. But still his legs didn't come over to me, didn't bend down, or show his face peering in at me. His legs just kept moving to and fro around the room. It was awfully hard, after all that running, to keep my breath down.

Finally he said out loud, "Chilly in here," and I could hear him rattling newspapers, getting them together. It didn't sink in for a minute what was going to happen next. I thought, "Has he forgotten me? Is he that crazy? Am I going to get away with it?" But there'd been a malicious snicker in his remark; he was crazy like a fox.

Suddenly his legs came over straight to me, without bending down to look he was stuffing the papers in beside me. I couldn't see out any more past them. I heard the scrape of a match against the floor boards. Then there was the momentary silence of combustion. I was sick, I wanted to die quick, but I didn't want to die that way. There was the hum of rising flame, and a brightness just before me, the papers all turned gold. I thought, "Oh, Nick! Nick! Here I go!"

I came plunging out, scattering sparks and burning newspapers.

He said, smiling, pleased with himself, casual, "Hello, Muriel. I thought you didn't have any more use for me? What are you doing in my house?" He still had the knife—with the cop's blood on it.

I said, "I'm not Muriel, I'm Ginger Allen from the Joyland. Oh, mister, please let me get out of here, please let me go!" I was so scared and so sick I went slowly to my knees. "Please!" I cried up at him.

He said, still in that casual way, "Oh, so you're not Muriel? You didn't marry me the night before I embarked for France, thinking I'd be killed, that you'd never see me again, that you'd get my soldier's pension?" And then getting a little more vicious, "But I fooled you, I was shellshocked but I didn't die. I came back even if it was on a stretcher. And what did I find? You hadn't even waited to find out! You'd married another guy and you were both living on my pay. You tried to make it up to me, though, didn't you, Muriel? Sure; you visited me in the hospital, bringing me jelly. The man in the next cot died from eating it. Muriel, I've looked for you high and low ever since, and now I've found you."

He moved backwards, knife still in hand, and stood aside, and there was an old battered relic of a phonograph standing there on an empty packing case. It had a great big horn to it, to give it volume. He must have picked it up off some ash heap, repaired it himself. He released the catch and cranked it up a couple of times and laid the needle into the groove.

"We're going to dance, Muriel, like we did that night when I was in my khaki uniform and you were so pretty to look at. But it's going to have a different ending this time."

He came back toward me. I was still huddled there, shivering. "No!" I moaned. "Not me! You killed her, you killed her over and over again. Only last month, don't you remember?"

He said with pitiful simplicity, like the tortured thing he was, "Each time I think I have, she rises up again." He dragged me to my feet and caught me to him, and the arm with the knife went around me, and the knife pressed into my side.

The horrid thing over there was blaring into the emptiness, loud enough to be heard out on the street: "Poor Butterfly." It was horrible, it was ghastly.

And in the candle-lit pallor, with great shadows of us looming on the wall, like two crazed things we started to go round and round. I couldn't hold my head up on my neck; it hung way back over my shoulders like an overripe apple. My hair got loose and went streaming out as he pulled me and turned me and dragged me around. . . .

"I just must die, poor butterfly!"

Still holding me to him, he reached in his pocket and brought out a palmful of shiny dimes, and flung them in my face.

Then a shot went off outside in front of the house. It sounded like right in the areaway where the knifed cop was. Then five more in quick succession. The blare of the music must have brought the stabbed cop to. He must've got help.

He turned his head toward the boarded-up windows to listen. I tore myself out of his embrace, stumbled backwards, and the knife point seemed to leave a long circular scratch around my side, but he didn't jam it in in time, let it trail off me.

I got out into the hall before he could grab me again, and the rest of it was just kind of a flight nightmare. I don't remember going down the stairs to the basement; I think I must have fallen down them without hurting myself—just like a drunk does.

Down there a headlight came at me from the tunnel-like passage. It must have been just a pocket torch, but it got bigger and bigger, then went hurling on by. Behind it a long succession of serge-clothed figures brushed by me.

I kept trying to stop each one, saying, "Where's Nick? Are you Nick?"

Then a shot sounded upstairs. I heard a terrible death cry. "Muriel!" and that was all.

When I next heard anything it was Nick's voice. His arm was around me and he was kissing the cobwebs and tears off my face.

"How's Ginger?" he asked.

"Fine," I said, "and how's Nick?"

LUCKY PENNY

Linda Barnes

Lieutenant Mooney made me dish it all out for the record. He's a good cop, if such an animal exists. We used to work the same shift before I decided—wrongly—that there was room for a lady P.I. in this town. Who knows? With this case under my belt, maybe business'll take a 180-degree spin, and I can quit driving a hack.

See, I've already written the official report for Mooney and the cops, but the kind of stuff they wanted: date, place, and time, cold as ice and submitted in triplicate, doesn't even start to tell the tale. So I'm doing it over again, my way.

Don't worry, Mooney. I'm not gonna file this one.

The Thayler case was still splattered across the front page of the *Boston Globe*. I'd soaked it up with my midnight coffee and was puzzling it out—my cab on automatic pilot, my mind on crime—when the mad tea party began.

"Take your next right, sister. Then pull over, and douse the lights. Quick!"

I heard the bastard all right, but it must have taken me thirty seconds or so to react. Something hard rapped on the cab's dividing shield. I didn't bother turning around. I hate staring down gun barrels.

I said, "Jimmy Cagney, right? No, your voice is too high. Let me guess, don't tell me—"

"Shut up!"

"*Kill* the lights, *turn off* the lights, okay. But *douse* the lights? You've been tuning in too many old gangster flicks."

"I hate a mouthy broad," the guy snarled. I kid you not.

"*Broad,*" I said. "Christ! *Broad?* You trying to grow hair on your balls?"

"Look, I mean it, lady!"

"*Lady's* better. Now you wanna vacate my cab and go rob a phone booth?" My heart was beating like a tin drum, but I didn't let my voice shake, and all the time I was gabbing at him, I kept trying to catch his face in the mirror. He must have been crouching way back on the passenger side. I couldn't see a damn thing.

"I want all your dough," he said.

Who can you trust? This guy was a spiffy dresser: charcoal-gray three-piece suit and rep tie, no less. And picked up in front of the swank Copley Plaza. I looked like I needed the bucks more than he did, and I'm no charity case. A woman can make good tips driving a hack in Boston. Oh, she's gotta take precautions, all right. When you can't smell a disaster fare from thirty feet, it's time to quit. I pride myself on my judgment. I'm careful. I always know where the police checkpoints are, so I can roll my cab past and flash the old lights if a guy starts acting up. This dude fooled me cold.

I was ripped. Not only had I been conned, I had a considerable wad to give away. It was near the end of my shift, and like I said, I do all right. I've got a lot of regulars. Once you see me, you don't forget me—or my cab.

It's gorgeous. Part of my inheritance. A '59 Chevy, shiny as new, kept on blocks in a heated garage by the proverbial dotty old lady. It's the pits of the design world. Glossy blue with those giant chromium fins. Restrained decor: just the phone number and a few gilt curlicues on the door. I was afraid all my old pals at the police department would pull me over for minor traffic violations if I went whole hog and painted "Carlotta's Cab" in ornate script on the hood. Some do it anyway.

So where the hell were all the cops now? Where are they when you need 'em?

He told me to shove the cash through that little hole they leave for the passenger to pass the fare forward. I told him he had it backwards. He didn't laugh. I shoved bills.

"Now the change," the guy said. Can you imagine the nerve?

I must have cast my eyes up to heaven. I do that a lot these days.

"I mean it." He rapped the plastic shield with the shiny barrel of his gun. I checked it out this time. Funny how big a little .22 looks when its pointed just right.

I fished in my pockets for change, emptied them.

"Is that all?"

"You want the gold cap on my left front molar?" I said.

"Turn around," the guy barked. "Keep both hands on the steering wheel. High."

I heard jingling, then a quick intake of breath.

"Okay," the crook said, sounding happy as a clam, "I'm gonna take my leave—"

"Good. Don't call this cab again."

"Listen!" The gun tapped. "You cool it here for ten minutes. And I mean frozen. Don't twitch. Don't blow your nose. Then take off."

"Gee, thanks."

"Thank *you,*" he said politely. The door slammed.

At times like that, you just feel ridiculous. You *know* the guy isn't going to hang around, waiting to see whether you're big on insubordination. *But,* he might. And who wants to tangle with a .22 slug? I rate pretty high on insubordination. That's why I messed up as a cop. I figured I'd give him two minutes to get lost. Meantime I listened.

Not much traffic goes by those little streets on Beacon Hill at one o'clock on a Wednesday morn. Too residential. So I could hear the guy's footsteps tap along the pavement. About ten steps back, he stopped. Was he the one in a million who'd wait to see if I turned around? I heard a funny kind of whooshing noise. Not loud enough to make me jump, and anything much louder than the ticking of my watch would have put me through the roof. Then the footsteps patted on, straight back and out of hearing.

One minute more. The only saving grace of the situation was the location: District One. That's Mooney's district. Nice guy to talk to.

I took a deep breath, hoping it would have an encore, and pivoted quickly, keeping my head low. Makes you feel stupid when you do that and there's no one around.

I got out and strolled to the corner, stuck my head around a building kind of cautiously. Nothing, of course.

I backtracked. Ten steps, then whoosh. Along the sidewalk stood one of those new "Keep Beacon Hill Beautiful" trash cans, the kind with the swinging lid. I gave it a shove as I passed. I could just as easily have kicked it; I was in that kind of funk.

Whoosh, it said, just as pretty as could be.

Breaking into one of those trash cans is probably tougher than busting into your local bank vault. Since I didn't even have a dime left to fiddle the screws on the lid, I was forced to deface city property. I got the damn thing open and dumped the contents on somebody's front lawn, smack in the middle of a circle of light from one of those snooty Beacon Hill gas streetlamps.

Halfway through the whiskey bottles, wadded napkins, and beer cans,

I made my discovery. I was doing a thorough search. If you're going to stink like garbage anyway, why leave anything untouched, right? So I was opening all the brown bags—you know, the good old brown lunch-and-bottle bags—looking for a clue. My most valuable find so far had been the moldy rind of a bologna sandwich. Then I hit it big: one neatly creased bag stuffed full of cash.

To say I was stunned is to entirely underestimate how I felt as I crouched there, knee-deep in garbage, my jaw hanging wide. I don't know what I'd expected to find. Maybe the guy's gloves. Or his hat, if he'd wanted to get rid of it fast in order to melt back into anonymity. I pawed through the rest of the debris. My change was gone.

I was so befuddled I left the trash right on the front lawn. There's probably still a warrant out for my arrest.

District One Headquarters is off the beaten path, over on New Sudbury Street. I would have called first, if I'd had a dime.

One of the few things I'd enjoyed about being a cop was gabbing with Mooney. I like driving a cab better, but, face it, most of my fares aren't scintillating conversationalists. The Red Sox and the weather usually covers it. Talking to Mooney was so much fun, I wouldn't even consider dating him. Lots of guys are good at sex, but conversation—now there's an art form.

Mooney, all six-foot-four, 240 linebacker pounds of him, gave me the glad eye when I waltzed in. He hasn't given up trying. Keeps telling me he talks even better in bed.

"Nice hat," was all he said, his big fingers pecking at the typewriter keys.

I took it off and shook out my hair. I wear an old slouch cap when I drive to keep people from saying the inevitable. One jerk even misquoted Yeats at me: "Only God, my dear, could love you for yourself alone and not your long red hair." Since I'm seated when I drive, he missed the chance to ask me how the weather is up here. I'm six-one in my stocking feet and skinny enough to make every inch count twice. I've got a wide forehead, green eyes, and a pointy chin. If you want to be nice about my nose, you say it's got character.

Thirty's still hovering in my future. It's part of Mooney's past.

I told him I had a robbery to report and his dark eyes steered me to a chair. He leaned back and took a puff of one of his low-tar cigarettes. He can't quite give 'em up, but he feels guilty as hell about 'em.

When I got to the part about the bag in the trash, Mooney lost his sense of humor. He crushed a half-smoked butt in a crowded ashtray.

"Know why you never made it as a cop?" he said.

"Didn't brown-nose enough."

"You got no sense of proportion! Always going after crackpot stuff!"

"Christ, Mooney, aren't you interested? Some guy heists a cab, at gunpoint, then tosses the money. Aren't you the least bit *intrigued?*"

"I'm a cop, Ms. Carlyle. I've got to be more than intrigued. I've got murders, bank robberies, assaults—"

"Well, excuse me. I'm just a poor citizen reporting a crime. Trying to help—"

"Want to help, Carlotta? Go away." He stared at the sheet of paper in the typewriter and lit another cigarette. "Or dig me up something on the Thayler case."

"You working that sucker?"

"Wish to hell I wasn't."

I could see his point. It's tough enough trying to solve any murder, but when your victim is *the* Jennifer (Mrs. Justin) Thayler, wife of the famed Harvard Law prof, and the society reporters are breathing down your neck along with the usual crime-beat scribblers, you got a special kind of problem.

"So who did it?" I asked.

Mooney put his size twelves up on his desk. "Colonel Mustard in the library with the candlestick! How the hell do I know? Some scumbag housebreaker. The lady of the house interrupted his haul. Probably didn't mean to hit her that hard. He must have freaked when he saw all the blood, 'cause he left some of the ritziest stereo equipment this side of heaven, plus enough silverware to blind your average hophead. He snatched most of old man Thayler's goddam idiot artworks, collections, collectibles—whatever the hell you call 'em—which ought to set him up for the next few hundred years, if he's smart enough to get rid of them."

"Alarm system?"

"Yeah, they had one. Looks like Mrs. Thayler forgot to turn it on. According to the maid, she had a habit of forgetting just about anything after a martini or three."

"Think the maid's in on it?"

"Christ, Carlotta. There you go again. No witnesses. No fingerprints. Servants asleep. Husband asleep. We've got word out to all the fences here and in New York that we want this guy. The pawnbrokers know the stuff's hot. We're checking out known art thieves and shady museums—"

"Well, don't let me keep you from your serious business," I said, getting up to go. "I'll give you the collar when I find out who robbed my cab."

"Sure," he said. His fingers started playing with the typewriter again.

"Wanna bet on it?" Betting's an old custom with Mooney and me.

"I'm not gonna take the few piddling bucks you earn with that ridiculous car."

"Right you are, boy. I'm gonna take the money the city pays you to be unimaginative! Fifty bucks I nail him within the week."

Mooney hates to be called "boy." He hates to be called "unimaginative." I hate to hear my car called "ridiculous." We shook hands on the deal. Hard.

Chinatown's about the only chunk of Boston that's alive after midnight. I headed over to Yee Hong's for a bowl of wonton soup.

The service was the usual low-key, slow-motion routine. I used a newspaper as a shield; if you're really involved in the *Wall Street Journal,* the casual male may think twice before deciding he's the answer to your prayers. But I didn't read a single stock quote. I tugged at strands of my hair, a bad habit of mine. Why would somebody rob me and then toss the money away?

Solution Number One: He didn't. The trash bin was some mob drop, and the money I'd found in the trash had absolutely nothing to do with the money filched from my cab. Except that it was the same amount—and that was too big a coincidence for me to swallow.

Two: The cash I'd found was counterfeit and this was a clever way of getting it into circulation. Nah. Too baroque entirely. How the hell would the guy know I was the pawing-through-the-trash type?

Three: It was a training session. Some fool had used me to perfect his robbery technique. Couldn't he learn from TV like the rest of the crooks?

Four: It was a frat hazing. Robbing a hack at gunpoint isn't exactly in the same league as swallowing goldfish.

I closed my eyes.

My face came to a fortunate halt about an inch above a bowl of steaming broth. That's when I decided to pack it in and head for home. Wonton soup is lousy for the complexion.

I checked out the log I keep in the Chevy, totaled my fares: $4.82 missing, all in change. A very reasonable robbery.

By the time I got home, the sleepiness had passed. You know how it is: one moment you're yawning, the next your eyes won't close. Usually happens when my head hits the pillow; this time I didn't even make it that far. What woke me up was the idea that my robber hadn't meant to steal a thing. Maybe he'd left me something instead. You know, something hot, cleverly concealed. Something he could pick up in a few weeks, after things cooled off.

I went over that backseat with a vengeance, but I didn't find anything besides old Kleenex and bent paperclips. My brainstorm wasn't too clever after all. I mean, if the guy wanted to use my cab as a hiding place, why advertise by pulling a five-and-dime robbery?

I sat in the driver's seat, tugged my hair, and stewed. What did I have to go on? The memory of a nervous thief who talked like a B movie and stole only change. Maybe a mad toll-booth collector.

I live in a Cambridge dump. In any other city, I couldn't sell the damned thing if I wanted to. Here, I turn real estate agents away daily. The key to my home's value is the fact that I can hoof it to Harvard Square in five minutes. It's a seller's market for tarpaper shacks within walking distance of the Square. Under a hundred thou only if the plumbing's outside.

It took me a while to get in the door. I've got about five locks on it. Neighborhood's popular with thieves as well as gentry. I'm neither. I inherited the house from my weird Aunt Bea, all paid for. I consider the property taxes my rent, and the rent's getting steeper all the time.

I slammed my log down on the dining room table. I've got rooms galore in that old house, rent a couple of them to Harvard students. I've got my own office on the second floor, but I do most of my work at the dining room table. I like the view of the refrigerator.

I started over from square one. I called Gloria. She's the late-night dispatcher for the Independent Taxi Owners Association. I've never seen her, but her voice is as smooth as mink oil and I'll bet we get a lot of calls from guys who just want to hear her say she'll pick 'em up in five minutes.

"Gloria, it's Carlotta."

"Hi, babe. You been pretty popular today."

"Was I popular at one-thirty-five this morning?"

"Huh?"

"I picked up a fare in front of the Copley Plaza at one-thirty-five. Did you hand that one out to all comers or did you give it to me solo?"

"Just a sec." I could hear her charming the pants off some caller in the background. Then she got back to me.

"I just gave him to you, babe. He asked for the lady in the '59 Chevy. Not a lot of those on the road."

"Thanks, Gloria."

"Trouble?" she asked.

"Is mah middle name," I twanged. We both laughed and I hung up before she got a chance to cross-examine me.

So. The robber wanted my cab. I wished I'd concentrated on his face instead of his snazzy clothes. Maybe it was somebody I knew, some jokester in mid-prank. I killed that idea; I don't know anybody who'd pull a stunt like that, at gunpoint and all. I don't want to know anybody like that.

Why rob my cab, then toss the dough?

I pondered sudden religious conversion. Discarded it. Maybe my robber was some perpetual screwup who'd ditched the cash by mistake.

Or . . . maybe he got exactly what he wanted. Maybe he desperately desired my change.

Why?

Because my change was special, valuable beyond its $4.82 replacement cost.

So how would somebody know my change was valuable?

Because he'd given it to me himself, earlier in the day.

"Not bad," I said out loud. "Not bad." It was the kind of reasoning they'd bounced me off the police force for, what my so-called superiors termed the "fevered product of an overimaginative mind." I leapt at it because it was the only explanation I could think of. I do like life to make some sort of sense.

I pored over my log. I keep pretty good notes: where I pick up a fare, where I drop him, whether he's a hailer or a radio call.

First, I ruled out all the women. That made the task slightly less impossible: sixteen suspects down from thirty-five. Then I yanked my hair and stared at the blank white porcelain of the refrigerator door. Got up and made myself a sandwich: ham, Swiss cheese, salami, lettuce and tomato, on rye. Ate it. Stared at the porcelain some more until the suspects started coming into focus.

Five of the guys were just plain fat and one was decidedly on the hefty side; I'd felt like telling them all to walk. Might do them some good, might bring on a heart attack. I crossed them all out. Making a thin person look plump is hard enough; it's damn near impossible to make a fatty look thin.

Then I considered my regulars: Jonah Ashley, a tiny blond southern gent; muscle-bound "just-çall-me-Harold" at Longfellow Place; Dr. Homewood getting his daily ferry from Beth Israel to MGH; Marvin of the gay bars; and Professor Dickerman, Harvard's answer to Berkeley's sixties radicals.

I crossed them all off. I could see Dickerman holding up the First Filthy Capitalist Bank, or disobeying civilly at Seabrook, even blowing up an oil company or two. But my mind boggled at the thought of the great liberal Dickerman robbing some poor cabbie. It would be like Robin Hood joining the sheriff of Nottingham on some particularly rotten peasant swindle. Then they'd both rape Maid Marian and go off pals together.

Dickerman *was* a lousy tipper. That ought to be a crime.

So what did I have? Eleven out of sixteen guys cleared without leaving my chair. Me and Sherlock Holmes, the famous armchair detectives.

I'm stubborn; that was one of my good cop traits. I stared at that log till my eyes bugged out. I remembered two of the five pretty easily; they were handsome and I'm far from blind. The first had one of those elegant bony faces and far-apart eyes. He was taller than my bandit. I'd ceased eyeballing him when I noticed the ring on his left hand; I never fuss with the married kind. The other one was built, a weight lifter. Not an Arnold

Schwarzenegger extremist, but built. I think I'd have noticed that bod on my bandit. Like I said, I'm not blind.

That left three.

Okay. I closed my eyes. Who had I picked up at the Hyatt on Memorial Drive? Yeah, that was the salesman guy, the one who looked so uncomfortable that I'd figured he'd been hoping to ask his cabbie for a few pointers concerning the best skirt-chasing areas in our fair city. Too low a voice. Too broad in the beam.

The log said I'd picked up a hailer at Kenmore Square when I'd let out the salesman. Ah, yes, a talker. The weather, mostly. Don't you think it's dangerous for you to be driving a cab? Yeah, I remembered him, all right: a fatherly type, clasping a briefcase, heading to the financial district. Too old.

Down to one. I was exhausted but not the least bit sleepy. All I had to do was remember who I'd picked up on Beacon near Charles. A hailer. Before five o'clock, which was fine by me because I wanted to be long gone before rush hour gridlocked the city. I'd gotten onto Storrow and taken him along the river into Newton Center. Dropped him off at the Bay Bank Middlesex, right before closing time. It was coming back. Little nervous guy. Pegged him as an accountant when I'd let him out at the bank. Measly, undernourished soul. Skinny as a rail, stooped, with pits left from teenage acne.

Shit. I let my head sink down onto the dining room table when I realized what I'd done. I'd ruled them all out, every one. So much for my brilliant deductive powers.

I retired to my bedroom, disgusted. Not only had I lost $4.82 in assorted alloy metals, I was going to lose fifty dollars to Mooney. I stared at myself in the mirror, but what I was really seeing was the round hole at the end of a .22, held in a neat, gloved hand.

Somehow, the gloves made me feel better. I'd remembered another detail about my piggy-bank robber. I consulted the mirror and kept the recall going. A hat. The guy wore a hat. Not like my cap, but like a hat out of a forties gangster flick. I had one of those: I'm a sucker for hats. I plunked it on my head, jamming my hair up underneath—and I drew in my breath sharply.

A shoulder-padded jacket, a slim build, a low slouched hat. Gloves. Boots with enough heel to click as he walked away. Voice? High. Breathy, almost whispered. Not unpleasant. Accentless. No Boston *r*.

I had a man's jacket and a couple of ties in my closet. Don't ask. They may have dated from as far back as my ex-husband, but not necessarily so. I slipped into the jacket, knotted the tie, tilted the hat down over one eye.

I'd have trouble pulling it off. I'm skinny, but my build is decidedly female. Still, I wondered—enough to traipse back downstairs, pull a chicken leg out of the fridge, go back to the log, and review the feminine possibilities. Good thing I did.

Everything clicked. One lady fit the bill exactly: mannish walk and clothes, tall for a woman. And I was in luck. While I'd picked her up in Harvard Square, I'd dropped her at a real address, a house in Brookline: 782 Mason Terrace, at the top of Corey Hill.

JoJo's garage opens at seven. That gave me a big two hours to sleep.

I took my beloved car in for some repair work it really didn't need yet and sweet-talked JoJo into giving me a loaner. I needed a hack, but not mine. Only trouble with that Chevy is it's too damn conspicuous.

I figured I'd lose way more than fifty bucks staking out Mason Terrace. I also figured it would be worth it to see old Mooney's face.

She was regular as clockwork, a dream to tail. Eight-thirty-seven every morning, she got a ride to the Square with a next-door neighbor. Took a cab home at five-fifteen. A working woman. Well, she couldn't make much of a living from robbing hacks and dumping the loot in the garbage.

I was damn curious by now. I knew as soon as I looked her over that she was the one, but she seemed so blah, so *normal*. She must have been five-seven or -eight, but the way she stooped, she didn't look tall. Her hair was long and brown with a lot of blond in it, the kind of hair that would have been terrific loose and wild, like a horse's mane. She tied it back with a scarf. A brown scarf. She wore suits. Brown suits. She had a tiny nose, brown eyes under pale eyebrows, a sharp chin. I never saw her smile. Maybe what she needed was a shrink, not a session with Mooney. Maybe she'd done it for the excitement. God knows, if I had her routine, her job, I'd probably be dressing up like King Kong and assaulting skyscrapers.

See, I followed her to work. It wasn't even tricky. She trudged the same path, went in the same entrance to Harvard Yard, probably walked the same number of steps every morning. Her name was Marcia Heidegger and she was a secretary in the admissions office of the college of fine arts.

I got friendly with one of her coworkers.

There was this guy typing away like mad at a desk in her office. I could just see him from the side window. He had grad student written all over his face. Longish wispy hair. Gold-rimmed glasses. Serious. Given to deep sighs and bright velour V necks. Probably writing his thesis on "Courtly Love and the Theories of Chrétien de Troyes."

I latched onto him at Bailey's the day after I'd tracked Lady Heidegger to her Harvard lair.

Too bad Roger was so short. Most short guys find it hard to believe that I'm really trying to pick them up. They look for ulterior motives. Not the

Napoleon type of short guy; he assumes I've been waiting years for a chance to dance with a guy who doesn't have to bend to stare down my cleavage. But Roger was no Napoleon. So I had to engineer things a little.

I got into line ahead of him and ordered, after long deliberation, a BLT on toast. While the guy made it up and shoved it on a plate with three measly potato chips and a sliver of pickle you could barely see, I searched through my wallet, opened my change purse, counted out silver, got to $1.60 on the last five pennies. The counterman sang out, "That'll be a buck eighty-five." I pawed through my pockets, found a nickel, two pennies. The line was growing restive. I concentrated on looking like a damsel in need of a knight, a tough task for a woman over six feet.

Roger (I didn't know he was Roger then) smiled ruefully and passed over a quarter. I was effusive in my thanks. I sat at a table for two, and when he'd gotten his tray (ham-and-cheese and a strawberry ice cream soda), I motioned him into my extra chair.

He was a sweetie. Sitting down, he forgot the difference in our height, and decided I might be someone he could talk to. I encouraged him. I hung shamelessly on his every word. A Harvard man, imagine that. We got around slowly, ever so slowly, to his work at the admissions office. He wanted to duck it and talk about more important issues, but I persisted. I'd been thinking about getting a job at Harvard, possibly in admissions. What kind of people did he work with? Were they congenial? What was the atmosphere like? Was it a big office? How many people? Men? Women? Any soulmates? Readers? Or just, you know, office people?

According to him, every soul he worked with was brain dead. I interrupted a stream of complaint with "Gee, I know somebody who works for Harvard. I wonder if you know her."

"It's a big place," he said, hoping to avoid the whole endless business.

"I met her at a party. Always meant to look her up." I searched through my bag, found a scrap of paper and pretended to read Marcia Heidegger's name off it.

"Marcia? Geez, I work with Marcia. Same office."

"Do you think she likes her work? I mean I got some strange vibes from her," I said. I actually said "strange vibes" and he didn't laugh his head off. People in the Square say things like that and other people take them seriously.

His face got conspiratorial, of all things, and he leaned closer to me.

"You want it, I bet you could get Marcia's job."

"You mean it?" What a compliment—a place for me among the brain dead.

"She's gonna get fired if she doesn't snap out of it."

"Snap out of what?"

"It was bad enough working with her when she first came over. She's one of those crazy neat people, can't stand to see papers lying on a desktop, you know? She almost threw out the first chapter of my thesis!"

I made a suitably horrified noise and he went on.

"Well, you know, about Marcia, it's kind of tragic. She doesn't talk about it."

But he was dying to.

"Yes?" I said, as if he needed egging on.

He lowered his voice. "She used to work for Justin Thayler over at the law school, that guy in the news, whose wife got killed. You know, her work hasn't been worth shit since it happened. She's always on the phone, talking real soft, hanging up if anybody comes in the room. I mean, you'd think she was in love with the guy or something, the way she. . . ."

I don't remember what I said. For all I know, I may have volunteered to type his thesis. But I got rid of him somehow and then I scooted around the corner of Church Street and found a pay phone and dialed Mooney.

"Don't tell me," he said. "Somebody mugged you, but they only took your trading stamps."

"I have just one question for you, Moon."

"I accept. A June wedding, but I'll have to break it to Mother gently."

"Tell me what kind of junk Justin Thayler collected."

I could hear him breathing into the phone.

"Just tell me," I said, "for curiosity's sake."

"You onto something, Carlotta?"

"I'm curious, Mooney. And you're not the only source of information in the world."

"Thayler collected Roman stuff. Antiques. And I mean old. Artifacts, statues—"

"Coins?"

"Whole mess of them."

"Thanks."

"Carlotta—"

I never did find out what he was about to say because I hung up. Rude, I know. But I had things to do. And it was better Mooney shouldn't know what they were, because they came under the heading of illegal activities.

When I knocked at the front door of the Mason Terrace house at 10:00 A.M. the next day, I was dressed in dark slacks, a white blouse, and my old police department hat. I looked very much like the guy who reads your gas meter. I've never heard of anyone being arrested for impersonating the gasman. I've never heard of anyone really giving the gasman a second look. He fades into the background and that's exactly what I wanted to do.

I knew Marcia Heidegger wouldn't be home for hours. Old reliable had left for the Square at her usual time, precise to the minute. But I wasn't 100 percent sure Marcia lived alone. Hence the gasman. I could knock on the door and check it out.

Those Brookline neighborhoods kill me. Act sneaky and the neighbors call the cops in twenty seconds, but walk right up to the front door, knock, talk to yourself while you're sticking a shim in the crack of the door, let yourself in, and nobody does a thing. Boldness is all.

The place wasn't bad. Three rooms, kitchen and bath, light and airy. Marcia was incredibly organized, obsessively neat, which meant I had to keep track of where everything was and put it back just so. There was no clutter in the woman's life. The smell of coffee and toast lingered, but if she'd eaten breakfast, she'd already washed, dried, and put away the dishes. The morning paper had been read and tossed in the trash. The mail was sorted in one of those plastic accordion files. I mean, she folded her underwear like origami.

Now coins are hard to look for. They're small; you can hide 'em anywhere. So this search took me one hell of a long time. Nine out of ten women hide things that are dear to them in the bedroom. They keep their finest jewelry closest to the bed, sometimes in the nightstand, sometimes right under the mattress. That's where I started.

Marcia had a jewelry box on top of her dresser. I felt like hiding it for her. She had some nice stuff and a burglar could have made quite a haul with no effort.

The next favorite place for women to stash valuables is the kitchen. I sifted through her flour. I removed every Kellogg's Rice Krispy from the giant economy-sized box—and returned it. I went through her place like no burglar ever will. When I say thorough, I mean thorough.

I found four odd things. A neatly squared pile of clippings from the *Globe* and the *Herald,* all the articles about the Thayler killing. A manila envelope containing five different safe-deposit-box keys. A Tupperware container full of superstitious junk, good luck charms mostly, the kind of stuff I'd never have associated with a straight-arrow like Marcia: rabbits' feet galore, a little leather bag on a string that looked like some kind of voodoo charm, a pendant in the shape of a cross surmounted by a hook, and, I swear to God, a pack of worn tarot cards. Oh, yes, and a .22 automatic, looking a lot less threatening stuck in an ice cube tray. I took the bullets; the loaded gun threatened a defenseless box of Breyers' mint chocolate-chip ice cream.

I left everything else just the way I'd found it and went home. And tugged my hair. And stewed. And brooded. And ate half the stuff in the refrigerator, I kid you not.

At about one in the morning, it all made blinding, crystal-clear sense.

The next afternoon, at five-fifteen, I made sure I was the cabbie who picked up Marcia Heidegger in Harvard Square. Now cabstands have the most rigid protocol since Queen Victoria; you do not grab a fare out of turn or your fellow cabbies are definitely not amused. There was nothing for it but bribing the ranks. This bet with Mooney was costing me plenty.

I got her. She swung open the door and gave the Mason Terrace number. I grunted, kept my face turned front, and took off.

Some people really watch where you're going in a cab, scared to death you'll take them a block out of their way and squeeze them for an extra nickel. Others just lean back and dream. She was a dreamer, thank God. I was almost at District One Headquarters before she woke up.

"Excuse me," she said, polite as ever, "that's Mason Terrace in *Brookline*."

"Take the next right, pull over, and douse your lights," I said in a low Bogart voice. My imitation was not that good, but it got the point across. Her eyes widened and she made an instinctive grab for the door handle.

"Don't try it, lady," I Bogied on. "You think I'm dumb enough to take you in alone? There's a cop car behind us, just waiting for you to make a move."

Her hand froze. She was a sap for movie dialogue.

"Where's the cop?" was all she said on the way up to Mooney's office.

"What cop?"

"The one following us."

"You have touching faith in our law-enforcement system," I said.

She tried a bolt, I kid you not. I've had experience with runners a lot trickier than Marcia. I grabbed her in approved cop hold number three and marched her into Mooney's office.

He actually stopped typing and raised an eyebrow, an expression of great shock for Mooney.

"Citizen's arrest," I said.

"Charges?"

"Petty theft. Commission of a felony using a firearm." I rattled off a few more charges, using the numbers I remembered from cop school.

"This woman is crazy," Marcia Heidegger said with all the dignity she could muster.

"Search her," I said. "Get a matron in here. I want my four dollars and eighty-two cents back."

Mooney looked like he agreed with Marcia's opinion of my mental state. He said, "Wait up, Carlotta. You'd have to be able to identify that four dollars and eighty-two cents as yours. Can you do that? Quarters are quarters. Dimes are dimes."

"One of the coins she took was quite unusual," I said. "I'm sure I'd be able to identify it."

"Do you have any objection to displaying the change in your purse?"

Mooney said to Marcia. He got me mad the way he said it, like he was humoring an idiot.

"Of course not," old Marcia said, cool as a frozen daiquiri.

"That's because she's stashed it somewhere else, Mooney," I said patiently. "She used to keep it in her purse, see. But then she goofed. She handed it over to a cabbie in her change. She should have just let it go, but she panicked because it was worth a pile and she was just baby-sitting it for someone else. So when she got it back, she hid it somewhere. Like in her shoe. Didn't you ever carry your lucky penny in your shoe?"

"No," Mooney said. "Now, Miss—"

"Heidegger," I said clearly. "Marcia Heidegger. She used to work at Harvard Law School." I wanted to see if Mooney picked up on it, but he didn't. He went on: "This can be taken care of with a minimum of fuss. If you'll agree to be searched by—"

"I want to see my lawyer," she said.

"For four dollars and eighty-two cents?" he said.

"It'll cost you more than that to get your lawyer up here."

"Do I get my phone call or not?"

Mooney shrugged wearily and wrote up the charge sheet. Called a cop to take her to the phone.

He got Jo Ann, which was good. Under cover of our old-friend-long-time-no-see greetings, I whispered in her ear.

"You'll find it fifty well spent," I said to Mooney when we were alone.

Jo Ann came back, shoving Marcia slightly ahead of her. She plunked her prisoner down in one of Mooney's hard wooden chairs and turned to me, grinning from ear to ear.

"Got it?" I said. "Good for you."

"What's going on?" Mooney said.

"She got real clumsy on the way to the pay phone," Jo Ann said. "Practically fell on the floor. Got up with her right hand clenched tight. When we got to the phone, I offered to drop her dime for her. She wanted to do it herself. I insisted and she got clumsy again. Somehow this coin got kicked clear across the floor."

She held it up. The coin could have been a dime, except the color was off: warm, rosy gold instead of dead silver. How I missed it the first time around I'll never know.

"What the hell is that?" Mooney said.

"What kind of coins were in Justin Thayler's collection?" I asked. "Roman?"

Marcia jumped out of the chair, snapped her bag open, and drew out her little .22. I kid you not. She was closest to Mooney and she just stepped up to him and rested it above his left ear. He swallowed, didn't say a word. I never realized how prominent his Adam's apple was. Jo Ann froze, hand on her holster.

Good old reliable, methodical Marcia. Why, I said to myself, *why* pick today of all days to trot your gun out of the freezer? Did you read bad luck in your tarot cards? Then I had a truly rotten thought. What if she had two guns? What if the disarmed .22 was still staring down the mint chocolate chip ice cream?

"Give it back," Marcia said. She held out one hand, made an impatient waving motion.

"Hey, you don't need it, Marcia," I said. "You've got plenty more. In all those safe deposit boxes."

"I'm going to count to five—" she began.

"Were you in on the murder from day one? You know, from the planning stages?" I asked. I kept my voice low, but it echoed off the walls of Mooney's tiny office. The hum of everyday activity kept going in the main room. Nobody noticed the little gun in the well-dressed lady's hand. "Or did you just do your beau a favor and hide the loot after he iced his wife? In order to back up his burglary tale? I mean, if Justin Thayler really wanted to marry you, there is such a thing as divorce. Or was old Jennifer the one with the bucks?"

"I want that coin," she said softly. "Then I want the two of you"—she motioned to Jo Ann and me—"to sit down facing that wall. If you yell, or do anything before I'm out of the building, I'll shoot this gentleman. He's coming with me."

"Come on, Marcia," I said, "put it down. I mean, look at you. A week ago you just wanted Thayler's coin back. You didn't want to rob my cab, right? You just didn't know how else to get your good luck charm back with no questions asked. You didn't do it for money, right? You did it for love. You were so straight you threw away the cash. Now here you are with a gun pointed at a cop—"

"Shut up!"

I took a deep breath and said, "You haven't got the style, Marcia. Your gun's not even loaded."

Mooney didn't relax a hair. Sometimes I think the guy hasn't ever believed a word I've said to him. But Marcia got shook. She pulled the barrel away from Mooney's skull and peered at it with a puzzled frown. Jo Ann and I both tackled her before she got a chance to pull the trigger. I twisted the gun out of her hand. I was almost afraid to look inside. Mooney stared at me and I felt my mouth go dry and a trickle of sweat worm its way down my back.

I looked.

No bullets. My heart stopped fibrillating, and Mooney actually cracked a smile in my direction.

So that's all. I sure hope Mooney will spread the word around that I helped him nail Thayler. And I think he will; he's a fair kind of guy. Maybe it'll get me a case or two. Driving a cab is hard on the backside, you know?

THE FUZZY THINGS

D. B. Olsen

The man took the long slim package from his coat pocket, put it on the table, and unwrapped it with hands that shook. He was a big man and there was something peculiarly childish about his fear. He was like a little boy afraid of the dark. "This came today—the second inside a week. You can see where the chocolates have been tampered with. The other box had strychnine in it."

Miss Rachel Murdock lifted one from its paper nest and examined the under side. There had been a picked-out hole refilled unskillfully with a chocolate mixture, unlike the coating put on by the candy maker. More like cake frosting, she thought.

"This wasn't addressed to you?"

"No. To my wife and her little girl, my stepdaughter." He took out a white handkerchief and mopped his forehead. "It was quite by accident that I noticed the tampering in the first box and kept Jenny from sampling one of them. She loves candy and we've spoiled her with it. My wife wasn't inclined to be afraid, but I had the filling tested just to be safe. All the candy was poisoned."

Miss Rachel pulled her lacy shawl closer as if she were suddenly cold. Her cat, a big black fluffy cat with amazingly green eyes, had been sleeping in her lap and, feeling the shiver, looked up. Miss Rachel said, "You went to the police, of course?"

"Oh, yes. Right away." He hesitated, staring at the open box. "I know I have to be completely frank if you're to help us. My wife didn't want me to go to the police and she absolutely forbade me to mention the man we suspect of sending the candy. She's sure that she can handle him. She doesn't know I've come to you. It was getting this second box, the inhuman boldness of it, that woke me up, that brought me here."

"This man you suspect—is it the child's father?"

He looked up, startled. "How did you know?"

"I just guessed," she admitted. "You'd better tell me about him."

They were seated in Miss Rachel's tiny parlor. Several unfinished bits of knitting lay about. Miss Jennifer, the elder and more sensible in her own opinion, had decided that it might settle Miss Rachel's nerves to be taught to knit; and Miss Rachel was realizing with relief that all she had needed had been some mystery to meddle with. Like this one, unpleasant as it was.

The big man with the childish fear in his eyes spoke slowly as if thinking out what he must say. "My wife married a man about whom she knew almost nothing. They met at a resort, Arrowhead, and because she was young and inexperienced she was impressed by his looks and his money. He had plenty of money. He was a counterfeiter."

The cat had gone back to sleep. The room was quiet, full of afternoon sunlight and the clean smell of the new wool Miss Rachel was supposed to be knitting on.

"When the law caught up with him a few months after their marriage, and he was sent to prison, she almost went insane. She bore their child alone, on charity. I would have helped, of course, but she didn't let me know. She worked, trained herself for a secretary, and came to me for a job. I'd been a friend of the family—I'm a lot older than she is, of course—but when we realized we were in love I helped her get a divorce and we were married. We've been very happy for nearly five years. You see, he's been where he couldn't hurt us, behind prison bars."

"And he's out now? Recently?"

"Two weeks, and already he's at work." His glance toward the open box of candy was savage and afraid.

She shook her head at the simplicity of his problem. "The police won't have any trouble tracing his purchase of the poison, or his mailing the package."

An expression of defeat settled about his mouth. "I'm hamstrung. She grows hysterical at the idea of setting the police after him."

"She still cares for him, then. Or pities him," Miss Rachel murmured thoughtfully.

"No one could love a crook like that. It's pity, of course."

Miss Rachel, from the advantage of her seventy years, reflected that he had a good deal to learn about women. Women could love the most awful crooks. Her own Aunt Lily, the one who had been a chorus girl in the nineties, had loved a confidence man who had, at the desperate end, run away on the money he got from hocking Aunt Lily's clothes, including her tights. Miss Rachel asked carefully, "Does anyone else know the truth?"

He hesitated a second. "My sister Dorothy. She lives with us. She's devoted to the child. Her terror over the poisoned candy is even greater than mine."

"Just what is it you wish me to do?"

"Try to convince my wife that she must, for the child's sake, turn this man in to the police. I suggest that you come for a day or two, this weekend, perhaps. In addition to convincing my wife of Jenny's danger, you may intercept some new attempt, something that we might not catch until it was too late." He clenched his hands together; the veins in his wrists stood out. "This man is an infernally clever criminal. He was a counterfeiter of the utmost skill and shrewdness. Only the slip of a subordinate finally gave him away."

"How strange, then," Miss Rachel pointed out, "that he works this attempted murder so openly, so clumsily."

He checked what he had been about to say. Some new thought, a strange fear, seemed to show for an instant in his eyes. Then he shook his head. "He's all the more dangerous. Like a mad animal. Will you come?"

"Oh, yes, I'll come."

He started to wrap up the package.

"Leave the chocolates, will you, please?"

His hand stumbled over their handling of the box. The contents spilled out suddenly into a heap upon the rug. In a seeming attempt to back away, his foot came down and crushed the candy into one lump of chocolate. He stood looking down at it blankly. "Damn it, I've spoiled them all."

Miss Rachel was looking at him calmly. "It's all right. We'll clean the rug." Her cat jumped to the floor and went to the crushed chocolates and sniffed with a delicate disdain. "I knew you were nosy," Miss Rachel scolded, pulling Samantha away, "but not downright stupid."

He was at the door, mopping perspiration again with the white handkerchief. "When will you come? Soon?"

"I'll be at your house tonight for dinner."

"Good. I'll see that the guest room is ready. I'm—I'm sorry about your rug."

"Don't worry about it."

Through the curtains at the window, she watched him walk down the steps, across the sidewalk and get into the long gray car at the curb. The air of nervousness seemed to have passed into dejection. The final glance he gave the house hadn't much hope in it.

He had come just after lunch, given his name as Thackley and his business with Miss Rachel as private. Miss Jennifer had been dressed to go out—it was the day for the Ladies' Aid meeting—and she had cautioned Miss Rachel before leaving that there must not be any more horrors.

Miss Rachel had peeped into the hall where Mr. Thackley waited. "He doesn't look like such a horror, Jennifer."

"You know what I mean," said Jennifer darkly. "Don't get off the subject."

The interview had started by Mr. Thackley saying that he needed help and didn't quite know how to get it. At first mention of the attempted poisoning, Miss Rachel had suggested a private guard. Mr. Thackley had explained, "It's not violence I fear. I can take care of anything like that. I need someone with an acute, wary intelligence." Miss Rachel had nodded graciously at the compliment. Then he had brought out the chocolates.

Miss Rachel called her housekeeper. "We've had an accident on the carpet. Will you get the most of it into a clean box and take it downtown to the police laboratories with a note?"

Miss Rachel had an old friend in the laboratory. She sat down and wrote briefly. Then she packed a small suitcase, called a cab, and picked up her cat. The cat looked eagerly at the door; she liked to travel.

"When my sister comes, tell her I'll be away for a day or two. Tell her I had a chance to . . . ah . . . go to the Wisteria Festival."

The housekeeper shook her head. No one was going to believe that story, least of all Miss Jennifer, who would get hopping mad at the idea of Rachel being involved in a new "horror."

The Thackley home was high on a bluff above the shore near Malibu. The cab pulled up through a long drive bordered with pink asters and blue lantana, to a massive door in a stark white wall. Miss Rachel stood on dark-red tiles and rang the bell. Below was the panorama of the sea, the headlands which fell away toward Santa Monica, the far blue smudge of Catalina Island. The air held a smell of roses and blossoming sage and the wet tang of the Pacific. The door opened silently. A woman looked out at her.

She was a tall woman, well over forty, with tight graying hair, sharp cheekbones, eyes of a peculiar metallic greenish-blue. The color, Miss Rachel recalled, of Mr. Thackley's eyes also. This must be his sister Dorothy. There seemed to be a starved look to her, somehow; something denied, taken away, snatched from her grasp. Not food. Love, perhaps. Miss Rachel smiled into the grim eyes. "I'm Miss Murdock. Your brother asked me to come."

The woman opened the door and showed a long sunny hall. "Come in, won't you? I'm Miss Thackley; guess you saw the resemblance. People do. May I take your cat?"

Miss Rachel decided to experiment. She tried to put Samantha into Dorothy's arms. The cat let fuzz grow up along her back; she put claws into Miss Rachel's bosom and clung, stubborn and unfriendly. "She'll take a little while to get used to you."

Dorothy Thackley took the rebuff indifferently. "I'm not much for cats, anyway. Here, let me take your bag. I'll show you your room."

On the stairs, Miss Rachel asked, "How much of my coming did your brother explain?"

"All of it," said Dorothy flatly. "I wanted him to go to the police with the truth at once—no reflection on your ability, of course—but we pay taxes and we might as well get some return for them. The police know how to handle fiends like *him*." Her heavy sensible shoes made a loud thumping on the polished stairs. "Our little Jenny—she's all we have. We can't be too careful." The starved, lonely quality was in her voice now. There was a yearning note when she mentioned the child's name.

She took Miss Rachel into a large simple bedroom. "We're very plain here, for all the size of the place," she explained. "We do all our own housekeeping. We got used to it during the war." She stopped in the act of opening the closet. "Here's our little Jenny now. Such a tease, she hid in here to see you."

Jenny came out of the closet. She was about six, a small girl with bright brown pigtails, merry eyes, a blue pinafore and white barefoot sandals. The effect she gave was of someone small and warm-hearted and very dearly loved. She came close and put a gently inquisitive hand on Samantha's head and said shyly, "Does he mind if I pet him? He's so soft. Like feathers."

"Her name is Samantha and she seems to like you very much," said Miss Rachel. She managed, without seeming to, to get a look at Dorothy while the child made a fuss over the cat. The woman's angular face seemed wistful, the greenish eyes more lonely than before.

Jenny put her ear against Samantha's and crooned softly.

It occurred to Miss Rachel that Jenny would be easy to love; and that sometimes love is a jealous emotion.

"May I take her to my room?" Jenny begged. "I'll give her my mouse to play with."

But Dorothy came forward firmly. "No, no, Jenny. Leave Miss Murdock's cat be. We have to wash for dinner now."

The child went, but regretfully. Fixing herself for dinner, Miss Rachel was thoughtful.

The dinner table had been set in a corner of the open patio, where bougainvillea on a trellis made a shade. A young woman who had been putting yellow plates out upon the redwood surface turned as Miss

Rachel came out of the house. She was very slender; her hair was the lively shining brown of Jenny's pigtails, curling softly to her shoulders; but her eyes were not merry and friendly as Jenny's were. They settled on Miss Rachel, examined her with displeasure and reserve. She put out a hand as if with effort. "I'm Mrs. Thackley."

"How do you do?" said Miss Rachel, finding the hand cool and unresponsive.

Mrs. Thackley's voice went on stiffly, "I hadn't been informed of my husband's visit to you, and your coming here, until a few minutes ago. As the wife, and supposed hostess of this home, you'd think I might know a bit more of who is invited here, wouldn't you?"

She was very young to be Mr. Thackley's wife, probably not more than twenty-three or -four. Her air of importance, of anger, gave her the look of a little girl who is playing at keeping house. Only the harsh displeasure in her eyes was adult and real, and made Miss Rachel acutely uncomfortable.

"I'm sorry if my coming has upset you," Miss Rachel murmured quietly. She waited courteously to be told to go away.

The girl's face turned pink. "I don't mean to seem rude. I—I guess you came because of Jenny."

"Yes, that's why I came. I can't imagine anyone vicious enough to try to poison a child."

"It happened," said Mrs. Thackley quickly. "I mean, it was true. The candy came by mail and it had been opened and poison put in it."

"For you alone, perhaps?"

She shook her head. "I don't care for candy. Jenny loves it."

"The handwriting on the package—"

"Had been disguised," Mrs. Thackley broke in bitterly. "He'd know so well how to do that. He had a thousand different ways of writing his own name."

"He was clever," Miss Rachel suggested.

"As the devil from hell."

The garden was quiet. There was a single blue jay in the bougainvillea vine. He had his eye on the basket of crackers in the center of the table. At Miss Rachel's feet, Samantha had opened her green eyes very wide. She had never been able to catch a jay, but this one might be different.

"You had word from him when he was released from prison?"

Mrs. Thackley moved a plate nervously. "He wasn't in prison, not during the last year. He was in an honor camp in the mountains. He didn't write to me, but to Jenny. He sent a short note that he wanted to see her and that he had a surprise for her. Then the candy came, the first box that Ray had analyzed." She moved to the other side of the table, covering what may have been a shudder.

"You didn't feel that you should tell the whole story to the police?"

The hands touching a yellow plate grew very still. "No. I—I feel that he'll straighten out. It's a kind of insanity. He's been shut up all these years, concentrating upon Jenny, upon me. His letters, the few he wrote that I opened, ignored my second marriage. But this blindness to the truth, his refusal to acknowledge that he has lost me, will pass. I want him to have the chance to get back to reality."

Jenny ran out into the patio. She wore a clean pinafore and her face and hands were shining. She scurried toward the cat. At this moment, feeling Samantha's attention off him, the jay swooped for the table. The cat leaped from under Jenny's hands. There was a wild flutter of blue. Then Samantha was standing alone, looking foolish and embarrassed, and the jay was in the vine with a cracker. A single big blue feather lay beside the table. Jenny pounced on it, held it by the quill and rubbed the downy part against her cheek. Her eyes laughed at Miss Rachel. "Feathers feel so good!" she chirped.

Her mother seized the feather and tore it apart as though something about it enraged her. "Nasty! Off that dirty bird! And just before dinner! Go wash your hands again."

Jenny went in soberly and Miss Rachel saw that Dorothy Thackley met her in the hall.

The meal went off quietly, under an air of restraint. When the dishes had been cleared, Mr. and Mrs. Thackley went into the living room to read. Dorothy Thackley and Jenny put on aprons and hurried to the kitchen. Miss Rachel tried to get interested in a book. She thought Mr. Thackley might wish to talk things over in the presence of his wife. When nothing happened, she decided that the kitchen might be livelier.

Jenny was on a stool, washing dishes at the sink. Dorothy was drying. There were laughter and splashings, and, on Dorothy's part, a wistful air of hoping the closeness, the fun, might never end.

"Jenny likes fuzzy soft things," Miss Rachel remarked, stroking her cat. She was in a kitchen chair, Samantha on her lap. "I remember how Samantha was as a kitten. Like a ball of wool."

Jenny smiled, turning from the sink. But Dorothy's face had stiffened, grown a little pale.

"I have a fuzzy ball," said Jenny. "When I'm through with the dishes I'll bring it for your cat."

The three of them went out into the patio when the dishes were done. The fuzzy ball was blue. In the pale twilight Jenny rolled the ball to and fro among the flowers and shrubbery and the cat ran after it, a little lazily, for Samantha had not been a kitten for a long time. Miss Rachel and Dorothy sat on one of the redwood benches beside the table. The fading light shone in Dorothy's anxious eyes as they followed the child.

Love can be like a cage, Miss Rachel thought. It can be too close, too possessive, suffocating. She was conscious that the evening air was growing chill, that the wind off the sea felt damp and salty. She had hoped that the woman beside her might talk about the problem which had brought her here, but Dorothy's attention seemed absorbed. She suddenly stood up, tense. The little girl had run out of sight behind a white brick wall. "Jenny, don't go far!"

There was an instant of utter blank silence during which Miss Rachel realized that it was almost dark. The light had faded, stars were out, and Jenny had disappeared behind a wall and now there was nothing. She rose, as Dorothy had, with sudden fear.

There came a scream, thin and terrified and childish.

Dorothy ran with a pounding hurry, Miss Rachel with the lightness of a wraith. They reached the garage at the same moment and found Jenny at its side door, staring in, shaking with fright. "There's a man inside!" Jenny shrieked. "He's on a rope!"

They stood as if rooted while inside in the deep gloom the body of the hanged man swung slowly around and around at the end of a rope tied to the rafters. Dorothy, though she was the bigger and sturdier of the two, clung to the door, her face gone sick. Miss Rachel had turned pale, but remained composed. She went in and had a look.

"Come out! Don't touch him! Oh, it's terrible!" cried Dorothy's voice.

Jenny said wonderingly, "She's very brave, isn't she?"

Miss Rachel touched the man's hand softly. "He's quite cold. There's nothing we can do for him." She looked into the dead man's face, not shudderingly but with quiet composure, and then at the dropped stuff about his feet. From among other things, little odd-colored stones and pressed fluffy flowers and bunches of downy leaves, she drew forth a small toy-man made of round knots of wood, on his head a crude mounting of feathers. The painted features on the knot forming the head had a look of humor, of wanting to be friendly. As she studied the toy a sudden expression of anger came into Miss Rachel's usually mild features. "I never believed it," she said half-aloud.

Dorothy Thackley had turned from the door, shielding the child from sight of the hanging figure. "What did you say?"

"I want you to get the police on the telephone at once," said Miss Rachel firmly. "I'll stay here until they arrive."

"But—but a lady shouldn't—" Dorothy's bulging greenish eyes seemed to take in for the first time the smallness, the frailness of Miss Rachel's figure. "You're so tiny, so helpless."

"I've got guts, though," Miss Rachel declared. She could practically hear Jennifer swoon, even at this distance.

As if spurred by this unusual declaration, Dorothy hurried away. Miss Rachel spent the next few minutes switching on the garage lights, taking one more painful look at the man who hung from the rafters, and picking up odds and ends from the floor. The dead man had been extremely handsome; even the sort of death he had endured had not erased the dark good looks, the even features, the exciting pirate dare-deviltry. The stuff upon the floor had the look of little treasures gathered for a child.

"It's what they are, of course," said Rachel to her cat, who followed her about with an air of walking softly so as not to be heard. Since her embarrassing failure with the jay, Samantha had been very quiet. Miss Rachel studied a leaf whose underside was golden and downy. "These were things he had picked up at the honor camp for his child. Bird feathers and bright stones, a toy-man he made of oak galls. A little Indian man for Jenny." The anger returned to burn deep in her eyes. "And so, of course, he didn't send the candy. I never believed he had."

She looked up suddenly toward the door, realizing the appearance there of Mr. Thackley.

He had the gasping, horrified look of someone who comes up from under a wave which has almost drowned him. "This is—is frightful! I didn't dream when I asked you here that there'd be anything like this."

"Probably not," Miss Rachel agreed coolly. "But he's here, though. Can your wife identify him?"

Mrs. Thackley glided forward from the darkness outside. She had put on a black coat, buttoned it high at the neck as if she were chilled. "It's Ted, Jenny's father. I couldn't ever forget how he looked, that clever inhuman slyness." She turned and clung to Mr. Thackley's coat, burying her face against his shoulder. "Did he come to kill Jenny and me? Did he lose his nerve at the last and commit suicide?"

Mr. Thackley's gaze avoided Miss Rachel's searching one. He put his arms about his wife clumsily, uncertainly. "It seems as if he had. At the end, perhaps, he woke up and saw what a monstrous thing he had planned. He couldn't face the knowledge of his own evil. Perhaps we should be glad. Jenny will be safe now. He won't send any more packages."

Miss Rachel had found a small crushed box from which the feathers and leaves had fallen. She straightened the cardboard, put in carefully all the things Jenny's father had brought with him. To Mr. Thackley she said quietly, "You might prepare yourself for other possibilities. The man may not be a suicide."

"Eh?" He peered at her from above his wife's bent shining head. "Not killed himself? Nonsense!"

"The police will decide, of course. My own theory is that he may have been knocked out or drugged, then hanged here to give the impression of suicide. Perhaps the real sender of that poisoned candy feared to be exposed."

Mrs. Thackley twisted away from her husband, raised her head starkly to look into his eyes. "You told me over and over that he must have sent it."

Mr. Thackley's mouth worked; an aching fright blazed in his face. "I—I thought he must have. Why would anyone else?"

Miss Rachel had put the lid on the small box. "Several reasons have occurred to me. Shall we go into the house? I hear the police siren; they'll want this place to themselves."

While they waited for the police investigation to be completed, Miss Rachel made a telephone call. Her friend at the police laboratory told her that the mass of crushed candy had contained an unnecessarily large amount of strychnine. The strychnine had been used in an easily available form, a household rat poison. The small openings in the bottoms of the chocolates had been refilled, he believed, by an uncooked mixture of powdered sugar and cocoa. Was that what she wished to know?

Miss Rachel asked him a couple of questions about oak galls. She listened carefully to what he said.

The telephone was in an alcove in the hall. Miss Rachel did not reenter the living room, where Mrs. Thackley stared at her husband in stony-eyed suspicion, where Mr. Thackley pretended to read a book and where Dorothy watched over Jenny with the anxiety of a mother hen. She went on quietly into the kitchen, snapped on lights, and explored the cupboards. She found several half-used boxes of powdered sugar, a large tin of cocoa and a tube of commercial rat poison. She searched further and came up with a tiny squeeze-gun pastry decorator. She was experimenting with a sugar-and-cocoa mixture, dampened to the proper consistency with cold coffee, and was squeezing out dots of the stuff upon the tiled sink when she heard a step behind her. She turned swiftly. Dorothy Thackley had come in quietly and now stood not three feet away. The lonely, lost expression tightened her mouth, made her eyes bitter. "What are you doing here?" she demanded.

"I wanted to make sure just how the candy had been filled with the poisoned mixture," Miss Rachel explained.

"It wasn't done here."

"Oh, yes, I think so. I never thought it was something a clever criminal would do; amateur, obviously, and needing the sort of tools you'd find only in a kitchen."

Dorothy's lean hands twitched. Her eyes searched over the sink, the drawers, the little box Miss Rachel had brought with her. "I won't let you torment my brother with this insanity. He's had all the worry, the strain, that he can stand."

"There won't be any happiness, any safety, until the truth comes out. By the way, have the police reported anything about the death of Jenny's father?"

Dorothy's jaw set itself. "One of them came in a moment ago and said that the man had been murdered. I don't believe it." Her voice shook. "Why would anyone kill him?"

"For jealousy? Because Jenny might have loved him?" Miss Rachel's glance had settled on the broken cardboard box into which she had put the feathers, the stones, and the little man made of oak galls. "You see, the truth was much different from what you three believed, or pretended to believe. Jenny's father had no wish to harm her. I think actually he loved her very much."

Dorothy began to back away. The pinched loneliness in her face gave it the baldness of a skull. She felt behind her for the door. "I won't stay and listen to you."

Miss Rachel opened the little box and held it toward her. "See what he brought, soft feathers, downy leaves, smooth little stones. Things with texture and softness which he knew Jenny would love because he loved them. You saw how she was with the jay's feather—"

A spasm of defeat crossed Dorothy's face before she turned and fled. When Miss Rachel went back to the living room, she found the woman lying on a couch, her eyes shut, her bleak face turned toward the wall. Mr. and Mrs. Thackley were listening to Lieutenant Davis.

Davis was a big, intelligent-looking cop. He was explaining the murder. "The man was tapped at the rear of the skull with some blunt tool, not a hard blow nor one which required much strength. Then he was strung up and allowed to strangle."

Mr. Thackley had his handkerchief out, wiping at his forehead. Mrs. Thackley said slowly, "The pulling up of that limp body would have taken strength, though. A lot of it."

"I think the rope was tied to a car. As the car backed, the body was raised toward the rafters. You're right about the job taking strength. Even a man might have trouble." His eyes were on Mr. Thackley, who flinched. "Who used the car around three o'clock today?"

"I—I did," Mr. Thackley stuttered. "I'd been to see Miss Murdock in the city."

"The car isn't in the garage now. It's in the courtyard," Davis pointed out. "Where did you leave it?"

"Uh—I'm not sure. I usually put it away." His eyes went everywhere but toward his wife's accusing, suspicious stare. "I didn't kill the man. I swear it."

"This story about the candy, now." Davis pursed his lips. "You came in a week ago to report the first box, but you declared you had no idea who would send such a thing."

"I was wrong, of course." Mr. Thackley looked down at his handkerchief as though he wished to weep into it. "Quite wrong. My wife thought the man would come out of it, come to his senses."

"I don't think that he ever lost them," Miss Rachel put in. The three turned toward her abruptly. Jenny, playing with the cat in a corner removed from earshot, looked up at the change in attention. "I think he came here, not to do any harm, but to see his child because he loved her. He brought her these little treasures. Whoever killed him scattered and trampled them in the garage." She held out the open box; a couple of downy leaves floated to the floor. Jenny left the cat, crossed the room curiously.

"He loved fuzzy, fluffy things," Mrs. Thackley said dully. "It's a quality Jenny has. I can't break her of it."

"You shouldn't try," said Miss Rachel. "Let her be as she is. And let her remember that her father brought her something, though he didn't live to deliver it." She lifted the toy-man with his Indian crest, and Jenny smiled and reached for it.

"What's that?" asked Davis.

"A toy he made of oak galls. An Indian man." She lifted the little figure suddenly from her palm, stared into her hand critically. "I'd forgotten. Oak galls are a strong source of tannic dye, a kind of natural ink." She raised her glance to Davis while all sound died in the room. "The person who murdered Jenny's father trampled all these little things he brought her—in jealousy, in rage. Why don't you just have a look at these three people's shoes for traces of tannic stain?"

The explosive moment lengthened; its breathless quiet hurt her ears. If she had done right, done it quickly enough and surprisingly enough, one of the three would break. She thought she knew which one it would be; someone whose jealous love had not contained itself, had crossed into madness.

Dorothy Thackley turned on the couch and writhed upright. Her face was set like stone. Only her eyes were alive.

"I don't mean jealousy over the love of Jenny," Miss Rachel explained.

Mrs. Thackley rose from her chair and stumbled toward the hall. She seemed blinded, feeling her way with outstretched hands. "Stop her!" cried Mr. Thackley. "Make her come back here and face it!"

For, of course, Miss Rachel thought, his air of being a little boy afraid of the dark stemmed from his unwilling belief that his own wife had made and sent the poisoned chocolates.

At the door, she flung around. Davis had risen to follow her. He said stolidly, "It won't work. My men are all over the grounds. You'll never get away."

She threw back the lovely shining hair, tugged the black coat higher. "I have a way out. You'll never stop me now."

"Let me see your shoes!" commanded Davis.

She laughed in his face. "Why should I? Of course, they're covered with the dye, or whatever it is came out of the oak galls. I wish I could have broken the thing into a thousand pieces!"

She was tense as a strung wire, her slim body turned, whiplike, against the jamb of the door.

"Wait a minute!" cried Miss Rachel. "There are things that only you can tell us. For Jenny's sake, tell us the truth about the candy. Wasn't it to throw your husband off any suspicion he may have had that you wanted to go back to Jenny's father?"

She laughed again, too high-pitched, too harshly. "He'd never dream that I was counting the minutes until Ted came. Not if I seemed to believe that Ted was sending us poisoned candy."

"Mr. Thackley wanted desperately to believe you," Miss Rachel agreed. "He wanted me to prove your innocence. But, you see, he wouldn't have had me come if he meant to do murder. And Dorothy had been warned. Only you, you see, *didn't know I was coming*."

She put up a hand to rub her temple. "It wouldn't have made any difference. I went crazy when he told me."

"When he told you what?" begged Mr. Thackley.

"When she knew that it was Jenny he came for, and not her. Her jealous love for him turned into madness," Miss Rachel said quietly.

Dorothy crept over to Jenny and put her arms about the child and covered the small ears with her hands.

The girl at the door snapped about at the sound of steps. Then she ran with an animal-like fear and swiftness. A door slammed; there were fading steps on the tile path of the patio. Mr. Thackley stood up, braced himself against his chair, looked at Miss Rachel wearily. "Where is she going? There's no escape that way."

"Keep the child's ears covered," Miss Rachel told Dorothy. She met Mr. Thackley's frantic stare. "The sea cliff," she said softly.

His lips moved for a moment before he got words out of them. "It's a horrible drop. More than a hundred feet. She wouldn't try to—"

The scream came, then. Everyone in the room flinched except Davis, who was running in the hall. Mr. Thackley shut his eyes and Dorothy made a muffled, horrified sound against Jenny's hair.

Miss Rachel sat down, shivering as if with a chill.

Mr. Thackley said stiffly, then, "She never did love me. It was all a hoax. A way to get a home for Jenny." He put out a big hand timidly and Jenny, who had been about to cry, clutched it and tried to smile. "I don't mind, once I get used to the idea. Jenny'll always have a home with us."

"I'm sure she will."

The starved look, the tension, was leaving Dorothy's face. She wouldn't have to worry about Jenny's ever leaving.

Miss Rachel bent over the little girl and offered her the tiny box. Jenny accepted gravely. The cat came forward to sniff interestedly at the headdress on the toy-man. There was in the room a sudden feeling of peace, of evil fading away, of hatred and passion burned out and gone.

Jenny giggled. "Your cat likes feathers, too."

"It's as close as she'll ever get to a jay," Miss Rachel explained.

COYOTE AND QUARTER-MOON

Bill Pronzini & Jeffrey Wallmann

With the Laurel County Deputy Sheriff beside her, Jill Quarter-Moon waited for the locksmith to finish unlatching the garage door. Inside, the dog—a good-sized Doberman; she had identified it through the window—continued its frantic barking.

The house to which the garage belonged was only a few years old, a big ranch-style set at the end of a cul-de-sac and somewhat removed from its neighbors in the expensive Oregon Estates development. Since it was a fair Friday morning in June, several of the neighbors were out and mingling in a wide crescent around the property; some of them Jill recognized from her previous visit here. Two little boys were chasing each other around her Animal Regulation Agency truck, stirring up a pair of other barking dogs nearby. It added to the din being raised by the Doberman.

At length the locksmith finished and stepped back. "It's all yours," he said.

"You'd better let me go in with you," the deputy said to Jill.

There was a taint of chauvinism in his offer, but she didn't let it upset her. She was a mature twenty-six, and a full-blooded Umatilla Indian, and she was comfortable with both her womanhood and her role in society. She was also strikingly attractive, in the light-skinned way of Pacific Northwest Indians, with hip-length brown hair and a long willowy body. Some men, the deputy being one of them, seemed to feel protective, if not downright chivalric, toward her. Nothing made her like a man less than being considered a pretty-and-helpless female.

She shook her head at him and said, "No thanks. I've got my tranquilizer dart gun."

"Suit yourself, then." The deputy gave her a disapproving frown and stepped back out of her way. "It's your throat."

Jill drew a heavy padded glove over her left hand, gripped the dart gun with her right. Then she caught hold of the door latch and depressed it. The Doberman stopped barking; all she could hear from inside were low growls. The dog sensed that someone was coming in, and when she opened the door it would do one of two things; back off and watch her, or attack. She had no way of telling beforehand which it would be.

The Doberman had been locked up inside the garage for at least thirty-six hours. That was how long ago it had first started howling and barking and upsetting the neighbors enough so that one of them had complained to the Agency. The owner of the house, Jill had learned in her capacity as field agent, was named Edward Benham; none of the neighbors knew him—he'd kept to himself during the six months he had lived here—and none of them knew anything at all about his dog. Benham hadn't answered his door, nor had she been able to reach him by telephone or track down any local relatives. Finally she had requested, through the Agency offices, a court order to enter the premises. A judge had granted it, and along with the deputy and the locksmith, here she was to release the animal.

She hesitated a moment longer with her hand on the door latch. If the Doberman backed off, she stood a good chance of gentling it enough to lead it out to the truck; she had a way with animals, dogs in particular—something else she could attribute to her Indian heritage. But if it attacked she would have no choice except to shoot it with the tranquilizer gun. An attack-trained, or even an untrained but high-strung, Doberman could tear your throat out in a matter of seconds.

Taking a breath, she opened the door and stepped just inside the entrance. She was careful to act natural, confident; too much caution could be as provoking to a nervous animal as movements too bold or too sudden. Black and short-haired, the Doberman was over near one of the walls—yellowish eyes staring at her, fangs bared and gleaming in the light from the open doorway and the single dusty window. But it stood its ground, forelegs spread, rear end flattened into a crouch.

"Easy," Jill said soothingly. "I'm not going to hurt you."

She started forward, extending her hand, murmuring the words of a lullabye in Shahaptian dialect. The dog cocked its head, ears perked, still growling, still tensed—but it continued to stay where it was and its snub of a tail began to quiver. That was a good sign, Jill knew. No dog wagged its tail before it attacked.

As her eyes became more accustomed to the half light, she could see that there were three small plastic bowls near the Doberman; each of them had been gnawed and deeply scratched. The condition of the bowls told her that the dog had not been fed or watered during the past thirty-six hours. She could also see that in one corner was a wicker sleeping basket about a foot and a half in diameter, and that on a nearby shelf lay a curry comb. These things told her something else, but just what it meant she had no way of knowing yet.

"Easy, boy . . . calm," she said. She was within a few paces of the dog now and it still showed no inclination to jump at her. Carefully she removed the thick glove, stretched her hand out so that the Doberman could better take her scent. "That's it, just stay easy, stay easy . . ."

The dog stopped growling. The tail stub began to quiver faster, the massive head came forward and she felt the dryness of its nose as it investigated her hand. The yellow eyes looked up at her with what she sensed was a wary acceptance.

Slowly she put away the tranquilizer gun and knelt beside the animal, murmuring the lullabye again, stroking her hand around its neck and ears. When she felt it was ready to trust her she straightened and patted the dog, took a step toward the entrance. The Doberman followed. And kept on following as she retraced her path toward the door.

They were halfway there when the deputy appeared in the doorway. "You all right in there, lady?" he called.

The Doberman bristled, snarled again low in its throat. Jill stopped and stood still. "Get away, will you?" she said to the deputy, using her normal voice, masking her annoyance so the dog wouldn't sense it. "Get out of sight. And find a hose or a faucet, get some water puddled close by. This animal is dehydrated."

The deputy retreated. Jill reached down to stroke the Doberman another time, then led it slowly out into the sunlight. When they emerged she saw that the deputy had turned on a faucet built into the garage wall; he was backed off to one side now, one hand on the weapon holstered at his side, like an actor in a B movie. The dog paid no attention to him or to anyone else. It went straight for the water and began to lap at it greedily. Jill went with it, again bent down to soothe it with her hands and voice.

While she was doing that she also checked the license and rabies tags attached to its collar, making a mental note of the numbers stamped into the thin aluminum. Now that the tenseness of the situation had eased, anger was building within her again at the way the dog had been abused. Edward Benham, whoever he was, would pay for that, she thought. She'd make certain of it.

The moment the Doberman finished drinking, Jill stood and faced the bystanders. "All of you move away from the truck," she told them. "And keep those other dogs quiet."

"You want me to get the back open for you?" the deputy asked.

"No. He goes up front with me."

"Up front? Are you crazy, lady?"

"This dog has been cooped up for a long time," Jill said. "If I put him back in the cage, he's liable to have a fit. And he might never trust me again. Up front I can open the window, talk to him, keep him calmed down."

The deputy pursed his lips reprovingly. But as he had earlier, he said, "It's your throat," and backed off with the others.

When the other dogs were still Jill caught hold of the Doberman's collar and led it down the driveway to the truck. She opened the passenger door, patted the seat. The Doberman didn't want to go in at first, but she talked to it, coaxing, and finally it obeyed. She shut the door and went around and slid in under the wheel.

"Good boy," she told the dog, smiling. "We showed them, eh?"

Jill put the truck in gear, turned it around, and waved at the scowling deputy as she passed him by.

At the Agency—a massive old brick building not far from the university—she turned the Doberman over to Sam Wyatt, the resident veterinarian, for examination and treatment. Then she went to her desk in the office area reserved for field agents and sat down with the Benham case file.

The initial report form had been filled out by the dispatcher who had logged the complaint from one of Benham's neighbors. That report listed the breed of Benham's dog as an Alaskan husky, female—not a Doberman, male. Jill had been mildly surprised when she went out to the house and discovered that the trapped dog was a Doberman. But then, the Agency was a bureaucratic organization, and like all bureaucratic organizations it made mistakes in paperwork more often than it ought to. It was likely that the dispatcher, in checking the registry files for the Benham name, had either pulled the wrong card or miscopied the information from the right one.

But Jill kept thinking about the sleeping basket and the curry comb inside the garage. The basket had been too small for the Doberman but about the right size for a female husky. And curry combs were made for long-haired, not short-haired dogs.

The situation puzzled as well as angered her. And made her more than a little curious. One of the primary character traits of the Umatilla was inquisitiveness, and Jill had inherited it along with her self-reliance and her way with animals. She had her grandmother to thank for honing her curiosity, though, for teaching her never to accept any half-truth or partial answer. She could also thank her grandmother, who had been born in the days when the tribe lived not on the reservation in northeastern Oregon but along the Umatilla River—the name itself meant "many rocks" or "water rippling over sand"—for nurturing her love for animals and leading her into her present job with the Agency. As far back as Jill could remember, the old woman had told and retold the ancient legends about "the people"—the giant creatures, Salmon and Eagle and Fox and the greatest of all, Coyote, the battler of monsters, who ruled the earth before human beings were created, before all animals shrank to their present size.

But she was not just curious about Benham for her own satisfaction; she had to have the proper data for her report. If the Agency pressed charges for animal abuse, which was what she wanted to see happen, and a heavy fine was to be levied against Benham, all pertinent information had to be correct.

She went to the registry files and pulled the card on Edward Benham. The dispatcher, it turned out, *hadn't* made a mistake after all: the breed of dog listed as being owned by Benham was an Alaskan husky, female. Also, the license and rabies tag numbers on the card were different from those she had copied down from the Doberman's collar.

One good thing about bureaucratic organizations, she thought, was that they had their filing systems cross-referenced. So she went to the files arranged according to tag numbers and looked up the listed owner of the Doberman.

The card said: *Fox Hollow Kennels, 1423 Canyon Road, Laurel County, Oregon.*

Jill had heard of Fox Hollow Kennels; it was a fairly large place some distance outside the city, operated by a man named Largo or Fargo, which specialized in raising a variety of purebred dogs. She had been there once on a field investigation that had only peripherally concerned the kennel. She was going to make her second visit, she decided, within the next hour.

The only problem with that decision was that her supervisor, Lloyd Mortisse, vetoed it when she went in to tell him where she was going. Mortisse was a lean, mournful-looking man in his late forties, with wild gray hair that reminded Jill of the dried reeds her grandmother had strung into ornamental baskets. He was also a confirmed bureaucrat, which meant that he loved paperwork, hated anything that upset the routine, and was suspicious of the agents' motives every time they went out into the field.

"Call up Fox Hollow," he told her. "You don't need to go out there; the matter doesn't warrant it."

"I think it does."

"You have other work to do, Ms. Quarter-Moon."

"Not as important as this, Mr. Mortisse."

She and Mortisse were constantly at odds. There was a mutual animosity, albeit low-key, based on his part by a certain condescension—either because she was a woman or an Indian, or maybe both—and on her part by a lack of respect. It made for less than ideal working conditions.

He said, "And I say it's not important enough for you to neglect your other duties."

"Ask that poor Doberman how important it is."

"I repeat, you're not to pursue the matter beyond a routine telephone call," Mortisse told her sententiously. "Now is that understood?"

"Yes. It's understood."

Jill pivoted, stalked out of the office, and kept right on stalking through the rear entrance and out to her truck. Twenty minutes later she was turning onto the long gravel drive, bordered by pine and Douglas fir, that led to the Fox Hollow Kennels.

She was still so annoyed at Mortisse, and preoccupied with Edward Benham, that she almost didn't see the large truck that came barreling toward her along the drive until it was too late. As it was, she managed to swerve off onto the soft shoulder just in time, and to answer the truck's horn blast with one of her own. It was an old Ford stakebed, she saw as it passed her and braked for the turn onto Canyon Road, with the words *Fox Hollow Kennels* on the driver's door. Three slat-and-wire crates were tied together on the bed, each of which contained what appeared to be a mongrel dog. The dogs had begun barking at the sound of the horns and she could see two of them pawing at the wire mesh.

Again she felt both her curiosity and her anger aroused. Transporting dogs in bunches via truck wasn't exactly inhuman treatment, but it was still a damned poor way to handle animals. And what was an American Kennel Club-registered outfit which specialized in purebreds doing with mongrels?

Jill drove up the access drive and emerged into a wide gravel parking area. The long whitewashed building that housed Fox Hollow's office was on her right, with a horseshoe arrangement of some thirty kennels and an exercise yard behind it. Pine woods surrounded the complex, giving it a rustic atmosphere.

When she parked and got out, the sound of more barking came to her from the vicinity of the exercise yard. She glanced inside the office, saw that it was empty, and went through a swing-gate that led to the back. There, beside a low fence, a man stood tossing dog biscuits into the concrete run on the other side, where half a dozen dogs—all of these purebred setters—crowded and barked together. He was in his late thirties, average-sized, with bald head and nondescript features, wearing Levi's and a University of Oregon sweatshirt. Jill recognized him as the owner, Largo or Fargo.

"Mr. Largo?" she said.

He turned, saying, "The name is Fargo." Then he set the food sack down and wiped his hands on his Levi's. His eyes were speculative as he studied both her and her tan Agency uniform. "Something I can do for you, miss?"

Jill identified herself. "I'm here about a dog," she said, "a male Doberman, about three years old. It was abandoned inside a house in Oregon Estates at least two days ago; we went in and released it this morning. The house belongs to a man named Benham, Edward Benham, but the Doberman is registered to Fox Hollow."

Fargo's brows pulled down. "Benham, did you say?"

"That's right. Edward Benham. Do you know him?"

"Well, I don't recognize the name."

"Is it possible you sold him the Doberman?"

"I suppose it is," Fargo said. "Some people don't bother to change the registration. Makes a lot of trouble for all of us when they don't."

"Yes, it does. Would you mind checking your records?"

"Not at all."

He led her around and inside the kennel office. It was a cluttered room that smelled peculiarly of dog, dust and cheap men's cologne. An open door on the far side led to an attached work room; Jill could see a bench littered with tools, stacks of lumber, and several slat-and-wire crates of the kind she had noticed on the truck, some finished and some under construction.

Along one wall was a filing cabinet and Fargo crossed to it, began to rummage inside. After a time he came out with a folder, opened it, consulted the papers it held, and put it away again. He turned to face Jill.

"Yep," he said. "Edward Benham. He bought the Doberman about three weeks ago. I didn't handle the sale myself; one of my assistants took care of it. That's why I didn't recognize the name."

"Is your assistant here now?"

"No, I gave him a three-day weekend to go fishing."

"Is the Doberman the only animal Benham has bought from you?"

"As far as the records show, it is."

"Benham is the registered owner of a female Alaskan husky," Jill said. "Do you know anyone who specializes in that breed?"

"Not offhand. Check with the American Kennel Club; they might be able to help you."

"I'll do that." Jill paused. "I passed your truck on the way in, Mr. Fargo. Do you do a lot of shipping of dogs?"

"Some, yes. Why?"

"Just curious. Where are those three today bound?"

"Portland." Fargo made a deliberate point of looking at his watch. "If you'll excuse me, I've got work to do. . . ."

"Just one more thing, I'd like to see your American Kennel Club registration on the Doberman you sold Benham."

"Can't help you there, I'm afraid," Fargo said. "There wasn't any AKC registration on that Doberman."

"No? Why not? He's certainly a purebred."

"Maybe so, but the animal wasn't bred here. We bought it from a private party who didn't even know the AKC existed."

"What was this private party's name?"

"Adams. Charles Adams. From out of state—California. That's why Fox Hollow was the first to register the dog with you people."

Jill decided not to press the matter, at least not with Fargo personally. She had other ways of finding out information about him, about Fox Hollow, and about Edward Benham. She thanked Fargo for his time, left the office, and headed her truck back to the Agency.

When she got there she went first to see Sam Wyatt, to check on the Doberman's health. There was nothing wrong with the animal, Wyatt told her, except for minor malnutrition and dehydration. It had been fed, exercised, and put into one of the larger cages.

She looked in on it. The dog seemed glad to see her; the stub of a tail began to wag when she approached the cage. She played her fingers through the mesh grille, let the Doberman nuzzle them.

While she was doing that the kennel attendant, a young redhead named Lena Stark, came out of the dispensary. "Hi, Jill," she said. "The patient looks pretty good, doesn't he?"

"He'll look a lot better when we find him a decent owner."

"That's for sure."

"Funny thing—he's registered to the Fox Hollow Kennels, but they say he was sold to one Edward Benham. It was Benham's garage he was locked up in."

"Why is that funny?"

"Well, purebred Dobermans don't come cheap. Why would anybody who'd pay for one suddenly go off and desert him?"

"I guess that is kind of odd," Lena admitted. "Unless Benham was called out of town on an urgent matter or something. That would explain it."

"Maybe," Jill said.

"Some people should never own pets, you know? Benham should have left the dog at Fox Hollow; at least they care about the welfare of animals."

"Why do you say that?"

"Because every now and then one of their guys comes in and takes most of our strays."

"Oh? For what reason?"

"They train them and then find homes for them in other parts of the state. A pretty nice gesture, don't you think?"

"Yes," Jill said thoughtfully. "A pretty nice gesture."

She went inside and straight to the filing room, where she pulled the Fox Hollow folder. At her desk she spread out the kennel's animal licensing applications and studied them. It stood to reason that there would be a large number and there were; but as she sifted through them Jill was struck by a peculiarity. Not counting the strays Fox Hollow had "adopted" from the Agency, which by law had to be vaccinated and licensed before being released, there were less than a dozen dogs brought in and registered over the past twelve months. For a kennel which claimed to specialize in purebreds, this was suspiciously odd. Yet no one else had noticed it in the normal bureaucratic shuffle, just as no one had paid much attention to Fox Hollow's gathering of Agency strays.

And why *was* Fox Hollow in the market for so many stray dogs? Having met Fargo, she doubted that he was the humanitarian type motivated by a desire to save mongrels from euthanasia, a dog's fate if kept unclaimed at the Agency for more than four days. No, it sounded as if he were in some sort of strange wholesale pet business—as if the rest of the state, not to mention the rest of the country, didn't have their own animal overpopulation problems.

But where did Edward Benham, and the Doberman, fit in? Jill reviewed the Benham file again, but it had nothing new to tell her. She wished she knew where he'd gone, or of some way to get in touch with him. The obvious way, of course, was through his place of employment; unfortunately, however, pet license applications did not list employment of owners, only home address and telephone number. Nor had any of his neighbors known where he worked.

Briefly she considered trying to bluff information out of one of the credit-reporting companies in the city. Benham had bought rather than rented or leased his house, which meant that he probably carried a mortgage, which meant credit, which meant an application listing his employment. The problem was that legitimate members of such credit companies used special secret numbers to identify themselves when requesting information, so any ruse she might attempt would no doubt fail, and might even backfire and land her in trouble with Mortisse.

Then she thought of Pete Olafson, the office manager for Mid-Valley Adjustment Bureau, a local bad-debt collection service. Mid-Valley could certainly belong to a credit-reporting company. And she knew Pete pretty well, had dated him a few times in recent months. There wasn't any torrid romance brewing between her and the sandy-haired bachelor, but she knew he liked her a good deal—maybe enough to bend the rules a little and check Benham's credit as a favor.

She looked up Mid-Valley's number, dialed it, and was talking to Pete fifteen seconds later. "You must be a mindreader, Jill," he said after she identified herself. "I was going to call you later. The University Theater is putting on 'Our Town' tomorrow night and I've wangled a couple of free passes. Would you like to go?"

"Sure. If you'll do me a favor in return."

Pete sighed dramatically. "Nothing is free these days, it seems. Okay, what is it?"

"I want to know where a man named Edward Benham is employed. Could you track down his credit applications and find out from them?"

"I can if he's got credit somewhere."

"Well, he owns his own home, out in Oregon Estates. The name is Benham. B-e-n-h-a-m, Edward. How fast can you find out for me?"

"It shouldn't take long. Sit tight; I'll get back to you."

Jill replaced the handset and sat with her chin propped in one palm brooding. If the lead to Edward Benham through Pete didn't pan out, then what? Talk to his neighbors again? Through them she could find out the name of the real estate agent who had sold Benham his home . . . but it was unlikely that they would divulge personal information about him, since she had no official capacity. Talk to Fargo again? That probably wouldn't do her any good either. . . .

The door to Lloyd Mortisse's private office opened; Jill saw him thrust his wild-maned head out and look in her direction. It was not a look of pleasure. "Ms. Quarter-Moon," he said. "Come into my office, please."

Jill complied. Mortisse shut the door behind her, sat down at his desk, and glared at her. "I thought," he said stiffly, "that I told you not to go out to Fox Hollow Kennels."

Surprised, Jill asked, "How did you know about that?"

"Mr. Fargo called me. He wanted to know why you were out there asking all sorts of questions. He wasn't pleased by your visit; neither am I. Why did you disobey me?"

"I felt the trip was necessary."

"Oh, you felt it was necessary. I see. That makes it all right, I suppose."

"Look, Mr. Mortisse—"

"I do not like disobedience," Mortisse said. "I won't stand for it again, is that clear? Nor will I stand for you harassing private facilities like Fox Hollow. This Agency's sole concern in the Benham matter is to house the Doberman for ninety-six hours or until it is claimed. And I'll be the one, not you, to decide if any misdemeanor animal-abuse charges are to be filed against Mr. Benham."

Jill thought that it was too bad these weren't the old days, when one of the Umatilla customs in tribal disputes was to hold a potlatch—a fierce social competition at which rival chiefs gave away or destroyed large numbers of blankets, coppers, and slaves in an effort to outdo and therefore vanquish each other. She would have liked nothing better than to challenge Mortisse in this sort of duel, using bureaucratic attitudes and red tape as the throwaway material. She also decided there was no point in trying to explain her suspicions to him; he would only have said in his supercilious way that none of it was Agency business. If she was going to get to the bottom of what was going on at Fox Hollow, she would have to do it on her own.

"Do you understand?" Mortisse was saying. "You're to drop this matter and attend to your assigned duties. And you're not to disobey a direct order again, under any circumstances."

"I understand," Jill said thinly. "Is that all?"

"That's all."

She stood and left the office, resisting an impulse to slam the door. The wall clock said that it was 4:10—less than an hour until quitting time for the weekend. All right, she thought as she crossed to her desk. I'll drop the matter while I'm on Agency time. But what I do and where I go on my own time is *my* business. Mortisse or no Mortisse.

It was another ten minutes, during which time she typed up a pair of two-day-old reports, before Pete Olafson called her back. "Got what you asked for, Jill," he said. "Edward Benham has a pretty fair credit rating, considering he's modestly employed."

"What does he do?"

"He's a deliveryman, it says here. For a kennel."

Jill sat up straight. "Kennel?"

"That's right," Pete said. "Place called Fox Hollow outside the city. Is that what you're after?"

"It's a lot more than I expected," Jill told him. Quickly she arranged tomorrow night's date with him, then replaced the receiver and sat mulling over this latest bit of news.

If she had needed anything more to convince her that something was amiss at Fox Hollow, this was it. Fargo had claimed he didn't know Edward Benham; now it turned out that Benham worked for Fargo. Why had he lied? What was he trying to cover up? And where was Benham? And where did the Doberman fit in?

She spent another half hour at her desk, keeping one eye on the clock and pretending to work while she sorted through questions, facts, and options in her mind. At ten minutes of five, when she couldn't take any more of the inactivity, she went out into the kennel area to see Lena Stark.

"Release the Doberman to me, will you, Lena?" she asked. "I'll bring him back later tonight and check him in with the night attendant."

"Why do you want him?"

"I like his looks and I want to get better acquainted. If it turns out neither Fox Hollow nor Benham decides to claim him, I may just adopt him myself."

"I don't know, Jill . . ."

"He's all right, isn't he? Sam Wyatt said he was."

"Sure, he's fine. But the rules—"

"Oh, hang the rules. Nobody has to know except you and me and the night attendant. I'll take full responsibility."

"Well . . . okay, I guess you know what you're doing."

Lena opened the cage and the Doberman came out, stubby tail quivering, and nuzzled Jill's hand. She led it out through the rear door, into the parking lot to where her compact was parked. Obediently, as if delighted to be free and in her company, the dog jumped onto the front seat and sat down with an expectant look.

Jill stroked its ears as she drove out of the lot. "I don't want to keep calling you 'boy'," she said. "I think I'll give you a name, even if it's only temporary. How about Tyee?" In the old Chinook jargon, the mixed trade language of Indians and whites in frontier days, *tyee* was the word for chief. "You like that? Tyee?"

The dog cocked its head and made a rumbly sound in its throat.

"Good," Jill said. "Tyee it is."

She drove across the city and into Oregon Estates. Edward Benham's house, she saw when she braked at the end of the cul-de-sac, looked as deserted as it had this morning. This was confirmed when she went up and rang the doorbell several times without getting a response.

She took Tyee with her and let him sniff around both front and back. The Doberman showed none of the easy familiarity of a dog on its own turf; rather, she sensed a wary tenseness in the way he moved and keened the air. And when she led him near the garage he bristled, made low growling noises. He was as much a stranger here as she was, Jill thought. But then why had he been locked in Benham's garage?

She would have liked to go inside for a better look around, but the locksmith had relocked the doors, as dictated by law, before leaving the premises that morning. The house was securely locked too, as were each of the windows. And drawn drapes and blinds made it impossible to see into any of the rooms from outside.

Jill took Tyee back to her compact. She sat for a time, considering. Then she started the engine and pointed the car in an easterly direction.

It was just seven o'clock when she came up the access drive to Fox Hollow Kennels and coasted to a stop on the gravel parking area near the main building. There were no other vehicles around, a *Closed* sign was propped in one dusty pane of the front door, and the complex had a deserted aura; even the dogs in the near kennels were quiet.

She got out, motioning for Tyee to stay where he was on the front seat. The setting sun hung above the tops of the pines straight ahead, bathing everything in a dark-orange radiance. Jill judged that there was about an hour of daylight left, which meant that an hour was all she would have to look around. Prowling in daylight was risky enough, though if she were seen she might be able to bluff her way out of trouble by claiming she had brought Tyee back to his registered owner. If she were caught here after dark, no kind of bluff would be worth much.

The office door was locked, but when she shook it, it rattled loosely in its frame. Jill bent for a closer look at the latch. It was a spring-type lock, rather than a deadbolt. She straightened again, gnawing at her lower lip. Detectives in movies and on TV were forever opening spring locks with credit cards or pieces of celluloid; there was no reason why she couldn't do the same thing. No reason, that was, except that it was illegal and would cost her her job, if not a prison term, were she to be caught. She could imagine Lloyd Mortisse smiling like the Cheshire Cat at news of her arrest.

But she was already here, and the need to sate her curiosity was overpowering. The debate with her better judgment lasted all of ten seconds. Then she thought: Well, fools rush in—and she went back to the car to get a credit card from her purse.

Less than a minute of maneuvering with the card rewarded her with a sharp click as the lock snapped free. The door opened under her hand. Enough of the waning orange sunlight penetrated through the windows, she saw when she stepped inside, so that she didn't need any other kind of light. She went straight to the filing cabinets, began to shuffle through the folders inside.

The kennel records were in something of a shambles; Jill realized quickly that it would take hours, maybe even days, to sort through all the receipts, partial entries, and scraps of paper. But one file was complete enough to hold her attention and to prove interesting. It consisted of truck expenses—repair bills, oil company credit card receipts, and the like—and what intrigued her was that, taken together, they showed that the Fox Hollow delivery truck consistently traveled to certain towns in Oregon, northern California, and southern Washington. Forest Grove, Corvallis,

Portland, McMinnville, Ashland, La Grande, Arcata, Kirkland. . . . These, and a few others, comprised a regular route.

Which might explain why Edward Benham was nowhere to be found at the moment; some of the towns were at least an overnight's drive away, and it was Benham's signature that was on most of the receipts. But the evident truck route also raised more questions. Why such long hauls for a small kennel? Why to some points out of state? And why to these particular towns, when there were numerous others of similar size along the way?

"Curiouser and curiouser," Jill murmured to herself.

She shut the file drawers and turned to the desk. Two of the drawers were locked; she decided it would be best not to try forcing them. None of the other drawers, nor any of the clutter spread across the top, told her anything incriminating or enlightening.

The door to the adjacent workroom was closed, but when she tried the knob it opened right up. That room was dimmer but there was still enough daylight filtering in to let her see the tools, workbench, stacks of lumber, finished and unfinished crates. She picked through the farrago of items on the bench; caught up slats and corner posts of an unassembled cage, started to put them down again. Then, frowning, she studied one of the wooden posts more carefully.

The post was hollow. So were the others; the inner lengths of all four had been bored out by a large drill bit. When fitted into the frame of a fully constructed cage the posts would appear solid, their holes concealed by the top and bottom sections. Only when the cage was apart, like now, would the secret compartments be exposed, to be filled or emptied.

Of what?

Jill renewed her search. In a back corner were three rolls of cage wire—and caught on a snag of mesh on one roll was a small cellophane bag. The bag was out of easy sight and difficult to reach, but she managed to retrieve it. It looked new, unopened, and it was maybe 3 × 5 inches in size. The kind of bag—

And then she knew. What the bag was for, why the corner posts were hollowed out, what Fox Hollow was involved in. And it was ugly enough and frightening enough to make her feel a chill of apprehension, make her want to get away from there in a hurry. It was more than she had bargained for—considerably more.

She ran out of the workroom, still clutching the cellophane bag in her left hand. At the office door she peered through the glass before letting herself out, to make sure the parking area remained deserted. Then she set the button-lock on the knob, stepped outside, pulled the door shut, and started across to her compact.

Tyee was gone.

She stopped, staring in at the empty front seat. She had left the driver's window all the way down and he must have jumped out. Turning, she peered through gathering shadows toward the kennels. But the dogs were still quiet back there, and they wouldn't be if the Doberman had gone prowling in that direction. Where, then? Back down the drive? The pine woods somewhere?

Jill hesitated. The sense of urgency and apprehension demanded that she climb into the car, Tyee or no Tyee, and drive away pronto. But she couldn't just leave him here while she went to tell her suspicions to the county sheriff. The law would not come out here tonight no matter what she told them; they'd wait until tomorrow, when the kennel was open for business and when they could obtain a search warrant. And once she left here herself she had no intention of coming back again after dark.

She moved away from the car, toward the dark line of evergreens beyond. It was quiet here, with dust settling, and sounds carried some distance; the scratching noises reached her ears when she was still twenty paces from the woods. She'd heard enough dogs digging into soft earth to recognize the sound and she quickened her pace. Off to one side was a beaten-down area, not quite a path, and she went into the trees at that point. The digging sounds grew louder. Then she saw Tyee, over behind a decayed moss-festooned log, making earth and dry needles fly out behind him with his forepaws.

"What are you doing?" she called to him. "Come here, Tyee."

The Doberman kept on digging, paying no attention to her. She hurried over to him, around the bulky shape of the log. And then she stopped abruptly, made a startled gasping sound.

A man's arm and clenched hand lay partially uncovered in the soft ground.

Tyee was still digging, still scattering dirt and pine needles. Jill stood frozen, watching part of a broad back encased in a khaki shirt appear.

Now she knew what had happened to Edward Benham.

She made herself move, step forward and catch hold of the Doberman's collar. He resisted at first when she tried to tug him away from the shallow grave and what was in it; but she got a firmer grip and pulled harder, and finally he quit struggling. She dragged him around the log, back out of the trees.

Most of the daylight was gone now; the sky was grayish, streaked with red, like bloody fingermarks on faded cloth. A light wind had come up and she felt herself shiver as she took the Doberman toward her compact. She was anything but a shrinking violet, but what she had found at Fox Hollow tonight was enough to frighten Old Chief Joseph or any of the other venerable Shahaptian warriors. The sooner she was sitting in the safety of the Laurel County Sheriff's office, the better she—

And the figure of a man came out from behind her car.

She was ten feet from the driver's door, her right hand on Tyee's collar, when the man rose up into view like Nashlah, the legendary monster of the Columbia River. Jill made an involuntary cry, stiffened into a standstill. The Doberman seemed to go as tense as she did; a low rumble sounded in his throat as the man came toward them.

Fargo. With a gun in his hand.

"You just keep on holding that dog," he said. He stopped fifteen feet away, holding the gun out at arm's length. "You're both dead if you let go his collar."

She was incapable of speech for five or six seconds. Then she made herself say, "There's no need for that gun, Mr. Fargo. I'm only here to return the Doberman. . . ."

"Sure you are. Let's not play games. You're here because you're a damned snoop. And I'm here because you tripped a silent alarm connected to my house when you broke into the office."

It was not in Jill's nature to panic in a crisis; she got a grip on her fear and held it down, smothered it. "The office door was unlocked," she said. "Maybe you think you locked it when you left but you didn't. I just glanced inside."

"I don't buy that either," Fargo said. "I saw you come out of the office; I left my car down the road and walked up here through the trees. I saw you go into the woods over there, too."

"I went to find the dog, that's all."

"But that's not what you found, right? He's got dirt all over his forepaws—he's been doing some digging. You found Benham. And now you know too much about everything."

"I don't know what you're talking about."

"I say you do. So does that cellophane bag you're carrying."

Jill looked down at her left hand; she had forgotten all about the bag. And she had never even considered the possibility of a silent alarm system. She had a lot to learn about being a detective—if she survived to profit by her mistakes.

"All right," she said. "It's drugs, isn't it? That's the filthy business you're in."

"You got it."

"Selling drugs to college kids all over the Pacific Northwest," she said. That was the significance of the towns on the Fox Hollow shipping route: they were all college or university towns. Humboldt State in Arcata, Lewis & Clark in Portland, Linfield College in McMinnville, Eastern Oregon College in La Grande. And the state university right here in this city. That was also why Fox Hollow had taken so many stray dogs from the Agency; they needed a constant supply to cover their shipment of drugs—cocaine and heroin, probably, the kind usually packaged and shipped in small cellophane bags—to the various suppliers along their network. "Where does it come from? Canada?"

"Mexico," Fargo said. "They bring it up by ship, we cut and package and distribute it."

"To kennels in those other cities, I suppose."

"That's right. They make a nice cover."

"What happens to the dogs you ship?"

"What do you think happens to them? Dogs don't matter when you're running a multi-million-dollar operation. Neither do snoops like you. Nobody fouls up this kind of operation and gets away with it."

Tyee growled again, shifted his weight; Jill tightened her grip on his collar. "Did Benham foul it up? Is that why he's dead?"

"He tried to. His percentage wasn't enough for him and he got greedy; he decided to hijack a shipment for himself—substitute milk sugar and then make off with the real stuff. When he left here on Wednesday for Corvallis he detoured over to his house and made the switch. Only one of the crates had the drugs in it, like always; he had to let the dog out of that one to get at the shipment and it turned on him, tried to bite him."

"This dog, the Doberman."

"Yeah. He managed to lock it up inside his garage, but that left him with an empty crate and he couldn't deliver an empty, not without making the Corvallis contact suspicious. So he loaded his own dog, the husky, inside the crate and delivered it instead. But our man checked the dope anyway, discovered the switch, and called me. I was waiting for Benham when he got back here."

"And you killed him."

Fargo shrugged. "I had no choice."

"Like you've got no choice with me?"

He shrugged again. "I forgot all about the Doberman, that was my mistake. If I hadn't, I wouldn't have you on my hands. But it just didn't occur to me the dog would raise a ruckus and a nosy Agency worker would decide to investigate."

"Why did you lie to me before about knowing Benham?"

"I didn't want you doing any more snooping. I figured if I gave you that story about selling him the Doberman, you'd come up against a dead-end and drop the whole thing. Same reason I called your supervisor: I thought he'd make you drop it. Besides, you had no official capacity. It was your word against mine."

"Lying to me was your second mistake," Jill said. "If you kill me, it'll be your third."

"How do you figure that?"

"I told somebody I came out here tonight. He'll go to the county sheriff if I disappear, and they'll come straight to you."

"That's a bluff," Fargo said. "And I don't bluff. You didn't tell anybody about coming here; nobody knows but you and me. And pretty soon it'll just be me." He made a gesture with the gun. "Look at it this way. You're only one person, but I got a lot of people depending on me: others in the operation, all those kids we supply."

All those kids, Jill thought, and there was a good hot rage inside her now. College kids, some of them still in their teens. White kids, black kids—Indian kids. She had seen too many Indian youths with drug habits; she had talked to the parents of a sixteen-year-old boy who had died from an overdose of heroin on the Umatilla reservation, of a seventeen-year-old girl, an honor student, killed in a drug raid at Trout Lake near the Warm Springs development. Any minority, especially its restless and sometimes disenchanted youth, was susceptible to drug exploitation; and Indians were a minority long oppressed in their own country. That was why she hated drugs, and hated these new oppressors, the drug dealers like Fargo, even more.

Fargo said, "Okay, we've done enough talking—no use in prolonging things. Turn around, walk into the woods."

"So you can bury me next to Benham?"

"Never mind that. Just move."

"No," she said, and she let her body go limp, sank onto her knees. She dropped the cellophane bag as she did so and then put that hand flat on the gravel beside her, keeping her other hand on Tyee's collar. The Doberman, sensing the increase of tension between her and Fargo, had his fangs bared now, growling steadily.

"What the hell?" Fargo said. "Get up."

Jill lowered her chin to her chest and began to chant in a soft voice—a Shahaptian prayer.

"I said get up!"

She kept on chanting.

Fargo took two steps toward her, a third, a fourth. That put less than five feet of ground between them. "I'll shoot you right where you are, I mean it—"

She swept up a handful of gravel, hurled it at his face, let go of Tyee's collar, and flung herself to one side.

The gun went off and she heard the bullet strike the ground near her head, felt the sting of a pebble kicked up against her cheek. Then Fargo screamed, and when Jill rolled over she saw that Tyee had done what she'd prayed he would—attacked Fargo the instant he was released. He had driven the man backward and knocked him down and was shaking his captured wrist as if it were a stick; the gun had popped loose and sailed off to one side. Fargo cried out again, tried to club the Doberman with his free hand. Blood from where Tyee's teeth had bitten into his wrist flowed down along his right arm.

Jill scrambled to her feet, ran to where the gun lay and scooped it up. But before she could level it at Fargo, he jacknifed his body backwards, trying to escape from the Doberman, and cracked his head against the front bumper of her compact; she heard the thunking sound it made in the stillness, saw him go limp. Tyee still straddled the inert form, growling, shaking the bloody wrist.

She went over there, caught the dog's collar again, talked to him until he let go of Fargo and backed off with her. But he stood close, alert, alternately looking at the unconscious man and up at her. She knelt and hugged him, and there were tears in her eyes. She disliked women who cried, particularly self-sufficient Indian women, but sometimes . . . sometimes it was a necessary release.

"You know who you are?" she said to him. "You're not Tyee, you're Coyote. You do battle with monsters and evil beings and you save Indians from harm."

The Doberman licked her hand.

"The Great One isn't supposed to return until the year 2000, when the world changes again and all darkness is gone; but you're here already and I won't let you go away. You're mine and I'm yours from now on—Coyote and Quarter-Moon."

Then she stood, shaky but smiling, and went to re-pick the lock on the office door so she could call the Laurel County sheriff.

At the Old Swimming Hole

Sara Paretsky

1

The gym was dank—chlorine and sweat combined in a hot, sticky mass. Shouts from the trainers, from the swimmers, from the spectators, bounced from the high metal ceilings and back and forth from the benches lining the pool on two sides. The cacophony set up an unpleasant buzzing in my head.

I was not enjoying myself. My shirt was soaked through with sweat. Anyway, I was too old to sit cheering on a bleacher for two hours. But Alicia had been insistent—I had to be there in person for her to get points on her sponsor card.

Alicia Alonso Dauphine and I went to high school together. Her parents had bestowed a prima ballerina's name on her, but Alicia showed no aptitude for fine arts. From her earliest years, all she wanted was to muck around with engines. At eighteen, off she went to the University of Illinois to study aeronautics.

Despite her lack of interest in dance, Alicia was very athletic. Next to airplanes, the only thing she really cared about was competitive swimming. I used to cheer her when she was NCAA swimming champ, always with a bit of irritation about being locked in a dank, noisy gym for hours at a time—swimming is not a great spectator sport. But after all, what are friends for?

When Alicia joined Berman Aircraft as an associate engineer, we drifted our separate ways. We met occasionally at weddings, confirmations, bar mitzvahs (my, how our friends were aging! Childlessness seemed to suspend us in time, but each new ceremony in their lives marked a new milestone toward old age for the women we had played with in high school).

Then last week I'd gotten a call from Alicia. Berman was mounting a team for a citywide corporate competition—money would be raised through sponsors for the American Cancer Society. Both Alicia's mother and mine had died of cancer—would I sponsor her for so many meters? Doubling my contribution if she won? It was only after I'd made the pledge that I realized she expected me there in person. One of her sponsors had to show up to testify that she'd done it, and all the others were busy with their homes and children, and come on, V.I., what do you do all day long? I need you.

How can you know you're being manipulated and still let it happen? I hunched an impatient shoulder and turned back to the starting blocks.

From where I sat, Alicia was just another bathing-suited body with a cap. Her distinctive cheekbones were softened and flattened by the dim fluorescence. Not a wisp of her thick black hair trailed around her face. She was wearing a bright red tank suit—no extra straps or flounces to slow her down in the water.

The swimmers had been wandering around the side of the pool, swinging their arms to stretch out the muscles, not talking much while the timers argued some inaudible point with the referee. Now a police whistle shrilled faintly in the din and the competitors snapped to attention, moving toward the starting blocks at the far end of the pool.

We were about to watch the fifty-meter freestyle. I looked at the hand-scribbled card Alicia had given me before the meet. After the fifty-meter, she was in a 4 × 50 relay. Then I could leave.

The swimmers were mounting the blocks when someone began complaining again. The woman from the Ajax insurance team seemed to be having a problem with the lane marker on the inside of her lane. The referee reshuffled the swimmers, leaving the offending lane empty. The swimmers finally mounted the blocks again. Timers got into position.

Standing to see the start of the race, I was no longer certain which of the women was Alicia. Two of the other six contenders also wore red tank suits; with their features smoothed by caps and dimmed lighting, they all became anonymous. One red suit was in lane two, one in lane three, one in lane six.

The referee raised the starting gun. Swimmers got set. Arms swung back for the dive. Then the gun, and seven bodies flung themselves into the water. Perfect dive in lane six—had to be Alicia, surfacing, pulling away from all but one other swimmer, a fast little woman from the brokerage house of Feldstein, Holtz and Woods.

Problems for the red-suited woman in lane two. I hadn't seen her dive, but she was having trouble righting herself, couldn't seem to make headway in the lane. Now everyone was noticing her. Whistles were blowing; the man on the loudspeaker tried ineffectually to call for silence.

I pushed my way through the crowds on the benches and vaulted over the barrier dividing the spectators from the water. Useless over the din to order someone into the pool for her. Useless to point out the growing circle of red. I kicked off running shoes and dove from the side. Swimming underwater to the second lane. Not Alicia. Surely not. Seeing the water turn red around me. Find the woman. Surface. Drag her to the edge where, finally, a few galvanized hands pulled her out.

I scrambled from the pool and picked out someone in a striped referee's shirt. "Get a fire department ambulance as fast as you can." He stared at me with a stupid gape to his jaw. "Dial 911, damn it. Do it now!" I pushed him toward the door, hard, and he suddenly broke into a trot.

I knelt beside the woman. She was breathing, but shallowly. I felt her gently. Hard to find the source of bleeding with the wet suit, but I thought it came from the upper back. Demanding help from one of the bystanders, I carefully turned her to her side. Blood was oozing now, not pouring, from a wound below her left shoulder. Pack it with towels, elevate her feet, keep the crowd back. Wait. Wait. Watch the shallow breathing turn to choking. Mouth-to-mouth does no good. Who knows cardiopulmonary resuscitation? A muscular young man in skimpy bikini shorts comes forward and works at her chest. By the time the paramedics hustle in with stretcher and equipment, the shallow, choking breath has stopped. They take her to the hospital, but we all know it's no good.

As the stretcher-bearers trotted away, the rest of the room came back into focus. Alicia was standing at my side, black hair hanging damply to her shoulders, watching me with fierce concentration. Everyone else seemed to be shrieking in unison; the sound re-echoing from the rafters was more unbearable than ever.

I stood up, put my mouth close to Alicia's ear, and asked her to take me to whoever was in charge. She pointed to a man in an Izod T-shirt standing on the other side of the hole left by the dead swimmer's body.

I went to him immediately. "I'm V. I. Warshawski. I'm a private detective. That woman was murdered—shot through the back. Whoever shot her probably left during the confusion. But you'd better get the cops here now. And tell everyone over your megaphone that no one leaves until the police have seen them."

He looked contemptuously at my dripping jeans and shirt. "Do you have anything to back up this preposterous statement?"

I held out my hands. "Blood," I said briefly, then grabbed the microphone from him. "May I have your attention, please." My voice bounced around the hollow room. "My name is V. I. Warshawski; I am a detective. There has been a serious accident in the pool. Until the police have been here and talked to us, none of us must leave this area. I am asking the six timers who were at the far end of the pool to come here now."

There was silence for a minute, then renewed clamor. A handful of people picked their way along the edge of the pool toward me. The man in the Izod shirt was fulminating but lacked the guts to try to grab the mike.

When the timers came up to me, I said, "You six are the only ones who definitely could not have killed the woman. I want you to stand at the exits." I tapped each in turn and sent them to a post—two to the doors on the second floor at the top of the bleachers, two to the ground-floor exits, and one each to the doors leading to the men's and women's dressing rooms.

"Don't let anyone, regardless of *anything* he or she says, leave. If they have to use the bathroom, tough—hold it until the cops get here. Anyone tries to leave, keep them here. If they want to fight, let them go but get as complete a description as you can."

They trotted off to their stations. I gave Izod back his mike, made my way to a pay phone in the corner, and dialed the Eleventh Street homicide number.

2

Sergeant McGonnigal was not fighting sarcasm as hard as he might have. "You sent the guy to guard the upstairs exit and he waltzed away, probably taking the gun with him. He must be on his knees in some church right now thanking God for sending a pushy private investigator to this race."

I bit my lips. He couldn't be angrier with me than I was with myself. I sneezed and shivered in my damp, clammy clothes. "You're right, Sergeant. I wish you'd been at the meet instead of me. You'd probably have had ten uniformed officers with you who could've taken charge as soon as the starting gun was fired and avoided this mess. Do any of the timers know who the man was?"

We were in an office that the school athletic department had given the police for their investigation-scene headquarters. McGonnigal had been questioning all the timers, figuring their closeness to the pool gave them the best angle on what had happened. One was missing, the man I'd sent to the upper balcony exit.

The sergeant grudgingly told me he'd been over that ground with the other timers. None of them knew who the missing man was. Each of the companies in the meet had supplied volunteers to do the timing and other odd jobs. Everyone just assumed this man was from someone else's firm. No one had noticed him that closely; their attention was focused on the action in the pool. My brief glance at him gave the police their best description: medium height, light, short brown hair, wearing a pale green T-shirt and faded white denim shorts. Yes, baggy enough for a gun to fit in a pocket unnoticed.

"You know, Sergeant, I asked for the six timers at the far end of the pool because they were facing the swimmers, so none of them could have shot the dead woman in the back. This guy came forward. That means there's a timer missing—either the person actually down at the far end was in collusion, or you're missing a body."

McGonnigal made an angry gesture—not at me. Himself for not having thought of it before. He detailed two uniformed cops to round up all the volunteers and find out who the errant timer was.

"Any more information on the dead woman?"

McGonnigal picked up a pad from the paper-littered desk in front of him. "Her name was Louise Carmody. You know that. She was twenty-four. She worked for the Ft. Dearborn Bank and Trust as a junior lending officer. You know that. Her boss is very shocked—you probably could guess that. And she has no enemies. No dead person ever does."

"Was she working on anything sensitive?"

He gave me a withering glance. "What twenty-four-year-old junior loan officer works on anything sensitive?"

"Lots," I said firmly. "No senior person ever does the grubby work. A junior officer crunches numbers or gathers basic data for crunching. Was she working on any project that someone might not want her to get data for?"

McGonnigal shrugged wearily but made a note on a second pad—the closest he would come to recognizing that I might have a good suggestion.

I sneezed again. "Do you need me for anything else? I'd like to get home and dry off."

"No, go. I'd just as soon you weren't around when Lieutenant Mallory arrives, anyway."

Bobby Mallory was McGonnigal's boss. He was also an old friend of my father, who had been a beat sergeant until his death fifteen years earlier. Bobby did not like women on the crime scene in any capacity—victim, perpetrator, or investigator—and he especially did not like his old friend Tony's daughter on the scene. I appreciated McGonnigal's unwillingness to witness any acrimony between his boss and me, and was getting up to leave when the uniformed cops came back.

The sixth timer had been found in a supply closet behind the men's lockers. He was concussed and groggy from a head wound and couldn't remember how he got to where he was. Couldn't remember anything past lunchtime. I waited long enough to hear that and slid from the room.

Alicia was waiting for me at the far end of the hall. She had changed from her suit into jeans and a pullover and was squatting on her heels, staring fiercely at nothing. When she saw me coming, she stood up and pushed her black hair out of her eyes.

"You look a mess, V.I."

"Thanks. I'm glad to get help and support from my friends after they've dragged me into a murder investigation."

"Oh, don't get angry—I didn't mean it that way. I'm sorry I dragged you into a murder investigation. No, I'm not, actually. I'm glad you were on hand. Can we talk?"

"After I put some dry clothes on and stop looking a mess."

She offered me her jacket. Since I'm five-eight to her five-four, it wasn't much of a cover, but I draped it gratefully over my shoulders to protect myself from the chilly October evening.

At my apartment Alicia followed me into the bathroom while I turned on the hot water. "Do you know who the dead woman was? The police wouldn't tell us."

"Yes," I responded irritably. "And if you'll give me twenty minutes to warm up, I'll tell you. Bathing is not a group sport in this apartment."

She trailed back out of the bathroom, her face set in tense lines. When I joined her in the living room some twenty minutes later, a towel around my damp hair, she was sitting in front of the television set changing channels.

"No news yet," she said briefly. "Who was the dead girl?"

"Louise Carmody. Junior loan officer at the Ft. Dearborn. You know her?"

Alicia shook her head. "Do the police know why she was shot?"

"They're just starting to investigate. What do you know about it?"

"Nothing. Are they going to put her name on the news?"

"Probably, if the family's been notified. Why is this important?"

"No reason. It just seems so ghoulish, reporters hovering around her dead body and everything."

"Could I have the truth, please?"

She sprang to her feet and glared at me. "It is the truth."

"Screw that. You don't know her name, you spin the TV dials to see the reports, and now you think it's ghoulish for the reporters to hover around? . . . Tell you what I think, Alicia. I think you know who did the shooting. They shuffled the swimmers, nobody knew who was in which lane. You started out in lane two, and you'd be dead if the woman from Ajax hadn't complained. Who wants to kill you?"

Her black eyes glittered in her white face. "No one. Why don't you have a little empathy, Vic? I might have been killed. There was a madman out there who shot a woman. Why don't you give me some sympathy?"

"I jumped into a pool to pull that woman out. I sat around in wet clothes for two hours talking to the cops. I'm beat. You want sympathy, go someplace else. The little I have is reserved for myself tonight.

"I'd really like to know why I had to be at the pool, if it wasn't to ward off a potential attacker. And if you'd told me the real reason, Louise Carmody might still be alive."

"Damn you, Vic, stop doubting every word I say. I told you why I needed you there—someone had to sign the card. Millie works during the day. So does Fredda. Katie has a new baby. Elene is becoming a grandmother for the first time. Get off my goddamn back."

"If you're not going to tell me the truth, and if you're going to scream at me about it, I'd just as soon you left."

She stood silent for a minute. "Sorry, Vic. I'll get a better grip on myself."

"Great. You do that. I'm fixing some supper—want any?"

She shook her head. When I returned with a plate of pasta and olives, Joan Druggen was just announcing the top local story. Alicia sat with her hands clenched as they stated the dead woman's name. After that, she didn't say much. Just asked if she could crash for the night—she lived in Warrenville, a good hour's drive from town, near Berman's aeronautic engineering labs.

I gave her pillows and a blanket for the couch and went to bed. I was pretty angry: I figured she wanted to sleep over because she was scared, and it infuriated me that she wouldn't talk about it.

When the phone woke me at 2:30, my throat was raw, the start of a cold brought on by sitting around in wet clothes for so long. A heavy voice asked for Alicia.

"I don't know who you're talking about," I said hoarsely.

"Be your age, Warshawski. She brought you to the gym. She isn't at her own place. She's gotta be with you. You don't want to wake her up, give her a message. She was lucky tonight. We want the money by noon, or she won't be so lucky a second time."

He hung up. I held the receiver a second longer and heard another click. The living room extension. I pulled on a dressing gown and padded down the hallway. The apartment door shut just as I got to the living room. I ran to the top of the stairs; Alicia's footsteps were echoing up and down the stairwell.

"Alicia! Alicia—you can't go out there alone. Come back here!"

The slamming of the entryway door was my only answer.

3

I didn't sleep well, my cold mixing with worry and anger over Alicia. At eight I hoisted my aching body out of bed and sat sneezing over some steaming fruit juice while I tried to focus my brain on possible action. Alicia owed somebody money. That somebody was pissed off enough to kill because he didn't have it. Bankers do not kill wayward loan customers. Loan sharks do, but what could Alicia have done to rack up so much indebtedness? Berman probably paid her seventy or eighty thousand a year for the special kinds of designs she did on aircraft wings. And she was the kind of client a bank usually values. So what did she need money for that only a shark would provide?

The clock was ticking. I called her office. She'd phoned in sick; the secretary didn't know where she was calling from but had assumed home. On a dim chance I tried her phone. No answer. Alicia had one brother, Tom, an insurance agent on the far south side. After a few tries I located his office in Flossmoor. He hadn't heard from Alicia for weeks. And no, he didn't know who she might owe money to.

Reluctantly Tom gave me their father's phone number in Florida. Mr. Dauphine hadn't heard from his daughter, either.

"If she calls you, or if she shows up, *please* let me know. She's in trouble up here, and the only way I can help her is by knowing where she is." I gave him the number without much expectation of hearing from him again.

I did know someone who might be able to give me a line on her debts. A year or so earlier, I'd done a major favor for Don Pasquale, a local mob leader. If she owed him money, he might listen to my intercession. If not, he might be able to tell me whom she had borrowed from.

Torfino's, an Elmwood Park restaurant where the don had a part-time office, put me through to his chief assistant, Ernesto. A well-remembered gravel voice told me I sounded awful.

"Thank you, Ernesto," I snuffled. "Did you hear about the death of Louise Carmody at the University of Illinois gym last night? She was probably shot by mistake, poor thing. The intended victim was a woman named Alicia Dauphine. We grew up together, so I feel a little solicitous on her behalf. She owes a lot of money to someone: I wondered if you know who."

"Name isn't familiar, Warshawski. I'll check around and call you back."

My cold made me feel as though I was at the bottom of a fish tank. I couldn't think fast enough or hard enough to imagine where Alicia might have gone to ground. Perhaps at her house, believing if she didn't answer the phone no one would think she was home? It wasn't a very clever idea, but it was the best I could do in my muffled, snuffled state.

The old farmhouse in Warrenville that Alicia had modernized lay behind the local high school. The boys were out practicing football. They were wearing light jerseys. I had on my winter coat—even though the day was warm, my cold made me shiver and want to be bundled up. Although we were close enough that I could see their mouthpieces, they didn't notice me as I walked around the house looking for signs of life.

Alicia's car was in the garage, but the house looked cold and unoccupied. As I made my way to the back, a black-and-white cat darted out from the bushes and began weaving itself around my ankles, mewing piteously. Alicia had three cats. This one wanted something to eat.

Alicia had installed a sophisticated burglar alarm system—she had an office in her home and often worked on preliminary designs there. An expert had gotten through the system into the pantry—some kind of epoxy had been sprayed on the wires to freeze them. Then, somehow disabling the phone link, the intruder had cut through the wires.

My stomach muscles tightened, and I wished futilely for the Smith & Wesson locked in my safe at home. My cold really had addled my brains for me not to take it on such an errand. Still, where burglars lead shall P.I.s hesitate? I opened the window, slid a leg over, and landed on the pantry floor. My feline friend followed more gracefully. She promptly abandoned me to start sniffing at the pantry walls.

Cautiously opening the door I slid into the kitchen. It was deserted, the refrigerator and clock motors humming gently, a dry dishcloth draped over the sink. In the living room another cat joined me and followed me into the electronic wonderland of Alicia's study. She had used built-in bookcases to house her computers and other gadgets. The printers were tucked along a side wall, and wires ran everywhere. Whoever had broken in was not interested in merchandise—the street value of her study contents would have brought in a nice return, but they stood unharmed.

By now I was dreading the trek upstairs. The second cat, a tabby, trotted briskly ahead of me, tail waving like a flag. Alicia's bedroom door was shut. I kicked it open with my right leg and pressed myself against the wall. Nothing. Dropping to my knees I looked in. The bed, tidily covered with an old-fashioned white spread, was empty. So was the bathroom. So was the guest room and an old sun porch glassed in and converted to a solarium.

The person who broke in had not come to steal—everything was preternaturally tidy. So he (she?) had come to attack Alicia. The hair stood up on the nape of my neck. Where was he? Not in the house. Hiding outside?

I started down the stairs again when I heard a noise, a heavy scraping. I froze, trying to locate the source. A movement caught my eye at the line of vision. The hatch to the crawl space had been shoved open; an arm swung down. For a split second only I stared at the arm and the gun in its grip, then leaped down the stairs two at a time.

A heavy thud—the man jumping onto the upper landing. The crack as the gun fired. A jolt in my left shoulder, and I gasped with shock and fell the last few steps to the bottom. Righted myself. Reached for the deadlock on the front door. Heard an outraged squawk, loud swearing, and a crash that sounded like a man falling downstairs. Then I had the door open and was staggering outside while an angry bundle of fur poured past me. One of the cats, a heroine, tripping my assailant and saving my life.

4

I never really lost consciousness. The football players saw me stagger down the sidewalk and came trooping over. In their concern for me they failed to tackle the gunman, but they got me to a hospital, where a young intern eagerly set about removing the slug from my shoulder; the winter coat had protected me from major damage. Between my cold and the gunshot, I was just as happy to let him incarcerate me for a few days.

They tucked me into bed, and I fell into a heavy, uneasy sleep. I had jumped into the black waters of Lake Michigan in search of Alicia, trying to reach her ahead of a shark. She was lurking just out of reach. She didn't know that her oxygen tank ran out at noon.

When I woke finally, soaked with sweat, it was dark outside. The room was lit faintly by a fluorescent light over the sink. A lean man in a brown wool business suit was sitting next to the bed. When he saw me looking at him, he reached into his coat.

If he was going to shoot me, there wasn't a thing I could do about it—I was too limp from my heavy sleep to move. Instead of a gun, though, he pulled out an ID case.

"Miss Warshawski? Peter Carlton, Federal Bureau of Investigation. I know you're not feeling well, but I need to talk to you about Alicia Dauphine."

"So the shark ate her," I said.

"What?" he demanded sharply. "What does that mean?"

"Nothing. Where is she?"

"We don't know. That's what we want to talk to you about. She went home with you after the swimming meet yesterday. Correct?"

"Gosh, Mr. Carlton. I love watching my tax dollars at work. If you've been following her, you must have a better fix on her whereabouts than I do. I last saw her around 2:30 this morning. If it's still today, that is."

"What did she talk to you about?"

My mind was starting to unfog. "Why is the Bureau interested in Miss Dauphine?"

He didn't want to tell me. All he wanted was every word Alicia had said to me. When I wouldn't budge, he started in on why I was in her house and what I had noticed there.

Finally I said, "Mr. Carlton, if you can't tell me why you're interested in Miss Dauphine, there's no way I can respond to your questions. I don't believe the Bureau—or the police—or anyone, come to that—has any right to pry into the affairs of citizens in the hopes of turning up some scandal. You tell me why you're interested, and I'll tell you if I know anything relevant to that interest."

With an ill grace he said, "We believe she has been selling Defense Department secrets to the Russians."

"No," I said flatly. "She wouldn't."

"Some wing designs she was working on have disappeared. She's disappeared. And a Soviet functionary in St. Charles has disappeared."

"Sounds pretty circumstantial to me. The wing designs might be in her home. They could easily be on a disk someplace—she did all her drafting on computer."

They'd been through her computer files at home and at work and found nothing. Her boss did not have copies of the latest design, only of the early stuff. I thought about the heavy voice on the phone demanding money, but loyalty to Alicia made me keep it to myself—give her a chance to tell her story first.

I did give him everything Alicia had said, her nervousness and her sudden departure. That I was worried about her and went to see if she was in her house. And was shot by an intruder hiding in the crawl space. Who might have taken her designs. Although nothing looked pilfered.

He didn't believe me. I don't know if he thought I knew something I wasn't telling, or if he thought I had joined Alicia in selling secrets to the Russians. But he kept at me for so long that I finally pushed my call button. When the nurse arrived, I explained that I was worn out and could she please show my visitor out? He left but promised me that he would return.

Cursing my weakness, I fell asleep again. When I next woke it was morning, and both my cold and my shoulder were much improved. When the doctors came by on their morning visit, I got their agreement to a discharge. Before I bathed and left, the Warrenville police sent out a man who took a detailed statement.

I called my answering service from a phone in the lobby. Ernesto had been in touch. I reached him at Torfino's.

"Saw about your accident in the papers, Warshawski. How you feeling? . . . About Dauphine. Apparently she's signed a note for $750,000 to Art Smollensk. Can't do anything to help you out. The don sends his best wishes for your recovery."

Art Smollensk, gambling king. When I worked for the public defender, I'd had to defend some of his small-time employees—people at the level of smashing someone's fingers in his car door. The ones who did hits and arson usually could afford their own attorneys.

Alicia as a gambler made no sense to me—but we hadn't been close for over a decade. There were lots of things I didn't know about her.

At home for a change of clothes I stopped in the basement, where I store useless mementos in a locked stall. After fifteen minutes of shifting boxes around, I was sweating and my left shoulder was throbbing and oozing stickily, but I'd located my high school yearbook. I took it upstairs with me and thumbed through it, trying to gain inspiration on where Alicia might have gone to earth.

None came. I was about to leave again when the phone rang. It was Alicia, talking against a background of noise. "Thank God you're safe, Vic. I saw about the shooting in the paper. Please don't worry about me. I'm okay. Stay away and don't worry."

She hung up before I could ask her anything. I concentrated, not on what she'd said, but what had been in the background. Metal doors banging open and shut. Lots of loud, wild talking. Not an airport—the talking was too loud for that, and there weren't any intercom announcements in the background. I knew what it was. If I'd just let my mind relax, it would come to me.

Idly flipping through the yearbook, I looked for faces Alicia might trust. I found my own staring from a group photo of the girls' basketball team. I'd been a guard—Victoria the protectress from way back. On the next page, Alicia smiled fiercely, holding a swimming trophy. Her coach, who also taught Latin, had desperately wanted Alicia to train for the Olympics, but Alicia had had her heart set on the U of I and engineering.

Suddenly I knew what the clanking was, where Alicia was. No other sound like that exists anywhere on earth.

5

Alicia and I grew up under the shadow of the steel mills in South Chicago. Nowhere else has the deterioration of American industry shown up more clearly. Wisconsin Steel is padlocked shut. The South Works are a fragment of their former monstrous grandeur. Unemployment is over thirty percent, and the number of jobless youths lounging in the bars and on the streets had grown from the days when I hurried past them to the safety of my mother's house.

The high school was more derelict than I remembered. Many windows were boarded over. The asphalt playground was cracked and covered with litter, and the bleachers around the football field were badly weathered.

The guard at the doorway demanded my business. I showed her my P.I. license and said I needed to talk to the women's gym teacher on confidential business. After some dickering—hostile on her side, snuffly on mine—she gave me a pass. I didn't need directions down the scuffed corridors, past the battered lockers, past the smell of rancid oil coming from the cafeteria, to the noise and life of the gym.

Teenage girls in blue shirts and white shorts—the school colors—were shrieking, jumping, wailing in pursuit of volleyballs. I watched the pandemonium until the buzzer ended the period, then walked up to the instructor.

She was panting and sweating and gave me an incurious glance, looking only briefly at the pass I held out for her. "Yes?"

"You have a new swimming coach, don't you?"

"Just a volunteer. Are you from the union? She isn't drawing a paycheck. But Miss Finley, the coach, is desperately shorthanded—she teaches Latin, you know—and this woman is a big help."

"I'm not from the union. I'm her trainer. I need to talk to her—find out why she's dropped out and whether she plans to compete in any of her meets this fall."

The teacher gave me the hard look of someone used to sizing up fabricated excuses. I didn't think she believed me, but she told me I could go into the pool area and talk to the swim coach.

The pool dated to the time when this high school served an affluent neighborhood. It was twenty-five yards long, built with skylights along the outer wall. You reached it through the changing rooms, separate ones with showers for girls and boys. It didn't have an outside hallway entrance.

Alicia was perched alone on the high dive. A few students, boys and girls, were splashing about in the pool, but no organized training was in progress. Alicia was staring at nothing.

I cupped my hands and called up to her, "Do you want me to climb up, or are you going to come down?"

At that she turned and recognized me. "Vic!" Her cry was enough to stop the splashing in the pool. "How—Are you alone?"

"I'm alone. Come down. I took a slug in the shoulder—I'm not climbing up after you."

She shot off the board in a perfect arc, barely rippling the surface of the water. The kids watched with envy. I was pretty jealous, myself—nothing I do is done with that much grace.

She surfaced near me but looked at the students. "I want you guys swimming laps," she said sharply. "What do you think this is—summer camp?"

They left us reluctantly and began swimming.

"How did you find me?"

"It was easy. I was looking through the yearbook, trying to think of someone you would trust. Miss Finley was the simple answer—I remembered how you practically lived in her house for two years. You liked to read *Jane Eyre* together, and she adored you.

"You are in deep trouble. Smollensk is after you, and so is the FBI. You can't hide here forever. You'd better talk to the Bureau guys. They won't love you, but at least they're not going to shoot you."

"The FBI? Whatever for?"

"Your designs, sweetie pie. Your designs and the Russians. The FBI are the people who look into that kind of thing."

"Vic. I don't know what you're talking about." The words were said with such slow deliberateness that I was almost persuaded.

"The $750,000 you owe Art Smollensk."

She shook her head, then said, "Oh. Yes. That."

"Yes, that. I guess it seems like more money to me than it does to you. Or had you forgotten Louise Carmody getting shot? . . . Anyway, a known Russian spy left Fermilab yesterday or the day before, and you're gone, and some of your wing designs are gone, and the FBI thinks you've sold them overseas and maybe gone East yourself. I didn't tell them about Art, but they'll probably get there before too long."

"How sure are they that the designs are gone?"

"Your boss can't find them. Maybe you have a duplicate set at home nobody knows about."

She shook her head again. "I don't leave that kind of thing at home. I had them last Saturday, working, but I took the diskettes back. . . ." Her voice trailed off as a look of horror washed across her face. "Oh, no. This is worse than I thought." She hoisted herself out of the pool. "I've got to go. Got to get away before someone else figures out I'm here."

"Alicia, for Christ's sake. What has happened?"

She stopped and looked at me, tears swimming in her black eyes. "If I could tell anyone, it would be you, Vic." Then she was jogging into the girls' changing room, leaving the students in the pool swimming laps.

I stuck with her. "Where are you going? The Feds have a hook on any place you have friends or relations. Smollensk does, too."

That stopped her. "Tom, too?"

"Tom first, last, and foremost. He's the only relative you have in

Chicago." She was starting to shiver in the bare corridor. I grabbed her and shook her. "Tell me the truth, Alicia. I can't fly blind. I already took a bullet in the shoulder."

Suddenly she was sobbing on my chest. "Oh, Vic. It's been so awful. You can't know . . . you can't understand . . . you won't believe . . ." She was hiccuping.

I led her into the shower room and found a towel. Rubbing her down, I got the story in choking bits and pieces.

Tom was the gambler. He'd gotten into it in a small way in high school and college. After he went into business for himself, the habit grew. He'd mortgaged his insurance agency assets, taken out a second mortgage on the house, but couldn't stop.

"He came to me two weeks ago. Told me he was going to start filing false claims with his companies, collect the money." She gave a twisted smile. "He didn't have to put that kind of pressure on—I can't help helping him."

"But Alicia, why? And how does Art Smollensk have your name?"

"Is that the man Tom owes money to? I think he uses my name—Alonso, my middle name—I know he does; I just don't like to think about it. Someone came around threatening me three years ago. I told Tom never to use my name again, and he didn't for a long time, but now I guess he was desperate—$750,000 you know. . . .

"As to why I help him . . . You never had any brothers or sisters, so maybe you can't understand. When Mom died, I was thirteen, he was six. I looked after him. Got him out of trouble. All kinds of stuff. It gets to be a habit, I guess. Or an obligation. That's why I've never married, you know, never had any children of my own. I don't want any more responsibilities like this one."

"And the designs?"

She looked horrified again. "He came over for dinner on Saturday. I'd been working all day on the things, and he came into the study when I was logging off. I didn't tell him it was Defense Department work, but it's not too hard to figure out what I do is defense-related—after all, that's all Berman does; we don't make commercial aircraft. I haven't had a chance to look at the designs since—I worked out all day Sunday getting ready for that damned meet Monday. Tom must have taken my diskettes and swapped the labels with some others—I've got tons of them lying around."

She gave a twisted smile. "It was a gamble: a gamble that there'd be something valuable on them and a gamble I wouldn't discover the switch before he got rid of them. But he's a gambler."

"I see. . . . Look, Alicia. You can only be responsible for Tom so far. Even if you could bail him out this time—and I don't see how you possibly can—there'll be a next time. And you may not survive this one to help him again. Let's call the FBI."

She squeezed her eyes shut. "You don't understand, Vic. You can't possibly understand."

While I was trying to reason her into phoning the Bureau, Miss Finley, swim coach-cum-romantic-Latin-teacher, came briskly into the locker room. "Allie! One of the girls came to get me. Are you all—" She did a double-take. "Victoria! Good to see you. Have you come to help Allie? I told her she could count on you."

"Have you told her what's going on?" I demanded of Alicia.

Yes, Miss Finley knew most of the story. Agreed that it was very worrying but said Allie could not possibly turn in her own brother. She had given Allie a gym mat and some bedding to sleep on—she could just stay at the gym until the furor died down and they could think of something else to do.

I sat helplessly as Miss Finley led Alicia off to get some dry clothes. At last, when they didn't rejoin me, I sought them out, poking through half-remembered halls and doors until I found the staff coaching office. Alicia was alone, looking about fifteen in an old cheerleader's uniform Miss Finley had dug up for her.

"Miss Finley teaching?" I asked sharply.

Alicia looked guilty but defiant. "Yes. Two-thirty class. Look. The critical thing is to get those diskettes back. I called Tom, explained it to him. Told him I'd try to help him raise the money but that we couldn't let the Russians have those things. He agreed, so he's bringing them out here."

The room rocked slightly around me. "No. I know you don't have much of a sense of humor, but this is a joke, isn't it?"

She didn't understand. Wouldn't understand that if the Russian had already left the country, Tom no longer had the material. That if Tom was coming here, she was the scapegoat. At last, despairing, I said, "Where is he meeting you? Here?"

"I told him I'd be at the pool."

"Will you do one thing my way? Will you go to Miss Finley's class and conjugate verbs for forty-five minutes and let me meet him at the pool? Please?"

At last, her jaw set stubbornly, she agreed. She still wouldn't let me call the Bureau, though. "Not until I've talked to Tom myself. It may all be a mistake, you know."

We both knew it wasn't, but I saw her into the Latin class without making the phone call I knew it was my duty to make and returned to the pool. Driving out the two students still splashing around in the water, I put signs on the locker room doors saying the water was contaminated and there would be no swimming until further notice.

I turned out the lights and settled in a corner of the room remote from the outside windows to wait. And go over and over in my mind the story. I believed it. Was I fooling myself? Was that why she wouldn't call the Feds?

At last Tom came in through the men's locker room entrance. "Allie? Allie?" His voice bounced off the high rafters and echoed around me. I was well back in the shadows, my Smith & Wesson in hand; he didn't see me.

After half a minute or so another man joined him. I didn't recognize the stranger, but his baggy clothes marked him as part of Smollensk's group, not the Bureau. He talked softly to Tom for a minute. Then they went into the girl's locker room together.

When they returned, I had moved part way up the side of the pool, ready to follow them if they went back into the main part of the high school looking for Alicia.

"Tom!" I called. "It's V. I. Warshawski. I know the whole story. Give me the diskettes."

"Warshawski!" he yelled. "What the hell are you doing here?"

I sensed rather than saw the movement his friend made. I shot at him and dived into the water. His bullet zipped as it hit the tiles where I'd been standing. My wet clothes and my sore shoulder made it hard to move. Another bullet hit the water by my head, and I went under again, fumbling with my heavy jacket, getting it free, surfacing, hearing Alicia's sharp, "Tom, why are you shooting at Vic? Stop it now. Stop it and give me back the diskettes."

Another flurry of shots, this time away from me, giving me a chance to get to the side of the pool, to climb out. Alicia lay on the floor near the door to the girls' locker room. Tom stood silently by. The gunman was jamming more bullets into his gun.

As fast as I could in my sodden clothes I lumbered to the hitman, grabbing his arm, squeezing, feeling blood start to seep from my shoulder, stepping on his instep, putting all the force of my body into my leg. Tom, though, Tom was taking the gun from him. Tom was going to shoot me.

"Drop that gun, Tom Dauphine." It was Miss Finley. Years of teaching in a tough school gave creditable authority to her; Tom dropped the gun.

6

Alicia lived long enough to tell the truth to the FBI. It was small comfort to me. Small consolation to see Tom's statement. He hoped he could get Smollensk to kill his sister before she said anything. If that happened, he had a good gamble on her dying a traitor in their eyes—after all, her designs were gone, and her name was in Smollensk's files. Maybe the truth never would have come out. Worth a gamble to a betting man.

The Feds arrived about five minutes after the shooting stopped. They'd been watching Tom, just not closely enough. They were sore that they'd let Alicia get shot. So they dumped some charges on me—obstructing federal authorities, not telling them where Alicia was, not calling as soon as I had the truth from her, God knows what else. I spent several days in jail. It seemed like a suitable penance, just not enough of one.

MOM SHEDS A TEAR

James Yaffe

"The pitter-putter of little feet," Mom said, managing to sigh sentimentally and point her finger at me accusingly, both at the same time. "It's one of the chief pleasures in life. I don't know what's the matter with you and Shirley, that you're not interested in this pleasure."

I smiled a little sheepishly, as I always do when Mom, in her sharp disconcerting way, brings up this subject. "Shirley and I are very anxious to have kids," I said. "As soon as I get my raise, and we can afford the down payment on a house in the suburbs—"

"Down payments! Raises!" Mom gave an angry toss of her head. "Young people nowadays, sometimes I think they got checkbooks where their feelings should be. Believe me, Davie, if your Papa and me worried our heads over down payments when we was your age, believe me you wouldn't be sitting here eating this pot roast right now."

It was Friday night. The next day was my day off from the Homicide Squad, so of course I was having my weekly dinner up in the Bronx with Mom. My wife Shirley wasn't with me tonight, though. She was out in Chicago for a week, visiting her folks. And as usual, Mom felt that Shirley's absence entitled her to get terribly personal—downright embarrassing, in fact—about my married life.

"Besides, Mom," I said, trying to turn the conversation into a joke, "aren't you the one who's always telling me that children are more trouble than they're worth? You know your favorite saying—'They break your furniture when they're babies, and they break your heart when they grow up.' "

"Who's denying it?" Mom snapped back at me. "And without such heartbreaks what would life be?"

"I wonder if you'd feel like that," I said, "if you were Agnes Fisher."

"Agnes Fisher? I don't know her. There's a Sadie Fishbaum on the third floor—"

"Agnes Fisher is involved in a case I started on yesterday. She's a widow, and she has a little boy five years old named Kenneth."

"And what's the matter with him, this little Kenny Fisher?"

"Nothing that we'll ever be able to prove. But all the indications are that little five-year-old Kenneth Fisher is a murderer."

Mom lowered her fork and glared at me. For a long time she glared, so hard that I had to turn my eyes away guiltily, even though I had no idea what I was feeling guilty about. Finally she gave a long sarcastic sigh: "It's finally happened. Haven't I been predicting it for years? Associating all the time with dope fiends and homopathic maniacs and drunk drivers, it finally went to your head. It only goes to show, when you had a chance to go into the shirt business with your Uncle Simon, why didn't you listen to your mother?"

"Take it easy, Mom. I'm not the one who's crazy. It's this Fisher case. I'll tell you about it, and you can judge for yourself."

Obviously unconvinced, Mom brought her fork to her lips again, took a ladylike mouthful, and settled down to hear my story.

"Agnes Fisher is in her early thirties," I said, "very pretty and breathless and a little absent-minded—in a nice attractive way, you understand. Her husband died a year ago—he was an Air Force pilot in Korea—and she lives with her little boy Kenneth in the house that her husband left her. It's a four-story house on Washington Square, one of the few oldtime red-brick houses of that type that's left on the Square. It's been in the Fisher family since the nineteenth century."

"He had money, this Mr. Fisher?" Mom said.

"The Fishers are a wealthy old New York family. Not so wealthy as they used to be, I guess, but still doing pretty well. So anyway, Agnes Fisher lived on Washington Square quite peacefully, getting along nicely with her friends and neighbors, apparently reconciling herself to her widowhood. But her little boy's life wasn't quite so calm and happy. The death of his father evidently upset him badly. He's a naturally shy, dreamy kid, and with his father gone he sort of went into his shell more than ever. He spent lots of time by himself. He seemed to prefer his own daydreams to the company of other kids. And then, a few months ago, somebody new came into the lives of the boy and his mother.

"The newcomer was Nelson Fisher, little Kenneth's uncle, his father's younger brother. Nelson Fisher was about thirty years old. Like his late brother he was an Air Force pilot. He had just been discharged from the service, not because he wanted to be—flying was his whole life—but because he had contracted malaria in the Pacific. He needed care and attention, and his sister-in-law Agnes is his only responsible relative. She's a kindhearted woman, and she was happy to take him in. She gave him the whole third floor of the old house, and so he moved in with his sister-in-law and his little nephew."

"And little Kenny was jealous maybe?" Mom said.

"At first he was jealous. He sulked in a corner, or he cried and carried on, or he looked daggers at his uncle. Nelson Fisher was still a sick man—he still had after-effects from his malaria, and what with his medicines, his dizzy spells, his chills, his weekly visits from the doctor, Agnes did a lot of fussing over him. Kenneth seemed to resent this. One day he even went into a tantrum over it. He jumped up and down and yelled hysterically, '*He's* not my father! I don't want *him* for my father!' He finally calmed down, but the incident upset his mother terribly. And it caused a lot of talk among the servants."

"This was only at first though?" Mom said. "Afterwards little Kenny changed his opinion of his uncle?"

"His antagonism lasted about a month. Then, all of a sudden, he developed a completely different attitude. One day he couldn't stand the sight of Nelson, the next day he couldn't stand to be *out* of Nelson's sight. Suddenly he had a case of genuine, full-fledged hero-worship. He dogged his poor uncle's heels. He trotted after him wherever he went. He bombarded him with questions, and whatever answers he got he believed them implicitly. He gaped in admiration at everything his Uncle Nelson did or said."

"So this is normal enough in little children," Mom said. "They change their minds for no logical reason. And incidentally, I've also known some grown-ups—"

"Oh, it was normal all right," I said. "Anyway, it seemed to be. It's only because of what happened later—But I won't get ahead of my story. For a few months everything was fine in the Fisher home. Nelson seemed to enjoy his nephew's company. He had never married and had any kids of his own, and he treated Kenneth like a younger brother. Very ideal relationship. And then, about a week ago, at the beginning of the summer, little Kenneth started to do peculiar things. Until a week ago, he had always been a fairly honest kid. And then, a week ago, he started to steal things."

"Steal things?" said Mom, poking her head forward. "So what did he steal?"

"Always the same kind of thing, Mom. Things that belonged to his dead father. For instance, it started with Agnes noticing that her husband's medal, a Silver Star, was missing. She kept it in the jewelry case in her dresser drawer, along with his cufflinks, wedding ring, and other things, but now it was gone. she sounded out the cook and the housemaid as indirectly as she could, but they both got very indignant and insisted that they weren't thieves. For a while she suspected that the man who had come to fix the plumbing was the guilty one. And then, the next morning, the housemaid came to her, very triumphantly, holding up the medal. She had found it, she said, while she was making up Kenneth's bed just a few minutes before. The medal was under Kenneth's pillow. Agnes was puzzled. She asked Kenneth about it, but he wouldn't give her any explanation. He just turned his eyes away, mumbling something, then ran off. And Agnes isn't the strong-willed, domineering type of mother who could keep pounding at the boy until she got the truth out of him.

"And then Kenneth did it again. In one of the hall closets Agnes keeps a lot of miscellaneous things stored away in boxes—some of her husband's old clothes, his books and papers, and so on. One day she was passing this closet when she heard a rattling inside. She opened the door and saw Kenneth. He had pulled down one of the boxes, torn it open, and was about to take away something from inside of it.

"Believe it or not, Mom, Kenneth was stealing one of those long, flowing old-fashioned opera capes that people used to wear fifty years ago. It had belonged to Kenneth's father. When he was an undergraduate at Princeton, he had appeared in a sort of Gay Nineties revue presented by the dramatic society. This old opera cape was part of his costume for that show."

"And little Kenny knew, definitely knew, that his Papa wore this opera cape once?"

"He couldn't help but know, Mom. There's a photograph of his father in the living room of the house—taken after the performance of the revue and showing him with the opera cape over his shoulders. Well, Agnes naturally made Kenneth put the opera cape back in the box. And the next day she looked into the same closet, found that the same box had been torn open again and the opera cape removed. She went right up to Kenneth's room. He wasn't there, but sure enough the opera cape was hanging up in his closet. So Agnes took it down and put it back in the box. And the next day—"

"Don't say it," Mom said.

"You're right," I said. "The opera cape was gone. It was too much for Agnes. She didn't want to spend all her time running after that opera cape. So she told herself Kenneth probably wanted it for some innocent game of his, and she shrugged off the whole thing.

"But Kenneth's stealing didn't stop there. Only two days later—about three days ago—he was at it again. The housemaid came to Agnes in great alarm, along with the cook. The night before, they had both heard strange noises coming from the top floor of the house. They both thought it was mice or the wind or something, and went to sleep. But this morning, when the housemaid went upstairs to clean, she found a terrible disorder that neither mice nor wind could have caused. There's a small storeroom on the top floor, and in this storeroom, packed away in mothballs, Agnes keeps all of her late husband's uniforms, his caps, his insignia, the rest of his civilian clothes, overcoats, shoes, and so on. The housemaid found this room looking as if a cyclone had hit it. Clothes and mothballs were scattered all over the place. And all her husband's uniforms, down to the last little insignia, were missing. The cook immediately announced that she was quitting her job. She wasn't going to stay in the same house with a wild little thief like Kenneth, and all Agnes's pleading wouldn't change her mind.

"Well, Agnes just didn't know what to make out of all this. She was really worried about the boy by now, so worried that she thought of taking him to a doctor or a child psychologist to find out what was wrong. But she isn't a very decisive person. She put off calling the doctor, and then yesterday morning it was too late. Yesterday morning the murder happened."

I could see the gleam of interest in Mom's eye. A certain perverse something in my nature made me pause, sigh, chew my food, and generally encourage the atmosphere of suspense.

Finally, to my immense satisfaction, Mom spoke up. "All right, all right, not so much *geschrei* and get to the point!"

"Yesterday morning," I went on, "right from the start Kenneth acted funny. He had breakfast as usual with his mother and his Uncle Nelson. Only Kenneth, who was ordinarily a big eater at breakfast, wouldn't touch a bit of food—not even a glass of water.

"After breakfast he went off to play. He had a favorite spot for his games, a small canvas canopy set up on the roof of the house. This was Kenneth's 'clubhouse'—but until Nelson's arrival, he didn't have any other 'club member' to go with it. So now, after breakfast, he went up to the roof with his Uncle Nelson. Only Kenneth didn't go up with his usual energy and high spirits. He climbed the stairs to the roof in a slow trudging way, glancing back over his shoulder, and with a sort of determined look on his face. His mother saw him on the way and wondered about it, but she was busy on the phone at the moment, so she put it out of her mind.

"Two hours later she heard the yell. A long agonized yell. The whole household heard it, and even though it was hard to tell exactly where it came from, everybody instinctively made for the roof. When they got there they found Kenneth standing by the ledge—a narrow stone ledge as high as his chin—looking down at the backyard four stories below. He was looking at his Uncle Nelson. Apparently Nelson had fallen from the roof, and his body was lying on the concrete below. They all rushed downstairs to help him, of course, and they found that he was still alive. Only for a few more seconds, though. During those few seconds, in his last painful breath, he kept repeating the same words. 'Kenny, why? Why, Kenny, why?' Then he died.

"Only one more thing to tell you, Mom. When the Homicide Squad arrived, we made a search of that roof. Underneath the canvas canopy, Kenneth's 'clubhouse,' we found—you guessed it, Mom—all those things Kenneth had stolen from the house. His father's uniforms, his father's opera cape, his father's insignia, even his father's Silver Star, which that kid had managed to sneak out of his mother's dresser for the second time!"

My voice came to a stop on a rising note. Frankly, I was pleased with myself. Very dramatically presented, I told myself. Now let Mom make sense out of this one!

"And the little boy?" Mom said, in a low voice.

"He went into a kind of shock," I said. "He grabbed hold of his mother and sobbed wildly for the rest of the day. But he won't say what happened up there on the roof. He just stares ahead when anybody asks him. The doctor says he'll get over the shock in a week or so. But after that his memory of the incident may be gone."

"And your opinion, Davie?" Mom said. "According to you and the police, what *did* happen on the roof?"

"It's not according to us, Mom. It's according to the facts. There are lots of different possibilities—we've considered them all—but only one of them seems to fit all the facts."

"So let's hear your possibilities."

"One possibility is that Nelson committed suicide. But this doesn't make sense. He was upset over being sick and leaving the Air Force, of course. But Agnes says he was just beginning to get *over* his illness, and to reconcile himself to civilian life. If he was going to kill himself because of his illness, why did he wait so long to do it? And what makes even less sense, why did he kill himself in the presence of his five-year-old nephew? People don't usually want witnesses to their suicides."

"Absolutely, I agree. Next possibility?"

"That Nelson's death was an accident. He was running, looking the wrong way, or something, and he tripped and fell over the ledge. But this is very unlikely. The ledge of the roof reached well above Nelson's waist. It's hard to imagine any sort of purely accidental force that would tumble him over so high a ledge."

"A good point. I'm applauding."

"Well, there's the possibility—after all, we have to consider everything—that Nelson tried to push his little nephew Kenneth off the ledge, that Kenneth kicked and struggled and knocked Nelson over instead. But this doesn't fit the facts, either. When Agnes got to the roof, Kenneth was neat as a pin—no sign at all of a struggle, nor any sign of physical exertion. Which leaves us with only one other possibility."

"And this is?"

"I mentioned it already, Mom. We hate to believe it. We're fighting against believing it. But the facts leave us no alternative. That little five-year-old kid must be mentally unbalanced. It's happened before, you know. Our official psychiatrist says he's come across dozens of cases of childhood psychosis, split personality, melancholia, and so on. So that's what it must be in this case. The death of his father, his lonely life, his dependence on his mother, the sudden arrival of his uncle to disrupt his routine—all this must have upset his feeling of security. It must have preyed on the kid's mind, and finally something snapped.

"The kid's crazy behavior before the murder tells us very clearly what was going on in his mind. By some peculiar twist—really not so peculiar—his uncle suddenly appeared to him as the rival of his dead father. His uncle was trying to take his father's place, and he, little Kenneth, had to prevent this for his father's sake. He had to get rid of this intruding uncle, remove the cause of his unhappiness, see to it that he and his father had his mother to themselves again.

"He didn't act the way an adult would, of course. It was just instinctive—the way a child steals or lies or kicks his nurse. But he did change his attitude toward his uncle. He pretended to feel affection for him. He pretended to worship him like a hero. Then, when he had completely gained his uncle's trust, he got ready for the big moment. Which brings us to the most interesting psychological phenomenon. Little Kenneth was now going to do his father's work, and so, with typical childish logic, he proceeded to steal his father's things. His father's uniforms, his father's opera cape, his father's medal—he took them all, slept on them or hid them away, in order to give himself his father's courage, his father's strength. By the time yesterday morning arrived, that poor kid had pushed himself into a real father fixation. In his own subconscious mind, he actually *was* his father.

"That's why he went up to the roof yesterday morning looking so determined. He had made up his mind what he was going to do. Once up there, he played with his uncle innocently for a while—the craftiness of little kids is really amazing, Mom! Finally, under some pretext, he persuaded his uncle to lean over the ledge. Remember that Nelson, even though he was a grown man, was weak and underweight and sick. Kenneth simply had to run up behind him, grab Nelson, lift, and then give him a push—the hardest push he could manage. Nelson toppled and screamed, and Kenneth went into shock.

"That's the story, Mom. And you can see another thing about it—it's the only theory that accounts for Nelson's last words. 'Why, Kenny, why?' Stunned, bewildered—even in his death throes, he just couldn't understand what had come over his little nephew."

"And this is your solution to the case?"

I nodded my head solemnly. "I'm afraid it is, Mom."

Mom was silent. She was looking thoughtful, abstracted, far away from our conversation and the dining room. This is peculiar behavior for Mom. On Friday nights, when I tell her about my latest case, she usually maintains a sharp, scornful attention. No sooner am I finished with my story than she pops out with cryptic questions, mysterious hints, sarcastic references to my thickheadedness. And finally, with great relish, she presents me with a complete, logical, inescapable solution based on her everyday experiences with scheming butchers, nosy neighbors, and selfish relatives. And so, this sudden frowning silence from Mom made me wonder.

A second later Mom's unusual mood vanished. Her head snapped up, a gleam of triumph was in her eye, and her voice sounded as vigorous as ever. "He's afraid it is. He *should* be afraid. He's got something to be afraid about. The whole police force of New York City—a bunch of grown-up men with pensions coming to them any day now—and all they can think of when they got a body on their hands is to blame it on a little five-years-old boy!"

I felt a pang of hurt pride. "I've given you all the facts, Mom. Who do *you* want to blame it on?"

"I'll tell you," Mom said, "right after you answer me three simple questions."

I sighed. Mom's "simple questions" are well known to me. Generally they're so "simple" that they leave me ten times more confused than I was before. "Ask away, Mom," I said.

"Question One," she said, raising her forefinger. "This little boy, Kenny—did he go in much for games? Was he the athletical type?"

"Oh, I see why you're asking that," I said. "You want to know if he was really strong and agile enough to push his Uncle Nelson off the roof. Well, the answer doesn't prove much. The kid didn't go in much for athletics, because he didn't have many friends. In the neighborhood where he lives, it just happens that most of the kids are older. He was too small to play games with them—in fact, that may be one reason for his shyness and loneliness. On the other hand, he's a husky kid for his five years. Strong muscles, lots of stamina, excellent health. And his Uncle Nelson, as I pointed out, was sick and rundown—"

"Yes, yes, this I know." Mom interrupted impatiently. "Now, Question Two." She raised two fingers this time. "Little Kenny, what sort of books did he read?"

"Books, Mom?"

"Books, books. You remember, what you used to open up now and then when you was at college—though God knows, with the crazy profession you decided to go into, you certainly didn't need them much. This little Kenny was shy and lonely, you say. He spent a lot of time by himself. So little boys like that, usually they do a lot of reading."

"I don't see the point of the question," I said, "but you're right. The kid is a big reader. His room was full of books. Comic books mostly. Superman, Batman, space travel, that sort of thing. He's a little too young yet for anything better."

"Good, good," Mom said, nodding her head. "Question Three. This is the most important question of all." She fixed her eyes on me hard for a moment, then brought it out: "Yesterday, when Uncle Nelson got killed, it was late in the morning. I was busy in the meat market all morning—a little misunderstanding over my lamb chops, which I had a discussion about with Perelman the butcher—so I didn't notice what the weather was like outside. Was it nice and sunny, or was it dark and cloudy?"

I just stared at her. "*That's* the most important question of all? Mom, what's the point of it?"

"Never mind the point. Only give me an answer."

"It was a bright sunny day yesterday. The hottest day so far this summer. But I don't see—"

"You don't," Mom said. "But I do." Then she nodded her head and went back to her food.

After a while I cleared my throat. "You do what, Mom?"

"I see. Exactly what I suspected. Exactly the solution that was in my head right at the beginning."

"You mean the little boy had nothing to do with it?"

"Who said so? The little boy had everything to do with it." Mom enjoyed my confusion for a few moments, then she gave a sigh and a shake of her head. "Davie, Davie, don't you see the the mistake you was making all along, you and the Homicide Squad? All this talk about little boys that want their Mama's affection, and they're jealous of their uncles, and they get a Papa fixation and steal things and it's just like kicking the nurse—this is very clever, only it isn't what goes on inside the head of a little boy. It's only what you personally think *ought* to go on inside the head of a little boy."

"And you know what does go on inside a little boy's head, Mom?"

"Why shouldn't I? For a lot of years didn't I have a little boy's head right under my nose here in this apartment? A lot of *tsooris* it gave me, that head, but believe me I found out what went on inside of it. And you yourself, you and Shirley, you could find this out too. If you stopped reading psychology books for a minute and—All right, all right, no propaganda, back to the case. The main thing you should remember about a five-years-old boy is that he's only five years old. Only five years he's been alive in this world, and half that time he was learning how to talk English.

"So how much can you expect such a little baby to find out about life in five years? What's true, what isn't true? If you put your finger into a candle flame, you get a burn. But you put your finger into a sunbeam, and it only feels nice and warm. So how can a little baby find out the difference till he tries it for himself? When Papa comes home, you can throw your arms around his neck and kiss him on the cheek. But what about the nice man on the television set—how come you can't throw your arms around *him* and kiss *his* cheek? Mama tells you a fairy story before you go to sleep—you hear Papa talking about a story from the newspapers about a little boy who got kidnapped. So which one of these stories is true? Which one is only for fun, and which one should you be frightened at? Which one really happened? Is there anything in this world that couldn't happen?

"It's like my baby brother Max, your Uncle Max, when he was seven years old and we came to America. Ever since he could remember, Max heard about the gangsters in America. Only what was a gangster? How old was a gangster? Did he look like other people? Anybody bigger than Max, who shouted at him and hit him, anybody like that, for Max at age seven could be a gangster. And wasn't it his bad luck, the first neighborhood we moved into, near Delancey Street, to meet a couple little boys ten years old that wasn't exactly the sweetest, kindest little boys in the world? So he asked them one day, 'What's a gangster, Sammy? Are you a gangster, Charlie?' So Sammy and Charlie winked at each other and said, 'Absolutely, we're a couple of gangsters, we're the worst gangsters in the whole city. We've got big guns in our pockets right now, and we're going to shoot you.'

"And didn't poor little Max believe them? Naturally he believed them. For weeks and weeks he was scared to death of them. He hid his face whenever a policeman passed by. He lost his appetite. He hated to step out of the house. And one time, when they told him they were going to come into his room in the middle of the night and kill him, he laid awake shivering in his bed, and when he heard the door squeak he practically jumped out of the window. Believe me, if the window had been opened a little farther, my brother Max wouldn't be your Uncle Max today."

"Mom, this is ridiculous," I broke in. "Are you saying that little Kenneth talked his Uncle Nelson into believing that he was a gangster, that a five-year-old kid scared a grown man into jumping off the roof?"

"Certainly I'm not saying this!" Mom drew herself up with dignity. "All I'm saying is—little children are so small and ignorant, they've got such a trust in people, such a willingness to believe anything you tell them, they're like little delicate china knickknacks that you keep on the hall table. They're so weak, and the rest of the world is so big and strong and clumsy, and cruel sometimes, that there's practically a million ways to break them into a million pieces."

"I still don't get it—"

"What I'm saying is this, Davie. If you wanted to get rid of a five-years-old boy, if he was in your way or you didn't like him, you wouldn't have to kill him and take the chance you'll get arrested for murder. You could be much smarter. You could work on him a little, tell him things, frighten him and confuse him, and eventually get him to do some crazy thing so he'd have an accident and get killed."

This statement stunned me. I didn't know how to take it. I felt there was a glimmer of meaning in Mom's words, but I couldn't quite see it.

"I'm talking, Davie," Mom said, "about all that stealing which little Kenny did. Nowadays there's so much talk from psychiatry, everybody you meets thinks he's another Dr. Sigmund Freed. Somebody does something we don't understand, so right away we say, 'Ha, ha! It's psychiatrical! It's a Papa fixation! It's an infra-red complex!' But sometimes Davie, things have got a simple, obvious explanation—if you only take a little trouble and look at them.

"This last week, before his Uncle Nelson gets killed, little Kenny spends all his time stealing his Papa's things. So naturally you come to the conclusion, he wants to take his Papa's place and get rid of his uncle. But one thing you're forgetting—little Kenny didn't just steal his Papa's things, he stole only certain *particular* things. When he tore open the box in the closet for his Papa's opera cape, he didn't touch his Papa's books or papers. When he went through the storeroom for his Papa's uniforms, he didn't bother about his Papa's civilian suits. When he opened up his Mama's jewel case, he didn't take away his Papa's cufflinks, he only took his Papa's medal. So isn't this interesting that he only takes a certain type thing belonging to his Papa? His Papa's *uniform,* his Papa's *insignia,* his Papa's *medal*—he only takes things which are connected with his Papa's work as an Air Force pilot."

"Yes, that's true, Mom. But what does it prove? Besides," I added suddenly, "he took the opera cape! What does the opera cape have to do with the Air Force?"

"The opera cape is the whole answer, Davie. A little boy is interested in stealing everything that his Papa used in the Air Force—but he also steals his Papa's opera cape. He steals it once, twice, three times. Such anxiousness to get hold of this opera cape! What's it so important for? A little idea comes into my head, and I ask you the question; what books does he read? The answer is like I expected. Comic books—but which comic books? Cowboy books? Detective books? Pirate treasure books? No. This little Kenny, he's interested in other subjects. Space traveling, Superman, Batman. And Superman and Batman, when they go flying through the air, what is it that they're always wearing, streaming away behind them, puffing out from the wind?"

"A big long flowing cape!" I cried—and the light dawned.

"What else? So it isn't such a mixed-up *kasha* any more, is it? It's as clear as a consommé now. A common, normal, boyish thing was going on in little Kenny's head, a thing which lots of little boys go through, a thing which causes plenty little accidents and some big ones every year. Little Kenny got it into his head that he was going to fly!"

"Of course," I said, almost with a groan. "I should've seen it all along. I remember, one summer when I was six, three of us climbed a tree in Uncle Dan's backyard—But we lost our nerve at the last minute."

"This I never heard before," Mom said, giving me a sharp look. Then she shrugged. "And such a natural thing for little Kenny. His Papa used to be an Air Force pilot. Flying was a regular topic of conversation in his house. And his Papa was a hero to him. And he's a boy who don't have many friends. A strong active boy, but too small to play with the other boys in the neighborhood. They laugh at him maybe. They tell him to go away, he's a midget, what good could *he* be on the team? It's a terrible torture to him. What else does he want in this world except a chance to show them how wrong they are, to do something absolutely wonderful even though he *is* small, so that from then on they'll be happy to have him on the team?

"Yesterday morning was the big moment, like you say. He was looking determined when he went up to the roof—not because he was going to kill somebody, but because he was finally going to put on his long cape, and maybe also part of his Papa's uniform and his Papa's insignia, and fly off from the roof. This was why he wouldn't eat breakfast or drink any water. Because he wanted to be as light as he could—"

"I get it, Mom. And then, just as he was about to climb up on the ledge, his Uncle Nelson realized what was happening. He tried to stop the kid. He rushed at him. Kenneth sidestepped. Nelson lost his balance and fell off the roof instead."

"Almost," Mom said. "Not exactly. You forgot the most important detail. A little boy gets a crazy idea in his head. 'I can fly,' he says. 'I'll go up to the roof and try it.' But little Kenny didn't get this idea all of a sudden. He got it over a week ago. He stole his Papa's uniform because he knew his Papa could never fly without it, and he wanted its mysterious power to come to him. He stole Papa's medal and slept with it under his pillow, the way little children sleep on a tooth—so he could have his wish to fly in the air like Papa. He stole Papa's long opera cape for his wings. So clever, so psychiatrical—to me this means only one thing. Little Kenny didn't get the idea all by himself.

"Oh, yes, he was *ready* for the idea. This I admit. He was lonely, he was full of imagination, his hero was his Papa the Air Force pilot. You and the Homicide Squad was closer than you thought, Davie, when you said that the whole case depended on the little boy's feelings for his Papa. What you didn't see was that somebody had to work on these feelings. Stealing the uniforms, using the opera cape, sleeping on the medal—these are schemes which would appeal to a little boy, but which a five-years-old boy wouldn't be able to think up himself. Somebody else—"

"But who is this somebody, Mom? Agnes Fisher herself? I can't believe it. Such a pretty scatterbrained woman—and she really loves her son. One of the servants maybe? How about the cook, the one who suddenly quit a few days before the accident?"

Mom gave a snort. "Foolishness. A cook who ups and leaves, nowadays it's a common occurrence. It would be a miracle if the cook *didn't* up and leave. The answer isn't so complicated, Davie. Look at it this way. The big day is here. Little Kenny is going to fly. He's nervous. He eats no breakfast. He goes up to the roof like a criminal going to the electrical chair. Two hours he's up there, but he can't bring himself to get started. The person who's put this idea in his head, he don't dare go away until he's sure little Kenny is really going to jump. So finally he says to the boy, 'It's very simple. Here, I'll show you exactly how you begin. I'll climb up on the ledge. I'll flap my arms like a bird. I'll do everything except fly—which I couldn't do, because I'm too big and heavy—' "

"Wait a second, Mom! Are you saying that Nelson Fisher was behind his nephew's crazy behavior?"

"Who else? Who acted very peculiar for a grown man, ignoring the company of people his own age and spending his time with a little five-years-old? Who was lonely and sick and in a terrible state because his life as a plane pilot was over? Who could think to himself, 'This sister-in-law of mine likes me already. She could be mine, along with her house and her money—if only this little brat was out of the way'? And who was it, after the first jealousy wore off, that had the most influence over little Kenny? Who did little Kenny hero-worship and believe everything he said—especially on the subject of flying, because wasn't his Uncle Nelson an Air Force pilot like his Papa used to be? And last but not littlest, who was up on the roof with little Kenny all morning? Nelson, exclusively Nelson. He climbed on the ledge, he flapped his arms, he shouted, 'Look, Kenny, see how easy it is? Why are you hesitating, Kenny? Why are you acting scared? *Why, Kenny, why?'*—and then he fell over himself."

The picture before my eyes fascinated me, kept me silent for a moment. Then I said, "But how did it happen, Mom? What made him lose his balance and fall from the ledge?"

Mom frowned. "This was a problem. For a while it bothered me. And then it came to me, and I asked you about the weather. It was bright, hot, sunny morning, you said. So I put myself in this no-good Nelson's place. I'm excited. I'm so close to what I've been wanting and working for. And I'm a man who had malaria, a man who still gets dizzy spells. I climb up on a ledge—a narrow ledge, four stories up, and when I look down I see how far it is to the ground. And the sun is so hot, and it is beating down on me, I flap my arms, I yell at the little boy, then everything begins to dance in front of me. It is one of my dizzy spells. My God, I'm falling—I'm flying—" And Mom let her voice trail off solemnly.

After a pause, I laughed out loud, I couldn't help myself. "Mom, you don't know how grateful I am. A five-year-old murderer—we've been hating the idea all day. What a relief for the boys down at Homicide!"

"What a relief for the Mama," said Mom, in a low voice.

I looked at her a moment. And then I thought I'd have a little fun with her. "But you still haven't proved your main point, Mom," I said, pretending to be very serious. "You still haven't proved that it's a good thing to have kids, that they aren't all little monsters."

Mom's head snapped up. "I haven't proved it? Who said so? Didn't I show you that this Kenny is a sweet, innocent, intelligent little child?"

"Yes, Mom. But what about Nelson? Nelson was somebody's child once."

"Nelson?" Mom gaped at me, almost at a loss for words. Then her voice grew very fierce. "Nelson don't mean nothing! What kind of talk is this, bringing up Nelson as an argument?"

"I don't know, Mom." I shrugged my shoulders elaborately. "Shirley and I will have to do a lot of thinking about this. We'd love to have a kid like Kenneth. But suppose that kid grew up to be like Nelson. It's quite a problem."

"It's no problem!" Mom shook her head back and forth energetically. "Don't talk like that—a son of mine! Don't get a prejudice against children, I beg you, Davie. Little children—little grandchildren—they're the most beautiful thing in the world. Sometimes I think they're the *only* beautiful thing in the world."

Then it happened—something I never thought I'd see. A mist came into Mom's eyes, a trembling over her lips, and while I stared in amazement, Mom shed a tear.

I was terribly ashamed of myself. "Please, Mom," I said, "I was only fooling."

She recovered herself instantly. She got to her feet, her eyes dry again. "So was I!" she snorted. Then she stamped out indignantly to fetch the nesselrode pie.

DAISY BELL

Gladys Mitchell

Daisy, Daisy, give me your answer, do!
I've gone crazy, all for the love of you!
It won't be a stylish marriage—
We can't afford a carriage—
But you'll look neat upon the seat
Of a bicycle made for two.

In the curved arm of the bay the sea lay perfectly still. Towards the horizon was reflected back the flashing light of the sun, but under the shadow of huge cliffs the dark green water was as quiet as a lake at evening.

Above, riding over a ridge between two small villages, went the road, a dusty highway once, a turnpike on which the coach had changed horses three times in twenty miles. That dusty road was within the memory of the villagers; in the post office there were picture postcards, not of the coaches, certainly, but of the horse-drawn station bus on the shocking gradients and hairpin bends of the highway.

The road was now slightly wider—not much, because every extra foot had to be hacked from the rocky hillside, for on one side the road fell almost sheer to the sea. A humped turf edge kept this seaward boundary (insufficiently, some said, for there had been motoring accidents, especially in the dark), and beyond the humped edge, and, treacherously, just out of sight of motorists who could see the rolling turf but not the danger, there fell away a Gadarene descent of thirteen hundred feet.

George took the road respectfully, with an eye for hairpin bends and (although he found this irksome) an occasional toot on the horn. His employer, small, spare and upright, sat beside him, the better to admire the rolling view. Equally with the moorland scenery she admired her chauffeur's driving. She was accustomed to both phenomena, but neither palled on her. In sixteen crawling miles she had had not a word to say.

At the County Boundary, however, she turned her head slightly to the right.

"The next turning, George. It's narrow."

His eyes on the road ahead, the chauffeur nodded, and the car turned off to the left down a sandy lane, at the bottleneck of which it drew up courteously in face of a flock of lively, athletic, headstrong moorland sheep. The shepherd saluted Mrs. Bradley, passed the time of day with the chauffeur, said it was a pity all they motors shouldn't have the same danged sense, and urged his charges past the car, and kept them within some sort of bounds with the help of a shaggy dog.

At the bottom of the slope, and wedged it seemed in the hollow, was a village with a very small church. Mrs. Bradley went into the churchyard to inspect the grave of an ancestress (she believed) of her own who had died in the odor of sanctity, but, if rumor did not lie, only barely so, for she had enjoyed a reputation as a witch.

Mrs. Bradley, looking (with her black hair, sharp black eyes, thin hands and beaky little mouth) herself not at all unlike a witch, spent an interesting twenty minutes or so in the churchyard, and then went into the church.

Its architectural features were almost negligible. A fourteenth-century chancel (probably built on the site of the earliest church), a badly restored nave, a good rood screen, and the only remaining bit of Early English work mutilated to allow for an organ loft, were all obvious. There seemed, in fact, very little, on a preliminary investigation, to interest even the most persistent or erudite visitor.

In the dark south wall, however, of what had been the Lady Chapel, Mrs. Bradley came upon a fourteenth-century piscina whose bowl had been carved in the likeness of a hideous human head. She took out a magnifying glass and examined the carving closely. Montague Rhodes James, with his genius for evoking unquiet imaginings and terrifying, atavistic fears, might have described the expression upon its horrid countenance. All that Mrs. Bradley could accomplish was a heathenish muttering indicative of the fact that, in her view, the countenance betrayed indications of at least two major Freudian complexes and a Havelock Ellis regression into infantile criminology.

"A murderer's face, mam," said a voice behind her. "Ay, as I stand, that be a murderer's face."

She turned and saw the verger with his keys. "Ay, they do tell, and vicar he do believe it, as carver was vouchsafed a true, just vision of Judas Iscariot the traitor, and carved he out for all to look upon."

He smiled at her—almost with the sinister leer of the carving itself, thought Mrs. Bradley, startled by the change in his mild and previously friendly expression. He passed on into the vestry, dangling his keys.

Shaking her head, Mrs. Bradley dropped some money into the offertory box on the pillar nearest to the porch, and took the long sloping path between the headstones of the graves to the lych-gate. Here she found George in conversation with a black-haired woman. George had always given himself (with how much truth his employer had never troubled herself to find out) the reputation of being a misogynist, and on this occasion, seated on the step of the car, he was, in his own phrase, "laying down the law" with scornful masculine firmness. The girl had her back to the lych-gate. She was plump and bareheaded, and was wearing brown corduroy shorts, a slightly rucked-up blouse on elastic at the waist, and—visible from the back view which Mrs. Bradley had of her—a very bright pink vest which showed between the rucked-up blouse and the shorts. For the rest she was brown-skinned and, seen face to face, rather pretty.

A tandem bicycle, built to accommodate two men, was resting against the high, steep, ivy-grown bank of the lane. The young woman, seeing Mrs. Bradley, who had in fact strolled round to get a view of her, cut short George's jeremiads by thanking him. Then she walked across the road, set the tandem upright, pushed it sharply forward, and, in spite of the fact that the slope of the road was against her, mounted with agility and ease on to the front saddle. Then she tacked doggedly up the hill, the tandem, lacking any weight on the back seat, wagging its tail in what looked to Mrs. Bradley a highly dangerous manner as it zigzagged up to the bend in the lane and wobbled unwillingly round it.

George had risen to his feet upon the approach of his employer, and now stood holding the door open.

"A courageous young woman, George?" suggested Mrs. Bradley, getting into the car.

"A foolish one, madam, in my opinion," George responded primly, "and so I was saying to her when she was asking the way. Looking for trouble I call it to cycle one of them things down these roads. Look at the hill she's coming to, going to Lyndale this route. Meeting her husband, she says; only been married a month, and having their honeymoon now and using the tandem between them; him having to work hereabouts, and her cycling that contraption down from London, where she's living with her mother while he gets the home for her. Taken three days to do it in, and meeting him on top of Lyndale Hill this afternoon. More like a suicide pact, if you ask me what I think."

"I not only ask you, George, but I am so much enthralled by what you think that I propose we take the same route and follow her."

"We were due to do so in any case, madam, if I can find a place to turn the car in this lane."

It took him six slow miles to find a suitable place. During the drive towards the sea, the big car brushing the summer hedgerows almost all the time, Mrs. Bradley observed,

"I don't like to think of that young woman, George. I hope you advised her to wheel the bicycle on all dangerous parts of the road?"

"As well advise an errand boy to fit new brake-blocks, madam," George austerely answered. "I did advise her to that effect, but not to cut any ice. She fancies herself on that jigger. You can't advise women of that age."

"Did you offer her any alternative route to Lyndale?"

"Yes, madam; not with success."

At the top of the winding hill he turned to the left, and then, at the end of another five miles and a quarter of wind and the screaming seabirds, great stretches of moorland heather, bright green tracks of little peaty streams, and, south of the moor, the far-off ridges and tors, he engaged his lowest gear again and the car crept carefully down a long, steep, dangerous hill. There were warning notices on either side of the road, and the local authority, laying special emphasis on the subject of faulty brakes, had cut a parking space from the edge of the stubborn moor. The gradient of the steepest part of the hill was one in four. The car took the slant like a cat in sight of a bird.

"What do you think of our brakes, George?" Mrs. Bradley enquired. George replied, in the reserved manner with which he received her more facetious questions, that the brakes were in order, or had been when the car was brought out of the garage.

"Well, then, pull up," said his employer. "Something has happened on the seaward side of the road. I think someone's gone over the edge."

Her keen sight, and a certain sensitivity she had to visual impressions, had not deceived her. She followed the track of a bicycle to the edge of the cliff, crouched, lay flat, and looked over.

Below her the seagulls screamed, and, farther down, the sea flung sullenly, despite the brilliant day, against the heavy rocks, or whirl-pooled, snarling, about the black island promontories, for the tide was on the turn and coming in fast. Sea-pinks, some of them brown and withered now, for their season was almost past, clung in the crevices or grew in the smallest hollows of the cliff-face. Near one root of them a paper bag had lodged. Had it been empty, the west wind, blowing freshly along the face of the cliff (which looked north to the Bristol Channel), must have removed it almost as soon as it alighted, but there it perched, not wedged, yet heavy enough to hold its place against the breeze. To the left of it, about four yards off, was a deep, dark stain, visible because it was on the only piece of white stone that could be seen.

"Odd," said Mrs. Bradley, and began to perform the feat which she would not have permitted to anyone under her control—that of climbing down to reach the dark-stained rock.

The stain was certainly blood, and was still slightly sticky to the touch. She looked farther down (having, fortunately, a mountaineer's head for heights) and thought that, some thirty feet below her, she could see a piece of cloth. It was caught on the only bush which seemed to have found root and sustenance upon the rocky cliff. It resembled, she thought, material of which a man's suit might be made.

She left it where it was and scrambled across to the bag.

"George," she said, when she had regained the dark, overhanging lip of the rough turf edge of the cliff and had discovered her chauffeur at the top, "I think I saw a public telephone marked on the map. Somebody ought to search the shore below these cliffs, I rather fancy."

"It would need to be by boat, then, madam. The tide comes up to the foot," replied the chauffeur. He began to walk back up the hill.

Mrs. Bradley sat down at the roadside and waited for him to return. While she was waiting she untwisted the top of the screwed-up paper bag and examined the contents with interest.

She found a packet of safety-razor blades, a tube of toothpaste half full, a face flannel, a wrapped cake of soap of the dimensions known euphemistically in the advertisements as "guest-size," a very badly worn toothbrush, a set of small buttons on a card, a pipe-cleaner, half a bicycle bell, two rubber patches for mending punctures, and a piece of wormlike valve-rubber.

"Calculated to indicate that whoever left the bag there was a cyclist, George," she observed, when her chauffeur came back from the telephone. "Of course, nobody may have fallen over the cliff, but—what do you make of the marks?"

"Palmer tires, gent's model—not enough clearance for a lady's—see where the pedal caught the edge of the turf?"

"Yes, George. Unfortunately one loses the track a yard from the side of the road. I should have supposed that the bicycle would have left a better account of itself if it had really been ridden over. Besides, what could have made anybody ride it over the edge? The road is wide enough, and there does not seem to be much traffic. I think perhaps I'll retrieve that piece of cloth before we go."

"I most seriously hope you will not, madam, if you'll excuse me. I've no head for heights myself or I would get it. After all, we know just where it is. The police could get it later, with ropes and tackle for their men, if it *should* be required at an inquest."

"Very true, George. Let us get on to the village to see whether a boat has put out. How much farther is it?"

"Another three miles and a half, madam. There's another hill after this—a smaller one."

The car descended decorously. The hill dropped sheer and steep for about another half mile, and then it twisted suddenly away to the right, so that an inn which was on the left-hand side at the bend appeared, for an instant, to be standing in the middle of the road.

So far as the black-haired girl on the smashed and buckled tandem was concerned, that was where it might as well have stood, Mrs. Bradley reflected. The tandem had been ridden straight into a brick wall—slap into it as though the rider had been blind or as though the machine she was riding had been completely out of her control. Whatever the cause of the accident, she had hurtled irrevocably to her death, or so Mrs. Bradley thought when first she knelt beside her.

"Rat-trap pedals, of all things, madam," said George. The plump large feet in the center-seamed cycling shoes were still caught in the bent steel traps. George tested the brakes.

"The brakes don't act," he said. "Perhaps a result of the accident, madam, although I shouldn't think so." He released the girl's feet and lifted the tandem away. Mrs. Bradley, first delicately and then with slightly more firmness, sought for injuries.

"George," she said, "the case of instruments. And then go and get some cold water from somewhere or other."

The girl had a fractured skull. Her left leg was slightly lacerated, but it was not bruised and the bone was not broken. Her face was unmarked, except by the dirt from the roadside. It was all a little out of the ordinary, Mrs. Bradley thought, seizing the thermos flask full of icy water which the resourceful George had brought from a moorland stream.

"She's alive, George, I think," she said. "But there have been some very odd goings-on. Are the tandem handlebars locked?"

"No, madam. They move freely."

"Don't you think the front wheel should have been more seriously affected?"

"Why, yes, perhaps it should, madam. The young woman can't go much less than ten or eleven stone, and with the brakes out of order . . ."

"And although her feet were caught tight in the rat-trap pedals, her face isn't even marked. It was only a little dirty before I washed it."

"Sounds like funny business, madam, to me."

"And to me, too, George. Is there a hospital near? We must have an ambulance if possible. I don't think the car will do. She ought to lie flat. That skull wants trepanning and at once. Mind how you go down the hill, though. I'll stay here with her. You might leave me a fairly heavy spanner."

Left alone with the girl, Mrs. Bradley fidgeted with her case of instruments, took out gouge forceps, sighed, shook her head, and put them back again. The wound on the top of the head was extremely puzzling. A fracture of the base of the skull would have been the most likely head injury, unless the girl had crashed head-first into the wall, but, from the position in which the body had been lying, this seemed extremely unlikely. One other curious point Mrs. Bradley noticed which changed her suppositions into certainty. The elastic-waisted white blouse and the shorts met neatly. It was impossible to believe that they could do so unless they had been pulled together after the girl had fallen from the saddle.

Mrs. Bradley made a mental picture of the girl leaning forward over the low-slung sports-type handlebars of the machine. She must, in the feminine phrase, have "come apart" at the back. That blouse could never have overlapped those shorts.

Interested and curious, Mrs. Bradley turned up the edge of the soiled white blouse. There was nothing underneath it but the bare brown skin marked with two or three darker moles at the waist. Of the bright pink vest there was no sign; neither had the girl a knapsack or any kind of luggage into which she could have stuffed the vest supposing that she had taken it off for coolness.

"Odd," said Mrs. Bradley again, weighing the spanner thoughtfully in her hand. "I wonder what's happened to the husband?"

At this moment there came round the bend an A.A. scout wheeling a bicycle. He saluted as he came nearer.

"Oh dear, madam! Nasty accident here! Poor young woman! Anything I can do?"

"Yes," said Mrs. Bradley very promptly. "Get an ambulance. I'm afraid she's dead, but there might be a chance if you're quick. No, don't touch her! I'm a doctor. I've done all that can be done here. Hurry, please. Every moment is important."

"No ambulance in the village, madam. Couldn't expect it, could you? I might perhaps be able to get a car. How did you get here? Was you with her when she crashed?"

"Go and get a car. A police car, if you like. Dead or alive, she'll have to be moved as soon as possible."

"Yes, she will, won't she?" said the man. He turned his bicycle, and, mounting it, shot away round the bend.

Mrs. Bradley unfolded an Ordnance Survey map of the district and studied it closely. Then she took out a reading glass and studied it again. She put out a yellow claw and traced the line of the road she was on, and followed it into the village towards which first George and then the A.A. scout had gone.

The road ran on uncompromisingly over the thin red contour lines of the map, past nameless bays on one side and the shoulder of the moor on a rising hill on the other. Of deviations from it there were none; not so much as the dotted line of a moorland track, not even a stream, gave any indication that there might be other ways of reaching the village besides crossing the open moorland or keeping to the line of the road. There was nothing marked on the map but the cliffs and the shore on the one hand, the open hilly country on the other.

She was still absorbed when George returned with the car.

"The village has no ambulance, madam, but the bus has decanted its passengers on to the bridge and is getting here as fast as it can. It was thought in the village, madam, that the body could be laid along one of the seats."

"I hope and trust that 'body' is but a relative term. The young woman will live, George, I fancy. Somebody has had his trouble for nothing."

"I am glad to hear that, madam. The villagers seem well disposed, and the bus is the best they can do."

He spoke of the villagers as though they were the aboriginal inhabitants of some country which was still in process of being explored. Mrs. Bradley gave a harsh little snort of amusement and then observed,

"Did the A.A. scout stop and speak to you? Or did you ask him for information?"

"No, madam, neither at all. He was mending a puncture when I passed him."

"Was that on your journey to the village or on the return here?"

"Just now, madam. I saw no one on my journey to the village."

"Interesting," said Mrs. Bradley, thinking of her Ordnance map. "Punctures are a nuisance, George, are they not? If you see him again you might ask him whether *Daisy Bell* met her husband on top of the hill."

Just then the bus arrived. Off it jumped a police sergeant and a constable, who, under Mrs. Bradley's direction, lifted the girl and placed her on one of the seats, of which the bus had two, running the whole of the inside length of the vehicle.

"You take the car to the hotel, George. I'll be there as soon as I can," said his employer. "Now, constable, we have to hold her as still as we can. Sergeant, kindly instruct the driver to avoid the bumps in the road, and then come in here and hold my coat to screen the light from her head. Is there a hospital in the village?"

"No, mam. There's a home for inebriates, though. That's the nearest thing. We're going to take her there, and Constable Fogg is fetching Doctor MacBain."

"Splendid," said Mrs. Bradley, and devoted herself thenceforward entirely to her patient.

One morning some days later, when the mist had cleared from the moors and the sun was shining on every drop of moisture, she sent for the car, and thus addressed her chauffeur:

"Well, did you give the scout my message?"

"Yes, madam, but he did not comprehend it."

"Indeed? And did you explain?"

"No, madam, not being instructed."

"Excellent child. We shall drive to the fatal spot, and there we shall see—what we shall see."

George, looking haughty because he felt befogged, held open the door of the car, and Mrs. Bradley put her foot on the step.

"I'll sit in front, George," she said.

The car began to mount slowly to the bend where the accident had come to their notice. George was pulling up, but his employer invited him to go on.

"Our goal is the top of the hill, George. That is where they were to meet, you remember. That is the proper place from which to begin our enquiry. Is it not strange and interesting to consider all the motives for murder and attempted murder that come to men's minds? To women's minds, too, of course. The greater includes the less."

She cackled harshly. George, who (although he would have found it difficult to account for his opinion) had always conceived her to be an ardent feminist, looked at the road ahead, and did not relax his expression of dignified aloofness.

Prevented, by the fact that he was driving, from poking him in the ribs (her natural reaction to an attitude such as the one he was displaying), Mrs. Bradley grinned tigerishly, and the car crawled on up the worst and steepest part of the gradient.

George then broke his silence.

"In my opinion, madam, no young woman losing her brakes on such a hill could have got off so light as *she* did, nor that tandem neither."

"True, George."

"If you will excuse the question, madam, what put the idea of an attempt on her into your mind?"

"I suppose the piscina, George."

George concluded that she was amusing herself at his expense and accepted the reply for what it was worth, which to him was nothing, since he did not know what a piscina was (and was habitually averse to seeking such information). He drove on a little faster as the gradient eased to one in seven and then to one in ten.

"Just here, George," said his employer. "Run off on to the turf on the right-hand side."

George pulled up very close to the A.A. telephone which he had used before. Here the main road cut away from the route they had traversed and an A.A. scout was on duty at the junction.

" '*Behind the barn, down on my knees,*' " observed Mrs. Bradley, chanting the words in what she fondly believed to be accents of their origin, " '*I thought I heard a chicken sneeze*'—and I did, too. Come and look at this, George."

It was the bright pink vest. There was no mistaking it, although it was stained now, messily and rustily, with blood.

"Not *her* blood, George; *his,*" remarked Mrs. Bradley. "I wonder he dared bring it back here, all the same. And I wonder where the young woman the first time fell off the tandem?" She looked again at the blood-stained vest. "He must have cut himself badly, but, of course, he had to get enough blood to make the white stone look impressive, and he wanted the vest to smear it on with so that he need use nothing of his own. Confused thinking, George, on the whole, but murderers do think confusedly, and one can feel for them, of course."

She sent George to fetch the A.A. scout, who observed,

"Was it the young woman as fell off bottom of Countsferry? Must have had a worse tumble just here by the box than Stanley seemed to think. He booked the tumble in his private log. Would you be the young woman's relatives, mam?"

"We represent her interests," said Mrs. Bradley, remarking afterwards to George that she thought they might consider themselves as doing so since they had saved her life.

"Well, he's left the log with me, and it do seem to show the cause of her shaking up. Must have been dazed like, and not seen the bend as was coming, and run herself into the wall. And Stanley, they do say, must have gone over the cliff in trying to save her, for he ain't been back on duty any more. Cruel, these parts, they be."

"Did her fall upset both her brakes, then?" Mrs. Bradley enquired. She read the laconic entry in the exercise book presented for her inspection, and having earned the scout's gratitude in the customary simple manner, she returned to the car with the vest (which the scout had not seen) pushed into the large pocket of her skirt.

"Stop at the scene of the accident, George," she said. "She seemed," said George admiringly later on to those who were standing him a pint in exchange for the story, "like a bloodhound on the murderer's trail."

"For a murderer he was, in intention, if not in fact," continued George, taking, without his own knowledge, a recognized though debatable ecclesiastical view. "She climbed up the bank and on to the moor as if she knew just what to look for, madam did. She showed me the very stone she reckoned he hit the young woman over the head with, and then where he sunk in the soft earth deeper than his first treads, because he was carrying the body back to the tandem to make out she crashed and fell off."

"And didn't she crash?" his hearers wanted to know.

"Crash? What, her? A young woman who, to give her her due (although I don't hold with such things), had cycled that tandem—sports model and meant for two men—all the way down there from London? No. He crashed the tandem himself after he'd done her in. That was to deceive the police or anybody else that found her. He followed her on his bike down the hill with the deed in his heart. You see, he was her husband.

"But he didn't deceive me and madam, not by a long chalk he didn't! Why, first thing I said to her, I said, 'Didn't it ought to be buckled up more than that if she came down that hill without brakes?' 'Course, that was his little mistake. That, and using her vest. I hope they give him ten years!

"Well, back we went up the hill to where madam found the paper bag and its etceteras. The only blood we could see was on the only white stone."

The barmaid at this point begged him to stop. He gave her the horrors, she said.

"So what?" one listener enquired.

"Well, the whole bag of tricks was to show that *someone,* and that someone a man and a cyclist, had gone over the cliff and was killed, like the other scout said. That was going to be our scout's alibi if the police ever got on his track, so madam thinks, but he hoped he wouldn't need to use that; it was just his standby, like. The other A.A. man had seen him go off duty. That was his danger, or so he thought, not reckoning on madam and me. He'd fixed the head of the young woman's machine while she stood talking to him at the A.A. telephone, so that when she mounted it threw her. That was to show (that's why he logged it, see?) as she mightn't have been herself when she took the bend. Pretty little idea."

Three days later Mrs. Bradley said to him,

"They will be able to establish motive at the trial, George. Bell—I call him that—was arrested yesterday evening. He had insured her life, it appears, as soon as they were married, and wished to obtain possession of the money."

"But what I would still like to know, madam," George observed, "is what put the thought of murder into your mind before ever we saw the accident or even the bag and the blood."

"The bag and the blood, for some reason, sounds perfectly horrible, George."

"But, madam, you spotted the marks he'd made on that edge with his push-bike as though you'd been *waiting* to spot them. And you fixed on him as the murderer, too, straight away."

"Ah, that was easy, George. You see, he never mentioned that he'd seen you go by in the car, and you told me that on your journey to the village to find assistance you had not seen him either. Therefore, since he must have been somewhere along that road, I asked myself why, even if he should have left the roadside himself, his bicycle should not have been visible. Besides, he was the perfect answer to several questions which, up to that time, I had had to ask myself. One was: why did they choose to meet at the top of that hill? Another was: why did he risk bending over the injured girl to fix her feet back in those rat-trap pedals we saw and out of which, I should imagine, her feet would most certainly have been pulled if she'd had such a very bad crash?"

"Ah, yes, the A.A. box and the A.A. uniform, madam. In other words, Mr. G. K. Chesterton's postman all over again."

"Precisely, George. The obvious meeting place, in the circumstances, and the conspicuous yet easily forgotten uniform."

"But, madam, if I may revert, what *did* turn your mind to murder?"

"The piscina, George," Mrs. Bradley solemnly reminded him. George looked at her, hesitated, then overrode the habit of years and enquired,

"What *is* a piscina, madam?"

"A drain, George. Merely a drain.

" 'Now, body, turn to air,
Or Lucifer will bear thee quick to hell!
O soul, be chang'd into little water drops,
And fall into the ocean, ne'er be found!' "

Solo Job

Paul Gallico

The so-called "Treasure Hunt" shooting in North Haverhill, New Jersey, had been a two-day story and a flop, and the authorities had had to turn the perpetrators loose in the face of considerable local indignation. There was nothing to hold them on. Legally, they were within their rights. And neither of the boys died.

Sally (Sherlock) Holmes Lane had been sent out to cover it for the *New York Standard.* She had filed one fair story on the two small boys who went on a treasure hunt and were digging on a farm in the hills west of North Haverhill, when the farmer's wife had come upon them suddenly and shot them both with charges from a double-barreled shotgun. Then Sally had come back to report to Pop Durant, her city editor.

Sally Holmes Lane—everybody called her "Sherlock"—was the best girl reporter on the *Standard,* and probably the best man, too. She had a fantastic nose for news, and a lot of theories. She was small, wiry, with a grave, thin face topped by a shaggy mop of silky platinum-colored hair. Only it was real. She rarely used makeup. Her eyes had a trick of shading from deep green to light gray. She had only recently become engaged to Ira Clarke, the big, ugly night editor, and they loved each other breathlessly. Pop was still wondering how their love affair would turn out, because he claimed that Sally hadn't been halter-broke—love or no love. She was a reporter first.

It was six o'clock in the evening. Pop was going over his schedules before turning them over to Ira Clarke. It was an hour before press time, and the city desk was fairly quiet. Clarke breathed a sigh of relief when Sally came swinging through the local room.

She came around to Ira's side of the desk and said, "Hello, dope," and patted him on the cheek; and then, noticing his expression, she asked quickly, "Anything wrong?"

Ira shook his head. "Uh-huh! Just damned glad to see you. I always get the jitters when you're away on a story."

Sally looked at him. So it was that again. "Oh, Ira," she said, "you know I can take care of myself. Don't be so silly." Then she turned to Pop, who said, "Hi, Sherlock! What do you know?" He was a little, round, fussy man who looked exactly like Foxy Grandpa, but he was the best city editor in town, and he could be a terror when he had to.

"Well," said Sally, "the kids aren't going to die. They were really more frightened than hurt. They got it in the legs. If one or both had died there would have been a lynching. The crowd was in a nasty temper. They turned the wife and her husband loose, and they went back to their farm with two state troopers. There was nothing they could hold 'em on."

"Ummmmm," said Pop, "I see. Legally—"

"Within their rights," said Sally. "The farm is posted with NO TRESPASS signs. And the man had a license for the gun."

Pop picked up a clipping and skimmed through it, mumbling, "Hmm. John Polonok, aged fifty-three; wife Bertha, aged fifty, held for the shooting of Joe Semaglino and Frank Morris, aged nine and eleven respectively. Woman came upon them digging on farm property, procured shotgun, fired both barrels at them. Screams heard by Anthony Pedani, truck farmer, who was driving by on the road adjoining the farm. Took them to North Haverhill Hospital. Pair threatened troopers, but submitted to arrest . . . Hmmmm, yes. What were the boys digging for?"

"Buried treasure," said Sally. "Pirates' treasure."

"Hmmm," said Pop. "What made them think there would be pirates' treasure on a farm back in the hills of New Jersey?"

"Well," began Sally, "you see—" Suddenly she checked herself, glanced at her fiancé and caught him gazing full at her. She flushed and went on, "You know how kids are, Pop."

"Hmmm. Yes. Well, I guess that washes it up. Thanks, Sherlock."

Sally remained standing there. She said, "Pop, I—I want to work on that story some more."

"I thought there wasn't any story," said the city editor.

"Well, not exactly that one—that is, yes and no—there *is* a story. I—I can't put my finger on it—yet. That woman was so—so horrible. Like a great, sour toad. I've never seen a face so brutal. She was all dressed in clothes—I mean, she must have had petticoats and petticoats on under her things, dirty ones. She was thick with clothing and venom—and there was something else, too. I could feel it. It was all through the courtroom. Something horrible was coming from her. Oh, I am telling it wretchedly."

"No. Oh, no," said Pop, leaning forward in his chair. "What is it?" Ira Clarke got up and came around to stand next to Sally.

The girl said, "I—I can't tell. I—" she made a little gesture with both hands—"I feel something. I want to go back there. Alone. In two or three days, when it's died down, I—she would have killed those boys if the man in the car hadn't happened along after she shot them the first time. The woman is loathsome, but it's more than that."

"Hunch?" asked Pop.

"Hunch," said Sally.

"Go to it," said Pop. "If you want any help, yell."

"N-no." Sally hesitated. "It's the kind of story—I mean, if it's anything, I'll be better alone."

Pop nodded. Moving away, Sally bumped into Ira.

His voice sounded husky as he said, "Dinner, lamb? I get out at eight tonight."

Sally nodded.

They went to eat in a little Italian restaurant down the street from the *Standard* offices. Ira was moody, and Sally knew what was coming.

Finally he said, "Are you going out on that story alone?"

Sally tried lightness. "Sure. A lot of big feet galumphing about will spoil it."

"Sherlock, don't. Please don't."

"What's the matter, Ira?"

"I—I don't know. I guess I just love you so much I can't bear to think of anything happening to you."

Sally placed a hand tenderly over Ira's big paw. "Now, now," she soothed, "nothing's going to happen to me. Nothing ever does."

"No," repeated Ira, a little bitterly, "nothing ever does, except getting gassed at strikes and missed by falling beams because you've got to get right up close to fires, and nearly being trampled to death in the subway panic. You're just a girl, Sally, after all, and—" He stopped there, because Sally suddenly drew her hand from his and straightened up. Then he said, "Well, aren't you?"

Sally shook her head. "No. No, Ira, I'm not. I'm a reporter." She stopped for a moment, then went on. "Ira, look! I love you, my dearest, and shall until I die. But I won't let it—let you make me weak. I've always worked alone. I can stand on my own feet, Ira. I won't let what we are to each other change what we are to ourselves."

"But Sherlock," said Ira, "haven't you ever thought that that is different now; that you don't have to work alone—I mean, inside—ever again; that you've got help? That's what I'm here for."

Sally shook her head. "No—no, our work is different."

Ira changed his tactics. He said, "Sherlock, you know more about that yarn than you told Pop, don't you?"

Sally hesitated, then looked her fiancé full in the face. There was a line of defiance about her mouth. "Yes, I do."

"Does anyone else?"

"N-no. I don't think so. You see, none of the others thought to ask them."

"Going to tell me?"

"No, Ira."

"Why not?"

"Because I work alone, Ira. I always have. You do understand?"

The man sighed and nodded. Then Sally caught an expression on his face. She pounced.

"Ira," she cried, "you won't try to interfere! Oh, you mustn't. Promise me you won't. Promise me, dear."

"All right," said Ira wearily, "I promise."

They left, and Ira walked Sally to her tiny apartment. Their goodnight kiss was strained. Sally's heart was heavy as she went upstairs. Ira's was, too, when he returned to the office. Later in the evening he had a long talk with little Mike Rocco, the assistant night city editor. Mike, a rolypoly Italian, was the office trouble shooter. Everyone told him everything.

Later still, Mike made a telephone call to Newark. He talked from a private wire in an office booth. Mike was known to have some queer friends in strange places. . . .

The rain was falling in curving curtains, lashed by the wind. Sally saw it as she passed the last lamplit pole on the muddy road. She had no watch, but she knew it must be nearing half-past nine at night. She had another half mile to go to reach the Polonok farm. It lay in a depression between two low hills and was reached by a narrow dirt road off the main road.

It was pitch dark, and Sally had to feel the road with her feet to keep to it. She was carrying a small suitcase. She was nervous because of what lay ahead of her, because of what she had to do, but not yet frightened. She wondered whether there would be a light burning in the farmhouse. She hoped there would be. If there was not, it would make her story a trifle less plausible.

She trudged on, her shoulders drooping with fatigue, her clothing soaked and muddy, water squelching from her flimsy shoes. Fortunately, it was a late spring rain and not cold. Nevertheless, she shivered from the wet. She felt her way around a bend in the road. Ahead, there was a minute tear in the darkness, a pinprick of light. Sally sighed. It was the farmhouse.

Here she paused. She had no time for forebodings. She knew she was heading into possible trouble, and she marshaled her mind the way a drill sergeant controls his squad. She set it in order and locked the compartments. Then she opened the one she had newly packed and prepared for the venture. At that point on the muddy, rain-drenched road, Sally Holmes Lane ceased to exist. When she picked up the paper suitcase and sloshed forward, she was another person.

The light disappeared for a moment and then reappeared, but higher up. The Polonoks had taken their lamp upstairs. Sally climbed a barred fence. A dog broke into a vicious bark, chilling her in spite of the fact that she had prepared herself for it. She let herself go limp on the ground on the other side of the fence. She knew that if she crouched there and remained immovable, there was little chance of being hurt if the dog were loose.

She waited. There was further barking. So the animal was chained up. As she rose to her knees, a window in the upper story of the house opened and she heard a woman's voice, low-pitched, coarse and hard.

"Shaddup! What's the matter with you? Lay down."

Sally let a sob burst from her. "Help!" she cried. "Oh, God, help!" She staggered across the yard and collapsed by the door, sobbing heavily. Then she rapped on it weakly with her knuckles.

She heard the woman's voice again. "Who's there? Is somebody there? Get out!"

"Oh, God," said Sally, "let me in. Please let me in. I can't go no more. Help!"

"Who is it? What do you want? Get out of there."

Then a man's voice said, "Who is it?"

Sally was lying against the door, her face turned up to the rain. She moaned softly. "Oh, let me in. Let me in."

She heard the woman say, "Get me the gun," and the man remonstrating. She had banked on her judgment that they would not want to go into court again for another shooting.

The woman bawled, "Get away from there or I'll shoot! D'ye hear? This is private property. I give ya warning. Get out of there or I'll shoot."

Sally knew there was still a chance that the woman would shoot. She had shot the boys without warning. But the very fact that she was giving a warning . . .

"Oh, I don't care," sobbed Sally. "I want to die. I can't go on."

The man said, "It's a woman." His wife: "I don't care what it is. Get her out of there." There was an argument.

Sally relaxed, closed her eyes, and leaned the upper half of her body against the door. When it was opened, she fell backwards and lay half across the threshold. The bravest thing she ever did in her life was to keep her eyes closed.

She heard the man say, "It's a girl. She's out."

The woman said, "She's faking. I'll show you."

Sally was aware of the movement even before she felt the stinging slap across her face.

The man said, "Nah, Bertha, don't do that. She's out. Look at her."

"We'll get her out of here, then," said the woman.

The man said, "Nah. Wait a minute. If she dies around here, ya gonna have them cops around again. Use ya head." The woman grunted, and Sally heard the man say, "Where's that bottle?"

She set her jaws rigidly and then felt them yanked open viciously and the neck of a bottle jammed against her teeth. The cheap, raw whisky burned the back of her throat and choked her, but she fought down the cough, gasped weakly and let the liquid dribble out of the corner of her mouth. Then she opened her eyes and gazed dully before her.

Mrs. Polonok said, "I thought that would bring her around. Come on, get up and get out."

Sally said nothing, but gazed vacantly from one to the other. Mrs. Polonok had a flannel wrapper around her shoulders, drawn at the waist with a string. She was thick and heavy and still bloated with skirts. From her came a fetid odor that made Sally sick. The woman's face was foul, with a pronounced mustache and vagrant black hairs. She had course, greasy black hair and a small mouth like a polyp. Her nose was flat, and her eyes were like shoe buttons sunk in swollen masses of flesh. Her frame was enormous.

The man who held the lamp was of middle height, but desiccated and stringy. He had sparse tow-colored hair, and his mustache was stained with tobacco juice. He was wearing a pair of overalls pulled on over a filthy nightshirt. Both their faces were hot with suspicion and hatred as they stared back at the girl lying on the floor.

What they saw, in turn, was an exhausted, terrified girl dressed in cheap clothing, wet and muddied. A mass of platinum-colored hair showed beneath a weather-stained felt hat. She had deep circles under her gray-green eyes. Her mouth sagged, and her complexion was the sallow deadish gray of utter fatigue, except for the red mark where she had been slapped. The whiteness of the face set off the tawdry crimson of a mouth painted into a bow, which made her hair look utterly false.

Sally had achieved these effects very simply by going without food and sleep for forty-eight hours. She had no patience with detective-story disguises. She had a simple theory that if you wished to give the idea that you were on the point of exhaustion, the most convincing thing was to get that way.

"Come on," repeated Mrs. Polonok. "Get up and get out of here."

Sally licked her lips before she spoke. She said, "I can't go on no more. I can't! Oh, why didn't I die?"

Polonok said, "What's the matter with you? What are you doing here?"

"I run away," said Sally. "I couldn't go no more. I took a bus as far as my money went. Then I walked. I got lost."

The woman said, "Yeah? Whaddaya running away from?"

"I—I'm in trouble," said Sally.

"Yeah? Feller?"

Sally began to sob again. "Oh, God, I don't know what to do! I run away from home. My old man would kill me if he found out. He'd kill Joe, too."

Mrs. Polonok suddenly dropped on her knees beside Sally and sank a thumb hard into each shoulder. Her rancid odor turned Sally sick again. The woman shook her. "Who sent you here?" she shouted. "Did somebody send you here?"

All Sally's nerve ends tingled. Her faculties became razor-sharp. Why had that question been asked? There were two possibilities. One was that the woman suspected that Sally was not what she pretended to be. But what if she believed her?

"Nobody sent me," said Sally. "I seen your light. I didn't know where I was going. I got as far as Kinnerly on the bus. I been walking since last night. I got lost in the dark. I ain't had anything to eat."

"What's your name?" asked Mrs. Polonok.

"Mary Donovan."

"Where are you from?"

"Jersey City."

"Got any money?"

"No."

Mrs. Polonok pounced upon Sally's handbag and turned out its contents. They consisted of a crumpled half packet of cigarettes, a paper of matches, a cheap lipstick and powder compact, celluloid comb, a latchkey, the stub of a bus ticket from Jersey City to Kinnerly, New Jersey, and three pennies. Sally had spent an hour choosing the contents.

The woman then opened her suitcase. It contained a skirt, a blouse, a night dress, stockings, underwear and a few toilet articles. It gave every evidence of having been thrown together hastily.

"I'll do anything," said Sally, "work, sweep, anything until I've earned enough to go on. I can't go back. I can't!"

The man and the woman exchanged quick glances. Then Mrs. Polonok said to her husband, "Get out!" He left the room. "Gimme your clothes," said Mrs. Polonok. "I'll give you something dry."

She went out. Sally felt it was a test. Sally Lane would not have removed her clothes in the presence of such a woman, but Mary Donovan did.

Mrs. Polonok returned. She carried a dirty wrapper and a glass of milk. "You can have this," she said. Her eyes wandered over Sally's body. Sally slipped into the wrapper and drank the milk gratefully. It was taking all her powers of concentration to keep locked those compartments of her mind that were Sally. The woman indicated a sofa. "You can sleep there," she said, and walked out.

Sally lay down on the couch. There was no necessity to fake sleep. She was tired to the point of exhaustion. She went to sleep immediately. She had no knowledge of the fact that after a while the man and the woman entered the room, bearing a lamp, gazed at her, conversed in whispers and went away again.

It was still dark, though turning to early gray, when Sally felt herself shaken. It was Mrs. Polonok. She said, "Get up!" and lighted a lamp.

Sally shook herself and arose. "Can I have my clothes?" she asked timidly.

"They ain't ready," said Mrs. Polonok. "Here, tie this around and put these on." She handed Sally a piece of string and a pair of large battered slippers.

From a doorway Mrs. Polonok called, "C'mere!" and Sally followed her into the farmhouse kitchen. It was in an indescribable state of filth. A sink was piled high with greasy pots and dishes.

"Pitch in," said Mrs. Polonok. "You keep your mouth shut and mind your own business and work, and you can stay here and have your brat." She went out into the yard, where John Polonok was already moving about.

Sally had little time to think that day. She worked until she ached. The Polonoks had some twenty acres connected with the ramshackle farmhouse. Little of it was under cultivation, though there was a large truck garden. They kept pigs, chickens and guinea fowl which apparently they raised for market, and Sally noted that the pigsties seemed to be the cleanest things about the place.

She never got her clothes back. The woman gave her a voluminous cotton overall and the slippers. Sally had time to note a few details: there was no telephone in the house; no delivery wagon ever drove up to the farmhouse; the gate was constantly barred. In the afternoon a grocery truck stopped in the road and honked. John Polonok went out and collected a few staples. There was a small rattletrap auto truck in the barn not far from the house, but John Polonok kept the ignition keys in his pocket. There was an R.F.D. box down the road near the gate, but the Polonoks received no newspapers.

Sally suddenly realized that she was completely cut off from the world. Once when a bakery delivery wagon pulled up in the road and honked she went out to meet it. Halfway to the gate she heard Mrs. Polonok's voice from the barn. "Hey, you! Get back in the house and mind your own business. If you do that again, I'll bust your head in."

Mary Donovan said, "I didn't mean no harm. I won't do it again." Sally said to herself, "You've run yourself into a nice trap, my girl. And for what?"

She had been asking herself that for some time. Outside of the isolation of the Polonoks' house and their apparent hatred of having their property invaded by an outsider—which might be set down to eccentricity or the fact that they were foreigners—she had come upon nothing suspicious. The Polonoks tended their stock, talked but little, seemed to live almost like the animals they raised. They ate together in the kitchen and rarely addressed a word to Sally, who did the cooking. They gave her a mattress to sleep on in a small empty room.

But Sally belonged to the school who saw evil in the appearance of evil and the unclean. It occasionally got her into trouble, as it had in the Stockwell trunk murder when she caused the arrest of an innocent postman because he had a squint, a scar and a limp. But it was not only the appearance but the aura of evil to which Sally was sensitive. She was convinced that something as foul as Mrs. Polonok could exist only for evil.

And there was something else she felt emanating from both the woman and her husband. But what? True, she had one other thing on which to base suspicion. She knew why the two boys had gone digging for pirate treasure on the Polonok farm. The explanation from the boys' point of view was simple. They had been out night fishing. Trudging home past the Polonok farm between ten and eleven, they had seen the farmer and his wife with a lantern out by a clump of trees some distance from the barn. They were digging.

It was when the slick-haired stranger with the flashy silk shirt and the flashy smile called at the farm one evening that Sally solved one of the things she wanted to know about the Polonoks.

It was after the evening meal. Sally was cleaning up in the kitchen. She could see Mrs. Polonok, bloated and toad-like, in the front room reading a movie magazine. Her husband was cleaning the shotgun. Outside, it was still light.

No one heard the car stop. No one heard the man approach the door—not even the dog—until he knocked and followed his knock by walking in. Usually the door was bolted. It wasn't then.

Sally, looking from the kitchen, saw Mrs. Polonok jump to her feet, her hand at her throat, her face livid. She saw, too, the expression on John Polonok's face, and then she knew what lived with the Polonoks night and day. Fear.

Out the window Sally could see a cream-colored roadster in the road. The stranger was young, and his black hair was greased and shiny.

He said, "Evening, folks. Sorry to bust in this way. Lost my way. Want to get to Morristown."

Mrs. Polonok found her voice. Sweat was standing out on her face. She broke into a scream. "Get out of here! What the hell do you want? John, give me that gun. Get out of here!"

"Now, now," said the stranger, "is that a way to talk?" He dropped his hand into his pocket. "Never mind the gun. Just tell me the way to Morristown. That's all I want."

"You get out or I'll blow you out!" screamed Mrs. Polonok.

The stranger smiled blandly. "Kind of jumpy, ain't you?"

It was Sally Lane rather than Mary Donovan who came out of the kitchen to get a closer look at the stranger.

Mrs. Polonok turned on her, livid again. She called her a foul name. "Get back in there, you——!" There was a china bowl on a near-by table. She picked it up and flung it at Sally's head. It smashed against the lintel of the door.

The stranger turned and looked at Sally, so that for a moment his back was turned to the Polonoks. "Nice people," he said. He winked at her, shrugged, and went through the door. A moment later they heard his car roar off.

Mrs. Polonok had gripped Sally's shoulders and was shaking her. "Who was he? Do you know him? Did you bring him here? Who was he?"

Sally could hardly answer because nearness to Mrs. Polonok always sickened her. But when she did and said, "I ain't never seen him before," it carried veracity because it was true. She never *had* seen the man.

Mrs. Polonok went back to her magazine grumbling and swearing. But Sally had learned something, too. The Polonoks had never seen the stranger before, either. Then what were they afraid of, and was it in any way tied up with their nocturnal digging? For what had they been digging? And Mrs. Polonok had shot two youngsters because they were digging. Was there a treasure angle?

But Sally's intuitive mind rejected that explanation because her instincts refused to connect it up with Mrs. Polonok. Fear had sat with the Polonoks all the time in the courtroom—not fear of what might happen to them as the result of the shooting, but fear of something else.

It was the next night that the Polonoks drugged her.

A letter had come for them in the morning, and with it tension. Inside and outside the drab farmhouse the Polonoks never let Sally out of their sight. Several times she caught them with their heads together, talking and looking at her.

Mary Donovan trudged about her duties, but Sally Lane was on edge. She knew that something was going to happen, but not what, except that she knew it was evil. The place became supercharged with it.

Not a word was spoken at dinner that night, but several times she saw the Polonoks exchange glances. They were watching her. She was alert but not yet afraid, because she felt that she was still supernumerary to what was about to occurr.

It was afterwards while she was doing the dishes that she suddenly felt faint and dizzy. She held onto the sink to keep from falling. Then she looked up to see Mrs. Polonok watching her from the doorway. But the woman seemed to have bloated to twice her size; she had become a horrible, grotesque balloon. And when she spoke, her voice came from somewhere far distant.

"Never mind those. Go to bed."

Then Sally knew she was drugged.

She began to fight almost immediately. If she could get out of the house for a moment . . . The drug must have been administered during dinner. How far had the action . . .

"Yes. I ain't feeling well. Wanna go to bed," Mary Donovan said. "Go outside a minute."

There was no plumbing in the farmhouse. She fought her way to the outhouse and stuck her finger down her throat. On the way back Mrs. Polonok met her halfway, coming after her. Sally staggered and the woman caught her by the arm, guided her to her room, pushed her in and slammed the door.

Sally fell on her couch. Her ears were singing, and her head felt as if it were compressed by shrinking steel bands. She did not know how much of the drug she had got rid of. She struck herself to try to keep awake. Something was going to happen that they did not want her to see. Something was going to happen . . . She lost consciousness.

There were nightmares, sinkings beneath rushing water, terrible struggles with unseen things that choked and suffocated, screams that were voiceless, all the horrid paraphernalia of the tortured stream of consciousness. Then during the night Sally awoke, shaking in a cold sweat. She was uncertain whether she was yet truly conscious, but the effects of the drug had worn off.

She felt terribly sick. She had no idea of the time. It was bright moonlight outside. Her window looked out onto the rear of the farm. She heard the noise of a car starting and listened to it drive away down the road. She wondered why she saw no reflection from its headlights.

Possibly it had none on. She lay there, temples throbbing, nerves jangling, wondering whether that which was to happen had already happened.

Then she heard heavy footsteps. She knew them for Mrs. Polonok's by the scuffing of her slippers. She heard the husband moving about, too. Then for a moment her heart seemed to stop, as she heard, or thought she heard, a faint cry. It was thin, and she could not tell whether it was human or animal. She listened, did not hear it again.

The heavy scuffing footsteps approached her door. Quickly she squirmed around and sprawled on her face, her limbs drawn up as though that were where she had first fallen in her drugged sleep. She could not see, but she felt the lamplight, and knew that Mrs. Polonok was standing in the doorway watching her. The light against her closed eyes increased. Her sense of smell told her that Mrs. Polonok was bending over her. She wondered what it would feel like to have a knife driven into her body.

But the light retreated, and she heard the door close and the footsteps recede. Then she heard Mrs. Polonok and her husband go out the back door. She had a desperate urge to follow them, but did not dare. She waited, trembling, until three or four minutes had passed. Then she crept to her window and looked out.

The moon had turned the roof of the barn to silver, and the leaves of the trees in the woods on the left had a silvery sheen. Some two hundred yards away by a clump of chestnut trees that stood just beyond the far edge of the truck garden she caught a slight movement. There was a dip in the ground there. The Polonoks were moving about in the dip.

Sally listened, straining her ears. The night was silent except for the peepers down in the pond, but occasionally they paused in their eternal chorus. Then she heard it, borne faintly but unmistakably on the light spring breeze; a *snick* . . . *snick* . . . of metal striking earth. The Polonoks were digging again.

Sally could have fled the house at that moment and perhaps escaped to town. But she had to know why they were digging—*had* to know. She knew she could never sleep again until she had stilled the fear and suspicion in her breast. She went back to her mattress and assumed the position in which she had been before. She knew there would be another visit. She waited. She heard a mantel clock strike: "One . . . two . . ."

After a little the Polonoks returned to the house. Sally regulated her breathing. The visit was repeated. She heard the Polonoks go upstairs, apparently satisfied. Sally decided to wait an hour.

When the little clock chimed three she arose quietly. She took her slippers off because she did not want to muddy them. She did not risk the door, but dropped out of her window, which was on the ground floor. The moon was still high in the sky, and she could see perfectly. She knew she could also be seen.

She slipped around the far side of the house and gained the barn. She was not afraid of the dog barking: it knew her now. She picked up a light spade and crept out of the barn and around it, keeping it between herself and the house. She reached the clump of chestnut trees where she had last seen the Polonoks.

There was newly turned earth there—a patch about three feet square. Sally attacked it slowly, inserting the spade into the soft, loose earth each time so that there would be no telltale snick. But now, curiously, she did not seem to care whether she was discovered or not. She knew that if she was, the last thing on earth she would know would be the roar of the shotgun. But she kept on. She always saw things through.

Her spade struck against something solid but soft. She probed its size. It was small. She had known long, long before that the Polonoks were not digging *for* something. She uncovered it and pulled back the cloth wrappings. For a while she knelt there and stared. Her senses, soul and body were reeling with sickness. The baby—not more than a week old—was dead. Its face was purple. Sally did not investigate further how it had died. She knew the marks that would be around its throat. She knew everything now. And she knew how close to death she was herself. For the first time in her life she was terribly frightened.

She swore at herself and pinched her arms and slapped her face. "Damn you! You're not going to faint. You're not! Hold it, Sally. Hold it!"

She conquered herself, covered the child and returned the earth. She spread it about as she had found it. She figured that the whole thing had taken not more than half an hour. Now she understood Mrs. Polonok's question: "Who sent you here?"

She returned to the house as she had come. There was no sound. She regained her room, where she fell onto her mattress again, shaking with terror and exhaustion. But there was still tomorrow to come. And Sally knew that she must not appear to wake by herself in the morning; that she must wait to be roused.

Somehow the time passed.

"Get up!" said Mrs. Polonok. "What's the matter with you?"

Sally said to herself, "Mary Donovan, Mary Donovan." Mary Donovan then said, "I—I don't know. I was sick last night. Is it morning?"

"Get up," said Mrs. Polonok. "You ain't sick."

The day was a desperate, losing fight for Sally. The compartments would not stay locked, and nausea was always at her throat. She had lost the nerve that never before had deserted her. She half suspected that it was the character of Mary Donovan that was whipped, but it was as Mary Donovan that she had to live if she were to survive.

Mrs. Polonok had become monstrous. Sally saw blood on her hands. She saw her dreadful hands at the throats of babies. John Polonok was a shadow who moved behind her. Sally would catch herself staring at Mrs. Polonok's pudgy hands, and if the fingers were moving it was almost more than she could bear.

She moved mechanically about the kitchen, and when Mrs. Polonok came near she would take a deep breath and hold it until she thought her lungs would burst. She knew she must get away. She didn't know how. She knew that when night fell she would not have the courage. She was trapped.

Sometimes she kept sane by thinking of Ira. Ira belonged to Sally, but not to Mary Donovan who would have a baby, and when she had had it, Mrs. Polonok would strangle it and then go out with her husband and dig. But Ira was lost to Sally, too. Ira wouldn't come. No one would come. She had cut herself off.

She suddenly thought of what Ira had said: "You don't have to work alone any more, Sherlock. That's what I'm here for." She had denied that. Now she saw what he had meant: that when two people loved each other they worked together always, two against the world, a little company. Joy was shared; trouble was split. You had an ally, somewhere, who was helping.

She knew that now. She knew that she would always know it thereafter, if there were to be any thereafter. She heard Mrs. Polonok moving about in the chicken yard and realized with a shock that for a few minutes she had been Sally Lane, and not Mary Donovan.

She watched Mrs. Polonok's huge feet treading about the yard. What lay beneath them? How many? How long had this dreadful land been the burial ground for the newborn unwanted? Sally saw them in rows beneath the soil. She cried to herself over and over, "Ira, Ira, Ira! Oh, Ira, don't leave me alone any longer."

The real horror began at night when she had to sit at table with the Polonoks. She had given up all thought of escape—ever. She knew in her terror that Mary Donovan was fading and Sally was gaining, and that soon she must give herself away. She was as white as the crockery, and her eyes were full of burning horror. She would catch herself staring at Mrs. Polonok's hands as she broke a piece of bread. Soon, soon those hands would be at her throat, and then the Polonoks would dig again.

Something was plucking at the inside of Sally's skull, and she knew she could stand no more. Mrs. Polonok had the leg joint of a chicken in her hands and was tearing at it with her fingers. The leg joint cracked, the way a little backbone would crack, and something in Sally cracked, too. She found herself standing suddenly, glaring at those hands.

"What's the matter with you, girl?" said Mrs. Polonok. "What are you standing there for? What are you up to?"

The woman rose and came around the table. Sally tried to invoke the vanished Mary Donovan, but she could not. Mrs. Polonok was at her side, her eyes wandering up and down Sally's rigid body.

"What's the matter with you? What's got into you?" Her coarse voice was rising. Her bloated face once more went livid with rage and suspicion. She said, "What have you been into? *Why have you got mud on your ankles?*" Then she reached for Sally with the hands that were dripping with blood.

Sally's scream rang through the house.

Then they all seemed to pour into the room at once. There was Ira Clarke, and Mike Rocco and Joe Seward, a photographer, with his camera and flash gun, and there was the stranger who had called at the house two nights before.

"*Ahhhh!*" Mrs. Polonok bellowed like a bull. "The gun, John! The gun."

The flashy stranger took his hand from his pocket, and in it he held a large pistol. He said, "Never mind the gun, or I'll let all the wind out of your belly."

Sally was in Ira's arms, clinging, moaning, babbling. "Oh, Ira, Ira, hold me. Oh, God, Ira—Ira dear. Ira. Don't let me go. Clean and dear and sweet. Ira, hold my head. Don't let my head go. Watch her fingers—her fingers, Ira. They'll put me where the others are. You came, Ira. The smell is blood and dead babies, Ira. Dig, Ira. You must all dig. Don't leave them there. Dig—down by the three chestnut trees. You'll find it—where I was last night . . . Oh, no more, Ira, no more, no more . . ."

The first thing Sally remembered consciously was waking up in a clean bed and screaming for Ira.

He was there immediately with his arms around her, stroking her head, murmuring, "Sally, Sally. Oh, my dear."

"Oh, you have me, haven't you, Ira?" Sally cried. "Yes, I'm close to you. You *are* holding me. I can close my eyes and open them and you're still here. Your face, Ira. Put it next to mine."

She noticed then that there was a nurse in white in the room and an elderly man. She looked from one to the other, and her face was once more full of intelligence.

"Oh, I see," she said. "How long, Ira?"

Ira looked at the elderly man, but he smiled and nodded. "Three weeks, Sherlock," he said. "You're all right now."

"Yes," said Sally. "I'm all right when you're holding me. Keep me close. I want to know things. How—how many were there, Ira?"

The big man hesitated, then said slowly, "Fourteen—so far. They're still digging over the farm. The Polonoks won't talk. They've been indicted for first degree. Some of the mothers have turned up. They would bring the babies to the Polonoks and pay them to look after them or find a home for them. Mrs. Polonok killed them the same night, or the next. If any of those poor women ever turned up again, which they probably never did, the Polonoks could say the child had been placed with a family and refuse to reveal the whereabouts."

Sally shuddered and buried her face in Ira's neck for a moment. Then she said, "Ira, who was the man with the slick black hair? The one with the gun."

Ira sighed. The nurse and the doctor had left the room. He said, "That was Little Sam Angy, one of Joe Colomimo's torpedoes. Newark racketeer. Friend of Mike Rocco's. He was keeping an eye on you. He drove into the office that afternoon and said maybe we'd better come out and take a look. He didn't like it."

"Who sent him, Ira?"

"Mike. I mean, I did. I got Mike to do it." Ira said it defiantly.

Sally looked at the big, ugly man out of the depths of her enormous eyes. Then she said, "Ira, tell me something. Why did you break your promise to me?" Ira Clarke held her off from him for a moment, but she said, "No, you don't," and struggled back into his arms again.

Then he answered her. He said, "Because I love you, you tow-headed idiot. Can you ever get that through your skull? And if you don't like it, you can walk out on me. I can't help myself. I'll always watch over you as long as I live. It's what I'm here for. So what?"

"Nothing, darling," Sally said meekly. "I just wanted to hear you say it. Never change. Never stop. Always watch over me. Oh, my darling, my darling!" Her joyous, living laugh rang out. "It *is* what you're here for."

Not Before My Morning Coffee

Susan Dunlap

Fog had covered Berkeley for the past week, lifting only long enough at four each afternoon to remind us what a decent day would have been like. Last night, it had thickened to a murky gray, dimming the streetlights till they seemed to draw their light back into themselves and abandon the sidewalks to darkness.

But some time in the night, the wind off the Pacific had gusted and grown stronger; it had slapped palm fronds against the bedroom window of the place where I was housesitting. I had woken briefly. Seth Howard had slept on. The gusts must have been powerful enough to sweep the fog to oblivion. And when the screech of tires outside the window woke me for good at nine A.M., I saw not the dull gray that is the normal beginning for even a good day here, but rivers of sunlight flowing in the window, dancing on the cobweb at its top corner. (I'm not much of a housekeeper. I'll get a maid in before the owners get back.) The sun glistened off the brass button of Howard's jeans on the floor where he'd tossed them (he's not exactly Mister Tidy, either).

Like the first day of spring in the east, this rare early morning sun is always a cause of celebration in Berkeley. It signals a day meant for walks in Tilden Park, or by the tables of the street vendors on Telegraph Avenue, or, I thought, glancing at Howard's shoulder as he wriggled it free of the blanket, other things. It was a day off work for both of us.

On such a day, I didn't mind being awakened at nine A.M. I didn't even mind it when Howard stretched, opened his eyes, and flicked on the police band radio. Turning on the radio first thing was something he had done occasionally when he was a patrol officer. With his promotion to Vice and Substance Abuse Detail, it had become a habit. All of us homicide detectives were addicted too. But I, at least, waited until I had had my first sip of coffee.

The radio hadn't been on two minutes when it spit out the call—a D.O.A. two blocks away. The ambulance would roll, code three (lights and sirens).

I wasn't "up"; it wouldn't be my case. But you don't lie in bed when one of your neighbors has been killed. Around here people congregated at Peet's Coffee Shop like villagers at the town well. There was a sense of camaraderie, even among those who merely stopped to fill their cups and strolled on home. But most of us had passed a few words, guessed whether today's coffee would be aged Indonesian decaf or Viennese roast, Sumatra or Mocha Java water-processed; we knew each other in that superficial way that skims the cream of pleasantry. It was too nice a day for one of us to die.

Howard raised himself up on an elbow. His curly red hair was matted on one side. "What was that address?"

"Two blocks down Walnut, past Walnut Square."

"Geez, I've got a snitch living there. Wilson, the little guy with the mole beside his nose."

I was out of bed now, pulling underwear from the drawer. "Wilson? Oh yeah. I see him waiting for coffee, weekends, I think. He reminds me of the ugliest puppy in the litter. The one cowering in the back of the box who snaps when you try to pet him."

"That's Wilson. Or at least, that's Wilson when he's straight. When he's had his snort, he doesn't cower before he nips. He's a penny-ante dealer."

"Well, he can't be too small time if he's living in this neighborhood."

"If he's *still* living."

By ten after nine we were headed toward Walnut Square, a rectangle of shops at the corner of Walnut and Vine. Ahead I could see the ambulance and patrol cars double-parked in the next block, flashers splashing red over the cars at both curbs and up onto the still-dewy leaves of the London plane trees.

In front of us, two of the morning regulars I'd met a couple of times strolled past the tree-shaded wooden houses toward Walnut Square, their bright purple, embroidered Thai shirts glaring in the sunlight. The woman bent to scratch a preening cat.

Already at their heels, Howard nearly fell over her. He hesitated, muttering an apology. But his expression said, "Get out of my way!" Before they could see that, I gave him a shove. "Go ahead." It was all he needed.

I turned to the couple to make amends. But they just shrugged; it was too nice a day to care. I could see Howard skirting dawdlers, running to the scene. Hope pulled him. *He* could get there and feel relief if he found the body was not Wilson the snitch's. But for me, if it wasn't Wilson, it was likely to be someone else I knew. As I crossed the street to Walnut Square, I realized I was cataloging faces, unconsciously pretending that if I could account for everyone I knew no one would have to be dead.

It was the smell of coffee coming from Peet's on the corner that brought me back to reality. But still, I mentally checked off the "regulars": the woman who always read a poetry book while she drank her coffee, the guy with the long curly blond beard, the woman with the cane—all survivors.

Had I been here fifteen minutes ago, at five to nine, the street would have been empty. Had I made my appearance at nine, twenty people would have been crowding at Peet's door. No one was here in a bathrobe, but clearly several of the regulars had been up no longer than I. A woman with a bandanna over her frizzy brown hair leaned back against the sunny doorway of the store, smiling and talking to a man in jeans and a holey T-shirt that proclaimed "McGovern for President." I had been here probably ten mornings, had seen her every time, and never without the bandanna. But in today's sun that worn bandanna looked festive. She had reason to rejoice at being alive, even if she didn't know it.

Nearby, a clutch of nylon-shorted joggers stood happily sweating, their T-shirts proclaiming their accomplishments in kilometers. Two of them were familiar.

And Henry—there he was, seated on "his" bench. Even without his regular nine A.M. coffee, he looked glad to be alive. I was ridiculously relieved to see him, even though I knew he didn't *live* here. Where he spent his nights was anybody's guess. His preference for street life didn't deter him from keeping an eye on foreign affairs (he was suspicious of countries that began with vowels), or from his daily ritual here. There was an admirable independence about Henry, something Berkeleyans responded to. He lived the life he'd chosen, made do with what it brought him. He had his standards and he kept them. By nine each morning he was in place on his bench, and had accepted the *Chronicle* from a man in khaki slacks and a beard who raced off to meet a friend for breakfast at nine. (Henry had dubbed him "Coffeehouse.") He'd gotten yesterday's *New York Times* from a woman running for the nine A.M. San Francisco bus. (He called her "Exec.") And his cup of coffee came via a gray-haired woman in a red Master's Swim Team sweatshirt ("Sporty"); she walked here right after the five-minute eight-fifty news ended. It was a coup for her when she could give Henry a late-breaking scoop. (Sporty swam, bicycled, played tennis, took two aerobics classes daily, and still had time to spend an hour or so here drinking her coffee every weekday morning. Henry worried about her having neither job nor other income. But his worry didn't keep him from accepting his morning cup of coffee.)

Others had offered him coffee or papers, but Henry accepted them only from those three proven benefactors. He had explained his criteria to me one morning as we sat on his bench. The people he came to count on had to live in the neighborhood; cars were unreliable. They had to own homes; renters moved. And most important, they had to be on time. Henry brooked no tardiness. As he said, if he could sleep in one of the parks or shelters and get himself here by nine, there was no reason why they couldn't. If they failed, there were others waiting. Plenty of people would have been honored to supply his three amenities. Doubtless, Wilson the snitch would have been delighted to attain that level of acceptance.

The arrangement was not one-sided. Henry paid with his own coin: his critique of the news, and more important, his familiarity with his corner. Once he arrived he rarely left his post. He knew who had come and who hadn't; he remembered messages. For the regulars he was better than an answering machine. Even now, the flashing lights of the patrol cars down the street hadn't lured him from his post.

I waved to Henry. Another patrol car passed, flashers pulsating in the sunlight. As I passed the door of Peet's the aroma of fresh-ground beans caught me anew. I inhaled long and deep.

I circled around the dog contingent by one of the sit-on planter boxes. Six dogs, and owners. There were usually more than that. Who was missing?

An old blue Cadillac inched down the street, the driver vainly searching for a parking spot.

The aroma of coffee hit me once more as I came to the crime house. Ten or twelve people had gathered at the sidewalk, cups in hand, every one. I skirted around them and hurried past the one reporter I recognized. The house was a brown shingle, one of those six-room, two-story dwellings with lots of dark wood, leaded-glass bookcases, and oriental carpets. Even though I expected it, the cold inside still made me shiver. And somehow, after the aroma of coffee the stench of death was that much worse.

The body was on the floor, holes in the chest and the stomach. It was Wilson. A Colt Diamondback revolver lay beside him.

Howard stood by the fireplace, holding a brick he had pulled loose. A sharp smell like that of chlorine clung to the brick. Howard was glaring into the dark empty hole behind it. "That's where Wilson kept his records," Howard said, his voice unsteady. "Damn! I knew it. I knew as soon as I heard the squeal. I just didn't want to believe it. He was such small fry. I almost didn't bother trying to turn him. It just never occurred to me that he'd know enough to be offed."

"Maybe he was killed for some other reason."

He slammed the brick back in its hole. "Other reasons! Wilson didn't have other reasons. I knew the guy, and I've seen enough here to know who offed him. Believe me. Nothing's gone but his records. And no one knew about them but his supplier and me."

"He showed *him* the hiding place?" I asked, amazed. "Why did he bother having a hiding place? He showed it to the good guys and the bad guys; who was left to hide stuff from?"

"Like I said, Jill, the guy was a twerp. I should have dragged him in when he first agreed to give me his supplier's name. Instead, I let him put me off till next week. If I had leaned on him more he'd be alive now."

"Okay," I said, anxious to change the subject. Kicking himself wasn't going to help Howard. "So the supplier realized Wilson was going to expose him."

Howard nodded. "Such a twerp, Wilson."

"The supplier killed Wilson to protect himself, right? So where is he?"

But Howard wasn't listening. He was staring down at Wilson. "Fool! Dealing was a game to him. Just covering expenses, that's what he told me, as if that made everything legit. Like he was ushering so he could get into the theater free. He never really believed he could go to jail, he was too middle-class. You know how people know things, but don't really *believe* them—like who really believes he's going to die?"

I shrugged.

"And he couldn't keep his mouth shut. God knows what he let slip. Fool! Dead fool."

I followed Howard's gaze down to Wilson's body. The blood had begun to drain from Wilson's face, making that mole beside his nose look all the darker. He really did look like the puppy nobody would buy, like a kid who'd sell coke to buy acceptance. Maybe, I thought, if Henry had taken him on as one of his honored three, Wilson wouldn't have had to get involved in coke. I shook my head. Dumb. The guy was a dealer; he knew the dangers.

Turning to the medic bent over his bag in the dining room, I said, "How long has he been dead?"

But it was Burke, the scene supervisor, who answered. "Woman in the house behind heard the shots. Call came at nine-oh-two. Pity he didn't run out back; she would have spotted him. Neighbors on either side are out of town."

"Convenient for the killer." I glanced questioningly at the medic.

"He's still warm," he said. "I got here at six after. Blood hadn't clotted."

"But the killer was gone, right?" Howard asked.

"Oh, yeah," Burke said. "Vanished."

I didn't ask Burke if he had anyone questioning the remaining neighbors. He would. To Howard I said, "Wilson lived alone?"

"Him and his habit."

Through the window I could see Raksen, the I.D. tech., climbing out of his double-parked car. In a minute he'd be poised over Wilson's body, camera ready. By then Eggs or Jackson, whichever would carry this case, would be here, holding him off till he'd gotten his own look at the corpse.

To Howard, I said, "Let's get these guys some coffee."

Before Howard could answer, Burke said, "Make it the real stuff, no decaf. And see if you can get some cream, okay?"

"You're on."

Eggs was just pulling up when we reached the sidewalk. I pointed to Peet's. "Darjeeling," he called. Eggs was off coffee this month.

Howard started through the crowd. It parted. Even strangers who didn't know how rare was the tautness in his face, this "blinders" walk, were keeping out of his way. I wanted to say something comforting to him, but there was nothing. I'd had informants go, too. Even when they went from natural causes it still stung. There was an odd symbiotic relationship between us and them, or at least some of them; it was one I could never bring myself to consider too deeply. But for now, there was nothing I could say.

Instead I walked toward the blue Cadillac that had been circling the block. It was triple-parked behind Raksen's car, the driver leaning across the front seat, peering out. He pulled himself back and was reaching for the gearstick by the time I got to the window. I held up a hand.

Releasing the gearstick, he said, "Hey, what's going on here?"

Ignoring his question, I pulled out my shield. "I'm Detective Smith. I saw you before. Looking for a parking spot, right?"

"*Looking* is right." His breath had that thick, sour smell of unbrushed teeth. "Might as well be panning for gold. You know you cops ought to do something about the parking in this city. You got all these two-hour zones, and one-hour zones, and neighborhood-only zones. It's worth your life to find a place to stash your car. And with this," he waved a hand at the length of the old Caddy, "I'm asking for a miracle."

"How early did you come?"

" 'Bout quarter of."

"Any spots then?"

"Hey, do you think I'd be driving around if there had been?" He favored me with a mouth-only smile. His teeth needed more than a brushing. The indentations between them could have doubled for little doggy-bags from last night's dinner.

"Maybe there were spots you missed."

"There's nothing I miss. I've lived in this town for ten years. I'm a pro. I can spot 'em a block away. Believe me, no one on this block or the ones on either side pulled out between quarter to nine and now."

"Are you sure? Maybe someone left while you were circling the far side of the block. Maybe someone else got the spot."

"Look, I told you, I'm a pro. If there's a guy walking, I spot him. I ask him if he's leaving, or I just wait until the guilt gets him. I can spot 'em. And I make 'em move. Listen, you guys should hire me on patrol. I'd cut your crime."

I thought: One trip in the car with you, with *that* breath, would pretty well do anybody in. To him I said, "So you saw no one in a car, no one in the street, no one in a yard, right? Nothing has changed?"

"I've driven around this block so many times I could describe every car on it. The people walking were headed to Peet's, and now to this show." He nodded toward the crowd by the house.

I got his name and told him to stick around. Then I motioned over one of the patrol officers on crowd control, and relayed the driver's story. Eggs would want to know.

I caught up with Howard halfway down the block and filled him in.

Howard nodded, more to himself than me. "Christ," he muttered, "if Wilson had only had the sense to give me a name when I asked, instead of putting it off."

I put a hand on his arm. "Look, Wilson was an adult. He made his choices. Your choice is you can think about him or think about his killer."

Howard scowled. "Hey, listen . . ." It was a moment before he shrugged, and said, "Yeah. Okay. So the guy didn't go out the back or the neighbor would have spotted him. He didn't drive off, either. If he was on foot, where would he go? You don't plan to kill a guy and wait for a bus to make your getaway."

"There's only one place open here at this time of morning, and that's Peet's," I said as we neared the crew outside it.

Taking in the size of the crowd, he sighed. "You think we should start with the joggers, or the dog people? Or more likely our perp's gone. If he had any sense, he got his coffee and wandered off."

Two dogs were circling each other half-heartedly, blocking the sidewalk. I stepped into the street. "It's not so bad as you think. If this were

Saturday or Sunday, we'd be in trouble. There'd be a line out the door here. But on Tuesday morning, what you'll find is pretty much just the regulars. And what Bad Gums is to parking spots, Henry is to the crowd here. If a stranger showed up, Henry will be able to tell us." I stepped back onto the sidewalk by the coffee shop door. "You get the guys' coffee and bring Henry a cup—" I said as we approached the bench. But Henry already had coffee.

Shifting the *New York Times,* I sat down next to him. "Anyone new here today?"

He put down the *Chronicle*. "Nope."

"No one?"

"Tuesday. People buy beans on Saturday. If they use up beans on the weekend, they get more Monday. By Tuesday they're set. Now Wednesdays—"

"You're sure there was no one at all who was not a regular?"

"Of course I'm sure," he said disgustedly. "I know this square."

I felt my shoulders slump. I stared through the window at Howard in line for the order. If the killer didn't drive off in a car, and didn't escape through the backyards, and didn't walk away from Walnut Square, and wasn't here. . . .

I looked down at Henry's cup of coffee. He always had his coffee promptly at nine. But today, he hadn't had it when I passed at nearly quarter after. He wouldn't accept his coffee from anyone but "Sporty," the wet-haired woman with the red Master's Swim Team sweatshirt, the woman who lived alone in an expensive house close by, who indulged her hobbies, and who had no visible means of support.

It took me a moment to spot her, standing near the dog group, as she did every morning. By then she had had her swim, stopped home to change and catch the news report that ended at eight fifty-five. That gave her five minutes to get here in time for Peet's opening, and to be in line for her coffee and Henry's. No one but Henry would realize she was ten minutes late getting here today. Ten minutes had been enough time to kill Wilson, but not enough time to both commit murder and buy coffee. And it explained the smell that had come from the brick at Wilson's place—chlorine drops from her pool-wet hair.

MRS. NORRIS OBSERVES

Dorothy Salisbury Davis

If there was anything in the world Mrs. Norris liked as well as a nice cup of tea, it was to dip now and then into what she called "a comfortable novel." She found it no problem getting one when she and Mr. James Jarvis, for whom she kept house, were in the country. The ladies at the Nyack library both knew and approved her tastes, and while they always lamented that such books were not written any more, nonetheless they always managed to find a new one for her.

But the New York Public Library at Fifth Avenue and Forty-second Street was a house of different entrance. How could a person like Mrs. Norris climb those wide marble steps, pass muster with the uniformed guard, and then ask for her particular kind of book?

She had not yet managed it, but sometimes she got as far as the library steps and thought about it. And if the sun were out long enough to have warmed the stone bench, she sometimes sat a few moments and observed the faces of the people going in and coming out. As her friend Mr. Tully, the detective, said of her, she was a marvelous woman for observing. "And you can take that the way you like, love."

It was a pleasant morning, this one, and having time to spare, Mrs. Norris contemplated the stone bench. She also noticed that one of her shoelaces had come untied; you could not find a plain cotton lace these days, even on a blind man's tray. She locked her purse between her bosom and her arm and began to stoop.

"It's mine! I saw it first!"

A bunioned pump thumped down almost on her toe, and the woman who owned it slyly turned it over on her ankle so that she might retrieve whatever it was she had found. Mrs. Norris was of the distinct opinion that there had been nothing there at all.

"I was only about to tie my shoelace," Mrs. Norris said, pulling as much height as she could out of her dumpy shape.

A wizened, rouged face turned up at her. "Aw," the creature said, "you're a lady. I'll tie the lace for you."

As the woman fumbled at her foot, Mrs. Norris took time to observe the shaggy hair beneath a hat of many summers. Then she cried, "Get up from there! I'm perfectly able to tie my own shoelace."

The woman straightened, and she was no taller than Mrs. Norris. "Did I hear in your voice that you're Irish?"

"You did not! I'm Scots-born." Then remembering Mr. Tully, her detective friend, she added, "But I'm sometimes taken for North of Ireland."

"Isn't it strange, the places people will take you to be from! Where would you say I was born? Sit down for a moment. You're not in a hurry?"

Mrs. Norris thought the woman daft, but she spoke well and softly. "I haven't the faintest notion," she said, and allowed herself to be persuaded by a grubby hand.

"I was born right down there on Thirty-seventh Street, and not nearly as many years ago as you would think. But this town—oh, the things that have happened to it!" She sat a bit too close, and folded her hands over a beaded evening purse. "A friend of mine, an actress, gave this to me." She indicated the purse, having seen Mrs. Norris glance at it. "But there isn't much giving left in this city. . . ."

Of course, Mrs. Norris thought. How foolish of her not to have realized what was coming. "What a dreadful noise the buses make," she commented by way of changing the subject.

"And they're all driven by Irishmen," the woman said quite venomously. "They've ruined New York, those people!"

"I have a gentleman friend who is Irish," Mrs. Norris said sharply, and wondered why she didn't get up and out of there.

"Oh, my dear," the woman said, pulling a long face of shock. "The actress of whom I just spoke, you know? She used to be with the Abbey Theatre. She was the first Cathleen Ni Houlihan. Or perhaps it was the second. But she sends me two tickets for every opening night—and something to wear." The woman opened her hand on the beaded purse and stroked it lovingly. "She hasn't had a new play in such a long time."

Mrs. Norris was touched in spite of herself: it was a beautiful gesture. "Were you ever in the theater yourself?" she asked.

The old woman looked her full in the face. Tears came to her eyes. Then she said, "No." She tumbled out a whole series of no's as though to bury the matter. She's protesting too much, Mrs. Norris thought. "But I have done many things in my life," she continued in her easy made-up-as-you-go fashion. "I have a good mind for science. I can tell you the square feet of floor space in a building from counting the windows. On Broadway, that naked waterfall, you know . . ." Mrs. Norris nodded, remembering the display. "I have figured out how many times the same water goes over it every night. Oh-h-h, and I've written books—just lovely stories about the world when it was gracious, and people could talk to each other even if one of them wasn't one of those psychiatrists."

What an extraordinary woman!

"But who would read stories like that nowadays?" She cast a sidelong glance at Mrs. Norris.

"I would!" Mrs. Norris said.

"Bless you, my dear, I knew that the moment I looked into your face!" She cocked her head, as a bird does at a strange sound. "Do you happen to know what time it is?"

Mrs. Norris looked at her wrist watch. The woman leaned close to look also. "A Gruen is a lovely watch," she said. She could see like a mantis.

"It's time I was going," Mrs. Norris said. "It's eleven-thirty."

"Oh, and time for me, too. I've been promised a job today."

"Where?" asked Mrs. Norris, which was quite unlike her, but the word had spurted out in her surprise.

"It would degrade me to tell you," the stranger said, and her eyes fluttered.

Mrs. Norris could feel the flush in her face. She almost toppled her new, flowered hat, fanning herself. "I'm sorry," she said. "It was rude of me to ask."

"Would you like to buy me a little lunch?" the woman asked brazenly.

Mrs. Norris got to her feet. "All right," she said, having been caught fairly at a vulnerable moment. "There's a cafeteria across the street. I often go there myself for a bowl of soup. Come along."

The woman had risen with her, but her face had gone awry. Mrs. Norris supposed that at this point she was always bought off—she was not the most appetizing of sights to share a luncheon table with. But Mrs. Norris led the way down the steps at a good pace. She did not begrudge the meal, but she would begrudge the price of it if it were not spent on a meal.

"Wait, madam. I can't keep up with you," the woman wailed.

Mrs. Norris had to stop anyway to tie the blessed shoelace.

Her guest picked at the food, both her taste and her gab dried up in captivity. "It's a bit rich for my stomach," she complained when Mrs. Norris chided her.

Mrs. Norris sipped her tea. Then something strange happened: the cup trembled in her hand. At the same instant there was a clatter of dishes, the crash of glass, the screams of women, and the sense almost, more than the sound, of an explosion. Mrs. Norris's eyes met those of the woman's across from her. They were aglow as a child's with excitement, and she grinned like a quarter moon.

Outside, people began to run across the street toward the library. Mrs. Norris could hear the blast of police whistles, and she stretched her neck, hoping to see better. "Eat up and we'll go," she urged.

"Oh, I couldn't eat now and with all this commotion."

"Then leave it."

Once in the street Mrs. Norris was instantly the prisoner of the crowd, running with it as if she were treading water, frighteningly, unable to turn aside or stem the tide. And lost at once her frail companion, cast apart either by weight or wisdom. Mrs. Norris took in enough breath for a scream which she let go with a piper's force. It made room for her where there had been none before, and from then on she screamed her way to the fore of the crowd.

"Stand back! There's nobody hurt but there will be!" a policeman shouted.

Sirens wailed the approach of police reinforcements. Meanwhile, two or three patrolmen were joined by a few able-bodied passers-by to make a human cordon across the library steps.

"It blew the stone bench fifty feet in the air," Mrs. Norris heard a man say.

"The stone bench?" she cried out. "Why, I was just sitting on it!"

"Then you've got a hard bottom, lady," a policeman growled. He and a companion were trying to hold on to a young man.

Their prisoner gave a twist and came face to face with Mrs. Norris. "That's the woman," he shouted. "That's the one I'm trying to tell you about. Let go of me and ask *her!*"

A policeman looked at her. "This one with the flowers on her hat?"

"That's the one! She looked at her watch, got up and left the package, then ran down the steps, and the next thing . . ."

"Got up and left what, young man?" Mrs. Norris interrupted.

"The box under the bench," the young man said, but to one of the officers.

"A box under the bench?" Mrs. Norris repeated.

"How come you were watching her?" the officer said.

"I wasn't especially. I was smoking a cigarette . . ."

"Do you work in the library?"

No doubt he answered, but Mrs. Norris's attention was suddenly distracted, and by what seemed like half the police force of New York City.

"I have a friend, Jasper Tully, in the District Attorney's office," she declared sternly.

"That's fine, lady," a big sergeant said. "We'll take a ride down there right now." Then he bellowed at the top of his lungs, "Keep the steps clear till the Bomb Squad gets here."

In Jasper Tully's office, Mrs. Norris tried to tell her interrogators about the strange little woman. But she knew from the start that they were going to pay very little attention to her story. Their long experience with panhandlers had run so true to pattern that they would not admit to any exception.

And yet Mrs. Norris felt sure she had encountered the exception. For example, she had been cleverly diverted by the woman when she might have seen the package. The woman had put her foot down on nothing—Mrs. Norris was sure of that. She remembered having looked down at her shoelace, and she would have seen a coin had there been one at her feet—Mrs. Norris was a woman who knew the color of money. Oh, it was a clever lass, that other one, and there was a fair amount of crazy hate in her. Mrs. Norris was unlikely to forget the venom she had been so ready to spew on the Irish.

She tried to tell them. But nobody had to button Annie Norris's lip twice. It was not long until they wished Jasper Tully a widower's luck with her, and went back themselves to the scene of the blast.

Mr. Tully offered to take her home.

"No, I think I'll walk and cogitate, thank you," she said.

"Jimmie gives you too much time off," Tully muttered. He was on close terms with her employer.

"He gives me the time I take."

"Is he in town now?"

"He is, or will be tonight. He'll be going full dress to the theater. It's an opening night."

"Aren't you going yourself?"

Mrs. Norris gave it a second's thought. "I might," she said.

The detective took a card from his pocket and wrote down a telephone number. "You can reach me through this at all hours," he said. "That's in case your cogitating gets you into any more trouble."

When he had taken her to the office door, Mrs. Norris looked up to his melancholy face. "Who was Cathleen Ni Houlihan?"

Tully rubbed his chin. "She wasn't a saint exactly, but I think she was a living person. . . . How the hell would I know? I was born in the Bronx!" A second later he added, "There was a play about her, wasn't there?"

"There was," said Mrs. Norris. "I'm glad to see you're not as ignorant as you make yourself out to be."

"Just be sure you're as smart as you think you are," Tully said, "if you're off to tackle a policeman's job again."

He had no faith in her, Mrs. Norris thought, or he wouldn't let her do it.

All afternoon she went over the morning's incidents in her mind. As soon as Mr. Jarvis left the apartment for dinner and the theater, she went downtown herself. The evening papers were full of the bombing, calling it the work of a madman. The mechanism had been made up of clock parts, and the detonating device was something as simple as a pin. It was thought possibly to have been a hatpin.

Well!

And there was not a mention of her in any account. The police were obviously ashamed of themselves.

Mrs. Norris took as her place of departure Forty-sixth Street and Seventh Avenue. Turning her back on the waterfall atop the Broadway building, she walked toward Shubert Alley. Anyone who could even guess at the number of times the same water went over the dam must have looked at it at least as often. And Cathleen Ni Houlihan—no stranger to the theater had plucked that name out of the air.

The beggars were out in droves: the blind, the lame, and the halt. And there were those with tin cups who could read the date in a dead man's eye.

Mrs. Norris was early, and a good thing she was. Sightseers were already congesting the sidewalk in front of the theater. New York might be the biggest city in the world, but to lovers of the stage a few square feet of it was world enough on an opening night.

She watched from across the street for five minutes, then ten, with the crowd swelling and her own hopes dwindling. Then down the street from Eighth Avenue, with a sort of unperturbed haste, came the little beggar-woman. She wore the same hat, the same ragged coat and carried the same beaded purse.

And she also carried a box about six inches by six which she carefully set down on the steps of a fire exit.

Mrs. Norris plunged across the street and paused again, watching the beggar, fascinated in spite of herself. Round and round one woman she walked, looking her up and down, and then she scouted another. The women themselves were well-dressed out-of-towners by their looks, who had come to gape at the celebrated first nighters now beginning to arrive. When the little panhandler had made her choice of victims, she said, and distinctly enough for Mrs. Norris to hear:

"That's Mrs. Vanderhoff arriving now. Lovely isn't she? Oh, dear, that's not her husband with her. Why, that's Johnson Tree—the oil man! You're not from Texas, are you, dear?"

Mrs. Norris glanced at the arrivals. It was her own Mr. Jarvis and his friend. A Texas oil man indeed! The woman made up her stories to the fit of her victims! She was an artist at it.

Mrs. Norris edged close to the building and bent down to examine the box. She thought she could hear a rhythmic sound. She could, she realized—her own heartbeat.

"Leave that box alone!"

Mrs. Norris obeyed, but not before she had touched, had actually moved, the box. It was empty, or at least as light as a dream, and the woman had not recognized her. She was too busy spinning a tale. Mrs. Norris waited it out. The woman finally asked for money and got it. She actually got paper money! Then she came for the box.

"Remember me?" Mrs. Norris said.

The woman cocked her head and looked at her. "Should I?"

"This morning on the Public Library steps," Mrs. Norris prompted.

The wizened face brightened. "But of course! Oh, and there's something I wanted to talk to you about. I saw you speaking to my young gentleman friend—you know, in all that excitement?"

"Oh, yes," Mrs. Norris said, remembering the young man who had pointed her out to the police.

"Isn't he a lovely young man? And to have had such misfortune."

"Lovely," Mrs. Norris agreed.

"You know, he had a scholarship to study atomic science and *those* people did him out of it."

"*Those* people?"

"All day long you can see them going in and out, in and out, carting books by the armful. Some of them have beards. False, you know. And those thick glasses—I ask you, who would be fooled by them? Spies! Traitors! And *they* can get as many books as they want."

"Oh, *those* people," Mrs. Norris said understandingly.

"And my poor young friend. They won't even give him a library card, and after I wrote him such a nice reference."

"Do you know where he lives?" Mrs. Norris said as casually as she could.

"No. But I know where he works. He fixes watches for a jeweler on Forty-seventh Street. I walked by there once and saw him working in the window. If you wait here for me, I'll walk over and show you the place tonight. He's not there now, of course, but I'm sure he'll be there in the morning. I hope you can help him."

"I'll try," Mrs. Norris said. A watchmaker.

The warning buzzer sounded within the theater. The lights flickered.

"Excuse me for a moment," the woman said, and picked up the box. "I've brought some violets for the leading lady. I want to take them in before curtain. Wouldn't it be nice if she invited us to see the play? I shan't accept unless she invites both of us."

Mrs. Norris followed the woman down the alleyway and then hung back as she handed the box in at the stage door. The woman waited and, observing Mrs. Norris, nodded to her confidently. Mrs. Norris was only reasonably sure the box was empty. She was beset by doubts and fears. Was there such a thing as a featherweight bomb? The doorman returned and put something in the woman's hand. She bowed and scraped and came along, tucking whatever she'd got into her purse.

With Mr. Jarvis in the theater, Mrs. Norris was not going to take any chances. "Wait for me out front," she said. "I want to have a look in there myself."

"Too late, too late," the woman crowed.

Mrs. Norris hurried.

"No one's allowed backstage now, ma'am," the doorman said.

"That box the old woman gave you . . ." It was sitting on a desk almost within her reach. "It could be dangerous."

"Naw. She's harmless, that old fraud. There's nothing in it but tissue paper. She comes round every opening night. 'Flowers for Miss Hayes,' or Miss Tandy or whoever. The company manager gives her a dollar for luck. I'm sorry, ma'am, but you'll have to go now."

Mrs. Norris beat a dignified retreat. The old woman was nowhere to be seen. But a watchmaker on Forty-seventh Street . . . Forty-seventh Street was also the diamond center of New York. What a lovely place for a leisurely walk-through with Mr. Tully!

THE PARKER SHOTGUN

Sue Grafton

The Christmas holidays had come and gone, and the new year was underway. January, in California, is as good as it gets—cool, clear, and green, with a sky the color of wisteria and a surf that thunders like a volley of gunfire in a distant field. My name is Kinsey Millhone. I'm a private investigator, licensed, bonded, insured; white, female, age thirty-two, unmarried, and physically fit. That Monday morning, I was sitting in my office with my feet up, wondering what life would bring, when a woman walked in and tossed a photograph on my desk. My introduction to the Parker shotgun began with a graphic view of its apparent effect when fired at a formerly nice-looking man at close range. His face was still largely intact, but he had no use now for a pocket comb. With effort, I kept my expression neutral as I glanced up at her.

"Somebody killed my husband."

"I can see that," I said.

She snatched the picture back and stared at it as though she might have missed some telling detail. Her face suffused with pink, and she blinked back tears. "Jesus. Rudd was killed five months ago, and the cops have done shit. I'm so sick of getting the runaround I could scream."

She sat down abruptly and pressed a hand to her mouth, trying to compose herself. She was in her late twenties, with a gaudy prettiness. Her hair was an odd shade of brown, like cherry Coke, worn shoulder length and straight. Her eyes were large, a lush mink brown; her mouth was full. Her complexion was all warm tones, tanned, and clear. She didn't seem to be wearing makeup, but she was still as vivid as a magazine illustration, a good four-color run on slick paper. She was seven months pregnant by the look of her; not voluminous yet, but rotund. When she was calmer, she identified herself as Lisa Osterling.

"That's a crime lab photo. How'd you come by it?" I said when the preliminaries were disposed of.

She fumbled in her handbag for a tissue and blew her nose. "I have my little ways," she said morosely. "Actually I know the photographer and I stole a print. I'm going to have it blown up and hung on the wall just so I won't forget. The police are hoping I'll drop the whole thing, but I got news for *them*." Her mouth was starting to tremble again, and a tear splashed onto her skirt as though my ceiling had a leak.

"What's the story?" I said. "The cops in this town are usually pretty good." I got up and filled a paper cup with water from my Sparklett's dispenser, passing it over to her. She murmured a thank you and drank it down, staring into the bottom of the cup as she spoke. "Rudd was a cocaine dealer until a month or so before he died. They haven't said as much, but I know they've written him off as some kind of small-time punk. What do they care? They'd like to think he was killed in a drug deal—a double cross or something like that. He wasn't, though. He'd given it all up because of this."

She glanced down at the swell of her belly. She was wearing a kelly green T-shirt with an arrow down the front. The word "Oops!" was written across her breasts in machine embroidery.

"What's your theory?" I asked. Already I was leaning toward the official police version of events. Drug dealing isn't synonymous with longevity. There's too much money involved and too many amateurs getting into the act. This was Santa Teresa—ninety-five miles north of the big time in L.A., but there are still standards to maintain. A shotgun blast is the underworld equivalent of a bad annual review.

"I don't have a theory. I just don't like theirs. I want you to look into it so I can clear Rudd's name before the baby comes."

I shrugged. "I'll do what I can, but I can't guarantee the results. How are you going to feel if the cops are right?"

She stood up, giving me a flat look. "I don't know why Rudd died, but it had nothing to do with drugs," she said. She opened her handbag and extracted a roll of bills the size of a wad of socks. "What do you charge?"

"Thirty bucks an hour plus expenses."

She peeled off several hundred-dollar bills and laid them on the desk.

I got out a contract.

My second encounter with the Parker shotgun came in the form of a dealer's appraisal slip that I discovered when I was nosing through Rudd Osterling's private possessions an hour later at the house. The address she'd given me was on the Bluffs, a residential area on the west side of town, overlooking the Pacific. It should have been an elegant neighborhood, but the ocean generated too much fog and too much corrosive salt air. The houses were small and had a temporary feel to them, as though the occupants intended to move on when the month was up. No one seemed to get around to painting the trim, and the yards looked like they were kept by people who spent all day at the beach. I followed her in my car, reviewing the information she'd given me as I urged my ancient VW up Capilla Hill and took a right on Presipio.

The late Rudd Osterling had been in Santa Teresa since the sixties, when he migrated to the West Coast in search of sunshine, good surf, good dope, and casual sex. Lisa told me he'd lived in vans and communes, working variously as a roofer, tree trimmer, bean picker, fry cook, and forklift operator—never with any noticeable ambition or success. He'd started dealing cocaine two years earlier, apparently netting more money than he was accustomed to. Then he'd met and married Lisa, and she'd been determined to see him clean up his act. According to her, he'd retired from the drug trade and was just in the process of setting himself up in a landscape maintenance business when someone blew the top of his head off.

I pulled into the driveway behind her, glancing at the frame and stucco bungalow with its patchy grass and dilapidated fence. It looked like one of those households where there's always something under construction, probably without permits and not up to code. In this case, a foundation had been laid for an addition to the garage, but the weeds were already growing up through cracks in the concrete. A wooden outbuilding had been dismantled, the old lumber tossed in an unsightly pile. Closer to the house, there were stacks of cheap pecan wood paneling, sunbleached in places and warped along one edge. It was all hapless and depressing, but she scarcely looked at it.

I followed her into the house.

"We were just getting the house fixed up when he died," she remarked.

"When did you buy the place?" I was manufacturing small talk, trying to cover my distaste at the sight of the old linoleum counter, where a line of ants stretched from a crust of toast and jelly all the way out the back door.

"We didn't really. This was my mother's. She and my stepdad moved back to the Midwest last year."

"What about Rudd? Did he have any family out here?"

"They're all in Connecticut, I think, real la-di-dah. His parents are dead, and his sisters wouldn't even come out to the funeral."

"Did he have a lot of friends?"

"All cocaine dealers have friends."

"Enemies?"

"Not that I ever heard about."

"Who was his supplier?"

"I don't know that."

"No disputes? Suits pending? Quarrels with the neighbors? Family arguments about the inheritance?"

She gave me a "no" on all four counts.

I had told her I wanted to go through his personal belongings, so she showed me into the tiny back bedroom, where he'd set up a card table and some cardboard file boxes. A real entrepreneur. I began to search while she leaned against the doorframe, watching.

I said, "Tell me about what was going on the week he died." I was sorting through cancelled checks in a Nike shoe box. Most were written to the neighborhood supermarket, utilities, telephone company.

She moved to the desk chair and sat down. "I can't tell you much because I was at work. I do alterations and repairs at a dry cleaner's up at Presipio Mall. Rudd would stop in now and then when he was out running around. He'd picked up a few jobs already, but he really wasn't doing the gardening full time. He was trying to get all his old business squared away. Some kid owed him money. I remember that."

"He sold cocaine on *credit?*"

She shrugged. "Maybe it was grass or pills. Somehow the kid owed him a bundle. That's all I know."

"I don't suppose he kept any records."

"Nuh-uh. It was all in his head. He was too paranoid to put anything down in black and white."

The file boxes were jammed with old letters, tax returns, receipts. It all looked like junk to me.

"What about the day he was killed? Were you at work then?"

She shook her head. "It was a Saturday. I was off work, but I'd gone to the market. I was out maybe an hour and a half, and when I got home, police cars were parked in front, and the paramedics were here. Neighbors were standing out on the street." She stopped talking, and I was left to imagine the rest.

"Had he been expecting anyone?"

"If he was, he never said anything to me. He was in the garage, doing I don't know what. Chauncy, next door, heard the shotgun go off, but by the time he got here to investigate, whoever did it was gone."

I got up and moved toward the hallway. "Is this the bedroom down here?"

"Right. I haven't gotten rid of his stuff yet. I guess I'll have to eventually. I'm going to use his office for the nursery."

I moved into the master bedroom and went through his hanging clothes. "Did the police find anything?"

"They didn't look. Well, one guy came through and poked around some. About five minutes' worth."

I began to check through the drawers she indicated were his. Nothing remarkable came to light. On top of the chest was one of those brass and walnut caddies, where Rudd apparently kept his watch, keys, loose change. Almost idly, I picked it up. Under it there was a folded slip of paper. It was a partially completed appraisal form from a gun shop out in Colgate, a township to the north of us. "What's a Parker?" I said when I'd glanced at it. She peered over the slip.

"Oh. That's probably the appraisal on the shotgun he got."

"The one he was killed with?"

"Well, I don't know. They never found the weapon, but the homicide detective said they couldn't run it through ballistics, anyway—or whatever it is they do."

"Why'd he have it appraised in the first place?"

"He was taking it in trade for a big drug debt, and he needed to know if it was worth it."

"Was this the kid you mentioned before or someone else?"

"The same one, I think. At first, Rudd intended to turn around and sell the gun, but then he found out it was a collector's item so he decided to keep it. The gun dealer called a couple of times after Rudd died, but it was gone by then."

"And you told the cops all this stuff?"

"Sure. They couldn't have cared less."

I doubted that, but I tucked the slip in my pocket anyway. I'd check it out and then talk to Dolan in homicide.

The gun shop was located on a narrow side street in Colgate, just off the main thoroughfare. Colgate looks like it's made up of hardware stores, U-haul rentals, and plant nurseries; places that seem to have half their merchandise outside, surrounded by chain link fence. The gun shop had been set up in someone's front parlor in a dinky white frame house. There were some glass counters filled with gun paraphernalia, but no guns in sight.

The man who came out of the back room was in his fifties, with a narrow face and graying hair, gray eyes made luminous by rimless glasses. He wore a dress shirt with the sleeves rolled up and a long gray apron tied around his waist. He had perfect teeth, but when he talked I could see the rim of pink where his upper plate was fit, and it spoiled the effect. Still, I had to give him credit for a certain level of good looks, maybe a seven on a scale of ten. Not bad for a man his age. "Yes ma'am," he said. He had a trace of an accent, Virginia, I thought.

"Are you Avery Lamb?"

"That's right. What can I help you with?"

"I'm not sure. I'm wondering what you can tell me about this appraisal you did." I handed him the slip.

He glanced down and then looked up at me. "Where did you get this?"

"Rudd Osterling's widow," I said.

"She told me she didn't have the gun."

"That's right."

His manner was a combination of confusion and wariness. "What's your connection to the matter?"

I took out a business card and gave it to him. "She hired me to look into Rudd's death. I thought the shotgun might be relevant since he was killed with one."

He shook his head. "I don't know what's going on. This is the second time it's disappeared."

"Meaning what?"

"Some woman brought it in to have it appraised back in June. I made an offer on it then, but before we could work out a deal, she claimed the gun was stolen."

"I take it you had some doubts about that."

"Sure I did. I don't think she ever filed a police report, and I suspect she knew damn well who took it but didn't intend to pursue it. Next thing I knew, this Osterling fellow brought the same gun in. It had a beavertail fore-end and an English grip. There was no mistaking it."

"Wasn't that a bit of a coincidence? His bringing the gun in to you?"

"Not really. I'm one of the few master gunsmiths in this area. All he had to do was ask around the same way she did."

"Did you tell her the gun had showed up?"

He shrugged with his mouth and a lift of his brows. "Before I could talk to her, he was dead and the Parker was gone again."

I checked the date on the slip. "That was in August?"

"That's right, and I haven't seen the gun since."

"Did he tell you how he acquired it?"

"Said he took it in trade. I told him this other woman showed up with it first, but he didn't seem to care about that."

"How much was the Parker worth?"

He hesitated, weighing his words. "I offered him six thousand."

"But what's its value out in the marketplace?"

"Depends on what people are willing to pay."

I tried to control the little surge of impatience he had sparked. I could tell he'd jumped into his crafty negotiator's mode, unwilling to tip his hand in case the gun showed up and he could nick it off cheap. "Look," I said, "I'm asking you in confidence. This won't go any further unless it becomes a police matter, and then neither one of us will have a choice. Right now, the gun's missing anyway, so what difference does it make?"

He didn't seem entirely convinced, but he got my point. He cleared his throat with obvious embarrassment. "Ninety-six."

I stared at him. "Thousand dollars?"

He nodded.

"Jesus. That's a lot for a gun, isn't it?"

His voice dropped. "Ms. Millhone, that gun is priceless. It's an A-1 Special 28-gauge with a two-barrel set. There were only two of them made."

"But why so much?"

"For one thing, the Parker's a beautifully crafted shotgun. There are different grades, of course, but this one was exceptional. Fine wood. Some of the most incredible scroll-work you'll ever see. Parker had an Italian working for him back then who'd spend sometimes five thousand hours on the engraving alone. The company went out of business around 1942, so there aren't any more to be had."

"You said there were two. Where's the other one, or would you know?"

"Only what I've heard. A dealer in Ohio bought the one at auction a couple years back for ninety-six. I understand some fella down in Texas has it now, part of a collection of Parkers. The gun Rudd Osterling brought in has been missing for years. I don't think he knew what he had on his hands."

"And you didn't tell him."

Lamb shifted his gaze. "I told him enough," he said carefully. "I can't help it if the man didn't do his homework."

"How'd you know it was the missing Parker?"

"The serial number matched, and so did everything else. It wasn't a fake, either. I examined the gun under heavy magnification, checking for fill-in welds and traces of markings that might have been overstamped. After I checked it out, I showed it to a buddy of mine, a big gun buff, and he recognized it, too."

"Who else knew about it besides you and this friend?"

"Whoever Rudd Osterling got it from, I guess."

"I'll want the woman's name and address if you've still got it. Maybe she knows how the gun fell into Rudd's hands."

Again he hesitated for a moment, and then he shrugged. "I don't see why not." He made a note on a piece of scratch paper and pushed it across the counter to me. "I'd like to know if the gun shows up," he said.

"Sure, as long as Mrs. Osterling doesn't object."

I didn't have any other questions for the moment. I moved toward the door, then glanced back at him. "How could Rudd have sold the gun if it was stolen property? Wouldn't he have needed a bill of sale for it? Some proof of ownership?"

Avery Lamb's face was devoid of expression. "Not necessarily. If an avid collector got hold of that gun, it would sink out of sight, and that's the last you'd ever see of it. He'd keep it in his basement and never show it to a soul. It'd be enough if he knew he had it. You don't need a bill of sale for that."

I sat out in my car and made some notes while the information was fresh. Then I checked the address Lamb had given me, and I could feel the adrenaline stir. It was right back in Rudd's neighborhood.

The woman's name was Jackie Barnett. The address was two streets over from the Osterling house and just about parallel; a big corner lot planted with avocado trees and bracketed with palms. The house itself was yellow stucco with flaking brown shutters and a yard that needed mowing. The mailbox read "Squires," but the house number seemed to match. There was a basketball hoop nailed up above the two-car garage and a dismantled motorcycle in the driveway.

I parked my car and got out. As I approached the house, I saw an old man in a wheelchair planted in the side yard like a lawn ornament. He was parchment pale, with baby-fine white hair and rheumy eyes. The left half of his face had been disconnected by a stroke, and his left arm and hand rested uselessly in his lap. I caught sight of a woman peering through the window, apparently drawn by the sound of my car door slamming shut. I crossed the yard, moving toward the front porch. She opened the door before I had a chance to knock.

"You must be Kinsey Millhone. I just got off the phone with Avery. He said you'd be stopping by."

"That was quick. I didn't realize he'd be calling ahead. Saves me an explanation. I take it you're Jackie Barnett."

"That's right. Come in if you like. I just have to check on him," she said, indicating the man in the yard.

"Your father?"

She shot me a look. "Husband," she said. I watched her cross the grass toward the old man, grateful for a chance to recover from my gaffe. I could see now that she was older than she'd first appeared. She must have been in her fifties—at that stage where women wear too much makeup and dye their hair too bold a shade of blonde. She was buxom, clearly overweight, but lush. In a seventeenth-century painting, she'd have been depicted supine, her plump naked body draped in sheer white. Standing over her, something with a goat's rear end would be poised for assault. Both would look coy but excited at the prospects. The old man was beyond the pleasures of the flesh, yet the noises he made—garbled and indistinguishable because of the stroke—had the same intimate quality as sounds uttered in the throes of passion, a disquieting effect.

I looked away from him, thinking of Avery Lamb instead. He hadn't actually told me the woman was a stranger to him, but he'd certainly implied as much. I wondered now what their relationship consisted of.

Jackie spoke to the old man briefly, adjusting his lap robe. Then she came back and we went inside.

"Is your name Barnett or Squires?" I asked.

"Technically it's Squires, but I still use Barnett for the most part," she said. She seemed angry, and I thought at first the rage was directed at me. She caught my look. "I'm sorry," she said, "but I've about had it with him. Have you ever dealt with a stroke victim?"

"I understand it's difficult."

"It's impossible! I know I sound hard-hearted, but he was always short-tempered and now he's frustrated on top of that. Self-centered, demanding. Nothing suits him. Nothing. I put him out in the yard sometimes just so I won't have to fool with him. Have a seat, hon."

I sat. "How long has be been sick?"

"He had the first stroke in June. He's been in and out of the hospital ever since."

"What's the story on the gun you took out to Avery's shop?"

"Oh, that's right. He said you were looking into some fellow's death. He lived right here on the Bluffs, too, didn't he?"

"Over on Whitmore . . ."

"That was terrible. I read about it in the papers, but I never did hear the end of it. What went on?"

"I wasn't given the details," I said briefly. "Actually, I'm trying to track down a shotgun that belonged to him. Avery Lamb says it was the same gun you brought in."

She had automatically proceeded to get out two cups and saucers, so her answer was delayed until she'd poured coffee for us both. She passed a cup over to me, and then she sat down, stirring milk into hers. She glanced at me self-consciously. "I just took that gun to spite *him,*" she said with a nod toward the yard. "I've been married to Bill for six years and miserable for every one of them. It was my own damn fault. I'd been divorced for ages and I was doing fine, but somehow when I hit fifty, I got in a panic. Afraid of growing old alone, I guess. I ran into Bill, and he looked like a catch. He was retired, but he had loads of money, or so he said. He promised me the moon. Said we'd travel. Said he'd buy me clothes and a car and I don't know what all. Turns out he's a penny-pinching miser with a mean mouth and a quick fist. At least he can't do that anymore." She paused to shake her head, staring down at her coffee cup.

"The gun was his?"

"Well, yes, it was. He has a collection of shotguns. I swear he took better care of them than he did of me. I just despise guns. I was always after him to get rid of them. Makes me nervous to have them in the house. Anyway, when he got sick, it turned out he had insurance, but it only paid eighty percent. I was afraid his whole life savings would go up in smoke. I figured he'd go on for years, using up all the money, and then I'd be stuck with his debts when he died. So I just picked up one of the guns and took it out to that gun place to sell. I was going to buy me some clothes."

"What made you change your mind?"

"Well, I didn't think it'd be worth but eight or nine hundred dollars. Then Avery said he'd give me six thousand for it, so I had to guess it was worth at least twice that. I got nervous and thought I better put it back."

"How soon after that did the gun disappear?"

"Oh, gee, I don't know. I didn't pay much attention until Bill got out of the hospital the second time. He's the one who noticed it was gone," she said. "Of course, he raised pluperfect hell. You should have seen him. He had a conniption fit for two days, and then he had another stroke and had to be hospitalized all over again. Served him right if you ask me. At least I had Labor Day weekend to myself. I needed it."

"Do you have any idea who might have taken the gun?"

She gave me a long, candid look. Her eyes were very blue and couldn't have appeared more guileless. "Not the faintest."

I let her practice her wide-eyed stare for a moment, and then I laid out a little bait just to see what she'd do. "God, that's too bad," I said. "I'm assuming you reported it to the police."

I could see her debate briefly before she replied. Yes or no. Check one. "Well, of course," she said.

She was one of those liars who blush from lack of practice.

I kept my tone of voice mild. "What about the insurance? Did you put in a claim?"

She looked at me blankly, and I had the feeling I'd taken her by surprise on that one. She said, "You know, it never even occurred to me. But of course he probably would have it insured, wouldn't he?"

"Sure, if the gun's worth that much. What company is he with?"

"I don't remember offhand. I'd have to look it up."

"I'd do that if I were you," I said. "You can file a claim, and then all you have to do is give the agent the case number."

"Case number?"

"The police will give you that from their report."

She stirred restlessly, glancing at her watch. "Oh, lordy, I'm going to have to give him his medicine. Was there anything else you wanted to ask while you were here?" Now that she'd told me a fib or two, she was anxious to get rid of me so she could assess the situation. Avery Lamb had told me she'd never reported it to the cops. I wondered if she'd call him up now to compare notes.

"Could I take a quick look at his collection?" I said, getting up.

"I suppose that'd be all right. It's in here," she said. She moved toward a small paneled den, and I followed, stepping around a suitcase near the door.

A rack of six guns was enclosed in a glass-fronted cabinet. All of them were beautifully engraved, with fine wood stocks, and I wondered how a priceless Parker could really be distinguished. Both the cabinet and the rack were locked, and there were no empty slots. "Did he keep the Parker in here?"

She shook her head. "The Parker had its own case." She hauled out a handsome wood case from behind the couch and opened it for me, demonstrating its emptiness as though she might be setting up a magic trick. Actually, there was a set of barrels in the box, but nothing else.

I glanced around. There was a shotgun propped in one corner, and I picked it up, checking the manufacturer's imprint on the frame. L.C. Smith. Too bad. For a moment I'd thought it might be the missing Parker. I'm always hoping for the obvious. I set the Smith back in the corner with regret.

"Well, I guess that'll do," I said. "Thanks for the coffee."

"No trouble. I wish I could be more help." She started easing me toward the door.

I held out my hand. "Nice meeting you," I said. "Thanks again for your time."

She gave my hand a perfunctory shake. "That's all right. Sorry I'm in such a rush, but you know how it is when you have someone sick."

Next thing I knew, the door was closing at my back and I was heading toward my car, wondering what she was up to.

I'd just reached the driveway when a white Corvette came roaring down the street and rumbled into the drive. The kid at the wheel flipped the ignition key and cantilevered himself up onto the seat top. "Hi. You know if my mom's here?"

"Who, Jackie? Sure," I said, taking a flyer. "You must be Doug."

He looked puzzled. "No, Eric. Do I know you?"

I shook my head. "I'm just a friend passing through."

He hopped out of the Corvette. I moved on toward my car, keeping an eye on him as he headed toward the house. He looked about seventeen, blond, blue-eyed, with good cheekbones, a moody, sensual mouth, lean surfer's body. I pictured him in a few years, hanging out in resort hotels, picking up women three times his age. He'd do well. So would they.

Jackie had apparently heard him pull in, and she came out onto the porch, intercepting him with a quick look at me. She put her arm through his, and the two moved into the house. I looked over at the old man. He was making noises again, plucking aimlessly at his bad hand with his good one. I felt a mental jolt, like an interior tremor shifting the ground under me. I was beginning to get it.

I drove the two blocks to Lisa Osterling's. She was in the backyard, stretched out on a chaise in a sunsuit that made her belly look like a watermelon in a laundry bag. Her face and arms were rosy, and her tanned legs glistened with tanning oil. As I crossed the grass, she raised a hand to her eyes, shading her face from the winter sunlight so she could look at me. "I didn't expect to see you back so soon."

"I have a question," I said, "and then I need to use your phone. Did Rudd know a kid named Eric Barnett?"

"I'm not sure. What's he look like?"

I gave her a quick rundown, including a description of the white Corvette. I could see the recognition in her face as she sat up.

"Oh, him. Sure. He was over here two or three times a week. I just never knew his name. Rudd said he lived around here somewhere and stopped by to borrow tools so he could work on his motorcycle. Is he the one who owed Rudd the money?"

"Well, I don't know how we're going to prove it, but I suspect he was."

"You think he killed him?"

"I can't answer that yet, but I'm working on it. Is the phone in here?" I was moving toward the kitchen. She struggled to her feet and followed me into the house. There was a wall phone near the back door. I tucked the receiver against my shoulder, pulling the appraisal slip out of my pocket. I dialed Avery Lamb's gun shop. The phone rang twice.

Somebody picked up on the other end. "Gun shop."

"Mr. Lamb?"

"This is Orville Lamb. Did you want me or my brother, Avery?"

"Avery, actually. I have a quick question for him."

"Well, he left a short while ago, and I'm not sure when he'll be back. Is it something I can help you with?"

"Maybe so," I said. "If you had a priceless shotgun—say, an Ithaca or a Parker, one of the classics—would you shoot a gun like that?"

"You could," he said dubiously, "but it wouldn't be a good idea, especially if it was in mint condition to begin with. You wouldn't want to take a chance on lowering the value. Now if it'd been in use previously, I don't guess it would matter much, but still I wouldn't advise it—just speaking for myself. Is this a gun of yours?"

But I'd hung up. Lisa was right behind me, her expression anxious. "I've got to go in a minute," I said, "but here's what I think went on. Eric

Barnett's stepfather has a collection of fine shotguns, one of which turns out to be very, very valuable. The old man was hospitalized, and Eric's mother decided to hock one of the guns in order to do a little something for herself before he'd blown every asset he had on his medical bills. She had no idea the gun she chose was worth so much, but the gun dealer recognized it as the find of a lifetime. I don't know whether he told her that or not, but when she realized it was more valuable than she thought, she lost her nerve and put it back."

"Was that the same gun Rudd took in trade?"

"Exactly. My guess is that she mentioned it to her son, who saw a chance to square his drug debt. He offered Rudd the shotgun in trade, and Rudd decided he'd better get the gun appraised, so he took it out to the same place. The gun dealer recognized it when he brought it in."

She stared at me. "Rudd was killed over the gun itself, wasn't he?" she said.

"I think so, yes. It might have been an accident. Maybe there was a struggle and the gun went off."

She closed her eyes and nodded. "Okay. Oh, wow. That feels better. I can live with that." Her eyes came open, and she smiled painfully. "Now what?"

"I have one more hunch to check out, and then I think we'll know what's what."

She reached over and squeezed my arm. "Thanks."

"Yeah, well, it's not over yet, but we're getting there."

When I got back to Jackie Barnett's, the white Corvette was still in the driveway, but the old man in the wheelchair had apparently been moved into the house. I knocked, and after an interval, Eric opened the door, his expression altering only slightly when he saw me.

I said, "Hello again. Can I talk to your mom?"

"Well, not really. She's gone right now."

"Did she and Avery go off together?"

"Who?"

I smiled briefly. "You can drop the bullshit, Eric. I saw the suitcase in the hall when I was here the first time. Are they gone for good or just for a quick jaunt?"

"They said they'd be back by the end of the week," he mumbled. It was clear he looked a lot slicker than he really was. I almost felt bad that he was so far outclassed.

"Do you mind if I talk to your stepfather?"

He flushed. "She doesn't want him upset."

"I won't upset him."

He shifted uneasily, trying to decide what to do with me.

I thought I'd help him out. "Could I just make a suggestion here? According to the California penal code, grand theft is committed when the real or personal property taken is of a value exceeding two hundred dollars. Now that includes domestic fowl, avocados, olives, citrus, nuts, and artichokes. Also shotguns, and it's punishable by imprisonment in the county jail or state prison for not more than one year. I don't think you'd care for it."

He stepped away from the door and let me in.

The old man was huddled in his wheelchair in the den. The rheumy eyes came up to meet mine, but there was no recognition in them. Or maybe there was recognition but no interest. I hunkered beside his wheelchair. "Is your hearing okay?"

He began to pluck aimlessly at his pant leg with his good hand, looking away from me. I've seen dogs with the same expression when they've done pottie on the rug and know you've got a roll of newspaper tucked behind your back.

"Want me to tell you what I think happened?" I didn't really need to wait. He couldn't answer in any mode that I could interpret. "I think when you came home from the hospital the first time and found out the gun was gone, the shit hit the fan. You must have figured out that Eric took it. He'd probably taken other things if he'd been doing cocaine for long. You probably hounded him until you found out what he'd done with it, and then you went over to Rudd's to get it. Maybe you took the L.C. Smith with you the first time, or maybe you came back for it when he refused to return the Parker. In either case, you blew his head off and then came back across the yards. And then you had another stroke."

I became aware of Eric in the doorway behind me. I glanced back at him. "You want to talk about this stuff?" I asked.

"Did he kill Rudd?"

"I think so," I said. I stared at the old man.

His face had taken on a canny stubbornness, and what was I going to do? I'd have to talk to Lieutenant Dolan about the situation, but the cops would probably never find any real proof, and even if they did, what could they do to him? He'd be lucky if he lived out the year.

"Rudd was a nice guy," Eric said.

"God, Eric. You *all* must have guessed what happened," I said snappishly.

He had the good grace to color up at that, and then he left the room. I stood up. To save myself, I couldn't work up any righteous anger at the pitiful remainder of a human being hunched in front of me. I crossed to the gun cabinet.

The Parker shotgun was in the rack, three slots down, looking like the other classic shotguns in the case. The old man would die, and Jackie would inherit it from his estate. Then she'd marry Avery and they'd all have what they wanted. I stood there for a moment, and then I started looking through the desk drawers until I found the keys. I unlocked the cabinet and then unlocked the rack. I substituted the L.C. Smith for the Parker and then locked the whole business up again. The old man was whimpering, but he never looked at me, and Eric was nowhere in sight when I left.

The last I saw of the Parker shotgun, Lisa Osterling was holding it somewhat awkwardly across her bulky midriff. I'd talk to Lieutenant Dolan all right, but I wasn't going to tell him everything. Sometimes justice is served in other ways.

Murder on Wheels

Stuart Palmer

A NOVEL

1

Jack-in-the-Box

Like the note of a pitch-pipe between the lips of some mad, unearthly chorus leader, the traffic officer's whistle sounded its earsplitting E above high C. Rush-hour traffic on the Avenue, which had just been granted a green light, stopped jarringly with a screech of brakes. All but the open Chrysler roadster, which, as Officer Francis X. Doody had noted from the corner of his vigilant blue eye, was veering crazily toward the left instead of keeping on south past the impassive stone lions of the Library as was its proper course. . . .

Officer Doody took the whistle out of his mouth and bellowed, "Hey!" But the echoes were still sounding back their flattened versions of his blast when there came a sickening crash of tortured glass and metal. The open blue Chrysler had come to rest with its front end inextricably entangled with the fender of a north-bound Yellow taxi.

"Where do you think you're goin'?" Doody spoke his piece by rote as he strode wearily over toward the scene of the smash. He jerked the white gloves from his big red hands as he went, remarking audibly that this was just about what he could have expected of his lousy luck, anyway. As if it wasn't enough, on the tag end of a dreary November afternoon, to have it start snowing just as the crowds were pouring out of shops and office buildings! To cap it all, some dumb driver had to pick the busiest corner in Manhattan to try a forbidden left turn in the middle of a *Go* light. "One damn thing after another!" Doody was mumbling.

Then he stopped suddenly, his arms akimbo. Swiftly the realization came over him that there was something decidedly wrong here, something "phony," as he himself would have expressed it. Mechanically his lips formed the words, "One damn thing after another. . . ."

It was at that moment that this accident began to be different from all other accidents. For there wasn't any driver behind the wheel of the Chrysler roadster. There wasn't anybody in the car at all. It was deserted, wandering, derelict.

Doody walked clear around the wreck, oblivious of the interrupted traffic and to the din of the sirens. His jaw was thrust forward belligerently, but his expedition drew a blank.

"Smart guy, huh?"

But nobody answered him. He rubbed his eyes, half blinded by the thick falling flakes of the sooty precipitate which passes for snow in Manhattan.

The driver of the wounded taxi scrambled down from his seat at Doody's command. His name, he insisted, was Al Leech. Doody had a hard time to get him to speak loudly enough to be heard. Somewhere in the vast reaches of his skinny throat his voice seemed to have a way of losing itself. He was naturally small and nervous, and his eyes were unnaturally wild.

Doody took the little man by the shoulder and shook him vigorously, for lack of a better victim.

"Come clean, you! Where did the driver of that Chrysler go?"

The cabdriver swallowed with obvious difficulty, and then pointed up the street. "I saw him, I tell yer! I saw him . . . he's there!"

Doody turned, and at that moment the street lights came on, slightly increasing the confusion, without adding greatly to the visibility. "You saw *who, where?*"

The cabbie pulled away from Doody's clutch, still pointing. His grimy finger indicated a spot perhaps thirty yards away, across Forty-second Street and up Fifth a little distance.

Doody rubbed at his eyes again. The snowfall was thickening, and this was the period between the dark and the daylight, which Longfellow, in an earlier age, dedicated as "the children's hour," and which has since been diverted from children to cocktails. The pale yellow glow of the street lamps fought the last of the winter daylight, and a nearby church clock was striking five-thirty.

Even Officer Doody could see that something lay quietly and still in the narrow lane between north- and south-bound traffic on the Avenue—something that vaguely resembled a sack, and was not.

Doody took several uncertain steps forward, and then remembered his post of duty. He drew his whistle, let forth a series of staccato blasts, and then waited a moment for an answer. There was no answer. He tried again, and drew another blank.

The street was already jammed enough to block traffic both ways. Let it stay that way for a while, Doody reflected. And hc set out on the run toward the gathering crowd which already had surrounded that shapeless sack on the pavement.

He fought his way through the mob, the little cabdriver directly in his rear. For the hundredth time the big cop wondered at the sudden appearance of the curious crowd which always seems to spring out of nowhere, like worms after the rain, at the first cry of an accident.

Halfway through the jam he whirled and caught the cabdriver by the shoulder. "It's an accident case, sure enough!" he yelled above the din. "You get to the nearest phone and get an ambulance, quick! Get Bellevue—no, Roosevelt is closer. Scram!"

Obediently the little man turned and dashed toward the corner. By means of a perfect off-tackle plunge, Doody came at last to the bull's-eye of the rapidly increasing circle.

"Get back, will yez? What's the trouble here?"

Nobody answered him. They were all looking down, down to the glistening asphalt where a young man lay sprawled out on his back . . . a big young man with fair hair. It was a face that would have been thought more than handsome under ordinary circumstances, but it was not handsome now.

He was dressed, this accident case of Doody's, in a thick overcoat of yellow camel's hair, with pigskin gloves on his somewhat small hands and bright tan shoes on his feet. The brim of a crushed felt hat protruded from beneath one shoulder, and a cigarette still burned merrily into the furry overcoat lapel where it must have dropped from lips now black and contorted.

A snappy dresser, this accident case. But there was one detail of his array which did not jibe with Doody's ideas of what the well-dressed young man will wear this season. Around his neck, just above the soft pinned collar and the blue-gold tie of printed silk, was another and heavier cravat—a noose of twisted hempen rope!

Doody blew his whistle again, a dozen short sharp blasts. Then he sank slowly to his knees, and touched the face, on which the snowflakes were still melting as they fell. The head rolled loosely, almost too loosely, to one side as he brought his reluctant fingers against the flesh. Then Doody got a grip on the knot in the half-inch rope, and worked it until it came loose in his hand. But as the rope came away it left a cruel red stigma around the throat of the young man who lay there on the asphalt.

From the knot this rope ran off somewhere under the encroaching feet of the multitude. Doody hauled on it vigorously, glad of something definite to get his hands on. With a certain amount of useless advice and assistance from the crowd the end was gathered in, not without an old lady or two being upset in the process.

He had expected to find something on the end of it. It stood to reason that a man can't be hanged unless he is hanged from something. But there was only a binding of fine silk thread, dark blue in color, to keep the end from raveling.

Doody kicked aside his landlubberly coil and stared again at that unlovely face which looked rather horribly up at the sky. "Another suicide," he said aloud. "Get back, all of yez! Why don't somebody hunt up the officer on this beat?"

He sent another series of blasts echoing above the howling sirens of the blocked autos, which now were jammed all the way down to the Empire State Building.

"Suicide or not, I got to get the street clear," decided Doody aloud. "Come on, some of you. Give me a hand, and we'll get him inside." He pointed to the nearest bystander. "You, there!"

An apple peddler shook his head vehemently and backed away out of sight. His place in the inner circle of the curious was taken by a youngish man in a derby, whose fingers tugged nervously at a yellow moustache as he saw what lay at his feet. He dropped his briefcase, and seemed to have some trouble in taking his eyes from the face of the man who lay in the street.

"Good God, it's Laurie Stait!" The words seemed torn from his lips.

"So? You know him, huh? Well, never mind." Doody motioned imperatively. "Grab his legs. We can't let him lay here in the street."

If the new arrival was willing, he hid it successfully. But Doody insisted. "Come on; if you know him you don't need no introduction. Grab his legs."

He bellowed at the crowd until a narrow lane was formed, and the two of them lifted the unhappy young man to the curb, across the sidewalk, and in through the wide doors of the Enterprise Trust Building.

"Here, you can't bring that man in here!" shouted the elevator starter. "You can't do it. . . ."

"Horsefeathers!" retorted Doody. "We did do it, see? And you'll like it."

The crowd in the lobby was closing in again. One woman screamed that she was about to faint, and then pressed forward for a better view.

The young man with the moustache stood irresolute. "Officer, is he dead?"

"I'm not the medical examiner," said Doody shortly. "This is the patrolman's job, not mine. I got to get back on my corner."

The stranger bent almost unwillingly for a moment over the body, his ear pressed against the heart. He fumbled a bit with the victim's coat. "That's nearer than I'd want to be," observed somebody in the crowd. The young man bent closer, and then suddenly stood up. "How did this happen?"

"Never mind that." Doody came closer. "You say you know this fellow?"

The stranger stood there, staring at the body.

"Come on, speak up! What's your name? Friend or relative of the deceased, if he is deceased? What did you say his name was?"

"I—I don't know, Officer."

"None of that. You said you knew him. Do you know him, or don't you?"

"I don't know if I know him or not!"

Doody's homely face wrinkled into a scowl. "Why, you—" He was interrupted by the speedily increasing wail of an approaching siren. The crowd surged toward the door as a Dodge special-built truck came lurching down the Avenue and skidded to a stop at the curb outside. Doody signaled vigorously with waves of his arm.

It wasn't the white ambulance that Doody had expected, but a black truck with the red initials P D on the side.

There were three men in the front seat. Two of them wore plain blue uniforms, and the other had on a Chesterfield with the collar turned up around his ears.

He slid down to the street and pushed through the crowd. "Heard you had a stiff up here," he said casually. "Where's it laying?"

"But I didn't send for you, Doc. I sent for the ambulance!"

"Yeah? Well, the guy who phoned in said there was a stiff up here. I happened to be down at the morgue and I thought I'd run up and get it over quick." He touched the body gently with his foot.

"Pretty, very pretty, Doody, my boy. Don't weep because you didn't get your ambulance. The intern wouldn't have taken this carcass aboard, anyways. It's cooling off already." He knelt down. "Well, I'm a son of a gun! As Doc Bloom's assistant medical examiner, I've seen plenty of hangings in this town, particularly since the bottom fell out of Wall Street, but I never saw a guy snap his own neck before. They have to drop 'em twenty feet on a gallows to do that."

He stood up and dusted his hands. "Where'd you cut him down from? Hang himself in the elevator shaft?"

Doody told him where they'd found the body. "Hung himself out of the window, I guess."

"Oh, yeah? Well, if he'd fallen from any window, he'd be bruised up worse than he is." The doctor signaled to his two stretcher bearers. "Take it away!" he yelled.

They came in with a strip of canvas stretched between two poles. The rope was coiled neatly on the dead man's chest, and they lifted their burden.

Just then an unforeseen interruption occurred.

A rasping voice, a voice that reeked with authority, came from behind them.

"Ixnay, you dopes, ixnay!"

A tall, gaunt man in a loose gray topcoat was pushing through the crowd. His lower lip protruded belligerently, and a dead cigar was clamped in one corner of his mouth.

"Put it down, you. You guys would have to go to night school for years before you'd get to be halfwits!"

The stretcher, gruesome burden and all, was dropped hurriedly to the floor again. A sheepish look came over the stretcher bearers' faces, and Officer Doody saluted.

"I didn't know you were here, Inspector. It's just another suicide, and I moved him in here so traffic could go on."

"That's too bad," said Inspector Oscar Piper. He lit his cigar methodically. "Don't you know that you ought to have a couple of plainclothes men on a mix-up like this before you can start carting the body around?" He swung around the crowded lobby. "Where's the patrolman on this beat?"

"I don't know," admitted Doody. "That's why I was blowing my whistle."

"You blew it so long that I had to leave a lady sitting over in Whyte's restaurant and dash out to find what was coming off. I figured it was a Red parade at the least." Inspector Piper shrugged his shoulders. "I guess it was a lot of fuss over nothing. It's a hell of a note when the Homicide Squad can't have a quiet cup of tea without picking up every two-for-a-dime suicide. Sorry I interrupted, Levin. You can cart the stiff off on my authority. Get him out of this mob, anyway. How'd he die?"

"Fracture of the first and second cervical vertebrae," said Dr. Levin. "A very neat job of hanging, I'll say. He's been dead not more than half an hour. I'd say less. Body temperature is—" he took out a little thermometer from the dead man's mouth—"just a little less than ninety-six."

"Okay. Doody, who cut him down?"

Doody told what he knew. Inspector Piper frowned. "That doesn't make sense, man. Well, never mind. Get back to your corner before all New York gets jammed bumper to headlight—hey, wait a minute. Did you find out who he is?"

Doody nodded. "His name is *Stait,* a fellow said. I didn't look in the pockets."

"A fellow said? What fellow?" Suddenly the Inspector was really interested.

Doody scratched his chin and stared around the crowded lobby. The air went out of him like a pricked balloon.

"There was a fellow here, Inspector. But he must have left without waiting to give his name. A tall guy, with a little moustache!"

"Never mind, never mind. Get back on your corner. Blowing a whistle is just your speed, Doody." Piper turned to the waiting morgue attendants. "Go ahead, take it away. I guess he must have jumped off the first-floor window upstairs, though it's funny nobody saw him commit suicide."

Doody took his departure with obvious relief.

"If this stiff was lying in the middle of the street he couldn't have jumped from a window," pointed out Dr. Levin. "They don't fall outwards, they fall straight down. Besides, he's hardly bruised."

"I guess I've seen enough hangings to know suicide when I run across it," said Oscar Piper testily. He leaned over the body and felt at the inside coat pocket. It was empty of wallet or of anything else. Swiftly his hands went through the other pockets. A ring of keys, a wafer-thin watch set in a transparent case of pure crystal, a linen handkerchief with the initials in blue, "L.S", three crumpled one-dollar bills and some silver. That was all.

"Now, that's funny," observed the Inspector. He was thoughtful. "That's damned funny. A guy who carries one of those five-hundred-dollar watches usually packs a wallet and some dough, not to speak of visiting cards and all that."

"Still think it's suicide, Oscar?"

The Inspector whirled around at the voice. Standing at his shoulder was a woman of perhaps thirty-nine or so, a woman possessed of a certain unusual determination of character, if her chin and the bridge of her nose were to be taken as evidence. She was dressed in the fashion of some years ago, if in any fashion at all, and she gripped a well-worn umbrella firmly in one hand. The crowd pushed back discreetly to let her through.

"Hildegarde Withers! I didn't know you followed me!"

"You didn't think I was going to sit there in Whyte's and eat your cinnamon toast as well as my own, did you?" Her voice was pitched low, but it had an edge on it. "The last time you heard a police alarm and walked out on me you left me sitting in a taxi outside City Hall until the marriage license bureau had closed. I'm not letting you get away from me again that way."

"This is just a vulgar suicide," explained the Inspector to his lady friend.

"Yes? Well, if there's any excitement I'm going to get in on it." Miss Withers' nostrils widened a trifle, increasing the resemblance between her face and that of a particularly well-bred horse. Her keen eyes, behind the gold-rimmed glasses, twinkled delightedly. "Notice the coat, Oscar, notice the coat," she whispered. "You may find out before we're done that this is the place for the Homicide Squad after all. And perhaps the place for me, too."

The Inspector's face was blank. "I don't get you!"

Miss Withers pointed silently to the cigarette, which had burned itself quite thoroughly into the furry softness of the dead man's coat lapel.

"Did you ever hear of a man's committing suicide while smoking a cigarette? Not while he was hanging himself, anyway. Hemp and tobacco don't go well together—although some people like to smoke cigars that are compounded that way." She sniffed at Piper's fuming perfecto.

The Inspector nodded slowly. "Maybe, just maybe, you're right. Well, this is a mess. The Commissioner will raise hell because we didn't leave the body in the middle of traffic until they'd taken photographs and fingerprinted the whole block and so forth. But there's nothing for it now. . . ."

He stopped short. Officer Doody, who had made a beginning at sorting out his badly entangled corner, appeared suddenly beside him again. Someone was with him.

"Beg your pardon, sir." Doody produced the cringing figure of the little cabdriver. "This is Al Leech, Inspector, Hackman's Badge 4588. It was him I sent to ring in for an ambulance. Instead of doing that, he phoned for the morgue wagon. It was him that saw whatever it was that happened. I just nabbed him as he was trying to untangle his cab from the wreck down there with the car that didn't have any driver."

"Good work, Doody," said the Inspector. He faced the little man.

"So you had a smash, huh? Did that have anything to do with this business up here? Where's the other driver?"

"The other driver? There wasn't any other driver!"

"You mean he beat it as soon as there was a crash? Or did he come running up here to rubberneck like the rest of these yawps?"

"Neither one," insisted Leech. "I'm telling you there wasn't any driver in that Blue Chrysler. That blue open job was running wild when she bumped me—because the driver jumped out away up the street. About here, I'm thinking. That's him there on the stretcher!"

"You're drunk, man!"

"I haven't had enough fares today to buy a glass of beer," insisted the driver. "I tell you, I saw it all. It wasn't so clear, on account of the darkness and the thick snow and all. But I saw him. He jumped out of the roadster, as if he was trying to grab the side of a bus that was sailing past. I was way over to the left, trying to pass the car in front of me, which is the only reason I saw anything. I saw it all. . . ."

"Go on, man. You saw what all?"

"I saw the guy in the yellow coat. He gave a sort of leap, like a fish going after the bait or a scared frog coming out of a puddle. I saw him rise right up out of the seat, his arms flopping. His car came on toward me, and the headlights were burning dim. But he . . . he . . . You'll say I'm lying. . . ."

"Go on!" Piper's teeth were clamped into his dead cigar. "What else did you see?"

"As God is my Judge," said Leech, the hackman, "I saw him go up into the air, over the rumble seat and down to the street . . . *backward!*"

2

Corpus Delicti

Twenty minutes later Patrolman Dan Kehoe came striding along the slush of Forty-second Street, his nightstick twirling gaily, and a broad smile on his face. He waved cheerfully at Doody through the rush of traffic, and then took advantage of a lull, and came up beside the traffic officer.

"It's a great night for ducks," he observed, knocking the wet snow from his shoulders.

"Yeah," said Doody shortly.

"What are you so grumpy about? Sore because you have to stand here in the slush? You ought to get yourself transferred, Doody."

"Maybe I will," said the traffic officer shortly. "There ought to be a job open walking pavements on this beat tomorrow or the next day, if I can tell anything from the look on the Inspector's face when he was here a minute ago."

"Huh?" Kehoe looked up quickly. "What Inspector?"

Doody stopped the east-west traffic with a determined hand. "Piper, of the Homicide Squad. We been having a three-ring circus here while you was wetting your whistle in a speak somewhere. A stiff laying in the street, with a rope around his neck, and everything else. Read about it in the papers. They just took him away to the Morgue; and, if you don't believe me, look up there and see if that's Helen Morgan leaning against the lamppost."

Kehoe looked, and saw a uniformed cop from his own precinct lounging idly on the sidewalk in front of the Enterprise Trust, guarding the scene of the disturbance.

"I'm a son of a gun," he remarked. "But, say, I ain't been in no speak. Lookit this eye of mine."

Doody looked, and saw that the flatfoot had a gorgeous shiner around his left eye, of that deep, rich shade of bluish black which comes from the impact of hard knuckles.

"What did they do—throw you out of Mike's Place for digging into the bologna dish too heavy?"

"They did not." Dan Kehoe looked hurt. "I was walking down Forty-fourth Street about three-quarters of an hour ago and I see some rough-necks haul a cabdriver out from behind his wheel and sock him a couple of times on the nose.

"So I tear up and I start to pull 'em apart, and what does the biggest of the toughs do but whale away and take a sock at me. So I socks back, and the other one jumps me. I'm going for my gun, when a third guy, a little guy, climbs out of the cab and knocks the feet out from under me. He yelled something about teaching me to interfere in a private argument between gentlemen."

"As if he could teach you anything," cut in Doody.

"Sure. Well, I was just getting my second wind, when out of the hotel comes a big guy in a fancy vest. He says his name is Carrigan, and he's the manager of the outfit, which happens to be a travelling rodeo that's over to the Garden this week. He explained that the boys ought to be forgiven on account of how they ain't used to gyp cabs out in Wyoming, where they hail from, and if I was to book any of the boys on disorderly conduct charges, why, the show would have to be called off, so I finally let him talk me into being soft-hearted. We all went into Mike's and had a beer or two, and he gave me these, for tonight. . . ."

Kehoe pulled a sheaf of pink pasteboards from his service coat. "Box seats, too!"

"Leave me see!" Doody grabbed a couple. "Damned if they ain't. Well, the missis and me will enjoy these, thanks to ye. She likes the western movies, and she ought to get a kick out of seeing real cowboys in action. By the looks of your eye, they got plenty action, too. You better ring up the station house and explain where you been while all the excitement was going on here, and then go and get your eye painted out."

"Okay," said Kehoe. "But first I'm going up and have a look at the spot where your boyfriend jumped out of his car with a rope around his neck."

"Find yourself a clue and solve the mystery," suggested Doody, his voice heavy with sarcasm. "Find the dropped cufflink and you'll get put on Piper's squad of masterminds in the Homicide Squad."

"Nerts," said Dan Kehoe. He cut through traffic, avoiding the broken glass which still littered the northeast corner of the crossing, and sauntered up to chat for a moment with the bored copper who had been assigned to watch over the "scene of the crime."

Then Kehoe plodded on north through the snow toward the callbox. There was a broken fountain pen lying in the gutter, half hidden by the slushy snow, and only a few inches from where his heavy brogans passed. But Dan Kehoe wasn't looking for clues.

If he had found that fountain pen, history would have been considerably different. But Dan Kehoe was busy thinking how to spend the yellowbacked twenty that Carrigan, manager of the rodeo, had slipped him to make up for the black eye.

That fountain pen was to be discovered about theater-time by a quick-witted young Jewish student who knew that its makers in their Thirty-fourth Street shop replaced all broken parts instantly and without charge. He smashed the barrel, therefore, until the etched name was obliterated, and the next day he had it repaired from point to cap—with a new name on the barrel.

Morris Miltberg was to write an almost perfect philosophy examination at CCNY with it in a few weeks, for which he was spending most of his evenings cramming at the present time. If he had only read the daily papers he might have recognized a name, and then the philosophy examination, and this story, might never have been written. But he didn't.

At this moment Miss Withers and the Inspector were rolling across Fifty-seventh in a taxi.

"Well, suppose it does happen to be one of *the* Staits who was found dead in the street," Miss Withers was saying. "Besides there having been a college athlete by that name a year or so ago, who are the Staits? I thought you said no more murder cases for you unless it was somebody in the public eye?"

"You probably wouldn't know about the Stait family," explained the Inspector wearily. "Naturally the old name doesn't mean anything out in Iowa where you come from. But here in New York . . ."

"Never mind where I come from," interrupted the schoolteacher, testily. It had always been a great sorrow to Miss Withers that her father and mother had moved from the intellectual fastness of Beacon Street to Des Moines a few months before her advent into this world.

"Anyway," continued the Inspector, "the Staits used to rate with the Vanderbilts and the Stuyvesants. The third mayor of New York was a Stait. Tammany Hall was built on land donated by old Roscoe Stait the First. And now one of his grandsons is found dead in the middle of a crowded thoroughfare which his grandfather used for a cow pasture. The family hasn't the money it used to have, but there's a bit in the till yet, I'm thinking. Anyway, the newspapers are going to raise merry hell until we find the inside of that circus of death that happened this afternoon. What's more, we're going to get the murderer, and get him quick."

Miss Withers smiled triumphantly. "Then you agree that it's murder and not suicide?"

"It's murder all right," insisted the Inspector. The cab slowed down for a red light at Seventy-second. "A nasty murder, too. Nothing to work from. No rhyme or reason to it. Here's a man found in the street with a rope around his neck. And an empty roadster. No place to search for fingerprints. No doorman to question. No eyewitnesses, just because there were too many people there."

"I don't get that," said his companion. "On Fifth Avenue . . . at the rush hour. . . ."

"Exactly. It was snowing hard, and everybody was looking to see where they walked, and nobody paid much attention to passing cars. The only eyewitness we've got gives us a cock-and-bull story about a man jumping backwards out of his car. And that's a physical impossibility."

"I wonder," murmured Miss Withers.

"The trouble with this case," said the Inspector, drumming his fingers impatiently against the window, "the trouble with this case is that it's too weird, too bizarre. My boys know just what to do when they find a round-heeled little chorus girl strangled in her apartment, or walk in on a missing judge dead in bed with the wife of his best friend. That's routine. All the same, even though there's nothing here but the rope to get our teeth into, it's the complicated murders that are solved easiest. If we found Walter Winchell with a bullet through his head we'd have to pick up a thousand suspects, but when we find somebody choked to death with butter we just look for a nut. See what I mean?"

The cab whirled round on to the Drive, and began to make better time. It was already dark, and the snow was falling so heavily that Miss Withers could hardly make out the lights of Jersey across the Hudson.

"We're almost there," Inspector Piper explained. "I want to be the one to break the news to that family, and see how they take it. I won't be but a few minutes; you'd better wait in the cab."

Miss Withers got her dander up in a second. "Wait in the cab? Oscar Piper, you had me wait in a cab once, and I waited there for nearly two hours while you chased a poor little Chinaman across Brooklyn Bridge."

"Yeah? Well, that poor little Chinaman was packing opium enough to keep the snow-birds happy all winter. I explained it all, Hildegarde!"

"Never mind. But I'm coming in the Stait house with you. I can be your stenographer again, and take down questions and answers. I want to be in it, if there's any excitement. And you do, too. You claim you're taking up this case personally because of the Stait name, but you're really doing it because it's a case that's different, and after the excitement we had on the Aquarium Murder desk work bores you. Isn't that true?"

Inspector Piper nodded. "But there's no need for you to get mixed up in this."

"If you shut me out of this case," promised Miss Withers decisively, "I won't even keep my promise to be a *sister* to you, Oscar Piper."

In the first flush of excitement at the successful culmination of the

Aquarium Murder, these two had decided to get married. A confirmed old bachelor and a determined old maid, they were both secretly relieved that an accidental alarm had prevented them from going through with it.

"All right, you can come along," said the Inspector grudgingly. "There's the house, you can see it from here. It's the big four-story gray stone tomb on the corner—the one with the light on the top floor." He tapped on the window. "Pull up here, driver."

They walked slowly along the sidewalk toward the Stait mansion, the snow muffling their footsteps.

"This is an errand I dislike," confessed Piper. "It's not so easy, even if you've been in the business as long as I have, to walk into a happy home and say, 'Excuse me, but I just sent your darling son to the morgue, and I want you to come down with me and identify him.' "

"There isn't a chance that they've already got the news?"

The Inspector shook his head. "Not a chance. The papers won't come out with an extra tonight, anyway. The first sheet to have it will be the morning rags, which will be on the street in about two hours. No, we're first with the tidings all right."

He pressed his gloved thumb against the button. From somewhere in the recesses of the house came the muffled peal of a bell.

There was a long delay, and then at last a shadow appeared on the door. It swung open, disclosing the well-rounded figure of a little maid who quite evidently had remained ignorant of the recent exodus of short skirts from the fashion pages. Her knees, the Inspector couldn't help noticing, were all that they should have been, beneath the insignificant little lace apron. There was a quantity of mussed blondish hair.

Miss Withers thought that the girl didn't look overly bright.

"Is Mr. Stait at home?"

The girl made a valiant effort to slam the door in their faces, but the Inspector's heavy brogan interposed just in time.

"You mean Mr. Lew Stait?" asked the maid, when she saw that these visitors were determined.

The Inspector hesitated. "I'm not sure who I want to see," he said. "It's about Mr. Lew." He showed his badge, cupped in the palm of his hand.

The vacant blue eyes widened, and then grew suddenly hard and brittle as turquoise, and much the same shade.

"I don't care who you are," she said defiantly. "I've instructions that Mr. Lew isn't at home to anybody!"

"All right, my girl. Now don't get hysterical, but I have some bad news and I have to break it to some member of the family."

"Tell me!" The girl's voice was rasping and hoarse. "What about Mr. Lew? You've got to tell me!" She had forgotten for a moment that she was a maid.

"Be a good, calm girl and don't scream," said Inspector Piper smoothly. "Mr. Lew Stait won't be at home at all. You see, he was murdered about an hour ago."

There was a moment's silence. Miss Withers thought to herself that it was just like a man to break it that way.

The girl screamed. But they were screams of laughter. She flung the door wide open, and pointed her finger at the figure of a young man who sat on the davenport in the first-floor living room, clearly visible through the dingy portières. He was a tall young man in a dark blue suit, a very handsome young man. Miss Withers noticed that he was reading a magazine upside down, and had just finished combing his hair.

His soft collar was open, which struck Miss Withers with a ghastly significance. For on the last occasion when she had seen that fair-haired young man he had worn the red stigma of a noose around his throat!

"That's him, right there! That's Mr. Lew!" proclaimed the girl in ringing soprano tones. "I ask you, does he look like a dead one?"

Her position forgotten, the girl stood with her back against the wall, her head turned toward the young man. He had risen from his chair and was coming, with an expression of polite distaste, toward the hall. He stopped in the doorway.

"I am Lewis Stait," he said calmly. "Is there something I can do for you?"

Piper's teeth met in his cigar with a dull click.

Miss Withers advanced a step. "Inspector, hadn't you better tell the young man that the newspapers are already printing his obituary?"

3

The Gray Goose

"You'd better come in," said Lew Stait. "Gretchen, that will do. If I need you, I'll ring." His voice held no touch of softness or romance.

This young man was pale, but otherwise seemed to be in pretty good control. With a flounce of her diminutive skirt, the little maid turned her back on him and started down the hall toward the servants' quarters.

"Don't leave the house," warned Inspector Piper. "I'll want to ask you some questions in a little while."

Then he went into the living room after their host, and Miss Withers followed. It was a high, long room, with an obsolete gas chandelier in the center of the ceiling and old-fashioned hot air registers in the floor. Bookcases ran around the walls, containing musty volumes which looked as if they had never been opened. The chair in which Miss Withers seated herself, like everything else in the room, was dark, and heavy and old . . . and vaguely uncomfortable.

The Inspector introduced himself, and pointed out Miss Withers as his assistant.

Lew Stait nodded. "About my obituary? . . ."

The Inspector was still staring at the smooth, unmarked throat of the young man who faced them. The words brought him up with a jerk.

"There seems to be some mistake here," he said slowly. "There was an accident about an hour ago on Fifth Avenue. The body of a young man in a camel's hair overcoat was found not far from a wrecked Chrysler roadster, and identified as that of a Lew Stait. We traced the auto registration and got this address. All I have to say is this, that your double, the closest double I've ever seen, lies down in the autopsy room of the city morgue at this moment."

Their host lost his aplomb for a second, and his eyes widened. Then by an obvious effort he regained his *savoir faire*. "Not my double, Inspector. It must be—it's my twin brother, Laurie!"

"Your *twin?*"

The boy nodded, his face white as death. "We're what they call *identical twins*. It only happens once in a thousand cases of twins that both are exactly the same in physical characteristics, I've heard. So it isn't strange that whoever saw Laurie's—Laurie's body after the auto wreck might mistake it for mine. You see, he was driving my car, and he'd slipped into my camel's-hair coat because of the storm. And now, you say he's . . . he's dead?"

"He's dead," agreed the Inspector. "But not in an auto crash. He was strangled. We don't just know how, but it looks like murder."

The boy was gripping the edge of his chair, but somehow Miss Withers felt that he wasn't really as surprised as he tried to be. Perhaps it was because of the countless inhibitions of his inbred, overcivilized stock, but he was too deeply entrenched behind his barriers to seem genuinely shocked.

"*Murder!*" He repeated the word several times, tasting it.

The Inspector nodded. "In a few minutes I want you to go down to the morgue with me or one of my men, and formally identify the body of your brother. But first, I must ask you some questions just as a matter of routine."

"But who did it? What happened? I don't understand!"

"You don't need to. Just answer these questions. First, when did you last see your brother Laurie alive?"

The boy swallowed, and considered for a moment. "It was about teatime this afternoon, I should say. Perhaps four-thirty, perhaps a little before. It was right here in this room. He came to get the key to my roadster. The car, you see, is mine, but we both used it a good deal. And now he won't ever use it again!"

"Do you know where he was driving? Any idea of why he wanted the use of the car?"

Lew Stait shook his head. "No—no, I don't know. Why should I know? He used it whenever he wanted it. He considered he had a right to, because there was only the one car. Gran gave it to me, but actually it was as much his as mine."

Miss Withers was jotting all this down in her little notebook, a fact that seemed to make Lew Stait vaguely uncomfortable.

"Would you mind telling me just who are the members of this household?"

"Not at all. First, there's Gran. My grandmother, you know. Mrs. Roscoe Stait. Gran is well over ninety, and she hardly ever comes downstairs. The attic has been done over for her. But all the same, she's the commanding officer in this family, and don't you forget it. You can order the rest of us around, but your badge won't mean a thing to Gran."

"Yes? And then, besides Gran?"

"Well, there's Aunt Abbie. She's a younger sister of my mother . . . my mother and father, you see, are dead. Aunt Abbie isn't a Stait, but she's been sort of in charge of our bringing up since father and mother went down in the *Titanic*. She—"

"Never mind. The rest of them?"

"Well, that's the list on the distaff side, barring the servants. You saw Gretchen, and the cook is Mrs. Hoff. She's been here forever I guess. Then there's cousin Hubert. He's a Stait, but more or less indirectly. He's really a second cousin, but he's an orphan, too, so this has been his home since he was a baby. He's the brains of the house, and Laurie and I have always been the brawn. Football, and all that, you know, while Hubert was making Phi Beta Kappa. Of course, we all went to Columbia. Gran wouldn't have us out of her sight."

"That's all?"

"All but the colored boy who comes in to tend the furnace and clip the grass in summer. He makes himself useful around the kitchen when there are guests, which is very seldom now."

"Good. Now can you get them all into one room for me? I'd like to question everybody for a few minutes, including the servants." The Inspector was warming up.

But Lew Stait shook his head. "I can't get them all into one room. Gran wouldn't come downstairs to please anybody. It's Mrs. Hoff's night out, and she won't be back for hours. And Aunt Abbie and Hubert are at a movie. Aunt Abbie gets a thrill out of the cinema. She loves to lose herself in a thriller, and she'd sit through an earthquake if she was seeing a love scene. She doesn't like to go alone, so we take turns in playing escort. She's been mighty good to us, and it's the least we can do for her."

"At a movie, huh? Happen to know which one?"

Lew Stait nodded. "It's the Cinemat, the modernistic theater on Fifty-seventh. I know because I heard Hubert say when he left here with Laurie that he was going to meet Aunt Abbie in the lobby. She's been shopping today. Hubert was going to take her to the movie and then to dinner, on account of this being the cook's night out."

The Inspector was puzzled. "You say that your cousin Hubert left here with Laurie?"

"Yes. Laurie was going to drop him off at the theater on his way down."

Piper nodded. "Fifty-seventh would lie on the direct route between here and where the accident happened. Hildegarde, will you get the theater on the phone and have those people paged, or an announcement made from the stage or something?"

Miss Withers looked at her watch. "It isn't necessary," she pointed out. "It's eight o'clock now, and those movies never run longer than two hours at the most. Even allowing an hour for dinner, they'll be here shortly if they come right home."

Piper nodded. "One thing more. Young man, I suppose you can account for your own time during the last three hours?" He lit his cigar, and eyed the surviving twin through the curls of smoke.

"I can account for it all right," said Lew Stait sullenly. "I was right here in this house. Gretchen will bear witness to that. She made some sandwiches for me, and took up Gran's toast and tea as usual. Why, do you insinuate that I'd have a hand in whatever you think happened to Laurie? My own twin? God, man, it would be like suicide to lay a hand on him. He was . . . he was like *myself!*"

His acting is improving, thought Miss Withers. Or else he wasn't acting. She didn't sense the insincerity of his feeling now.

Instead of the Inspector's own gruff, professional tones, her own voice took up the questioning. "Young man, who do you think it was that killed your brother Laurie?"

He looked up, startled. "How should I know?"

"Twins are generally supposed to be closer together than other people, even than brothers and sisters, aren't they? Murder always casts its shadow ahead. Didn't you notice anything in your brother Laurie's actions these past few days?"

He hesitated for a long second. "No—no, of course not. Nothing definite, I mean. Except that Laurie has been a bit worried, upset a little, during the last month or so. Particularly since Monday."

"This is Friday," Miss Withers pressed the point. "How do you mean that he acted 'upset'?"

Lew Stait took up a cigarette, but instead of lighting it, he carefully broke it into halves, and then quarters, and then eighths. "Well, just little things, you know. We've always shared a room here, you see. We've been together ever since we were boys. The first time we were ever separated longer than a weekend was this summer, when Laurie went out to a dude ranch in Wyoming, and I stayed here in town."

"Why didn't you go?"

"I had a job. Have it yet. In the Brunnix Agency, advertising. I'll have to quit it now, though, because Gran will want me around home after what's happened. Anyway, since Laurie got back from that ranch near Medicine Hat he's been acting strangely. He got letters from a girl out there, for one thing."

Miss Withers had stepped out of character for a supposed police stenographer. "You said he seemed worried. What did he do?"

Lew Stait was staring at the open fire, his eyes cloudy. "It was the worst when Laurie was alone," admitted the young man. "He used to sit there in that big dark room upstairs for hours and hours, chewing away at the mouthpiece of his pipe, and staring at the brick walls across the alley until I thought he was going crazy or something."

A question was on the tip of Miss Withers' tongue, but she didn't ask it. For just at that moment the lights of a taxicab flashed against the window, and then came to a standstill along the curb. The tension in the room was broken.

"There's Aunt Abbie and Hubert now," said Lew Stait. His voice was steadier, and it was clear that he welcomed the relief.

He moved toward the hall, but the Inspector raised his hand. "Wait a minute. I'll answer the door. Miss Withers, will you use that phone in the hall under the stairs to get in touch with Headquarters and have Sergeant Taylor and a couple of the boys come up here on the double? Stait, I wish you'd get your hat and wait until I call you. Just a matter of routine, you know, this identification stuff."

Hesitatingly, Lew Stait moved toward the stair.

"Mind, you're not to talk to anybody about this, now or later," instructed the Inspector. Then he went swiftly toward the foyer door, in which a key was already being inserted. Evidently members of the Stait family did not put much trust in Gretchen's promptness, but used their own latchkeys.

Miss Withers stood alone in the center of the big living room for a moment, and revolved a few fundamental facts in her mind. Nothing definite and yet—

Then she remembered that she was supposed to be on the telephone now. She went toward the instrument slowly enough to catch a glimpse of two new faces at the other end of the hall—the round, cherubic visage of a plump young man in glasses and a sloppy fedora, and behind him the placid, vacuous stare of a woman of Miss Withers' own age, but painted and powdered and bedecked with a Eugenie hat and three long feathers.

Cousin Hubert and Aunt Abbie. . . . "Give her another feather, Lord, and let her take wing," whispered Miss Withers, remembering the anecdote.

Inspector Piper was already introducing himself. He always put a good deal of faith in the effect of bad tidings, Miss Withers knew. He loved to blurt out the news and then watch out for changes of expression on the faces of his audience.

"Spring 7-3100," said Miss Withers into the mouthpiece. As she waited for the operator to complete the call, she found herself absent-mindedly humming an old tune—a tune vaguely reminiscent of something that she had sung Sunday after Sunday in the third pew on the left in St. Luke's Episcopal Church back in Des Moines. . . .

No, that wasn't it, either. It wasn't a hymn tune. It was something that Hildegarde Withers had learned at, or rather on, the knee of her own grandmother. The schoolteacher shivered a little as she realized its weird significance now. For the words to the senseless thing began, "Go tell Aunt Abbie, go tell Aunt Abbie . . . Go tell Aunt Abbie that her gray goose is dead. . . ."

Aunt Abbie's voice rose, very much like the cry of that same gray goose, from the living room. She had got the news.

4

Miss Withers Freezes

Miss Withers was about to leave the phone and return to the living room when suddenly she drew back into the shadows under the stairway.

Someone was coming down the stairs, someone who quite evidently did not wish to make any noise. The muffled tread was cautious and light, as if whoever was descending those steps was prepared to turn and run at the sound of a dropped pin.

But Miss Withers wasn't dropping any pins these days. She had dropped a pin on a stairway once, and a man was sitting in the death house at Ossining for the strange use he had put it to—in the pool of the black penguins.

There was only one light in the long hall, and that was up in the front toward the little vestibule. It was years ago that Miss Withers had learned to be silent and invisible. She might have been standing in the doorway of her third-grade classroom during a furious spitball battle, or looming up over the shoulder of a hapless youth who preferred a lurid copy of *Weird Tales* to the more prosaic reading of his geography, and had got the happy idea of enclosing the former within the covers of the latter. Naturalists call it "the ability to freeze"—and a just-hatched partridge chick can do it perfectly. Miss Withers froze now, shrinking back into the extreme corner. She was there and yet she was not there. A spider might have used her shoulder for one corner of his web, and a mouse might have run across her shoes without fright—at least on the part of the mouse.

And as she waited there, hardly drawing breath into her lungs, Miss Withers saw the figure of a man pass quickly past her, back toward the domain of the servants. A door closed upon him—but not too soon for Miss Withers to make sure who this man was. It was Lew Stait, in his hat and overcoat, and he had a dark and indistinguishable oblong in his hand!

She went on, into the living room. "Aunt Abbie" was seated on a chaise longue, having a mild case of the vapours. Closer scrutiny confirmed Miss Withers' first impression of the lady. She was as empty of ideas as a drum. Her dress was a little on the tea gown order, and a worn sealskin cape lay beside her. She was sniffing into her handkerchief about "poor dear Laurie." She shook her head sadly. "And to think how we all treated him, too!"

Behind her, "cousin Hubert" peered through his thick lenses like a startled owl. Inspector Piper, who had learned to identify people by their clothes and bearing, put Hubert Stait down as a nondescript poor relation. Miss Withers was sorry for him, and later events justified her feeling.

The Inspector was quizzing Hubert. "You say that you rode down as far as the Cinemat Theater with your cousin Laurie?"

"I did." Hubert chose his words carefully. "He dropped me off there because I had an appointment to take Aunt Abbie to see the new German musical film 'Zwei Herzen im Deudelsac Takt.' . . ."

"What time did you see Laurie last?"

Hubert looked at his watch. "I met Aunt Abbie outside the theater at five. You see, we always go to the films at that hour because the matinée prices are still in effect, and we dine late anyway. I must have left Laurie a minute or two before five. . . ."

"I see." The Inspector added. "That is very important. I was anxious to find if Laurie had time to pick anyone else up, or to visit anyone, before the time he met his end, which was at five-thirty or a few seconds before. But with traffic as it is at that hour, he must have kept on a straight course to have reached Forty-second Street in half an hour. Young man, do you realize that you must have been the last person, except of course the murderer, to see Laurie Stait alive?"

Hubert nodded. "Perhaps you're right, officer—I beg your pardon,

Inspector. He seemed in high spirits as he left us, however. He didn't seem to have any warning of what was waiting for him when he waved good-bye to Aunt Abbie and me."

"We none of us do," said the Inspector grimly. "So you went to the moving picture show with your aunt?"

Hubert nodded. "It's a pretty good picture, Inspector. The Germans understand the nuances of production so much better than our Hollywood technicians, don't you think?"

"I like Clara Bow," said Piper gruffly.

"Well, in this picture there's a bourgeois girl who falls in love with a musician—"

"Never mind, never mind. I don't want a rehash of the plot. I believe you were there, all right."

"If you don't, here's our ticket stubs," said Hubert with a faint grin. He offered two bits of red cardboard. Each bore a serial number and the monogram of the theater in big block letters. The Inspector put them in his vest pocket.

He turned to Aunt Abbie. "Did you like the movie?"

"Oh yes, Inspector. But to think we were sitting there, laughing and enjoying ourselves, when poor Laurie was being killed in the street!"

"I notice that Hubert here is nearsighted," observed the Inspector casually. Almost too casually, in fact. "I suppose he has to sit down in front while you, like most older persons, prefer to sit in the back rows?"

Aunt Abbie shook her head. "No, we usually sit in the middle rows, just as we did tonight. I hate to sit alone in a theater, even though I do get pretty engrossed in the story. A girl never knows who may come and sit beside her and . . . you understand. . . ."

The Inspector nodded. "And after the show?"

"After the show we had dinner at a little restaurant near the theater, and then we came home. And it's a good thing we did, let me tell you. I don't know exactly how Gran is going to stand the shock. Of course, it's not as if it was Lew—her favorite, you know. But Gran is so old that there's no telling what she'll do or how she'll take on, and she's used to my taking care of her, you know. I'd better run up and see." Aunt Abbie gathered herself together.

"She doesn't know yet," the Inspector admitted. "There'll be time enough, before this night is over. If she's likely to take it hard, you'd better get a trained nurse over here."

"Trained nurse?" Hubert was almost laughing. "You don't know Gran. She'd throw a trained nurse out of the window, would Gran. She's a despot, and not so benevolent a one, either. I'd hate to cross her. And she hasn't let even the maid into her bedroom in years and years. If you got a trained nurse without her consent, or did anything else against her orders,

Gran would be perfectly capable of cutting your throat. She's so old she doesn't care what happens."

"Yeah? I'm looking forward to meeting this old lady." Piper dropped his air of cross-examination. "This will be all for tonight. You can go to your rooms, but I'll want to ask some more questions of both of you any time. Remember, no discussing this between yourselves. I don't suppose either of you has any idea of who might have had reason to strangle Laurie Stait?"

"It was just what I'd have expected of him," Aunt Abbie declared. "Laurie was always getting into scrapes. He wasn't a bit like Lew, except in looks. That's why they always called him 'the bad twin' and Lew 'the good twin.' You know, doctors claim that twins have only enough moral stamina for one person, and usually it's all on one side."

Aunt Abbie paused for breath. "All the same, I can't think who could have done it. It would have been more like Laurie to have committed suicide."

"Why couldn't it have been suicide?" Cousin Hubert took the floor. "You said that Laurie was found in the street with a rope around his neck, and that the car he'd been driving was empty and wrecked a little distance ahead. Couldn't he have tied the rope to something inside the car, and slipped the noose around his own neck—then jumped overboard and let his car go on and hang him?"

Miss Withers objected. "What about the rope? It wasn't tied to the car when they found it. It was hanging loose."

"It could have been pulled loose with the shock if it wasn't tied tight," the Inspector suggested, musingly. "We'll see what the medical examiner says in his report tomorrow."

He stopped, watching Miss Withers, who was sniffing. "Something burning in the kitchen," she observed.

"But what could be burning? It's cook's night out, and nobody ate in except Gran with her toast and tea a while ago, and whatever cold snack Gretchen was willing to dish up for Lew," Aunt Abbie cut in.

"Maybe it isn't the kitchen," Miss Withers conceded. "Probably the drains in these old houses aren't what they should be."

The sound of a car horn came from outside, again and again. "That must be Taylor and the boys," said the Inspector. "Miss Withers, will you wait here while I arrange to have Lew Stait taken down to the morgue to identify his twin? I don't understand why, if that is the Sergeant outside, he doesn't come on in. . . ."

Suddenly Aunt Abbie clapped her hands. "I remember! The terrible, terrible news you told me when I came in made me forget. That's our cabman out there. Poor dear Hubert never has any money because he spends his allowance for books, and I spent more than I meant to spend shopping. I told the man to wait while I got some money."

She moved toward the hall. "I'll run upstairs and get some change."

She almost ran into Lew Stait, who was waiting with hat and coat on, to make the trip down to the morgue. "How lucky," cried Aunt Abbie. "You've saved me a climb upstairs, Lew. I need a dollar, perhaps two, for my cabman. Have you got it to spare?"

"Of course, Auntie." Lew's hand went to his inside coat pocket, fumbled a moment, and then dropped to his hip.

While the four of them watched, he went through his pockets one by one. "Of all the things to happen!" he said in a dazed whisper. "My pocket's been picked!"

"Maybe you left it up in your room?" Aunt Abbie was comforting.

"No, I had it this afternoon. There wasn't but fifteen or twenty dollars in it. That's funny."

He looked thoughtful. "Maybe I lost it somewhere—though I haven't been out all afternoon. I distinctly remember having it at noon, though. I wonder—"

Lew stopped short. "I wonder if Laurie could have needed some money and picked the wallet up off my dresser? We often borrowed back and forth, you know. At least, Laurie did."

"I don't like to speak ill of the dead," said Aunt Abbie. "But Laurie Stait was untrustworthy about money, and there's no use hiding it. Oh, he *wasn't* dishonest. But he was always running short, and always borrowing and forgetting to return it. . . ."

"So there was only fifteen or twenty dollars in the wallet? Well, if Laurie did borrow it, that might establish a motive for murder, though a slim one. Because his wallet was missing when his body was found." Inspector Piper made the announcement boldly, and it seemed to stagger Lew Stait.

"You mean that my brother might have been killed for what money was in that wallet?"

Piper nodded. "You see, nobody need have known how much or how little was in the notecase. And he looked as if he had money, you know. Only the means used in this murder don't make sense with a robbery angle." He scratched his head—and down the street the wail of a police siren rose as the cabdriver honked his signal again imploringly.

The Inspector took two dollars from his own pocket. "I'll take care of your cab, ma'am," he promised Aunt Abbie. "You can pay me tomorrow. I've got some friends of mine outside. Wait here, the rest of you, while I arrange for Mr. Lew Stait to take a little trip in a squad car."

He beckoned to the surviving twin. "You might as well get it over with," he said kindly. "You're the nearest male relative."

Lew Stait followed the Inspector out of the door, and a moment later Miss Withers heard the rising wail of the siren again, bearing Stait and one of the plainclothes men down to the gray building with the marble mattresses.

She herded Aunt Abbie and Hubert up the stairs, warning them that the Inspector would not want them to carry the news to the old lady on the top floor.

It was about ten minutes before Inspector Piper reappeared. Sergeant Taylor was with him, and behind the wiry little sergeant loomed the bulk of McTeague, the biggest and the dumbest-appearing detective on the force. He had dull, lifeless blue eyes that blinked often. Every blink printed a clear photograph on the sensitized paper that was the memory of McTeague.

Miss Withers nodded to the newcomers, who separated—one to each entrance of the house. Then she drew Piper aside. "What about some dinner, Oscar? All you've had since lunch is tea and cinnamon toast, and you must be starved." She showed him her little address book, its pages filled with curlicues. "I'm running out of paper."

"Never mind dinner," said Inspector Piper. She sensed that something had happened. "And never mind your shorthand notes, either. Look what McTeague just discovered, outdoors. The snow's stopped, and there's not a breath of wind. He saw something on the snow beside the pavement that looked like a drop or two of blood. But it wasn't blood. And we scouted around until we found all of it."

The Inspector showed Miss Withers four or five bits of red pasteboard that he had wrapped carefully between the pages of an old letter in his pocket. The pieces fitted together.

They bore a serial number and the monogram of a theater. Miss Withers had seen that monogram before.

"Exhibit B," said the Inspector. He took from his vest pocket the two ticket stubs that Cousin Hubert had handed over to him.

They matched perfectly, all three of them. Except that Hubert's stubs bore the serial numbers R44557 and R44558—while the torn fragments when pieced together read R44601.

"And this means? . . ."

"It means that someone in this house went to that movie this afternoon—someone who wanted to make sure that Hubert and Aunt Abbie were there, I'll bet. Someone who threw the stub away at the last minute, realizing that it might be dangerous to him—or herself—and trusted to the snowfall to cover it."

Miss Withers shook her head slowly. "But I don't see what it means!"

"When you do see what it means," grinned Inspector Piper, "this case will be all washed up!"

"Right now it could stand a lot of washing," agreed Miss Withers.

5

Bull in the China Shop

The routine investigation went on, a little more swiftly now. Gretchen, the pert little blonde maid, was brought into the living room again. Her hair was combed, and she had put on a fresh apron and an air of defiance which wilted a little at the sight of Piper's best third-degree glare.

"Your name?"

"Gretchen Gilbert, sir. . . ."

"*Born* Gilbert?" Inspector Piper was lighting a fresh cigar.

"Yes, sir. No, sir. The name used to be Gilbrecht."

"How long have you had your job here?"

"It will be two years next September . . . no, August." Gretchen was sitting on the very edge of the sofa, her ridiculously naked-looking legs crossed at the slim ankles.

"Like your job?"

"Oh yes, sir."

"What are your duties, exactly?"

"Well, sir, I take care of the upstairs, all but old Mrs. Stait's rooms, you know. She won't let anybody in there. And I wait on the table at meals and answer the door and make myself generally useful."

"Generally useful to Mr. Lew now and then, also?" The Inspector's voice was dry and quizzical, although Miss Withers looked up from her notebook with a start, and Sergeant Taylor choked a guffaw.

Gretchen never batted an eye. "You mean this afternoon? Well, a girl has to get ahead, Mister Policeman. I wouldn't expect you to understand. You've never been an upstairs maid."

"Never," admitted the Inspector. "Would you mind telling us just what your movements were this afternoon?"

Gretchen batted both eyes this time. "Huh?"

"The Inspector means, what did you do this afternoon?" Miss Withers helped out.

"Oh. Well, I helped Mrs. Hoff with the luncheon dishes because it was her afternoon off and she was anxious to get away. Then I got the linen ready for the laundry, which we do every Friday. It takes about an hour or so, I guess. About three o'clock Mr. Lew came home, and half an hour later Mr. Laurie and Mr. Hubert. Mr. Lew leaves his office early quite often, because business is so slow, he says."

"And then?"

"Then I took Mrs. Stait her tea as usual, and shortly after that Mr. Lew rang from the living room and said that he didn't want to go out for dinner because of the snow and would I get him a cold snack in the kitchen, which I did. I brought him some sandwiches in this room here, in front of the fireplace."

"And this time?"

"It must have been six o'clock, or a little before."

"And you are able to swear that Mr. Lew wasn't out of the house between three, when he came home from the office, and six, when you took him some sandwiches?"

"Why"—she hesitated. "Why, yes, sir. I mean, I don't think he went out. I didn't see him go."

"Very good. When did you see Mr. Laurie last?"

"Why, this afternoon, about four-thirty. He and Mr. Lew and Mr. Hubert were in the living room here having a drink. Mr. Hubert told me in the hall that he wouldn't be home to dinner because he was riding with Mr. Laurie to the movie. Mr. Lew stayed in the living room, reading."

Inspector Piper nodded slowly. "Tell me, Gretchen. Were there any telephone calls here today?"

"Oh yes, sir, lots. The florist called about his bills, and a lady called about some contribution to the Hundred Neediest Cases, and—"

"No, never mind that. I mean, any telephone calls that were out of the ordinary!"

Gretchen was thoughtful. "No, sir. I don't think so."

"Nothing at all? No calls from anyone you didn't know?"

"Oh yes. That man called again."

Miss Withers sat up straight in her chair, and the Inspector's voice bore an edge. "What man?"

"Why, the man who's always calling Mr. Laurie. The man who's called every day this week. You said out of the ordinary, but that's got to be the ordinary thing in this house. It's a man with a sort of southern accent."

"What did he say? Come on, tell us."

"Why, he asked for Mr. Laurie. You see, Mr. Laurie gave instructions last Monday that he was always out, no matter who phoned or called. So I gave the message."

"What did the man *say?*"

"He said—" She was thoughtful. "He said: 'Tell that so-and-so of a tenderfoot that I'm going to have a talk with him right soon, OR ELSE!' He yelled the last two words, and then hung up like to deafen me the way he banged the receiver."

"Ah ha! Now we're getting someplace!" The Inspector looked at Miss Withers triumphantly.

"You don't know this man's name?" Gretchen admitted that she didn't. She also admitted that she only answered the phone if she happened to be near it.

"Very good. Now, Gretchen, I want you to give me some information about this house. This is official, you understand, and you'll find it to your best interests to be frank with us."

Gretchen was nervous and willing. "Yes, sir."

"Tell me, frankly. Were any of the members of this household enemies? I mean, was there ever any strife, any unpleasantness?"

Gretchen's eyes widened again. "Oh, no, sir. Mrs. Stait is a little—well, a little peculiar, sir. But she's all right when she has her own way, and she always has her own way. There was never any unpleasantness, sir."

"Did the twins, Mr. Lew and Mr. Laurie, get along perfectly?"

"Oh yes, sir. They were very close, sir. It's only natural, seeing they were as like as two peas in a pod, sir. In looks, that is."

"Excuse me for interrupting," cut in Miss Withers, "but how did you manage to tell them apart? They wore each other's clothes, they shared a room. It must have been difficult.

Gretchen smiled dreamily. "Oh, not for me, ma'am. Mr. Lew, he's always bright and cheerful and full of energy, with a kind word for anybody. They looked alike, but that was as far as it went. Mr. Laurie, he was always sort of standoffish and quiet—a regular hermit sort. That's why he wasn't popular, ma'am. I'll admit that when I first came here it gave me a start sometimes to see one of the twins here and then the other one come in from somewhere all of a sudden, but I soon got used to it. And even at first I found out a sure way. If it was Mr. Laurie, he'd pass by without a word, but if it was Mr. Lew, he'd pinch my cheek or rumple my hair."

Gretchen was blushing a little around the neck and ears, and Miss Withers nodded sagely. "I see."

"Mr. Lew is always singing or humming or whistling, and Mr. Laurie was always gloomy. He liked to be by himself."

"Thank you, Gretchen. And Mr. Hubert?" The Inspector took up the round again. "How did Mr. Hubert get along with Mr. Lew and Mr. Laurie?"

"Just perfect, sir. Oh, they were just like big brothers to Mr. Hubert. Cook tells me that in all the five years that Mr. Hubert's lived here in this house, she's never seen anything sweeter than the way the twins took to their cousin from the first. He's never been very strong, you know. He's always been a little queer. But they saw to it that he got out and played games instead of reading all the time. Why, it was Mr. Lew who practically made Mr. Hubert take boxing lessons so they could all spar together in the basement. And when they were seniors at the University here, and Mr. Hubert was a sophomore, they made him go and play football. Why, they wouldn't take no for an answer, and it did him worlds of good, cook says."

"I see. Then the three boys seemed to enjoy one another's company?"

"Oh yes, sir. Why, Mr. Laurie and Mr. Lew wouldn't think of going anywhere without taking Mr. Hubert along. They were so much alike they got tired of each other, I guess, and wanted a third. Why, they bought Mr. Hubert a full dress suit out of their own allowances when Gran—I mean Mrs. Stait—said that his dinner jacket was good enough with times as bad as they are. Though if I do say it as shouldn't, he looked a sight in those long tails, with his skinny neck and his legs that don't meet at the knees by half an inch." She giggled wickedly.

"That will do, Gretchen. You can go to your room, and as soon as Mrs. Hoff comes in, tell her that I want to talk to her here."

"Yes, sir." Gretchen made a willing exit from the scene of the inquisition.

Inspector Piper shook his head after her. "There goes a tough little mug if I ever saw one," he observed.

Miss Withers shook her head. "Nonsense, Oscar. Didn't you ever hear of the flapper? Well, Gretchen's just learned about flapperdom. In five years she'll have a husband and a flat full of Grand Rapids furniture by the month, and a couple of hostages to fortune into the bargain. You're old-fashioned, Oscar."

"I'm surprised at you," Piper told her. "Well, let's get back to business. There's only the old lady and the cook left for us to quiz. Got your notebook full?"

"When I have, I'll throw it away and write the shorthand on my cuff," said Miss Withers acidly. "You aren't getting anywhere, Inspector. You aren't even 'getting to foul ball,' as the boys say. . . ."

"You probably mean 'first base,' " put in the Inspector mildly. "But I don't see why I'm not getting anywhere. This is all part of the routine."

"Routine fiddlesticks," said the schoolteacher. "Why don't you find out where Laurie Stait was bound for when he borrowed his brother's car and started down Fifth Avenue? Why don't you find out that?"

"But—"

"Somebody knew," she reminded him tartly.

"Maybe the old lady will tell us," suggested Piper thoughtfully. "I sort of look forward to the chat with her. She sounds like something out of Godey's Book. Here goes—"

The telephone in the hall broke into a shrill crescendo. Sergeant Taylor moved swiftly from the front door to answer it, but the Inspector halted him.

"You go, Miss Withers," he said softly. "It would seem more natural for a woman's voice to answer at this house than a man's. We might just possibly learn something."

She went. For a moment she held the receiver against her ear. Then she said "Hello" in a low voice.

"Is Mr. Lew Stait there?"

It was a girl's voice, a deep, warm mezzo-soprano. There was a thin note of worry somewhere, buried deep.

Miss Withers knew what she was supposed to say. "Who is calling, please?"

"Oh, is that you, Aunt Abbie? This is Dana. Is Lew there . . . or Laurie?"

"They're out just now . . . is there any message?" Miss Withers hated to tell the lie, even though it was regular procedure in such cases.

"Oh . . . I see." The voice was disappointed.

"Shall I have him call you back when he comes in? Where are you now?"

The girl at the other end of the wire wasn't suspicious. "Where should I be? Here at home, at the apartment, of course . . . where I've been waiting for Lew hours and hours. . . . Has anything happened?"

"You say you're at the apartment *where?*" Miss Withers made a good cast, but the trout didn't rise to the fly. There was a long silence, and then the receiver clicked softly at the other end of the line.

Miss Withers left the phone and rejoined the Inspector. She told him what had happened.

"A dame with a soft, sweet voice asking for Mr. Lew, huh?" The Inspector permitted himself the luxury of a fresh, unchewed cigar and a smile. "Strike up the chamber music, boys. Hearts and Flowers from now on in this case; we've found our love interest. I was hoping that we could do better than Gretchen." He cast a glance at the schoolteacher. "Just like the Aquarium Murder, Hildegarde. Still looking for the happy ending?"

"I'm off romance for the present," Miss Withers told him stiffly. "I suppose you're all full of ideas about how to track down the poor child who just talked to me, yes? It's comparatively simple, of course."

"Yeah?" The Inspector stopped dead in his tracks and looked at her. "How is it so easy? It'll be no cinch to trace that call—most of the phones are on the dial system now anyway, and there's not a chance to trace a call from one of those jiggers."

Miss Withers shook her head. "You don't need to trace that call. That girl who called herself Dana hung up when she realized I was a fraud as Aunt Abbie—and she knew I was a fraud because I asked where her apartment was. Which means that Aunt Abbie, and probably the rest of the household here, know her pretty well and where she lives."

"Right. I'll put the screws to Aunt Abbie." He went toward the hall. "Taylor, hop up those stairs and get me the dame who was down here a minute ago. Hurry up!"

The Sergeant's heavy tread mounted the stairs and died away in the upper hall. "My theory about this case—" began the Inspector heavily. "Good God!"

From somewhere in the rear of the house there came a crash, of such proportions as to suggest a young earthquake.

Voices, dim and muffled through the intervening doors, rose in furious altercation, and then another explosion, louder than the first, brought silence to the old house. Too much silence.

That was all. Miss Withers looked at the Inspector, and he looked back at her. His hand instinctively hovered over the hip on which he had carried no weapon since the memorable day eleven years before when he had taken off his uniform.

Then a square of light showed at the end of the long hall—and was immediately blotted out by something large, imposing, and formidable.

Someone was coming up from the rear, past the dark corner under the stair, out into the full light of the front hall.

It turned out to be a woman, a large woman, built on the general proportions of Grant's Tomb.

She was wearing somewhat askew a hat that was more reminiscent of Mary of England than of Eugenie of France. Wisps of glossy red hair shone from beneath it, and there was a glint of redder fire in her eye. Her fur-trimmed coat was disarrayed.

In one hand she gripped an iron skillet, and as she advanced she kept it poised in readiness to thrust or parry. She stopped at the foot of the stairs, legs wide apart and eyes narrow.

"You cutthroats!" she offered. "Come on one at a time and I'll give you what-for!"

Neither Miss Withers nor the Inspector accepted the invitation. At that opportune moment Aunt Abbie appeared at the head of the stair with the Sergeant behind her.

"Amanda!"

The lady with the skillet took a deep breath. "Yes'm?"

"Amanda Hoff, what in the world is the matter? These people are from the police."

The skillet resumed its place as a culinary tool rather than as a weapon.

"The police, ja? Well, it's about time. Why don't you come back and arrest the dead corpse in my kitchen?"

6

A Mummy Song

"What in heaven's name . . ." Inspector Piper snapped out of his coma as if a spring had suddenly been released. "Come on!"

He led the way on the run down the long hall toward the kitchen, followed by the belligerent Mrs. Hoff and the Sergeant. Aunt Abbie was close behind.

Miss Withers lagged for a moment. It was not that she dreaded whatever she might see in the kitchen. She had no fear of death, at least not when it struck somewhere else.

But something troubled her mind, some subtle sixth sense clamored in the back of her head for attention, crying, "See here! See here!"

It was not the faintly tainted odor of something burning which still pervaded the old house. That she had noticed before.

For a long moment she stood alone, and then all of a sudden the realization came to her. From somewhere in this ancient, decaying mansion there came a contralto voice of exceeding purity, faint but clear. Perhaps it was a radio set or a gramophone—whatever it was, the voice was strangely eerie. It was sweet and haunting, and not altogether human.

There were loud exclamations in the kitchen, Mrs. Hoff's gutturals among them. But Miss Withers did not hear. She was straining her ears to identify the strange yet hauntingly familiar melody.

She knew it for the solo portion of the duet between Azucena, the old gypsy woman, and her son when both lay in the shadow of death, during the third act of Verdi's hackneyed *Il Trovatore*. ". . . ai nostri monti . . ." came the faint contralto in the age-old song of sorrow. "Home to our mountains. . . ."

Even as Miss Withers exclaimed at the quality of that voice, it cracked terribly, harshly—and then continued with a dreadful cacophony to the end of the phrase, a quarter of a note flat!

It was unthinkable that any musically trained ear could have permitted that grotesque parody to continue—yet continue it did, on to the last warped quaver. There was a long moment of stillness, and then Miss Withers went thoughtfully on toward the door of the kitchen.

After all, she supposed, the death of a man was more important than the death of a voice.

However, as luck would have it, this man was not entirely and completely dead—perhaps irrevocably is the word, since every sleep is a little death, and McTeague was as sound asleep as he had ever been in his life.

He was still stretched out on the kitchen floor where he had fallen under the crushing weight of Mrs. Hoff's skillet, and there was a sizable lump on his forehead.

Aunt Abbie, with a bustling ineffectiveness, was dribbling water on his wrists and neck, and the breath of life was beginning to suck again through his blue lips.

The Inspector and Mrs. Hoff were facing each other like a couple of bantam roosters—or rather, like a bantam rooster and an ostrich. Honors at present were all to the bantam, as the Inspector let his temper carry him on. Sergeant Taylor had drawn back in admiration.

"Woman, do you realize what you've let yourself in for? Assaulting an officer with a deadly weapon, resisting an officer in the course of his duty, mayhem . . . why, you're lucky if you get out of Auburn in time to celebrate your hundredth birthday, you meddling old battle-axe!" He pushed a lean jaw almost into the fat face of the German cook. "Come on, answer me! What in the name of God made you try to murder my best operative?"

The woman shook her head dumbly. "By the back door into mine own kitchen I'm coming, and stands in the middle of the room holding a gun in his fist this man! And a racketeer he was, I'm saying. Ja. I know about these bad ones."

The Inspector grunted. "Can you prove where you have been for the past three hours?"

"Oh, ja, ja. To the Strand I was." Mrs. Hoff had definitely decided to get hysterical. "Ach, Gott, and now I haf to burn in what they call the Hot Squat, ja?" She was quivering like a jellyfish.

The Inspector moved his eyebrows a quarter of an inch, and nodded slowly. He turned to Miss Withers. "Hildegarde, what movie is playing at the Strand this week?"

Miss Withers didn't know. But Aunt Abbie stopped doing the Florence Nightingale. "It's a wonderful picture, Inspector. I saw it last night. It's *What Price Gangster,* with Chester Morris."

"Ah ha!" The Inspector grinned at Mrs. Hoff. "So you were going to knock poor McTeague for a public enemy, huh?" He leaned forward suddenly. McTeague, under the momentary respite from Aunt Abbie's sprinkling, was coming round. "Hello, Mike!"

The cloudy blue eyes opened, and gradually came into their normal focus. McTeague shook his head savagely for a moment, and then looked up at the Inspector.

"Come on, Mike. Get up on your pins, you're okay. The old lady took you for Scarface Capone. Come on, this isn't getting us anywhere."

Mike still lay there, staring up at the Inspector. Slowly one eyelid dropped and raised again.

"Huh?" Piper almost dropped his cigar. Then McTeague winked again, twice. It was the old operative's signal, meaning, "I can't talk here—don't recognize me—sit on your cards—"

"Come on, back into the other room, all of you!"

Piper pointed to the door. "All right, Taylor, take everybody into the front room and keep 'em there."

Then the Inspector was alone with his operative. "What is it, Mike? What's on your mind besides a lump like a hen's egg?"

"Come down here." McTeague's lips formed the words, almost soundlessly. But the big detective made no effort to rise to his feet.

"What's wrong, Mike? Come on, you're all right. Snap out of it."

"Come down here, Inspector!"

Piper got down on his knees, wondering if the operative had gone off his trolley from that crack on the forehead.

McTeague was looking up at the underside of the kitchen table. Piper followed the line of his eyes, and then drew a quick breath.

Pinned to the wooden frame in which the drawer was supposed to slide, the Inspector saw a whitish oblong with a black dot in the center. The dot proved to be a common drawing-pin that yielded to the blade of a penknife, and the white oblong was a letter.

"Now what sort of foolishness is this?"

The envelope had been folded twice, and showed signs of wear and tear along the folds. Someone had carried it around for quite a while. Piper smelled it, and then offered it to McTeague.

"What do you make of that, Mike?"

The big detective sniffed. "Hmmmm—not a dame, Inspector. Smells as if it had been toted around in the pocket of a leather suit for a while."

"Right—it's calfskin, that odor. Now let's see what it says."

The handwriting on the envelope was in a slanting feminine script. It was addressed to "Mr. Laurie Stait, Keeley's Lazy Y Ranch, Medicine Hat, Wyoming." The postmark was dated "New York, July 18th"—of the previous summer.

The Inspector had no scruples about drawing out the single sheet of expensive notepaper, which also showed signs of much handling. Whoever had carried the envelope had read and re-read its contents often, he figured. The note itself was short and to the point.

> *Dearest* (it began),
> *I am writing to tell you that you were right and I was very wrong, not only about us but about Lew. The only reason I ever loved him was because he is so much like you. For that reason I can't hurt him by telling him, there must be a better way.*

"Now we're getting somewhere," said McTeague cheerfully, forgetting his bump as he stared over the Inspector's shoulder.

The Inspector read on:

> *But I say now, as I refused to say when we parted, I love you more than anybody else in this world, and nobody, not even Lew, is going to stand in our way.*
>
> *Always,*
> *Your Dana.*

Painstakingly the Inspector folded it back into the envelope. His face was grave.

So a girl had loved both the Stait twins—and sworn that nobody was going to stand in the way of her getting Laurie! Well, it looked as if something *had* stood in the way. That something was a length of limber hemp.

"You know, Chief, it's smart to think of planting a letter there," McTeague pointed out. "There wasn't a chance in a million that we'd find it, but we got a lucky break." McTeague grinned and rubbed his forehead.

"Yeah. Well, Mike, don't ever let anybody tell you that this business isn't just full of lucky breaks. Now get back on your post, and try to keep your thick skull out of the way of falling kitchenware."

Piper started back up the hall, wondering just what the letter in his pocket was going to mean. He noticed as he came out of the kitchen that another door opened into the rear of the hall. Probably the rear stair—no, upon investigation it proved to be the passage to the musty-smelling cellar. Evidently this house, like so many of its kind, had no servants' stair. Well, that simplified a few things.

Sergeant Taylor was just putting down the phone. "Oh, Inspector, Headquarters on the wire. Doc Bloom's assistant reports that Stait could not have taken his own life, and the case goes down in the Medical Examiner's records as murder. Death caused by snapping the vertebra, and it was instantaneous. Preliminary autopsy showed no sign of drugs, either a dose or habitual. Brain showed a trace of alky, though. That's all, I guess—I knew you were busy, so I took the message. Oh yes, they found in the morgue that the pelvis was cracked, too. But only minor abrasions of the skin."

"Okay, Taylor. Where's everybody?"

The Sergeant nodded toward the living room. "Aunt Abbie whatshername and the cook are in there. Your lady friend spent some time comforting the cook, and then went upstairs."

"Upstairs! What did Miss Withers do that for? I'm saving the upstairs for later."

Piper turned and ran up the steps. "I never knew it to fail," he was muttering. "Women can do more damage in ten minutes . . ."

There was no sign of Miss Withers when he reached the second-floor hallway. The lights of the Drive were shining through the open door of the front bedroom, and the Inspector came down the hall and gave it a once over. Aunt Abbie's room, beyond a doubt. Ribbons held back the white curtains, doilies lay primly on every table, there was a stupid-looking canary in a gilt cage—a frowsy, slightly bald-looking canary—and on the bureau a framed photograph of that remarkable Hollywood thespian, Mr. Clark Gable, no doubt signed by his secretary.

"Hrrmp," remarked the Inspector. He retraced his steps. The next door opened into a vast and uncomfortable-looking bath, with much exposed piping and a tremendous tub set in oak. There were four prim guest towels on a rack. "I'd hate to live in this dump," Piper told himself.

He came out of the bathroom, and ran almost head on into Miss Withers. He seized her arm. "Hildegarde! Where have you been, and what in God's name started you poking around up here? We haven't got any search warrant for this house!"

"One question at a time," the schoolteacher said calmly. "First, I've been rambling through the halls trying to trace down a phantom voice that I heard, or thought I heard. I went way up to the attic floor, too, but I didn't hear anything more. There's a light showing under the door of the top floor, and two bedrooms on the floor above us. I suppose that's Cousin Hubert in one, and the maid in the other. Nobody heard me and I didn't disturb anything, so don't get such an annoyed look on your face."

The Inspector stuck out his lower lip. "It's just like a woman to upset the routine procedure," he informed her. "I don't suppose you happen to know which would be the bedroom of the dead twin, do you? It's the only one we have a right to search."

Miss Withers shook her head. "We might try that door there in the rear," she said sagely. "It's the only unexplored territory."

They came into a long room with two windows facing on the backyard, a room with twin bookcases, twin bureaus, and, of course, twin beds—of ancient walnut. Miss Withers went at once to the bookcase, while Piper surveyed the rest of the place.

The only decorations in the room were a collection of pipes—meerschaum, student, clay and briar—between the beds, and on a peg above the bookcase a well-worn saddle of the McClellan type, with an imitation silver-mounted pommel. Attached to it by means of the end of a rawhide quirt were a couple of spurs, likewise silvered.

Two heavy leather chairs completed the furnishings. Miss Withers sank into one of them gratefully, a book in her hand which brought back her own childhood. It was *Toby Tyler—or Ten Weeks With a Circus,* and the title page bore a boyish scrawl—"To Laurie from Lew—Xmas 1921."

"I think Sherlock Holmes' brother had the right idea about this detective business," she remarked. "Remember him? He sat in an armchair all the time."

"Nonsense," the Inspector told her, testily. "That theory stuff is silly. You can't get anywhere in an armchair. You can't see anything from an armchair. Put away the book, and we'll get somewhere." He stuck his head out of the closet where he had been rummaging. "The main thing in this business is to keep rustling around."

He disappeared again. A few minutes later he reappeared, dusty and disgruntled.

Miss Withers, smarting under his remarks, let her voice have the slightest suggestion of a barb in it. "Well, did your rustling around discover any clues in that closet as to why Laurie Stait appeared on Fifth Avenue wearing a rope?"

"No, there's nothing in there but a lot of clothes, mostly duplicates, some shoes, and some old magazines and junk."

"By any chance did there happen to be an empty picture frame twelve inches by fifteen or thereabouts?" Miss Withers was casual.

The Inspector almost jumped. "You've been snooping in there!"

"I have not," said Miss Withers triumphantly. "But I knew it was there. From where I sit in this chair I can see a light square on the wall, over there between the bureaus. See it?"

"See what?"

"Well, doesn't that suggest to you that perhaps someone took down a picture recently? There's enough dust in this town so that it must have been recently."

"But why must the frame be empty?" The Inspector was humbler.

"That was a wild guess," admitted Miss Withers, conscious of her victory. "But it seemed natural that if someone wanted a picture off the wall he'd keep the frame, at least, and throw away the picture." Her forehead wrinkled. "Or suppose he didn't throw away the picture?"

There was a wastebasket by the door, but it was empty. The picture hadn't gone there—at any rate, not today. And Miss Withers had an idea that very few hours had passed since that strangely clean spot on the wall was covered.

"Oscar—suppose you wanted to hide a picture, in a room like this. Where would you put it?"

The Inspector was thoughtful. "Let me see. Behind the wallpaper? No, that would be difficult to get loose and more difficult to get stuck on again. Under a carpet—but there's only scatter rugs in this room."

"We've got to do better than this," Miss Withers reminded him. "Could it be in one of those books—no, they're all too small for a picture that size. Under the lining of one of the bureau drawers?"

"I've got an idea!" The Inspector was galvanized into action. Swiftly, while Miss Withers watched, he drew out the drawers of both bureaus. He didn't look under the linings, but hoisted each drawer up over his head and stared intently at the under side.

He found what he was looking for under the next to the last drawer, pinned with four drawing pins against the bottom.

"Somebody is smart," he observed. "Most people think of hiding an article on top of something, not underneath it. We're all accustomed to laying things down, not sticking them up." But he didn't explain how the idea had come to him.

Nor did Miss Withers give him the congratulations he was angling for. She was staring at the photograph in his hand.

It showed the head of a striking-looking young woman of twenty or thereabouts, a girl with light tawny hair curled at the ends, above whose wide eyes were stuck two ridiculously diminutive eyebrows. The mouth was firm and resolute, for all the sculptured softness of the lips.

"She looks to me like a girl who'd get anything she wanted, or *else,*" observed Miss Withers.

The Inspector nodded slowly. A single sentence rang through his brain. "I love you more than anybody else in the world and nobody . . . is going to stand in our way." Those were the words written on that sheet of crisp notepaper tucked away in his pocket.

There was writing on the bottom of the photograph, writing that was vaguely familiar to the Inspector.

"To Lew, with all my love," it read. It was signed "Your Dana."

7

Abaft the Mizz'mast

"Well, this is the door," said Miss Withers in a whisper. She and the Inspector were standing on the attic-floor landing, in semidarkness. "Though I wish you'd tell me what you expect to find out from the old lady."

"You'll see," Piper told her. He rapped on the door. The only answer was a thick, almost gummy silence.

He knocked again, this time with the heel of his hand. There was a booming echo inside, together with faint thumpings and stirrings and rustlings that betokened someone's stealthy presence.

"May I trouble you a moment, Mrs. Stait?"

A shrill cackle of inhuman, uncanny laughter answered him. But no one came to the door.

"Hello in there! Mrs. Stait, this is the police. We must ask you a few questions!" Piper knocked again, this time with a clenched fist. He had had no dinner this night, and he had exhausted his stock of patience.

"I say, Inspector!" a voice interrupted from the foot of the stairs. "It's no use with Gran. She'll do just as she pleases."

It was Hubert outside the door of his room, in dressing gown and slippers. "She'll send for you when she's willing to see you."

"Oh yes? Well, she'll see me now. I represent the law here in this house. And besides, something may have happened to the old lady." The Inspector rapped again. "Mrs. Stait, if you don't open this door I'm going to kick it in."

"Why don't you try the knob first?" Miss Withers suggested.

Automatically the Inspector dropped his hand to the knob, and it turned easily. The door opened inward—and a thick, musty odor struck their faces. The room was black as pitch. "There ought to be a light switch just inside the door here," said Piper, fumbling through the darkness.

His fingers collided with something which was not a light switch, and there was the smash of breaking glass as something toppled to the floor.

"What in the devil . . . a lamp in this place? . . ."

But the Inspector didn't get a fair start with what he was intending to say. From across the room there burst an avalanche of purple language, double strength and hundred-proof, that sizzled around his ears.

"Hell fire! Hell fire and brimstone! Batten down your hatches and stand by to repel boarders, you stinking lubbers! . . . Where's the Skipper, the Skipper? . . . Here, Fido, here, Fido, sic'em, Fido! . . . Bloody, bloody boogies, all of you!"

"Great Scott, what's that?"

The harsh old voice went on without pausing to draw breath. "Hell and damnation . . . stowaways, Skipper, stowaways . . . feed the sharks, Skipper! . . . Belay me for a bloody lubber! . . . Rats, Fido, rats! . . . Help, murder, bloody murder!"

Miss Withers had firm hold of the Inspector's arm. She could see nothing, not even the glow of light from a window . . . nor could she hear anything except that rush of full-flavored language.

At that moment a further door, across the room, opened suddenly, disclosing the tall, gaunt figure of an old woman in a red shawl. Beneath the shawl, Miss Withers could see by the flickering light of a kerosene lamp held in the old lady's hand, she wore a dress that had once been black silk, but that now was a purplish green with dust and age.

Her face was as seamed and wrinkled as a dried russet apple, and her little beady eyes gleamed out of dark caverns in her skull.

She spoke in a voice that was strangely younger than herself. "That dratted parrot! Quiet, Skipper!"

Sitting on a perch across the impossibly cluttered room, a fat, featherless monstrosity squawked once and then subsided obediently.

In all her thirty-nine years Miss Withers had never seen a dodo, except in one of Sir John Tenniel's fantastic drawings. But this unspeakably evil, fat, naked slug, with its tremendous hooked beak and its expression of cheerful malevolence, was as close to being that extinct horror of the Indian Ocean as anything she could imagine.

"Policemen are always the same," said the old lady none too pleasantly. "Always a lot of blackguards, bursting their way into decent people's homes and shooting innocent bystanders while the footpads flourish and wax fat."

"Excuse the intrusion, madam, but it was necessary. It's about your grandson Laurie."

"I will *not* bail him out if he's in trouble again, and that's final!" The old lady stalked towards the inner door. "Laurie has been a disgrace to this family since his birth."

"He'll never be a disgrace to this family again," cut in the Inspector hastily. "You see, Mrs. Stait, your grandson has been killed!"

She turned round, a look of polite incredulity. "Killed? Don't be silly. The Staits don't have such things happen to them. He's not dead. Pour water on him. Probably he's been scorching at the cocktail bar down at the Haymarket."

"But you don't understand, Mrs. Stait. Your grandson has been *murdered!*"

"Rats, rats, Fido—rats! Bloody murder, boys!" The parrot caught his gnarled claws around his perch and hung head downwards, swinging merrily. "Bloody murder abaft the mizz'mast! Belay him good, Skipper! Skrrrrrrrrrrr!"

"Hush, Skipper!" The elderly bird cocked one eye and leered horribly at Miss Withers.

His mistress carefully lowered the wick of her lamp. "Murdered, hey? Well, he can't say I didn't warn him. I always said that boy would come to no good end. And it's a happy day for the Stait family that he's gone, that's all I say. Always going out with low companions. Late hours and too many girls. Nothing like my younger grandson, Lew."

"Younger? But aren't they *twins?*" The Inspector's jaw dropped.

Mrs. Stait glared at him. "Yes, younger. I'm old, but *I'm* not in my second childhood, young man. Did you think twins came into the world neck and neck, like racehorses on the home stretch? Laurie was born at midnight some twenty-four years ago, and Lew came at one o'clock. Like as two pins, they were, only Laurie was always yelling and Lew never did anything more than snivel. Twins have only morals enough for one, and Lew got 'em all."

"I just want to ask you a few questions, Mrs. Stait." The Inspector coughed hesitantly, and Miss Withers got out her notebook. "Have you any idea as to who had a reason to kill your grandson?"

"Why should I tell you if I did?" The heartless old lady was heading again for the door of her bedroom. "I'm not being paid to play Hawkshaw, mister policeman. That worthless grandson of mine deserved just what he got, besides. Now get out of here, and take your typewriter with you."

Miss Withers realized, after a moment's wonder, that she was the "typewriter" referred to.

"But, Mrs. Stait, won't you tell me what you mean when you say that Laurie deserved what happened to him?"

"*Girls,*" said the old lady. "Too many girls. Always in trouble. Only the other day a man was here. I didn't see him, but he was here. Said his sister was in trouble—told it to our family lawyer, who happened to be downstairs. Blamed Laurie. Unpleasant man with very bad accent, so Charles says. Charles Waverly—a distant branch of our family, and a fine barrister. He's going to settle the case if it's possible. Ask questions of him from now on. I don't choose to be disturbed. I bid you a very good evening. Now get out of here."

"Bloody murder!" yelled Skipper from his perch. "Below decks, ye bloody scum! Give 'em the cat-o'-nine-tails, Skipper! Hell and damnation!"

"Nice bird that," said Inspector Piper. His hand was on the doorknob.

"He's more of a gentleman than you are, for all his language," said the old lady tartly. "Skipper is well along on his second century, and he's learned a-plenty in his day. He's been round the world three times on a Baltimore clipper, that parrot has. And he's lived here in this room for twenty years without breaking a lamp chimney, as you did the first minute you got inside. You could learn manners from him, mister policeman."

"One thing more, madam. Do you know any girl named Dana?"

"Dana? You mean Dana Waverly? Of course I know Dana. Fine girl. Going to marry Lew one of these days. It's been arranged since before she was born. Engaged for the past two years. None of that silly modern stuff about her. She'd fight for her man with tooth and claw. But you leave Dana out of this mess of Laurie's, d'you hear? Now get out of my rooms before I throw you out."

Frail and trembling, the gaunt old lady raised the lamp as if to hurl it across the room. The parrot took up the cry.

"Shiver my timbers, but they're a bunch of bloody sons-a-sluts! Yeeeeek, yeeeeek, buckets of blood, buckets of blood! Sling him from the stern at a rope's end, Skipper! Hell fire!"

With that final farewell from the irate Skipper, who was jumping up and down on his perch and waving his featherless flippers, the door closed behind Miss Withers and the Inspector.

They looked at each other, wordlessly. Then they went down the stair. The phone was ringing in the lower hall, ringing with a persistent nagging note that was somehow like the screaming "Skrrrrrr" of the parrot upstairs.

"I'll take it," called out Piper as he saw the Sergeant moving down the hall.

The voice at the other end was a familar one—that of the cop on special duty in his own office at Headquarters.

"Hello, Inspector? Just got something that'll interest you. Yeah. The boys went over the Chrysler, but no prints except the stiff's. Yeah.

Nothing else that didn't belong. Ignition key in the dashboard. No marks on the cushions. No sign of any place where the rope could have been tied, and then pulled loose."

"Well, what else?"

"The post office sent over a wallet that they found in the outgoing mail about ten minutes ago, Inspector. One of the collectors got it in a late round this afternoon, stuck away in one of the letterboxes. He's not sure which building, but it's in the general district where the Stait guy was bumped. Yeah, that's what pickpockets always do with a wallet. Lift the dough and then drop it through the slot so it won't pin a rap on them later. Only this one had twenty-five bucks still in it . . . and what's more, it has a half a dozen swell engraved cards with the name Lewis Maitland Stait. Yeah. That's the brother of the stiff, ain't it?"

Piper said, "Yes," and rubbed his chin thoughtfully. "Anything else, Joe?"

"No, nothing else, Inspector—oh, wait a minute. Here comes a messenger from Van Donnen's office with the rope you wanted him to look over."

"Good! What's the expert testimony in the rope? Read it quick."

"Dr. Van Donnen says it's not a rope at all, it's a lariat or *reata*. Belongs out west somewhere. Signs of animal hair, probably shorthorn cattle. Tensile strength three hundred pounds or more. The binding of the blue thread at the end is from Woolworth's, though. Yeah, Woolworth's. Well, he says he's sure. And the knot isn't a hangman's noose at all, it's just a running slip-knot spliced into place. That's all."

"That's plenty, Joe. See you tomorrow morning." The Inspector hung up.

He told Miss Withers the latest news. "Laurie Stait goes out west to a dude ranch this summer, and we find him with a lariat around his neck a few months later. You don't suppose that we've got a tangible clue of this hodgepodge, do you? Putting two and two together . . ."

"The trouble with you, Oscar, is that you always put two and two together and make a baker's dozen out of it," Miss Withers told him.

The Inspector nodded. "Maybe. But when you put the dude ranch and the lariat together with the fact that there's been a rodeo at the Madison Square Garden all week . . ."

"And what is a rodeo?" They were preparing to leave. Miss Withers yawned politely.

"Oh, a bunch of crazy hoodlums put on a Wild West show, with a lot of riding wild horses and bulldogging steers and rope tricks."

"You don't suppose," said Miss Withers casually, "that there was a gentleman at the rodeo who knew some rope tricks that weren't part of the program?"

McTeague had gone home to nurse the lump on his forehead, and Sergeant Taylor was relaxed in a chair in the front hall, on special duty for the rest of the night. Miss Withers and the Inspector came down the front steps together, and paused for a moment to look between the houses at the full moon, which hung like a great white skull in the sky.

"The police have this case well in hand and an arrest is expected hourly," quoted the Inspector bitterly. From somewhere in the decaying mansion they had just left came the muffled sound of shrill derisive laughter. It might have been from the little maid Gretchen or the lewd centenarian parrot that Mrs. Stait called Skipper.

Miss Withers thought it a fitting end for the first day of this mad murder case.

8

The Valkyrie Gets Taken for a Ride

The Inspector arose an hour earlier than was his custom next morning. It was entirely too early for Mrs. McFeeters, the amiable but light-fingered shoplifter who "did" for him. She had reformed, insofar as shoplifting went, but she still snatched forty winks whenever she could. He made himself a quick cup of under-strong and over-hot coffee, slipped into his heaviest ulster, and let himself out into the knifelike air of the New York morning.

"And right here is where little Oscar pulls a fast one and gets hot on the trail—alone," he said to himself happily. "I'll show Hildegarde Withers!"

Instead of taking his usual course downtown toward his office, with its miniature Chamber of Horrors around the wall-cases, he headed straight west, across town. The Inspector was in a good humor. The crisp air, more like January than November, put the Stait murder case in a new light. Last night it had seemed—well—involved to say the least. What with the cook and the naked parrot and that inhuman old lady in the attic. All that would be washed up in short order this morning, and Miss Withers would have demonstrated before her eyes the power of the organized police.

The first cigar of the day was always the best for Inspector Piper. It was, as a rule, the only one he ever managed to smoke through. He blew the smoke in twisting rings from his mouth as he strode up Fifty-seventh Street.

By the time he reached Eighth Avenue, and turned down toward the looming gray atrocity which is called Madison Square Garden because it is not anything like a garden and is several miles from Madison Square, the Inspector was able to pass the newsboy's ramparts of morning papers without wincing at "STRANGLER STILL AT LARGE—POLICE POWERLESS" or "NOOSE KILLER SLAYS PLAYBOY."

He strode gaily in at the main entrance of the Garden, past the arcade with its windows full of snappy suits and snappier wristwatches. Except for a couple of cats who evidently were still set on making a night of it, and a cleaning man with a mop who was presumably posing for slow-motion pictures, there was no sign of life in the open-roofed lobby.

The box office kiosk, of course, was locked. It would be at this ungodly hour of seven-thirty. The cleaning man, poking dully at endless little islands of dried chewing gum, answered his inquiries with a jerk of the thumb toward the inner doors.

Inspector Piper had his hand against the panel when the door swung violently toward him and Miss Withers stepped out, her umbrella under her arm and a belligerent look on her face—a look which changed to pained surprise.

"Oscar! Excuse me! Did I hurt you?"

The Inspector wasn't hurt. He murmured something. Then he took out his flavorless cigar, glared at it, and hurled it in the direction of the nearest cat, who dodged without taking her attention from what she hoped would develop into an interesting relic of bologna skin. The morsel turned out to be cellophane, but that is neither here nor there.

"You needn't look so unglad to see me," Miss Withers told the Inspector. "Anyway, I've saved you fifteen minutes traipsing around inside there. I had plenty of trouble finding out what we want to know, but I finally got hold of a sort of janitor. And he told me what I ought to have known in the first place—that the cowboys don't come around here except for rehearsal or when the rodeo is actually on in the afternoon and evening. The horses and cattle are stabled in a warehouse three blocks away on Eleventh Avenue, and the riders are at the Hotel Senator."

"The Senator? Why, that's on Forty-fourth Street over near Fifth Avenue. . . ."

"Exactly. And it's a couple of stone's throws from where Laurie Stait met with an accident last night. I thought of that, too. In case you're interested, the manager of the outfit is a Mr. Carrigan. And here is a program of the show, which I picked out of the janitors' trash basket."

The Inspector took the gaudy sheet, printed in red and black on a luminous yellow paper. "Well, here we are. All about Carrigan's Annual Rodeo—a thousand thrills of daring and skill, according to the blurb. Wild West at its best—a poetical fellow, this Carrigan, if he writes his own advertising. Riding, roping, bulldogging—throwing and tying contests, bronco-busting, chariot races, fancy sharpshooting."

"Have they got Eliza Crossing the Ice, too?" inquired Miss Withers.

"Probably, though they don't mention any bloodhounds." Suddenly the

Inspector pressed a stubby forefinger against a note halfway down the sheet. "Will you get a load of this!"

"If you mean look at it, I shall be glad to do so," reprimanded Miss Withers. "Let me see. . . . 'Third Event—Fancy Shooting—Mr. Laramie White assisted by Miss Rose Keeley. Fourth Event—Roping Three-horse Team in Full Gallop (Horses for this Event by Lazy Y ranch)—Mr. Buck Keeley. Fifth Event—Roping Contest with Wild Yearling Steer—Entries, Mr. Laramie White, Mr. Sam Gowdy, Mr. Buck Keeley. . . .' Is that what you mean?"

Inspector Piper was triumphant. "That's it. Ever hear that last name before?"

Miss Withers was thoughtful. "No, not that I remember. I don't follow the sporting pages to any considerable extent."

The Inspector was in good humor again. "Naturally you wouldn't catch this, being a woman. That shows the power of the trained detective mind, Hildegarde. You've been lucky, and clever, too. I won't argue against that. But this isn't any chess game of wits with a would-be mastermind criminal. And in this case it's the little things that a trained mind remembers that will bring the murderer to justice."

"Oscar Piper! What in heaven's name are you talking about?"

They had gravitated toward a little Coffee Potte in the arcade of the Garden entrance. "Sit down and have a poached egg with me, and I'll point out the detail you missed," said the Inspector.

"On the force," he began, "we learn very early the importance of remembering names. We do it by hooking them up with other names, see? Suppose a fellow's name is Moses, I ask myself if he doesn't play pool, see? Remember Moses in the pool of bulrushes? And then if I want to remember his name months later I think of pool and then of Moses. Simple, isn't it?"

Miss Withers was visibly unimpressed. "That's no deep police secret," she informed him. "That little trick is known as 'association of ideas,' and it dates back to William James and probably before. But go on, why should I remember the name Jack Keeley or whatever it was?"

"Buck, Buck Keeley," corrected the Inspector. "When I saw the name on the letter last night I remembered the old-fashioned idea about taking the Keeley-cure for drunks, see? Well, that ticketed the name in the back of my mind, and now when I see it again on the program here, I put two and two together."

He stopped suddenly at the look on Miss Withers' face. She wasn't attacking her poached egg.

"Oscar Piper, are you holding out on me?"

He felt guilty. All too late he remembered that he hadn't intended mentioning the letter under the kitchen table.

"Why, no, Hildegarde. I . . ."

"If that isn't like a man! The superior sex, huh? So you had to look to your laurels this time? Just to prove to me that a woman can't be a detective!"

The Inspector was nettled. But Miss Withers wouldn't let him speak.

"All right, Oscar Piper. I was going to send a substitute down to my third-grade classes for the rest of the month. But if that's the way you feel about it, you can just go blundering ahead alone. And to think I very nearly married you!"

"But, Hildegarde . . ."

Miss Withers shoved her egg away as if it had mortally offended her patrician nose, and seized her umbrella.

"Be reasonable, will you? I meant to tell you about that letter sometime. We'll work on the case together."

"I never want to work on another case anyhow," Miss Withers informed him. "I hope I never hear of another murder nor meet another flatfooted detective as long as I live. I'm through, and I mean it. I haven't the slightest interest in sleuthing. . . ."

She was moving toward the door. But she stopped suddenly, her cotton umbrella gripped tensely in her hand.

From somewhere within the vast expanses of the Garden, muffled by the intervening walls, there came a couple of dull *thump-thumps* . . . another. . . .

It might have been the slamming of a door, or the backfiring of a dirty truck engine.

But it was neither of the two, and both Miss Withers and the Inspector knew it. There is something about the staccato bark of a forty-five caliber revolver that, once heard, is never confused with anything else.

The sound of shots came again, a regular fusillade.

Miss Withers raised her umbrella like a crouched lance. "What in heaven's name are you waiting for? Oscar, come on!"

The Inspector came on, swinging in the long stride that had won a silver cup or two in earlier police Field Days. But all the same, Miss Withers, who had no interest in sleuthing, beat him through the entrance to the Garden by at least two lengths.

There was no sign of the janitorlike individual who had grudgingly given out information a few minutes before. The main entrance hall of the Garden was empty and almost dark, though a dim glow showed through an entrance marked "M to Q."

They ran up a short slope of concrete, and came out high above the great bowl—the bowl which was more like a saucer now. The wide rim consisted of row upon row of board seats, and the oval in the center was bare, and scattered with tanbark. They stopped to take in a puzzling panorama.

The Inspector had never been in the Garden before when this center space was not filled with seats optimistically labelled "Ringside" and faced toward a squared bit of canvas platform beneath glaring floodlights.

The floodlights were on full blast, and in their glare sat a big blonde girl on a big white horse, both of them as rigid as if cut out of marble. There was some sort of a dark screen or background behind them, against which smoke curled lazily upward from a cigarette between the lips of the girl. She wore pink tights and short boots, and in spite of the costume she might have posed as one of the Valkyrie.

As they watched, she raised her gloved hand in a quick signal, and from the shadows at the far end of the auditorium another horse and rider appeared, at full gallop.

This horse was a plump little red and white paint, and he ran by bunching up his body and kicking viciously at the ground as it passed by. His rider was a lean and lanky young man dressed only in shirt, black trousers, and high-heeled boots. With his left hand he held the reins loosely, and his right gripped a massive but businesslike revolver.

As he swung past the waiting girl he leaned forward in the saddle and discharged his weapon in her general direction.

She did not, as Miss Withers had half expected, fall into a crumpled heap. She only took the cigarette out of her mouth, looked at it thoughtfully, and made an unprintable observation. The white horse switched his tail impatiently.

The male rider pulled his mount on its haunches and lit a cigarette of his own.

A small man in a derby rose suddenly from one of the front seats at the edge of the tanbark.

"Lousy," he gave as his verdict. "Plenty lousy. You didn't come within a mile of it, Laramie. Try it again."

Laramie shrugged his shoulders and looked at the girl. "Rose moved her head," he suggested, in the tone of one who does not expect to be believed.

"I moved nothing," she said, in a soft yet penetrating drawl. "You're getting the jitters worser every day, Laramie. Can't you see out of the *good* eye, even? That slug was a good five inches away from the hot end of the cigarette. I could hear it go by."

"All right, all right," broke in the nervous man in the derby. "Try it again. You've either got to get a better average than one in three or else we'll have to cut the number entirely—unless we go back to the way it was last year. We can't go on using the fake cigarette on the thread. Somebody is going to catch on, the way they did about the cactus burrs under the saddles on those broncs in Chi, and we'll get the razz in the papers."

"All right, we'll try it again," said Laramie, reining up the paint. "But I tell you this for the last time, Carrigan, I ain't going back to the act the way it was last year. If we do the number at all, I'm holding the gun and Rose is holding the cigarette, see? I ain't going to let any dame throw lead at me."

"Well, why not? Rose is as good a shot as you, and she doesn't get rattled as easy. I don't see why, after two years of it, you have to switch places with her."

"Neither do I, for that matter," said Rose, her red lips curled scornfully. Miss Withers and the Inspector by this time had crept down unnoticed almost to the ring itself. And the little schoolteacher couldn't help noticing that a glance was exchanged between the sharpshooter on the horse and the human target, which was not altogether professional jealousy. There was a mutual understanding, and a mutual antagonism, hidden there.

"All right, get on with it. The rest of the boys will be here in a little while, and then we'll have to quit monkeying with your number. All set?" He slid back into his seat again, but then he noticed that the girl was looking over his shoulder.

"*Rubes,* Carrigan!" sang out Rose, in a voice that was all too clear. "They must have left those front doors on the latch again."

Carrigan whirled around to face the intruders. "Look here," he said belligerently, "this is a private rehearsal, not a public park. The performance doesn't start until two o'clock this afternoon. If you want to come back then, buy a ticket."

"He's wrong," said Miss Withers softly. "The performance has already begun."

"Go on, scram," yelled Carrigan. "Find your way out the way you came in or I'll call a cop and have you thrown out."

Inspector Piper smiled faintly, and squared his shoulders. "Oh, so you'll call a cop and have us thrown out?"

"That's what I said! An' maybe I won't bother to call a cop!"

The Inspector flashed his badge in the palm of his hand. "If you want to call a cop, you don't need to strain your voice, Mr. Carrigan. I'm Inspector Piper of the Homicide Squad, and this is my assistant. I came up here to ask you some questions."

"Why, sure, Inspector! Howdy, ma'am. Have yourself a couple of seats. I didn't get you at first. Anything I can do. . . . I suppose this is about licenses for the guns we use in the show? They told us it would be all right as long as the boys didn't wear 'em in the street."

"No," admitted Inspector Piper. "I'm not bothering with the Sullivan Law these days. I just wanted to ask you a question or two about a man named Keeley, Buck Keeley."

The girl suddenly galvanized into action, slid out of her saddle. She strode toward the little group, her fists clenched and her eyes blazing. For the first time Miss Withers realized what a formidable person this Valkyrie of the plains could be.

"What do you want to know about my brother?" she demanded fiercely.

The Inspector stared at her. "So Buck Keeley of the Lazy Y ranch is your brother, eh? Well, maybe you can tell me where he was between five-thirty and seven o'clock last night."

She didn't hesitate for the fraction of a second. "I sure can, Marshal. I don't know what you want him for, but my brother wasn't into any mischief last night. Because he was with me, in my room at the Senator. I was feeling low, 'count of some hard luck I've had lately, and Buck had chuck with me up in my room on the tenth floor. He bunks downstairs with the boys, but he most generally chows with me."

"I see. What time did your brother join you?"

"We went over from here together as soon as the afternoon show was done and the horses put back in the corral we rigged up in an old warehouse down the road. That must have been about five."

"And your brother was with you all the time until after dinner?"

"That's what I said, Marshal. All the time. Just ask the rest of the boys. Ask Laramie here. Hey, Laramie, wasn't Buck with me for dinner at the hotel last night?"

The lean and lanky young man came cantering up on the paint, wiping his face. "Huh?" Miss Withers noticed that he had sticking-plaster over his left eye.

"I asked you, wasn't Buck with me in the hotel at five-thirty last night?"

"Him? Why er–yes, of course he was. Sure he was." Laramie turned to Carrigan, and his good eye dropped a quarter of an inch. Miss Withers pretended not to notice it.

"Hey, Tom, wasn't Buck with his sister last night around chow time?"

Up to this time Carrigan had stood there, chewing at his moustache. "Why, sure he was. He went right over to the hotel after the show. You must be thinking of somebody else, Inspector." He was a little more eager to agree than seemed necessary to Miss Withers.

"Good," grunted Inspector Piper. He faced the girl again. "By the way," he said casually, "are you any relation to the Keeley family that runs a dude ranch out at Medicine Hat, Wyoming?"

She shook her head. "Our ranch isn't at Medicine Hat, Marshal. That's where we get our mail, but the ranch is a long drive from the railroad . . . up in the Johnson's Hole country on the edge of the Tetons."

"But you and your brother run a dude ranch there?"

She nodded. "Why not? This rodeo business only is good for a few months in the spring and fall. Everybody does it out there."

"I was just asking," said the Inspector heavily. "A young fellow I know was out there this summer. Laurie Stait was the name."

If he expected her to show any emotion, the Inspector was disappointed. "Yeah, he was with us for a while. Guess he had a good time, too."

"Heard from him since he came back to the city?" The Inspector's voice was thick with sarcasm.

But the blonde Valkyrie shook her head. "No, I haven't heard from him. Nor my brother either."

"You're lying," said the Inspector soberly. "You see, we've found your letters in Laurie Stait's bureau—yours and your brother's, too. Don't you think you'd better talk?" He let his voice become wheedling and persuasive.

Her eyes were narrow. "Marshal, you think I'm a hick, don't you? You're trying to bluff me, and you aren't getting anywhere. You didn't find any letters, or you wouldn't be trying to trap me into saying something about them. Come on, let's see the letters you think I wrote to that tenderfoot of a Stait kid. I don't see what difference it makes, though. Is it any skin off *your* back porch?"

If this was a bluff she was carrying it through, Miss Withers decided. Good heavens, hadn't the girl even seen the newspapers that blared from every corner this morning?

The Inspector asked her that. Rose Keeley shook her head. "We don't truck much with newspapers where I come from," she admitted. "Why should I ought to have read the paper this morning particular? The only reading material I got any use for is the Montgomery Ward catalogue and *True Story*. Besides, we got something to do besides read newspapers—or stand around here and talk to you, either."

The Inspector, by adroit manipulation on the part of his tongue, pushed his dead cigar from one corner of his mouth to the other. His lower lip slid out a little farther than was necessary.

"Then you didn't read the papers or hear the news, eh? I suppose it'll come as a considerable shock to you to know that Laurie Stait was murdered last night!"

The girl's eyes widened, in what Miss Withers swore to be honest surprise. "Laurie Stait *murdered* . . . last night?"

"Yes, murdered," said the Inspector savagely. He was angry that he had shot his bolt without securing any damaging admission from the girl in the moment of shock. "He was riding along in his brother's roadster, and somebody dropped a lariat over his head, slick and pretty."

The Inspector didn't need to finish. He'd secured his effect, after all. Miss Withers cried out as she saw the blood drain from the girl's blank face. Then Rose Keeley's splendid big body suddenly went lifeless as an empty sack.

She fell face down in the tanbark, and for a long moment the rest of them watched her, powerless to move. Even at that moment Miss Withers could not help noticing the look of utter unbelief on the faces of Carrigan and the rider Laramie. They could not have been more nonplussed if Rose Keeley had suddenly disappeared in a pillar of smoke.

But she had not disappeared. She was sprawled like an empty sack in the tanbark.

Miss Withers moved to pick her up, but Laramie White was quicker.

9

Hubert Cries "Wolf!"

"I'll . . . I'll get some water. . . ." gasped Miss Withers. But Carrigan elbowed her aside.

"We'll take care of Rose," he said roughly. "Haven't you done harm enough already? Take your hands off her!"

"Young man, I . . ."

But Inspector Piper nodded to her. "Come on, Hildegarde." The girl who had fainted so unexpectedly was already murmuring something, and showing signs of life. "She's all right. Let's get out of here."

She followed him up the ramp. "But what's the hurry? We might have found out something."

"We did find out something," he told her. "Plenty. And those fellows will see that she doesn't say anything else now. We'll take another try when her precious brother is here, unless we pick him up first. I've got to get back to my office; there's plenty to settle."

"There is," agreed Miss Withers grimly, as she climbed into a taxicab. "And the first thing is this, Oscar Piper. We were discussing a little matter in the restaurant when we heard that shooting."

He was thoughtful. "Yes, Hildegarde, we'll settle that. So you really want to quit the case, huh?"

"You know that isn't true," she contradicted him swiftly. "But I'm not going to butt in where I'm not wanted, unless it's for a person's own good."

"You know how much I value your help—"

"All right then. But why didn't you tell me about the letter you found in thc Stait house?"

The Inspector was very uncomfortable. "Why . . . I was going to tell you about that—a little later."

"You were? Oscar Piper, you wanted to demonstrate your masculine superiority, that's all. You thought I was getting too sure of myself after my luck in the last case we did together, and so you handed yourself a handicap. You held back some evidence so that I wouldn't beat you too badly!"

"But, Hildegarde . . ."

"Yes, and you got up early this morning to try and beat me to a few facts over here, didn't you?"

"But, Hildegarde, you did the same thing . . ."

"Never mind. Oscar Piper, it's all or nothing. Maybe you don't like to have the other officers see you tagging around with a woman all the time. All right, we'll work separately. And we'll see which one of us gets to the truth of this mess first. I'll bet you—I'll bet you a week's salary, mine against yours, that I find out who killed Laurie Stait before you do. You can have all the power of the police department, and I'll work alone, and I'll show you what your masculine superiority is worth."

Miss Withers was raging, and the Inspector had bitten through his cigar. "All right, you're on with that bet," he said. "And what's more, I'll give you a better break than that. I'll tell you every concrete fact I establish and give you the advantage of everything that the police have or can get on the case. And you don't have to tell me anything you don't wish to. That makes it even, and we'll just prove once and for all how far an amateur can get against a trained operative."

"Fair enough." They shook hands. "And now, what about that letter?"

Piper told her.

Miss Withers was silent while the taxi coursed southward a couple of blocks. "So this girl Dana was engaged to Lew and in love with Laurie? Lew stayed in New York and Laurie went out to a ranch, and then he came back and got himself murdered! I'm trying to fit it all together."

"Not much fitting to do," grunted the Inspector. "Brothers have killed brothers before over a girl."

Miss Withers shook her head. "It doesn't fit. Besides, Lew Stait had an alibi. He was at home when the thing happened."

The Inspector laughed bitterly. "In the first place, we don't know what happened. A body in the street with a rope around its neck. But that's nothing. How did it get out of the car and into the street? Who threw the noose? Why didn't anybody see it? Besides, what is Lew's alibi worth? The maid was upstairs, and she couldn't swear that he didn't go out when she was taking the old mummy her tea in the attic rooms, or when she was checking the laundry. Besides, by the looks of the situation when we came, little Gretchen is sweet on Mister Lew anyway. So why shouldn't she lie to protect him?"

"But there's another reason why it isn't as simple as that," Miss Withers thought aloud. "This business in the Garden . . ."

"You mean the girl's fainting when I told her Laurie Stait was dead?"

Miss Withers shook her head again. "I do not. I mean the girl's fainting when she heard that Laurie Stait had died from being strangled with a lariat! There's a difference, you remember. She took your first sentence calmly enough. It was the second that knocked her over."

"You mean, you think she was involved with Laurie last summer when he was out at the dude ranch, and that she had something to do with the fact that he was murdered?"

"I don't know. One thing just occurred to me. Is there any way of finding out if the rodeo had a parade last night on Fifth Avenue, or if they were moving horses through the streets?"

"That's easy. I happen to know that no permit for a parade was granted them, and that none would be. Besides, the thing is impossible at the rush hour. No, there was no parade."

"So Laurie Stait was not murdered by a lasso in the hands of a cowboy. Well, I just wanted to know. I've seen movies of that sort of thing."

"Well, this isn't a movie, nor was the end of that rope held by any man on horseback. It would have been seen; besides, because a cowboy on horseback would have attracted as much attention as a knight in armor on that Avenue. No, it was a simpler method."

"Out of a window?" Miss Withers polished her glasses. "Somebody might have made a successful cast from a second-story window and snagged him. It would have to be an expert with a rope to have that accurate an aim."

"Well, doesn't it strike you as fairly obvious that the town is full, right now, of the smartest experts in fancy roping that all the Wild West can offer?"

They rode on in silence. "How's this?" offered the Inspector. "Laurie Stait was a handsome chap. Suppose that he went out west because he knew his brother's girl had fallen for him, and he wanted to play fair. Then this Rose Keeley also gets hipped over him, and they fix it up to get married. Only her brother Buck doesn't like the city slicker and forbids it, so she waits until the rodeo brings them here, and starts seeing Laurie again. And the brother gets wise and knocks the boy off. How's that?"

"Too easy," objected Miss Withers. "Besides, you saw Rose Keeley. Did she strike you as the kind of a girl who would let a brother tell her what to do? More likely she tells him what to do. She looks like the kind of woman who gets what she wants, or knows the reason why."

"Suppose she wanted Laurie Stait . . . and he didn't want her?"

"Oscar, I do believe you're improving," Miss Withers congratulated him. "Well, here we are at the abode of justice."

"You'd better come on up," suggested the Inspector.

"But what about our agreement? I was going to keep in the background."

"There's a lot of routine matters that ought to be settled by now," he explained. "There's the report of the auto expert who went over the wrecked Chrysler, and the pictures from the photographer, and so forth. Take a look at them, and then you can go out sleuthing all you like on your own. . . ."

"I don't think I'll . . . oh yes, I will." Miss Withers exercised the ancient prerogative of her sex and changed her mind. For she had noticed a young man going up the flight of stone steps ahead of them, toward the main entrance of the building.

It was a young man she had seen before. In spite of his wearing a nondescript hat and overcoat, she recognized him quite clearly. It was Hubert Stait, the odd little cousin of the dead twin, and he was going somewhere in a considerable hurry.

That somewhere proved to be the Inspector's own office, or as close to that sanctum sanctorum as was possible with Lieutenant Keller barring the door.

"I tell you, I've got to see the Inspector," Hubert Stait was demanding as they came down the hall.

"Well, if you turn around you can see him all right," the Lieutenant informed him drily. "But as for his seeing you, I can't say."

Miss Withers watched Hubert as he turned to face them. He looked even more like a startled owl than ever, now. His tie had not been tied carefully, and it failed to match his shirt—or even to harmonize. His voice showed evidence of a considerable amount of excitement.

"May I see you alone, Inspector?"

"Certainly." Inspector Piper led the way to the inner door. As he held it open for Hubert Stait, his eyes sought Miss Withers' for a second, and then dropped meaningly toward a low padded chair. "Will you wait *there,* Hildegarde?"

She was vaguely annoyed, having hoped to hear the inside of this, whatever it was. But she dropped obediently into the padded chair.

Lieutenant Keller came back into the office, and busied himself at some file cases near the window. For a few minutes Miss Withers amused herself by trying to figure out where the murderer could have stood to cast a noose over the head of a man in an open roadster on Fifth Avenue.

In the car? That wasn't likely. He would have had to jump out, which wasn't easy, and then brace himself with the rope in his hands. No, that was out.

From a window of one of the buildings? That was more likely, but though, as the Inspector had pointed out, a cowboy trained in the use of a lariat might have made the cast of the rope, yet how would a stranger in town have ingress to a front office on the Avenue, and how would he know Laurie Stait was driving past at that hour? Miss Withers knew that there was a saying that if you wait on the corner of Forty-second Street at Fifth Avenue long enough, you will meet everyone you ever knew. She had always doubted the usefulness of meeting everyone she'd ever known, and besides, there wasn't a high degree of probability that one of the cowboys had taken up such a vigil. Much less Rose Keeley, who didn't appear a highly patient person.

It was from such reveries that Miss Withers was rudely jerked when she realized that there was a low buzzing somewhere close by. It annoyed her, and she looked over the desk top to see what it was.

The buzzing came in starts and stops, and gradually as her ears became accustomed to it she made out that she was listening to the human voice . . . to Inspector Piper's voice, dim and far away. But it did not come through the door.

Lieutenant Keller was watching her. "Top drawer to the left," he suggested. She opened it, and found a radio headset of earphones, as well as a pad of paper and a dozen sharpened pencils.

The Lieutenant nodded encouragingly. She put on the headset, and then suddenly her pencil started flying across the pad in a weird line of hieroglyphics which neither Mr. Pitman nor Mr. Gregg would have owned. But her own brand of shorthand had come in handily before, and it was handy now.

With the headset over her ears, she could hear every word that was spoken in the next room. The Inspector was talking, crisply and clearly.

". . . you'll have to explain the reason," he was finishing. "It's not the custom for us to furnish an officer as a bodyguard in a case of this kind. What are you afraid of? As it happens, there was an officer in the hall last night, but I'm taking him off today. Why do you want a bodyguard?"

"Because there's *danger* in that house," broke in Hubert Stait, his voice raised above its usual cautious calm. "I'm entitled to police protection, aren't I?"

"My dear young man, the murder is already committed. Laurie Stait is dead. It's unlikely . . ."

"It is not unlikely that something else will happen. I know! Inspector, I tell you that nobody's life is safe if you don't keep a guard in our house at night. That's like the police. You come round and ask questions and make life miserable for the innocent bystanders, but when a person knows that there is the greatest danger you pooh-pooh it until it's too late. Laurie is dead, though he might not be if he'd come to the police when he started to be worried over whatever it was. We all knew he was in trouble—worse trouble than usual. All week he'd been staying home and he wouldn't let anyone else answer the phone . . . though he seemed to dread it. But he is dead . . . and I'm not going to be the next one."

"Why should anyone want to murder you?"

"I don't know, I tell you! But I think somebody is trying to wipe out every male member of our family. Laurie was first, he's the eldest. But why do you think it's going to stop there?"

"Why not? Any reason why you think all the men in the family are doomed? Who are they, by the way—besides the late Laurie Stait, and Lew, and yourself?"

There was a moment's silence, and Miss Withers heard the creak of the Inspector's easy chair.

Then Hubert's careful voice came over the wire. "The next in line would be Charlie, that's Charles Waverly, the New York attorney. He's a fourth cousin or something to the twins, while I'm a first cousin. The next relatives are farther removed, both by blood and by actual distance. They're out in Kansas or somewhere."

"I see. And why would anyone start to knock off the whole family? Is there a large estate?"

"I . . . I don't think so. Gran always is preaching economy, although there's money enough to keep things running. Gran never entertains, you know, and two servants keep the place. The house itself ought to be worth a good deal."

"Doesn't look like motive for murder to me," said the Inspector. "Even a house on Riverside Drive isn't worth more than twenty or thirty thousand in these times. Nobody would start wholesale murder for that."

"Then why was Laurie killed?"

"We'll have an answer for that question one of these days," said Inspector Piper slowly. "It may be an answer that certain people don't like, but it will be the right one. No, Mr. Hubert Stait, I'm afraid I'll have to refuse your request to have an officer play wet nurse for you unless you can give me a better reason than this fantastic story of a deep-laid plot. . . ."

"Then I'll give you a better reason than that, Inspector." Hubert's voice cracked. "Last night someone tried to kill me!"

10

"Or Forever Hold His Peace"

There was a silence during which Miss Withers might have counted ten. Then the Inspector's voice rose, raspingly.

"Someone what?"

"Yes, sir. That's why I'm down here. I'll begin at the beginning. I couldn't sleep last night, after all that had happened. After you and your lady friend went away I lay in my bed listening to that parrot of Gran's chattering up on the floor above. The house seemed to be full of noises.

My room, as you know, is on the front of the house, and I lay there in bed and waited for the first signs of daylight to show on the Jersey shore across the river. Then I heard somebody coming stealthily along the hall. . . ."

"Heavy or light tread? Sound like a man or a woman?"

There was a little hesitation. "Honestly, I can't say, Inspector. It was very light and cautious, just a 'hush-hush' sound along the carpet. That was what made me suspicious. The sounds stopped just outside my door."

"Which was locked?"

"Yes, sir. The locks in that house are all old-fashioned, however, and they can be opened with any skeleton key. So I'd pushed a chair against the knob on the inside. Well, I lay there for what must have been fifteen minutes, waiting for whatever it was to go on past. But it didn't. I tried to keep myself from dozing off, and then something happened that will keep me from dozing off for a week. I swear that I hadn't heard a key turn in the lock, nor a squeak from the chair-back that was against the door. But as I lay there, staring into the darkness, I saw that the door was ajar, perhaps eight inches. My chair-back didn't fit tightly enough under the knob, I guess. Anyway, I could see a dim panel of light which must have come from the lamp at the head of the stairs."

"But there was the Sergeant down in the lower hall! Why didn't you call out to him?"

"You forget, Inspector. I didn't know he was there. You sent me to my room, and you said nothing about leaving an operative on duty. I thought that I was the only man in the house, except for Lew."

"Oh yes, of course. So what did you do?"

"I sat on the edge of the bed and said, 'Who's there?' There wasn't any answer. I thought I saw something in the air, like a bat flying, but then I lost it. And then I saw that the door had closed again. I got up and moved a bureau in front of it. Then I came back to bed and found the pillow pinned against the headboard of the bed with . . . this!"

There was a metallic rattle as something was laid on the Inspector's desk. Miss Withers realized for the first time the disadvantages of her listening post. Television would have helped. She was curious to know what it was that had pinned the pillow of Hubert Stait to the headboard of his bed.

"Very nice," came the Inspector's voice. "A nasty little toadsticker, this. Ever see it before you saw it sticking through your pillow?"

"I . . . I don't like to say!"

"Come, come. You'll have to answer. Where did you see it before?"

"It was part of the camping outfit that Laurie took west with him last summer. He was figuring on making an expedition into the Tetons alone with a frying pan and a book and a dog that he picked up out there, he wrote us. I don't know whether he ever did or not."

"Did he bring this knife back with him?"

"I think so . . . though I don't remember seeing it after he returned."

"Very well. Now, Hubert, tell me one thing more. Have you any idea who it was who stood outside your door and tossed cold steel at you last night?"

"I . . . no, sir."

"Not even a suspicion?"

"No, sir."

"Man or woman?"

"I'm not sure . . . but I think it must have been a man. To throw that hard."

"You say the only other man in the house, besides the Sergeant, was your cousin Lew?"

"Yes, sir."

"Do you think it was Lew who threw that knife at you?"

"Don't make me answer that, Inspector. I don't know. I just want to be protected, that's all."

"Against Lew Stait?"

"Well . . . yes."

"Tell me, do you think your cousin Lew was responsible, then, for what happened to Laurie?"

"I don't know, Inspector. He'd kill me if he knew . . . that I'm talking to you. They've always called Lew the good twin, and Laurie the bad one. It should have been the other way round. Laurie was open and free in what he did, but Lew was the sanctimonious one, always playing up to Gran and then getting into scrapes. Everybody but Gran and Aunt Abbie knew about Lew and the maid. But if she'd seen it with her own eyes Gran would have said it was Laurie. Laurie always has taken the blame for everything bad Lew did. If Lew comes in drunk, it's Laurie. If Lew gets in a fight in a Harlem brothel, it's Laurie. They always stood up for each other, you see. When they were in school they used to share the work, each studying what was easiest for him and then reciting for whichever name was called. You see, no teacher could tell them apart. Laurie used to write Lew's English and history exams, while Lew did the math for both of them. Their writing was enough alike so nobody could be sure."

"Hmmm. So Laurie, you say, was the scapegoat. And he stood for it?"

"Always. You see, they don't think as two persons, entirely. I mean they didn't. They always agreed, for instance, on what they were going to wear that day . . . always the same thing. Perhaps Laurie resented the burden of bearing Lew's sins, but he never showed it."

"Very good." Miss Withers heard the sound of the Inspector's chair being pushed back. "I'll consider what you say, young man."

"I tell you, my life—nobody's life—is safe in that house unless you do something, Inspector."

"I'll do something, never fear." The Inspector's voice faded as he moved away from the concealed microphone. "Good morning."

Then the knob of the inner office door turned noisily, giving Miss Withers a second or two in which she might slip off the headphones and close the drawer. She was fixing her hat when the Inspector ushered Hubert Stait through the office again and out toward the hall.

Then Piper came over to where she was sitting. "There's a badly scared young man, or I'm no judge," he said.

"Excited, anyway," Miss Withers agreed. "I could tell that much by his voice. He's a strange person, very. I got everything but the beginning, Oscar. What did he want you to do?"

"He asked permission to get away, out of town, or at least out of the Stait house. And I told him again, as I did last night, that there wasn't a chance. Because every member of that household and every friend and relative of the dead man is a suspect until we get a little farther with the case. He acted as if my decision was no surprise to him, and then he wanted me to station a plainclothes man to guard him—you heard that. He's a nervous, over-intellectual type, and he's scared silly of his cousin. Under the circumstances I don't blame him, though we haven't got evidence enough to make an arrest."

"May I see that knife?" Miss Withers drew back as the Inspector whipped from his pocket nine inches of gleaming steel, with a heavy handle of polished horn. It was a wicked-looking thing, more like a bayonet than a hunting knife.

"So that knife belonged to the dead man, eh?" Miss Withers hefted it. "Looks like the knives they throw in vaudeville."

The Inspector nodded. "That's what it is. Evidently Laurie Stait liked to practice tossing this little toy. Evidently his brother—or somebody—also had the habit. You see, it's balanced to whirl end over end so that the thrower can gauge the number of revolutions to impinge the blade wherever he takes a fancy."

"I see." Miss Withers fingered the glittering thing casually. "Oscar, any objection to my keeping this knife overnight? Unless of course you want to photograph it for fingerprints."

"There aren't any," she was told. "I dusted it with powder in my office, and there wasn't a single print. Hubert picked it up with a handkerchief, being a sensible young man for all his Phi Beta Kappa key, and the thrower evidently handled it the same way. But why do you want it?"

"I just want it, that's all."

"Going to put it under your pillow and then dream the name of the person who threw it?" The Inspector permitted himself a mild smile.

"Something like that. You can have it tomorrow, Oscar. By the way, are you going to do what Hubert asked you to, and post a man in the Stait house?"

"I don't know. Maybe it would be the wise thing. I'd hate to see what the papers would say if there was another member of that family bumped off. Wait a minute—"

The telephone on the Inspector's desk was buzzing merrily, and he moved to answer it himself. Miss Withers followed him into the inner office. He shouted "Hello" into the mouthpiece.

"Sergeant Taylor reporting, sir, from the Stait house. It's nine o'clock, and I'm leaving as per orders, sir."

"All right, Sergeant. Anything happen in the night?"

"Not a thing, sir. I stayed there at the foot of the stairs, and nothing happened except the milkman's arrival. A little while ago Mr. Hubert Stait went out, in a hurry."

"Yes, I know about that. Oh, by the way, Sergeant. What time did Lew Stait get back from identifying his brother at the morgue?"

"Get back? But . . . but, Inspector, nobody came in the house at all, I tell you! I was right at the front door, and there's no back stairs, so anybody coming in the back way would have had to pass by me to get upstairs. I didn't see hide nor hair of Lew Stait. I thought he'd come in before you left, and that he was safe in his bed."

"Good lord, man! Then Lew Stait has made his getaway!" The Inspector looked up at Miss Withers. "I meant to have somebody tail him, but I didn't because I took it for granted that the boys who drove him down to the morgue would bring him back home. And he just walked out and disappeared!"

He turned to the phone again. "Hello, Sergeant? I suppose you're anxious to get some shut-eye, so you can go home . . . Wait a minute. . . ."

Miss Withers whispered a suggestion and the Inspector nodded. "Oh, before you go off duty, Sergeant, I want you to do something for me. Go upstairs to the front room on the third floor and have a look at the pillows. That's all . . . and phone me back here at Headquarters."

He put down the phone. "Damn the luck! So Lew Stait has slipped out of our fingers, huh? Right when we were beginning to get something on him. Well, he won't get far. We'll have him dragged back, if he took a train or a boat or even went by air. Even if he's out of our jurisdiction there's no trouble getting extradition for murder. . . ."

"It's not so easy to manage it in all cases," Miss Withers put forward drily. "Didn't Hubert say something about all men of the Stait family being marked for death? How is the extradition from the next world, Oscar?"

"You mean—you think he's been killed?"

She shrugged her shoulders. "If it could happen to one twin it could happen to the other. They always shared share and share alike, you know."

Inspector Piper nodded heavily. "But that screws everything up. If Lew Stait wasn't in that house last night, and I'm pretty sure that Taylor is telling the truth when he says Lew wasn't, then who opened the door of Hubert's room and tossed the cutlery at him? He didn't like to say so, but he was sure it was Lew."

Miss Withers nodded. "Have you considered this, Oscar? Hubert is a nervous, over-intellectual type. Suppose he got it into his head that Lew was after him, not knowing that Lew was out of the house all night, and then imagined the whole thing?"

"Imagined the knife, too?"

"He might have picked that up somewhere, to make his delusion seem real. Or perhaps he is just frightened half to death and trying to get something which will impel you to protect him with a detective in the house. A sort of hysteria, perhaps."

"For that matter, somebody might have thrown that knife besides Lew," Piper pointed out. "The old lady, or that tough Dutch cook. . . ." He slapped his knee. "That's it. The cook was used to knives, in the kitchen."

"She peeled potatoes with them, certainly. But did you ever see a cook peel a potato by *throwing* knives at it?" Miss Withers shook her head. "Oscar Piper, there's something here we don't see."

"There's damn little that we do see," said the Inspector, trying vainly to relight his dead cigar. "But the first thing I'm going to do is to send out the alarm for Lew Stait. Can't you see the newspaper headlines if the other twin has been bumped off?" He reached for the telephone, but even as he lifted the receiver it burst into a shrill ringing.

"Hello—Taylor?"

It was.

"Listen, Inspector, I went up and had a look at those pillows the way you asked me."

"Go on, what did you find?"

"Well, the one on the left had a slit, like a razor cut, about three-quarters of an inch long, in both back and front of the linen slip and the pillow itself. There was a nick in the headboard of the bed, too."

The Inspector nodded. "Good, Taylor. Now you can get home. What's that?"

He listened for a moment, and his mouth dropped open with astonishment. "You say it happened when you were upstairs? Well, I'll be . . ."

"What is it, for heaven's sake?" Miss Withers leaned toward him, across the desk. "Tell me, Oscar! Is Lew Stait dead?"

He put down the phone slowly, and looked up at her. "Not exactly, Hildegarde."

"What do you mean—not exactly?"

"He's married," said the Inspector. "Right at this moment he's standing in the front hall of the Stait house, according to the Sergeant, and making the announcement to the family. The girl is with him—they just got back from Greenwich, Connecticut. The girl is—"

"Dana Waverly, of course," interrupted Miss Withers. "Oscar, isn't there a statute in this state which prevents a wife from taking the witness stand against her husband?"

Inspector Piper nodded his head, and his pugnacious lower lip thrust itself forward.

11

'Twas Brillig

The Inspector reached for his hat and overcoat. "Where are you rushing to?" Miss Withers wanted to know. "Going up to Riverside Drive to give the young couple your blessing?"

"I am not." He stopped beside the file case to take down a bound copy of the latest Manhattan telephone book. "Let's see . . . U—V—W . . . here we are. Waverly, B. O.—perfumer. . . . Waverly, Dr. Bruce. . . . Waverly, Charles M.—attorney, 555 Enterprise Trust Building—LAckawanna 4-4333 . . . hmmm. . . . Here we are. Waverly, Miss Dana E., 23 Minetta Lane—SPring something or other. . . ."

He looked up. "I'm off for 23 Minetta Lane," he announced. "Coming, Hildegarde?"

She stared at him without answering.

"Coming?"

She shook her head. "Wait a minute, Oscar. What was the name you read aloud just before you found Dana Waverly's?"

"You mean Charles M. Waverly, the attorney? I know what you're thinking. Yes, it's undoubtedly the family lawyer old Mrs. Stait was talking about—and the next in line of the Stait men. You might make a note of the address. I'll need to see him."

"I did make a note of the address. Enterprise Trust Building, number 555. Doesn't that mean anything to you?"

"Mean anything? What should it mean? . . . Oh, Great Scott! Wasn't it the lobby of the Enterprise Trust Building where Laurie Stait's body was carried by that dumb traffic cop Doody?"

"It was. Still going down to Minetta Lane, Oscar?"

"More than ever," he told her. "If there isn't some connection between Charles Waverly the lawyer and Dana Waverly the new Mrs. Lew Stait, I'll eat my badge, and my buttons too. Lieutenant, phone Swarthout and have him meet me downstairs in a hack. Come on, Hildegarde."

"I'm not coming," Miss Withers informed him. "I've got other plans. First I'm going to go home and do my setting-up exercises, and then I'm going to look in at the rodeo at Madison Square Garden again. I'd like to meet this Buck Keeley, or at least have a look at him. That ought to be an interesting matinée today, particularly if Rose Keeley feels well enough to perform."

"But I thought . . ."

"Never you mind, Oscar Piper. We agreed that we were going to work this case out separately and see which one was right. We might meet this evening and have dinner, if you like. In a sort of armed neutrality, perhaps."

"Right you are. I'll be seeing you."

He was almost at the door when there was the sound of heavy footsteps in the hall outside, and in walked a massive gentleman in blue, with the nightstick and uniform cap of a patrolman in his hand. One eye was puffed and in mourning.

"Dan Kehoe reporting, sor, by permission . . ."

"Kehoe? Reporting for what?" The Inspector was in a hurry. "Out with it."

"It's like this, Inspector. There was a killing on my beat last night, sor." Kehoe swallowed with difficulty. "The Stait fellow that was strangled."

"I know that," the Inspector told him. "So you're the dummy who didn't show up all evening, huh? And why not?"

"That's what I come to tell you about, sor. I reported it to the Captain last night at the precinct station when he bawled me out for not being there on duty. He thought nothing of it at the time, but since then I've been wondering if maybe there wasn't some connection, sor. He told me to report it in person."

"Some connection between what?" The Inspector jammed his hat down on his ears. "I'm in a hurry, Kehoe."

"Yes, sor. A connection between the killing of this Stait fellow and the fight I got in. It was at five-thirty o'clock, sor. And I was coming down Forty-fourth Street near the Avenue when I saw a cab pull up in front of the Hotel Senator. Some fellows got out and started to argue with the driver, Inspector. It was about the fare. And I catch a glimpse of them pulling him out from behind the wheel so he'd be the handier for taking a sock at. So I got up to them and I warn them to stop making a nuisance and I ask the driver if he wants to prefer a charge of disorderly conduct.

And just then one of the roughnecks hauls off and gives me this in the eye, Inspector."

"Well, what did you do? Warn him again?"

"No, sor. I punched him in the jaw. His big hat rolled halfway acrost the street."

"So he had an opera hat on? A swell, huh? And drunk at that hour, too."

"No, sor. Not an opry hat. It was one of them ten-gallon hats that Tom Mix wears in the movies. They all of them had hats like that. And then another guy jumps me, and a third climbs out of the cab and kicks at my shins, and we mix into it pretty hot and heavy. And just as I'm getting my second wind there comes a little guy in a derby out of the hotel and separates us."

"What did he do, throw a pail of water on the whole dogfight of you?"

"No, sor. But he seemed to have some control over the cowboys. For that's what they were. He was the manager, he said. And he explained that they weren't really used to taxicabs and such, and that they didn't mean any harm. And he said that if I booked any of the boys on disorderly conduct they'd have to call off the rodeo, and half the kids in town would be disappointed. So I let 'em go, and he gave me some box seats for the show, and that was all. Nice fellow he was, name of Carrigan. Then I reported back to the station house, and explained to the Captain why I didn't know about the killing on my own beat, Inspector. Only last night I got to wondering."

"About what?"

"Well, the boys said that this Stait was killed with a rope, and those cowboys are good with ropes. I've seen 'em before. It seemed funny, things happening all at the same time like that."

"Very good, Kehoe. Now you can stop wondering, and let us do that. If you were involved in an emergency call on your beat, there's no reason why you need to fear any disrating for missing the killing. You can go."

The big patrolman turned a blue back.

"Oh, Kehoe. You might keep your mouth shut about this."

"Yes, sor. 'Sealed-lips Kehoe,' they calls me." He saluted, a broad smile on his face and his good eye twinkling. Then he was gone.

Miss Withers wanted to know what the Inspector thought of that. He admitted that he didn't think much of anything of it.

"If Buck Keeley was one of the cowboys who got in a brush with Kehoe, then he didn't bump off Laurie Stait, and if he wasn't, well—what does the brawl mean?"

"You go on down to Minetta Lane and let me worry over what it means," Miss Withers told him.

But she spent the next couple of hours, as it happened, in an entirely different pursuit—one which would have surprised the Inspector considerably if he could have seen her, though he was not easily surprised.

The Inspector came down the stone steps outside Headquarters and looked up the street and down for signs of the operative who was supposed to be waiting for him here.

"Hey, Swarthout!"

A ruddy, boyish face presented itself above the spare tire of a waiting Yellow. "Yes, Inspector?"

"Come on, snap out of it!" The driver of the Yellow climbed swiftly behind the wheel, and the Inspector climbed in beside his youngest operative.

The young man offered his chief a cigarette, unsuccessfully. "Didn't see you coming," he admitted.

Piper gave the driver the Minetta Lane address. "What were you doing behind this cab when I came down?"

Swarthout looked innocent. "Nothing, Inspector. Nothing but passing the time away." There was the slightest accent on the word "passing."

"Oh, yeah? You're a fine example to the public, Swarthout. The crap-shooting detective, huh? Gambling in public!"

Swarthout took a pair of pink cubes from his pocket and rattled them lovingly. "I don't mind telling you in confidence, Inspector, that with these dice there isn't any gambling in it at all. I found 'em on Tony the Wop last week, and they take the chance out of games of chance. By the way, what are we doing down in Greenwich Village—attending a drag?"

Piper grunted. "I want to have a little look at a girl's apartment down there," he admitted. "I sent for you because you're handy with tools, and we may have to break into the place. Besides, you don't look as much like a stage dick as most of the boys, and I want to keep this little visit quiet, see?"

"Right, Inspector." Georgie Swarthout patted his little pocket kit of tools. He was one of the few men attached to Headquarters who had not risen from the police ranks, but had been taken on during the past spring when a new Commissioner had started a campaign for "higher education" in the cohorts of the city's defenders. Most of the "college cops" had not lasted as long as the shine of their first brass buttons, but because he looked and acted so much like anything in the world except a detective, this one had made something of a niche for himself. The Inspector disapproved of him and liked him.

"You know, Angel-face, I love the Village less than any other section of this town," the Inspector confessed as they rolled around a corner. "I'll never forget a night when we had to call out the reserves. I was a Precinct Captain then. The usual complaints of a noisy party came in, but this wasn't the usual party. The people in a basement apartment on Bedford Street complained that their ceiling was coming down.

"Well, as it turned out later a crazy poet above them was throwing a lease-breaking party. As a climax some of the boys had kidnapped a milkman's horse and somehow led it up four steps and into the ground-floor living room. When we got there they'd all ducked out, and all we picked up was a lonesome white horse surrounded by empty gin bottles."

They had no difficulty in finding the building. It stood out among the tumbledown houses of the Lane like a buyer's order on a broker's desk. There were flowerboxes outside the front windows, empty now, but sure to blossom with red geraniums as soon as April brought the flower hucksters to the street.

In the lobby was a set of push-buttons, with one at the bottom labeled "Supt.—out of order."

The Inspector ran his thumb down the line of cards in brackets. There it was. "Third floor front—Miss Dana Waverly." Above the engraved name "Waverly" had been neatly lettered with a fountain pen the addition "B. Doolittle."

So Dana Waverly had a roommate, huh? Well, that either simplified or complicated things. Piper knew that there might be difficulties in getting the janitor to let him roam through the place. After all, they had no search warrant with them. He pressed hard on the bell opposite "Third floor front."

Nothing happened. Evidently not even the roommate was in. There was still a trick or two up his sleeve. Waving Swarthout away from the lock of the inner door, Piper jammed his thumb against every doorbell in the house. There'd be somebody home in one apartment or another. There was. The inner door clicked alarmingly, and Swarthout caught it, opened it a few inches, and shot the night lock. Then the two of them marched out of the building, allowed time enough for whoever had answered the ring to give up waiting for the unexpected visitor, and then returned. With no hesitation the Inspector led the way through the unlocked door, up the two flights of stairs, and then along the corridor to the third floor front. Nobody was in the hall.

The lock, unfortunately, was of the Yale variety. The Inspector searched the mantel and under the carpet, as a matter of form, but there was no key parked anywhere. "Do your stuff, kid," he ordered.

The young operative became deadly serious as he went over the lock. His hands made a few deft motions, involving the use of a long coiled spring, a screwdriver, and the blade of a knife. Then he placed his shoulder against one side of the doorframe, his right foot against the other, and pressed inward.

There was a sharp click, and then the door opened. Swarthout looked at his wristwatch. "One minute and forty-five seconds," he announced. "I wish the professor who flunked me in mechanical engineering could have seen that."

The lock was scarred, but a few turns of a screwdriver tightened it again and made what had happened fairly unnoticeable. The Inspector had a look round the room. This was not, he realized, the typical Greenwich Village apartment.

In the first place, there were a good many comfortable places to sit down. Between the front windows was a large radio-gramophone combination, and against one wall appeared an antique chest of drawers that was out of the ordinary. The floor was covered with gay rag rugs.

The general effect was one of moderate luxury. Small cases scattered here and there held a good many books.

"Quite a library," suggested Swarthout. The Inspector joined him in front of one of the shelves.

"I don't object to books in themselves," said Piper. "But I wish you'd tell me sometime the excuse for all this poetry."

Swarthout held no brief for poetry himself, not having read any since he had waded through a semester of required English Lit. But he felt it necessary to uphold the cause of verse on account of the academic background for which he was kidded so unmercifully by his fellow detectives.

"Here's something you'd go for, Inspector." He drew from the shelf a worn copy of *Alice in Wonderland*. The title page, he noted, was inscribed "To Dana from Lew and Laurie, Christmas 1921. . . ."

He fanned the pages. "Get a load of this. . . . ''Twas brillig, and the slithy toves did gyre and gimble in the wabe—all mimsy were the borogoves. . . .' "

"Thanks. I'll stick to Zane Grey and W. Clark Russell for my reading," Piper told him. "That door there leads to the kitchenette, I see. You hop in and have a look at the place. Sometimes you can learn a lot about people from their kitchens. You might make an inventory of the icebox. I'll go through the bedroom."

"Right, Inspector." The younger man disappeared through the nearer of the two doors in the rear wall of the room, and the Inspector chose the other. Somewhat to his surprise he found himself in a large combined dressing room and bath. This told him nothing except that Dana Waverly or her roommate had used Fracy's lavender soap, and that a large number of clean towels had been recently hung on the racks.

A door at the farther end of the bath led into the bedroom proper—or improper, if you like. There were too many gimcracks here for the Inspector's taste. Three ridiculous French dolls watched him gravely from the pillows, and everything seemed covered with taffeta. A single bed, a vanity table, a chest of sweet-smelling cedar, and three chintz chairs made up the furnishings of the room. It was not hard to figure that this was occupied by only one person. Probably Dana Waverly slept here and her roommate used the day bed in the living room, Piper guessed.

He crossed at once to the vanity table, avoiding his own image in the myriad mirrors and bending over the drawers. Here were an unholy number of creams and powders, all of exquisite makes and manufacture. But there were no letters, none of the personal and revelatory material that he desired.

He went on swiftly through the drawers, now and then jabbing his fingers on a hairpin. He wasn't quite sure what he was looking for anyway, but it was a cinch that he wasn't finding it.

There were two cupboards opening into the room. The first contained four dresses of the type known as "useful all-round," a pair of galoshes, a pair of rubbers, an evening dress of somewhat flighty taffeta trimmed with what the Inspector called "jittery ribbons," two hats, both well rained upon, and on a floor was a strange object which the Inspector realized, upon closer inspection, was a reducing girdle.

There was, strangely enough, no baggage of any kind in the cupboard or on the shelves.

The next cupboard was a different story. A whiff of mingled perfume, sachet, and good leather struck the Inspector's delicate nose as he opened the door. The rod was jammed with dresses—light dresses and dark dresses—silks and satins and lace and everything else under the sun. The floor was littered with shoes, and more shoes hung everywhere on the inside of the door.

The shelf held a Boston bag, two overnight bags, and a suitcase—all empty. This, the Inspector decided, was Dana Waverly's cupboard, and the other must be that of Miss "B. Doolittle."

It was then that the Inspector noticed the black leather bag which lay half concealed by a heap of shoes. Someone had been through this cupboard in a hurry, Piper decided. Unless this young lady believed in putting her belongings away by throwing them up in the air and letting them fall.

The bag was almost empty, or seemed so on first sight. There was a crumpled package of Camels, a leather lighter without any wick in it, seven pennies, and a Geranium lipstick, well past its prime.

The Inspector was about to cast it aside as impertinent to his search when he heard something crackle in the lining. There was another pocket, a narrow compartment, just wide enough for a letter or two.

The white corner of an envelope showed . . . an envelope which, when finally held in the Inspector's thumb and finger, showed itself as a little less white than when it had come from the stationer's.

For the second time in this case someone had carried an envelope around until it showed signs of wear and tear.

12

Stale Sidecars

But this was no letter. There was no address on the envelope, and it was heavily lined and lightly scented. One of Dana's own, the Inspector guessed.

When he had learned everything that was to be learned from the envelope, he lifted the unsealed flap and drew out the contents.

It was a photograph, a postcard size snapshot, amateurishly printed. The subjects were a young man who bore an uncanny resemblance to Lew Stait and a large collie dog still in the gawkiness of puppyhood. The young man—it must have been Laurie Stait because of the mountains in the background—was holding a stick high in the air, and the dog was caught in the act of hurling himself after it.

"A nice pup, that," observed the Inspector. Then he reversed the picture. On the other side, in somewhat erratic typescript, was this message:

> *You asked for a picture of me, Dana darling, so here it is. The dog is Rowdy, and he has adopted me. He belongs to the ranch, but it will be tough to leave him when I come back. Love—Laurie.*

The Inspector scratched his head. First a letter from Dana to Laurie at the ranch, declaring her love. Then this picture, which evidently Dana Waverly had carried about with her for months, concealed in the envelope. Somehow, this did not fit in with Dana's marrying Lew, even if she had been engaged to him for years. With Laurie dead, did she try to find him in the twin who was so like him, or was there a darker significance?

The Inspector put the photograph back in the envelope, and the envelope into his pocket. No telling what use he could put it to later. It might be revealing to confront Dana Waverly—Dana Stait now—with it.

The Inspector gave a look round the bedroom. Nothing more here, at any rate. For that matter, there was no sign that anyone had slept here in this apartment last night, although he realized that an efficient maid could have made it look that way. The fresh towels in the bathroom gave evidence of some sort of maid service. They were folded too neatly, and hung too beautifully—and uselessly—on the racks to have been put there by the two tenants of the place.

Inspector Piper came back into the living room and proceeded to ignite a cigar with leisurely puffs, at the flame of a table lighter in the shape of a silver cannon ball.

At that moment the hall door opened quickly and a large tan suitcase entered, followed by a somewhat largish girl in a Eugenie hat and a coonskin coat.

As her eyes met the Inspector's she dropped the tan suitcase, and her mouth opened like the gaping rent of an earthquake, displaying a great deal of teeth.

The scream, which was meant to be something notable in the way of noise, "died a-borning," as Miss Withers would have said. The Inspector beat her to it with a swift "How do you do, Miss Doolittle!"

"I—I'm Bertha Doolittle. But what are you-all doing here? Where's Dana? How did you know my name?"

"It is the business of the police to know everything," the Inspector told her. At the same moment he displayed his shield.

Well, he had to think quickly. He had no more business in the apartment than a sneak thief, and he knew it.

Miss Doolittle had covered all of her teeth except the two front incisors, which glittered with an unpleasant whiteness at the Inspector.

"Your apartment, young lady," he said swiftly, "your apartment has been—er—burgled. Fortunately, nothing of value seems to be missing." He pointed out to her the faint scratches on the door jamb which Georgie Swarthout's tools had made.

"We were just having a look round," the Inspector explained. "It seems that the prowlers were frightened away before they could do any damage."

Miss Doolittle did not seem entirely satisfied with his explanation. "But where's Dana? She was heah when I left yesterday morning to spend the week with some kinfolks of mine on Long Island . . . tell me, did anything happen to Dana?"

"Yes and no," said the Inspector. "Tell me, what brought you back so soon, Miss Doolittle, if you intended to stay away a week?"

The girl opened her purse and took out a clipping. From where he stood the Inspector could make out the usual headlines. It was the story of the murder of Laurie Stait on the previous evening. "Strangler Still at Large" declared the headline.

"And just why did that clipping bring you back?"

"You-all just don't understand," declared Miss Doolittle in a Dixie accent that struck the Inspector as being laid on with a trowel. "Dana is ma roommate, and she's such a sweet child she needs somebody to take care of her. And a dreadful thing like this happenin' to her! Why, *Laurie*—not Lew—Stait was the man she loved, though she was engaged to his brother. The families arranged that, you know. His grandmother and Dana's brother Charlie, a no-good if I ever saw one. He's just white trash, that's all, even if he is Dana's brother. They thought a good deal of each other, though. I expect that's where Dana is right now, she's with Charlie. . . ."

The Inspector nodded as if all this did not interest him vitally. "So Dana Waverly loved Laurie Stait, huh?"

"Oh yes, suh. But she didn't love Lew. Those twins were as like as two peas, but after she got to know 'em both she loved Laurie. All the family were down on him, and I'll bet you that they're glad he's daid. But all the same, he was the best of the two."

"I see. Did Dana break her engagement to Lew Stait?"

"I don' think so. No, I know she didn't. But she tol' me when I went away yesterday morning that by the time I got back she'd have some news for me. Lew was comin' to dinner last night. I think she meant that after dinner she was going to muster up her courage and tell him that it was just no use waitin' around. She hated to give back that diamond, too. Such a beauty that ring was!"

Suddenly the girl was galvanized into action. "I wonder if she did give it back! Or maybe the sneak-thieves got it when they broke in here. Wait a minute!"

She ran toward the bedroom, the Inspector close behind. What had happened to Swarthout he could not guess, but the boy was not in evidence. Probably he had caught a flash of the teeth, and decided to stay out of it.

Miss Doolittle was down on the floor in Dana Waverly's cupboard. "She never wears the ring, you know. Except when she sees Lew, and that's been getting less and less often lately. We've got a little hiding place—"

As she spoke she put her hand on a silver slipper slightly more battered than the rest. Her fingers seized upon a wad of tissue paper jammed into the toe. Inside the toe was a string of near-pearls, a class ring marked, "Savannah High School 1922," and a small blue box. Inside the box was a diamond of moderate size and more than moderate perfection, glittering and unflawed.

"They *didn't* find it," said Bertha Doolittle with a certain satisfaction. "It was my idea that we hide our jewelry this way. Nobody would think of looking here."

"Quite right," agreed the Inspector. "All the same it's strange that the ring is here now. Particularly since Lew Stait gave it, as you say, to Dana Waverly some time ago. It's strange, don't you think, that she didn't wear it to be married in?"

The teeth came out again, and the Dixie accent went out of her speech. "Wha-a-a-a-a-t? Dana married?"

"This morning, in Greenwich," Piper said quietly. "To Lew Stait. Very romantic, what? An elopement and all that sort of thing—special license and so forth. And with Laurie Stait, the man you say she loved, not yet thoroughly chilled out down on his marble slab."

Bertha Doolittle sat down in one of the chintz chairs, hard. "I don't believe it," she insisted.

"Why not?"

"Roommates get to know each other pretty well. Dana used to tell me everything and I told her everything. And I tell you, I know that she didn't have the slightest idea of ever marrying Lew Stait as long as she lived. She loved Laurie and he loved her, and I guess I ought to know. I've gone out to enough movies so they could be alone here together." There was a shade of bitterness in Miss Doolittle's voice at this point. The Inspector guessed that Bertha's trips to the movies had not been entirely her own idea.

"Charlie Waverly wanted his sister to marry Lew Stait, and so did Lew's grandmother. But I tell you this right now, if Dana married Lew this morning she did it at the point of a gun! She didn't love him."

"There's other reasons for marrying than love," the Inspector observed. "But right now I can't think of any reason for leaving off your engagement ring when you are married. It's supposed to be bad luck or something, isn't it?"

Bertha Doolittle was of the opinion that he was right. "Maybe she forgot it," she suggested. "No, Dana wouldn't forget it. She's not like that." She shook her head again.

"Mister Policeman, I tell you this right now. I'll never believe that Dana Waverly married a poor white trash like Lew Stait, not if she tells me so herself. Unless she was drunk or drugged. Why, it was only last week that she heard indirectly about Lew's being seen kissing the maid up at his home. Charlie Waverly tried to make light of it, and Cousin Hubert—he's a nice chap, but very deep—Cousin Hubert told Dana that it must have been a mistake, and Laurie instead of Lew that somebody saw. Which made it all the worse, you see, because she really didn't care a hang what foolishness Lew was up to, but she did love Laurie."

"Tell me this," said the Inspector. "Were Lew and Laurie really so much alike?"

"Alike? I never could tell which was which, even when I saw them together!"

"But Dana, could she tell them apart?"

Bertha Doolittle was thoughtful. "If anybody could, Dana could," she said slowly. "They looked awfully alike, and they acted alike on the surface. But in spite of the great closeness between them, they were absolutely different underneath. What they thought, I mean. Lew was gay and loud and always taking what he wanted, and Laurie was shy and willing to take the blame for most of the things that Lew did. He was like that."

"I see." The Inspector tossed his cigar out of the open window into the flowerbox. "Well, Miss Doolittle, you've been a great help. I'm glad that nothing is missing in the apartment."

At that moment there was a tremendous crash in the kitchenette. Bertha Doolittle seized a pair of nail scissors and charged through the door. "There's the sneak-thief now! Come on, policeman, don't let him get away!"

The Inspector came on, quickly enough to save young Swarthout from complete annihilation. He explained that this was one of his assistants.

"Well, I'd like to know what he's been doing in the kitchenette all this time," insisted Bertha Doolittle belligerently.

The Inspector nodded. "I'm inclined to see your point of view. I've been too busy chatting with you to notice the passage of time, but now that you bring it up, I too wonder what he's been doing." He faced the "college cop" inquiringly. Swarthout stood half sheltered by the swinging door of the kichenette, ready to duck out of range if Bertha showed any signs of opening fire with the scissors.

"By the way, Georgie, what in hell have you been doing there in that kitchenette for half an hour?"

With an air of terribly injured dignity, Georgie Swarthout produced a notebook. "Inspector, you yourself told me to make an inventory of the contents of the icebox. You said—"

"Never mind what I said." The Inspector took the notebook impatiently. "I still don't see why it took you this long. . . ."

His voice died away, and his lower lip slid forward alarmingly. This was the inventory that met his eye, begun in Swarthout's neat script:

One quart of milk, unopened.
Two avocado pear salads, with dressing, untouched.
Two cup custards with strawberries.
Two baked potatoes (cold).
One pound of butter, with two butter balls beside it.
Four lamb chops, uncooked.
One shaker full of cocktails. . . .

As an afterthought, the words "*Sidecars—stale*" appeared after the last item. An addition had been made to the line—the word *three-quarters* inserted neatly after *shaker,* and before *full.*

Evidently the urge for absolute scientific accuracy had smitten the operative, for the word *three-quarters* had itself been struck out, and *half* written in above it, in a script that was no longer neat, but somewhat wavering.

Across the bottom of the page, in letters half an inch high, wobbly as the trail of a seasick serpent, appeared the final notation—"*Not so very stale. . . .*"

13

Gray Goose Feathers

It was almost two-thirty that afternoon when Miss Withers stopped her experiment for the time being, and hurriedly snatched up her overcoat and hat. She had been so engrossed in what she had been doing, or trying to do, that she had forgotten the passage of time, and leaving the apartment on West 76th Street she hailed the first south-bound taxicab which came along. The apartment could stay as it was until she got back, and if the two other teachers who shared it with her didn't like the looks of it now, they could straighten up for themselves. She had bigger plans afoot, plans which necessitated the opera glasses which she gripped firmly in her hand.

For the second time that day she strode in at the main entrance of Madison Square Garden. The same newspapers blared their headlines at her, reworded from the forenoon editions but still announcing that the strangler was "at large." Indeed, the *American* went so far as to suggest that "STRANGLER TERRORIZES CITY," which seemed to Miss Withers something of an overstatement. Hubert Stait seemed about the only person terrorized so far.

The two cats still hovered aimlessly about the door of the little Coffee Potte, but they were spending more time and energy dodging the footsteps of the crowd of passersby than had been required of them that morning. The ticket kiosk in the center of the foyer was open now, and there was a line before it. Miss Withers made no effort to get in on the weight of her official connection, whatever that might be, but put down her dollar fifty for a box seat, and passed through the big doors that a janitor had left on the latch that morning. She was relieved of half her ticket and sent round the bowl to a distant aisle.

The Garden was about half full of spectators, a good matinée crowd in this year of A.D.—Awful Depression, as the Inspector called it.

Directly across the circus-like area of tanbark Miss Withers could see a line of high, boarded pens. Around the gateways of these pens a number of young men were moving busily. Most of them wore large Stetson hats, of the type known as two-gallon, handkerchiefs around their necks, and each displayed trousers strangely fabricated of sheepskin, with the wool left on and the seat left out.

Suddenly loudspeakers all over the vast auditorium announced the fact that the next event on the program would be an exhibition of fancy shooting—"Executed, ladeez an' gemmun, by Mr. Laramie White with the assistance of the brave and fearless Miss Rose Keeley. I thank you. . . ."

It was the voice of the manager, Carrigan, Miss Withers realized as she saw him step away from a microphone located near the north barrier. He had replaced his derby with one of the inevitable Stetsons, she noticed. And then two huskies came running out with the dark screen background which she and the Inspector had noticed that morning, setting it up carefully under the floodlights and bracing the back so that it couldn't tip over under the shock of the punishment it was about to take.

The two men ran back toward the barrier, and at the same moment a door in one of the high board pens opened, and a girl rode out on a white horse.

The crowd demonstrated its approval by a smattering of applause. She was dressed all in silver-white, from the wide-brimmed hat to the high-heeled boots. Her low-bosomed shirt was of white satin, worked with designs in blue. A white leather belt, dotted with extra cartridges and weighted with a blue and gold-worked holster from which a pearl-handled gun protruded, held up her white silk trousers and the snow-white chaps which covered most of them.

The big white horse came out with its head held high, prancing and mincing, and lifting its feet high above the tanbark at every step. As the applause died away, the girl lifted her Stetson, displaying a mass of light blonde hair, and bowed to her public.

It was Rose Keeley, sure enough. But Miss Withers hardly recognized her. The daring costume had changed her—but more than that, the girl's face seemed strangely paler than it had looked that morning. It might have been the dead white of her dress, but all the same Miss Withers started wondering. It was her business to wonder.

The white horse took up his stand, as if he, at least, knew his business, directly in front of the background drop, and stood steady as a rock. Rose Keeley, in the saddle, brought out a cigarette, displayed it to the crowd, and struck a match.

Only Miss Withers, because of the powerful glasses before her eyes, and the word of argument which she had overheard that morning, distinguished the fact that Rose Keeley did not draw that cigarette from the pack which she held in her other hand, but slipped it out of her palm as if it were thin and breakable glass.

Only Miss Withers noticed that the business of lighting it was a clever fake, and that no smoke came from the girl's pale lips.

Rose Keeley raised her hand, and the crowd was silent. Then suddenly one of the gates across the area was opened, and there danced into the ring a fat little red and white horse whose colors seemed to have been put on by the accidental crash of a painter's ladder. He bucked once or twice, as if to reassure himself that his rider was able to stick on in all kinds of weather, and then suddenly bunched himself up and set out down the tanbark at a full gallop.

The rider, a lean and lanky young man, gripped the reins loosely, and round his right forefinger he spun a heavy Colt.

The little red and white horse ran as if he had a personal grudge against the ground which bumped his heels—all the same his gait steadied as he passed the white horse and rider at a range of some hundred feet.

The Colt spat noisily in the hand of the lanky young man. But Miss Withers had her glasses trained on the blonde Valkyrie who waited, like a silver statue. Therefore she saw the short jerk of the girl's other arm which, at the end of the connecting thread which Miss Withers could only guess must have been there, tore the largest part of the dummy cigarette from between her pale lips.

The bit of white paper fluttered to the ground, and Rose Keeley leaped down from her steed and displayed the fraction of an inch of butt which remained.

The crowd roared its approval, whether of the stunt itself, or of the somewhat voluptuous figure displayed, Miss Withers could only guess. Rose Keeley ran a good bit to bosom and hips, and the tight silk shirt and the somewhat sketchy chaps did not bury her light under a bushel.

Laramie White was standing beside her, his Stetson waving in the air. Miss Withers turned the glasses on him, and saw that he had replaced the plaster over his eye with a narrow bit of flesh-tint adhesive tape. She also saw something else.

As the two turned to each other, on their second bow, and shook hands, Miss Withers noticed to her astonishment an interchange of looks between them which, in her own words, was enough to blister an andiron.

There was hearty dislike in Laramie's eyes, and something more that Miss Withers could not understand. But it needed no mind reader to see what Rose Keeley thought of her partner. If he had been a particularly noxious rattlesnake she could not have flashed contempt, hatred, and disgust any more clearly . . . for that second. Then they faced the crowd again, and Rose Keeley's lips were curved in a wooden smile.

The number was continued with Laramie's blazing away at some colored glass balls which the girl tossed in a continuous parabola before the bulletproof screen, and here the cowboy's shooting must have been better, for he managed to explode four out of five of them.

But Miss Withers did not remain in her seat to watch the second half of the event. Next on the program, she saw by the bill in her hand, was "Roping a three-horse team in full gallop—Mr. Buck Keeley."

For some reason or other, Miss Withers wanted very much to get a close view of this Buck Keeley. There were still a few seats vacant in the boxes at the other side of the area. By a judicious combination of bullying and bribing, she managed to plant herself in a seat at the very ringside edge of the barrier, almost within reaching distance of the end pen. From its direction came the strong smell of horse, together with a muffled oath or two, and the rattle of shod heels against timber.

One of the two handymen who had carried the backdrop for the shooting event now appeared on the scene bearing a big silver-mounted saddle on his shoulder and a couple of coiled ropes under his arm. He entered the end pen, and immediately reappeared.

Laramie White and the girl had already made their exit, and the manager was approaching the loud-speaker again. "Ladeez and gemmun, the next event . . ."

The handyman dropped the saddle and the ropes and ran along the pens. "Keeley!" he called. "Hey, Buck! Here's yer props, come saddle yer hoss. . . ."

Somebody else took up the cry. . . . "Where's Keeley?" Cowboys appeared in the exit ways, and sombreros were shoved up above the tops of the pens. "Buck! Time to get on!"

They kept up the cry for a few minutes, and then a messenger ran toward where Carrigan was still orating into the microphone.

In a moment his voice was booming again through the vast auditorium, informing the assembled devotees of sport that a slight readjustment of the program had been found necessary, and that instead of fancy roping by Mr. Buck Keeley, the next event would be a roping contest, involving another artist and a wild yearling steer.

But Miss Withers did not remain to observe the subjugation of the wild yearling steer, who was already bellowing in one of the farther pens. She was making a fast sneak for the exit, with a shapeless something bundled beneath her coat.

Perhaps Mr. Buck Keeley had done his last job of fancy roping. But tucked to her bosom the schoolteacher held the lariat which he was to have used—the lariat which the handyman had dropped beside the saddle in amazement at not finding Keeley in the pen with his horse.

Once more her cotton umbrella had stood Miss Withers in good stead, for the crooked handle had been just long enough to snag a loop of the rope. The saddle did not matter, she had seen one like it before, decorated with the same silver mountings and blue working. It had been hanging on the wall of the room shared by Lew and Laurie Stait.

She thought that she had seen a facsimile of the lariat, too. But that had not been in the room shared by Lew and Laurie . . . it had been wound firmly round the neck of a fair-haired young man who had leaped backwards into the air one evening at dusk . . . and had thereafter lain still. Laurie Stait had worn a rope like this for a cravat.

There was the same kind of running knot here as in the death noose, and somewhat similar blue thread binding the other end to keep it from fraying. Perhaps it didn't mean anything. But Miss Withers was wondering.

All the way up to Seventy-sixth Street she wondered. There wasn't any sense in going ahead with this case until they knew how Laurie Stait had been killed. In spite of the medical examiner's report after listening to the Inspector's coaching, there was no real evidence here that a murder had been committed. If it was a murder, *How?*—not *Who?*—was the first question to ask.

Could an especially prepared noose have been dropped over the victim's head as his car passed another, bound in the opposite direction? Perhaps. Only it would take a true expert to drop a noose with such deadly accuracy. And there were circumstances here which made Miss Withers wonder if that were possible.

Besides, if the noose had been hurled from another car, why would the dead or dying man have been seen by the one observer to leap *up* in the air before falling to the pavement? Miss Withers resolved to refer once more to her early notes on the testimony of the little taxidriver, Leech.

She had had time to type out only a few of her notes as yet, and the sheets were lying on her desk in her apartment.

She unlocked the door with her own key, and saw Inspector Oscar Piper, taking the privileges of a regular caller, and seated in the one comfortable easy chair of her living room. In his mouth was a fuming perfecto, in his hands were the notes which she had begun to transcribe, and all round him was the sea of feathers which Miss Withers had not had time to clean up before she left.

"Good evening, Hildegarde," he said cheerfully. She tossed the coiled rope which she had stolen into the clothes cupboard, and hoped he had not seen it—yet. There would be time enough for that later.

"Do you know," the Inspector observed with heavy sarcasm as she entered the room, smoothing her hair, "do you know, there's nothing, after all, like a little spick-and-span nest where a man can relax! Hildegarde, do you mind telling me why in the name of all that's holy you choose to carpet your floor with these nasty feathers? I've got feathers in my nose, feathers in my eyes, feathers in my pockets. Have you girls varied the monotony of spinsterhood by having a duel to the death with pillows, or what?"

"I'll show you what," she told him. "I spent three hours today making a little experiment, Oscar Piper. I failed, which in a way I consider success. Now I want you to try it. Here!"

She opened a table drawer and suddenly whipped a gleaming blade out at him.

"I don't suppose you noticed," she said with a certain acidity in her tone, "that the pillows up at the Stait house were all stuffed with the best and softest goose down. Well, I've been trying to throw this knife through one of my own goose pillows that my mother took west with her from Boston before I was born, and I haven't got anywhere."

She indicated a pillow which she had propped up against the wall on a sofa across the room. There were a dozen or so slits in the linen slip, and feathers were spewed everywhere around.

"I'm not a knife thrower," she told the Inspector. "See what you can do."

He hefted the knife carefully, and then took it with the blade gripped firmly between his thumb and first finger. "A wop sergeant once showed me how it's done," he observed. "I'll see if I remember. . . ."

His first try sent the knife whirling beautifully through the air, but only slapped the pillow with the handle instead of the blade. Miss Withers said nothing, but her attitude implied that he was worse at it than she had been herself. He tried again, and this time the blade flew unerringly toward its mark.

Rip it went through the pillow slip, and that was all. For a second it hung in the air against the pillow, and then dropped to the sofa. The Inspector tried again, with the same result.

"Now try it closer," Miss Withers suggested. "Get right in front of it. And if you can pin that pillow to the wall, even at that range, or if you can manage to cut a tiny slit in the back of the pillow, I'll buy a box of cigars and smoke half of them myself."

The Inspector took off his coat and put down his cigar. Then he walked up to within three feet of the pillow and hurled the knife as if into the heart of his deadliest enemy. Once more the weapon penetrated no more than a quarter of an inch, and then dropped back.

Ten minutes later the Inspector gave it up as a bad job. Not even by laying the pillow down flat and stabbing at it with the knife gripped firmly in his hand could he penetrate the feathers.

He wiped the perspiration from his face. "Lord, woman, it's like trying to stab a jellyfish. No resistance, but you don't get anywhere."

She was triumphant. "Exactly. I had an idea it would be this way. That's why I insisted that you lend me the knife that nearly killed Hubert Stait, according to his own story. You see, I've helped stuff pillows, and I know that feathers are both the softest and the most obstinate things in the world. And whatever *did* happen last night in Hubert's room, nobody threw this knife through his pillow, pinning it to the head of the bed!"

"Hmmm," said the Inspector. "But the Sergeant found a slit in the back of the pillow, and a mark on the woodwork of the bed?"

"It's possible that somebody took the knife and slit one of those holes . . . or both of them, for that matter."

They both sat in silence for a moment.

"Now what do you know about that?" the Inspector said softly. "So nice little Hubert up and told us a lie!"

"He told us what looks like a lie," Miss Withers reminded him. "But so have a lot of other people in this case."

14

"Bury Me Not on the Lone Prairee"

"I think I'm on the track at last," the Inspector was saying. He had relaxed in Miss Withers' big armchair, a sandwich in one hand and a glass of milk in the other, in lieu of dinner.

The schoolteacher was attacking the feathers with a whisk broom, and succeeding only in scattering them like thistledown. "On the track of what? Or whom, if you prefer."

"The murderer of Laurie Stait, of course. In spite of all your trouble in proving that poor little Hubert was faking, I don't think that trail leads anywhere. Hubert was at the movie when the murder was committed, with the stupid but estimable Aunt Abbie. But I think I know—"

Miss Withers stopped bustling about with her broom. "You mean?"

"I mean the brother of Dana Waverly, that's who I mean. Charles Waverly, the distant relative and next male heir of the Stait family. He's a lawyer, and therefore in a position to know just what loot there would be in the Stait fortune."

"Lawyers usually have better ways of getting loot than committing murder for it," Miss Withers suggested dryly. "They play safe, as a rule."

"I found out some other things today, though." The Inspector, warmed by food, opened up and told the events which had transpired down in the Village. "Don't you see? Dana was engaged to Lew and she loved Laurie. But her brother was all for her marrying the so-called 'good twin.' Charles Waverly is much older than his sister, and they're orphans, so I suppose he's her natural guardian. Anyway, she had it all set to break the news to Lew Stait after dinner that night—the stuff in the icebox showed that she had planned on a guest—and she didn't look forward to the task as an easy job, because she undoubtedly tipped off her roommate to stay out of town for the weekend, and she'd laid her plans very carefully. What was the natural thing for her to do before making the plunge? See her brother, of course. I'll wager you anything you like that Dana called at Charles' office yesterday afternoon and told him the news."

"Suppose she did?"

"Well, you remember that his office is in the Enterprise Trust Building. It might be just accident that it was outside that building that Laurie Stait got his, but I doubt it. I think that smart lawyer was foolish enough to take things in his own hands. He wanted Dana to marry Lew, perhaps for business reasons. Perhaps he knew that old Mrs. Stait was leaving her money to Lew. We can check that later. Anyway, he hated to see Laurie Stait supplant the other twin in his sister's nuptial couch, and he took steps to see that it didn't happen. By removing Laurie Stait from this scheme of things."

"Perfect," Miss Withers told him icily. "You have a perfect case there against Charles Waverly. Except that you haven't shown how he knew that Laurie Stait was driving by at that particular hour. He might have known that Lew had a date with his sister—but where does Laurie come in?" Miss Withers stopped suddenly. "Tell me, Oscar, has it occurred to you that Lew Stait didn't make any effort to keep his dinner date with Dana the night of the murder? We found him playing around with the maid, you remember, and it was past the dinner hour."

"Maybe she'd called the dinner off?"

"No, she hadn't. Because she phoned, don't you remember, to ask for Lew, last night?"

The Inspector nodded. "Maybe Lew knew what the bad news was going to be and he dodged it. Yet that doesn't fit, somehow, with his marrying the girl early the next morning."

His face brightened. "Well, anyway, I've been thinking it over and I'm going to send a couple of the boys to bring Charlie Waverly in for questioning. I've got a sneaking suspicion that the murder rope was dropped out of his office window."

Miss Withers shook her head. "You're barking up the wrong tree, Oscar. I think I see a glimmer of light, though."

"Yeah? What is it?"

"I'm not telling you yet," she informed him. "But I'll give you a hint. There's something mighty interesting in that little Exhibit A you brought back with you from Dana Waverly's apartment!"

The Inspector was surprised. "You mean the snapshot of Laurie and the collie dog taken last summer on the ranch?"

"Well, not exactly." Miss Withers studied it for a moment. "A nice dog, that. But I was talking about something else. The diamond ring, Oscar. I never heard before of a bride who left her engagement ring at home during the ceremony."

The Inspector reached for the phone. "All the same," he said calmly, "I'm going to pick up this Waverly fellow. Not an arrest, exactly, just bring him in for questioning." He spoke into the mouthpiece. "Spring 3100—all right, sister, have it your own way. Spring *seven* three one hundred. . . ."

Miss Withers sprung her surprise. "While your bloodhounds are out, you'd better have them pick up that wild cowboy Buck Keeley," she suggested. She ducked into the cupboard for a moment, and came out with the rope which she had picked up at the rodeo.

"Keeley? Oh, I don't think he had anything to do with the murder." And then the Inspector saw what she held in her hand. She told him where and how she had found it.

"Don't forget," she said, "that members of the Stait family testified that Laurie had been worried and upset since Monday, and that he had answered the phone himself and had denied himself to callers—everybody. Doesn't it seem a coincidence that—"

"That the rodeo opened here in town on Monday? Good Lord, maybe you're right. Laurie Stait might have been threatened by Keeley. Maybe they had a fight out at the ranch this summer." He gave rapid orders into the mouthpiece.

"Maybe they did have a fight," Miss Withers agreed. "I've got a hunch what it was about, too. Wasn't Laurie Stait supposed to be loose with women—and wasn't Rose Keeley out there?"

"That beautiful iceberg?"

"Maybe she wasn't an iceberg last summer," Miss Withers insinuated. "Remember, Laurie got some letters from Wyoming after he returned to New York. And his brother testified that Laurie had been sitting alone in their room and staring at a brick wall across the court."

"Scared or worried, huh? I'll just bet you that Keeley had been threatening him. Well, we'll soon find out. I sent a couple of the boys over to the Hotel Senator with instructions to pick him up."

Miss Withers nodded absent-mindedly. "Oscar, do you happen to remember just what that little taxidriver said he saw on Fifth Avenue last night—you know, the eyewitness? I've been trying to think."

"Sure I remember," Piper told her. "He said that there wasn't any driver in the Chrysler. And he went on to explain that although the weather was pretty thick with snow and everything, he saw somebody jump out of the roadster, backwards!"

She shook her head. "There was something else. I didn't take it down in shorthand because I didn't think it was important. But we can't get any farther in this case until we know how Laurie Stait was killed. Oscar, you're supposed to have the trained memory. Didn't Leech say something else, something important?"

The Inspector shook his head. "I don't remember anything. Oh yes, he did say something about seeing the figure of a man rise right up out of the seat, with both arms flopping, like a scared frog jumping out of a puddle. He said it looked as if the fellow was trying to grab the side of a bus that was passing. . . ."

"Eureka!" shouted Miss Withers. "Now I know how the murder was committed. It wasn't from a window of the Enterprise Trust. I'll bet that Charlie Waverly's offices are in the rear somewhere. Anyway, it couldn't happen from a window, nor from a rodeo parade, because there wasn't any . . . nor from a car passing in the opposite direction, because the body would not have been pulled up out of the seat that way, at least not high enough so that it looked like a backward leap." She was flushed with excitement.

"It was the bus I was trying to think of! The top of a bus is the only place from which that murder could have been committed."

The Inspector stared at her. "But my dear lady, it's . . ."

"It's not impossible, I tell you." She snatched up a pencil and a sheet of typewriter paper. "It's as clear as daylight, Oscar Piper. Wait until I sketch it for you. . . ."

The Inspector studied it at length. "You see? I put in the rope, to make it clearer, although of course Leech wouldn't notice it. The rope was light in color, remember, and it would blend with the snow. The murderer dropped it over Laurie Stait's head as the bus going north passed the southbound roadster. The motion of the two cars was enough to jerk the victim out of his seat and into the air to crash on the pavement. It must have been a man, too, because it would take a lot of strength to withstand the shock."

"Not if the murderer took a hitch of the rope's end around the edge of the bus rail," pointed out the Inspector. "He could let go of the rope when his job was done, and let the body lie there in traffic while he sailed north on the bus top! Good lord, woman, you've got it! We may be able to trace the murderer through the Fifth Avenue bus company. Although heaven knows there were probably fifty buses through that street at approximately five-thirty!"

"Look for an open bus," Miss Withers suggested.

"Why open? The murderer could have dropped his noose out of a side window just as well."

She shook her head. "If it had been a roofed bus, there'd have been other people up on the bus top, and the murderer would have run too great a risk. He—or she, for it could have been a woman, you know—undoubtedly chose an open top bus. They still run some of them at this time of year, although there's few enough people who venture up there in a snowstorm. The murderer counted on that, you see."

The Inspector pursed his lips. "We'll find the conductor of that bus. He must have collected the fare from that passenger, whoever he was."

"Not necessarily. If the murderer was as smart as I think, he slipped aboard the bus when the conductor was collecting fares inside, and sneaked up the stairs. Ten to one the conductor wouldn't think it likely that anyone was up on top in that snowstorm."

"Maybe you're right, Hildegarde. But it's something to work with, anyway. I'll start the wheels rolling first thing in the morning. I'll have Taylor or one of the boys interview every driver who had an open bus on the street at that hour. Maybe they did see something, after all."

He was rudely interrupted by the shrill clatter of Miss Withers' phone. It was Lieutenant Keller calling the Inspector, who listened for a moment, his brows narrowing.

"What? What's that? When did he go? Who? Oh, never mind about the dame. Start the dragnet working. Broadcast his description to all outgoing ships. Cover all exits to the city and don't forget the flying fields. Right."

He hung up the phone a bit wearily. "What happened, Oscar? Did the smart Mr. Charles Waverly give you the slip?" Miss Withers moved closer.

Piper shook his head. "Who? No, they found him all right, and he is on his way down to Headquarters now. But your cowboy friend, Buck Keeley, has blew the town." The Inspector made a vague gesture.

"Lieutenant Keller says that they went busting up to the Hotel Senator and found only Buck's sister, Rose. And when she heard who they were, she flopped in a faint!"

Miss Withers' eyebrows showed surprise. "Oscar, has it occurred to you that Rose Keeley isn't the blushing violet type? She's been fainting a good deal oftener than seems natural to me, unless—"

The Inspector suddenly interrupted.

"I've got it! At last we've discovered a decent motive! They called Laurie Stait the bad twin, didn't they? He was supposed to be a bit on the make with the fair sex? Well, he and this Rose Keeley got a case on each other out at the ranch this summer. But brother Buck didn't approve of his sister marrying any Eastern playboys, so he broke it up. And then when they left the ranch for the rodeo tour and came to New York, he discovered that his sister was seeing Laurie again here, and he bumped him off with his own rope from the top of a bus, just like you said. And the sister knows or suspects, only she won't squawk on her brother. That's why she faints so easy!" He looked at the schoolteacher for approval.

Miss Withers surveyed him thoughtfully. "Closer Oscar. But still you don't win a baby doll. Why should Buck Keeley object to his sister marrying an Easterner with money? Surely it would be just the kind of a marriage he would like to arrange."

"You're wrong, Hildegarde. Naturally, Buck Keeley would object to his sister's getting involved with a weak-kneed dude from the city. He'd want her to marry a son of the sagebush."

"Laurie Stait doesn't look so weak-kneed to me. He played football at Columbia, you know. And I think you've been reading too much Zane Grey. People are pretty much alike, east or west. A rancher who tours with a rodeo every winter isn't apt to keep his natural simplicity very long."

"That's all very well. But Buck Keeley lammed, didn't he? He took a runout powder, and that's a pretty good confession of guilt. We'll have him, though, inside of a few hours. Then we'll see what story he tells when the boys put the sweat on him. Maybe he'll have an excuse to offer why his rope got around Laurie Stait's neck, but, believe me, it had better be good." The Inspector rubbed his hands together, and he did not conceal the fact that in his opinion things were picking up.

"Are you going to throw the sister into jail, too?"

He shook his head. "Of course not. We'll just put somebody on the job of tailing her. Maybe the brother will try to get in touch with her, or she'll try to make a break and go to him if he's still in town. Rose Keeley ought to make a good decoy, what?"

Miss Withers started suddenly. "A decoy? Maybe you're right, Oscar. And maybe someone thought of that before. Perhaps she's had practice at the job!"

"Meaning?"

"Meaning whatever you like. There's something here that doesn't meet the eye."

The Inspector laughed. "All right, all right. I know that you're still suspecting Lew Stait of killing his brother. Or maybe you think the human rabbit, Hubert, got up courage enough to do the job? I suppose that Aunt Abbie was his accomplice?"

Miss Withers shook her head. "I didn't say I suspected Hubert, or the surviving twin, either. It doesn't seem likely that a boy could kill his own twin in cold blood, it would be like suicide. But Lew Stait hasn't explained a lot of things. He had no good alibi, in spite of the little maid. He made no effort to keep his date with Dana that night. And why did he hurry so to marry her the next morning? Why did he sneak past me in the hall in the Stait house last night, and why was the letter from Dana to Laurie pinned against the bottom of the kitchen table?"

She got no answer to her questions.

The Inspector was struggling into his coat. "I'll take this rope along with me," he told Miss Withers. "I've got to get down and have my little chat with Charlie Waverly. I may learn something about the Stait family, even if I've changed my mind about the possibility of Waverly's being involved. Want to come along?"

She shook her head. "I'm very tired," she informed him. "Besides, I want to get up early tomorrow and make a little visit to the Stait house."

"What for? Going to congratulate the young married couple? Or have you got a sudden desire to hear the old lady's parrot swear a few more swears?"

"It might be both," Miss Withers told him. "But it doesn't happen to be either. I just want to borrow a book."

The Inspector stared at her, and then shrugged his shoulders. "I must be dashing, Hildegarde. Go up to Stait's if you like, but I think I'll have this case settled before you get there. Buck Keeley will be dragged back to town before he gets very far, and then we'll see. Good night, and pleasant dreams."

"Good night," Miss Withers said softly. But when the Inspector was gone she did not seek her couch. She left a note for her roommates saying that she was going to be out late and please not to shoot the night bolt, and shortly afterward she was striding vigorously along Central Park West.

There were two men lounging in the lobby of the Hotel Senator whom Miss Withers recognized, but she did not speak to them, nor did they acknowledge her. Operatives on duty never greet each other, she knew.

Unannounced, she rang the bell of room number 1012. There was a long delay, and then a low, throaty voice answered from behind the panel. "Go away!"

Miss Withers rang the bell again, and then the door was suddenly thrown open. Rose Keeley stood there, dressed in mules and a ridiculous pink wrapper. Her eyes were red-rimmed, and her hair was tousled.

When she saw who it was she tried to swing the door shut, but Miss Withers interposed an agile oxford.

"You'd better talk to me," she suggested.

"I'll talk to nobody," said Rose Keeley hysterically. "If you want to arrest me, come on and arrest me. But I won't talk."

"I'm not a regular member of the police force," Miss Withers explained. "I'd like to help you, young woman. This visit is unofficial."

"You expect me to believe that? You're a spy, I know it! A police spy! Leave me alone, I tell you!"

"Calm yourself, Rose," advised Miss Withers. "Don't you know that in your condition it's dangerous to work yourself into hysteria?"

The girl's eyes widened, and she stepped back. "You . . . you know?"

Miss Withers came into the hotel room, and seated herself in a chair near the bed. "Of course I know," she admitted. "A girl like you doesn't faint at the drop of a hat unless she's in what they call an interesting condition."

"Interesting? Well, it didn't interest the ones it should have, let me tell you!" Rose pulled herself up short. "What do you want to know? Why did you come here?"

"I came here to find out the truth," Miss Withers told her. "I think it's high time we got some truth into this business. Tell me, Rose, was it Laurie Stait?"

The girl hesitated, and a hard, almost calculating look came into her eyes. "Yes, it was." Then she suddenly regretted herself. "No, if you must know the truth, it wasn't. I . . . ."

She threw herself on the bed. "I'll tell you one thing, though. My brother had nothing to do with what happened to Laurie Stait. I know what you're thinking. I know what the police are thinking. Maybe Buck did threaten Laurie, but he didn't mean anything by it. I swear he didn't. If he's gone away it's only because somebody used a rope to kill that Stait fellow, and Buck knew they'd try to pin it on him. He has a horror of being behind bars, even overnight."

"Did you love Laurie Stait?" Miss Withers asked the question softly.

Rose Keeley laughed in her face. "Me? I should say not! Love him? I'll never love any man as long as I live. They're all alike. Not that he wasn't a nice enough kid out at the ranch last summer. . . ."

Miss Withers remembered something. "Didn't Laurie have a dog out there, a young collie dog?"

"Oh, you mean Rowdy! We got him from the kennels at Butte early in the summer because Buck thought it would be nice for the dudes to have a pup to play with. Only Rowdy attached himself to Laurie Stait and wouldn't pay any attention to anybody else. I guess blooded dogs are thataway. It pretty near broke poor Rowdy's heart when Mr. Stait—I mean Laurie—had to leave the ranch and come back east. He wanted to buy him, but he didn't have any place here to keep him, he said. Rowdy wouldn't chow for a week, he was so lonesome after Mr. Stait left. He's never been the same dog since—he still meets the station wagon every day expecting to see his pard come back."

"And he never will," put in Miss Withers. "Because the man he learned to love is going to be laid away in a vault day after tomorrow. Murder is bad business, Rose. I hope your brother didn't have anything to do with it, but you realize that it looks bad for him. Unless he can prove where he was at the time of the murder."

"But he can! He told me all about it. Buck has a perfect alibi. He was with Carrigan and some of the boys, and they got into a fight with a policeman outside the hotel here, over a taxicab bill. They'll all bear witness. . . ."

"But they have," Miss Withers told her grimly. "Don't you remember? You claimed earlier today that Buck was with you in the hotel here at that hour, and Carrigan, and that Mr. Laramie White insisted that he wasn't with them. Isn't that right?"

Rose Keeley nodded her head, miserably. Her eyes were clouded, and she seemed to be torn between a desire to say something and the necessity for keeping quiet. Miss Withers rose to her feet.

"One thing more, young lady. When was the last time you saw Laurie Stait?"

"Him? Why, when he left the ranch last summer. . . ."

"You didn't see him here in New York?"

She shook her head. "I tried to phone him, but he wouldn't see me. I . . . Oh, there's no use. I won't say anything more, and you can't make me."

Miss Withers patted her shoulder. "I'd like to help you, child," she said. "And the best advice I can give you is to go down and tell the whole story to Inspector Piper in the morning. If you know where your brother is, you'd better advise him to come back and face the music. If he isn't guilty, nothing can happen to him. The sooner you get it over with, the sooner you can go back to your own country, and be happy. . . ."

She drew a blank on that one. Rose Keeley sat up on the bed, eyes wide and lips twisted in a sneer.

"Go back west, and be happy? Say, you don't think I like it out there, do you?"

"But I thought . . ."

"You've never lived through a Wyoming winter," Rose Keeley told her savagely. "Snowdrifts up to your armpits, blizzards three days a week, and mail about twice a month. You've never lived a day's drive from the nearest town, where you can't buy anything or go anywhere or have any fun! I hate it, I tell you!"

"But the summers . . ."

"The summers are great for the dudes that have money. They come out and howl about the air and the sun and the mountains. But for us it's just a lot of damned hard work. Playing bellhop for a lot of tourists. Say, the only good times I ever have are on these tours with the rodeo, and there's no money in them. The only advantage of it is that we get away from that damned prairie for a while, and see a little city life!"

"If you feel that way about it, why don't you leave the ranch and get a job here?"

Rose Keeley laughed again, with a bitter ring in her voice. "What would I do here? Who wants a girl who can shoot and ride a horse? The only way I could ever leave the ranch is to marry somebody from the city.

That's my only chance for happiness. Otherwise I'll be buried out there on the prairie all my life!"

"I see," said Miss Withers. And she was beginning to, at that.

15

Giving the Bride Away

A youngish man sat in the none-too-easy chair of Inspector Piper's sanctum, and tugged at the wisp of yellow moustache which adorned his upper lip. His general air was that of a crisp and decisive young business man, as indeed he had shown himself.

"Mr. Charles Waverly," began the Inspector heavily, "I'm sorry to trouble you at this hour of the evening. But there are a few little questions I'd like to ask you in regard to the murder of Laurie Stait. We're trying to investigate every angle of the case, and as the family lawyer you can be of the utmost assistance to us if you wish."

Charles Waverly intimated with a wave of his hand that he would be only too delighted to aid the Inspector.

"Very well. You are related to the Stait family yourself, are you not?"

The lawyer nodded. "I happen to be a grandnephew of the late Roscoe Stait, husband of the present Mrs. Stait."

"That's the old lady with the naked parrot?" Waverly grinned momentarily, and nodded.

The Inspector made much ado about lighting up a cigar, though he seemingly forgot to offer his guest one. "Just what is the condition of the family fortune? The old lady is pretty rich, isn't she?"

"Yes and no," the young lawyer answered, without hesitation. "The Stait fortune was at one time very large. Most of it is invested in New York real estate, which at the present time is sadly depreciated in value. I should say that the yearly income is in the neighborhood of thirty thousand dollars, or slightly more. However, it is not correct to say that Mrs. Stait, or Gran as we call her, is particularly wealthy, because according to the terms of her husband's will she only controls the income during her lifetime. The property is in trust, entail is the legal term, and on Mrs. Stait's death it devolves upon the nearest male heir of the Stait family."

The Inspector nodded. "That would be Lew Stait?"

"What? Oh yes, yes, of course. Laurie was the elder twin, then Lew of course would be the next in line."

"And after Lew?" The question was almost too casual.

Charles Waverly looked surprised. "In the event of Lew's dying without male heirs of his body—that is, without a son—the estate would devolve upon Hubert Stait, his cousin."

"And after Hubert?"

The lawyer smiled again. "I'm afraid I'll have to confess that I myself would be the lucky one in that event, Inspector. Roscoe Stait made explicit directions in his will that his property should never go outright to a woman, and he tried in every possible way to make sure that the male line would continue. If I were to inherit, I should have legally to adopt the name of Stait, however."

"I see. Tell me, what was the reason for the estate's being entailed in this fashion? It's not usual, is it?"

The lawyer shook his head. "Old Roscoe Stait didn't trust women, you see. He lived all his life under a sort of shadow. His married life was happy enough, I guess, but he never slept at night very soundly. It's a sort of skeleton in the family closet, Inspector, but I suppose you have the right to know. You have heard, perhaps, of Eva Montelli?"

The Inspector frowned. "Eva Montelli? It has vague associations, but I'm not sure. Wasn't she the housewife over in Jersey who poisoned her husband a few years back? Or was she the Washington Lure?"

"Neither one. It was a long time before your day or mine, Inspector. Eva Montelli was what she called herself, and if she ever had another name she succeeded in losing it. Those were the gay days just after the Civil War when New York society discovered opera. Eva Montelli was the Mary Garden of her day, a contralto with a voice, they said, like a houri. She certainly had the looks, and some of the habits, of one. She was the darling of the gay young bloods, and it was from her slipper that champagne tasted best, so the stories run. I've seen a few pictures of her, and although she had an hourglass figure and too much dignity for my taste, she was a beautiful woman all the same."

"And old Roscoe Stait got himself involved with this Montelli opera singer?"

"Worse than that. It seems that she had been having an affair with the director of the opera company, a broken-down Wagnerian tenor named Havemeyer. How serious an affair nobody knows. But she was no puritan. Then she met Roscoe Stait, and married him."

"So? The old man was married twice?" The Inspector was interested.

"No, only once. But my story isn't over. Eva Montelli married the old millionaire after a romantic elopement sort of business, and there was much rejoicing. Perhaps she loved him. I don't know why the idea has grown up that women can marry only poor men for love. Anyway, this thick-skulled Prussian of a Havemeyer brooded over things until he got himself into a fine temperamental rage, and then he called on the happy bridegroom with a pocketful of Eva's letters, as well as some other evidence to prove or insinuate that she was not what her new husband hoped. It was a pretty rotten thing for him to do, and that's why when he was found riddled with bulletholes the jury freed Eva Montelli Stait after fifteen minutes' deliberation. The story goes that each juryman kissed her hand when she thanked them. Roscoe Stait did the gentlemanly thing and took his wife back with open arms—then he locked her in the upper floors of his house and kept her there."

"And she stood for that?"

"Evidently she did. Maybe she got used to being shut away from other men. Her husband had the idea, you see, that her beauty was fatal. Anyway, even after his death she went on expiating her 'justifiable homicide' in the same way, living in the attic of the Stait house with only a parrot for company. That was where her two sons were born—both dead now. Oh, she's been known to come downstairs, and she rules that family with an iron hand, though there's nobody left but her two grandsons now, and Hubert and Aunt Abbie who've found a home there. You can figure it out as you like. Personally, I think she's a trifle touched. Sometimes she sings to herself up there at night, and it's weird enough, God knows. But you can't make her believe that she's paying more than that worthless fat tenor was worth, and there she stays, drying up a little more every year."

The Inspector shook his head. "It's unhealthy to be shut up anywhere, for anything. She'd have been better off if they'd sent her up the river for that killing. But tell me, why did she hate Laurie?"

"Laurie? I don't think she did hate him, exactly. Of course, she gave that car to Lew, but she knew he'd let his brother use it. But she was fanatical about sex, partly on account of her own early experience, I suppose. And she had the idea that Laurie was a rounder with women, and intimate with the maid."

"I saw *Lew* Stait with the little Dutch maid," confessed the Inspector. "The night of the murder. Maybe Laurie was blamed for the sins of his twin?"

And that remark surprised Charles Waverly all out of proportion to its significance. The Inspector pretended not to notice anything.

"One more question," he began. "Mrs. Stait said something about your having a chat with a man some time last week who came to see Laurie, a man with an accent, she said."

Charles Waverly nodded. "It was a westerner, a big, hearty fellow with one of those trick hats in his hand. He wanted to talk to Laurie, and I finally got out of him that he was appearing on behalf of his sister. Laurie had spent the summer at their ranch out west, and it appeared that the sister was in a family way.

"I pointed out to him the legal aspects of the case, and then he was bold enough to demand that if Laurie wouldn't marry his sister, he should make a cash settlement, which put the whole thing in the light of blackmail to me, and I told him so. I made it clear that Laurie Stait would have all the protection that his family position could give him, and the cowboy went away using pretty strong language."

"Yeah?" The Inspector rose to his feet. "And you didn't come and give me this information when you heard that Laurie Stait had been strangled with a western lariat? My God, man, that's a clear motive for murder!"

Charles Waverly shrugged his shoulders. "I don't think so. It seemed to me that this Keeley fellow was more put out at not getting some easy money than he was about his sister."

"But why have you kept this to yourself for all this time?"

"I hoped it would never come out," admitted the young lawyer. "For my sister's sake, mostly."

"But how would it affect your sister Dana? She married Lew Stait, and it wouldn't hurt the dead twin to have a scandal attached to his name."

"What? Oh, quite right, Inspector. I was in error, I know. But as the family lawyer, I wished to keep it all back if possible. Because Dana's unfortunate marriage this morning—"

The Inspector leaped into the breach. "Unfortunate? Why, I understood that you were in favor of her marrying Lew, and that you were afraid of her marrying Laurie?"

"Of course. I meant that the marriage was unfortunate in the time chosen, and not in itself. You see, I love my sister Dana more than anything else in the world, and I'd do anything short of murder to see her happy."

The Inspector nodded. "Tell me, Waverly. At what time the afternoon of the murder did your sister Dana come to your office? It was early, wasn't it?"

Charles Waverly did not flinch. "You can't trap a lawyer, Inspector."

"But she was at your office? She came there to tell you that she wouldn't marry Lew, didn't she?"

Charles Waverly did show a start at that. "Damn that stenographer of mine. Did Mildred tell you that? She must have, because I know Dana wouldn't. . . ."

"Dana didn't," the Inspector announced. "She's avoided being questioned, so far." He stood up, and stepped toward the door of the outer office. "Excuse me a moment, will you?"

A night man in uniform was waiting in the outer office, and the Inspector gave quick, explicit instructions. "Remember—a girl named Mildred something." Then he was back at his desk.

"You haven't answered my question, Mr. Waverly."

"I don't think I need to answer it. My sister did call on me that afternoon, and she did discuss with me her problem. She was engaged to Lew Stait, and infatuated with his twin brother. That's all I care to say at this time."

"Very well." The Inspector leaned closer to his guest. "You couldn't hazard a guess as to who might have killed Laurie Stait, could you?"

"I'm sorry, Inspector. It's a mystery to me."

"Of course it is. And you wouldn't care to suggest who the man might have been who identified the body of Laurie Stait in the lobby of the Enterprise Trust Building, and then retracted his identification and slipped away in the crowd? The officer in charge said that it was a tall man with a little moustache—and your office happens to be in that building."

Charles Waverly shook his head. "That will not get you anywhere, Inspector. There are several thousand tenants in that building, and it is only natural that there should be a good many persons on the busiest corner in the world who happen to be tall and have moustaches. It really won't do . . . and unless you have something awfully important to ask me now, I'd like to run along home. It's a long subway ride up to my little apartment on East Seventieth."

The Inspector apologized for the inconvenient location of Headquarters. "It's too bad," he said, "that we aren't closer to Fifth Avenue. Buses are a lot more comfortable than subways—don't you agree with me?"

Waverly nodded. "I always take a bus in preference to any other mode of travel," he admitted. "I ride down every morning to my office on an open bus, if the weather permits, and it peps me up for the day. Usually I go home the same way. Well, good night, Inspector. If there's anything else I can tell you—"

"If there's anything else you can tell me, you're smart enough not to," the Inspector said under his breath. But he let the smart young lawyer pass out of the office.

The Inspector relaxed into his chair again and crossed his feet on his desk. "I wonder how good an actor this Waverly fellow is?" he said softly. "Never batted an eye when I mentioned the bus. If he'd had an ounce of guilty conscience he would have denied ever using the buses—supposing that Hildegarde is right about the way the job was done. I wonder—"

He was still wondering an hour or two later when he got a report over the telephone.

"I found her, Inspector," came Swarthout's excited tenor. "Name's Mildred Hotchkiss. Lives in the Bronx, which is where I am at the moment, calling from a drugstore. She's worked for Charlie Waverly as stenog—she calls it secretary—for a couple of years, and with a little pressure I got one thing out of her, though I don't think she knows that it means anything, and I'm not sure what it means myself. But anyway, Dana Waverly and her brother had a hell of a quarrel that afternoon of the murder. It was something about a promise she'd made to him in the past. Waverly sent Mildred on an errand, but she came back in time to hear the girl say to her brother: 'Those stories are all lies, and he loves me. I know he loves me, because he carries the only love letter I ever wrote him around in his wallet right now!' She's a cute little trick, Inspector. Want me to stick on the job?"

"I do not. You'd better come back to town and get yourself some sleep. Get it in bed, your own bed, and not under a table in some speakeasy. It'll do you more good."

The Inspector crashed the receiver and debated whether or not to allow himself just one more cigar before going home. The cigar won the decision, and when it was burning merrily, he pulled a pad of paper out of his drawer and made a number of markings which partook of the nature of a cryptogram. He drew a square, quartered it, blocked in the quarters, and then added a decoration of a chimney and a roof to the top. He followed this masterpiece of surrealism with a fresco of automobile wheels, and a couple of somewhat shaky triangles. Then he wrote:

> *Wallet—Lew's—missing when his aunt wanted money for taxi but discovered that same night in a post office collection box, with the dough intact.*
> *Wallet—Laurie's—missing from the corpse.*
> *Wallet—Somebody's—contained a love letter of Dana Waverly's.*

Inspector Piper then drew a large question mark, added legs and a silk hat to it, and went home to bed.

16

Coffee For Newlyweds

Long experience as a teacher had given Miss Withers the pet theory that the time to find out anything that someone doesn't want to tell is early in the morning. She knew that a large majority of the world's citizens awaken by slow degrees, with resistance at a low ebb, and whenever she found it necessary to determine a culprit among her pupils at Jefferson School she made the accusation bright and early the next morning as the boys and girls were filing into their seats.

Grade Three at Jefferson School was now being administered—undoubtedly very badly—by a substitute, but in her avocation of sleuthing Miss Withers applied the same technique. Thus it was that she rang the bell at the servants' entrance of the Stait house a few minutes after eight o'clock the next morning.

A clatter of pans died away inside, but otherwise there was no answer. Miss Withers rang again, and suddenly the door was flung open and a large and shining butcher's knife was presented before her maidenly breast.

"Hands up!" demanded a highly nervous voice. It was Mrs. Hoff, but her vast bulk was trembling like Jello in a high wind.

Miss Withers put up, not her hands, but her eyebrows. Slowly the weapon was withdrawn.

"You can come in," said Mrs. Hoff grudgingly. "I not know who it wass. The way things happen in this house, I take no chances."

"You certainly do not, but anyone who comes near you takes a good many," said Miss Withers. She advanced into the kitchen, but stopped short on seeing Gretchen, the little blonde maid, also with a large and glittering knife.

Gretchen proceeded to bisect an orange and add it to a bowl of yellow semisphere beside her. Then she rose to her feet and made a beeline for the hall.

"Never mind her," Miss Withers told the cook. "It's you I want to talk to. You realize, of course, that it is to your best interest to aid the police in every possible way? You could be arrested, if that detective wanted to press the charge, for resisting an officer, mayhem, assault and battery, attack with a deadly weapon and the intent to kill. . . ."

"I not do any of those things," Mrs. Hoff said weakly. "I only hit him with a skillet." But her resistance was ebbing away. She subsided into a rocking chair and stared out of the window.

Miss Withers wasn't sure how to begin. She surveyed the preparations for breakfast. A dozen slices of bacon lay on a plate beside the stove. On the table stood a large and formidable device which resembled a mammoth hourglass with an aluminum band in the narrow neck. Above, boiling water slowly subsided to reappear in the crystal-clear compartment at the bottom as golden brown coffee.

"That's a French dip machine," volunteered the cook. "Mrs. Stait is very fussy about her coffee. So is the whole family, except Mr. Lew, of course. Until last night he never drank a cup in his life, willingly."

Miss Withers had her lead. "Yes? Then Mr. Lew's tastes have changed since the—the accident to his brother?"

Mrs. Hoff nodded. "Ja, in a way. Mr. Laurie never drank coffee, either, though. You see, as boys both the twins used to have to take their castor oil in coffee, and they always said that the two tasted just alike to them after they got grown up."

"Oh!" Miss Withers was disappointed. "But you said that Mr. Lew drank some last night?"

Mrs. Hoff nodded. "Strange it wass for him. But marriage changes everybody, I guess. Last night late he and his new wife send down twice for coffee, each time two cups. And they say I don't make it strong enough." The cook's fat face widened into a Rabelaisian smile. "When I was first married I didn't need coffee at night to keep from going to sleep, let me tell you! But these young people today—"

"Yes, yes, of course." Miss Withers changed the subject. "Do you think the young couple are happy, Mrs. Hoff?"

"Happy? Why not? They are young, they should be happy."

"But do you think they're in love? It was unusual, for them to marry the way they did, just after what happened to Mr. Lew's twin brother."

Mrs. Hoff frowned. "I wonder about that, too. Maybe Mr. Lew was lonesome after his brother die, and he was not able to stand it alone. Anyway, they act like a couple of lovers, I know that. Sad and happy all at the same time. When I bring up the coffee last night, they are both excited, and she is crying. But they hold hands, all the same."

Miss Withers filed that away for future reference.

"Do you notice any other change in Mr. Lew since he got married?"

"Change? No, I don't see any change. He's not eat much these days, but that is not so strange. Mr. Hubert is the only one of the family who has his appetite these dark days. And the aunt, of course, when she remembers to come to the table. She is so absent-minded that she gets reading a book or a magazine and she doesn't know the passing of time."

Mrs. Hoff sighed and shook her head at the idea of anyone missing a meal from forgetfulness.

"I haf to get the breakfast now," she reminded her caller. "Mrs. Stait will want her tray in a minute. And the rest of them come down soon."

"Tell me," said Miss Withers. "Do all the members of the family eat together? Is everything friendly? Have they accepted Dana, Mr. Lew's new wife?"

The cook nodded. "Of course. Miss Dana has been a guest here for many a meal, and they've been engaged for a long time. All members of the family eat together, except this morning. I think Mr. Lew goes out early. . . ." A bell buzzed dully above the cabinet, and Mrs. Hoff leaped out of her chair. "There!" she announced triumphantly. "I knew it! Mrs. Stait wants her tray, and it isn't ready."

Bacon sizzled into a frying pan, and then a bell down the hall tinkled alarmingly. "That's the family in the dining room," wailed Mrs. Hoff. "I shall lose my job for this!"

"Say nothing about it," warned Miss Withers, and she strode out into the hall. She ran into Gretchen, who was lurking outside the open door of the dining room. The girl looked at her with wide, angry eyes. "Don't let her tell you that Mr. Lew hasn't changed," whispered Gretchen. "He's not the same at all, and I ought to know. He's stiff and formal and different since he married that . . . that girl. He's not his old free, cheery self at all!"

Miss Withers nodded. "Tell me, Gretchen, are all the family in there?" She pointed to the dining room.

"Everybody that's coming down, yes, mam. Mrs. Stait never comes downstairs, you know, and Mr. Lew went out early without his breakfast. Shall I show you into the living room until they get through?"

"Gretchen!" Mrs. Hoff's voice, low but insistent, sounded from the kitchen. "Gretchen, carry in the coffee!"

"Never mind announcing me," Miss Withers decided. "I'll find my way by myself." Gretchen ran toward the kitchen, and Miss Withers tiptoed up the hall.

She paused just outside the dining room door. There was much rattling of newspapers inside, but very little conversation, and that little was strained. Hubert clinked his coffee cup, and mumbled something, probably to Dana. Whatever it was that Miss Withers had hoped to hear, she did not hear it.

She drew a deep breath, and stepped quickly past the doorway, catching a quick glimpse of the three who sat at one end of the long refectory table. Hubert and Aunt Abbie were deep in *The Times,* and the girl who had been Dana Waverly was tracing a design on the tablecloth with her fork. Even at this ungodly hour Dana was good-looking, there was no denying that. Very much like her picture—the picture that the Inspector and Miss Withers had discovered hidden away beneath a bureau in the upstairs room, only with an added touch of emotional strain that was not hard to understand.

The hall was dark, and as Miss Withers had hoped, no one recognized her, although Aunt Abbie called petulantly, "Gretchen, whatever is keeping you?" after her.

But she did not wait in the living room, after all. With a cautious glance behind her, she turned and went up the stairs.

This time Miss Withers wasted no precious seconds in a survey of Aunt Abbie's room, nor in the bath which opened into the hall. She went quickly to the large room at the rear of the house—the room which had been shared by the twins, and which now was quite evidently shared by Lew Stait and his bride. It was a strange, almost terrible, setting for a honeymoon, and Miss Withers was not surprised that the young couple needed coffee at midnight.

The atmosphere of this room had been subtly and femininely changed, somehow, overnight. She noticed that the saddle and spurs had been taken down from the wall. But the bookcase was still there. Miss Withers thumbed the titles for a moment, and at last found what she was seeking, and tucked it, without a qualm, inside her dress. It was only a small, tan volume with a crude drawing of a boy and a monkey on the cover, but it was suddenly important to her.

The position of sneak thief was abhorrent to Miss Withers, and she turned to leave the room as quickly as she had come. But something caught her eye.

It was not the incongruously feminine pajamas of cerise silk which had been flung across the footboard of the bed that Laurie Stait would never sleep in again. The room was littered with such garments. But on the mirror was a square of white paper. Miss Withers decided that she wanted to know what it meant.

She soon found out. It was a rough scrawl in pencil:

> *Dearest darlingest Dana* [it began]. *I've got an idea, and I don't want to wake you, so I'm slipping out early. I'll be back in about an hour with the ring and things you left at the apartment downtown in the Village—if the police find them it means trouble. Eleven million kisses.* It was signed with a scrawled letter "L."

Miss Withers stared at it as if she meant to commit it to memory, every line, and then suddenly tucked it away inside the pages of the book she had taken from the case. A suspicion which had been worming its way around the corners of her mind suddenly widened into a hunch, and Miss Withers believed in playing her hunches.

"I'll be in a fine kettle of fish if anyone finds me here," she said to herself softly.

Someone did. At that moment the alarm was sounded shrilly behind her.

"Thieves! Thieves! Robbers! Get a gun, get a gun! Sic 'em, sic 'em!"

She whirled, her hand at her throat, to see the loathsome white body of the naked parrot, Skipper, in the doorway. He waddled forward a step or two, waving his featherless wings, and then burst into a flood of the foulest profanity that Miss Withers had ever heard, ending up with a word positively Chaucerian.

"I'd like to wash your mouth out with soap," Miss Withers told him bitterly.

But Skipper only leered at her. "Birdseed, boys, birdseed! Hell and damnation!" He flopped closer, his beak snapping unpleasantly like the jaws of a trap. To Miss Withers he looked like a weird Hebrew penguin.

"Don't you come near me, you filthy beast," she implored, and then suddenly turned and ran past him out of the room and down the stairs.

Skipper hopped after her as far as the landing and said unprintable things. He was in reality only annoyed because he, like the rest of the inmates of the house, had been unreasonably delayed in breakfasting, but Skipper was cursed with an unfortunate upbringing spent at sea, and a physical appearance which made him look like a witch's familiar spirit.

Miss Withers was barely in the living room, perched in the shadow of a high-backed chair, when she heard the outer door open and someone come in. She caught a flash of Lew Stait's face, white and drawn, as he passed toward the dining room, and as always Miss Withers had the momentary and revulsive sensation that here was a dead man walking. For she had first seen that face blackened and twisted above a noose of hemp. . . .

Miss Withers remained alone with her thoughts for only a few minutes, and then Aunt Abbie, pale and fluttering, hastened into the room, followed by Hubert Stait.

"Oh, how do you do?" Aunt Abbie wanted to know. "Gretchen just told me you were here, or we wouldn't have kept you waiting. You're the lady from the police, aren't you?"

Miss Withers laid claim to a somewhat remote connection with officialdom. "I came here this morning to ask you if by any chance you had remembered anything which might shed light on the murder of your nephew," she explained. "Sometimes there are details which come out only after a day or two's thinking."

Aunt Abbie nodded. "Yes, yes, of course. But I'm sure I don't remember anything, do you, Hubert? I think it's terrible that the police haven't been able to make an arrest in all this time. What are we paying taxes for, I'd like to know? I'm sure we've given all the help we can, and the police ought to be able to find out who Laurie's enemies were. Of course, the poor dear boy was his own worst enemy, that's what I've always said. . . ."

Aunt Abbie walked up and down the room nervously. "I'm sure that if I remember anything which might have a bearing on the case I'll telephone the police at once. You'll excuse me now—I must go in to breakfast."

"But, Aunt Abbie," Hubert interposed, "you've just come from breakfast, don't you remember?"

Aunt Abbie stopped short. "Breakfast? Have I, really? Yes, yes, of course. The terrible events of the past few days have quite upset me, I'm sure. I believe I'll go to my room and lie down. I really don't feel like any more of this."

Neither did Miss Withers, and she let the fluttery lady go without protest. Hubert remained, staring at Miss Withers through his thick-lensed glasses.

"Tell me," he said suddenly. "Are the police getting anywhere? Have they got any idea who killed Laurie?"

"I think so," Miss Withers informed him. "I think we're on the track of the murderer all right. It's only a question of time."

Hubert came closer. "I'm glad of that. I was afraid that this was one of those perfect crimes we read about. Of course you know about the cowboy who was threatening Laurie all week. Is it he whom you suspect? I won't feel safe until I know that the killer is behind bars where he belongs. Is it the cowboy?"

"Perhaps," Miss Withers told him. "And perhaps it's someone else."

"Who else?" Hubert didn't look very surprised. But before Miss Withers could answer his question there were voices in the hall, and Lew Stait, followed by Dana, entered the room. They kept very close together.

Perhaps Miss Withers imagined it, but she thought that Lew's eyes caught Hubert's in a quick, questioning glance. The latter spoke, quickly.

"As you know, Miss Withers, I'll do anything in my power to aid the police in any way," he assured her. "I only want to see this terrible business settled before it ruins all our lives." He turned to the newcomers. "Dana, this is Miss Withers, who is making an investigation of the case for the police. Have you two met?"

Miss Withers got her first good look at the girl who had been Dana Waverly, and who was now Mrs. Lewis Stait by the grace of God and the authority of the State of Connecticut.

The wide eyes met hers without wavering, and their smoky depths betrayed no secrets. "How do you do?" said Dana softly, as if the answer to her question was quite immaterial. Miss Withers did not answer it.

"I'll be running along, because I know you have some questions to ask," Hubert said meaningly. He stopped in the doorway to flash Miss Withers a somewhat hunted smile, and then climbed sedately up the stair.

Lew Stait faced the schoolteacher. "I don't see why we can't be let alone," he said bitterly. "I suppose it seems strange to you that we—that we got married when we did?"

Dana's hand reached for his, and caught it.

Miss Withers shook her head. "It isn't any of my business," she said.

"I wish the newspapers felt that way about us," Lew said. "They've been raising a most terrible hullabaloo. But we love each other, and I wanted to be where I could protect Dana from this unpleasantness as much as possible."

"I see," said Miss Withers. "You must forgive me if I seem impertinent. But the only chance we have of solving the murder of your brother is to ask a lot of questions and follow up every clue. Tell me, who do you think killed Laurie Stait?"

Lew sank into a chair, and his young wife planted herself on the arm, with her hand on his shoulder.

"I know who killed my brother." He said the words dully. "It was that roughneck Keeley, who ran the ranch where Laurie spent the summer. The police must know by now that he came here threatening Laurie, and that my brother was killed with one of Keeley's ropes."

"And why would Buck Keeley want to kill your brother? Was it because of the condition his sister is in?"

She realized that she had said the wrong thing—the very wrong thing.

"It is not!" Lew half rose in his chair. "The man is crazy, I tell you. He's a homicidal maniac. Because I know that nothing happened at that ranch which Laurie should have been ashamed of. That girl meant nothing to him, I tell you, and never did. He never laid a hand on her. . . ."

It was a delicate subject, but Miss Withers pressed it. "Such things have a way of happening," she pointed out. "Rose Keeley is going to have a baby, you know. How can you be so sure?"

"I'm as sure of it as I'm sure of—of anything," said Lew proudly. "Because—well—well, because Laurie told me!" His voice was strained and nervous now, pitched too high.

Dana Waverly turned her wide eyes on her young husband, and their bodies moved imperceptibly apart.

"Whatever that girl says about Laurie is a *lie,*" Lew insisted. "He was innocent of any charge she can make!"

"But she doesn't say anything," Miss Withers informed him. "I talked to her last night, and she avoided the subject. But never mind that. Suppose, just for the sake of argument, that the cowboy had nothing to do with it." She lowered her voice. "Do you think that, for any reason in the world, your cousin Hubert's alibi could have been faked, and he might have committed the murder?"

There was a long pause, and if Lew Stait was not honestly surprised he was a better actor than Miss Withers gave him credit for.

"Hubert? Good heavens, no! Why, we twins have always been his best pals. I didn't know he had an alibi—the Inspector told us not to discuss this case among ourselves, and we've steered off the subject here in the household. But Hubert doesn't need an alibi. He couldn't have had anything to do with the murder. It's unthinkable. . . ."

"But—" Dana started to speak, and then thought better of it. Miss Withers wondered if the young bride had been about to disagree with her husband, and waited a moment, but no more information came forth.

"That's all I wanted to know," Miss Withers decided. "I'm sorry to have intruded like this. May I say that I wish you very good luck?"

Lew Stait thanked her, and Dana smiled a crooked little smile. "We'll need all the good luck we can get," she said. They passed on toward the stair, but not arm in arm as when they had come in. Miss Withers paused in the hallway to button her overcoat before braving the chill wind of the riverfront.

A hand touched her shoulder, startling the good lady considerably. It was Hubert again, his eyes wide and blinking behind the glasses.

"I want a word with you," he whispered. "I know you think that the cowboy killed my cousin. Maybe he did, but I doubt it. It was somebody closer to Laurie than that, somebody who knew he was driving down

Fifth Avenue at that hour—somebody who pretended to be his friend. Perhaps closer than a friend!"

"Yes? Who do you think that could be?" Miss Withers was casual.

Hubert looked behind him before he spoke. Then he came closer. "I'm afraid for my life," he whispered. "The deaths in this family aren't over yet, by a long way. And . . . if you want to find out who killed Laurie Stait, *watch his twin brother, Lew!*"

With that Hubert turned suddenly and scuttled up the stair as if his own shadow threatened him.

17

An Ellinson Never Forgets

The Inspector put down his telephone and crossed his feet luxuriously on his desk.

"Hildegarde," he announced, "you may be the first to congratulate me."

Miss Withers closed the door behind her and came into his office. "And just why did you think I should congratulate you? I suppose that you've solved the Stait murder? Or maybe you found Charlie Ross and Judge Crater all at once?"

"Your first guess was correct," he informed her, letting two beautiful smokerings rise in undulating whirls above his head.

Miss Withers had a quick thrill of apprehension. "You solved it? How?"

"Well, I just got word that my men have picked up Buck Keeley."

"Oh!" Miss Withers subsided into a chair with a distinct sigh of relief.

"Well, you don't seem very excited?"

"I'm not. I was afraid for a moment that you'd beaten me, Oscar Piper. But you and your Buck Keeley!"

"Yeah? Well, if Buck Keeley didn't kill Laurie Stait, I'd like to know who did! He had the motive, didn't he—with his sister like you said, in a family way? He had the rope, and the skill to use it. And he'd been making threats, everybody knew that."

"Yes," agreed Miss Withers. "Everybody knew that Buck Keeley was in town making threats. That's just the trouble." She saw the bewilderment on Piper's face. "Oh, I don't say that I can prove Keeley didn't do it. Maybe he did, although his sister claims Buck was having a brawl with some of the other cowboys and an officer at that moment, three blocks away from the scene of the murder."

"Sure she does. And Carrigan and the cowboys swear now that Keeley was with them. Only if you remember they talked differently when we first went to the rodeo. Then Rose Keeley insisted that Buck was with her at dinner in the hotel, and the boys bore her up."

"Maybe they were lying then because they thought Buck was being arrested for something in connection with the fight." Miss Withers shrugged her shoulders. "Anyway, it doesn't matter. Oscar, I said that I was going ahead on this case as a free-lance, to show you that a woman can be a sleuth. But I've got an idea that will take your official position to work out. Forget poor Buck Keeley, and look at these."

She passed a book across the desk to the Inspector, who stared at it blankly. "*Toby Tyler, or Ten Weeks with a Circus*—by James Otis. Thirty-fourth Printing—" He looked at her. "So what is this, another Peter Rabbit?"

"Look at the flyleaf," she suggested. "It happens to be a grand old classic among children's books, but I suppose you never read anything but Deadwood Dick when you were at the right age for it."

The Inspector looked at the flyleaf, and raised his brows. "To Laurie from Lew, Xmas, 1921." He nodded. "So you've been up at the Stait house again, have you? Well, what am I supposed to deduce from this, except that the twins used to exchange presents under the Christmas tree in a happier day than this?"

"Maybe nothing, maybe a great deal," Miss Withers informed him. "Notice anything about the writing?"

He looked at the flyleaf again. "Sort of a childish scrawl, but that's not so strange. Laurie and Lew Stait were hardly twelve years old then. Even the ink has faded out to a sort of dull brown. But as for any meaning . . ."

Miss Withers gave him Exhibit B. It was the note from Lew Stait to his young wife, the note which Miss Withers had lifted from the mirror in the bedroom at the Stait house that morning.

"It's not the context I'm interested in," she announced. "Though that's at least revealing. If that young man went down to the apartment after the engagement ring his wife somewhat absent-mindedly left there, he had his trip for nothing. But apart from that, does anything strike you about these two handwritings?"

"I'm no handwriting expert," the Inspector insisted. "They look alike, if that's what you mean. I suppose that a man's writing changes with the years."

"I'm no expert either," Miss Withers said coldly. "And therefore I think we'd better call in one. In this book inscription we have a genuine sample of Lewis Stait's writing before the murder, and in this note we have a sample of his writing after the murder."

"But why all this interest in Lew Stait's handwriting? This isn't a forgery case!"

"Maybe it is," Miss Withers told him solemnly. She hesitated as if about to take the plunge.

Then she thought better of it. "Oscar, I don't want to explain yet. I want you to submit these samples of handwriting to the best expert you know, and ask him if they are actually written by the same person. Perhaps it isn't possible to tell, but I understand that they can do wonderful things with a microscopic enlargement. Will you get the expert for me?"

"Of course, of course, if you think it means anything. I suppose you're trying to see if Lew Stait's early handwriting shows any traces of homicidal mania, or some such silliness. But I'll send them out to our expert, never fear." He pressed the buzzer on his desk.

"How soon will he make a report?"

"He happens to be a 'she,' " Piper informed her. "Mrs. Korn has officiated as technical witness in many a forgery and fraud case, and she can spot a poison-pen letter a mile away. She lives over in Jersey somewhere, but I'll have a messenger take these to her and bring back the reply within a few hours. If there's any secrets hidden away in Lew Stait's childish scrawl or in his note to lovey-dovey, Lolly Korn will ferret them out, even if she is bedridden."

He handed the exhibits to Sergeant Taylor, with brief and explicit instructions. Then he relit his cigar. "You needn't sit back and look like the cat who swallowed the canary, Hildegarde."

Miss Withers was wearing a self-satisfied smile. "I have a feeling that this case is going to be settled, and settled soon," she ventured.

The Inspector agreed, heartily. "Give me a couple of hours with this Buck Keeley, and I'll have a signed confession of the Stait murder," he promised. "I wish they'd bring him in. The boys must have picked him up in a wheelbarow instead of the wagon."

But before the Inspector's cigar had gone out again he heard the wail of a siren, and then a somewhat disheveled-looking young man was brought up the hall. His clothes gave evidence that he had slept in them, and slept none too well at that. There was a bristle of beard on his face, and his small, pig-like eyes held an expression of injured innocence which was alien to his hangdog air and the manacles which adorned either wrist.

On each side of the stocky westerner loomed the tall blue figure of a uniformed policeman, and in the rear Mike McTeague strode along in plainclothes, with one hand on the holster which bulged under his coat.

"And here's your roughneck," announced McTeague breezily. The Inspector, standing in the door of his inner office with Miss Withers behind him, shook his head.

"Mike, who do you think you're arresting? Terrible Tommy O'Connor? Take those bracelets off him."

McTeague rattled his keys.

"Where did you pick him up?"

"Down in the Municipal Lodging House, sir. He was there on the bum, with a hundred bucks in his pocket. One of the bums saw his wad, and when he couldn't lift it he squealed and they ganged up on him. That's how it came out."

"I see. Well, Keeley, you see it's no good." The Inspector's voice was calm and gentle. He might have been a father-confessor. "Don't you think you'd better tell us all about it?"

Buck Keeley raised a whiskery but pugnacious jaw. "Tell you all about what? Am I here under arrest?"

Inspector Piper shook his head. "Of course not. We just wanted to ask you a few questions, and the boys were a little over-eager, that's all."

"I'm answering no questions, and I'm leaving right now," objected Buck Keeley. But he did not get far.

"In that case we'll exercise our privilege and hold you overnight as a suspicious character associating with known criminals," the Inspector told him. "But I hope it won't be necessary. I'm sure you'll be able to explain everything satisfactorily, including the reason why you slipped up and used one of your own ropes to bump off Laurie Stait." Piper turned to the two uniformed men. "Take him down the hall, boys, and I'll be there in a minute. Make him comfortable."

Buck Keeley muttered a word worthy of old Mrs. Stait's parrot in his more bawdy moments, and then went down the hall without offering resistance.

"He's going to be easy," the Inspector promised Miss Withers. "You watch me. Wait here and I'll be back with a confession before you can say 'Jack Robinson.' " Then he, also, went down the hall.

The hands of the clock crawled on toward noon, swung past the meridian and down on the afternoon side. And still the Inspector did not show up with his confession.

When he did arrive, coatless and tieless, he was mopping his brow. He poured himself something that may have been water from a carafe on his desk, and then shook his head at Miss Withers.

"I stopped saying 'Jack Robinson' because I lost count," she informed him acidly. "It would seem that you over-estimated the third degree. Another hour and Buck Keeley will have *you* signing a confession of the murder."

"He's stubborn, all right," Piper agreed. "I've worn out a couple of my best detectives on him, and there's a new shift shooting questions at him now. He's a pig-headed sort, the kind of a mug who fixes a story and then sticks to it."

"I don't suppose it occurred to you that his story might possibly be true?"

"It can't be," Piper told her. "He claims that he tried to hide out only because he knew he'd be blamed for the bumping. And he says that at the hour of the murder he was having a fistfight with a cop on Forty-fourth Street."

"Well? Couldn't he have?" Miss Withers was thoughtful. "Why don't you have the policeman in here to identify him? Kehoe ought to recognize the men who gave him that beautiful black eye."

"I thought of that," confessed the Inspector. "And I tried it. But identifications aren't always sure fire, you know. There was a case only a few months ago when we nearly sent a little punk to the Hot Squat up the river because he looked a lot like Two-gun Crowley, and happened to be in the courtroom when witnesses to a holdup were pointing out who they imagined had done it. Well, that's the way it was with Kehoe. We had him down here about an hour ago, and walked Keeley down the other corridor with five court attaches, so Kehoe could get a flash at him. But what does that dumb Irishman do but pick out the City Recorder of Deeds, who happened to be passing through, as one of the guys who had socked him in the fistfight and then had a drink with him afterward! So what does it prove?"

Miss Withers nodded thoughtfully. "You say they had a drink together?"

"Yeah. Of course Kehoe didn't tell me that, but the rodeo manager, Carrigan, did. As far as that goes, I'd rather a cop would have a drink with a citizen now and then, than arrest everybody he brushes up against. The court calendar is full enough as it is, and the less arrests the better. Only of course I couldn't tell Kehoe that, for the sake of discipline."

He suddenly clapped his fist against his palm. "I've got it! I'll bet you that the whole thing was a frame. The fight and all that was faked, in order to furnish Keeley with an alibi. He got his friends to pull the thing, and then swear he was there, only it went askew somehow."

"You'd have got further with the identification stunt if you'd walked a squad of policemen past Keeley, and had him point out the one he'd taken a sock at," Miss Withers suggested. "He's no prize, but I think he's smarter than Kehoe. All the same, I hate to think of you poor policemen wearing out yourselves in a third degree, so I'll offer a suggestion." And she did.

The Inspector nodded, slowly. "Not a bad idea. A damn good idea. If the guy can be reached . . ."

He seized the telephone, asked to be connected with a certain office in the Criminal Courts Building. "Hallo, Max? Got something right up your alley. Tell me, what speakeasies are there on West Forty-fourth Street?"

There was a pause. "No, no, I don't mean that. Just in one block, say within a few doors of the Hotel Senator, on the south side of the street not far from Fifth Avenue." He began scribbling. "Okay. Thanks."

"Well, this ought to settle Buck Keeley's hash, one way or the other," he told Miss Withers. He reached for the phone again.

By the time Miss Withers and the Inspector had finished a sketchy luncheon consisting of ham sandwiches and malted milks, the scene was set.

"You've never seen the morning lineup, have you, Hildegarde?" He opened the door of a large room on the top floor of the building. "Well, it's the only place large enough for what we plan to try, so we'll have a little lineup of our own. At eight o'clock every morning all the previous day's arrests are paraded along that platform there, where you see the horizontal lines, with the floodlights on them. In these chairs sit the plainclothes men and a few uniformed men on special duty, getting a slant at the bright and smiling faces of the lads they're going to meet up with later in the course of duty. It's a great invention. Now you sit here in the front row, and I'll be back with the boys."

Evidently the Inspector routed out every plainclothes operative, desk clerk, and innocent bystander in the building. The chairs were soon filled, and the crowd awaited the show, whatever it was. Behind her was Buck Keeley, between two guards. Miss Withers realized that she was the only woman there, but nobody else seemed to think it strange.

At that moment the Inspector appeared in the doorway, talking affably with a small gentleman who wore a derby crammed down upon his cauliflowered ears. "I'll consider it a great favor, Mr. Ellinson," he was saying.

"Just call me Moe," said Mr. Ellinson cheerily. Then he saw the brightly lit platform with its telltale black lines against the wall, and recoiled noticeably.

"I ain't going to get up on there for nobody," he announced. "A favor I'll do for you, Inspector, but I'm no crook and I'm not going to be mugged."

"Wait a minute, Moe. I just want you to pick out one or more of the men whose faces you recognize in this crowd. It won't take a minute."

"Sure I'll pick 'em out," agreed Moe Ellinson. "But I don't get up on that platform. I've got an honest business, Inspector. I run a speakeasy, not anything illegal. Ask anybody on Forty-fourth Street if I'm not on the level."

He scratched his head. "Tell you what I'll do, Inspector. I couldn't see anything from that platform anyway. But you walk the gents across it, and let me stand here, and I'll pick out the one you want. Agreeable?"

It was definitely not agreeable to the crowd. But the Inspector was pleadingly insistent. After all, they were all friends here, he said. And Mr. Ellinson was doing the Police Department a favor. . . .

So, after much argument, it was settled. Moe Ellinson remained in the shadow of the door, beside the Inspector, and a line of gentlemen filed across the stage, most of them looking particularly self-conscious and silly. The Inspector realized for the first time how extremely criminal some of his aides looked when seen under these conditions.

"You don't think you'll have any trouble in recognizing him?" he said to the little man in the derby.

"I run my business by recognizing faces, right off the bat," pointed out Moe Ellinson. "This is between friends, Inspector, and I don't mind telling you that if I made any mistakes in who I let through that grilled door of mine, I'd be closed up quick. Once a man comes in my place, he needs no card to get there again. I remember him."

He was staring at the gentlemen on the stage. "Oh, hello, Mr. Hennessy. How's the sweet little wife? We haven't seen you around lately."

Chief-clerk Hennessy flushed brick red and moved off the stage. There was a scattering of applause from those in the confraternity who remembered that Hennessy had a wife out in Queens somewhere who could never under any circumstances be described as either "little" or "sweet."

Several more figures filed across the stage, and then Moe Ellinson spoke again. "How d'do, Mr. Wegman? I haven't seen you up at my place since the first of October. That check, Mr. Wegman, it was rubber. Thirteen dollars, it was. . . ."

Mr. Wegman, who spent his days in serving subpoenas, likewise betook himself off in a hurry. There were protests, and several gentlemen changed their minds about aiding Piper in his little experiment.

Miss Withers was enjoying herself. And then, all of a sudden, it was over. The last man had passed across the stage. Miss Withers knew that the Inspector was, as he would say, pulling a fast one.

Piper turned to Moe Ellinson. "As I explained to you, Mr. Ellinson, we asked you to come here because a certain gentleman in this room maintains that he came into your place for a drink with some friends on last Friday afternoon. You say you never forget a face. Which of the men who passed across the stage was that man?"

Moe Ellinson shook his head. "Some of the gentlemen are my customers," he said. "But I haven't seen any of them for a few weeks. Business has been bad since the depression."

Piper nodded. "Then you haven't seen the gentleman here at all? His name was Keeley, although you may not have given him a card to your place."

"Sure I've seen him," said Moe Ellinson easily. "But you tried to put something over on me. He didn't come up on the stage at all. The gent you mention came into my place with four others at about five-thirty Friday afternoon, and after he'd washed the blood off his face I served 'em up a couple of rounds of beer. Then they left."

"Can you pick him out?"

Every eye in the room was on Moe Ellinson now. He enjoyed the limelight.

"Sure I can pick him out for you, Inspector. The gent you're referring to just went up the aisle on his hands and knees, and he's going through the hall door right now. Don't mention it."

Miss Withers whirled around, and saw an empty chair behind her, with two surprised-looking guards gripping empty air. Buck Keeley had given them the slip!

They started for the door, but the Inspector held them back. "My experiment has been a success," he said calmly. "Let him go; he's been handed a sure-fire alibi."

Miss Withers and the Inspector went slowly down the hall toward his office. "I said that my experiment was a success," he told her. "It was, from Keeley's point of view. But it was a flat failure from mine."

Miss Withers caught sight of the familiar face of Sergeant Taylor down the hall. "There's the report from your handwriting expert, Mrs. Korn," she cried excitedly. "Your experiment was a failure, but watch and see how *mine* turns out!"

The report from Jersey was brief and to the point. "Whether because they were written under different emotional conditions, or because of change of development in the writer, these two samples of handwriting differ slightly in obvious characteristics. But *beyond the shadow of a doubt* they were written by the same person!"

"I guess the day leaves us both right behind the eight ball," the Inspector told her unkindly.

But Miss Withers was unconvinced.

18

The Finger of Scorn

Miss Withers returned to the Inspector's office later that same day to find that worthy minion of the law bidding farewell to a group of gentlemen who appeared too indigent and uninterested to be anything but members of what is sometimes laughingly called "the Fourth Estate." Inspector Piper was talking.

"Just say that Buckner Keeley, rodeo star rider, was arrested this morning on charges arising from the Stait murder, but that he was released this afternoon when he cleared himself of suspicion by the proving of a well-supported alibi. Will you print that, as a favor to me?"

There were several grunts of assent. "But look here, Inspector, it's not news if you discover that somebody *didn't* do the murder. There must be a lot of people in town who're innocent of snagging the candy playboy out of his go-cart the other evening."

"Yeah," another voice rose up. "This little story is all right, but my city editor says he has a bellyful of listening to announcements that an arrest is expected before nightfall."

"Is it true that you suspect Laurie Stait of having been the center of a smuggling ring?"

"Is it true that the twin brother's girlfriend is unable to account for—"

"D'you think this murder is the work of a homicidal maniac?"

"Will you announce . . ."

The Inspector herded them desperately past Miss Withers and out into the hall. "I think that this murder and every other murder is the work of a homicidal maniac," he admitted. "Now scram back to your desks, boys. I'll let you know as soon as there is anything doing. When we get our hands on the murderer—"

"He'll have already cheated the chair by dying of senile dementia," suggested an irreverent baritone.

The Inspector came back mopping his brow. This had not been a notably comfortable day.

"All the same," he explained to Miss Withers. "I had to release that story. We've nothing against Buck Keeley now, and the poor devil may as well know it. He probably thinks that he's being hunted down with rifle squads, but he'll read the morning newspapers in a few hours and find out it's all fixed."

"He knows it's all fixed," said Miss Withers quietly.

"You mean he waited here long enough to hear what Ellinson said before he walked out from between those two dumb flatties I had guarding him?"

"No, not exactly. But I saw him about half an hour ago, and I told him."

Inspector Piper frowned. "You saw him? Where?"

"If you must know, it was up in his sister's room at the Hotel Senator," Miss Withers explained. "He was under the bed, with a revolver in each hand, and I was afraid he'd start shooting before I could explain why I came up there. But I talked first, luckily."

"That's good," said the Inspector absent-mindedly. "Say, by the way. Just why did you go up there? How did you know he was there?"

"I didn't know he was there. I knew his sister Rose was there. Remember our bargain, Oscar. I want to play a lone hand on this, because I'm pretty sure I've got a full flush—"

"You probably mean a full house?"

"Have it your way, Oscar. Anyway, I think I've got what we're looking for. Only I can't prove it, as yet. That's why I went to see Rose

Keeley. I had to ask her help." Miss Withers leaned back in the easiest chair.

"But what in the world do you need Rose Keeley's help for?" The Inspector did not conceal his amazement.

Miss Withers smiled enigmatically. "I needed her help in sending a telegram, Oscar. What this case cries out for is a character witness capable of making an identification. I sent for one."

"A character witness for Buck Keeley?"

"Hardly." And that was all the Inspector could get out of his co-worker. Finally she changed the subject.

"I came back here hoping to interest you in having tea with me somewhere," she informed him. "You realize, don't you, that we had hardly any lunch? I thought that there might be a place near here."

The Inspector welcomed the suggestion. "Just around the corner is the Diavolo Rosso," he informed her. "Best Italian food in the city, though it's something of a dump outside. And the *vino* is swell."

"Where I was brought up, out in Dubuque, spaghetti and red wine weren't served at teatime," Miss Withers observed acidly. "Besides, so far as it is possible I try to observe the laws of our great, if somewhat depressed, nation. It's probably a silly old-fashioned habit that I've grown into from trying to live as an example to the younger generation in my classes. I realize that I'm behind the times, and that while I'm in Rome I ought to burn Roman candles, but—"

The rest of Miss Withers' little homily was drowned out by the skirl of the telephone.

The Inspector discovered that a gentleman named Waverly would like to speak with him on important business.

"Go ahead, put him on," was the decision.

"Hello, Inspector Piper? This is Charles Waverly. You remember our little chat of last evening?"

Inspector Piper admitted that he did.

"You remember asking me why I considered the marriage of my sister to the surviving Stait twin as unfortunate?"

Again the Inspector assented, impatiently.

"Well, I thought you ought to know this. They had some kind of a dreadful row this morning, and my sister moved away from the Stait house. My prediction was right, Inspector."

"Well, what if it was? Do you want to set up as a clairvoyant and give me as a reference? Go on, man. Why did she leave him?"

There was a pause over the line. Then: "Really, I don't know. She won't talk to me, Inspector. She won't talk to anybody, she says. But she's left her husband and moved back to her apartment in the Village and she says that she's going to sail for Bermuda on Friday's boat."

"You tell her for me that if she tries to sail on that boat I'll have her dragged off by the scruff of her neck," Inspector Piper shouted into the telephone. "And you tell her another thing—"

"I can't," cut in Charles Waverly. "She phoned me to tell me what had happened, and hung up before I could ask her why. And she's not answering the phone at her apartment."

"She'll do some answering for me," the Inspector promised. And he hung up the phone.

Miss Withers listened in silence to what the message had been. "Why are you putting on your hat, Oscar?"

"I'm going down there and find out why Dana walked out on her husband, of course."

Miss Withers shook her head. "It wouldn't do any good, Oscar."

"And why not?"

"Because she won't be there," the schoolteacher informed him. "If Dana Waverly doesn't want to talk, she won't put herself in a position where she has to talk. She's enough of a sport so that, even if she's leaving her husband, she won't say anything against him until this has blown over somehow. She's the type."

"But I've got to find out why she left him!"

"I've got an idea," Miss Withers suggested. "You'll have a terrible time locating Dana this afternoon, because evidently she wants to keep out of this, and she'll know you'll be looking for her. But I know where you'll be able to find her tomorrow."

"Huh? Where will she be tomorrow?"

"Mr. Frank Campbell is having belated funeral services for Laurie Stait tomorrow afternoon at two," Miss Withers reminded him. "Dana is such a close friend of the family that she won't dare stay away, particularly in the light of all the newspaper publicity that there's been. She'll appear at the chapel, certainly, even if she doesn't go on out to the burial vault with the family afterward. Dana is the type who would consider that part of her code. Why don't you seize her there, and ask your questions, if you think you must?"

The Inspector nodded slowly. "Maybe you're right, at that. I'd rather go to the dentist than to a funeral, but sometimes you can learn something even there. I suppose that even the old lady herself will leave her parrot and put in an appearance; she's just the type to get a big thrill out of the party."

He reached for his coat. "Come on, it's late enough so we can pretend this is dinner, and you shouldn't object to spaghetti for dinner. Let's forget about sleuthing for tonight, and take on a movie."

It was, as the Inspector pointed out next morning, a great day for a funeral. No funeral director could have arranged, or even imagined, a more fitting setting for the last grim rites. Gray, ghostly clouds hung low over the temples and minarets of Manhattan, shrouding the city and cutting off the top of the Empire State Building as if with a pair of shears. Little, scudding winds through the storied canyons, chill and bleak, howling of a winter that was no longer a promise but a bitter actuality.

The threat of rain or snow did not deter the Inspector from showing up at Headquarters in accordance with his custom at eight o'clock, in time for the daily roundup. When his major social event of the day was completed, and the crop of gangsters and auto thieves and degenerates had been returned to their cells, he descended the stairs to his own sanctum.

Sergeant Taylor was on duty in the outer office. "Phone call just came for you," he announced. "Lady left a message—Miss Withers. She says she's expecting you to pick her up at one-thirty, in time for the funeral. She can't come down this morning because she has to go out to the school where she teaches."

"Huh? Okay, thanks." Inspector Piper broke open a new box of cigars, and busied himself for a while in trying to pry the first one loose.

The Sergeant poked his head in at the door. "Somebody wants to see you, Inspector."

Piper looked up, annoyed. "All right, tell 'em to wait. I'm busy." He went on digging until at last a cellophane-wrapped panatella leaped into his hand. He made a religious rite of removing the wrapper and getting the cigar burning well. Long ago the Inspector had discovered that his mental processes worked smoothest when his teeth were clamped hard upon one of these moist and aromatic bundles of weed.

At last he came to a decision. "Hey, Sergeant!"

Taylor appeared in the doorway.

"Sergeant, I got a job for you. It's a hard job and an important one. Take one of the boys and go pick up Lew Stait, wherever he is."

The Sergeant grinned. "That's not such a hard job as you think, Inspector." He stepped to one side and jerked his thumb toward the outer office behind him. "That guy who's waiting to see you says his name is Lew Stait. And he says he's in a hurry."

The early visitor was in a hurry, and likewise in something of a nervous state. He had neglected to shave, and his yellow hair was unkempt under his derby. He had not slept in his clothes, but that was because quite evidently he had not slept at all.

The Inspector did not offer to shake hands, but he pointed out a chair by the window, where such light as there was fell directly on the young man's face.

Stait pulled a newspaper clipping from his pocket and shoved it across at the Inspector. "I want to know what that means," he said.

The Inspector studied it. "COWBODY RODEO STAR WINS FREE-

DOM". . . . It was a reasonably correct version of the statement he had issued to the press yesterday afternoon.

"It means just what it says. Why?"

"Because you've turned loose the murderer of my brother, that's why!"

"Nonsense." The Inspector shook his head. "Mr. Stait, we've proved beyond the possibility of a doubt that Buck Keeley could not have been the murderer of your twin brother. He's got an unbreakable alibi!"

"Can't alibis be faked?"

"Sometimes. But not this one." The Inspector stared at his caller. "Why are you so anxious to see Keeley indicted? He didn't have any motive, did he?"

"Of course he had a motive. He was trying to force my brother into marrying his slut of a sister, although I swear to you that there was no reason under heaven why he should have married her."

"How can you be so sure of that, young man? Your brother was out at the Wyoming ranch and you were here in town last summer."

"I tell you, that makes no difference. I know that nothing happened which should not have happened. They were trying to marry that girl off to what they thought was a rich man. I'll swear it on a stack of Bibles."

The Inspector shrugged his shoulders. "I'd like to settle this case and forget it just as much, or probably more, than you would. But I tell you frankly, Buck Keeley convinced us of his innocence."

"But it was his rope!"

The Inspector rose to his feet and passed over to one of the glass cases which lined the wall, and twisted a tiny key into the lock.

The panel swung open, then he fumbled among the assorted weapons there until he found what he wanted. It was a coil of soft, light rope, bound at the end with blue silk thread. He drew it out from among the sash-weights and revolvers and stilettos which had been Exhibit A's in the most important murder cases of the last decade and others slated for impending trials.

He threw the rope on the table under his visitor's eyes, and the young man drew back with a violent start.

"Pretty, isn't it?" The Inspector fingered the noose at the end. "This is what jerked the life out of your brother," he observed affably. "This part here cut into his throat. It's a bad death to die, hanging is. Worse than the chair, in some ways, they say."

He pretended not to notice the evident agitation of his caller, and passed quickly over to his desk, where he drew a second rope from a bottom drawer.

This also he threw upon the table, beside the first. "And now, since you want to know, I'll show you just why we are sure Buck Keeley didn't kill your brother," he said roughly. "Notice this second rope? In the first place, it's more than twice as long as the murder weapon."

He pointed out the difference, and Lew Stait nodded slowly.

"The full-length lariat was too long and awkward to use for that little job," said the Inspector heartily. "So the murderer cut it off, not wanting to have any more rope to conceal under his coat than was absolutely necessary. He cut it off, and then found he had to bind the end to keep it from unwinding. . . ."

The younger man fingered the end of the rope. "But this blue thread is Buck Keeley's special mark. He uses it to distinguish all his ropes and saddles and so forth."

"Just how do you know?"

"Why—because Laurie, my brother, brought back souvenirs of his trip out there. When he left the ranch he bought his saddle and spurs. . . ."

"And a rope?"

"No, not a rope. But he told me about them."

"Well, it's true that Buck Keeley used a blue thread to mark his riding gear and his ropes," the Inspector confided. "This longer rope here is one that he used in the rodeo at the Garden. Notice the blue thread. It would take a laboratory expert to tell the difference in those two different threads, but one is common silk and the other is a silk-rayon combination sold only at the excellent notion counters of Mr. Woolworth's stores. In other words, the rope that hanged your brother was bound with thread that Buck Keeley would have had to travel across two states to buy. We have a laboratory expert, you see. What's more, we find that whoever bound the murder rope did an awkward and slipshod job on it. He wasn't a cowboy, Stait."

"Who was he, then?"

The Inspector didn't answer that. "Maybe you can tell me that?"

Lew Stait thought for a moment. "Maybe I . . ." His jaw closed like a trap, and there was the gleam of a sudden determination in his eye. The Inspector guessed that his caller had made up his mind about something or other—a decision which had evidently been a difficult one.

"May I ask you one more question, Inspector?"

"What is it?" The Inspector had some questions of his own to ask, but he was wondering if this was the time to ask them.

"Tell me one thing," begged the surviving Stait twin, as he leaned across the table. "Tell me this. Your ladyfriend, Miss Withers, said something about Hubert's having an alibi for the time of the murder. You warned us not to discuss the case at home, and even if you hadn't the subject is such a sore one that nobody has mentioned it. Where was Hubert when my brother was killed?"

The Inspector considered for a moment, and then decided that there could be no harm in letting that secret out.

"Your cousin Hubert was at a movie with your Aunt Abbie," he announced. "They left together; you knew that."

"Yes, I knew that. But—let me think. Listen, Inspector, if you want to solve this case, break down that alibi! Hubert must have been involved. . . ."

"Why?"

"I—I can't tell you. It's . . ."

"You're making a pretty strong accusation, young man. Your cousin Hubert had no motive for the killing, remember. He wasn't in love with the same girl as the dead man. He stood to inherit only after *your* death as well as your brother's. And he has the ticket stubs and your Aunt Abbie to prove where he was at the time of the murder. No, you're not in a position to accuse him. It might even make someone suspect *you* of murdering Laurie Stait!"

For some unknown reason, that remark struck home. "Me murder Laurie Stait?" The young man burst forth into paroxysms of laughter. He laughed until he was weak. The Inspector suddenly rose and left him there.

He spoke briefly to the Sergeant. "When this young man leaves my office, put a tail on him and keep it there day and night, see? I want him free for the funeral this afternoon, and if things break right we'll have our arrest for the afternoon papers tomorrow!"

He returned to his office to find his visitor in a new mood. Lew Stait was in control of himself now, and the Inspector realized that he had missed an opportunity of striking while the iron was hot. There was a rigidity about the disheveled young man with the yellow hair that told of his nervous and wrought-up condition. His eyes were narrow, and a vein throbbed visibly in his temple.

"Thank you, Inspector," he was saying. "I've got an errand to perform now. If you want me you know where to find me."

"If we should want to question your wife, do you know where we could find her?" asked the Inspector gently.

Lew Stait shook his head. "She's gone. Do you blame her? So what matters now?" His hands were plunged deep into the pockets of his overcoat, and he was breathing heavily.

Then he whirled suddenly toward the door, as if making up his mind again. "I've got to get out of here," he shouted, and then was gone.

The Inspector watched as the young man went down the hall, and saw a lounger in a brown overcoat detach himself from a pillar and stroll idly along behind him. Then Piper returned to his office, locked up the murder rope along with the other murder tools in his exhibition cases, and lit a fresh cigar.

Sergeant Taylor appeared in the doorway with a batch of mail. "On second thought," said the Inspector cheerfully, "on second thought we may have that arrest in time for the evening papers."

19

Alarums and Excursions

The Inspector and Miss Withers sat in the shelter of a taxicab outside the funeral chapel and watched the people pass from curb to doorway. It was not a big funeral, as funerals go. There was no blocking of the street with frenzied mourners, as at Valentino's last rites. No solid silver coffin bore the bones of this unfortunate man to his last resting place, for this was no gangster funeral. But the Staits were people who had once mattered in this rapidly changing city, and there were those who had not forgotten.

They saw figures prominent in the social and intellectual life of the city pass under the canopy and into the wide chapel, gloomy as a stage setting for the last act of Romeo and Juliet.

Here and again Miss Withers nudged the Inspector to point out the arrival of one or two of the figures associated with the murder investigation itself. Mrs. Hoff and Gretchen arrived early, the former clad in sober black but the little maid arrayed in a white coat of rabbit fur and wide net stockings as her contribution to the ceremony. Charles Waverly was there, in formal mourning clothes. Miss Withers had a quick suspicion that he had even blackened his frivolous yellow moustache for the ceremony.

Then there came Dana, red-eyed and leaning on the arm of the buxom Bertha Doolittle. She might have been the widow, Miss Withers thought. There was a look in her eyes as if something she had loved was dead.

Last of all the figures in this panorama, and most theatrically imposing, was Gran—Mrs. Roscoe Stait herself. Wrinkled as a mummy, old as the mouldering horse and carriage which deposited her at the curb, the old lady scorned Aunt Abbie's proffered arm and stalked across the sidewalk to the door of the chapel. It might have been her first sight of the outdoors and the faces of her fellow men in a dozen years, but Gran looked neither to right nor left. The poise which had stood her in such good stead on opera stage and in the courtroom did not desert her now. This was her hour, and she disappeared inside with a great rustling of mouldy silks. The Inspector turned nervously to see whether or not the naked parrot was hopping down from the carriage door to follow her, but that, at least, was spared him.

"You aren't going in, are you?" Miss Withers wanted to know. He shook his head.

"It wouldn't look well for a member of the Force to intrude at a time like this," he admitted. "But I did want to get a glimpse of the arrivals, and we've got that."

"All members of the family are here except Lew Stait and Cousin Hubert," Miss Withers pointed out. "They're already beginning inside—I can hear the organ."

"I don't know about Hubert," the Inspector admitted. "Probably he doesn't like funerals, and I don't blame him. But I don't mind telling you that I doubt very much if Lew Stait will show up at all. It's a hunch of mine that that young man is trying at this moment to step out of the picture, and it won't do him any more good than it did Buck Keeley. And Lew Stait has no alibi that's worth a tinker's damn."

"Oscar," said Miss Withers suddenly, "I've got something to tell you. I know who committed this murder." There was a sudden lessening of the tension between them.

The Inspector grinned. "Of course you do. And so do I. I promised Taylor an hour ago that we'd have our arrest in time for the home edition of the afternoon papers. And I mean to— Wait a minute, who's that?"

A boyish-faced usher in cutaway and striped trousers was calling something from the doorway. Then he came running across the sidewalk.

"Are you Inspector Piper of the Police?"

The Inspector pleaded guilty.

"Well, your office is on the phone and they say it's a matter of life and death. They want to relay a call that just came in. . . ."

"Get out of my way!" Piper shouted, and sprinted for the doorway.

Miss Withers cooled her heels for what seemed like half an hour, and what was probably as long as five minutes. Then the Inspector came out, still on the run, and leaped into the taxi beside her.

"The Stait house—203 Riverside Drive—and step on it!"

The driver whined. "But, mister, if the cops sees me . . ."

Piper flashed his gold badge. "I *am* the cops," he shouted, unconsciously paraphrasing a *bon mot* of one of the less fortunate Louises. And the machine leaped forward up Broadway as if shot from a bow.

"It was Hubert Stait," explained the Inspector, hanging on to the strap for dear life as the taxi ducked round a truck.

Miss Withers was all ears.

"He spoke so low into the phone I could hardly hear him," continued Piper. "Says he knows now who killed his cousin; not only knows but can prove it. He's scared green over something, and his voice quavered like an old man's, but he's game, Hildegarde. Says he's at last got evidence that'll convict the murderer—"

"And that is—?"

"He wouldn't say over the phone. Afraid he'd be overheard, I guess. But he begged me to hurry. I guess he's afraid he'll lose his nerve."

"I don't think that young man will ever lose his nerve," said Miss Withers dryly. And her fingers slowly polished the already worn handle of her umbrella.

The taxicab skidded round a corner and then spurted up the Drive, passing red lights, ducking between oncoming cars, and otherwise giving Miss Withers a mild case of nervous prostration.

The Stait house came into view, gaunt and gloomy against the heavy gray sky. The taxi skidded to a stop, and Miss Withers glanced at her watch. It was exactly two-thirty-five—the trip from Broadway at 67th had taken something less than fifteen minutes. Miss Withers was of the opinion that this was a record for the distance. If it wasn't, she was quite content to let the old record stand.

But the Inspector did not race up the steps as she had expected. Down the street he noticed the figure of a young man in a brown overcoat idly chatting with a doorman of a new apartment building. He waved his arm, and the man in the brown overcoat came running up the street.

"Sure the Stait twin is in there," said Swarthout. "I tailed him round to four sporting-goods stores where he tried to buy cartridges, and then he came here. About half an hour ago. Nobody's been in or out. I guess he's alone in the house—the doorman says that he saw them all leave a while back to go some place. Even the old lady."

"Follow me," ordered the Inspector. "Maybe Stait isn't alone in there. Come on, Hildegarde."

He pressed his thumb against the bell and waited. There was no answer. He pressed it again, excitedly, impatiently, so that the hall rang with sound, but still nothing happened.

The Stait house stood vacant and gloomy and bare, silent as a tomb. Silent as the new abode of one twin, Miss Withers thought.

"What's wrong here?" The Inspector beat with the heel of his hand on the door. "Georgie, you duck to the back door. If it's open, come through and let us in. If it isn't, you stay there and don't let anybody in or out. I smell trouble."

He drew back, ready to try kicking in the front door, when it was suddenly jerked away from them, and the half-naked figure of a tall young man appeared, a big bath towel wrapped around him.

It wasn't, as Miss Withers had supposed for a moment, Cousin Hubert. It was the surviving Stait twin, water running from his sturdy althlete's body and forming pools on the carpet.

They had but a glimpse of his pale, startled face, and then their host made an effort to slam the door. The Inspector caught it with his shoulder just in time, and pushed through into the hall, his hand instinctively on the hip that had once borne a service revolver.

Miss Withers, scandalized but still game, hung in his wake.

"W-what do you want?"

The young man drew the bathsheet more closely around his body, and looked desperately past the intruders as if he was planning to bolt for it. He was trembling, whether from chill or from fear Miss Withers could only guess.

"Come clean, Lew! Where is your cousin Hubert?"

"Hubert?" Lew spoke the name as if it was new to him. "Hubert?"

"Yes, *Hubert!* Where is he?"

"I don't know. Why should I know?"

"Quit stalling. We want to find your cousin."

Lew drew a deep breath. "Why, you'll find Hubert at the funeral, I guess. He must be down at the funeral chapel. Why not look for him there? I couldn't stand seeing my own twin buried, but the rest went—"

He tried to lead them toward the door. "It's on Broadway above the Circle," he pointed out. "Only a short drive from here. Why—"

"You won't get rid of us that easy," Piper told him. "Come on, we're going up to your cousin's room."

"But he isn't there, I tell you!"

"How do you know?" put in Miss Withers.

The young man set his jaw. "I know damn' well. I came home figuring that Hubert wouldn't have the face to show up at the funeral. I wanted to talk to him. But he's gone out, and his door is locked."

They were going up the stairs, the Inspector pausing on the landing long enough for Lew Stait to get into a dressing gown and slippers. The butt of a revolver showed in the pocket of the dressing gown. Piper snatched it in silence. He exchanged a long look with Miss Withers. They went on—the young man white and still shivering. Miss Withers noticed that his hands were shrunken with the thousands of tiny wrinkles that come when soaked too long in over-hot water. They were not attractive hands, to her.

Then the three of them stood outside Hubert's door. The Inspector rapped loudly, but there was no answer.

He tried the knob, but the door was locked. He turned to Lew. "Have you got a key for this door?"

The young man denied it. "This is an old-fashioned lock," the Inspector observed. "I could pick it with a hairpin—or any ordinary skeleton would open it. But we won't wait for that."

He drew back, as if he intended to hurl his shoulder against the stout oak barrier, but instead he swung the heel of his right foot against the door near the knob, crashing it so that panels cracked and hinges screeched.

Again—and the door swung inward, disclosing the long narrow room which was Hubert Stait's bedroom and study. It was dim in the half-light of the winter afternoon, and there was a singularly musty odor in the air, which may have emanated from the rows of books which hung on both walls.

A clock on the mantel ticked monotonously, its slow beat pounding in Miss Withers' ears as she saw who was staring at them from a high wing chair near the fireplace.

It was Hubert Stait, but he did not seem surprised, or even interested, at their rude invasion of his privacy. He simply sat there, and stared.

"Hello, there!" said Piper, and there was a cracked ring in his voice. For somehow he knew that he would receive no answer to his greeting—knew, even before his fumbling fingers found the light switch beside the door.

As the lights went on, everything in the room was suddenly white and glaring, with one wide black shadow like a bar sinister across the carpet. That shadow was cast by the high back of the fireside chair in which Hubert Stait was resting.

His eyes, strangely naked without the habitual spectacles, were bulging in their sockets, and his body had been lifted a few inches from the cushion by means of a strangling cord which gripped the thick neck and ran up and over the high back of the chair.

On the floor beside his feet lay, face down, a copy of *Le Côté de Guermantes,* its leaves twisted and crumpled.

The noose, which had pulled savagely at the skin of his throat, was made of a rope familiar to all of them. It was of half-inch hemp, which ran up and over the high back and down where it was knotted around one foot of the chair. That end was bound with blue thread.

Miss Withers looked at her watch, instinctively. It was five to three—less than forty minutes since the Inspector had heard this man's voice over the telephone, imploring him to make haste.

They had not, for all their hurry, been quick enough. Hubert Stait was still warm, but he was quite completely and finally dead.

20

The Spilling of the Beans

"Am I to consider myself under arrest?"

The surviving Stait twin was dressing himself, under the eagle eye of two detectives from the local precinct station. The Inspector stood in the doorway, and behind him the old house bustled with ghoulish activity.

"You can consider whatever you please," said Piper. "And my advice to you is the less you say the better."

"I've told you the truth," Lew Stait protested. "I came home here to have a talk with Hubert—"

"After scouring the town in an attempt to buy .44 shells for the revolver you stole from my collection of murder weapons!"

"What if I did? I didn't get any cartridges, did I? I came home because I knew that Hubert wouldn't be at the funeral, and when I found his door locked I came downstairs and took a bath. I thought it would calm my nerves."

"You probably wanted to wash yourself clean of the stain of murder, like Macbeth in the play," suggested one of the detectives, who prided himself on a literary background.

"You can't get by with that story," Piper went on. "I talked to Hubert on the telephone at twenty minutes after two, and we've traced that call from this house. You can't tell me that he sneaked out of his room and used the telephone without your knowing he was here."

"But I was in the bath, with the water running."

"You'll have a hard time making a jury believe that, young man. You nearly got away with it, didn't you?"

"Away with what?"

"You killed your brother," the Inspector accused. "I always felt that your alibi that the little maid gave you wouldn't hold water. You dropped a noose over the head of your twin brother because you knew that the girl who was engaged to you really loved him. But your cousin Hubert got wise to you, and when you heard him telephone me that he had definite proof of the murderer, you sneaked up the stairs to his room—didn't you?"

Lew Stait refused to talk.

"You concealed yourself in the cupboard, or in the corner behind the bookcase. And when Hubert came back to his room to wait for my arrival, and sat down in his big chair in front of the fireplace, he thought he was safe. He thought he had a locked door between himself and you. He sat down in the big easy chair and picked up a book—and you pounced on him!"

The Inspector shoved his jaw almost in the young man's face. "The jig is up, Stait. You thought you'd inherit your brother's share of the property. You thought you'd cinch the girl you both loved, although that didn't work, either, because she got wise to you and left you a couple of days after you made her marry you. Oh, we're wise to you. You don't need to sign any confession.

"We know where you got the rope. Your brother Laurie brought it back from the west with him as a souvenir, along with the other cowboy paraphernalia. It was too long for the little strangling job you planned from the top of the bus, so you cut it off and hid the remainder of it somewhere in the house here. Then you bound the end with blue thread—the wrong blue thread, but you didn't know that—so that it would appear that Buck Keeley did the job. You knew he was in town and you knew that he was trying to get your brother to marry his sister, who was in trouble.

"Then Buck Keeley proved an alibi that took the wind out of your sails. And then your cousin got wise to you. Hubert had the brains of the family. I remember you told me that the first night I questioned you. But you didn't realize how true that was.

"So when he was sitting in the fireside chair up in his room you crept out of the shadows, probably in your stocking feet, and made use of the remainder of the lariat. You dropped a noose over his head as you stood behind his chair, and before he could move or cry out you drew it tight, throwing your whole weight on the rope. While he was dying, you tied the other end around the bottom leg of the chair, and left him there. Don't try to lie now, Stait. The key to your room fits his door, we found that out. You locked the door and came downstairs. Whatever made you get the idea of taking a bath is a mystery to me, but all you murderers are crazy."

"I'm not a murderer, I tell you. If Hubert didn't commit suicide, somebody else killed him!"

"Suicide? There was no key in that room, young man, and the door was locked. Besides, a man can hang himself, but how can he tie the other end of the rope to the back of the chair he's sitting in? Hubert was afraid of you. He thought you might try to give him what you gave your twin brother, and you did. You'll burn in the chair for it, Stait."

The boy's eyes were hunted, but he did not speak.

"Bravo, Oscar," came a voice from the hallway. "That's a fine speech all right. Masterly statement of the case. Only it's all wrong."

There stood Miss Withers. She was holding a key in her hand. "I saw something twinkling out in the street, and picked this up. I think if you try it you'll find it's the key to Hubert's room. . . ."

"Aha! So he threw it away to try and make it look as if the murderer had dropped it!" The Inspector was facing Lew, who now stood completely dressed except for his necktie. He seemed to hesitate in drawing the noose of silk round his throat.

"But it won't work, Stait! You can't get by with trying to make out that somebody besides you and Hubert was in this house this afternoon. Because I've had a man outside since you came in, and he swears that nobody passed in or out since then, either through the back or front. You were alone with Hubert Stait, and you're going to pay for what you did to him."

There was the sound of something bumping on the stair. Miss Withers drew back in instinctive dread of what was being carried down to the waiting ambulance from the morgue.

"That means that the photographers and the print men have finished," Piper announced. He stepped out into the hallway and shook hands with an assistant' medical examiner who was following the body downstairs. "Hello, doc. That was quick work. Anything new?"

Levin shook his head. "Pretty job of strangling," he announced. "You seem to run to those, Inspector. This beats the one we had on Fifth Avenue last week."

"You agree that it couldn't have been suicide?"

"I don't see any signs of it. He's been dead about two hours. Must have croaked about two-thirty. . . ."

"Five minutes after I talked to him on the phone," said Piper. "Oh, it's open and shut, all right. And this washes up the other murder, too."

"Which is a relief for everybody concerned," agreed the doctor. "Well, I'll see you around. Now that you've nabbed the wily gent in the bedroom, I suppose we'll have a rest from stranglings for a while. Good night, Inspector—'night, Miss Withers."

He passed on down the stairs.

"Well," announced the Inspector, happily, "I guess this washes up the Stait Murder. I don't see how you can maintain that my little résumé was wrong."

"Don't you?" Miss Withers was restless, with an undercurrent of excitement. "Well, I'll agree that this settles the Stait murder all right. But there's something else. . . ."

"That something else can wait," the Inspector told her. "Well, I guess this case proves that the official methods can sometimes win out ahead of amateurs, huh?"

Miss Withers was thoughtful. "What are you going to do now, Oscar?"

"What am I going to do? I'm going to take this Stait kid down to the station and have him committed for the grand jury on the charge of strangling his twin brother Laurie and his cousin Hubert, that's what I'm going to do."

Miss Withers looked at her watch. "Oscar, will you wait about ten minutes?"

"Ten minutes? Why should I wait? I've kept him here an hour or two longer than was necessary because I wanted to stick around myself until everything was washed up. I've rushed things through so that I could get the body out of the house before the whole family gets back from the funeral of the other twin. The shock might kill the old lady if she'd come in and found the stiff here."

"Wait a little longer, for your own sake," pleaded Miss Withers. "I've planned a little surprise, and he's on his way up here in a taxi now. But it takes quite a while to come in from Roosevelt Field. Oscar, this may make a tremendous difference, not only to your own career, but to the lives of innocent people. I can't tell you any more, because you won't believe me, but will you wait?"

"My dear lady, I can't wait! Do you want me to miss getting this arrest in the morning papers?"

"There'll be something in the morning papers that you won't be caring for if you make that arrest right now," Miss Withers warned him. "I tell you— Stop, maybe that's what I'm waiting for, now."

There was the sound of the front door being opened and of low voices in the lower hall. The Inspector leaned over the balustrade and saw what he had feared.

The Stait family, or what was left of it, was there in the hall. A harrowing ten minutes ensued, after which Gran was led upstairs in a state of near-collapse, Aunt Abbie on one side and Charles Waverly on the other. There were sounds of wailing from the kitchen, where Mrs. Hoff and Gretchen were playing the part of old family retainers, and one lone figure stood in the lower hall, dry-eyed, stiff, and somehow pitiful.

It was Dana Waverly—now Dana Stait—and Miss Withers could not forbear going down to her.

"I suppose you think it's strange, my being here," Dana said dully. "But I couldn't help coming, unless I told Gran everything, and I couldn't do that. She doesn't know that we're separated, you see." She put her hand on Miss Withers' arm. "Do you think I ought to go to—him?"

Miss Withers spoke a name. The girl drew back. "But—then you know?"

The schoolteacher nodded, and put her finger to her lips. "I think you ought to go to him," she said softly. "I think you ought to stay with him."

Dana shook her head. "You don't understand everything," she said. "Oh, I'd believe in him in spite of all this if it weren't for one thing . . . the Unforgivable!"

"There's very few sins that the Lord won't forgive under the right circumstances," Miss Withers pointed out. "At least, so I was taught as a child. Besides, I've also heard that it's better not to know anything than to know a lot of things that aren't so."

Dana looked at her, wonderingly. "I wish I knew what you mean," she whispered.

"You will, before you're an hour older," Miss Withers promised. She heard a taxicab drawing up outside, and she knew who it was.

"You go up and see him," she urged the girl. "He needs a friend right now worse than anything in the world. Maybe there'll be two of you soon."

"I—I'll do what you say," promised Dana. And she ran toward the stairs.

Ten minutes later Miss Withers came up the stairs, a conspirator's smile on her lips. She was risking everything on one throw of the dice.

She stopped in the doorway of the bedroom. The two detectives were staring out of the window, and Inspector Piper was jingling a ring of keys impatiently. A boy sat on the edge of the bed, and Dana knelt beside him, her arms pressing his head against her shoulder.

But he held himself rigid. "I know—I know you didn't do it!" she was saying.

He shook his head mechanically. The barrier between them was too high for her to pass. Dana moved away from him, and he looked up at the Inspector. "Come on, get it over with, will you?"

"I'm afraid I'll have to," Piper said. "I've stalled around now for hours. Sorry, Hildegarde, but whatever you had up your sleeve will have to come later." He faced the prisoner again.

"Lewis Maitland Stait, I hereby place you under arrest for the willful and premeditated murder of your cousin, Hubert Stait, and of your brother, Laurie Stait. . . ."

The Inspector's neat little speech was rudely interrupted. "Oscar," cut in Miss Withers, "isn't there something in the law which says that no man can be convicted of a murder unless the *corpus delicti* is proved?"

He turned on her, rapidly losing patience. "Good God, Hildegarde! At a time like this! Yes, of course there's such a law."

"And the *corpus delicti* means the actual proof that a crime has been committed—not only a crime in general, but in this case a murder against a specific person?"

"Yes, of course. Any fool knows that. . . ."

"And if the police don't know the identity of the corpse they have no murder case?"

"Of course not. But—"

"Well," said Miss Withers triumphantly, "you'll get yourself into hot water if you arrest Lew Stait for the murder of Laurie. You're arresting the wrong suspect for the murder of the wrong corpse, Oscar. I tried to tell you, but you wouldn't let me."

"What in heaven's name are you talking about?"

Miss Withers didn't answer, but accusingly faced the boy on the bed. "That's *Laurie* Stait over there," she said. "Aren't you Laurie?"

The prisoner looked up at her and shook his head dully. "I've nothing to say," he told her.

"Nothing? Remember, I know everything, young man." But he still kept his stolid silence.

Miss Withers drew the Inspector out into the hall.

"Explain yourself!" he objected. "I knew you had this crazy idea when you insisted that I send out the samples of handwriting to be tested. But remember what Mrs. Korn reported? That inscription in the old book and the note of Lew's were both in the same hand!"

"I know. But there were other things, Oscar, which made me keep on the track. Listen to me now, before you make a dreadful mistake. Hasn't it been clear to you that the living twin has been impersonating the dead one? They were *identical* twins, you know, and nobody could tell them apart but Dana."

"Yes, but—why, the first night when we came up here we found the boy you say is Laurie monkeying round with the maid, which was supposed to be Lew's idea of pleasure."

"That's true. But I've got a hunch he was already acting the part of his brother!"

"He couldn't have known, unless he killed him," said Piper.

"There might be a way he could have found out. But there were countless things. The missing wallets, for instance. You know and I know that the one identification most men carry is the card or two in their notecase. Well, I don't know how the dead man lost his, but remember I saw this boy in here go down the hall of this house that night to the cellar stair with something in his hand, and then we smelled burning leather? Well, he destroyed his own notecase, in case he should be searched. He wanted it to appear that he himself was dead."

"Why?"

"Because he was afraid, that's why. Probably of Buck Keeley, who had been making threats. Remember, the boy who was supposed to be Lew told us about what his brother had stared at *when he was alone*. And then Dana's marrying him when she did—it seemed more likely that she'd marry the man she loved that way than the man she was engaged to and hated. But, of course, she wouldn't wear Lew's ring when she married Laurie!"

"Suppose it is true? I don't see . . ."

"Wait. Don't you see how it fits together? Lew, not Laurie, had a date for dinner with Dana that night, at which she intended to break the sad news to him. Lew, not Laurie, started off in the roadster to keep his date, driving down Fifth Avenue. It didn't make sense, to me—the idea that Lew, who had the date, stayed home, and Laurie, who hadn't, took the car out and got himself strangled in the street."

"It's all a wild theory," the Inspector objected. "Hildegarde, I've been very patient with you because I have the highest regard for your intelligence, but—"

"Then listen a little more. Can't you see what a chance this was for Laurie, the so-called 'bad' twin, to step into his brother's shoes, to be the babied one of the family, to have them aid him in marrying the girl he loved and who loved him? And at the same time he freed himself from whatever entanglements, real or fancied, he had with the Wyoming girl . . . and her brother."

"It's a wild guess, Hildegarde, as I said before. What difference does it make?"

"Suppose you arrest that boy in there as Lew Stait, and he is really

Laurie. He'll be released, and you know it, because he'll prove his real identity. And you can't send a man to the chair for killing himself."

"But how can you prove what you're saying? If you can, you've got an iron-bound case against our prisoner!"

"I thought I'd done it with the book I discovered," Miss Withers admitted. "But the handwriting came out wrong. Laurie Stait was smart enough to realize that his handwriting might be tested, so he made sure that the only example of 'Lew's' writing round the house would be done by himself. He burned that Toby Tyler book, then bought another from Harpers and inscribed it to himself."

"But the ink was old and faded. . . ."

"That's where the coffee came in," Miss Withers pointed out. "Remember how Mrs. Hoff took up two or three cups late at night? Dana and Laurie were experimenting to get just the right shade of faded brown. It's a perfect imitation of aged ink. I should have wondered when I saw that line on the title page of the Toby Tyler book—'Thirty-fourth Printing'—but I didn't. Laurie Stait picked up somewhere a worn copy of the book, probably figuring that somebody round the house might miss the old one if it wasn't there, but he got a much more recent edition of the old classic."

"You make a good lawyer," the Inspector told her. "But in spite of all you say, that boy in there has got to go to jail. After all, you can't prove whether he's Lew or Laurie. I'll arrest him as John Doe. . . ."

"I can prove it," Miss Withers promised. She opened the door of the bedroom again. Dana was walking up and down the floor, and the boy on the bed was waiting.

"Do you still claim to be Lewis Stait?" she asked him.

"Yes, I'm Lew Stait. Go ahead. . . ."

"You're not Laurie Stait? You didn't go out to Keeley's dude ranch last summer?"

He shook his head, angrily. "Do I have to stand all this? Why . . ."

Miss Withers went to the head of the stairs. "Mr. Swarthout, will you go out to the taxi and tell Isidore Marx that it's time? He's the little Jewish boy with the red hair—just say Miss Withers sent word that he could come in." The door slammed, and she came back in the bedroom.

"I've got a surprise," she said calmly.

It was even more of a surprise than she had bargained for. There was the sound of the front door opening and closing, and then silence for a moment.

"Arrest me and get this over with," the boy begged. As he spoke there came a shrill whining sound from the lower hall, followed by the surprised exclamations of a little boy who called somebody a *schmutzick hund,* and the patter of feet on the stair.

A yellow whirlwind burst into the room, almost upsetting Miss Withers, who had been ill advised enough to stand in the doorway. It resolved itself into a big collie dog, still somewhat in the awkward age but already glorying in the fullness of a snowy white ruff and milky paws. A broken leash dangled from his collar.

His great plumed tail waved from side to side like a semaphore, and hiw nose wrinkled itself up into a snarling smile. He was making sure of his welcome. He took two steps toward the young man who sat, thunderstruck, on the bed, and then sniffed delightedly.

He gathered himself on his toes, and launched his body into the air, full at the throat of the single remaining Stait twin.

But the snarling whine was one of unaffected delight, and the great jaws opened only to let a long red tongue caress the face of the prisoner.

"Down, Rowdy, down!" The young man on the bed spoke without thinking.

"You see?" said Miss Withers. "This is a present from Rose Keeley, who is a little sorry for her part in this. We wired the ranch manager to ship the dog air mail. I sent one of my best pupils out to the flying field to get him here as quickly as possible. And now does anybody doubt that this boy was out at Keeley's ranch last summer, and adopted this dog?"

Nobody did. Rowdy was in the heights, prancing round his newly recovered master. Every second or two he stood up on his hind legs to place his forepaws on the shoulders of the boy whom they all knew now to be Laurie Stait. His nervous and delighted whine filled the room.

Laurie was stroking the silky head. "Rowdy, you've spilled the beans for me, old fellow." He turned to the Inspector. "Will you take me out of this? It doesn't make it any easier to see that pup, and know that I've got to go where I can't take him."

The Inspector nodded to his two aides, one of whom took a grimly glittering pair of bracelets from his coat pocket.

At this point there was a considerable interruption. From out in the hall came weird and raucous sounds. "Here, here, here—sic 'em, sic 'em! Rats!"

Rowdy deserted his master and dashed through the door in answer to the stern summons, only to wind up foolishly in the hall. Above him, perched on the balustrade, was the dumpy figure of the naked parrot. Someone, in ministering to the old lady, had left the door of her attic apartment open.

"Sic 'em, boy!"

Rowdy ran in circles for a moment, trying to find out who was calling him. It was evident that he took no stock in the ability of birds as conversationalists.

"Hell's bells, boys! Belay 'em with a nine-tailed cat! Rats, Fido, rats! Skrrrrr, skreeeeeeeeeeeee . . ."

Skipper relapsed into parrot language. The collie, suddenly realizing that he had been duped, returned to the bedroom with his ears drooping. He was shamefaced at having been taken in.

What he saw there made him forget all about the parrot, and spring to his master's side, with white teeth bared and his eyes a pale smoky yellow. He sensed that the two men who approached Laurie, one on either side, were not friends.

The detectives, who were ready with their handcuffs, drew back. "Hadn't I better use the butt of a gun on the pooch?" one of the operatives wanted to know.

"You won't need that," said Laurie Stait. "I'll go along without any fuss. All right, Rowdy, old boy, lie down."

Rowdy couched instantly upon all fours, ears cocked and his tongue panting.

His eyes were fixed on Laurie Stait with a world of love and admiration—something of the look that had been in Dana's eyes when first Miss Withers had seen the young couple together. But she had done all she could for them.

"Take him down to the station, boys. I'll be down there in a few minutes." The Inspector looked at Miss Withers uneasily.

"It's the only thing I can do," he pointed out.

"Of course," she agreed. They were standing in the hall, Miss Withers watching Dana's struggles to hold the leash which kept Rowdy from following his master to jail, or anywhere else in this world or the next.

"I'll keep him safe for you," she had told Laurie before he went through the door and down the steps. He did not answer her.

Miss Withers faced the Inspector. "Where are you going now, Oscar?"

"Where do you suppose? I'm going down to the precinct station and see that Laurie Stait is booked for the murder of Lew Stait and of Hubert Stait. Why?"

"You've got the wrong man," Miss Withers told him.

He shook his head. "You're off the track for once, dear lady. Hubert and Laurie were alone in this house. Nobody left the place until we got here. . . ."

"Exactly," Miss Withers agreed. "But afterward?"

"Why, I've got men stationed at both front and rear doors!"

"All the same, the murderer of Lew Stait—and of Hubert, for that matter—went out of here a little while ago. And you gave your official permission."

"What? Why, nobody left this house!"

"Somebody did," Miss Withers told him triumphantly. "Somebody left—feet first!"

21

Somersault

The Inspector stared at Miss Withers. "Suppose you explain?"

"I don't know whether I can explain or not, Oscar. It's like the jokes in *Punch,* or the meaning in James Joyce's *Ulysses*. If you see it, all right. If you don't, there's not much use analyzing. This whole thing has been a warped, twisted sort of puzzle—a game that we had to play according to the rules devised by a madman. It's as if a chess opponent arbitrarily decided to have his castles move diagonally, and his bishops control the files. It's mad, every bit of it. As mad as the court scene in Wonderland, and evil as sin besides."

"I don't see all that," Piper told her. "I think you've let your sympathies run away with you again."

"I'm not letting anything run away with me, if I can help it. There's been too much running already, and not enough thinking. I want to tell you a story, Oscar, and when I finish perhaps you'll see what I mean."

Miss Withers sat down on a bench on the first flight landing, and the Inspector joined her, a dead cigar between his teeth and a deep wrinkle between his eyes.

"It all goes back to that Friday afternoon, Oscar. The afternoon when Hubert and Lew Stait—you'll admit it was Lew, now?—left Laurie in this house after a friendly cocktail and drove off in the Chrysler roadster.

"Lew was going to see Dana for dinner, without the slightest suspicion of what news she had for him. Laurie knew his brother was going, and so did Hubert. You take that as being incriminating for Laurie. Because he had a very apparent motive for wanting his brother out of the way. But wait!

"Hubert was going to the movie, and his cousin dropped him off on the curb. We have Aunt Abbie as a witness to that, for she was waiting outside the lobby. Hubert knew, and Aunt Abbie knew, just where Lew was going, and the natural route he would take. You'll admit that?"

"Of course I'll admit that. But I still don't see how you can involve either one of them in the death of Lew. They went into the movie, and Lew drove on!"

Miss Withers smiled. "Of course! That's what fooled us for so long. Hubert went into the movie with Aunt Abbie. Remember, she isn't very bright, Oscar. She's movie mad, and absent-minded besides. They found seats, and then in a moment Hubert excused himself and got up—ostensibly to go to the men's room. He left Aunt Abbie engrossed in the picture, and—"

"And what? All this is mere guessing, Hildegarde. Suppose Hubert did leave the theater. He couldn't come out in time to catch his cousin in the roadster. He couldn't reach across the city and touch a man who was miles away!"

"You forget New York traffic conditions at the rush hour, Oscar. And you forget the dirty weather of that afternoon, which always jams things up even worse. Lew wasn't miles away. He wasn't even very many blocks away, and whoever murdered him counted on that fact."

"But I still don't see how—"

"Wait. The Cinemat Theatre is half a block from Carnegie Hall, where there's a station of the BMT. Suppose a young man were to get aboard a subway train there, and get off at Thirty-fourth Street five minutes later. He could walk over to Fifth Avenue, take a north-bound bus, and still be far ahead of the Chrysler.

"He'd pick an open top bus, as I explained to you some days ago, hoping to be alone up there. But if he wasn't, it wouldn't matter so terribly. He'd be in the rear seat, and the whole operation wouldn't take but a second or two. And the other passengers up on top would be with their backs to him, remember that.

"He ran a great risk, that murderer. Too great a risk to be sane. Because there were better and more secret ways of killing Lew Stait. But our murderer wanted the thrill of pulling the wool over the eyes of everybody. He wanted to feel that he was smarter than the world, and that he could murder his enemy on the busiest corner of the city."

"How did this murderer of yours know that the bus would pass close to the southbound auto?"

"He didn't, of course. Heaven only knows how many times he had tried it before, or was willing to try it again. But he knew that buses usually try to make time by keeping toward the middle of the street in rush hour, and knowing Lew Stait's temperament he figured that the driver of the Chrysler would also be in the outer lane. And he was not mistaken."

"But the rope, Hildegarde! You can't tell me that the murderer had time to go to the rodeo and steal a lariat."

"No. He had it wound round his waist, under his topcoat. And that rope, as I hinted before, was one of the trophies brought back from Wyoming by Laurie Stait. It hung in his room along with the saddle and the spurs. And it was where every member of the Stait family had access to it.

"So far so good. The murderer was crouched in the rear outside seat on top of that bus, and he knew that in the midst of that rush hour crowd, he was taking a terrible risk. And yet not as bad as it seems, for in that hurrying multitude everyone had to keep his eyes down to see where he was going. And so it was that only one person, the driver of the taxi far in the rear, saw what happened, or a part of it.

"There was a moment when the northbound bus swung past the southbound open roadster, and at that moment the murderer dropped his noose. The cast was not farther than ten feet, and he had been practicing. The contrary motion of the two vehicles snapped Lew's neck like a clay pipestem, and the murderer cast off the rope which had been caught round the rail of the bus, and let it go, body and all.

"Nobody would connect the body in the street behind them with the bus which sped northward. He counted on that, Oscar. I'll wager the murderer continued on his journey, all innocence, and only left the bus when he was well out of danger. Perhaps he even stayed on until the bus turned up Fifty-seventh.

"Then he bought another ticket—remember the extra red stub that you picked up out on the snow! That was where Hubert made his first mistake. He put the ticket stub automatically into his pocket and rejoined Aunt Abbie, and only thought of getting rid of it when he was almost home."

"But you mean to tell me that she wouldn't have missed him?"

"I doubt it. She's mad about the films, and the other morning, as I told you, she forgot whether she'd had her breakfast or not. Suppose she did miss him, I don't think she could tell whether he'd been gone three minutes or thirty. But wait—I think I see a little more light." Miss Withers pursed her lips.

"I've got it! Hubert—suppose for a while that it was Hubert—delayed a moment in a telephone booth before he went into the theater again. He had to send the news to Laurie!"

"Then Laurie was an accomplice?"

"In a way. You see, it was all part of the plan. Hubert phoned Laurie that he had just learned—never mind how—that Lew had been killed by a lariat. Laurie, already in hiding from Buck Keeley, naturally thought that his twin had been killed by mistake for himself. Hubert played on that. And he pointed out that Laurie had here a clear way out of his own difficulties, a chance to switch identities and start over again. It must have been Hubert's suggestion that Laurie try to ape Lew and make love to the little maid. He did it badly, and after that evening he didn't fool her at all. Remember how she warned me that Lew had changed since the death of his brother?

"Laurie has that respect for intellect, even for twisted intellect, that most healthy young morons have. He was in a panic, perhaps a panic that Hubert had helped to foment, and he clutched at any straw to rid himself of the incubus of Rose Keeley. Hubert warned him to get rid of identifying papers, and to say that his notecase had been stolen. Ergo, when a notecase marked Lew Stait was found in the dead man's pocket, we were supposed to take that only as evidence that Laurie had borrowed his brother's wallet.

"Laurie missed fire when he got rid of his papers, however, because he didn't have the heart to burn Dana's letter. He sneaked past me to the cellar to burn his wallet and smell up the house with leather, but he hid the love letter under the kitchen table on his way down because it was precious to him."

Miss Withers paused for breath, and then plunged on. "That letter, Oscar! Doesn't that suggest anything to you? Remember what Charles Waverly's stenographer overheard? Dana bragged about the love letter of hers that Laurie carried next to his heart. And that explains why no wallet was found on the dead body in the street.

"You suspected yourself, Oscar, that Charles Waverly was the man who identified the body. But at the same moment as he blurted out his identification in front of Doody, he realized the scandal that would ensue if Dana's letter were found. For of course he thought the body was Laurie's. Everybody took it for granted that if one of the Stait twins got into a scrape, it was Laurie.

"Charles Waverly did a brave thing, Oscar. He leaned over, pretending to listen to the dead man's heart to see if there was some spark of life. I've got that much from Doody. But what he really did was to pick the corpse's pocket. Charles Waverly would do anything to keep his little sister out of a murder investigation. As soon as he got away and looked at the wallet, he knew it was Lew who was dead. But then it was too late for him to come forward, so he dropped the wallet in a mail box and kept his own counsel. For Dana's sake."

"What have you proved? What is there in this fantastic yarn you've given me that wouldn't apply to Laurie as well as Hubert—Laurie who had a real motive?"

"Only this. You forget that perhaps Hubert had a motive. If he killed one twin and the other died to pay for it, he was the next in line. But the motive lies deeper than that. I'm guessing that it was revenge!"

"Revenge for what?" The Inspector was becoming exasperated.

"The twins were everything that Hubert wasn't, Oscar. They were big and handsome and strong and cheerful and uninhibited. They teased him and rallied him and probably despised him a little. Remember what the maid said about the twins forcing Hubert to take up boxing and football?

"It was the plan for the perfect murder, Oscar. But Hubert damned himself with one thing. I'll point it out later.

"We were supposed to arrest Keeley—free him, and arrest Laurie. The marriage and the handwriting test stalled off the evil day for Laurie, and Hubert began to worry. Then the police announced that Buck Keeley had been exonerated, and Hubert worried some more. Dana had left Laurie when she discovered why Rose Keeley was after him, but Laurie was discovering some things for himself. It was all right as long as he thought

Keeley had killed his brother, but when he learned that Keeley had an alibi, and remembered about Hubert's phoning him about the murder when Hubert couldn't have known it honestly, Laurie Stait went berserk. Hence the stolen gun and his search for shells. He intended to kill Hubert. But Hubert was waiting locked in his room, for he had prepared for this possibility, too.

"The wise man is always prepared for possible failure. But Hubert was faced by failure on every side. He had matched his cleverness against society, and was losing.

"Ahead of him was retribution . . . and the jeers of the multitude. Laurie was already suspecting him, and there was worse to follow. The Perfect Crime was a failure—almost!

"There was just one way, and Hubert Stait took it. Remember, he's an introspective, abnormal type. He crouched behind the door of his room, and heard Laurie outside banging on it. He knew the jig was up—he had known ever since the notice appeared in the morning papers about Keeley's alibi.

"There was just one way to make his deep-laid plan a success, and Hubert Stait took it!" Miss Withers paused, not only for effect, but also for breath. "Can't you see?"

The Inspector rose to his feet. "It's Greek to me," he admitted. "You've made a great case of it, and you're better than any lawyer Laurie Stait can get to save his neck. But so far you haven't offered a word of definite proof. And you ask me to believe that a man committed suicide for spite. And what's more, committed suicide by an impossible method." The Inspector shook his head. "Show me how a man can sneak up behind his own chair and strangle himself, and I'll release Laurie Stait."

"He's as good as released," Miss Withers said slowly. "Lend me one of your men who's about Hubert Stait's height, will you? We'll now make an attempt to run the film of Hubert's exit from this world in reverse."

The Inspector called down the stairs. "Send Swarthout up here, Sergeant."

The Inspector and Miss Withers stood once more before the room which had been Hubert Stait's. Nothing had been touched, except the removal of the body itself, of course. A big copper leaned against the doorpost and chewed Juicy Fruit, noisily.

As soon as the young man entered the room, Miss Withers directed him to the murder chair, which still cast its bar of sinister shadow across the polished floor. The noose lay near by, on the same table with Hubert's glasses.

"Put that round your neck," ordered Miss Withers.

Swarthout hesitated. "Hurry up, it won't bite you!"

"It bit somebody else this afternoon," the young man reminded her. But he gingerly dropped the noose over his own neck.

"Now stand behind the chair and tie the end of that rope round the lower leg, as it was before."

Swarthout knelt down and made the rope fast. Then he stood up for as far as the rope's length would let him. His shoulders came just above the high back of the chair.

"I'll have nightmares tonight," he complained.

"Never mind nightmares. Let me see. I've got an idea how this thing could be worked. All right," she nodded. "Take off the noose, but remember just how much leeway it gave you."

George Swarthout slipped the rope from his neck with a certain understandable alacrity.

"Now stand as you were before, when the rope was stretched tight between your neck and the leg of the chair," instructed Miss Withers. "Now! Is it possible for you to rest your chin on the back of the chair there and then give a kick with your legs and a lift with your hands . . . over the back and down into a normal sitting position?"

Swarthout was of the opinion that he was not enough of an athlete. Then, in deference to the Inspector's nod, he gave a tentative heave.

His body, pivoting against the chair back, made a complete circle in the air, feet whirling after him, and came down with a thud in the cushion of the chair, disheveled but sound. His heels dug into the floor as they struck.

The Inspector knelt to examine the floor beside them, and his square thumb explored two other corresponding gouges that were there. He nodded, thoughtfully.

"There are easier ways to sit down," Swarthout announced.

"The man who invented that method didn't pick it for its ease," Miss Withers told him. "Notice, Oscar, that the noose is about six inches above his neck, now? Suppose a man turned that somersault with the rope round his neck? He'd come down just like this, but with his weight six inches off the seat, and he'd strangle slowly but surely. The appearance of the thing would suggest that somebody had strangled him in his chair. And that was what he wanted!"

"Somebody?"

"Laurie, of course. They were alone in the house. Hubert had failed in his previous attempts to implicate Laurie. The story about the knife and pillow, and so forth. He was resolved not to fail now. He crept out of his room, while Laurie was running a bath to quiet his nerves, and phoned you. Then confident that you'd come posthaste, he went back to his room, locked himself in and threw the key out of the window, and prepared the scene. The book was supposed to signify that he was reading when it happened. But he had to take off his glasses at the last minute, or they'd have been crushed against the top of the chair as he started the somersault."

"Now I know you're crazy," the Inspector burst in. "Why, you can't make me believe that a man intent on suicide would care about his glasses."

"No? Men have hanged themselves before, but few men care for jagged splinters of glass forced into their eyes as they die. Besides—wait, Oscar. Suppose he didn't commit suicide!"

"That's what I'm telling you . . . Laurie killed him. . . ."

"Nonsense. Laurie couldn't have killed him. I'll show you why in a moment." Miss Withers removed her spectacles and polished them furiously, as if thus to see better into the workings of this dead man's mind.

"Oscar, there's a queer twist to this that just occurred to me! Did you tell Hubert, over the phone, where you were at the time?"

"Why, yes, I did. . . ."

"Well, then! Hubert knew that you were at the funeral parlors, and that you'd come up here on the double-quick. He knew that you weren't more than fifteen minutes away—and Oscar, he knew that it takes almost half an hour to strangle!"

"But I don't see . . ."

"Wait! Even if the murderous attack supposedly made on him by Laurie, who was the only other person in the house at the time, turned out to be unsuccessful, it would still damn Laurie, wouldn't it? It would point out that Laurie had killed his twin, too, because the job would be done with the missing half of the murder rope! Don't you see, Oscar? Hubert gambled with his life, but he hedged his bet!"

"You mean he expected us to get here in time to cut him down?" The Inspector whistled, silently. "Then he forgot to figure on my stopping to talk to the operative I had stationed outside!"

"You may go to the head of the class," Miss Withers told him.

22

Fanfare of Trumpets

The Inspector made one last weak effort to support his own broken lines of defense.

"Admitting all this," he objected. "You say you've got definite proof of the innocence of Laurie Stait? If you have, I don't see what it can be. Even if you prove Hubert's death a suicide, or a pretense at suicide, that still doesn't necessarily clear Laurie of suspicion in the death of his brother."

"I'll take your second point first," Miss Withers explained. "The rope in my hands, the fragment of a lariat used to choke the life out of Hubert

Stait. What's more, it's got the genuine blue thread on the end, where the other had a faked version. Notice how the binding is smooth and even and expert here? And the thread is silk, not rayon. Where did Hubert get this rope? Where he'd had it hidden since he used the rest of it to kill Lew! If he could lay hands on it whenever he wanted to, even you won't try to maintain that he was innocent of the murder of Lew.

"But never mind that. You ask me how I know Laurie had no complicity in the death of Hubert. I'll tell you."

Miss Withers tossed the noose across the room, and presented a firm palm to the Inspector. "Look at my hand, Oscar."

He looked at her hand. "So what?"

"Oscar, did you ever take a bath and soak and soak for a long time?"

"Are you insinuating—"

"Not at all. But you take showers, don't you? Cold ones? You're just the bustling type who would. All right, but I used to take hot baths, before I learned that while it steadies your nerves it plays havoc with your energy.

"When we got here, just a little less than half an hour after Hubert's phone call, we found Laurie steaming from the bath tub. He was dripping wet, you saw that. But did you notice his hands?"

"Why should I?"

"After about twenty minutes or more in sudsy hot water your hands get all wrinkled and water-soaked as the blood leaves them. It happens when I wash dishes, Oscar. It doesn't happen when you read in the tub, because the hands have to be immersed continuously for some time. Well, therefore I knew that since Laurie's hands were all water-soaked, he couldn't have just come downstairs from finishing off his cousin. And there wasn't time for him to have strangled Hubert before he took the bath, Oscar."

She paused, weary but triumphant.

"That's the weirdest alibi I've ever run across," agreed the Inspector slowly. "But I'll admit it seems to hold water. You win a week's salary."

"It was something weirder than all of Hubert's fantastic plotting," Miss Withers insisted. "Now you'd better go let Laurie Stait out of jail."

Miss Withers and the Inspector came slowly down the stairs of the Stait mansion. "Look there!" The Inspector caught his companion's arm and pointed toward the open door of the living room. It was already evening, but Dana Waverly had not troubled to turn on the lights. She sat there, staring into the empty fireplace.

Close beside her, with his white muzzle resting on her knee, stood Rowdy, the collie. Except for him, she was alone. Her brother Charles had long since gone away, after expressing his wonder and disgust at her remaining in his house. Aunt Abbie and the two servants were up in the attic with old Mrs. Stait. The old lady had accepted the death of Hubert with much the same calmness as she had met the news about Laurie's supposed death, but she was much perturbed over the wetness of the day in which she had had the temerity to go out of doors, and the consequent danger to what was left of her voice.

Dana sat alone, her profile white and marble-like in the gloom. "You tell her," whispered the Inspector. "Go ahead, you've earned it, Hildegarde. Go on and tell her that her husband is free."

But Miss Withers shook her head. "I'll do nothing of the kind," she said. "There's only one person she'll want to hear that news from, Oscar. It may be cruel to keep her suffering another half-hour, but it will be all the more wonderful when her lover tells her. Come on, we've got to get down to the station house."

They paused in the lower hall, but Dana did not look up. Rowdy, unsure as to whether these were friends or foes, waved the plume of his tail inquiringly, and then took his cue from his newfound mistress. If she had no greeting for these strangers, he would show them the supercilious stare of which only a pedigree collie is capable. Rowdy pretended not to notice them at all, and he sniffed, audibly.

His demonstration of poise was spoiled, suddenly, by a raucous interruption. "Here, boy, here! Sic 'em! Rats, boys, rats!"

Impulsively plunging to obey the summons, Rowdy dashed by the two who waited in the hall, and bounded up the stairs.

Fast as his white paws moved, the centenarian parrot was faster. The obscene bird scrambled, by dint of using feet, flippers, and his enormous hooked bill, to the lofty eminence of a cabinet which stood on the second floor landing, whence he launched volley after volley of unprintable curses at the excited collie.

Rowdy, furious with himself for having been tricked again into obeying this strange object, made a few tentative leaps at the bird without achieving his righteous purpose, and then descended the stairs again, followed by screeches of derisive laughter coupled with expressions of disfavor which the collie pretended neither to hear nor understand.

He stalked past the Inspector and Miss Withers without taking any notice of them whatever, and returned to his place beside Dana, the stiff hairs along his backbone bristling. He watched them go without moving his muzzle from the knee of the girl. Rowdy knew that something was wrong, and he was ashamed of himself for having, even temporarily, deserted his post.

There was a great hullabaloo at the station house of the Twenty-fourth Precinct, on 100th Street. The Inspector, with Miss Withers close at his heels, forced his way into the crowded room. He was immediately set upon by reporters, court attachés, and idle bystanders.

"Is it true that Lew Stait has confessed to the murder?"

"Will you let us quote you as saying that you consider Laurie Stait as the cleverest murderer of modern times?"

"Inspector, will you pose for a picture?"

"Will you sign a story on the way you deduced the case?"

"Will you please take off your hat and let us flash you beside your prisoner?"

"Scram," answered the Inspector succinctly, and shoved his way forward toward the desk.

His arm was seized from behind. It turned out to be a hanger-on from the D.A.'s office.

"Mr. Roche wants you to phone him at once!"

"You can tell Tom Roche, for me, that he can jump in the East River."

"But he wants to know what it's all about. Who are you arresting, and for what? Some of them say the prisoner is one twin, and the rest of them say he's the other, and the D.A. is going batty. . . ."

"He hasn't far to go, if you ask me," the Inspector remarked.

"But Mr. Roche wants to know when you're going to have the hearing before the magistrate. He wants to be on hand. He . . ."

The Inspector pressed closer to the bench. "Hello, Captain. Got my prisoner here safe and sound?"

"Sure have. And if I may say so, it's great work! I'm glad you got here, though. The prisoner won't talk, and there seems to be some question as to what his name is. Are you arresting Lew Stait for the murder of Laurie and Hubert Stait, or are you arresting Laurie Stait for the murder of Lew and Hubert Stait? I don't know how to book him." The Captain rubbed his nose.

"You don't need to bother," the Inspector informed him savagely. "There is only one charge against Laurie Stait, that I know about. And that isn't exactly criminal. I'm withdrawing the charge of murder!"

The Inspector crooked his thumb. "Go on, get Stait out of the cell!" He turned to the crowd. "You newspaper boys can release a story saying that the Stait Murderer cheated the electric chair via suicide at two-thirty this afternoon. Now scram out of here, all of you. The only charge against the prisoner is the *ownership of a dog without a license!*"

It took a good deal of strong arm work to get Laurie Stait through the crowd. "We'll run you home in a squad car," Piper told him when the first shock of surprise was over. "It'll keep the reporters off you, and it's the least we can do under the circumstances."

Laurie Stait was silent all the way home, although he drew into his lungs the over-chill and none-too-clean air of Manhattan as if he could never get enough of it. But there was still one dark cloud in his sky, and Miss Withers knew what it was.

"I guess you didn't understand what I meant when I said that Rose Keeley was making you a present of the collie because she was sorry for her part in this business. I had a little talk with her yesterday, and she gave me this note to give you."

Laurie took it as the squad car drew up before the entrance to the Stait house, and held the scribbled note in the light of the street lamp.

> *Dear Mr. Stait* (it began),
> *I'm sorry about it all. It wasn't Buck's fault, because I lied to him about who the man was. I was crazy to get away from the ranch and live in the east. But Miss Withers found out it was a put up job, and so I'm marrying Laramie White and going back where I belong.*
>
> *Yours respectfully, Rose Keeley.*

"Show that to Dana," suggested Miss Withers gently. "I think it will make your reunion a happier one."

Inspector Piper stared at his partner. "Will you tell me how you knew that?"

"Of course. Remember how at the rodeo we heard Carrigan, the manager, wondering why Rose and Laramie had reversed their act, so that he shot at her instead of vice-versa? The act wasn't as good that way, but Laramie wouldn't trust her to shoot at him day in and day out . . . and I knew there must be a reason. He had got her in trouble, that's why. When he didn't do anything about it, the girl got the idea of framing this kid here, and she convinced her brother that the honor of the family had been stained and so forth. But when she fainted that day at Madison Square Garden, Laramie White leaped to catch her, and I had an idea that things could be fixed up with a little firm talking to, and they were."

"You're a wonder, Hildegarde," admitted the Inspector.

But Laurie Stait had not waited to hear the details of how the plot of Rose Keeley had been exploded. He was running up the steps of the Stait mansion.

He thrust the note before the astonished eyes of the girl who was still staring into the fireplace, and then there was a long silence. It was broken, first by the roar of the auto outside which bore the Inspector and Miss Withers away, and then by the low growls of Rowdy, who had at last cornered the loathsome naked parrot in Aunt Abbie's bedroom, and who proceeded to make short work of it, squawk and all, beneath the bed.

He confidently expected to be punished for the deed, but, much to his relief, the body of the thing was not discovered until, in company with his master and his new mistress, he was aboard a Bermuda-bound liner.